FALLING FOR YOU

Married by Morning

AND

Love in the Afternoon

FALLING FOR YOU

Two Novels in One

Married by Morning

AND

Love in the Afternoon

LISA KLEYPAS

St. Martin's Paperbacks

Published in the United States by St. Martin's Paperbacks, an imprint of St. Martin's Publishing Group

FALLING FOR YOU

For information, address St. Martin's Publishing Group, 120 Broadway, New York, NY 10271.

www.stmartins.com

ISBN: 978-1-250-84903-8

Our books may be purchased in bulk for promotional, educational, or business use. Please contact your local bookseller or the Macmillan Corporate and Premium Sales Department at 1-800-221-7945, ext. 5442, or by email at MacmillanSpecialMarkets@macmillan.com.

Printed in the United States of America

St. Martin's Paperbacks edition / May 2022

10 9 8 7 6 5 4 3 2 1

Married by Morning

To my dear, elegant, wise Connie
Because a good friend is cheaper than therapy.
Love always,
L.K.

Chapter One

Anyone who had ever read a novel knew that governesses were supposed to be meek and downtrodden. They were also supposed to be quiet, subservient, and obedient, not to mention deferential to the master of the house. Leo, Lord Ramsay, wondered in exasperation why they couldn't have gotten one of *those*. Instead the Hathaway family had hired Catherine Marks, who, in Leo's opinion, cast an unflattering shadow upon the entire profession.

It wasn't that Leo found fault with Marks's actual abilities. She had done an excellent job of instructing his two youngest sisters, Poppy and Beatrix, in the finer points of social etiquette. And they had needed an inordinate amount of help, since none of the Hathaways had ever expected to mingle in the upper circles of British society. They had been reared in a strictly middle-class environment, in a village west of London. Their father, Edward Hathaway, had been a medieval history scholar, considered a man of good blood but hardly an aristocrat.

However, after a series of unlikely events, Leo had inherited the title of Lord Ramsay. Although he had trained to be an architect, he was now a viscount with land and tenants.

The Hathaways had moved to the Ramsay estate in Hampshire, where they had struggled to adjust to the demands of their new life.

One of the greatest challenges for the Hathaway sisters had been to learn the absurd multitude of rules and graces expected of privileged young ladies. Had it not been for Catherine Marks's patient instruction, the Hathaways would have rampaged through London with all the finesse of stampeding elephants. Marks had done wonders for all of them, especially Beatrix, who was undoubtedly the most eccentric sister of an already eccentric family. Although Beatrix was happiest romping through the meadows and woods like a wild creature, Marks had managed to impress on her that a different code of behavior was required in the ballroom. She had even written a series of etiquette poems for the girls, with such literary gems as:

> *Young ladies must display restraint*
> *When speaking with a stranger*
> *Flirtations, quarrels, or complaints*
> *Put our reputations in danger*

Naturally Leo hadn't been able to resist mocking Marks's poetic abilities, but he had to admit privately that her methods had worked. Poppy and Beatrix had successfully navigated a London season, at last. And Poppy had recently married a hotelier named Harry Rutledge.

Now only Beatrix was left. Marks had assumed the role of chaperone and companion to the energetic nineteen-year-old. As far as the rest of the Hathaways were concerned, Catherine Marks was practically a member of the family.

Leo, for his part, couldn't abide the woman. She aired her opinions at will and dared to give orders to him. On the rare occasions when Leo tried to be friendly, she snapped at him or turned away in scorn. When he stated a perfectly rational opinion, he could hardly finish a sentence before Marks had listed all the reasons why he was wrong.

Faced with the immutable fact of her dislike, Leo couldn't help but respond in kind. All during the past year he had tried to convince himself that it didn't matter if she despised him. There were many women in London who were infinitely more beautiful, engaging, and appealing than Catherine Marks.

If only she didn't fascinate him so.

Perhaps it was the secrets she guarded so zealously. Marks never talked about her childhood or her family, or why she had taken a position with the Hathaways. She had taught at a girls' school for a short time, but she refused to discuss her academic tenure or explain why she had left. There were rumors, passed on by former students, that she might have been a poor relation of the headmistress, or that she was a fallen woman whose loss of status had obliged her to go into service.

Marks was so self-contained and tenacious that it was often easy to forget she was still a young woman in her early twenties. When Leo had first met her, she had been the perfect embodiment of a dried-up spinster, with her spectacles and forbidding scowl and her stern hyphen of a mouth. Her spine was as unbending as a fireplace poker, and her hair, the dull brown of apple moths, was always pinned back too tightly. The Grim Reaper, Leo had nicknamed her, despite the objections of the family.

But the past year had wrought a remarkable change in Marks. She had filled out, her body slender but no longer matchstick thin, and her cheeks had gained color. A week and a half ago, when Leo had arrived from London, he had been absolutely astonished to see Marks with light golden locks. Apparently she had been dyeing her hair for years, but after an error on the part of the apothecary, she had been forced to abandon the disguise. And whereas the darker brown locks had been too severe for her delicate features and pale skin, her own natural blond was stunning.

Which had left Leo to grapple with the fact that Catherine Marks, his mortal enemy, was a beauty. It wasn't really the altered hair color that made her look so different . . . it was more that Marks was so uncomfortable without it. She felt vulnerable, and it showed. As a result, Leo wanted to strip away more layers, literal and physical. He wanted to *know* her.

Leo had tried to keep his distance while he pondered the ramifications of this discovery. He was confounded by his family's reaction to Marks, which amounted to nothing more than a collective shrug. Why weren't any of them even a fraction as curious about her as he was? Why had Marks deliberately made herself unattractive for so long? What the devil was she hiding from?

On a sunny Hampshire afternoon when Leo had ascertained that most of the family was otherwise occupied, he went in search of Marks, reasoning that if he confronted her in private, he would get some answers. He found her outside in a hedged garden filled with flowers. She occupied a bench at the side of a graveled path.

She was not alone.

Leo stopped at twenty yards' distance, drawing into the shade of a heavily foliated yew.

Marks was sitting beside Poppy's new husband, Harry Rutledge. They were engaged in what appeared to be an intimate conversation.

Although the situation wasn't precisely incriminating, neither was it appropriate.

What in God's name could they be talking about? Even from this remote vantage, it was clear that something of significance was being said. Harry Rutledge's dark head was inclined over hers protectively. Like a close friend. Like a lover.

Leo's mouth fell open as he saw Marks reaching beneath her spectacles with a delicate hand, as if to wipe away a tear.

Marks was *crying,* in the company of Harry Rutledge.

And then Rutledge kissed her on the forehead.

Leo's breath stopped. Holding still, he sorted through an emulsion of emotions and separated them into layers . . . amazement, worry, suspicion, fury.

They were hiding something. Plotting something.

Had Rutledge once kept her as a mistress? Was he blackmailing her, or was she perhaps extorting something from him? No . . . the tenderness between the pair was evident even at this distance.

Leo rubbed the lower half of his jaw as he considered what to do. Poppy's happiness was more important than any other consideration. Before he went dashing over to beat his sister's new husband to a bloody pulp, he would find out exactly what the situation was. And *then*, if circumstances warranted, he would beat Rutledge to a bloody pulp.

Taking slow, measured breaths, Leo watched the pair. Rutledge stood and went back to the house, while Marks remained seated on the bench.

Without making a conscious decision, Leo approached her slowly. He wasn't certain how he was going to treat her, or what he was going to say. It depended on which impulse leaped out most strongly the moment he reached her. It was entirely possible that he would throttle her. It was equally likely that he would pull her to the sun-warmed grass and ravish her. He found himself stewing in a hot, unpleasant rush of feeling that wasn't at all familiar. Was it jealousy? Christ, it was. He was jealous over a skinny termagant who insulted and nagged him at every opportunity.

Was this some new level of depravity? Had he developed a spinster fetish?

Perhaps it was her very reserve that Leo found so erotic . . . he had always been fascinated by the question of what it would take to demolish it. Catherine Marks, his fiendish little adversary . . . naked and moaning beneath him. There was nothing he'd ever wanted more. And that made sense, actually: When a woman was easy and willing, there was no challenge in it. But taking Marks to bed, making it last a long time, tormenting her until she begged and screamed . . . now, *that* would be fun.

Leo walked toward her casually, not missing the way she stiffened at the sight of him. Her face became pinched and unhappy, her mouth strict. Leo imagined taking her head in his hands, kissing her for long lascivious minutes, until she was limp and gasping in his arms.

Instead he stood with his fists in his coat pockets, surveying her without expression. "Care to explain what that was all about?"

The sun glinted on the lenses of Marks's spectacles, momentarily obscuring her eyes. "You've been spying on me, my lord?"

"Hardly. Whatever spinsters do in their personal time doesn't interest me in the least. But it's difficult not to notice when my brother-in-law is kissing the governess out in the garden."

One had to give Marks credit for composure. She showed no reaction except for the tightening of her hands in her lap. "One kiss," she said. "On the forehead."

"It doesn't matter how many kisses, or where they landed. You're going to explain to me why he did it. And why you let him. And try to make it credible, because I'm this close"—

Leo held his thumb and forefinger a mere quarter inch apart—
"to dragging you bodily to the coach road and putting you
on the next cart bound for London."

"Go to the devil," she said in a low voice, and sprang to
her feet. She had taken only two strides before he caught her
from behind. "Don't touch me!"

Leo turned her to face him, controlling her easily. His
hands closed over her slender upper arms. He could feel the
warmth of her skin through the thin muslin of her sleeves.
As he held her, the innocent scent of lavender water rose to
his nostrils. There was a faint dusting of talc at the base of
her throat. The fragrance of her reminded Leo of a freshly
made bed with pressed sheets. And oh, how he wanted to slip
into her.

"You have too many secrets, Marks. You've been a thorn
in my side for more than a year, with your sharp tongue and
your mysterious past. Now I want some answers. What were
you discussing with Harry Rutledge?"

Her fine brows, several shades darker than her hair, gathered in a scowl. "Why don't you ask him?"

"I've asked *you*." Met with her mulish silence, Leo decided
to provoke her. "Were you a different kind of woman, I'd suspect you of casting your lures at him. But we both know you
don't have any lures, don't we?"

"If I did, I certainly wouldn't use them on you!"

"Come, Marks, let's attempt a civil conversation. Just this
once."

"Not until you take your hands off me."

"No, you'd only run. And it's too hot to chase after you."

Catherine bristled and pushed at him, her palms flattening
against his chest. Her body was neatly packaged in stays and
laces and countless yards of muslin. The thought of what
was beneath . . . pink and white skin, soft curves, intimate
curls . . . aroused him instantly.

A shiver ran through her, as if she could read his thoughts. Leo stared down at her intently. His voice softened. "Are you afraid of me, Marks? You, who bludgeon and cut me down to size at every opportunity?"

"Of course not, you arrogant ass. I only wish you would behave like a man of your station."

"You mean like a peer?" He raised his eyebrows mockingly. "This is how peers behave. I'm surprised you haven't noticed by now."

"Oh, I've noticed. A man fortunate enough to inherit a title should have the decency to try and live up to it. Being a peer is an obligation—a responsibility—but instead you seem to regard it as a license to engage in the most self-indulgent and disgusting behavior imaginable. Moreover—"

"Marks," Leo interrupted in a velvety tone, "that was a perfectly wonderful attempt at distracting me. But it's not going to work. You're not getting away from me until you tell me what I want to know."

She swallowed hard and tried to look everywhere but at him, which wasn't easy when he was standing right in front of her. "The reason I was talking privately with Mr. Rutledge . . . the scene you witnessed . . ."

"Yes?"

"It was because . . . Harry Rutledge is my brother. Half brother."

Leo stared at her downbent head, trying to absorb the information. The sense of being duped, betrayed, ignited a bonfire of rage. Holy hell. Marks and Harry Rutledge were *siblings*?

"There could be no good reason," Leo said, "for such information to have been kept secret."

"The situation is complicated."

"Why have neither of you said anything before now?"

"You don't need to know."

"You should have told me before he married Poppy. You were obligated."

"By what?"

"Loyalty, damn you. What else do you know that might affect my family? What other secrets are you hiding?"

"It's none of your business," Catherine shot back, now twisting in his grip. "Let me go!"

"Not until I find out what you're plotting. Is Catherine Marks even your real name? Who the hell are you?" He swore as she began to struggle in earnest. "Hold still, you little she-devil. I just want to—*ouch*!" This last as she turned and jabbed a sharp elbow in his side.

The maneuver gained Marks the freedom she sought, but her spectacles went flying to the ground. "My spectacles!" With an aggravated sigh, she dropped to her hands and knees and began feeling for them.

Leo's fury was instantly smothered by guilt. From the looks of it, she was practically blind without the spectacles. And the sight of her crawling on the ground made him feel like a brute. A jackass. Lowering to his knees, he began to hunt for them as well.

"Did you see the direction they went in?" he asked.

"If I did," she said, fuming, "I wouldn't need spectacles, would I?"

A short silence. "I'll help you find them."

"How kind of you," she said acidly.

For the next few minutes the two of them traversed the garden on their hands and knees, searching among the daffodils. They both chewed on the gristly silence as if it were a mutton chop.

"So you actually need spectacles," Leo finally said.

"Of course I do," Marks said crossly. "Why would I wear spectacles if I didn't need them?"

"I thought they might be part of your disguise."

"My disguise?"

"Yes, Marks, disguise. A noun describing a means of concealing someone's identity. Often used by clowns and spies. And now apparently governesses. Good God, can *anything* be ordinary for my family?"

Marks glared and blinked in his direction, her gaze not quite focused. For a moment, she looked like an anxious child whose favorite blanket had been set out of reach. And that caused an odd, painful twinge in Leo's heart.

"I'll find your spectacles," he said brusquely. "You have my word. If you like, you can go into the house while I keep searching."

"No, thank you. If I tried to find the house on my own, I'd probably end up in the barn."

Seeing a metallic glimmer in the grass, Leo reached out and closed his hand around the spectacles. "Here they are." He crawled to Marks and faced her in an upright kneeling position. After polishing the spectacle lenses with the edge of his sleeve, he said, "Hold still."

"Give them to me."

"Let me do it, hardhead. Arguing comes to you as naturally as breathing, doesn't it?"

"No, it doesn't," she said immediately, and colored as he gave a husky laugh.

"It's no fun to bait you when you make it so easy, Marks." He placed the spectacles on her face with great care, running his fingers along the sides of the frame, viewing the fit with an assessing glance. Gently he touched the tips of the earpieces. "They're not fitted well." He ran an exploring fingertip over the upper rim of one ear. She was remarkably pretty in the sunlight, her gray eyes containing glimmers of blue and green. Like opals. "Such small ears," Leo continued, letting his hands linger at the sides of her fine-boned face. "No wonder your spectacles fall off so readily. There's hardly anything to hang them on."

Marks stared at him in bewilderment.

How fragile she was, he thought. Her will was so fierce, her temperament so prickly, that he tended to forget she was only half his size. He would have expected her to slap his hands away by now—she hated being touched, especially by him. But she didn't move at all. He let his thumb brush the side of her throat, and felt the tiny undulation of her swallow. There was something unreal about the moment, something dreamlike. He didn't want it to end.

"Is Catherine your real name?" he asked. "Will you at least answer that?"

She hesitated, fearful of yielding any part of herself, even that scrap of information. But as his fingertips slid along her neck, the light caress seemed to disarm her. A bloom of color rose from her throat.

"Yes," she choked out. "It's Catherine."

They were still kneeling together, her skirts having billowed and settled everywhere. Folds of flower-printed muslin had been caught under one of Leo's knees. His body reacted strongly to her nearness, heat sliding beneath his skin and gathering in inconvenient places. Muscles tightened, thickened. He would have to put an end to this, or he was going to do something they would both regret.

"I'll help you up," Leo said brusquely, making to rise. "We'll go inside. I warn you, however, I'm not through with you yet. There's more I—"

But he broke off, because as Marks had tried to struggle upward, her body had brushed against his. They went still, caught front to front, their breath mingling in uneven surges.

The dreamlike feeling intensified. The two of them were kneeling in a summer garden, the air weighted with the

perfume of hot crushed grass and scarlet poppies . . . and
Catherine Marks was in his arms. Her hair shimmered in the
sunlight, her skin petal-soft. Her upper lip was nearly as full
as the lower, the curves as delicate and smooth as a ripe per-
simmon. Staring at her mouth, he felt the hairs on the back
of his neck lift in reflexive excitement.

Some temptations, Leo decided hazily, should not be resisted. Because they were so persistent that they would only
keep returning, time and again. Therefore such temptations
absolutely *had* to be yielded to—it was the only way to be
rid of them.

"Damn it," he said raggedly, "I'll do it. Even knowing I'll
be annihilated afterward."

"You'll do what?" Marks asked, her eyes huge.

"This."

And his mouth descended to hers.

At last, every muscle in his body seemed to sigh. At last.
The sensation was so pleasurable that for a moment Leo
couldn't even move, just felt her mouth with his mouth. Sinking into the feeling, Leo let it take him. He stopped thinking
altogether and did everything and anything he wanted . . .
tugging at her upper lip and then her lower one, sealing their
mouths together, touching his tongue to hers, playing with
her. One kiss started before another had finished, a chain of
erotic strokes and skims and nudges. The delight of it went
all through him, echoing in every vein and nerve.

And God help him, he ached for more. He was dying to put
his hands inside her clothes, and feel every inch of her body.
He wanted to drag his mouth over her in intimate trails, kiss
and taste every part of her. Marks responded helplessly, curling her arm around his neck. She moved against him as if
sensation were coming from all directions. And it was. They
both struggled to press closer, tighter, their bodies pursuing
a new and unsteady rhythm. Had they not been separated by

so many layers of clothing, it would have been outright love-making.

Leo continued to kiss her long after he should have stopped, not only for the sheer pleasure of it, but also because he was reluctant to face what would happen afterward. Their cantankerous relationship could not resume as usual after something like this. It had been set on a new track with an unknown destination, and Leo was certain that neither of them were going to like where it led.

Finding that he couldn't release her all at once, he did it by degrees, letting his mouth nuzzle the edge of her jaw, following to the vulnerable hollow behind her ear. Her pulse was swift and vibrant against his lips.

"Marks," he said on a rough breath, "I was afraid of this. Somehow I knew . . ." Breaking off, he lifted his head and looked down at her.

She squinted through the mist that had accumulated on her lenses. "My spectacles . . . I've lost them again."

"No, you haven't. There's steam on the lenses."

As the fogged spectacles cleared, Marks shoved at him. She struggled to her feet, frantically swatting away his efforts to help.

They stared at each other. It was hard to say which one of them was more appalled.

But judging from her expression, it was probably Marks.

"This never happened," she snapped. "If you have the gall ever to mention it, I'll deny it to my last breath." She gave her skirts a few agitated whacks to remove the bits of leaves and grass, and shot Leo a fierce warning glance. "I'm going to the house now. And don't follow me!"

Chapter Two

Their paths didn't intersect again until dinner, a crowded affair that included his sisters Amelia, Win, and Poppy, and their respective husbands Cam Rohan, Kev Merripen, and Harry Rutledge. Catherine Marks sat with Beatrix at the far end of the table.

So far none of Leo's sisters had chosen conventional men to wed. Rohan and Merripen were both Roma, which accounted in part for their ability to fit in easily with the off-kilter Hathaways. And Poppy's husband, Harry Rutledge, was an eccentric hotelier, a powerful man whose enemies reputedly liked him more than his friends did.

Could it be true that Catherine Marks was Harry's sister?

Leo glanced from one to the other of them at dinner, searching for similarities. *Damned if I can't see a resemblance,* he thought. The high cheekbones, the straight lines of the brows, the slight feline tilt at the outward corners of the eyes.

"I need to speak to you," Leo said to Amelia as soon as dinner had concluded. "In private."

Her blue eyes widened with curiosity. "Of course. Shall we walk? It's still light outside."

Leo gave her a curt nod.

As the two oldest Hathaway siblings, Leo and Amelia had had their share of arguments. However, she was his favorite person in the world, not to mention his closest confidant. Amelia had a great deal of common sense, and she never hesitated to say what she thought.

No one had ever expected the pragmatic Amelia to be swept off her feet by Cam Rohan, a dashing Rom. But Cam had managed to seduce and marry Amelia before she had quite known what was happening. And as it had turned out, Cam was able to provide the levelheaded guidance the Hathaways had needed. With his black hair worn a trifle too long and a diamond stud glittering in one ear, he was hardly the image of a staid family patriarch. But it was Cam's unconventionality that allowed him to manage the Hathaways so adeptly. Now he and Amelia had a nine-month-old son, Rye, who had his father's dark hair and his mother's blue eyes.

Walking leisurely along the private drive with Amelia, Leo cast a proprietary glance at their surroundings. In summer, the Hampshire sun lingered until at least nine o'clock, illuminating a mosaic of woodland, heath, and grass meadows. Rivers and streams scored the landscape, feeding bogs and wet meadows teeming with prolific wildlife. Although the Ramsay estate was certainly not the largest in Hampshire, it was one of the more beautiful, with an ancient timber forest and three thousand acres of arable land.

In the past year Leo had come to know the estate tenants, he had made improvements in irrigation and drainage, repaired fences, gates, and buildings . . . and the devil knew he had learned far more than he'd ever wanted to know about farming. All part of Kev Merripen's merciless instructions.

Merripen, who had lived with the Hathaways since childhood, had undertaken to learn as much as possible about estate management. Now he was intent on teaching this accumulated knowledge to Leo.

"It's not really your land," Merripen had told him, "until you've put some of your own blood and sweat into it."

"Is that all?" Leo had asked sarcastically. "Only blood and sweat? I'm certain I can find one or two other bodily fluids to donate if it's that important."

But privately he acknowledged that Merripen had been right. This feeling of ownership, of connection, couldn't be acquired any other way.

Shoving his hands in his pockets, Leo let out a taut sigh. Dinner had left him restless and irritable.

"You must have had a row with Miss Marks," Amelia remarked. "Usually you're slinging arrows at each other across the table. But tonight you were both quiet. I don't think she looked up from her plate even once."

"It wasn't a row," Leo said curtly.

"Then what was it?"

"She told me—under duress—that Rutledge is her brother."

Amelia glanced at him suspiciously. "What kind of duress?"

"Never mind that. Did you hear what I just said? Harry Rutledge is—"

"Miss Marks has been under quite enough duress without you adding to it," Amelia said. "I do hope you weren't cruel to her, Leo. Because if so—"

"*I*, cruel to *Marks*? I'm the one you should worry about. After a conversation with her, I usually walk away with my entrails dragging behind me." His indignation doubled as he saw his sister trying to suppress a grin. "I gather you already knew Rutledge and Marks were related."

"I've known for a few days," she admitted.

"Why didn't you say anything?"

"She asked me not to, and I agreed out of respect for her privacy."

"The devil knows why Marks should have privacy when no one else around here does." Leo stopped in his tracks, obliging her to stop as well. They faced each other. "Why is it a secret that she's Rutledge's sister?"

"I'm not certain," Amelia admitted, looking perturbed. "All she would say is that it's for her protection."

"Protection from what?"

She shook her head helplessly. "Perhaps Harry might tell you. But I doubt it."

"By God, someone's going to explain it to me, or I'll throw Marks out on her arse before she can blink."

"Leo," she said in astonishment. "You wouldn't."

"It would be my pleasure."

"But think of Beatrix, and how upset she would be—"

"I am thinking of Beatrix. I won't have my youngest sister being looked after by a woman with a possibly dangerous secret. If a man like Harry Rutledge, who has ties to some of the most nefarious characters in London, can't acknowledge his own sister . . . she may be a criminal. Has that occurred to you?"

"No," Amelia said stonily, beginning to walk again. "Honestly, Leo, even for you this is a bit dramatic. She is not a criminal."

"Don't be naïve," he said, following her. "No one is exactly who he or she pretends to be."

After a curtailed silence, Amelia asked warily, "What are you going to do?"

"I'm leaving for London on the morrow."

Her eyes widened. "But Merripen is expecting you to take part in the turnip planting, and the fertilizing, and—"

"I know what Merripen expects. And I do hate to miss his

fascinating lectures on the wonders of manure. All the same, I'm going. I want to spend some time with Rutledge and pry some answers out of him."

Amelia frowned. "Why can't you talk to him here?"

"Because he's on his honeymoon, and he won't be willing to spend his last night in Hampshire chatting with me. Besides, I've decided to take on a small commission to design a conservatory for a house in Mayfair."

"I think you want to be away from Catherine. I think something happened between you."

Leo glanced at the last brilliant orange and purple vestiges of daylight. "The light is going," he remarked in a pleasant tone. "We should head back."

"You can't run from your problems, you know."

His mouth twisted in annoyance. "Why do people always say that? Of course you can run from your problems. I do it all the time, and it never fails."

"You're obsessed with Catherine," Amelia persisted. "It's obvious to everyone."

"Now who's being dramatic?" he asked, striding back toward Ramsay House.

"You watch everything she does." Amelia stubbornly kept pace with him. "Whenever her name is mentioned, you're all ears. And lately, every time I see you talking or arguing with her, you seem more alive than you have since . . ." She paused, seeming to think better of what she'd been about to say.

"Since when?" Leo asked, daring her to continue.

"Since before the scarlet fever."

It was a subject they never discussed.

The year before Leo had inherited the viscountcy, a fatal epidemic of scarlet fever had swept through the village where the Hathaways had lived.

The first to go had been Laura Dillard, Leo's fiancée.

Laura's family had let him stay at her bedside. For three days he had watched her die in his arms, hour by hour, until she had slipped away.

Leo had gone home and collapsed with the fever, and so had Win. By some miracle they had both survived, but Win had been left an invalid. And Leo had emerged an entirely different man, scarred in ways that even he couldn't fully catalog. He had found himself in a nightmare he couldn't wake from. He hadn't cared if he lived or died. The most unforgivable part was that in his torment, he had hurt his family and caused no end of problems for them. At the worst of it, when Leo had seemed bent on destroying himself, the family had made a decision. They had sent Win to recover at a clinic in France, with Leo accompanying her.

While Win's weak lungs had regained their strength at the clinic, Leo had spent hours walking through the heat-drowsed pantiled villages of Provence, up switchback footpaths scattered with flowers, across arid fields. The sunshine, the hot blue air, the *lenteur,* or slowness of life, had cleared his mind and calmed his soul. He had stopped drinking except for a single glass of wine at dinner. He had sketched and painted, and finally he had grieved.

When Leo and Win had returned to England, Win had wasted no time in achieving her heart's desire, which had been to marry Merripen.

Leo, for his part, was trying to make amends for the way he had failed his family. And above all, he was determined to avoid falling in love ever again. Now that he was aware of the fatal depth of feeling he was capable of, he would never give another human being such power over him.

"Sis," he told Amelia ruefully, "if you have some lunatic notion that I have any kind of personal interest in Marks, forget it at once. All I intend to do is find out what skeleton she has in her closet. Knowing her, it's probably a literal one."

Chapter Three

I didn't even know about Cat's existence until I was twenty," Harry Rutledge said, stretching out his long legs as he and Leo sat in the Rutledge Hotel's clubroom. The quiet and luxurious spot, with its numerous octagonal apses, was a popular gathering place in London for foreign nobility, travelers of means, aristocrats and politicians.

Leo regarded his brother-in-law with thinly veiled skepticism. Of all the men he would have chosen to marry one of his sisters, Rutledge would certainly not have topped the list. Leo didn't trust him. On the other hand, Harry had his good points, among them his obvious devotion to Poppy.

Harry drank from a snifter of warmed brandy, considering his words carefully before he continued. He was a handsome man, capable of great charm, but he was also ruthless and manipulative. One would expect no less from a man of his achievements, among them creating the largest and most opulent hotel in London.

"I'm reluctant to discuss Cat for several reasons," Harry said, his green eyes guarded. "Among them the fact that I've never been particularly kind to her, nor did I protect her when I should have. And I regret it."

"We all have regrets," Leo said, taking a sip of brandy, letting the velvet fire slide down his throat. "It's why I cling to my bad habits. One doesn't have to start regretting something unless one stops doing it."

Harry grinned, but sobered quickly as he stared into the flame of a small candle lamp that had been set on the table. "Before I tell you anything, I want to ask what the nature of your interest in my sister is."

"I'm asking as her employer," Leo said. "I'm concerned about the influence she may have over Beatrix."

"You never questioned her influence before," Harry shot back. "And from all accounts she's done an excellent job with Beatrix."

"She has. However, the revelation of this mysterious connection to you has me worried. For all I know, the two of you have been hatching some kind of plot."

"No." Harry stared at him directly. "There's no plot."

"Then why all these secrets?"

"I can't explain without telling you something of my own past—" Pausing, Harry added darkly, "Which I hate doing."

"So sorry," Leo said without a trace of sincerity. "Go on."

Harry hesitated again, as if weighing the decision to tell him anything. "Cat and I had the same mother. Her name was Nicolette Wigens. She was British by birth. Her family moved from England to Buffalo, New York, when she was still an infant. Because Nicolette was an only child—the Wigens had her fairly late in life—it was their desire to see her married to a man who would take care of her. My father Arthur was more than twice her age, and fairly prosperous. I suspect the Wigens forced the match—there was certainly no love in it. But Nicolette married Arthur, and I was born soon after. A bit too soon, actually. There was speculation that Arthur wasn't the father."

"Was he?" Leo couldn't help asking.

Harry smiled cynically. "Does one ever know for certain?" He shrugged. "In any case, my mother eventually ran off to England with one of her lovers." Harry's gaze was distant. "There were other men after that, I believe. My mother wasn't one for limiting herself. She was a spoiled, self-indulgent bitch, but very beautiful. Cat looks very much like her." He paused reflectively. "Only softer. More refined. And unlike our mother, Cat has a kind and caring nature."

"Really," Leo said sourly. "She's never been kind to me."

"That's because you frighten her."

Leo gave him a disbelieving glance. "In what possible way could I frighten that little virago? And don't claim that she's nervous around men, because she's perfectly amiable to Cam and Merripen."

"She feels safe with them."

"Why not with me?" Leo asked, offended.

"I believe," Harry said thoughtfully, "it's because she's aware of you as a man."

The revelation caused Leo's heart to jolt. He examined the contents of his brandy snifter with studied boredom. "Did she tell you that?"

"No, I saw it for myself, in Hampshire." Harry turned wry. "One has to be particularly observant where Cat is concerned. She won't talk about herself." He tossed off the rest of his brandy, set down the glass with care, and leaned back in his chair. "I never heard from my mother after she left Buffalo," he said, lacing his fingers together and resting them on his flat midriff. "But when I reached the age of twenty, I received a letter bidding me to come to her. She had contracted a wasting disease, some form of cancer. I assumed that before she died, she wanted to see what had become of me. I left for England at once, but she died just before I arrived."

"And that was when you met Marks," Leo prompted.

"No, she wasn't there. Despite Cat's wishes to stay with her mother, she had been sent to stay with an aunt and grandmother on her father's side. And the father, apparently unwilling to keep vigil by the sickbed, had left London altogether."

"Noble fellow," Leo said.

"A local woman had taken care of Nicolette during the last week of her life. It was she who told me about Cat. I gave a brief thought to visiting the child, but I decided against it. There was no place in my life for an illegitimate half sister. She was nearly half my age, and in need of female guidance. I assumed she was better off in her aunt's care."

"Was that assumption correct?" Leo brought himself to ask.

Harry gave him an inscrutable glance. "No."

An entire story was contained in that one bleak syllable. Leo wanted very much to hear it. "What happened?"

"I decided to stay in England and try my hand at the hotel business. So I sent Cat a letter, telling her where to send word if she ever needed anything. Some years later, when she was fifteen, she wrote to me, asking for help. I found her in . . . difficult circumstances. I wish I had reached her a little sooner."

Feeling a tug of unaccountable concern, Leo found it impossible to maintain his usual veneer of carelessness. "What do you mean, difficult circumstances?"

Harry shook his head. "I'm afraid that's as much as I can tell you. The rest is up to Cat."

"Damn it, Rutledge, you're not leaving it there. I want to know how the Hathaways got involved in this, and why I had the misfortune to end up as the employer of the most illtempered and interfering governess in England."

"Cat doesn't have to work. She's a woman of independent means. I settled enough money on her to allow her the freedom to do anything she wished. She went to boarding school for four years, and stayed to teach for another two. Eventually she came to me and said she'd accepted a position as a governess for the Hathaway family. I believe you were in France with Win at the time. Cat went for the interview, Cam and Amelia liked her, Beatrix and Poppy clearly needed her, and no one seemed inclined to question her lack of experience."

"Of course not," Leo said acidly. "My family would never bother with something so insignificant as job experience. I'm sure they started the interview by asking what her favorite color was."

Harry was trying unsuccessfully not to smile. "No doubt you're right."

"Why did she go into service, if she had no need of money?"

Harry shrugged. "She wanted to experience what a family was like, if only as an outsider. Cat believes she'll never have a family of her own."

Leo's brows drew together as he tried to make sense of that. "Nothing is stopping her," he pointed out.

"You think not?" A hint of mockery varnished Harry's hard green eyes. "You Hathaways would find it impossible to understand what it's like to be brought up in isolation, by people who don't give a damn about you. You have no choice but to assume it's your fault, that you're unlovable. And that feeling wraps around you until it becomes a prison, and you find yourself barricading the doors against anyone who wants to come in."

Leo listened intently, perceiving that Harry was talking about himself as well Catherine. Silently he acknowledged that Harry was right: even in the worst despair of Leo's life, he had always known that his family loved him.

For the first time he understood fully what Poppy had done

for Harry, how she had broken through the invisible prison he had described.

"Thank you," Leo said quietly. "I know it wasn't easy for you to talk about this."

"Certainly." And in absolute seriousness, Harry murmured, "One thing I should make clear, Ramsay: If you hurt Cat in any way, I will have to kill you."

DRESSED IN HER NIGHTGOWN, POPPY SAT IN BED WITH A novel. She heard someone enter the elegantly appointed private apartments, and she looked up with a smile as her husband came into the room. Her pulse quickened pleasurably at the sight of him, so dark and graceful. Harry was an enigmatic man, dangerous even in the view of those who professed to know him well. But with Poppy, he relaxed and showed his gentle side.

"Did you talk with Leo?" she asked.

"Yes, love." Harry shrugged out of his coat, draped it over the back of a chair, and approached the bedside. "He wanted to discuss Cat, as I expected. I told him as much about her past—and mine—as I could."

"What do you make of the situation?" Poppy knew that Harry was brilliant at discerning other people's thoughts and motives.

Harry untied his cravat, letting it hang on either side of his neck. "Ramsay is more concerned for Cat than he'd like to be, that's clear. And I don't like it. But I won't interfere unless Cat asks for help." He reached down to the exposed line of her throat, drawing the backs of his fingers over her skin with a sensitive lightness that caused her breath to quicken. His fingertips rested on the rapid tattoo of her pulse, and caressed softly. Watching a delicate tide of pink rise in her face, he said in a low voice, "Put the book aside."

Poppy's toes curled beneath the bed linens. "But I've reached a very interesting part," she said demurely, teasing him.

"Not half so interesting as what's about to happen to you." Drawing the covers back with a deliberate sweep that left her gasping, Harry lowered his body over hers . . . and the book dropped to the floor, forgotten.

Chapter Four

Catherine hoped that Leo, Lord Ramsay, would stay away from Hampshire for a good long while. Perhaps if enough time passed, they would be able to pretend the kiss in the garden had never happened.

But in the meantime, she couldn't help but wonder . . . why had he done it?

Most likely he had merely been amusing himself with her, finding a new way to set her off balance.

If life were at all fair, she thought dourly, Leo would have been pudgy, pockmarked, and bald. But he was a handsome man with a strapping six-foot build. He had dark hair and light blue eyes and a dazzling smile. The worst part was that Leo didn't look at all like the rogue he was. He looked wholesome and clean and honorable, the nicest gentleman one could ever hope to meet.

The illusion was dispelled as soon as he opened his mouth. Leo was a thoroughly wicked man, articulate in all circumstances. His irreverence spared no one, least of all himself. In the year since they had first met, he had exhibited nearly every objectionable quality a man could possess, and any attempt to correct him only made him worse. Especially if that attempt had been made by Catherine.

Leo was a man with a past, and he didn't even have the decency to try and hide it. He was frank about his dissolute history, the drinking and skirt-chasing and brawling, the self-destructive behavior that had nearly brought catastrophe to the Hathaway family on more than one occasion. One could only conclude that he liked being a scoundrel, or at least being known as one. He played the part of jaded aristocrat to perfection, his eyes glinting with the cynicism of a man who, at the age of thirty, had managed to outlive himself.

Catherine wanted nothing to do with any man, least of all one who radiated such dangerous charm. One could never trust such a man. His darkest days might still be ahead of him. And if not . . . it was entirely possible that hers were.

APPROXIMATELY A WEEK AFTER LEO HAD LEFT HAMPSHIRE, Catherine spent an afternoon outside with Beatrix. Unfortunately these outings were never the kind of well-regulated walk that Catherine preferred. Beatrix didn't walk, she explored. She liked to go deep into the forest, investigating flora, fungi, nests, webs, and holes in the ground. Nothing delighted the youngest Hathaway so much as the discovery of a black newt, a lizard's nest, or a rabbit warren, or the tracking of badgers' marks.

Injured creatures were caught, rehabilitated, and set free, or if they could not fend for themselves, they became part of the Hathaway household. And the family had become so accustomed to Beatrix's animals that no one so much as batted an eye when a hedgehog waddled through the parlor or a pair of rabbits hopped past the dinner table.

Pleasantly tired after the long ramble with Beatrix, Catherine sat at her dressing table and took down her hair. She scrubbed her fingers over her scalp and through the loose blond waves, soothing the little aches left from tight braids and hairpins.

A happy chatter came from behind her, and she turned to see Beatrix's pet ferret, Dodger, emerging from beneath her dresser. His long, sinuous body arced gracefully as he loped toward her with a white glove in his teeth. The mischievous thief liked to filch things from drawers and boxes and closets, and hide them in secret piles. To Catherine's frustration, Dodger especially loved *her* possessions. It had become a ritual humiliation to go through Ramsay House in search of her own garters.

"You overgrown rat," Catherine told him as he stood tall and braced his tiny paws on the edge of her chair. She reached out to pet his sleek fur, tickled the top of his head, and carefully pried the glove from his teeth. "Having stolen all my garters, you're moving on to gloves, are you?"

He regarded her affectionately, his eyes bright in the dark stripe that formed a mask across his face.

"Where have you hidden my things?" she asked, setting the glove on the dressing table. "If I don't find my garters soon, I'll have to keep my stockings up with pieces of old string."

Dodger twitched his whiskers and appeared to grin at her, displaying tiny pointed teeth. He wriggled invitingly.

Smiling reluctantly, Catherine picked up a hairbrush and drew it through the loose locks of her hair. "No, I don't have time to play with you. I'm getting ready for dinner."

In a liquid and lightning-fast movement, the ferret leaped to her lap, snatched the glove from the table, and streaked from the room.

"Dodger," Catherine exclaimed, dashing after him. "Bring that back!" She went out into the hallway, where maids were rushing back and forth with unusual haste. Dodger disappeared around the corner.

"Virgie," Catherine asked one of the maids, "what is happening?"

The dark-haired girl was breathless and smiling. "Lord Leo has just come from London, miss, and the housekeeper told us to ready his room and set another place for dinner, and unpack the luggage when the footmen bring it up."

"So soon?" Catherine asked, feeling the color drain from her face. "But he didn't send word. No one expected him."

I didn't expect him, was what she meant.

Virgie shrugged and hurried away with an armload of folded linens.

Catherine put a hand to her midriff, where nerves were leaping, and retreated into her room. She wasn't ready to face Leo. It wasn't fair that he had come back so soon.

Of course, it *was* his estate. But still . . .

She paced in a tight circle and tried to marshal the chaos of her thoughts. There was only one solution: She would avoid Leo. She would plead a headache and stay in her room.

In the midst of her turmoil, there was a tap on the door. Someone entered without waiting for a response. Catherine nearly choked on her own heartbeat as she saw Leo's tall, familiar form.

"How dare you come into my room without . . ." Her voice faded as he closed the door.

Leo turned to face her, his gaze sweeping over her. He was travel-rumpled and a bit dusty. His hair wanted a good brushing, the dark brown locks disheveled and falling over his forehead. He looked self-possessed but cautious, the ever-present mockery in his eyes replaced by something she couldn't identify. Something new.

Catherine's hand drew into a fist against her midriff, and she struggled to catch up with her own breathing. She held still as he approached her, while her heart pounded with a dizzying mixture of dread and excitement.

Leo's hands went on either side of her shrinking body and gripped the edge of the dressing table behind her. He was too close, his masculine vitality surrounding her. He smelled like outside air, like dust and horses, like a healthy young male. As he leaned over her, one of his knees pressed gently into the mass of her skirts.

"Why did you come back?" she asked weakly.

He stared directly into her eyes. "You know why."

Before Catherine could stop herself, her gaze dropped to the firm contours of his mouth.

"Cat . . . we have to talk about what happened."

"I don't know what you mean."

He inclined his head slightly. "Would you like me to remind you?"

"No, no . . ." She shook her head for emphasis. "No."

His lips twitched. "One 'no' is enough, darling."

Darling?

Filled with anxiety, Catherine fought to keep her voice steady. "I thought I made it clear that I wanted to ignore what happened."

"And you expect that will make it go away?"

"Yes, that's what one does with mistakes," she said with difficulty. "One sets them aside and moves on."

"Really?" Leo asked innocently. "My mistakes are usually so enjoyable that I tend to repeat them."

Catherine wondered what was wrong with her that she was tempted to smile. "This one will not be repeated."

"Ah, there's the governess voice. All stern and disapproving. It makes me feel like a naughty schoolboy." One of his hands lifted to caress the edge of her jaw.

Her body raced with conflicting impulses, her skin craving his touch, her instincts warning her to move away from him. The result was a kind of stunned immobility, every muscle drawing up taut. "If you don't leave my room this instant," she heard herself say, "I'll make a scene."

"Marks, there is nothing in the world I would enjoy more than watching you make a scene. In fact, I'll help you. How shall we start?" Leo seemed to enjoy her discomfiture, the wash of uncontrollable color over her face.

The pad of his thumb stroked the thin, soft skin beneath her jaw, a coaxing motion that caused her head to tilt back before she quite knew what she was doing. "I've never seen such eyes," he said almost absently. "They remind me of the first time I saw the North Sea." His fingertips followed the edge of her jaw. "When the wind chases the waves before it, the water is the same green-gray your eyes are now . . . and then it turns to blue at the horizon."

Catherine could only assume that he was mocking her again. She scowled at him. "What do you want from me?"

Leo took a long time to answer, his fingers trailing to her earlobe, massaging lightly. "I want your secrets. And I'll get them out of you one way or another."

That gave her the impetus to swat his hand away. "Stop this. You're amusing yourself at my expense, as usual. You are a dissipated scoundrel, an unprincipled cad, and—"

"Don't forget 'lecherous libertine,'" he said. "That's one of my favorites."

"Get *out*!"

He pushed away lazily from the dressing table. "All right. I'll go. Obviously you fear that if I stay, you won't be able to control your desire for me."

"The only desire I have for you," she said, "involves maiming and dismemberment."

Leo grinned and went to the door. Pausing at the threshold, he glanced over his shoulder. "Your spectacles are fogging again," he said helpfully, and slipped through the door before she could find something to throw.

Chapter Five

"Leo," Amelia said as Leo entered the breakfast room the next morning, "you have to get married."

Leo gave her a warning glance. His sister knew better than to start a conversation with him so early. He preferred to ease his way into the day, whereas Amelia liked to fling herself at it full tilt. Moreover, he'd slept badly the night before, plagued by erotic dreams involving Catherine Marks.

"You know I'll never marry," he said.

Marks's voice came from the corner. She was perched on a small chair, a sunbeam glancing off her fair hair and causing dust motes to glitter around her. "Just as well, since no rational woman would have you."

Leo took up the challenge without hesitation. "A rational woman . . ." he mused aloud. "I don't believe I've ever met one of those."

"How would you know if you did?" she asked. "You wouldn't be interested in her character. You would be far too busy examining her . . . her . . ."

"Her what?" he prompted.

"Her dress measurements," she finally said, and he laughed at her prudishness.

"Is it really so impossible for you to name ordinary body parts, Marks? Breasts, hips, legs—why is it indecent to talk about the human anatomy in a straightforward manner?"

Her eyes narrowed. "Because it leads to improper thoughts."

Leo smirked at her. "Mine already are."

"Well, mine aren't," she said. "And I would prefer them to remain that way."

His brows lifted. "You don't have improper thoughts?"

"Hardly ever."

"But when you do, what are they?"

She gave him an indignant glance.

"Have I ever been involved in your improper thoughts?" Leo persisted, causing her face to flame.

"I told you I didn't have any," she protested.

"No, you said 'hardly ever.' Which means one or two are rattling around in there."

Amelia broke in. "Leo, stop tormenting her."

Leo barely heard her, his attention fixed on Catherine. "I wouldn't think badly of you at all if you did," he said. "In fact, I'd like you much better for it."

"No doubt you would," Catherine shot back. "You probably prefer women with no virtues at all."

"Virtue in a woman is like pepper in the soup. A little makes for a nice seasoning. But overdo it, and no one wants very much of you."

Clamping her mouth shut, Catherine pointedly looked away from him, putting an end to the rapid-paced argument.

In the silence, Leo became aware that the entire family was staring at him with collective bemusement.

"Have I done something?" he demanded. "What's going on? And what the devil are you all reading?"

Amelia, Cam, and Merripen had spread papers over the

table, while Win and Beatrix appeared to be looking up words in a massive legal tome.

"A letter was just delivered from our London solicitor, Mr. Gadwick," Merripen said. "It seems there are legal issues that weren't made clear when you inherited the estate."

"No surprise there," Leo said. He went to the sideboard, where breakfast had been laid out. "The estate and title were tossed in my direction like used fish wrappings. Along with the Ramsay curse."

"There is no Ramsay curse," Amelia said.

"Oh?" Leo smiled darkly. "Then why did the last half-dozen Lord Ramsays die in quick succession?"

"Pure coincidence," she replied. "Obviously that particular branch of the family was clumsy and inbred. It's a common difficulty for bluebloods."

"Well, we certainly don't have that problem." Leo returned his attention to Merripen. "Tell me about our legal issues. And use small words. I don't like to think at this hour of the morning. It hurts."

Looking none too happy, Merripen sat at the table. "This house," he said, "and the parcel of land it stands on—about fourteen acres in total—were not part of the original Ramsay estate. It was added later. In legal terms, it's a copyhold portion, which is a separate property within the main estate. And unlike the rest of the estate, the copyhold can be mortgaged, bought, or sold at the will of the lord."

"Good," Leo said. "Since I'm the lord, and I don't want to mortgage or sell anything, it's all fine, isn't it?"

"No."

"*No?*" Leo scowled. "According to the rules of entailment, the lord always retains his land and manor home. It's nonpartible. And nothing can change that."

"That's right," Merripen said. "You are entitled to the

ancient manor home. The one on the northwest corner of the estate where two streams meet."

Leo set down his half-filled plate and stared at him blankly. "But that's a pile of rubble covered with scrub. It was built at the time of Edward the Confessor, for God's sake."

"Yes," Merripen said in a matter-of-fact tone. "That's your true home."

Becoming more and more irritated, Leo said, "I don't want that bloody wreckage, I want *this* house. Why is there a problem with that?"

"May I tell him?" Beatrix asked eagerly. "I've looked up all the legal words, and I know it better than anyone." She sat up with her pet ferret Dodger draped around her shoulders. "You see, Leo, the original manor home was left to ruin a few centuries ago. And one of the ancient Lord Ramsays acquired this fourteen-acre parcel and built a new home on it. Ever since then, Ramsay House has been handed down to each new viscount by special custom in the manor. But the last Lord Ramsay—the one just before you—found a way to leave all partible property, including the copyhold, to his widow and daughter. It's called an award of enfranchisement, and it's theirs for life. So Ramsay House and the fourteen-acre parcel it stands upon have been left to Countess Ramsay, and her daughter Vanessa Darvin."

Leo shook his head incredulously. "Why haven't we learned of this before?"

Amelia answered in a glum tone. "It seems that the widow had no previous interest in the house, because it was a shambles. But now that it's been restored so beautifully, she has informed our solicitor that she intends to move in and take possession."

Leo was filled with outrage. "I'll be damned if I'll let anyone take Ramsay House from the Hathaways. If necessary, I'll bring this to chancery at Westminster."

Merripen pinched the corners of his eyes wearily. "Chancery won't take it."

"How do you know?"

"Our solicitor has talked to the copyhold specialist at his firm. Unfortunately, there was never an entail placed on Ramsay House, only on the original manor home."

"What about purchasing the copyhold from the widow?"

"She has already stated that no amount of money would induce her to part from it."

"Women's minds are frequently changed," Leo said. "We'll make her an offer."

"Very well. But if she refuses to negotiate, there's only one way for us to keep this house."

"I can't wait to hear this," Leo said.

"The last Lord Ramsay made a provision that you would retain the copyhold, including the house, if you married and produced legitimate male issue within five years of ennoblement."

"Why five years?"

Win answered gently. "Because in the last three decades, no Ramsay has managed to live longer than five years after receiving the title. Nor have any of them sired a legitimate son."

"But the good news, Leo," Beatrix said brightly, "is that it's been four years since you became Lord Ramsay. If you can stay alive for just one more year, the family curse will be broken."

"And furthermore," Amelia added, "you have to marry and sire a son as soon as possible."

Leo stared at them all blankly in the expectant silence. A disbelieving laugh escaped him. "You're all mad if you think I'm going to be forced into a loveless marriage just so the family can continue living at Ramsay House."

Coming forward with a placating smile, Win handed him

a piece of paper. "Of course we would never want to force you into a loveless marriage, dear. But we have put together a list of prospective brides, all of them lovely girls. Won't you take a glance and see if any of them appeals to you?"

Deciding to humor her, Leo looked down at the list. *"Marietta Newbury?"*

"Yes," Amelia said. "What's wrong with her?"

"I don't like her teeth."

"What about Isabella Charrington?"

"I don't like her mother."

"Lady Blossom Tremaine?"

"I don't like her name."

"Oh, for heaven's sake, Leo, that's not her fault."

"I don't care. I can't have a wife named Blossom. Every night I would feel as if I were calling in one of the cows." Leo lifted his gaze heavenward. "I might as well marry the first woman off the street. Why, I'd be better off with Marks."

Everyone was silent.

Still tucked in the corner of the room, Catherine Marks looked up slowly as she realized that she was the focus of the Hathaways' collective gaze. Her eyes turned huge behind the spectacles, and a tide of pink rushed over her face. "That is *not* amusing," she said sharply.

"It's the perfect solution," Leo said, taking perverse satisfaction in annoying her. "We argue all the time. We can't stand each other. It's like we're already married."

Catherine sprang to her feet, staring at him in outrage. "I would *never* consent to marry you."

"Good, because I wasn't asking. I was only making a point."

"Do not use me to make a point!" She fled the room, while Leo stared after her.

"You know," Win said thoughtfully, "we should have a ball."

"A ball?" Merripen asked blankly.

"Yes, and invite all the eligible young women we can think of. It's possible one of them will strike Leo's fancy, and then he could court her."

"I'm not going to court anyone," Leo said.

They all ignored him.

"I like that idea," Amelia said. "A bride-hunting ball."

"It would be more accurate," Cam pointed out dryly, "to call it a groom-hunting ball. Since Leo will be the item of prey."

"It's just like Cinderella," Beatrix exclaimed. "Only without the charming prince."

Deciding to calm the brewing squabble, Cam lifted his hand in a staying gesture. "Easy, all of you. If it happens that we lose Ramsay House—God forbid—we can build another one on the freehold portion of the estate."

"That would take forever, and the cost would be enormous," Amelia protested. "And it wouldn't be the same. We've spent too much time restoring this place, and putting our hearts into it."

"Especially Merripen," Win added quietly.

Merripen gave her a slight shake of his head. "It's only a house."

But they all knew it was more than a structure of brick and mortar . . . it was their home. Cam and Amelia's son had been born there. Win and Merripen had been married there. With all its haphazard charm, Ramsay House was a perfect expression of the Hathaway family itself.

And no one understood that better than Leo. As an architect, he knew well that some buildings had an inherent character that was far more than the sum of their parts. Ramsay House had been damaged and restored . . . it had gone from a neglected shell to a thriving, happy home, all because one family had cared. It was a crime that the Hathaways would be displaced by a pair of women who had invested nothing in it, through what amounted to nothing more than a legal sleight of hand.

Swearing beneath his breath, Leo dragged his hand through his hair. "I want to have a look at the ruins of the old manor home," he said. "Merripen, what's the best way to reach it?"

"I'm not certain," Merripen admitted. "I rarely go out that far."

"I know," Beatrix volunteered. "Miss Marks and I have ridden there to sketch the ruins. They're very picturesque."

"Would you like to ride there with me?" Leo asked.

"I'd love to," she said.

Amelia frowned. "Why do you want to visit the ruins, Leo?"

He smiled in a way he knew would annoy her. "Why, to measure for curtains, of course."

Chapter Six

"Thunderbolts," Beatrix exclaimed, entering the library where Leo had been waiting, "I can't go with you to the ruins after all. I've just checked on Lucky, and she's about to have her babies. I can't leave her at such a time."

Leo smiled quizzically, replacing a book on a shelf. "Who's Lucky?"

"Oh, I forgot you hadn't met her. She's a three-legged cat who used to belong to the cheesemaker in the village. The poor thing got her paw caught in a rat trap, and it had to be amputated. And now that she's no longer a good mouser, the cheesemaker gave her to me. He never even named her, can you imagine?"

"Given what happened to her, the name 'Lucky' is something of a misnomer, isn't it?"

"I thought it might improve her fortunes."

"I'm sure it will," Leo said, amused. Beatrix's passion for helping vulnerable creatures had always worried and touched the other Hathaways in equal measure. They all recognized that Beatrix was the most unconventional person in the family.

Beatrix was always sought after at London social events.

She was a pretty girl, if not classically beautiful, with her blue eyes, dark hair, and tall, slender figure. Gentlemen were attracted by her freshness and charm, unaware that she showed the same patient interest to hedgehogs, field mice, and misbehaving spaniels. And when it came time for active courtship, men reluctantly left Beatrix's engaging company and turned to more conventional misses. With each successive season, her chances at marriage diminished.

Beatrix didn't seem to care. At the age of nineteen—nearly twenty—she had yet to fall in love. It was universally agreed among the Hathaways that few men would be able to understand or handle her. She was a force of nature, unhampered by conventional rules.

"Go take care of Lucky," Leo said gently. "I don't expect to have any difficulty finding the ruins by myself."

"Oh, you're not going alone," she told him. "I arranged for Miss Marks to accompany you."

"You did? And she was willing?"

Before Beatrix could answer, Catherine entered the library, her slim figure dressed in riding clothes, her hair pulled back in a tight braided chignon. A sketchbook was clasped beneath her arm. She stopped short at the sight of Leo, who was wearing a gentleman's riding coat, close-fitting breeches, and well-worn boots.

Her wary gaze went to Beatrix. "Why haven't you changed into your riding habit, dear?"

Beatrix replied apologetically, "I'm sorry, Miss Marks, I can't go after all. Lucky needs me. But it's just as well—you can show Leo the way even better than I." Her sunny smile encompassed them both. "It's a fine day for riding, isn't it? Have a good outing!" And she left the library in her long, lithe stride.

Catherine's slender brows rushed downward as she looked at Leo. "Why do you want to visit the ruins?"

"I just want to look at them. Hang it all, do I have to explain myself to you? Just refuse if you're afraid to go somewhere alone with me."

"Afraid of *you*? Not in the least."

Leo gestured to the doorway in a parody of gentlemanly manners. "After you, then."

AS A RESULT OF THE STRATEGIC IMPORTANCE OF THE PORTS of Southampton and Portsmouth, Hampshire was filled with ancient castles and picturesque ruins of forts and Saxon dwellings. Although Leo had known that there were remains of an old manor on the Ramsay estate, he hadn't yet found the opportunity to visit them. Among the concerns of farming, the accounting of rents, rates, and labor, the timber cutting and the architectural commissions Leo took on occasion, there hadn't been much time left for idle touring.

Together he and Catherine rode past fields of flowering turnips and wheat, and clover pastures where fat white sheep grazed. They crossed through the timber forest to the northwest of the estate, where heavy streams cut through green hills and limestone crags. The ground was less arable here, more rock than loam, but its location was a solidly defensible position for an ancient fortified manor home.

As they ascended a hill, Leo took covert glances at Catherine. She was slim and graceful on horseback, guiding the horse with a smooth economy of motion. An accomplished woman, he mused. Poised, articulate, competent in nearly everything she did. And yet when another woman would have advertised such qualities, Catherine went to great lengths to keep from drawing attention to herself.

They reached the site of the original manor, where the remains of ancient walls protruded from the ground like the vertebrae of fossilized creatures. Inequalities in the scrub-covered ground marked the locations of the manor's outbuildings. A shallow circular ring, approximately twenty-five feet wide, revealed the dimensions of the moat that had surrounded a sixty-square-foot elevation of land.

After dismounting and tethering his horse, Leo went to assist Catherine. She disengaged her right leg from the pommel and took her foot from the stirrup, letting Leo control her descent. She alighted on the ground, facing him. Her face lifted, the brim of her riding hat partially shadowing her opalescent eyes.

They stood together with her hands on his shoulders. Her face was flushed with exertion, her lips parted . . . and all at once Leo knew how it would be to make love to her, her body light and supple beneath his, her breath rushing against his throat as he moved between her thighs. He would bring her to ecstasy, slowly and ruthlessly, and she would claw and moan and sigh his name . . .

"Here it is," Catherine said. "Your ancestral home."

Tearing his gaze from her, Leo regarded the crumbling ruins. "Charming," he said. "A little dusting and sweeping, and the place will be as good as new."

"Will you go along with the family's plan to find a bride for you?"

"Do you think I should?"

"No, I don't think you have the makings of a decent husband. You haven't the character for it."

Leo's sentiments exactly. Except that it rankled to hear her say it.

"What makes you a fit judge of my character?" he asked.

Her shoulders lifted in an uncomfortable shrug. "One can't help hearing about your exploits when all the dowagers and matrons are together at the balls."

"I see. And you believe every rumor you hear?"

She was silent. Leo expected her to argue, or insult him. To his surprise, however, she stared at him with something like remorse. "You have a point. And whether the rumors are true or false, it was wrong of me to listen."

Leo waited for her to follow that with some stinging insult, but she appeared genuinely chastened. Which was a surprise. It made him realize there was much he didn't know about her, this solitary and serious young woman who had hovered at the edge of his family for so long.

"What do the gossips say about me?" he asked casually.

She gave him a wry glance. "Your prowess as a lover is much vaunted."

"Oh, well, those rumors are definitely true." He clucked his tongue as if shocked. "Do dowagers and chaperones really prattle about such things?"

Her slender brows arched. "What did you imagine they talked about?"

"Knitting. Jelly recipes."

She shook her head and bit back a smile.

"How tedious these affairs must be for you," Leo said. "Standing at the side of the room, listening to gossip and watching everyone else dance."

"I don't mind it. I don't like dancing."

"Have you ever danced with a man?"

"No," she admitted.

"Then how can you be sure you wouldn't like it?"

"I can have an opinion about something even if I haven't done it."

"Of course. It's so much easier to form opinions without being troubled by experience or facts."

She frowned but kept silent.

"You've given me an idea, Marks," Leo went on. "I'm going to allow my sisters to plan the ball they mentioned earlier. Only for this reason: I'm going to come to you in the middle of it and ask you to dance with me. In front of everyone."

She looked appalled. "I would refuse."

"I'm going to ask nevertheless."

"To make a mockery of me," she said. "To make fools of us both."

"No." His voice gentled. "Just to dance, Marks."

Their gazes locked in a long, fascinated stare.

And then to Leo's surprise, Catherine smiled at him. A sweet, natural, brilliant smile, the first she had ever given him. Leo felt his chest tighten, and he went hot all over, as if some euphoric drug had gone straight to his nervous system.

It felt like . . . happiness.

He remembered happiness from a long time ago. He didn't want to feel it. And yet the giddy warmth kept washing over him for no reason whatsoever.

"Thank you," Catherine said, the smile still hovering on her lips. "That is kind of you, my lord. But I will never dance with you."

Which, of course, made it the goal of Leo's life.

Catherine turned to retrieve a sketchbook and roll of pencils from the saddle pouch.

"I didn't know you sketched," Leo said.

"I'm not very good at it."

He gestured to the book in her hands. "May I see that?"

"And give you reason to mock me?"

"I won't. My solemn promise. Let me see." Slowly Leo extended his hand, palm up.

Catherine glanced at his open hand, and then his face. Hesitantly she gave the book to him.

Opening the book, he glanced through the sketches. There was a series of the ruins from different angles, perhaps too careful and disciplined in places where a bit of looseness would have given the sketch more vitality. But on the whole it was very well done. "Lovely," he said. "You have a nice feeling for line and form."

She colored, seeming uncomfortable with the praise. "I understand from your sisters that you are an accomplished artist."

"Competent, perhaps. My architectural training included a number of art classes." Leo gave her a casual grin. "I'm especially good at sketching things that stay still for long periods of time. Buildings. Lampposts." He leafed through the book. "Do you have any of Beatrix's drawings?"

"On the last page," Catherine said. "She began to sketch a protruding section of the wall, over there, but she became preoccupied with a squirrel that kept hopping into the foreground."

Leo found a perfectly rendered and detailed portrait of a squirrel. He shook his head. "Beatrix and her animals."

They exchanged a grin.

"Many people talk to their pets," Catherine said.

"Yes, but very few understand the replies." Closing the sketchbook, Leo gave it back to her and began to walk the perimeter of the manor enclosure.

Catherine followed, picking her way among the gorse studded with yellow flowers and shiny black pods. "How deep was the original moat, do you estimate?"

"I would guess no more than eight feet where it cuts into the higher ground." Leo shielded his eyes as he surveyed their surroundings. "They must have diverted one of the streams to fill it. You see those mounds over there? They were probably farm buildings and serf quarters, made of clay and stud."

"What was the manor home like?"

"The central keep was almost certainly made of stone, with the rest a combination of materials. And it was likely crowded with sheep, goats, dogs, and serfs."

"Do you know the history of the original overlord?" Catherine sat on a portion of the exposed wall and arranged her skirts.

"You mean the first Viscount Ramsay?" Leo stopped at the edge of the circular depression that had once been the moat. His gaze traveled across the broken landscape. "He started as Thomas of Blackmere, known for his lack of mercy. Apparently he had a talent for pillaging and burning villages. He was regarded as the left arm of Edward the Black Prince. Between them, they virtually destroyed the practice of chivalry."

Glancing over his shoulder, he smiled at the sight of Catherine's wrinkled nose. She sat with schoolgirl straightness, the sketchbook in her lap. He would have liked to snatch her off the wall and do some pillaging of his own. Reflecting that it was a good thing she couldn't read his thoughts, he continued the story.

"After fighting in France and being held prisoner for four years, Thomas was released and returned to England. I suppose he thought it was time to settle down, because he subsequently rode on this keep, killed the baron who had built it, seized his lands and ravished his widow."

Her eyes were wide. "Poor lady."

Leo shrugged. "She must have had some influence on him. He married her afterward and sired six children by her."

"Did they live to a peaceful old age?"

Leo shook his head, approaching her leisurely. "Thomas went back to France, where they put an end to him at Castillon. But the French were quite civilized about it and raised a monument to him on the field."

"I don't think he deserved any kind of tribute."

"Don't be too hard on the fellow—he was only doing what the times demanded."

"He was a barbarian," she said indignantly. "Regardless of the times." The wind had teased a lock of light golden hair loose from her tight chignon, and sent it straying over her cheek.

Unable to resist, Leo reached out and stroked the tendril back behind her ear. Her skin was baby-fine and smooth. "Most men are," he said. "It's only that they have more rules now." He removed his hat, set it on the wall, and stared into her upturned face. "You may put a man in a cravat, teach him manners, and make him attend a soiree, but hardly any of us are truly civilized."

"From what I know of men," she said, "I agree."

He gave her a mocking glance. "What do you know of men?"

She looked solemn, the clear gray irises now tinged with ocean green. "I know not to trust them."

"I would say the same of women." He shed his coat, tossed it over the wall, and went to the hill at the center of the ruins. Surveying the surrounding land, Leo couldn't help wondering if Thomas of Blackmere had stood on this exact spot, looking over his property. And now, centuries later, the estate was Leo's to make of what he would, his to shape and order. Everyone and everything on it was his responsibility.

"How is the view from up there?" he heard Catherine's voice from below.

"Exceptional. Come see it, if you like."

She left the sketchbook on the fence and began up the slope of the mound, lifting her skirts as she climbed.

Turning to watch Catherine, Leo let his gaze linger on her slender, pretty figure. She was fortunate that medieval times were long past, he thought with a private smile, or she would have found herself snapped up and devoured by some marauding lord. But the touch of amusement faded quickly as he imagined the primitive satisfaction of claiming her, picking her up and carrying her to a soft patch of ground.

For just a moment he let himself dwell on the idea . . . lowering himself to her writhing body, tearing her dress, kissing her breasts—

Leo shook his head to clear it, troubled by the direction of his thoughts. Whatever else he was, he was not a man to force himself on a woman. And yet the fantasy was too potent to ignore. With an effort, he bludgeoned the barbaric impulses back into submission.

Catherine was halfway up the slope when she gave a low cry and seemed to stumble.

Concerned, Leo started for her immediately. "Did you trip? Are you—*bloody hell*." He stopped in place as he saw that the ground had partially given way beneath her. "Stop, Cat. Don't move. *Wait*."

"What's happening?" she asked, her face bleached of color. "Is it a sinkhole?"

"More like a bloody architectural miracle. We seem to be standing on a portion of a roof that should have caved in at least two centuries ago."

They were approximately five yards apart, with Leo on higher ground.

"Cat," he said with great care, "slowly lower yourself to the ground to redistribute your weight over a greater surface. Easy. Yes, like that. Now you're going to crawl back down the slope."

"Can you help me?" she asked, and the tremor in her voice wrenched his heart.

He answered in a thick voice that didn't sound like his own. "Sweetheart, I would love nothing more. But joining my weight to yours could collapse the roof entirely. Start moving. If it makes you feel better, with all the debris in there, it can't be too far to fall."

"Actually, that doesn't make me feel better at all." White-faced, she moved slowly on her hands and knees.

Leo stayed in place, not taking his gaze from Catherine. The ground that seemed so solid beneath his feet was possibly nothing more than a layer of earth and ancient rotted timber. "You'll be fine," he said in a soothing tone, while his heart pounded with anxiety for her. "You weigh no more than a butterfly. It's my weight that's put a strain on what's left of the beams and bridging joints."

"Is that why you're not moving?"

"Yes. If I cause a collapse when I try to get off, I'd like you to be out of harm's way first."

They both felt the ground shift beneath them.

"My lord," Catherine asked, her eyes wide, "do you think this has anything to do with the Ramsay curse?"

"Actually, that hadn't occurred to me yet," Leo said. "Thank you so much for bringing it to my attention."

The roof collapsed, and they simultaneously plunged amid a torrent of earth, rock, and timber into the dark space below.

Chapter Seven

Catherine stirred and coughed. There was grit in her mouth and eyes, and she was sprawled on a wretchedly uncomfortable surface.

"Marks." She heard Leo shove debris aside as he made his way to her. His voice was unsteady and urgent. "Are you hurt? Can you move?"

"Yes . . . I'm all in one piece . . ." She sat up and rubbed her face. Evaluating the collection of aches and pains in her body, she decided they were all insignificant. "Just a bit bruised. Oh, dear. My spectacles are gone."

She heard him swear. "I'll try to find them."

Disoriented, she tried to make out what she could of their surroundings. Leo's lean form was a dark blur nearby as he searched the rubble. Dust clouded the air, settling slowly. From what little she could see, they were in a pit, perhaps six feet deep, with sunlight drizzling in through the broken roof. "You were right, my lord. It wasn't far to fall. Is this the keep?"

Leo's breathing sounded strained as he replied, "I'm not sure. It could be an undercroft beneath the keep. I see the remains of a stone partition over there . . . and hollows in the side wall where transverse joints would support—"

In a burst of fresh terror, Catherine launched herself at his indistinct form, scrabbling to reach him in the dimness.

"What is it?" Leo's arms closed around her.

Gasping, she buried her face against the solid surface of his chest. They were half sitting, half lying amid heaps of rotted timber, stone, and earth.

One of his hands came to her head, curving over her skull protectively. "What happened?"

Her voice was muffled in his shirt. *"Undercroft."*

He smoothed her hair and pressed her even closer into the protection of his body. "Yes. Why does that frighten you?"

She could hardly speak between panting breaths. "Isn't that . . . where they keep the bodies?"

The tremulous question hung in the air as Leo puzzled over it. *"Oh.* No, it's not that kind of undercroft." A quiver of rueful amusement ran through his voice, and she felt his mouth touch the rim of her ear. "You're thinking of one of the rooms beneath modern churches, where the deceased are put away. But a medieval undercroft is different. It's only a storeroom beneath the keep."

Catherine didn't move. "There are no s-skeletons in here?"

"No. Nor skulls, nor coffins." His hand continued to stroke tenderly over her hair. "Poor darling. It's all right. Nothing fearsome down here. Take a deep breath. You're safe."

Catherine continued to lie in his arms as she caught her breath. She tried to take in the fact that Leo, her enemy and tormentor, was calling her "poor darling" and petting her. His lips brushed her temple and lingered gently. Holding still, she absorbed the sensation. She had never been attracted to men of his size, preferring those of less intimidating stature. But he was strong and comforting, and he seemed so genuinely concerned, and his voice was like dark velvet wrapping around her.

How perplexing.

Had anyone told her that she would one day be trapped alone in a filthy pit with Leo, Lord Ramsay, she would have said that was her worst nightmare. And yet it was turning out to be a rather agreeable experience. No wonder Ramsay was so sought after by the ladies of London . . . If this was how he set about seducing them, all this lovely soothing and stroking, Catherine could easily understand how he got his way with them.

To her regret, he gently eased her away from him. "Marks . . . I'm afraid I'm not going to be able to find your spectacles in this wreckage."

"I have another pair at home," she ventured.

"Thank God." Leo sat up with a quiet grunt of discomfort. "Now, if we stand on the highest pile of debris, it's only a short distance to the surface. I'm going to hoist you up, get you out of here, and then you're going to ride back to Ramsay House. Cam trained the horse, so you won't need to guide him. He'll find his way back home with no trouble."

"What are you going to do?" she asked, bewildered.

He sounded rather sheepish. "I'm afraid I'm going to have to wait here until you send someone for me."

"Why?"

"I have a—" He paused, searching for a word. "Splinter."

She felt indignant. "You're going to make me ride back alone and unescorted and virtually blind, to send someone to rescue you? All because you have a splinter?"

"A large one," he volunteered.

"Where is it? Your finger? Your hand? Maybe I can help to . . . Oh, *God*." This last as he took her hand and brought it to his shoulder. His shirt was wet with blood, and a thick shard of timber protruded from his shoulder. "That's not a splinter," she said in horror. "You've been *impaled*. What can I do? Shall I pull it out?"

"No, it might be lodged against an artery. And I wouldn't care to bleed out down here."

She crawled closer to him, bringing her face close to his to examine him anxiously. Even in the shadows, he appeared pale and gray, and when she pressed her fingers to his forehead, she felt cool moisture.

"Don't worry," he murmured. "It looks worse than it is."

But Catherine didn't agree. If anything, it was worse than it looked. She was infused with panic as she wondered if he were going into shock, a condition in which the heart did not pump enough blood to maintain the body. It had been described as a "momentary pause in the act of death."

Stripping off her riding coat, she tried to lay it over his chest.

"What are you doing?" he asked.

"Trying to keep you warm."

Leo plucked the garment off his chest and made a scoffing sound. "Don't be ridiculous. First, the injury isn't that bad. Second, this tiny thing is not capable of keeping any part of me warm. Now, about my plan—"

"It is obviously a significant injury," she said, "and I do not agree to your plan. I have a better one."

"Of course you do," he replied sardonically. "Marks, *for once* would you do as I ask?"

"No, I'm not going to leave you here. I'm going to pile up enough debris for both of us to climb out."

"You can't even see, damn it. And you can't move these timbers and stones. You're too small."

"There is no need to make derogatory remarks about my stature," she said, lurching upward and squinting at her surroundings. Identifying the highest pile of debris, she made her way to it and hunted for nearby rocks.

"I'm not being derogatory." He sounded exasperated.

"Your stature is absolutely perfect for my favorite activity. But you're not built for hauling rocks. Blast it, Marks, you're going to hurt yourself—"

"Stay there," Catherine said sharply, hearing him push some heavy object aside. "You'll worsen your injury, and then it will be even more difficult to get you out. Let me do the work." Finding a heap of ashlar blocks, she picked one up and lugged it up the pile, trying not to trip over her own skirts.

"You're not strong enough," Leo said, sounding aggravated and out of breath.

"What I lack in physical strength," she replied, going for another block, "I make up for in determination."

"How inspiring. Could we set aside the heroic fortitude for one bloody moment and dredge up some common sense?"

"I'm not going to argue with you, my lord. I need to save my breath for"—she paused to heft another block—"stacking rocks."

SOMEWHERE AMID THE ORDEAL, LEO DECIDED HAZILY THAT he would never underestimate Catherine Marks again. Ounce for ounce, she was the most insanely obstinate person he had ever known, dragging rocks and debris while half blind and hampered by long skirts, diligently crossing back and forth across his vision like an industrious mole. She had decided to build a mound upon which they could climb out, and nothing would stop her.

Occasionally she stopped and put her hand on his forehead or throat, checking his temperature and pulse. And then she would be off again.

It was maddening not to be able to help her—humiliating to let a woman do such work without him—but every time he tried to stand, he became dizzy and disoriented. His shoulder was on fire, and he couldn't use his left arm properly. Cold sweat dripped from his face and stung his eyes.

He must have drifted off for a few minutes, because the next thing he was aware of was Catherine's urgent hands shaking him awake.

"Marks," he said groggily. "What are you doing here?" He had the confused impression that it was morning, and she wanted him to awaken before his usual hour.

"Don't sleep," she said with an anxious frown. "I've built the pile high enough that we can climb out now. Come with me."

His body felt as if it had been encased in lead. He was overwhelmed with weariness. "In few minutes. Let me doze a bit longer."

"*Now,* my lord." Clearly she would bully and badger him until he obeyed. "Come with me. Up with you. *Move.*"

Leo complied with a groan, lurching until he had staggered to his feet. A cold burst of pain radiated from his shoulder and arm, and a few helpless curses slipped out before he could stop himself. Oddly, Catherine didn't rebuke him.

"Over there," she said. "And don't trip—you're too heavy for me to catch."

Profoundly irritated but aware that she was trying to help him, he concentrated on placing his feet and maintaining his balance.

"Is Leo short for Leonard?" she asked, confusing him.

"Confound it, Marks, I don't want to talk now."

"Answer me," she persisted.

He realized she was trying to keep him alert. "No," he said, breathing heavily. "It's just Leo. My father loved the constellations. Leo is the . . . constellation of high summer. The brightest star marks his heart. Regulus." He paused to stare blearily at the pile she had made. "Well. How efficient you are. The next time I take an architectural commission—" He paused to catch his breath. "I'll recommend you as the contractor."

"Just think if I'd had my spectacles," she said. "I could have made proper stairs."

He let out a huff of laughter. "You go first, and I'll follow."

"Hold on to my skirts," she said.

"Why, Marks, that's the nicest thing you've ever said to me."

They climbed out together laboriously, while Leo's blood turned to ice and his wound ached and his brains went to mush. By the time he'd flopped to the ground in an awkward sideways sprawl, he was infuriated with Catherine for making him go to such effort when he'd wanted to stay in the pit and rest. The sun was blinding, and he felt hot and strange. A ferocious ache had settled behind his eyes.

"I'll fetch my horse," Catherine said. "We'll ride back together."

The prospect of mounting a horse and riding to Ramsay House was exhausting. But faced with her ruthless insistence, he had no choice but to comply. Very well. He would ride. He would bloody well ride until he expired, and Catherine would appear at the house with his corpse seated behind her.

Leo sat there fuming and boiling until Catherine brought the horse. The anger gave him the strength for one last massive effort. He swung up behind her, sat the horse, and put his good arm around her slim body. He held on to her, shivering with discomfort. She was small but strong, her spine a steady axis that centered them both. Now all he had to do was endure. His resentment evaporated, dispersed by thrills of pain.

He heard Catherine's voice. "Why have you decided never to marry?"

His head bobbed closer to her ear. "It isn't fair to ask personal questions when I'm nearly delirious. I might tell you the truth."

"Why?" she persisted.

Did she realize she was asking for a piece of him, of his

past, that he never gave to anyone? Had he been feeling even a little less wretched, he would have cut her off at once. But his usual defenses were no more effective than the broken stone wall surrounding the manor-house remains.

"It's because of the girl who died, isn't it?" Catherine stunned him by asking. "You were betrothed. And she perished from the same scarlet fever that afflicted you and Win. What was her name . . . ?"

"Laura Dillard." It seemed impossible that he could share this with Catherine Marks, but she seemed to expect that he would. And somehow he was obliging her. "Beautiful girl. She loved to watercolor. Few people are good at that, they're too afraid of making mistakes. You can't lift the color or hide it, once it's put down. And water is unpredictable—an active partner in the painting—you have to let it behave as it will. Sometimes the color diffuses in ways you don't expect, or one shade backruns into another. That was fine with Laura. She liked the surprises of it. We had known each other all during childhood. I went away for two years to study architecture, and when I came back, we fell in love. So easily. We never argued—there was nothing to argue over. Nothing in our way. My parents had both died the previous year. My father had a heart ailment. He went to sleep one night and never woke up. And my mother followed him just a few months later. She couldn't stop mourning him. I hadn't known until then that some people could die of grief."

He was quiet then, following the memories as if they were leaves and twigs floating on a stream. "When Laura caught the fever, I never thought it would be fatal. I thought I loved her so much that the power of it would be greater than any illness. But I held her for three days and felt her dying a little more each hour. Like water trickling through my fingers. I held her until her heart stopped beating, and her skin finally turned cool. The fever had done its work and left her."

"I'm sorry," she said softly, when he fell silent. She covered his good hand with her own. "Truly sorry. I . . . oh, what an inadequate thing to say."

"It's all right," Leo said. "There are some experiences in life they haven't invented the right words for."

"Yes." Her hand remained over his. "After Laura died," she said in a moment, "you fell ill with the same fever."

"It was a relief."

"Why?"

"Because I wanted to die. Except that Merripen wouldn't let me. It took a long time to forgive him for that. I hated him for keeping me alive. Hated the world for spinning without her. Hated myself for not having the bollocks to end it all. Every night I fell asleep begging Laura to haunt me. I think she did for a while."

"You mean . . . in your mind? Or literally, as a ghost?"

"Both, I suppose. I put myself and everyone around me through hell until I finally accepted that she was gone."

"And you still love her." Catherine's voice was bleak. "That's why you'll never marry."

"No. I have an extraordinary fondness for her memory. But it was a lifetime ago. And I can't ever go through that again. I love like a madman."

"It might not be like that again."

"No, it would be worse. Because I was only a boy then. And now who I am, what I need . . . it's too damned much for anyone to manage." A sardonic laugh rustled in his throat. "I overwhelm even myself, Marks."

Chapter Eight

By the time they reached the timber yard, set a short distance from Ramsay House, Catherine was desperately worried. Leo had become monosyllabic, and he was leaning on her heavily. He was shivering and sweating, his arm a cold weight across her front as he held on to her. A portion of her dress stuck to her shoulder where his blood had soaked it. She saw a blurry group of men preparing to unload a timber wagon. *Please, dear God, let Merripen be among them.*

"Is Mr. Merripen with you?" she called out.

To her vast relief, Merripen's dark, lean form emerged. "Yes, Miss Marks?"

"Lord Ramsay has been injured," she said desperately. "We took a fall—his shoulder was pierced—"

"Take him to the house. I'll meet you there."

Before she could reply, he had already begun to run to the house with smooth, ground-eating speed.

By the time Catherine had guided the horse to the front entrance, Merripen was there.

"There was an accident at the ruins," Catherine said. "A shard of timber has been lodged in his shoulder for at least an hour. He's very cold, and his speech is disoriented."

"That's my usual way of talking," Leo said behind her. "I'm perfectly lucid." He tried to descend from the horse in a kind of slow topple. Reaching up for him, Merripen caught him deftly. He wedged his shoulder beneath Leo's and guided his good arm around his neck. The pain jolted Leo and caused him to grunt. "Oh, you sodding filthy whoreson."

"You are lucid," Merripen said dryly, and he looked at Catherine. "Where is Lord Ramsay's horse?"

"Still at the ruins."

Merripen gave her an assessing glance. "Are you injured, Miss Marks?"

"No, sir."

"Good. Run into the house and find Cam."

Accustomed as the Hathaways were to emergencies, they managed the situation with brisk efficiency. Cam and Merripen helped Leo into the manor and up the stairs, one on either side of him. Although a bachelor's house had been built beside the estate for Leo's use, he had insisted that Merripen and Win live there instead, pointing out that as a fairly recently married couple, they needed the privacy far more than he. When he came to Hampshire, he stayed in one of the guest rooms in the main house.

They formed a fairly harmonious triad, Cam and Merripen and Leo, each with his own area of responsibility. Although Leo was the holder of the estate, he had no objection to sharing authority. Upon returning from France after a two-year absence, Leo had been grateful to see how Cam and Merripen had rebuilt the Ramsay estate in his absence. They had turned the ramshackle property into a thriving and prosperous enterprise, and neither of them had asked for anything in return. And Leo had recognized that he had much to learn from both of them.

Running an estate required far more than lounging in the library with a glass of port, as the aristocrats in novels did.

It took extensive knowledge of agriculture, business, animal husbandry, construction, timber production, and land improvement. All that added to the responsibilities of politics and Parliament was more than one man could undertake. Therefore, Merripen and Leo had agreed to share the timber and agricultural concerns, while Cam handled the estate business and investments.

In medical emergencies, although Merripen was competent in such matters, Cam usually took charge. Having learned the healing arts from his Romany grandmother, Cam was relatively experienced at treating illness and injury. It was better, safer even, to let him do what he could for Leo rather than send for a doctor.

The established practice in modern medicine was for doctors to bleed their patients for every imaginable ailment, despite controversies within the medical community. Statisticians had begun to track case history to prove that bloodletting did no good whatsoever, but the procedure persisted. Sometimes bloodletting was even used to treat hemorrhaging, in accordance with the belief that it was better to do something than nothing at all.

"Amelia," Cam said as he and Merripen settled Leo into his bed, "we'll need cans of hot water sent up from the kitchen, and all the toweling you can spare. And Win, perhaps you and Beatrix might take Miss Marks to her room and help her?"

"Oh, no," Catherine protested, "thank you, but I don't need assistance. I can wash by myself and—"

Her objections were overridden, however. Win and Beatrix would not relent until they had overseen her bath and helped to wash her hair and change her into a fresh gown. The extra pair of spectacles was found, and Catherine was relieved to have her vision restored. Win insisted on tending Catherine's hands and applying salve and bandages to her fingers.

Finally Catherine was allowed to go to Leo's room, while Win and Beatrix went to wait downstairs. She found Amelia, Cam, and Merripen all crowded around the bedside. Leo was shirtless, and heaped with blankets. It shouldn't have surprised her that he was arguing simultaneously with the three of them.

"We don't need his permission," Merripen said to Cam. "I'll pour it down his throat if necessary."

"The hell you will," Leo growled. "I'll kill you if you try—"

"No one is going to force you to take it," Cam interrupted, sounding exasperated. "But you have to explain your reasons, *phral,* because you're not making sense."

"I don't have to explain. You and Merripen can take that filthy stuff and shove it up your—"

"What is it?" Catherine asked from the doorway. "Is there a problem?"

Amelia came out into the hallway, her face taut with worry and vexation. "Yes, the problem is that my brother is a pigheaded idiot," she said, loudly enough for Leo to hear. She turned to Catherine and lowered her voice. "Cam and Merripen say the wound isn't serious, but it could become very bad indeed if they don't clean it properly. The piece of timber slipped in between the clavicle and the shoulder joint, and there's no way of knowing how deep it went. They have to irrigate the wound to remove splinters or clothing fibers, or it will fester. In other words, it's going to be a bloody mess. And Leo refuses to take any laudanum."

Catherine regarded her with bafflement. "But . . . he must have something to dull his senses."

"Yes. But he won't. He keeps telling Cam to go ahead and treat the wound. As if anyone could do such painstaking work when a man is screaming in agony."

"I told you I wouldn't scream," Leo retorted from the bedroom. "I only do that when Marks starts reciting her poetry."

Despite her consternation, Catherine almost smiled.

Peering around the doorjamb, she saw that Leo's coloring was terrible, his sun-browned complexion lightened to an ashy pallor. He was trembling like a wet dog. As his gaze met hers, he looked so defiant and exhausted and miserable that Catherine couldn't stop herself from asking, "A word with you, my lord, if I may?"

"By all means," came his sullen reply. "I would so love to have someone else to argue with."

She entered the room, while Cam and Merripen moved aside. With an apologetic expression, she asked, "If I might have a moment of privacy with Lord Ramsay . . . ?"

Cam gave her a quizzical glance, clearly wondering what influence she thought she could have with Leo. "Do what you can to persuade him to drink that medicine on the bedside table."

"And if that doesn't work," Merripen added, "try a hard knock on the skull with that fireplace poker."

The pair went out into the hallway.

Left alone with Leo, Catherine approached the bedside. She winced at the sight of the stake embedded in his shoulder, the lacerated flesh oozing blood. Since there was no bedside chair to sit on, she perched carefully on the edge of the mattress. She stared at him steadily, her voice soft with concern. "Why won't you take the laudanum?"

"Damn it, Marks . . ." He let out a harsh sigh. "I can't. Believe me, I know what it's going to be like without it, but I have no choice. It's . . ." He stopped and looked away from her, setting his jaw against a new spate of shivering.

"Why?" Catherine wanted so badly to reach him, to understand, that she found herself touching his hand. When no resistance was offered, she became emboldened and slid her bandaged fingers beneath his cold palm. "Tell me," she urged. "Please."

Leo's hand turned and enclosed hers in a careful grip that sent a response through her entire body. The sensation was one of relief, a feeling of something fitting exactly into place. They both stared at their joined hands, warmth collecting in the sphere of palms and fingers.

"After Laura died," she heard him say thickly, "I behaved very badly. Worse than I do now, if you can conceive it. But no matter what I did, nothing gave me the oblivion I needed. One night I went to the East End with a few of my more depraved companions, to an opium den." He paused as he felt Catherine's hand tighten in reaction. "You could smell the smoke all down the alley. The air was brown with it. They took me to a room filled with men and women all lying pell-mell on pallets and pillows, mumbling and dreaming. The way the opium pipes glowed . . . it was like dozens of little red eyes winking in the dark."

"It sounds like a vision of hell," Catherine whispered.

"Yes. And hell was exactly where I wanted to be. Someone brought me a pipe. With the first draw, I felt so much better, I almost wept."

"What does it feel like?" she asked, her hand clutched fast in his.

"In an instant, all is right with the world, and nothing, no matter how dark or painful, can change that. Imagine all the guilt and fear and fury you've ever felt, lifting away like a feather on a breeze."

Perhaps once Catherine would have judged him severely for indulging in such wickedness. But now she felt compassion. She understood the pain that had driven him to such depths.

"But the feeling doesn't last," she murmured.

He shook his head. "No. And when it goes, you're worse off than before. You can't take pleasure in anything. The people you love don't matter. All you can think of is the opium smoke and when you can have it again."

Catherine stared at his partially averted profile. It hardly seemed possible that this was the same man she had scorned and disdained for the past year. Nothing had ever seemed to matter to him—he had seemed utterly shallow and self-indulgent. When in truth, things had mattered far too much. "What made you stop?" she asked gently.

"I reached the point at which the thought of going on was too damned exhausting. I had a pistol in my hand. It was Cam who stopped me. He told me the Rom believe that if you grieve too much, you turn the spirit of the deceased into a ghost. I had to let Laura go, he said. For her sake." Leo looked at her then, his eyes a riveting blue. "And I did. I have. I swore to leave off the opium, and since then I've never touched the filthy stuff. Sweet Christ, Cat, you don't know how hard it was. It took everything I had to turn away. If I went back to it even once . . . I might find myself in the bottom of a pit I could never climb out of. I can't take that chance. I won't."

"Leo . . ." She saw him blink in surprise. It was the first time she had ever used his name. "Take the laudanum," she said. "I won't let you fall. I won't let you turn into a degenerate."

His mouth twisted. "You're offering to take me on as your responsibility."

"Yes."

"I'm too much for you to manage."

"No," Catherine said decisively, "you're not."

He let out a mirthless laugh, followed by a long, curious stare. As if she were someone he ought to know but couldn't quite place.

Catherine could hardly believe that she was perched on the

edge of his bed, holding the hand of a man she had battled so fiercely and for so long. She had never imagined that he would willingly make himself vulnerable to her.

"Trust me," she urged.

"Give me one good reason."

"Because you can."

Leo shook his head slightly, holding her gaze. At first she thought he was refusing her. But it turned out that he was shaking his head in rueful wonder at his own actions. He gestured for the small glass of liquid on the bedside table. "Give it to me," he muttered, "before I have a chance to think better of it." She handed the glass to him, and he downed it in a few efficient gulps. A shudder of revulsion swept through him as he gave the empty glass back to her.

They both waited for the medicine to take effect.

"Your hands . . ." Leo said, reaching for her bandaged fingers. The tip of his thumb brushed gently over the surface of her nails.

"It's nothing," she whispered. "Just a few scrapes."

The blue eyes turned hazy and unfocused, and he closed them. The pained grooves of his face began to relax. "Have I thanked you yet," he asked, "for hauling me out of the ruins?"

"No thanks are necessary."

"All the same . . . thank you." Lifting one of her hands, he cradled her palm against his cheek while his eyes remained closed. "My guardian angel," he said, the words beginning to slur. "I don't think I ever had one until now."

"If you did," she said, "you probably ran too fast for her to keep up with you."

He made a quiet sound of amusement.

The feel of his shaven cheek beneath her hand filled her with astonishing tenderness. She had to remind herself that the opium was exerting its influence on him. This feeling between them wasn't real. But it seemed as if something new were emerging from the wreckage of their former conflict. A thrill of intimacy went through her as she felt the ripple of his swallow in the space beneath his jaw.

They stayed like that until a noise from the doorway caused Catherine to start.

Cam entered the room, glanced at the empty glass, and gave Catherine an approving nod. "Well done," he said. "This will make it easer on Ramsay. And more importantly, on me."

"Bugger you," Leo replied mildly, slitting his eyes open as Cam and Merripen went to the bedside. Amelia followed with an armload of clean rags and toweling. Reluctantly, Catherine pulled away from Leo and retreated to the doorway.

Cam looked down at his brother-in-law with a mixture of concern and affection. The abundant sunlight from the window slid over the shiny black layers of his hair. "I can take care of this, *phral*. But we could send for a *gadjo* doctor if you prefer."

"God, no. Anything he did would be far worse than your blundering. And he'd start with his damned jar of leeches."

"No leeches here," Cam replied as he eased the pillows from behind Leo's back. "I'm terrified of them."

"Are you?" Amelia asked. "I didn't know that."

Cam helped Leo to lower to the mattress. "When I was a boy still living with the tribe, I went wading in a spring-fed pond with a few of the other children. We all came out with leeches attached to our legs. I would say I screamed like a girl, except the girls were much quieter."

"Poor Cam," Amelia said, smiling.

"Poor Cam?" Leo echoed, sounding indignant. "What about me?"

"I'm reluctant to give you too much sympathy," Amelia replied, "in light of my suspicion that you've only done this to get out of the turnip planting."

Leo replied with two choice words that made her grin.

Pulling the bed linens to her brother's waist, Amelia carefully tucked towels beneath his injured shoulder and side. The sight of his lean, smoothly muscled torso—and that intriguing dusting of hair on his chest—caused Catherine's stomach to dive in an odd little swoop. She retreated farther behind the door, not wanting to leave and yet knowing it was improper for her to stay.

Cam dropped a kiss atop his wife's head and nudged her away from the bed. "Wait over there, *monisha*—we need room to work." He turned to the nearby tray of supplies.

Catherine blanched as she heard the rattle of knives and metal implements.

"Aren't you going to sacrifice a goat or perform a tribal dance?" Leo asked woozily. "Or at least chant something?"

"We did all that downstairs," Cam said. He handed a piece of leather strap to Leo. "Put this between your teeth. And try not to make too much noise while we're working on you. My son is napping."

"Before I put this in my mouth," Leo said, "you might tell me the last place it's been." He paused. "On second thought . . . never mind. I don't want to know." He put the strap between his teeth, then removed it temporarily to add, "I'd rather you didn't amputate anything."

"If we do," Merripen said, swabbing carefully around the injured shoulder, "it won't be intentional."

"Ready, *phral*?" she heard Cam ask gently. "Hold him still, Merripen. All right. On the count of three."

Amelia joined Catherine in the hallway, her face tense. She wrapped her arms around her middle.

They heard Leo's low groan, followed by a voluble flow

of Romany between Cam and Merripen. The foreign language was brisk but soothing.

It was clear that despite the effects of the opium, the procedure was difficult to endure. Every time Catherine heard a grunt or pained sound coming from Leo, she tensed all over and knotted her torn fingers together.

After two or three minutes had passed, Amelia looked around the doorway. "Did it splinter?" she asked.

"Only a little, *monisha*," came Cam's reply. "It could have been much worse, but—" He paused at a muffled sound from Leo. "Sorry, *phral*. Merripen, take the tweezers and—yes, that part right there."

Amelia's face was pale as she turned back to Catherine. And she astonished her by reaching out and drawing her close in the same way she might have hugged Win, Poppy, or Beatrix. Catherine stiffened a little, not in aversion but awkwardness. "I'm so glad you weren't harmed, Catherine," Amelia said. "Thank you for taking care of Lord Ramsay."

Catherine nodded slightly.

Drawing back, Amelia smiled at her. "He'll be fine, you know. He has more lives than a cat."

"I hope so," Catherine said soberly. "I hope this isn't a result of the Ramsay curse."

"I don't believe in curses, or spells, or anything of the sort. The only curse my brother faces is self-imposed."

"You . . . you mean because of his grief over Laura Dillard?"

Amelia's blue eyes turned round. "He talked to you about her?"

Catherine nodded.

Amelia seemed caught off guard. Taking Catherine's arm, she drew her further along the hallway, where there was less risk of being overheard. "What did he say?"

"That she liked to watercolor," Catherine replied hesitantly.

"That they were betrothed, and then she caught the scarlet fever, and died in his arms. And that . . . she haunted him for a time. Literally. But that couldn't be true . . . could it?"

Amelia was silent for a good half minute. "I think it might be," she said with remarkable calmness. "I wouldn't admit that to many people—it makes me sound like a lunatic." A wry smile crossed her lips. "However, you've lived with the Hathaways long enough to know of a certainty that we are indeed a pack of lunatics." She paused. "Catherine."

"Yes?"

"My brother never discusses Laura Dillard with anyone. *Ever.*"

Catherine blinked. "He was in pain. He'd lost blood."

"I don't think that is why he confided in you."

"What other reason could there have been?" Catherine asked with difficulty.

It must have shown in her face, how much she dreaded the answer.

Amelia stared at her closely, and then shrugged with a rueful smile. "I've already said too much. Forgive me. It's only that I desire my brother's happiness so greatly." She paused before adding sincerely, "And yours."

"I assure you, ma'am, one has nothing to do with the other."

"Of course," Amelia murmured, and went back to the doorway to wait.

Chapter Nine

After the wound had been cleaned and bandaged, Leo was left gray-faced and exhausted. He slept for the rest of the day, waking occasionally to find broth or fever tea being poured down his throat. The family was merciless in their efforts to take care of him.

As he had expected, the opiate sent him into nightmares, filled with creatures rising from the earth to claw and pull at him, tugging him down below the surface where red glowing eyes blinked at him in the dark. Trapped in a narcotic daze, Leo couldn't fully awaken from the dreams, only struggled in the heat and misery, and subsided into more hallucinations. The only respite was when a cool cloth was applied to his forehead, and a gentle, comforting presence hovered beside him.

"Amelia? Win?" he mumbled in confusion.

"Shhhh . . ."

"Hot," he said with an aching sigh.

"Lie still."

He was vaguely aware of two or three other times when the cloth was changed . . . merciful coolness applied to his brow . . . a light hand curving against his cheek.

When he awoke in the morning, he was tired, feverish, and in the grip of a profound gloom. It was the usual aftermath of opium, of course, but the knowledge hardly helped to alleviate the overwhelming dreariness.

"You have a mild fever," Cam told him in the morning. "You'll need to drink more yarrow tea to bring it down. But there's no sign of festering. Rest today, and I expect you'll feel much better by tomorrow."

"That tea tastes like ditch water," Leo muttered. "And I'm not going to stay in bed all day."

Cam looked sympathetic. "I understand, *phral*. You don't feel ill enough to rest, but you're not well enough to do anything. All the same, you have to give yourself a chance to heal, or—"

"I'm going downstairs for a proper breakfast."

"Breakfast is done. They've already cleared the sideboard."

Leo scowled and rubbed his face, wincing at the fiery pull of his shoulder. "Have Merripen come up here. I want to talk to him."

"He is out with the tenants, drilling turnip seed."

"Where is Amelia?"

"Taking care of the baby. He's teething."

"What about Win?"

"She's with the housekeeper, taking inventory and ordering supplies. Beatrix is carrying baskets to elderly cottagers in town. And I have to visit a tenant who's two months lacking in his rent. I'm afraid there is no one available to entertain you."

Leo greeted this statement with surly silence. And then he brought himself to ask for the person he truly wanted. The person who hadn't bothered to look in on him or ask after his welfare even after she'd promised to safeguard him. "Where's Marks?"

"The last time I saw her, she was busy with needlework. It seems the mending has piled up, and—"

"She can do it here."

Cam's face was carefully blank. "You want Miss Marks to do the mending in your room?"

"Yes, send her up here."

"I'll ask if she's willing," Cam said, looking doubtful.

After Leo had washed and dragged on a dressing robe, he went back to bed. He was sore and infuriatingly unsteady. A housemaid brought a small tray with a solitary piece of toast and a cup of tea. Leo ate his breakfast while staring morosely at the empty doorway.

Where was Marks? Had Cam even bothered to tell her that she was wanted? If so, she had evidently decided to ignore the summons.

Callous, coldhearted harpy. And this after she had promised to be responsible for him. She had persuaded him to take the laudanum, and then she had deserted him.

Well, Leo didn't want her now. If she decided to appear after all, he would send her away. He would laugh scornfully and tell her that no company at all was better than having her there. He would—

"My lord?"

His heart gave a leap as he saw her at the doorway, dressed in a dark blue gown, her light golden hair caught up and pinned in its usual stern confinement.

She held a book in one hand and a glass of pale liquid in the other. "How are you this morning?"

"Bored out of my wits," Leo said with a scowl. "Why did you take so long to see me?"

"I thought you were still asleep." Entering the room, Catherine left the door wide open. The long, furry form of Dodger the ferret came loping in after her. After standing tall to view his surroundings, Dodger scurried beneath the dresser. Catherine watched the ferret suspiciously. "Probably one of his new hiding places," she said, and sighed. She brought Leo a glass of cloudy liquid, and gave it to him. "Drink this, please."

"What is it?"

"Willowbark, for your fever. I stirred in some lemon and sugar to improve the flavor."

Leo drank the bitter brew, watching as Catherine moved about the room. She opened a second window to admit more of the outside breeze. Taking his breakfast tray out to the hallway, she gave it to a passing housemaid. When she returned to Leo, she laid her fingers on his forehead to test his temperature.

Leo caught her wrist, staying the motion. He stared at her in dawning recognition. "It was you," he said. "You came to me last night."

"I beg your pardon?"

"You changed the cloth on my forehead. More than once."

Catherine's fingers curled lightly around his. Her voice was very soft. "As if I would enter a man's bedroom in the middle of the night."

But they both knew she had. The weight of melancholy lifted considerably, especially as Leo saw the concern in her eyes.

"How are your hands?" he asked, turning her scraped fingers to inspect them.

"Healing nicely, thank you." She paused. "I am told you require companionship?"

"Yes," he said promptly. "I'll make do with you."

Her lips curved. "Very well."

Leo wanted to pull her against him and inhale her scent. She smelled light and clean, like tea and talcum and lavender.

"Shall I read to you?" she asked. "I brought a novel. Do you like Balzac?"

The day was improving rapidly. "Who doesn't?"

Catherine occupied the chair by the bedside. "He meanders a bit too much for my taste. I prefer novels with more plot."

"But with Balzac," Leo said, "you have to give yourself over fully. You have to wallow and roll in the language . . ." Pausing, he looked more closely at her small oval face. She was pale, and there were shadows beneath her eyes, no doubt as a result of having visited him so many times in the night. "You look tired," he said bluntly. "On my account. Forgive me."

"Oh, not at all, it wasn't you. I had nightmares."

"What about?"

Her expression turned guarded. Forbidden territory. And yet Leo couldn't help pressing. "Are the nightmares about your past? About whatever situation it was that Rutledge found you in?"

Drawing in a sharp breath, Catherine stood, looking stunned and slightly ill. "Perhaps I should go."

"No," Leo said quickly, making a staying gesture with his hand. "Don't leave. I need company—I'm still suffering the aftereffects of the laudanum that *you* convinced me to take." Seeing her continuing hesitation, he added, "And I have a fever."

"A mild one."

"Hang it, Marks, you're a companion," he said with a scowl. "Do your job, will you?"

She looked indignant for a moment, and then a laugh burst out despite her efforts to hold it in. "I'm Beatrix's companion," she said. "Not yours."

"Today you're mine. Sit and start reading."

To Leo's surprise, the masterful approach actually worked. Catherine resumed her seat and opened the book to the first page. She used the tip of a forefinger to push her spectacles into place—a meticulous little gesture that he adored. "*Un Homme d'Affaires,*" she read. "*A Man of Business.* Chapter one."

"Wait."

Catherine glanced at him expectantly.

Leo chose his words with care. "Is there *any* part of your past that you would be willing to discuss?"

"For what purpose?"

"I'm curious about you."

"I don't like to talk about myself."

"You see, that's proof of how interesting you are. There's nothing more tedious than people who like to talk about themselves. I'm a perfect example."

She looked down at the book as if she were trying very hard to concentrate on the page. But after just a few seconds, she looked up with a grin that seemed to dissolve his spine. "You are many things, my lord. But tedious is not one of them."

As Leo gazed at her, he felt the same inexplicable flourish of warmth, of happiness, that he'd experienced yesterday, before their mishap at the ruins.

"What would you like to know?" Catherine asked.

"When did you first learn that you needed spectacles?"

"I was five or six. My parents and I lived in Holborn, in a tenement at Portpool Lane. Since girls couldn't go to school at the time, a local woman tried to teach a few of us. She told my mother that I was very good at memorization, but I was slow-witted when it came to reading and writing. One day my mother sent me on an errand to fetch a parcel from the butcher. It was only two streets away, but I got lost. Everything was a blur. I was found wandering and crying a few streets away, until finally someone led me to the butcher's shop." A smile curved her lips. "What a kind man he was. When I told him I didn't think I could find my way home, he said he had an idea. And he had me try on his wife's spectacles. I couldn't believe how the world looked. Magical. I could see the pattern of bricks on walls, and birds in the air, and even the weave of the butcher's apron. That was my problem, he said. I just hadn't been able to see. And ever since then I've worn spectacles."

"Were your parents relieved to discover their daughter wasn't slow-witted after all?"

"Quite the opposite. They argued for days about which side of the family my weak eyes had come from. My mother was quite distressed, as she said spectacles would mar my appearance."

"What rot."

She looked rueful. "My mother did not possess what one would call a great depth of character."

"In light of her actions—abandoning a husband and son, running to England with her lover—I wouldn't have expected a surfeit of principles."

"I thought they were married, when I was a child," she said.

"Was there love between them?"

Considering that, she chewed her lower lip, drawing his attention to the enticing softness of her mouth. "They were attracted to each other in a physical sense," she admitted. "But that's not love, is it?"

"No," he said softly. "What happened to your father?"

"I'd rather not discuss that."

"After all I've confided in you?" He gave her a chiding glance. "Be fair, Marks. It can't be any more difficult for you than it was for me."

"All right." Catherine took a deep breath. "When my mother fell ill, my father felt it as a great burden. He paid a woman to look after her until the end, and sent me away to live with my aunt and grandmother, and I never heard from him again. He may be dead, for all I know."

"I'm sorry," Leo said. And he was. Genuinely sorry, wishing he could somehow have gone back in time to comfort a small girl in spectacles, who had been abandoned by the man who should have protected her. "Not all men are like that," he felt the need to point out.

"I know. It would hardly be fair of me to blame the entire male population for my father's sins."

Leo became uncomfortably aware that his own behavior hadn't been any better than her father's, that he had indulged in his own bitter grief to the point of abandoning his sisters. "No wonder you've always hated me," he said. "I must remind you of him. I deserted my sisters when they needed me."

Catherine gave him a clear-eyed stare, not pitying, not censorious, just . . . appraising. "No," she said sincerely. "You're not at all like him. You came back to your family. You've worked for them, cared for them. And I've never hated you."

Leo stared at her closely, more than a little surprised by the revelation. "You haven't?"

"No. In fact—" She broke off abruptly.

"In fact?" Leo prompted. "What were you going to say?"

"Nothing."

"You were. Something along the lines of liking me against your will."

"Certainly not," Catherine said primly, but Leo saw the twitch of a smile at her lips.

"Irresistibly attracted by my dashing good looks?" he suggested. "My fascinating conversation?"

"No, and no."

"Seduced by my brooding glances?" He accompanied this with a waggish swerving of his brows that finally reduced her to laughter.

"Yes, it must have been those."

Settling back against the pillows, Leo regarded her with satisfaction.

What a wonderful laugh she had, light and throaty, as if she had been drinking champagne.

And what a problem this could become, this madly inappropriate desire for her. She was becoming real to him, dimensional, vulnerable in ways he had never imagined.

As Catherine read aloud, the ferret emerged from beneath the dresser and climbed onto her lap. He fell asleep in an upside-down circle, his mouth open. Leo didn't blame Dodger in the slightest. Catherine's lap looked like a lovely place to rest one's head.

Leo feigned interest in the complex and detailed narrative, while his mind occupied itself with the question of what she would look like naked. It seemed tragic that he would never see her so. But even by Leo's dilapidated code of ethics, a man did not take a virgin unless he had serious intentions. He had tried it once, letting himself fall madly in love, nearly losing everything as a result.

And there were some risks a man couldn't take twice.

Chapter Ten

It was past midnight. Catherine woke to the sound of a baby's whimpering. Little Rye was teething, and the usually sweet-natured cherub had been fretful of late.

Catherine stared sightlessly in the darkness, kicked the bed linens away from her legs, and tried to find a more comfortable position in which to sleep. Her side. Her stomach. Nothing felt right.

After a few minutes, the baby's crying stopped. No doubt he was being soothed by his attentive mother.

But Catherine was left awake. Lonely, aching. The worst kind of awake.

She tried to occupy herself with old Celtic sheep-counting words, still used by rural farmers in place of modern numbers . . . *yan, tan, tethera, pethera* . . . One could hear the echo of centuries in the ancient syllables. *Sethera, methera, hovera, covera* . . .

Her mind summoned an image of singular blue eyes, striated light and dark, like strips of sky and ocean. Leo had watched her while she had read to him, and while she had done the mending. And underneath their banter, and his relaxed façade, she had known that he wanted her. *Yan, tan, tethera* . . .

Perhaps Leo was awake at this very moment. His fever had dissipated earlier in the evening, but it might have rekindled. He might need water. A cool cloth.

Catherine left the bed and snatched up her dressing robe before she could think twice. Finding her spectacles on the dressing table, she placed them precisely on her nose.

Her bare feet crossed the wood floors of the hallway as she went on her charitable mission.

The door to his room was partially open. She slipped in without a sound, like a thief, tiptoeing to the bed just as she had the previous night. The darkness of the room was penetrated by a few runnels of light from the open window, as if the shadows were a sieve. She could hear the soft and steady flow of Leo's breathing.

Making her way to his side, Catherine reached out tentatively, her heartbeat thickening as she laid her fingers on his forehead. No fever. Only smooth, healthy warmth.

Leo's breathing fractured as he awakened. "Cat?" His voice was sleep-thickened. "What are you doing?"

She shouldn't have gone to him. Any excuse she gave would sound false and ridiculous, because there was no rational reason to have bothered him.

Awkwardly she mumbled, "I . . . I came to see if . . ." Her voice died away.

She began to draw back but he caught her wrist with remarkable dexterity, considering that it was night and he was barely awake. They both went still as she was caught poised over him, her wrist imprisoned in his grip.

Leo exerted tension on her arm, forcing her to lean farther over him, farther, until her balance was compromised and she fell on him in a slow topple. Terrified of hurting him, she scrabbled to brace her hands on the mattress, and he used every movement to lever her more fully onto his body. She started as she encountered bare flesh tightly knit with muscle, his chest covered with a soft, crisp fleece.

"My lord," she whispered, "I didn't—"

His long hand curved around the back of her head, and he brought her mouth down to his.

It wasn't a kiss, it was a possession. He took her fully, the heat of his tongue thrusting inside her, draining her of volition and thought. The masculine incense of his skin filled her nostrils. Erotic. Delicious. Too many sensations to take in at once . . . the hot silk of his mouth, the assured grip of his hands, the hard masculine contours of his body.

The world revolved slowly as Leo turned with her in his arms, half pinning her to the bed. His kisses were rough and sweet, kisses involving lips and teeth and tongue. Gasping, she reached around his neck and bandaged shoulder. He moved over her, big and dark, kissing her as if he wanted to devour her.

The folds of her dressing gown listed open, the hem of her nightgown rising to her knees. Leo's mouth broke from hers to begin a luscious search of her throat, following tender nerve paths down to the place where her neck and shoulder met. His fingers worked at the front of her nightgown, unmooring tiny buttons, spreading the thin fabric.

His head lowered, his lips slowly ascending the trembling slope of her breast until he reached the tip. Taking her into his mouth, he warmed the cool bud with lambent strokes of his tongue. Ragged moans rose in her throat, mingling with the gusts of his breath. Leo settled more heavily between her thighs, giving her his weight until she felt the hard length of him press her intimately. He sought her other breast, closing his mouth over the peak and tugging wetly, creating waves of involuting pleasure.

With every movement, more sensation was uncovered, the soft edges of arousal wearing away to exquisite rawness. Leo took her mouth with long, drugging kisses, while lower down he had begun a subtle rhythm, nudging and sliding, using himself to arouse her. She twisted beneath him, desperately trying to follow that teasing hardness. Their bodies pressed together like the pages of a closed book, and it felt so right, so wildly pleasurable, that it frightened her.

"No," she gasped, pushing at him. "Wait. Please—"

One of her hands pressed heedlessly against his injured shoulder, and Leo rolled off her with a curse.

"My lord?" She scrambled from the bed and stood there, shaking in every limb. "I'm sorry. Did I hurt you? What can I—"

"Go."

"Yes, but—"

"*Now*, Marks." His voice was low and guttural. "Or else come back to bed, and let me finish."

She fled.

Chapter Eleven

After a wretched night, Catherine fumbled for her spectacles and realized she had lost them sometime during her visit to Leo's room. Groaning, she sat at her dressing table and buried her face in her hands.

A stupid impulse, she thought dully. A moment of madness. She should never have given in to it.

There was no one to blame but herself.

What remarkable ammunition she had given to Leo. He would torture her with this. He would take every opportunity to humiliate her. She knew him well enough not to doubt it.

Catherine's ill humor was not helped by the appearance of Dodger, who emerged from the slipper box by her bed. The ferret pushed the lid open with his head, clucked in cheerful greeting, and tugged her slipper out of the box. Heaven knew where he intended to take it.

"Stop that, Dodger," she said wearily, laying her head on her arms as she watched him.

Everything was blurry. She needed her spectacles. And it was awfully difficult to go looking for something when you couldn't see more than two feet in front of your face. Moreover, if one of the housemaids found the spectacles in

Leo's room, or God help her, in his bed, everyone would find out.

Abandoning the slipper, Dodger trotted to her and stood tall, bracing his long, slender body against her knee. He was shivering, which Beatrix had told her was normal for ferrets. A ferret's temperature lowered when he was sleeping, and shivering was his way of warming himself upon awakening. Catherine reached down to stroke him. When he tried to climb into her lap, however, she nudged him away. "I don't feel well," she told the ferret woefully, although there was nothing wrong with her physically.

Chattering in annoyance at her rejection, Dodger turned and streaked out of the room.

Catherine continued to lie with her head on the table, feeling too dreary and ashamed to move.

She had slept late. She could hear the sounds of footsteps and muffled conversation coming from the lower floors. Had Leo gone down to breakfast?

She couldn't possibly face him.

Her mind returned to those blistering minutes of the previous night. A fresh swell of desire rolled through her as she thought of the way he had kissed her, the feel of his mouth on the intimate places of her body.

She heard the ferret come back into the room again, chuckling and hopping as he did whenever he was especially pleased about something. "Go away, Dodger," she said dully.

But he persisted, coming to her side and standing tall again, his body a long cylinder. Glancing at him, Catherine saw that something was clamped carefully in his front teeth. She blinked. Slowly she reached down and took the object from him.

Her spectacles.

Amazing, how much better a small gesture of kindness could make one feel.

"Thank you," she whispered, tears coming to her eyes as she stroked his tiny head. "I do love you, you disgusting weasel."

Climbing onto her lap, Dodger flipped upside down and sighed.

CATHERINE DRESSED WITH PAINSTAKING CARE, PUTTING extra pins in her hair, tying the sash of her gray dress a bit tighter than usual, even double-knotting the laces of her sensible ankle boots. As if she could contain herself so thoroughly that nothing could stray loose. Not even her thoughts.

Entering the breakfast room, she saw Amelia at the table. She was feeding toast to baby Rye, who was gumming it and drooling copiously.

"Good morning," Catherine murmured, going to pour a cup of tea at the samovar. "Poor little Rye . . . I heard him cry in the night. The new tooth hasn't come yet?"

"Not yet," Amelia said ruefully. "I'm sorry he disturbed your sleep, Catherine."

"Oh, he didn't bother me. I was already awake. It was a restless night."

"It must have been for Lord Ramsay as well," Amelia remarked.

Catherine glanced at her quickly, but thankfully there seemed to be no arch meaning in the comment. She tried to keep her expression neutral. "Oh? I hope he is well this morning."

"He seems well enough, but he's unusually quiet. Preoccupied." Amelia made a face. "I suppose it didn't improve his disposition when I told him that we are planning to hold the ball in one month's time."

Stirring sugar into her tea with great care, Catherine asked, "Will you tell people that the event is for the purpose of finding a bride for Lord Ramsay?"

Amelia grinned. "No, even I am not that indelicate.

However, it will be obvious that a great many eligible young women have been invited. And of course, my brother is a prime matrimonial target."

"I'm sure I don't know why," Catherine muttered, trying to sound offhand, when inside she was filled with despair.

She realized she would not be able to stay with the Hathaway family if or when Leo married. She literally wouldn't be able to bear the sight of him with another woman. Especially if she made him happy.

"Oh, it's simple," Amelia said impishly. "Lord Ramsay is a peer with a full head of hair and all his teeth, and he is still in his procreating years. And if he weren't my brother, I suppose I would consider him not bad-looking."

"He's very handsome," Catherine protested without thinking, and flushed as Amelia gave her an astute glance.

She applied herself to drinking her tea, nibbled at a breakfast roll, and left in search of Beatrix. It was time for their morning studies.

Catherine and Beatrix had settled on a pattern, beginning their lessons with a few minutes on etiquette and social graces, and then spending the rest of the morning on subjects such as history, philosophy, even science. Beatrix had long mastered the "fashionable" subjects that were taught to young ladies merely for the purpose of making them suitable wives and mothers. Now Catherine felt that she and Beatrix had become fellow students.

Although Catherine had never had the privilege of meeting the Hathaway parents, she thought that both of them, particularly Mr. Hathaway, would have been pleased by their children's accomplishments. The Hathaways were an intellectual family, all of them easily able to discuss a subject or issue on an abstract level. And there was something else they shared—an ability to make imaginative leaps and connections between disparate subjects.

One evening, for example, the discussion at dinner had centered on news of an aerial steam carriage that had been designed by a Somerset bobbin maker named John Stringfellow. It didn't work, of couse, but the idea was fascinating. During the debate about whether or not man might ever be able to fly in a mechanical invention, the Hathaways had brought up Greek mythology, physics, Chinese kites, the animal kingdom, French philosophy, and the inventions of Leonardo da Vinci. Trying to follow the discussion had very nearly been dizzying.

Privately Catherine had worried about whether such conversational pyrotechnics would put off potential suitors for Poppy and Beatrix. And in the case of Poppy, it had indeed turned out to be problematic. At least until she had met Harry.

However, when Catherine had tried to delicately raise the issue with Cam Rohan early on in her employment, he had been very decided in his reply.

"No, Miss Marks, don't try to change Poppy or Beatrix," Cam had told her. "It wouldn't work, and it would only make them unhappy. Just help them learn how to behave in society, and how to talk about nothing, as the *gadjos* do."

"In other words," Catherine had said wryly, "you want them to have the appearance of propriety, but you don't wish for them to actually *become* proper?"

Cam had been delighted by her understanding. "Exactly."

Catherine understood now how right Cam had been. None of the Hathaways would ever be like the denizens of London society, nor would she want them to be.

She went to the library to procure some books for her studies with Beatrix. As she entered the room, however, she stopped with a gasp as she saw Leo leaning over the long library table, writing something on a set of spread-out drawings.

Leo turned his head to glance at her, his eyes piercing. She went hot and cold. Her skull throbbed in the places where she had pinned her hair too tightly.

"Good morning," she said breathlessly, falling back a step. "I didn't mean to intrude."

"You're not intruding."

"I came to fetch some books, if . . . if I may."

Leo gave her a single nod and returned his attention to the drawings.

Acutely self-conscious, Catherine went to the bookshelves and hunted for the titles she had wanted. It was so quiet that she thought the pounding of her heart must have been audible. Needing desperately to break the pressing silence, she asked, "Are you designing something for the estate? A tenant house?"

"Addition for the stables."

"Oh."

Catherine gazed sightlessly along the rows of books. Were they going to pretend that the events of the previous night had never happened? She certainly hoped so.

But then she heard Leo say, "If you want an apology, you're not going to get one."

Catherine turned to face him. "I beg your pardon?"

Leo was still contemplating the set of elevations. "When you visit a man in his bed at night, don't expect tea and conversation."

"I wasn't visiting you in your bed," she said defensively. "That is, you were in your bed, but it was not my desire to find you there." Aware that she was making no sense at all, she resisted the urge to smack herself on the head.

"At two o'clock in the morning," Leo informed her, "I can nearly always be found on a mattress, engaged in either of two activities. One is sleeping. I don't believe I need to elaborate on the other."

"I only wanted to see if you were feverish," she said, turning crimson. "If you needed anything."

"Apparently I did."

Catherine had never felt so extraordinarily uncomfortable. All her skin had become too tight for her body. "Are you going to tell anyone?" she brought herself to ask.

One of his brows arched mockingly. "You fear I'm going to tattle about our nighttime rendezvous? No, Marks, I have nothing to gain from that. And much to my regret, we didn't do nearly enough to warrant decent gossip."

Blushing, Catherine went to a pile of sketches and scraps at the corner of the table. She straightened them into a neat stack. "Did I hurt you?" she managed to ask, recalling how she had inadvertently pushed on his wounded shoulder. "Does it ache this morning?"

Leo hesitated before replying. "No, it eventually eased after you left. But the devil knows it wouldn't take much to start up again."

Catherine was overcome with remorse. "I'm so sorry. Should we put a poultice on it?"

"A poultice?" he repeated blankly. "On my . . . *oh*. We're talking about my shoulder?"

She blinked in confusion. "Of course we're talking about your shoulder. What else would we be discussing?"

"Cat . . ." Leo looked away from her. To her surprise, there was a tremor of laughter in his voice. "When a man is aroused and left unsatisfied, he usually aches for a while afterward."

"Where?"

He gave her a speaking glance.

"You mean . . ." A wild blush raced over her as she finally understood. "Well, I don't care if you ache *there*, I was only concerned about your wound!"

"It's much better," Leo assured her, his eyes bright with amusement. "As for the other ache—"

"That has nothing to do with me," she said hastily.

"I beg to differ."

Catherine's dignity had been mowed down to nothing. Clearly there was no option but retreat. "I'm leaving now."

"What about the books you wanted?"

"I'll fetch them later."

As she turned to depart, however, the edge of her bell-shaped sleeve caught the stack of sketches she had just straightened, and they went spilling to the floor. "Oh, dear." Instantly she went to her hands and knees, gathering up papers.

"Leave them," she heard Leo say. "I'll do it."

"No, I'm the one who—"

Catherine broke off as she saw something among the drafts of structures and landscapes and the pages of notes. A pencil sketch of a woman . . . a naked woman reclining on her side, light hair flowing everywhere. One slender thigh rested coyly over the other, partially concealing the delicate shadow of a feminine triangle.

And there was an all-too-familiar pair of spectacles balanced on her nose.

Catherine picked up the sketch with a trembling hand, while her heart lurched in hard strikes against her ribs. It took several attempts before she could speak, her voice high and airless.

"That's me."

Leo had lowered to the carpeted floor beside her. He nodded, looking rueful. His own color heightened until his eyes were startlingly blue in contrast.

"Why?" she whispered.

"It wasn't meant to be demeaning," he said. "It was for my own eyes, no one else's."

She forced herself to look at the sketch again, feeling horribly exposed. In fact, she couldn't have been more embarrassed had he actually been viewing her naked. And yet the rendering was far from crude or debasing. The woman had been drawn with long, graceful lines, the pose artistic. Sensuous.

"You . . . you've never seen me like this," she managed to say, before adding weakly, "Have you?"

A self-deprecating smile touched his lips. "No, I haven't yet descended to voyeurism." He paused. "Did I get it right? It's not easy, guessing what you look like beneath all those layers."

A nervous giggle struggled through her mortification. "If you did, I certainly wouldn't admit it." She put the sketch onto the pile, facedown. Her hand was shaking. "Do you draw other women this way?" she asked timidly.

Leo shook his head. "I started with you, and so far I haven't moved on."

Her flush deepened. "You've done other sketches like this? Of me unclothed?"

"One or two." He tried to look repentant.

"Oh, please, *please* destroy them."

"Certainly. But honesty compels me to tell you that I'll probably only do more. It's my favorite hobby, drawing you naked."

Catherine moaned and buried her face in her hands. Her voice slipped out between the tense filter of her fingers. "I wish you would take up collecting something instead."

She heard his husky laugh. "Cat. Darling. Can you bring yourself to look at me? No?" She stiffened but didn't move as she felt his arms draw around her. "I was only teasing. I won't sketch you like that again." Leo continued to hold her, carefully guiding her face to his good shoulder. "Are you angry?"

She shook her head.

"Afraid?"

"No." She drew a trembling breath. "Only surprised that you would see me that way."

"Why?"

"Because it's not like me."

He understood what she meant. "No one ever sees himself—or herself—with perfect accuracy."

"I'm certain that I never lounge about completely naked!"

"That," he said, "is a terrible shame." He took a ragged breath. "You should know that I've always wanted you, Cat. I've had fantasies so wicked, it would send us both straight to hell if I told them to you. And the way I want you has nothing to do with the color of your hair, or the appalling fashions you wear." His hand passed gently over her head. "Catherine Marks, or whoever you are . . . I have the most profane desire to be in bed with you for . . . oh, weeks, at least . . . committing every mortal sin known to man. I'd like to do more than sketch you naked. I want to draw directly on you with feather and ink . . . flowers around your breasts, trails of stars down your thighs." He let his warm lips brush the edge of her ear. "I want to map your body, chart the north, south, east, and west of you. I would—"

"Don't," she said, scarcely able to breathe.

A rueful laugh escaped him. "I told you. Straight to hell."

"This is my fault." She pressed her hot face against his shoulder. "I shouldn't have gone to you last night. I don't know why I did it."

"I think you do." His mouth grazed the top of her head. "Don't come back to my room at night, Marks. Because if it happens again, I won't be able to stop."

His arms loosened, and he released her to stand up from the floor. Reaching for her hand, he pulled her up with him. The sheaf of fallen papers was retrieved, and Leo took up the sketch of her. The parchment was neatly ripped, the pieces folded together, and ripped again. He gave her the shreds of paper and molded her fingers around them. "I'll destroy the others as well."

Catherine stood without moving as he left the room. And her fingers tightened over the strips of parchment, crushing them into a damp knot.

Chapter Twelve

In the month that followed, Leo deliberately kept himself too busy to see much of Catherine. Two new tenant farms required irrigation schemes. It was a subject on which Leo had developed a certain amount of expertise while Cam worked with the horses and Merripen supervised the timber harvesting. Leo had designed water meadows that would be irrigated with rills and ditches leading from the nearby rivers. In one place where the channel would run too low to be let out naturally, they would require a waterwheel. The wheel, provided with buckets, would lift out the necessary amount of water and send it along a manmade canal.

Shirtless and sweating under the soft blaze of the Hampshire sun, Leo and the tenants dug ditches and drainage canals, moved rock, and hauled soil. At the end of the day Leo ached in every muscle, nearly too tired to stay awake during dinner. His body toughened and became so lean that he was obliged to borrow trousers from Cam while the village tailor altered his clothes.

"At least work keeps you from your vices," Win quipped one evening before supper, rubbing his hair affectionately as she joined him in the parlor.

"I happen to like my vices," Leo told her. "That's why I went to the trouble of acquiring them."

"What you need to acquire," Win said gently, "is a wife. And I'm not saying that out of self-interest, Leo."

He smiled at her, this gentlest of sisters, who had fought so many personal battles for the sake of love. "You don't possess a molecule of self-interest, Win. But as sound as your advice usually is, I'm not going to take it."

"You should. You need a family of your own."

"I have more than enough family to contend with. And there are things I would much rather do than marry."

"Such as?"

"Oh, cut out my tongue and join the Trappist Monks . . . roll naked in treacle and nap on an anthill . . . Shall I go on?"

"That won't be necessary," Win said, smiling. "However, you *will* marry someday, Leo. Both Cam and Merripen have said that you have a very distinct marriage line on your hand."

Bemused, Leo looked down at his palm. "That's a crease from the way I hold my pen."

"It's a marriage line. And it's so long, it practically wraps around both sides of your hand. Which means you will someday marry a fated love." Win raised her fair brows significantly, as if to say, *What do you think of that?*

"Romas don't really believe in palm reading," Leo informed her. "It's nonsense. They only do it to extract money from fools and drunkards."

Before Win could reply, Merripen entered the parlor. "*Gadjos* certainly know how to complicate matters," he said, handing a letter to Leo and lowering to the settee.

"What is this?" Leo asked, glancing at the signature at the bottom. "Another letter from the solicitor? I thought he was trying to *un*complicate matters for us."

"The more he explains," Merripen said, "the more confusing it is. As a Rom, I still have trouble understanding the concept of land ownership. But the Ramsay estate . . ." He shook his head in disgust. "It's a Gordian knot of agreements, grants, customs, exceptions, additions, and leases."

"That's because the estate is so old," Win said wisely. "The more ancient the manor, the more complications it's had time to acquire." She glanced at Leo. "By the way, I've just learned that Countess Ramsay and her daughter Miss Darvin wish to come for a visit. We received a letter from them earlier today."

"The devil you say!" Leo was outraged. "For what purpose? To gloat? Take inventory? I've still got a year left before they can lay claim to the place."

"Perhaps they wish to make peace and find an acceptable solution for all of us," Win suggested.

Win was always inclined to think the best of people and believe in the essential goodness of human nature.

Leo didn't have that problem.

"Make peace, my arse," he muttered. "By God, I'm tempted to get married just to spite that pair of witches."

"Do you have any candidates in mind?" Win asked.

"Not one. But if I ever did marry, it would be to a woman I was certain never to love."

A movement at the doorway caught his attention, and Leo watched covertly as Catherine entered the room. She gave the group a neutral smile, carefully avoiding Leo's gaze, and went to a chair near the corner. With annoyance, Leo noticed that she had lost weight. Her breasts were smaller, and her waist was reed slender, and her complexion was wan. Was she deliberately avoiding proper nourishment? What had caused her lack of appetite? She was going to make herself ill.

"For God's sake, Marks," he said irritably, "you're getting as scrawny as a birch branch."

"Leo," Win protested.

Catherine shot him a look of outrage. "*I'm* not the one whose trousers are being taken in."

"You look half dead from malnourishment," Leo went on with a scowl. "What's the matter with you? Why aren't you eating?"

"Ramsay," Merripen murmured, evidently deciding a boundary had been crossed.

Catherine shot up from her chair and glared at Leo. "You're a bully, and a hypocrite, and you have no right to criticize my appearance, so . . . so . . ." She cast about wildly for the right phrase. *"Bugger you!"* And she stormed from the parlor, her skirts rustling angrily.

Merripen and Win watched with open mouths.

"Where did you learn that word?" Leo demanded, hard on her heels.

"From you," she said vehemently over her shoulder.

"Do you even know what it means?"

"No, and I don't care. Stay away from me!"

As Catherine stormed through the house, and Leo went after her, it occurred to him that he had been craving an argument with her, any kind of interaction.

She went outside and partway around the house, and soon they found themselves in the kitchen garden. The air was pungent with the smell of sun-warmed herbs.

"Marks," he said in exasperation. "I'll chase you through the parsley if you insist, but we may as well stop and have it out right here."

She whirled to face him, bright flags of color high on her cheeks. "There's nothing to discuss. You've hardly said a word to me in *days,* and then you make offensive personal remarks—"

"I didn't mean to be offensive. I merely said—"

"I am not scrawny, you despicable oaf! Am I less than a person to you, that you dare to treat me with such contempt? You are the most—"

"I'm sorry."

Catherine fell silent, her breath coming hard.

"I shouldn't have spoken to you that way," Leo said gruffly. "And you are not less than a person to me, you're a person whose well-being I care about. I would be angry with anyone who didn't treat you well—which in this case happens to be you. You're not taking care of yourself."

"Neither are you."

Leo parted his lips to reply, but he couldn't think of an effective rebuttal. He opened and closed his mouth again.

"Every day you work yourself into exhaustion," Catherine said. "You've dropped half a stone, at least."

"The new farms need irrigation systems. I'm the one best suited to design and implement them."

"You don't have to dig trenches and move rocks."

"Yes, I do."

"Why?"

Leo stared at her, considering whether or not to tell her the truth. He decided to be blunt. "Because working to the point of exhaustion is the only way I can keep from coming to you at night and seducing you."

Catherine gave him a round-eyed glance. Her mouth opened and closed in the same way his had just a moment earlier.

Leo stared back at her with a mixture of wary amusement and growing heat. He could no longer deny that he found nothing in the world more entertaining than talking to her. Or just being near her. Cantankerous, stubborn, fascinating creature . . . completely unlike his past lovers. And at times like this, she had all the cuddlesome appeal of a feral hedgehog.

But she challenged him, met him as an equal, in a way that no other woman ever had. He wanted her beyond reason.

"You couldn't seduce me," Catherine said testily.

They were both motionless, their gazes locked.

"You deny the attraction between us?" Leo's voice was pitched deeper than usual. He saw a shiver run through her before she set her jaw in determination.

"I deny that one's rational will can be undermined by physical sensation," she said. "One's brain is always in charge."

Leo couldn't prevent the mocking smile that rose to his lips. "Good God, Marks. Obviously you've never participated in the act, or you would know that the major organ in charge is *not* the brain. In fact, the brain ceases working altogether."

"I find it easy to believe that a man's would."

"A woman's brain is no less primitive than a man's, especially when it comes to physical distraction."

"I'm sure you'd like to think so."

"Shall I prove it to you?"

Catherine's delicate mouth twisted skeptically. But then, as if she couldn't resist, she asked, "How?"

Taking her arm, Leo drew her to a more secluded area of the kitchen garden, behind a pair of pergolas covered with scarlet runner beans. They stood next to a glass forcing house, which was used to compel plants into flower before they might have otherwise. A forcing house allowed a gardener to grow plants and flowers irrespective of the prevailing weather.

Leo glanced at their surroundings to make certain they were not being observed. "Here's a challenge for your higher brain function. First, I'll kiss you. Directly afterward, I'll ask you a simple question. If you answer correctly, I'll concede the argument."

Catherine frowned and looked away from him. "This is ridiculous," she said to no one in particular.

"You certainly have the right to refuse," Leo told her. "Of course, I'll take that as a forfeiture."

Folding her arms across her chest, Catherine gazed at him with narrowed eyes. "One kiss?"

Leo spread his hands palm up, as if to demonstrate that he had nothing to hide. His gaze never left her. "One kiss, one question."

Slowly her arms loosened and lowered. She stood before him uncertainly.

Leo hadn't actually expected her to agree to the challenge. He felt his heart begin to beat in concentrated thumps. As he stepped closer to her, anticipation tightened his insides into knots.

"May I?" he asked, reaching for her spectacles, easing them from her face.

She blinked but didn't resist.

Leo folded the spectacles and tucked them in his coat pocket. Very gently he tilted her face upward with both hands He had made her nervous. *Good,* he thought darkly.

"Are you ready?" he asked.

She nodded within the careful bracket of his palms, her lips trembling.

Leo brought his mouth lightly to hers, kissing her with careful, undemanding pressure. Her lips were cool and sweet. Teasing them apart, he deepened the kiss. His arms slid around her, bringing her fully against him. She was slender but compact, her body as supple as a cat's. He felt her begin to mold against him, a slow and helpless relaxing. Concentrating on her mouth, he explored her with tender fire, searching with his tongue until he felt the vibration of her soft moan between their lips.

Lifting his head, Leo looked into her flushed face. He was so mesmerized by the drowsy green-gray of her eyes that it was a struggle to remember what he'd meant to ask her.

"The question," he reminded himself aloud, and shook his head to clear it. "Here it is. A farmer has twelve sheep. All but seven die. How many are left?"

"Five," she said promptly.

"Seven." A grin spread across his face as he watched her puzzle it out.

Catherine scowled. "That was a trick. Ask me another one."

"That wasn't the bargain," he said.

"Another one," she insisted.

A husky laugh escaped him. "God, you're stubborn. All right." He reached for her and lowered his head, and she stiffened.

"What are you doing?"

"One kiss, one question," he reminded her.

Catherine looked martyred. But she yielded to him, her head tilting back as he pulled her against him once more. This time he was not so tentative. His kiss was firm and urgent, his tongue sinking into the sweet, warm interior of her mouth. Her arms lifted around his neck, her fingers groping delicately in his hair.

Leo went dizzy with desire and pleasure. He couldn't pull her body close enough, he needed parts of her he couldn't reach. His hands shook with the need to find the sweet pale skin beneath the heavy fabric of her bodice. He kept trying to feel more of her, kiss her more deeply, and instinctively she tried to help him, sucking on his tongue with a little sound of pleasure. The hair on the back of his neck lifted as a chill of delight climbed up his spine to the base of his skull.

He broke the kiss, gasping.

"Ask me a question," she reminded him thickly.

Leo could barely remember his own name. All he wanted to concentrate on was the way she fit against him. But somehow he obliged her. "Some months have thirty-one days, some have thirty. How many months have twenty-eight days?"

A perplexed furrow appeared between her fine brows. "One."

"All of them," came his gentle reply. He tried to look sympathetic as he saw her incredulous outrage.

"Ask me another one," Catherine said, furious and determined.

Leo shook his head, breathless with laughter. "I can't think of any more. My brain is deprived of blood. Accept it, Marks, you lost the—"

She grabbed the lapels of his coat and dragged him back to her, and Leo's mouth fastened on hers before he knew what he was doing. The amusement vanished. Staggering forward with her in his arms, he put out one hand to brace himself against the glass forcing house. And he possessed her lips with rough, wholehearted ardor, reveling at the feel of her body arching against his. He was dying of lust, his flesh heavy and aching with the need to take her. He kissed her without restraint, sucking, almost gnawing, stroking the inside of her mouth in ways almost too delicious to bear.

Before he lost all semblance of self-control, Leo tore his lips from hers and held her tightly against his chest.

Another question, he thought dimly, and forced what was left of his mind to come up with something.

His voice was hoarse, as if he'd just tried to breathe in fire. "How many animals of each species did Moses take into the ark?"

Her answer was muffled in his coat. "Two."

"None," Leo managed to say. "It was Noah, not Moses."

But he no longer found the game amusing, and Catherine no longer seemed to care about winning. They stood together, gripped tight and close. Their bodies cast a single shadow that stretched along a garden path.

"We'll call it a draw," Leo muttered.

Catherine shook her head. "No, you were right," she said faintly. "I can't think at all."

They waited a little longer, while she leaned into the wild rhythm of his heart. They were both in a daze, mutually occupied with a question that couldn't be asked. An answer that couldn't be given.

Letting out an unsteady sigh, Leo eased her away. He winced as the fabric of his trousers chafed his aroused flesh. Thank God the cut of his coat was long enough to conceal the problem. Extracting her spectacles from his pocket, he replaced them carefully on her nose.

He offered his arm in wordless invitation—a truce—and Catherine took it.

"What *does* 'bugger' mean?" she asked unevenly, as he led her out of the kitchen garden.

"If I told you," he said, "it would lead to improper thoughts. And I know how you hate those."

LEO SPENT MUCH OF THE NEXT DAY AT A STREAM ON THE WEST side of the estate, determining the best site for a waterwheel and marking the area. The wheel would be approximately sixteen feet in diameter, equipped with a row of buckets that would empty into a trough from which the water would course along a series of wooden flumes. Leo estimated that the system would irrigate approximately one hundred and fifty acres, or ten generously sized tenant farms.

After laying out plots with the tenants and laborers, hammering wooden stakes into the ground, and wading through a cold, muddy stream, Leo rode back to Ramsay House. It was late afternoon, the sun a condensed yellow, the meadows still and breezeless. Leo was tired, sweat-soaked, and annoyed from battling gadflies. Wryly he thought that all the romantic poets who waxed rhapsodic about being out in nature had certainly never been involved in an irrigation project.

His boots were so caked with mud that he went to the kitchen entrance, left them by the door, and went inside in his stocking feet. The cook and a maid were busy slicing apples and rolling dough, while Win and Beatrix sat at the worktable, polishing silver.

"Hello, Leo," Beatrix said cheerfully.

"Heavens, what a sight you are," Win exclaimed.

Leo smiled at both of them, then wrinkled his nose as he detected a bitter stench in the air. "I didn't think it was possible for any odor to eclipse mine at the moment. What is it? Metal polish?"

"No, actually it's . . ." Win looked guarded. "Well, it's a kind of dye."

"For cloth?"

"For hair," Beatrix said. "You see, Miss Marks wants to darken her hair before the ball, but she was afraid of using dye from the apothecary, since he got it so wrong last time. So Cook suggested a recipe that her own mother used. You boil walnut shells and cassia bark together with vinegar and—"

"Why is Marks dyeing her hair?" Leo asked, striving to keep his tone ordinary, even as his soul revolted against the idea. That beautiful hair, gleaming gold and pale amber, covered with a dull, dark stain.

Win replied cautiously. "I believe she wishes to be less . . . visible . . . at the ball, with so many guests in attendance. I didn't press her for answers, as I felt she was entitled to her privacy. Leo, please don't distress her by mentioning it."

"Does no one find it odd that we have a servant who insists on disguising herself?" Leo asked. "Is this family so bloody eccentric that we accept any manner of strangeness without even asking questions?"

"It's not all that strange," Beatrix said. "Many animals change their colors. Cuttlefish, for example, or certain species of frogs, and of course chameleons—"

"Excuse me," Leo said through clenched teeth. He left the kitchen with purposeful strides, while Win and Beatrix stared after him.

"I was leading to some very interesting facts about chameleons," Beatrix said.

"Bea, darling," Win murmured, "perhaps you'd better go out to the stables and find Cam."

CATHERINE SAT AT HER DRESSING TABLE, CONTEMPLATING her own tense reflection in the looking glass. Several articles were neatly arranged in front of her: folded toweling, a comb, a pitcher and basin, and a pot filled with a strained dark sludge that looked like boot blacking. She had painted a single lock of hair with the stuff, and was waiting for it to take effect, to see what color had been imparted. After her last disaster with colorant, when her hair had turned green, she was taking no chances.

With the Hathaway ball only two days away, Catherine had no choice but to drab down her appearance as much as possible. Guests from surrounding counties would attend, as well as families from London. And as always, she was afraid of being recognized. However, as long as she obscured her appearance and kept to the corners, no one ever noticed her. Chaperones were most often spinsters or poor widows, undesirable women who had been assigned the task of watching over young girls who still had their best years ahead of them. Catherine was scarcely older than those girls, but she felt as if there were decades between herself and them.

Catherine knew that her past would catch up with her someday. And when it did, the time she had spent with the Hathaways would be over. It had been the only period of real happiness in her life. She would grieve to lose them.

All of them.

The door was flung open, shattering Catherine's quiet contemplation. She turned in her chair and saw Leo in remarkable disarray. He was sweaty and rumpled and filthy, standing there in his stocking feet.

She jumped up to face him, recalling too late that she wore nothing but a crumpled chemise.

His hard gaze raked over her, missing no detail, and Catherine turned red in outrage. "What are you doing?" she cried. "Have you gone mad? Leave my room this instant!"

Chapter Thirteen

Leo closed the door and reached Catherine in two strides. He hauled her forcibly to the pitcher and basin.

"Stop it," she screeched, flailing at him, while he pushed her head over the basin and poured water over the lock of hair she had saturated with dye. She spluttered furiously. "What is *wrong* with you? What are you doing?"

"Washing this slime from your hair." He dumped the rest of the water on her head.

Catherine yelped and struggled, managing to slosh water over him as well, until there were puddles on the floor and the carpet was soaked. They fought until Catherine found herself on the wet layer of wool covering the floor. Her spectacles had flown off, leaving the room a blur. But Leo's face was only inches above her own, his hot blue eyes staring into hers. He subdued her without effort, pinning her wrists, her torso, as if she had no more substance than a garment rippling on a clothesline. He was very heavy on her, muscle and weight and masculinity supported in the cradle of her thighs.

She twisted helplessly. She wanted him to let her go, and at the same time she wanted him to lie on her forever, his hips pressing hers harder, deeper. Her eyes turned wet.

"Please," she choked out. "Please don't hold my wrists."

As he heard the note of fear in her voice, his face changed. He released her arms at once. She was gathered up against him, her dripping head clasped to his shoulder.

"No," he muttered, "don't be afraid of me. I would never—" She felt him kiss the side of her face, the edge of her jaw, the frantic working of her throat. Waves of warmth slid over her, sensation rising in the places where they pressed. She let her arms remain limp and outstretched on the floor, but her knees tightened on his body, holding him instinctively.

"What does it matter to you?" she asked against his damp shirt. "What do you care what color my h-hair is?" She felt the hard wall of his chest beneath his shirt, and she wanted to delve beneath the garment, rub her mouth and cheeks through the dark fleece.

His voice was soft and fierce. "Because it's not you. It's not right. What are you hiding from?"

She shook her head weakly, her eyes swimming. "I can't explain. There's too much . . . I can't. If you knew, I would have to go. And I want to stay with you. Just a little longer." A sob slipped from her throat. "Not you, I meant your family."

"You can stay. Tell me, so I can protect you."

She swallowed back another sob. There was a hot, irritating trickle on the side of her face. A tear had slid into her hairline. She lifted a hand to brush at it, but he had already put his mouth there, his lips absorbing the trail of wet salt. Her trembling hand curved around his head. She hadn't meant to encourage him, but he took it as such, his mouth finding hers hungrily. And she moaned, lost in a flood of urgent feeling.

He slid an arm beneath her neck, supporting her as he kissed her. She felt the excitement in him, heard it in the rasp of his breathing as he searched and teased and licked deep. His weight lifted from her, his warm hand settling on the damp fabric covering her midriff. She might as well have been naked for all the concealment the chemise provided, her nipples rising tightly against the transparent chill of fabric. He kissed her over the wet muslin, his mouth fastening over the rosy veiled point. Impassioned, he tugged at the tie of her chemise and spread the garment to reveal the shapes of her breasts, high and small and round.

"Cat . . ." The rush of his breath against her damp skin made her shiver. "I could die of wanting you, you're so lovely . . . sweet . . . *God* . . ." He drew a flushed bud into his mouth, circling it with his tongue, tugging softly. At the same time his fingers went to her intimate flesh, tracing the delicate slit, stroking until she was open and wet. She felt the gentle pass of his thumb over a place of excruciating sensation, the caress sending fire up to the base of her throat. Her hips lifted into the soft stroking, and he teased her lightly, tenderly, until pleasure hummed through every part of her and an extraordinary promise of relief hovered just out of reach.

His touch deepened, a finger nudging the entrance of her body. The gentle invasion caused her to shrink backward in surprise. Except that she was on the floor on her back, and there was no place to retreat. She reached down reflexively, her hand going to his.

Leo nuzzled the side of her neck. "Innocent darling. Relax and let me touch you, let me . . ." She felt the intricate workings of bone and tendon in the back of his hand as his finger slid farther into the fluid softness. She caught her breath, her body grasping helplessly at the careful intrusion.

Leo's heavy lashes lowered over smoldering eyes, the color of the pale blue heart of a flame. A flush had crossed his cheeks and the bridge of his nose. "I want to be inside you," he said thickly, caressing her. "Here . . . and deeper . . ."

An incoherent sound climbed in her throat as the subtle inner teasing drew her knees up and caused her toes to curl.

She was suffused with desperate heat, craving things she had no words for. Drawing his head down to hers, she kissed him frantically, needing the voluptuous pressure of his mouth, the thrust of his tongue—

A series of determined raps on the door broke through the lurid haze of sensation. Leo cursed and pulled his hand from between her thighs, and tucked her body beneath his. Cat whimpered, her heart pounding madly.

"Who is it?" Leo called out brusquely.

"Rohan."

"If you open that door, I will kill you." The statement was uttered with the vicious sincerity of a man who had been pushed to his limits. Apparently it was enough to give even Cam Rohan pause.

After a long moment, Cam said, "I want a word with you."

"Now?"

"Definitely now," came the inexorable reply.

Closing his eyes, Leo drew in a taut breath and expelled it slowly. "Downstairs in the library."

"Five minutes?" Cam persisted.

Leo stared at the closed door with an expression of incredulous wrath. *"Go,* Rohan."

As Cam's footsteps retreated, Leo looked down at Catherine. She couldn't seem to stop writhing and trembling, her nerves jangling with agitation. Murmuring quietly, he held her close and rubbed circles on her back and hips. "Easy, love. Let me hold you." Gradually the frantic need faded, and she lay still in his arms, her cheek pressed against his.

Leo stood and scooped her up easily, and carried her to the bed. He set her half-naked body on the mattress. While she perched on the edge of the bed and fumbled to draw the counterpane around herself, he hunted for her spectacles. Finding them in the corner of the room, he brought them back to her.

The spectacles were beginning to look rather the worse for wear, she thought ruefully, straightening the battered wire frames and polishing the lenses with a corner of the counterpane.

"What are you going to say to Mr. Rohan?" she asked hesitantly, putting the spectacles on.

"I don't know yet. But for the next two days, until the damned ball is over, I'm going to put some distance between us. Because our relationship seems to have become a bit too flammable for either of us to manage. Afterward, however, you and I are going to talk. No evasions, no lies."

"Why?" she asked through dry lips.

"We have to make some decisions."

What kind of decisions? Was he planning to dismiss her? Or was some kind of indecent proposition in the making? "Perhaps I should leave Hampshire," she said with difficulty.

Leo's eyes glinted dangerously. Taking her head in his hands, he bent down to whisper in her ear, in what could have been either a promise or a threat. "Anywhere you go, I'll find you."

He went to the door, and paused before leaving. "Incidentally," he said. "When I drew those sketches of you, I didn't begin to do you justice."

AFTER LEO HAD WASHED AND CHANGED INTO DECENT attire, he went to the library. Cam was waiting there, looking no happier than Leo felt. Even so, there was a calmness about him, a quality of relaxed tolerance that helped to blunt the edge of Leo's temper. There was no man on earth whom Leo trusted more.

When they had first met, Leo would never have chosen a man like Cam Rohan for Amelia. It just wasn't done. But the temperament of the man, his patience, humor, and inherent decency, was impossible to deny.

In a relatively short time, Cam had become a brother to Leo. He had seen Leo at his worst, and he had offered steady support as Leo had fought to reconcile himself to a life bereft of innocence or hope. And somehow, in the past few years, Leo had regained a little of both.

Standing at the window, Cam leveled a shrewd stare at him.

Wordlessly Leo went to the sideboard, poured a brandy, and let the snifter warm in his fingers. To his surprise, he saw that his hand wasn't quite steady.

"I was called in from the stables," Cam said, "to find your sisters worried and the housemaids in hysterics, because you decided to close yourself in a bedroom with Miss Marks. You can't take advantage of a woman in your employ. You know that."

"Before you tread the moral high ground," Leo said, "let's not forget that you seduced Amelia before you married her. Or is debauching an innocent acceptable as long as she's not working for you?"

There was a flash of annoyance in Cam's hazel eyes. "I knew I was going to marry her when I did it. Can you say the same?"

"I haven't slept with Marks. Yet." Leo scowled. "But at this rate I'll have bedded her by week's end. I can't seem to stop myself." He raised his gaze heavenward. "Lord, please smite me." When it appeared there would be no response from the Almighty, he tossed back a swallow of brandy. It went down his throat in a rush of smooth fire.

"You think if you take her," Cam said, "it would be a mistake."

"Yes, that's what I think." Leo took another swallow of liquor.

"Sometimes you have to make a mistake to avoid making an even worse one." Cam smiled slightly as he saw Leo's baleful expression. "Did you think you could avoid this forever, *phral*?"

"That was the plan. And I've managed quite well until recently."

"You're a man in his prime. It's only natural to want your own woman. What's more, you have a title to pass on. And from what I understand of the peerage, your primary responsibility is to produce more of yourselves."

"Good God, are we back to that again?" Scowling, Leo finished his brandy and set the glass aside. "The last thing I want to do is sire brats."

Cam lifted a brow, looking amused. "What's wrong with children?"

"They're sticky. They interrupt. They cry when they don't have their way. If I want that kind of company, I have my friends."

Settling in a chair, Cam stretched out his long legs and regarded Leo with deceptive casualness. "You're going to have to do something about Miss Marks. Because this can't continue. Even for the Hathaways, it's . . ." He hesitated, searching for a word.

"Indecent," Leo finished for him. He paced across the room and back. Stopping at the cold, dark hearth, he braced his hands on the mantel and lowered his head. "Rohan," he said carefully. "You saw what I was like, after Laura."

"Yes." Cam paused. "The Rom would say you were a man who grieved too much. You trapped your beloved's soul in the in-between."

"Either that, or I went mad."

"Love is a form of madness, isn't it?" Cam asked prosaically.

Leo let out a humorless chuckle. "For me, undeniably."

They were both silent. And then Cam murmured, "Is Laura still with you, *phral*?"

"No." Leo stared into the empty fireplace. "I've accepted that she's gone. I don't dream about her anymore. But I remember what it was like, trying to live while I was dead inside. It would be even worse now. I can't go through it again."

"You seem to think you have a choice," Cam said. "But you have it backward. Love chooses you. The shadow moves as the sun commands."

"How I enjoy Romany sayings," Leo marveled. "And you know so many of them."

Rising from the chair, Cam went to the sideboard and poured himself a brandy. "I hope you're not entertaining any thought of making her your mistress," he said matter-of-factly. "Rutledge would have you drawn and quartered, no matter that you're his brother-in-law."

"No, I wouldn't, in any case. Taking her as a mistress would create more problems than it would solve."

"If you can't leave her alone, you can't keep her as a mistress, and you won't marry her, the only option is to send her away."

"The most sensible option," Leo agreed darkly. "Also my least favorite."

"Has Miss Marks indicated what she wants?"

Leo shook his head. "She's terrified to face that. Because, God help her, she may possibly want *me*."

Chapter Fourteen

For the next two days, the Hathaway household was a hive of activity. Vast quantities of food and flowers were brought in, furniture was temporarily stored, doors were taken off their hinges, rugs were rolled up, and the floors were waxed and polished.

Guests from Hampshire and surrounding counties would attend the ball, as well as families of distinction from London. To Leo's disgruntlement, the ball invitations had been eagerly accepted by a multitude of peers with daughters in marriageable circumstances. And as the lord of the manor, his duty was to act as host and dance with as many women as possible.

"This is the worst thing you've ever done to me," he told Amelia.

"Oh, not at all, I'm sure I've done worse things to you."

Leo considered that, running through a long list of remembered offenses in his mind. "Never mind, you're right. But to be clear . . . I'm only tolerating this to humor you."

"Yes, I know. I do hope you'll humor me further, and find someone to marry so you can produce an heir before Vanessa Darvin and her mother take possession of our home."

He gave his sister a narrow-eyed glance. "One could almost infer that the house means more to you than my future happiness."

"Not at all. Your future happiness means at least as much to me as the house."

"Thank you," he said dryly.

"But I also happen to believe that you'll be much happier when you fall in love and get married."

"If I ever fell in love with someone," he retorted, "I certainly wouldn't ruin it by marrying her."

The guests began to arrive early in the evening. Women were dressed in silk or taffeta, jeweled brooches glittering at low rounded necklines, hands covered with wrist-length white gloves. Many feminine arms were adorned with matching bracelets in the new fashion.

Gentlemen, by contrast, were dressed with severe simplicity in black coats and matching creaseless trousers, and cravats in either white or black. The clothes were tailored with a touch of welcome looseness, making natural movement far easier than it had been in the constricting garments of the recent past.

Music floated through rooms abundantly dressed with flowers. Tables draped in gold satin nearly creaked beneath pyramids of fruit, cheese dishes, roast vegetables, sweetbreads, puddings, joints of meat, smoked fish, and roast fowl. Footmen moved through the circuit of public rooms, bringing cigars and liquor to men in the library, or wine and champagne to the card rooms.

The drawing room was crowded, with clusters of people all around the sides and couples dancing in the center. Leo had to admit, there was an uncommon number of attractive young women present. They all looked pleasant, normal, and fresh-faced. They all looked the same. But he proceeded to dance with as many of them as possible, taking care to include wallflowers, and he even persuaded a dowager or two to take a turn with him.

And all the while he hunted for glimpses of Catherine Marks.

She was wearing a lavender gown, the same one she'd worn at Poppy's wedding. Her hair was caught in a smooth, tight chignon at the back of her neck. She watched over Beatrix while remaining discreetly in the background.

Leo had seen Catherine do the same thing countless times before, stand quietly among the dowagers and chaperones as girls only a little younger than herself flirted and laughed and danced. It was absurd that Catherine should not be noticed. She was the equal of any woman there, background be damned.

Somehow Catherine must have felt his gaze on her. She turned and glanced at him, and she couldn't seem to look away any more than he could.

A dowager captured Catherine's attention, asking a question about something, and she turned to the dratted woman.

At the same time, Amelia came up to Leo's side and caught at his sleeve.

"My lord," she said tensely. "We have a situation. Not a good one."

Glancing at his sister with instant concern, Leo saw that she wore a false smile for the benefit of anyone who might be watching. "I had despaired of anything interesting happening this evening," he said. "What is it?"

"Miss Darvin and Countess Ramsay are here."

Leo's face went blank. "Here? Now?"

"Cam, Win, and Merripen are talking to them in the entrance hall."

"Who the devil invited them?"

"No one. They prevailed on mutual acquaintances—the Ulsters—to bring them as guests. And we can't turn them away."

"Why not? They're not wanted."

"As improper as they've been in coming without invitations, it would be even worse for us to reject them. It would make us appear *exceedingly* ungracious, and to say the least, it wouldn't be good manners."

"Far too often," Leo reflected aloud, "good manners stand in direct opposition to what I want to do."

"I know that feeling well."

They shared a grim smile.

"What do you suppose they want?" Amelia asked.

"Let's find out," Leo said curtly. Offering her his arm, he escorted her out of the drawing room to the entrance hall.

More than a few curious gazes attended them as they joined the other Hathaways, who were speaking to a pair of women dressed in sumptuous ballgowns.

The older, presumably Countess Ramsay, was a woman of average appearance, a bit plump, neither attractive nor plain. The younger woman, Miss Vanessa Darvin, was a raving beauty, tall with an elegantly turned figure and a lavish bosom, all nicely displayed in a gown of blue-green trimmed with peacock feathers. Her midnight hair was arranged in a perfect mass of pinned-up curls. Her mouth was small and full, the color of a ripe plum, and her eyes were sultry, dark and heavily lashed.

Everything about Vanessa Darvin advertised sexual confidence, which Leo had certainly never held against a woman, except that in this girl it was a bit off-putting. Probably because she looked at him as if she expected him to fall at her feet and start panting like a pug dog with a respiratory ailment.

With Amelia on his arm, Leo approached the pair. Introductions were made, and he bowed with impeccable politeness.

"Welcome to Ramsay House, my lady. And Miss Darvin. What a pleasant surprise."

The countess beamed at him. "I hope our unexpected arrival does not inconvenience you, my lord. However, when Lord and Lady Ulster made it known that you were giving a ball—the first at Ramsay House since its restoration—we felt certain that you wouldn't mind the company of your nearest relations."

"Relations?" Amelia asked blankly. The kinship between the Hathaways and the Darvins was so distant as to hardly warrant the word.

Countess Ramsay continued to smile. "We are cousins, are we not? And when my poor husband passed on to his reward, may God rest his soul, we found consolation in the knowledge that the estate would pass into capable stewardship as yours. Although . . ." Her gaze flickered to Cam and Merripen. "We had not expected such a colorful variety of in-laws as you seem to have accumulated."

Fully comprehending the unsubtle reference to the fact that both Cam and Merripen were Roma, Amelia scowled openly. "Now see here—"

"How refreshing it is," Leo interrupted, trying to stave off an explosion, "to finally be able to communicate without the interference of solicitors."

"I agree, my lord," Countess Ramsay replied. "The solicitors have made the situation regarding Ramsay House quite complex, have they not? But we are only women, and therefore much of what they relate goes right over our heads. Isn't that right, Vanessa?"

"Yes, Mama," came the demure reply.

Countess Ramsay's pillowy cheeks puffed out with another smile. Her gaze encompassed the entire group. "What matters most is the bond of familial affection."

"Does that mean you've decided not to take the house away from us?" Amelia asked bluntly.

Cam settled a hand at his wife's waist and gave her a warning squeeze.

Looking taken aback, Countess Ramsay regarded Amelia with wide eyes. "Goodness me. I'm not at all able to discuss legalities—my poor little brain fairly collapses when I try."

"However," Vanessa Darvin said in a silky voice, "as we understand, there is a chance we may not be entitled to Ramsay House, if Lord Ramsay marries and sires offspring within a year." Her gaze slid boldly over Leo, traveling from head to toe. "And he seems well equipped to do so."

Leo arched a brow, amused by the delicate emphasis she placed on the term "well equipped."

Cam intervened before Amelia could utter a scathing reply. "My lady, do you have need of lodging during your stay in Hampshire?"

"Thank you for your kind concern," Vanessa Darvin replied, "but we are staying at the residence of Lord and Lady Ulster."

"Some refreshments would be welcome, however," Countess Ramsay suggested brightly. "I think a glass of champagne would revive me nicely."

"By all means," Leo said. "May I escort you to the refreshment tables?"

"How delightful," the countess said, beaming. "Thank you, my lord." She came forward to take his proffered arm, and Vanessa went to his other side. Summoning a charming smile, Leo led the pair away.

"What dreadful people," Amelia said dourly. "They're probably here to inspect the house. And they'll monopolize Leo all evening, when he should be talking and dancing with eligible young women."

"Miss Darvin is an eligible young woman," Win said, looking troubled.

"Good heavens, Win. Do you think they came here so that

Miss Darvin could meet Leo? Do you think she might set her cap for him?"

"There would be advantages to both sides if they married," Win said. "Miss Darvin would become Lady Ramsay and gain the entire estate instead of just the copyhold. And we could all continue living here, whether or not Leo fathers a child."

"The thought of having a sister-in-law like Miss Darvin is intolerable."

"One can't judge her on first acquaintance," Win said. "Perhaps she's a nice person on the inside."

"Doubtful," Amelia said. "Women who look like that never have to be nice on the inside." Noticing that Cam and Merripen were speaking to each other in Romany, she asked her husband, "What are you talking about?"

"There are peacock feathers on her gown," Cam remarked, in the same tone he might have said, *There are poisonous flesh-eating spiders on her gown.*

"It's a very dashing effect." Amelia looked at him quizzically. "You don't like peacock feathers?"

"To the Rom," Merripen said soberly, "a single peacock feather is an evil omen."

"And she was wearing *dozens* of them," Cam added.

They watched Leo walk away with Vanessa Darvin as if he were heading toward a pit filled with vipers.

LEO ESCORTED VANESSA DARVIN TO THE DRAWING ROOM, while Countess Ramsay remained near the refreshment tables with Lord and Lady Ulster. After a few minutes of conversation with Vanessa, it was obvious that she was a young woman with adequate intelligence and a highly flirtatious nature. Leo had known and bedded women like Vanessa before. She inspired little interest in him. However, it might benefit the Hathaway family to become acquainted with Vanessa Darvin and her mother, if only to learn their plans.

Chattering lightly, Vanessa confided how dreadfully dull it had been to spend a year in mourning after her father had passed away, and how eager she had been to finally have a season in London the following year. "But how charming this estate is," she exclaimed. "I remember visiting it once when my father had the title. It was a pile of rubbish, and the gardens were barren. Now it's a gem."

"Thanks to Mr. Rohan and Merripen," Leo said. "The transformation was entirely due to their efforts."

Vanessa looked puzzled. "Well. One would never have guessed. Their people aren't usually so industrious."

"Romas are highly industrious, actually. It's only that they're nomadic, which limits their interest in farming."

"But your brothers-in-law are not nomadic, it seems."

"They have each found good reason to stay in Hampshire."

Vanessa shrugged. "They give the appearance of being gentlemen, which I suppose is all one could ask."

Leo was annoyed by her disdainful tone. "They're both related to nobility, as a matter of fact, being only half Romany. Merripen will inherit an Irish earldom someday."

"I had heard something to that effect. But . . . Irish nobility," she said with a little moue of distaste.

"You consider the Irish inferior?" Leo asked idly.

"Don't you?"

"Yes, I've always found it so crass when people refuse to be English."

Either Vanessa chose to ignore the comment, or it sailed over her head. She exclaimed with pleasure as they approached the drawing room, with its rows of glittering windows, cream-painted interior, and steep tray ceiling. "How lovely. I believe I will enjoy living here."

"As you remarked earlier," Leo pointed out, "you may not have the chance. I have a year left to marry and procreate."

"You have a reputation as an elusive bachelor, which leaves

some doubt as to whether you will achieve the former." A provocative gleam appeared in her dark eyes. "The latter, I'm
sure you're very good at."

"I would never make that claim," Leo said blandly.

"You don't have to, my lord. The claim has often been
made on your behalf. Will you deny it?"

It was hardly a question one would have expected from
a well-bred miss upon first acquaintance. Leo gathered that
he was supposed to be impressed by her audacity. However,
after participating in an infinite number of such conversations in London parlors, he no longer found such remarks
intriguing.

In London, a little sincerity was far more shocking than
audacity.

"I wouldn't claim to be accomplished in the bedroom," he
said. "Merely competent. And women usually don't recognize the difference."

Vanessa giggled. "What makes one accomplished in the
bedroom, my lord?"

Leo glanced at her without smiling. "Love, of course.
Without it, the entire business is merely a matter of techni-
calities."

She looked disconcerted, but the flirtatious mask swiftly
reappeared. "Oh, la, love is a passing thing. I may be young,
but I'm hardly naïve."

"So I've gathered," he said. "Would you care to dance,
Miss Darvin?"

"That depends, my lord."

"On what?"

"On whether you're competent or accomplished at it."

"Touché," Leo said, smiling despite himself.

Chapter Fifteen

Upon being told by Amelia of the unanticipated arrival of Countess Ramsay and Vanessa Darvin, Catherine was filled with curiosity.

Followed soon thereafter by gloom.

Standing at the side of the room, she and Beatrix watched as Leo waltzed with Miss Darvin.

They were a striking pair, Leo's dark handsomeness perfectly balanced by Miss Darvin's vibrant beauty. Leo was an excellent dancer, if a bit more athletic than graceful as he guided his partner around the room. And the skirts of Miss Darvin's blue-green gown swirled most becomingly, a fold of her skirts occasionally wrapping against his legs from the motion of the waltz.

Miss Darvin was quite beautiful, with glowing dark eyes and rich sable hair. She murmured something that elicited a grin from Leo. He looked charmed by her. Absolutely charmed.

Catherine had a peculiar feeling in her stomach as she watched them, as if she had just swallowed a handful of ten-penny nails. Beatrix stood beside her and touched her back briefly, as if to offer comfort. Catherine felt a reversal of their usual roles, that instead of being the wise older companion, she was the one in need of reassurance and guidance.

She tried to school her features into blankness. "How attractive Miss Darvin is," she commented.

"I suppose," Beatrix said noncommittally.

"In fact," Catherine added in a glum tone, "she's enchanting."

Beatrix watched Leo and Miss Darvin with thoughtful blue eyes as they executed a perfect turn. "I wouldn't say *enchanting* . . ."

"I can't see one flaw."

"I can. Her elbows are knobby."

Squinting through her spectacles, Catherine thought that perhaps Beatrix was right. They *were* a bit knobby. "That's true," she said, feeling a tiny bit better. "And doesn't her neck seem rather too long?"

"She's a giraffe," Beatrix said with an emphatic nod.

Catherine strained to see Leo's expression, wondering if he had noticed the abnormal length of Miss Darvin's neck. It didn't appear that he had. "Your brother seems taken with her," she muttered.

"I'm sure he's merely being polite."

"He's never polite."

"He is when he wants something," Beatrix said.

But that only sent Catherine plummeting into deeper gloom. Because the question of what Leo might want from the dark-haired beauty had no palatable answer.

A young gentleman came to ask Beatrix to dance, and Catherine gave her permission. Sighing, she leaned back against the wall and let her thoughts wander.

The ball was an unqualified success. Everyone was having a lovely time, the music was delightful, the food delicious, the evening neither too warm nor too cool.

And Catherine was miserable.

However, she was hardly going to let herself crumble like a dry teacake. Forcing a pleasant expression to her face, she turned to make conversation with a pair of elderly woman standing next to her. They were involved in an animated debate over the comparative merits of a chain stitch or a split stitch in outlining crewel embroidery. Trying to listen attentively, Catherine stood with her gloved fingers laced together.

"Miss Marks."

She turned to the familiar masculine voice.

Leo was there, breathtaking in the formal evening scheme of black and white, his blue eyes sparkling wickedly.

"Would you do me the honor?" he asked, gesturing to the whirl of waltzing couples. He was asking her to dance. As he had once promised.

Catherine blanched as she became aware of the multitude of gazes on them. It was one thing for the host of the evening to confer briefly with his sister's companion. It was something else entirely for him to dance with her. He knew it, and he didn't give a damn.

"Go away," she said in a sharp whisper, her heart beating wildly.

A faint smile touched his lips. "I can't. Everyone's watching. Are you going to give me a public setdown?"

She could not embarrass him that way. It was a violation of etiquette to refuse a man's invitation to dance if it could have been construed that she didn't wish to dance with him personally. And yet to be the focus of attention . . . to set tongues wagging . . . it was contrary to every instinct for self-preservation. "Oh, why are you doing this?" she whispered again, desperate and furious . . . and yet somewhere in the midst of her inner tumult, there was a tingle of delight.

"Because I want to," he said, his smile widening. "And so do you."

He was unforgivably arrogant.

He also happened to be right.

Which made her an *idiot*. If she said yes, she deserved whatever happened to her afterward.

"Yes." Biting her lip, she took his arm and let him lead her toward the center of the room.

"You could try smiling," Leo suggested. "You look like a prisoner being led to the gallows."

"It feels more like a beheading," she said.

"It's just one dance, Marks."

"You should waltz with Miss Darvin again," she said, wincing inwardly as she heard the sullen note in her own voice.

Leo laughed quietly. "Once was enough. I've no wish to repeat the experience."

Catherine tried, without success, to smother the ripple of pleasure that went through her. "You didn't get on?"

"Oh, we got on marvelously, as long as we didn't stray from the topic of utmost interest."

"The estate?"

"No, herself."

"I'm sure that with maturity, Miss Darvin will become less self-involved."

"Perhaps. It's of no importance to me."

Leo took her into his arms, his hold firm and supportive, and inexplicably right. And an evening that had seemed so dreadful only moments before became so wonderful that Catherine was light-headed.

He held her, his right hand precisely against her shoulder blade, his left hand securing hers. Even through the layers of their gloves, she felt the thrill of contact.

The dance began.

In the waltz, the man was thoroughly in control of the timing, the pace, the sequence of steps. And Leo left Catherine no opportunity to falter. It was easy to follow him, every movement nonnegotiable. There were moments in which they seemed almost to hover before sweeping into another series of turns. The music was an audible ache of yearning. Catherine was silent, afraid to break the spell, focusing only on the blue eyes above hers. And for the first time in her life, she was wholly happy.

The dance lasted three minutes, perhaps four. Catherine tried to collect every second and commit it to memory, so that in the future she could close her eyes and bring it all back. As the waltz ended on a sweet, high note, she found herself holding her breath, wishing it would go on just a little longer.

Leo bowed and offered her his arm.

"Thank you, my lord. It was lovely."

"Would you like to dance again?"

"I'm afraid not. It would be scandalous. I'm not a guest, after all."

"You're part of the family," Leo said.

"You are very kind, my lord, but you know that's not true. I am a paid companion, which means—"

She broke off as she became aware that someone, a man, was staring at her. Glancing in his direction, she saw a face that had haunted her in nightmares.

The sight of him, a figure from the past she had managed to evade for so long, extorted every bit of calm she possessed and sent her into full-scale panic. Only her grip on Leo's arm kept her from doubling over as if she'd been kicked in the stomach. She tried to take a breath, and could only wheeze.

"Marks?" Leo stopped and turned her to face him, looking down at her bleached face in concern. "What is it?"

"A touch of the vapors," she managed to say. "It must have been the exertion of the dance."

"Let me help you to a chair—"

"*No.*"

The man was still staring at her, recognition dawning on his features. She had to get away before he approached her. She swallowed hard against the biting pressure of tears welling in her eyes and throat.

What might have been the happiest night of Catherine's life had abruptly become the worst.

It's over, she thought with bitter grief. Her life with the Hathaways had come to an end. She wanted to die.

"What can I do?" Leo asked quietly.

"Please, will you see to Beatrix . . . tell her . . ."

She couldn't finish. Shaking her head blindly, she walked out of the drawing room as quickly as possible.

THE EXERTIONS OF THE DANCE, MY ARSE, LEO THOUGHT darkly. This was a woman who had moved a pile of rocks so that he could climb out of a pit. Whatever was bothering Catherine, it had nothing to do with the vapors. Glancing around the room with narrowed eyes, Leo saw a stillness amid the chattering crowd.

Guy, Lord Latimer, was watching Catherine Marks as intently as Leo was. And as she left the drawing room, Latimer began to make his way to the open doorway as well.

Leo scowled with the irritable awareness that the next time his family planned a ball or soirée, he was going to personally inspect the guest list. Had he known that Latimer would be invited, he would have drawn through the name with the darkest of ink.

Latimer, at the age of approximately forty, had reached the stage of life at which a man could no longer be called a rake, which implied a certain youthful immaturity, but instead a roué, which had the flavor of middle-aged unseemliness.

As next in line to an earldom, Latimer had little to occupy him, other than to wait for his father to die. In the meantime he had dedicated himself to the pursuit of vice and perversion.

He expected others to clean up his messes, and he cared for no one's comfort but his own. The place in his chest where a heart should have been was as empty as a calabash gourd. He was wily, clever, and calculating, all in service of satisfying his own boundless needs.

And Leo, in the depths of his despair over Laura Dillard, had tried his best to emulate him.

Recalling the escapades he had been involved in with Latimer and his cadre of dissipated aristocrats, Leo felt distinctly unclean. Since his return from France, he had scrupulously avoided Latimer. However, Latimer's family was from the neighboring county of Wiltshire, and it would have been impossible to steer clear of him forever.

Seeing Beatrix approaching the side of the drawing room, Leo reached her in a few impatient strides and took her arm.

"No more dancing for now, Bea," he murmured close to her ear. "Marks isn't available to watch over you."

"Why not?"

"I intend to find out. In the meantime, don't get into trouble."

"What should I do?"

"I don't know. Go to the refreshment table and eat something."

"I'm not hungry." Beatrix heaved a sigh. "But I suppose one doesn't need to be hungry to eat."

"Good girl," he muttered, and left the room swiftly.

Chapter Sixteen

S top! Stop right there, I say!"
Catherine ignored the summons, keeping her head down as she hurried along a hallway toward the servants' stairwell. She was drowning in shame and fear. But she was also infuriated, thinking how monstrously unfair it was that this one man should keep ruining her life, over and over. She had known this would happen someday, that even though Latimer and the Hathaways moved in different circles, they would inevitably meet. But it had been worth the risk to be with the Hathaways, to feel that just for a little while, she had been part of a family.

Latimer grabbed her arm with bruising force. Catherine whirled to face him, her entire body shaking.

It surprised her to see the extent to which he had aged, his features blighted by coarse living. He was heavier, thick around the middle, and his ginger-colored hair was thinning. Most telling, his face had acquired the wizened look of habitual self-indulgence.

"I don't know you, sir," she said coolly. "You are importunate."

Latimer didn't let go of her arm. His devouring gaze made

her feel polluted and ill. "I've never forgotten you. I looked for years. You went to another protector, didn't you?" His tongue emerged to swipe moistly over his lips, and his jaw worked as if he were preparing to unhook it and swallow her whole. "I wanted to be your first. I paid a bloody fortune for it."

Catherine took a shivering breath. "Release me at once, or I'll—"

"What are you doing here, dressed in a spinster's garb?"

She looked away from him, battling tears. "I am employed by the Hathaway family. By Lord Ramsay."

"*That* I can believe. Tell me what services you provide for Ramsay."

"Let go of me." Her voice was low and strained.

"Not on your life." Latimer drew her stiff body closer, his wine-soured breath wafting in her face. "Revenge," he said softly, "is the act of a despicable and petty character. Which is no doubt why I've always enjoyed it so much."

"What do you want revenge for?" Catherine asked, despising him to the bottom of her soul. "You lost nothing because of me. Except perhaps the merest fragment of pride, which you could easily afford."

Latimer smiled. "There's where you're mistaken. Pride is all I have. I'm quite sensitive about it, really. And I won't be satisfied until it's returned with interest. Eight years of compounded pride is a tidy sum, wouldn't you say?"

Catherine stared at him coldly. The last time she had seen him, she had been a fifteen-year-old girl with no resources, and no one to protect her. But Latimer had no idea that Harry Rutledge was her brother. Nor did it seem to have occurred to him that there might be other men who would dare to stand between him and what he wanted. "You disgusting lecher," she said. "I suppose the only way you can have a woman is to purchase one. Except that I'm not for sale."

"You were once, weren't you?" Latimer asked idly. "You

were a costly piece, and I was assured that you were worth it. Obviously you're no virgin, being in service to Ramsay, but I'd still like a sample of what I paid for."

"I owe you nothing! Leave me alone."

Latimer stunned her by smiling, his face softening. "Come now, you do me a disservice. I'm not such a bad fellow. I can be generous. What does Ramsay pay you? I'll triple it. It would be no hardship, sharing my bed. I know a thing or two about pleasing a woman."

"I'm sure you know a great deal about pleasing yourself," she said, twisting in his grasp. "Let *go*."

"Don't struggle, you'll make me hurt you."

They were both so involved in their conflict that neither of them noticed the approach of a third party.

"Latimer." It was Leo's voice, severing the air like the quiet arc of a steel blade. "If anyone were going to molest my servants, Latimer, it would be me. And I certainly wouldn't require your assistance."

To Catherine's measureless relief, the brutal grip loosened and fell away. She backed up so hastily that she nearly stumbled. But Leo came to her swiftly, using a hand on her shoulder to arrest her momentum. The lightness of his grip, of a man mindful of fragility, was in stark contrast to Latimer's.

She had never seen Leo wear such an expression, a murderous glitter in his eyes. He wasn't at all the same man who had danced with her just minutes before.

"Are you all right?" he asked.

Catherine nodded, staring up at him in dazed misery. How closely acquainted was he with Lord Latimer? Dear God, was it possible they were friends? And if so . . . given the chance, might Leo have done the same thing to her that Latimer once had, all those years ago?

"Leave us," Leo murmured, removing his hand from her shoulder.

Glancing at Latimer, Catherine shivered in revulsion and fled from the pair, as her life came crashing down around her.

LEO STARED AFTER CATHERINE, RESISTING THE URGE TO follow her. He would go to her later, and try to soothe or repair what damage had been done. And it was considerable damage—he had seen it in her eyes.

Turning to Latimer, Leo was powerfully tempted to slaughter the bastard where he stood. Instead he made his face implacable. "I had no idea you'd been invited," he said, "or I would have advised the housemaids to go into hiding. Really, Latimer, must you force yourself on unwilling females with all the available ones to be had?"

"How long have you had her?"

"If you're referring to Miss Marks's period of employ, she's been with the family not quite three years."

"There's no need to maintain the pretense that she's a servant," Latimer said. "Clever lad, installing your mistress in the family household for your own convenience. I want a go at her. Just for one night."

Leo found it increasingly difficult to restrain his temper. "What in God's name gave you the idea that she's my mistress?"

"*She's the girl,* Ramsay. The one I told you about! Don't you remember?"

"No," Leo said curtly.

"We were in our cups at the time," Latimer conceded. "But I thought you were paying attention."

"At your sober best, Latimer, you're irrelevant and annoying. Why would I have paid attention to anything you said when you were drunk? And what the devil do you mean, 'she's the girl'?"

"I purchased her from my old madam. I won her in a private auction of sorts. She was the most charming thing I'd ever seen, no more than fifteen, with those golden curls, and such remarkable eyes. The madam assured me the girl was absolutely untouched, and yet she had been told all the ways to pleasure a man. I paid a fortune to have the girl at my service for the period of a year, with an option to continue the arrangement if I desired."

"How convenient," Leo said, his eyes narrowed. "I suppose you never bothered to ask the girl if she desired the arrangement?"

"Irrelevant. The agreement was all to her benefit. It was her fortune to be born a beauty, and she would learn how to profit from it. Besides, they're all prostitutes, aren't they? It's only a question of circumstance and price." Latimer paused, smiling quizzically. "She told you none of this?"

Leo ignored the question. "What happened?"

"On the day Catherine was delivered to my house, before I'd sampled the goods, a man forced his way in and took her. Literally abducted her. One of my footmen tried to stop him and took a bullet in the leg for his pains. By the time I realized what was happening, the man had already taken Catherine past the front threshold. I can only assume that he had lost the private auction and decided to take what he wanted by force. Catherine disappeared after that. I've wanted her for eight years." Latimer gave a low laugh. "And now she's turned up in your possession. I don't know that I'm surprised, really. You've always been a devious bastard. How did you manage to acquire her?"

Leo was momentarily silent. His chest was filled with searing anguish for Catherine's sake. Fifteen. Betrayed by those who should have protected her. Sold to a man without morals or mercy. The thought of what Latimer would have done to Catherine made Leo ill. Latimer's depravities wouldn't have stopped at mere physical violation—he would have destroyed her soul. No wonder Catherine found it impossible to trust anyone. It was the only rational response to impossible circumstances.

Leveling a cold stare at Latimer, Leo reflected that if he were just a bit less civilized, he would have killed the bastard on the spot. However, he would have to settle for keeping him away from Catherine, and doing whatever was necessary to keep her safe.

"She is owned by no one," Leo said with care.

"Good. Then I'll—"

"She is under my protection, however."

Latimer arched a brow, amused. "What am I to infer from that?"

Leo was deadly serious. "That you are to go nowhere near her. That she'll never have to endure the sound of your voice or the insult of your presence ever again."

"I'm afraid I can't oblige you."

"I'm afraid you'll have to."

A coarse laugh erupted. "Surely you're not threatening me."

Leo smiled coldly. "Much as I always tried to ignore your inebriated ravings, Latimer, a few things did stick in my memory. Some of your confessions of misconduct would make more than a few people unhappy. I know enough of your secrets to land you in Marshalsea prison without so much as a chum ticket. And if that's not enough, I would be more than willing to resort to bashing your skull in with a blunt object. In fact, I'm becoming quite enthused about the idea." Seeing the astonishment in the other man's eyes, Leo smiled without humor. "I see you grasp my sincerity. That's good. It might save us both some inconvenience." He paused to give his next statement greater impact. "And now I'm going to instruct my servants to escort you off my estate. You're not welcome."

The older man's face went livid. "You'll regret having made an enemy of me, Ramsay."

"Not nearly as much as I've regretted having once made a friend of you."

"WHAT HAPPENED TO CATHERINE?" AMELIA ASKED LEO when he returned to the drawing room. "Why did she leave so suddenly?"

"Lord Latimer accosted her," he said shortly.

Amelia shook her head in bewildered outrage. "That repulsive goat—why would he dare?"

"Because that's what he does. He's an affront to polite company and every standard of moral decency. A better question would be why the devil we invited him."

"We didn't invite him, we invited his parents. Obviously he came in their stead." She threw him an accusing glance. "And he's an old acquaintance of yours."

"From now on, let's assume that every old acquaintance of mine is either a lecher or a criminal and should be kept far away from the estate and the family."

"Did Lord Latimer harm Catherine?" Amelia asked anxiously.

"Not physically. But I want someone to see to her. I expect she's in her room. Will you go to her, or send Win?"

"Yes, of course."

"Don't ask questions. Just make certain she's all right."

A half hour later, Win came to Leo with the information that Catherine had declined to say anything other than she wished to retire undisturbed.

It was probably for the best, Leo thought. Although he wanted to go up to her and offer comfort, he would let her sleep.

On the morrow, they would sort everything out.

LEO AWAKENED AT THE HOUR OF NINE AND WENT TO CATHerine's door. It was still closed, and there was no sound from within. It took all his self-control to keep from opening the door and waking her. However, she needed to rest . . . especially in light of what he intended to discuss with her later.

It seemed to Leo as he went downstairs that the entire household, including servants, was practically sleepwalking. The ball hadn't ended until four in the morning, and even then some of the guests had been reluctant to leave. Sitting in the breakfast room, Leo drank a mug of strong tea and watched as Amelia, Win, and Merripen came in. Cam, always a late riser, was still absent.

"What happened to Catherine last night?" Amelia asked quietly. "And what of Lord Latimer's precipitate departure? More than a few tongues were wagging."

Leo had considered whether or not to discuss Catherine's secrets with the rest of the family. They would have to be told something. And although he would not go into detail, he felt it would be easier for Catherine if someone else gave the explanation. "As it turns out," he said carefully, "when Cat was a girl of fifteen, her so-called family made an arrangement with Latimer."

"What kind of arrangement?" Amelia asked. Her eyes widened as Leo sent her a speaking glance. "Dear Lord."

"Thankfully Rutledge intervened before she was forced to—" Leo broke off, surprised by the note of fury in his own voice. He struggled to moderate it before continuing. "I needn't elaborate. However, it's obviously not a part of Cat's past that she's fond of dwelling on. She's been in hiding for the past eight years. Latimer recognized her last evening, and upset her badly. I'm sure she'll awaken this morning with some notion of leaving Hampshire."

Merripen's features were stern, but his dark eyes were warm with compassion. "There's no need for her to go anywhere. She's safe with us."

Leo nodded, rubbing the edge of the teacup with the pad of his thumb. "I'll make that clear when I talk with her."

"Leo," Amelia said carefully, "are you certain that you're the best one to manage this? With your history of quarreling . . ."

He gave her a hard look. "I'm certain."

"Amelia?" A hesitant voice came from the doorway.

It was Beatrix, wearing a ruffled blue dressing gown, her dark hair trailing in wild locks. Worry had creased her forehead.

"Good morning, dear," Amelia said warmly. "There's no need to rise early, if you don't wish to."

Beatrix replied in a tumble of words. "I wanted to see how the injured owl I'm keeping in the barn is faring. And I was also looking for Dodger, because I haven't seen him since yesterday afternoon. So I opened Miss Marks's door just a sliver, to see if he was in there. You know how he likes to sleep in her slipper box—"

"But he wasn't there?" Amelia asked.

Beatrix shook her head. "And neither was Miss Marks. Her bed is made, and her carpetbag is gone. And I found this on the dressing table."

She handed a piece of folded paper to Amelia, who opened it and scanned the written lines.

"What does it say?" Leo asked, already on his feet.

Amelia handed it to him without a word.

Please forgive me for leaving without saying good-bye. There is no other choice. I can never express the gratitude I feel for your generosity and kindness. Hopefully you will not think it presumptuous of me to say that although you are not my family in truth, you are the family of my heart.

I will miss all of you.

Ever your
Catherine Marks

"Good God," Leo growled, tossing the folded paper to the table, "the drama in this household is more than a man can tolerate. I would have assumed that we could have had a reasonable discussion in the comfort of Ramsay House, but instead she flees in the dark of night and leaves a letter filled with sentimental twaddle."

"It's not twaddle," Amelia said defensively.

Win's eyes filled with compassionate tears as she read the note. "Kev, we must find her."

Merripen slid a hand over hers.

"She's gone to London," Leo muttered. To his knowledge, Harry Rutledge was the only person Cat could turn to. Although Harry and Poppy had been invited to the ball, hotel business had kept them in London.

Anger, urgency, exploded inside Leo from nowhere. He tried not to show it, but the discovery that Cat had left . . . left *him* . . . had filled him with a possessive fury unlike anything he had ever felt before.

"The mail coach usually leaves Stony Cross at five-thirty," Merripen said. "Which means you have a fair chance of overtaking her before she reaches Guildford. I'll go with you, if you like."

"So will I," Win said.

"We should all go," Amelia declared.

"No," Leo said grimly. "I'm going alone. When I catch up with Marks, you won't want to be there."

"Leo," Amelia asked suspiciously, "what are you planning to do to her?"

"Why do you always insist on asking questions when you know you won't like the answers?"

"Because, being an optimist," she said tartly, "I always hope I'm wrong."

Chapter Seventeen

The coach schedule was limited, now that the mails were most often loaded onto locomotive trains. Catherine had been fortunate to obtain a seat inside a coach bound for London.

She didn't feel all that fortunate, however.

She was miserable and chilled, even in the stuffy interior of the coach. The vehicle was filled with passengers outside and in, with parcels and luggage tied precariously up top. The whole thing felt dangerously top-heavy as it rumbled over rough patches of road. Ten miles per hour, one of the gentleman passengers had estimated, admiring the strength and endurance of the team of massive drays.

Morosely Catherine stared out the window as the meadows of Hampshire rolled into the heavy woodland and bustling market towns of Surrey.

There was only one other woman inside the coach, a plump and well-dressed matron who was traveling with her husband. She dozed in the opposite corner from Catherine's, emitting delicate snores. Whenever the coach jolted, it caused the objects on her hat to rattle and quiver. And quite a hat it was, adorned with clusters of artificial cherries, a plume, and a small stuffed bird.

At midday the coach stopped at an inn where a new team would be put to, in preparation for the next stretch of road. Groaning in relief at the prospect of a brief respite, the passengers poured out of the vehicle and into the tavern.

Catherine carried her tapestry carpetbag, afraid to leave it in the coach. The bag was a weighty affair containing a nightgown, undergarments and stockings, an assortment of combs and pins and a hairbrush, a shawl, and a voluminous novel with a mischievous inscription from Beatrix . . . "This story is guaranteed to entertain Miss Marks without improving her in the least! With love from the incorrigible B.H."

The inn appeared moderately well appointed but hardly luxurious, the kind of place that stablemen and workingmen frequented. Catherine glanced disconsolately at a wooden yard wall covered with posting bills, and turned to watch a pair of ostlers change the team.

She nearly dropped the carpetbag at the side of the carriage yard as she felt a rustle of independent movement within. Not as if something had shifted around . . . it was more like . . . something was alive in there.

Her heartbeat became rapid and disorganized, like the bobbing of small potatoes in boiling water. "Oh no," she whispered. Turning to face the wall, trying desperately to keep the bag out of view, she unlooped the fastener and opened the bag a mere two inches.

A sleek little head popped out. Catherine was aghast to behold a familiar pair of bright eyes and a set of twitching whiskers.

"Dodger," she whispered. The ferret chattered happily, the corners of his mouth curling in his perpetual ferret smile. "Oh, you *naughty* boy!" He must have slipped into the bag while she had been packing. "What am I to do with you?"

she asked in despair. Pushing his head back down into the bag, she stroked him to keep him quiet. There was no choice but to take the dratted creature all the way to London, and give him into Poppy's keeping until he could be returned to Beatrix.

As soon as one of the ostlers shouted, "All ready!" Catherine went back into the coach and settled the carpetbag at her feet. Opening the top once more, she peeked at Dodger, who was coiled in the folds of her nightgown. "Be quiet," she said sternly. "And don't cause trouble."

"I beg your pardon?" came the matron's voice as she entered the carriage, her hat plume trembling with indignation.

"Oh, ma'am, I wasn't speaking to you," Catherine said hastily. "I was . . . lecturing myself."

"Indeed." The woman's eyes narrowed as she plopped into the opposite seat.

Catherine sat stiffly. She waited for a telltale rustling of the carpetbag or a betraying noise. However, Dodger remained quiet.

The matron closed her eyes and lowered her chin to the high, mounded shelf of her bosom. In a matter of two minutes, she appeared to be dozing again.

Perhaps this wouldn't be difficult after all, Catherine thought. If the woman remained asleep, and the gentlemen resumed their newspaper reading, she might be able to smuggle Dodger to London unnoticed.

But just as Catherine allowed herself to teeter on the brink of hope, the entire situation went tumbling out of her control.

Without warning Dodger poked his head out, surveyed his interesting new surroundings, and slithered from the bag. Catherine's lips parted in a silent cry, and she froze with her hands arrested in midair. The ferret ran up the upholstered seat to the matron's beckoning hat. A nibble or two, and his sharp teeth had severed a cluster of artificial cherries from the hat. Triumphantly he scrambled down the seat and leaped into Catherine's lap with his prize. He did a happy ferret war dance, a series of hops and wriggles.

"No," Catherine whispered, grabbing the cherries from him and trying to shove him back into the carpetbag.

Dodger protested, squeaking and chattering.

The woman spluttered and blinked, waking irritably at the noise. "Wha . . . what . . ."

Cat went still, her pulse thundering in her ears.

Dodger streaked up around Cat's neck and hung limply, playing dead.

Like a scarf, Cat thought, struggling to repress a burst of demented giggles.

The matron's indignant gaze arrowed to the bunch of cherries in her lap. "Why . . . why, those are from *my hat*, aren't they? Were you attempting to *steal* those while I was napping?"

Catherine sobered immediately. "No, oh no, it was an accident. I'm so—"

"You *ruined* it, and this was my best hat, it cost two pounds and six! Give it back to me at—" But she broke off with a strangled sound, her mouth rounding into a calcified O as Dodger leaped to Catherine's lap, seized the cherries, and disappeared into the safety of the carpetbag.

The woman screamed with earsplitting force, exiting the coach in a full-rigged tumult of skirts.

Five minutes later, Catherine and the carpetbag had been unceremoniously ejected from the coach. She stood at the verge of the carriage yard, assaulted by a concurrence of strong smells: dung, horses, urine, combining queasily with scents of cooked meat and hot bread coming from the tavern.

The coachman mounted to the box, ignoring Catherine's outraged protests.

"But I paid to go all the way to London!" she cried.

"You paid for one passenger, not two. Two passengers get half the journey."

Incredulously Catherine looked from his stony expression to the carpetbag in her hand. "*This* is not a passenger!"

"We're a quarter hour behind time because of you and your rat," the coachman said, squaring his elbows and cracking the whip.

"He's not my rat, he's . . . wait, how am I to get to London?"

One of the ostlers replied implacably as the coach set out. "Next mails come tomorrow morning, miss. Maybe they'll let you and your pet ride up top."

Catherine glared at him. "I don't want to ride up top, I paid to ride *inside,* all the way to London, and I consider this a form of larceny! What am I to do until tomorrow morning?"

The ostler, a young man with a long-handled mustache, shrugged. "You might ask if there's a room available," he suggested. "Although they probably won't take kindly to guests with rats." He looked beyond her as another vehicle came into the yard. "Out of the way, miss, or you'll get thrown down by the carriage."

Infuriated, Catherine stomped to the entrance of the inn. She looked into her carpetbag, where Dodger was playing with the cherries. Was it not enough, she thought in frustration, that she'd just had to leave a life she had loved, that she'd been through an entire night of nearly ceaseless crying and was now exhausted? Why had an unkind fate also seen fit to deposit Dodger in her care? "*You,*" she fumed aloud, "are the last feather that broke the horse's back. You have plagued me for *years,* and stolen all my garters, and—"

"Pardon," came a polite voice.

Catherine looked up with a scowl. In the next moment she swayed, her balance momentarily off.

Her thunderstruck eyes beheld Leo, Lord Ramsay, who

looked amused. He kept his hands tucked in his pockets as he approached her in a relaxed stride. "I'm sure I shouldn't ask. But why are you shouting at your luggage?"

Despite the negligence of his manner, his gaze went over her thoroughly, taking careful inventory.

The sight of him had knocked the breath from her. He was so handsome, so beloved and familiar, that Catherine was nearly overcome by the impulse to fling herself at him. She couldn't fathom why he had come after her.

How she wished he hadn't.

Fumbling to close the carpetbag, she decided that it probably wouldn't do to advertise Dodger's presence before she managed to secure a room for herself. "Why are you here, my lord?" she asked unsteadily.

A leisurely shrug. "When I awakened this morning after a mere four and a half hours of sleep, I thought it would be just the thing to hop in the carriage and go for a picturesque drive to Haslemere and visit the"—Leo paused to glance at the sign above the door—"Spread Eagle Inn. What a fortuitous name." His lips twitched at her bewildered expression, but his eyes were warm. His hand came up to her face, gently lifting her unwilling chin. "Your eyes are swollen."

"Travel dust," Catherine said with difficulty, swallowing hard at the sweetness of his touch. She wanted to push her chin harder against his hand, like a cat hungry to be stroked. Her eyes stung with the portent of tears.

This would not do. Her reaction to him was nothing short of appalling. And if they stood out in the carriage yard even a moment longer, she would lose her composure altogether.

"Did you have difficulty with the coach?" he asked.

"Yes, and there won't be another till morning. I need to arrange for a room."

He wouldn't release her from his gaze. "You could come back to Hampshire with me."

The suggestion was more devastating than Leo could have known.

"No, I can't. I'm going to London, to see my brother."

"And after that?"

"After that, I'll probably travel."

"Travel?"

"Yes, I'll . . . I'll tour the Continent. And settle in France or Italy."

"By yourself?" Leo didn't bother to hide his skepticism.

"I'll hire a companion."

"You can't hire a companion, you *are* a companion."

"I've just left the position," she shot back.

For just a moment, there was an alarming intensity in his gaze. Something predatory. Something dangerous. "I have a new position for you," he said, and a little chill went down her spine.

"No, thank you."

"You haven't heard it yet."

"I don't need to." Blindly she turned and walked into the building.

Finding the innkeeper's table, she waited resolutely until a short, stocky man came to greet her. Although his head was shiny and bald, he had a thick gray beard and muttonchop sideburns. "May I help you?" he asked, looking from Catherine to the man just behind her.

Leo spoke before she could say a word. "I'd like to arrange a room for my wife and myself."

His *wife*? Catherine twisted to give him an offended glance. "I want my own room. And I'm not—"

"She doesn't, really." Leo smiled at the innkeeper, the rueful, commiserating smile of one put-upon man to another. "A marital squabble. She's cross because I won't let her mother visit us."

"Ahhh . . ." The innkeeper made an ominous sound and

bent to write in the registry book. "Don't give in, sir. They *never* leave when they say they will. When my mother-in-law visits, the mice throw themselves at the cat, begging to be eaten. Your name?"

"Mr. and Mrs. Hathaway."

"But—" Catherine began, nettled. She broke off as she felt the carpetbag quiver in her grasp. Dodger wanted to get out. She had to keep him hidden until they were safely upstairs. "All right," she said shortly. "Let's hurry."

Leo smiled. "Eager to make up after our quarrel, darling?"

She gave him a look that should have slayed him on the spot.

To Catherine's fidgety impatience, it took another ten minutes for the arrangements to be made, including securing lodging for Leo's driver and footman. Moreover, Leo's luggage—*two* sizable traveling bags—had to be brought in. "I thought I might not reach you until London," Leo said, having the grace to look slightly sheepish.

"Why did you arrange for only one room?" she whispered sharply.

"Because you're not safe by yourself. You need me for protection."

She glared at him. "You're the one I need protection from!"

They were shown to a tidy but sparsely furnished room, with a brass bed in need of polishing, and a faded, much-laundered quilt. Two chairs were poised by the tiny hearth, one upholstered, the other small and bare. A battered washstand occupied one corner, a small table in another. The floor was swept and the white-painted walls were vacant except for a framed work consisting of a motto embroidered on heavy perforated paper: "Time and tide wait for no man."

Mercifully there was a lack of strong odor in the room, only a slight whiff of roasted meat from the tavern below, and an ashy tang from the cold hearth.

After Leo had closed the door, Catherine set her carpet-bag on the floor and opened it.

Dodger's head emerged and did a complete swivel as he surveyed the room. He leaped out and scurried beneath the bed.

"You brought Dodger with you?" Leo asked blankly.

"Not voluntarily."

"I see. Is that why you were forced off the coach?"

Glancing at him, Catherine felt her insides rearrange themselves, a warm lifting and resettling as she saw him remove his coat and cravat. Everything about the situation was improper, and yet propriety no longer seemed to matter.

She told him the story then, about the rustling in the bag, and how the ferret had stolen the cherries off the matron's hat, and by the time she got to the part about Dodger pretending to be a scarf around her neck, Leo was gasping with laughter. He looked so thoroughly tickled, so boyish in his amusement, that Catherine didn't care if it was at her expense or not. She even laughed with him, breaking into helpless giggles.

But somehow her giggling dissolved into sobs, and she felt her eyes welling even as she laughed, and she put her hands over her face to hold the giddy emotions back. Impossible. She knew she looked like a madwoman, laughing and crying all at once. This kind of emotional unhinging was her worst nightmare.

"I'm sorry," she choked, shaking her head, covering her eyes with a sleeved forearm. "Please leave. Please."

But Leo's arms went around her. He collected the quivering bundle of her against his hard chest, and he held her firmly. She felt him kiss the hot, exposed curve of her ear. The scent of his shaving soap drifted to her nostrils, the masculine fragrance comforting and familiar. She didn't realize that she had continued to gasp out the word "sorry" until he answered, his voice low and infinitely tender. "Yes, you should be sorry . . . but not for crying. Only for leaving me without a word."

"I l-left a letter," she protested.

"That maudlin note? Surely you didn't think that would be enough to keep me from coming after you. Hush, now. I'm here, and you're safe, and I'm not letting go. I'm here." She realized that she was struggling to press closer to him, trying to fight her way deeper into his embrace.

When her crying broke into watery hiccups, she felt Leo tug the jacket of her traveling habit from her shoulders. In her exhaustion she found herself complying like an obedient child, pulling her arms from the sleeves. She didn't even protest as he took the combs and pins from her hair. Her scalp throbbed sharply as the tight coiffure was undone. Leo removed her spectacles and set them aside, and went to fetch a handkerchief from his discarded coat.

"Thank you," Catherine mumbled, mopping her sore eyes with the square of pressed cotton, wiping her nose. She stood with childlike indecision, the handkerchief balled in her fingers.

"Come here." Leo sat in the large hearthside chair and drew her down with him.

"Oh, I can't—" she began, but he hushed her and gathered her on his lap. The mounds of her skirts spilled heavily over them both. She rested her head on his shoulder, the agitated workings of her lungs gradually matching the measured rhythm of his. His hand played slowly in her hair. Once she would have shrunk away from a man's touch, no matter how innocuous. But in this room, removed from the rest of the world, it seemed neither of them were quite themselves.

"You shouldn't have followed me," she finally brought herself to say.

"The entire family wanted to come," Leo said. "It seems

the Hathaways can't do without your civilizing influence. So I've been charged with bringing you back."

That nearly started her crying again. "I can't go back."

"Why not?"

"You already know. Lord Latimer must have told you about me."

"He told me a little." The backs of his fingers stroked the side of her neck. "Your grandmother was the madam, wasn't she?" His tone was quiet and matter-of-fact, as if having a grandmother who owned a house of prostitution was a perfectly ordinary circumstance.

Catherine nodded, swallowing miserably. "I went to live with my grandmother and Aunt Althea when Mother took ill. At first I didn't understand what the family business was, but after a while I realized what working for my grandmother meant. Althea had finally reached the age when she was no longer as popular among the customers. And then I turned fifteen, and it was supposed to be my turn. Althea said that I was lucky, because she'd had to start when she was twelve. I asked if I could be a teacher or a seamstress, something like that. But she and my grandmother said I'd never make enough money to repay what had been spent on me. Working for them was the only profitable thing I could do. I tried to think of somewhere to go, some way to survive by myself. But there was no position I could get without recommendations. Except for a factory job, which would have been dangerous and the wages would have been too low to pay for a room anywhere. I begged my grandmother to let me go to my father, because I knew he would never have left me there, had he known of their plans. But she said—" Catherine stopped, her hands fisting in his shirt.

Leo disentangled her fingers and meshed his own with them, until their hands were caught together like the clasp of a bracelet. "What did she say, love?"

"That he already knew, and approved, and he would receive a percentage of the money I earned. I didn't want to believe it." She let out a broken sigh. "But he had to have known, didn't he?"

Leo was silent, his thumb softly rubbing into the cup of her palm. The question needed no answer.

Catherine set her jaw against a quiver of grief, and resumed. "Althea brought gentlemen to meet me one at a time, and she told me to be charming. She said that of all of them, Lord Latimer had made the highest offer." She made a face against his shirt. "He was the one I liked least of all. He kept winking and telling me there were naughty surprises in store for me."

Leo uttered a few choice words beneath his breath. At her uncertain pause, he ran his hand along her spine. "Go on."

"But Althea told me what to expect, because she thought I would fare much better if I knew. And the acts she described, the things I was supposed to . . ."

His hand went still on her back. "Were you required to put any of it in practice?"

She shook her head. "No, but it all sounded *dreadful*."

A note of sympathetic amusement warmed his voice. "Of course it did, to a fifteen-year-old girl."

Lifting her head, Catherine looked into his face. He was too handsome for his own good, and for hers as well. Although she wasn't wearing her spectacles, she could see every breathtaking detail of him . . . the dark grain of shaved whiskers, the laugh lines at the outer corners of his eyes, little pale whisks against the rosewood color of his skin. And most of all the variegated blue of his eyes, light and dark, sunlight and shadow.

Leo waited patiently, holding her as if there were nothing else in the world he would have preferred doing. "How did you get away?"

"I went to my grandmother's desk one morning," Catherine

said, "when the household was still asleep. I was trying to find money. I planned to run away and find lodging and a decent position somewhere. There wasn't a single shilling. But in one of the nooks in the desk, I found a letter, addressed to me. I'd never seen it before."

"From Rutledge," Leo said rather than asked.

Catherine nodded. "A brother I'd never known existed. Harry had written that if I were ever in need, I should send word to his address. I dashed off a letter to let him know the trouble I was in, and I gave it to William to deliver—"

"Who is William?"

"A little boy who worked there . . . he carried things up and down the stairs, cleaned shoes, went on errands, whatever he was told to do. I think he was the child of one of the prostitutes. A very sweet boy. He delivered the note to Harry. I hope Althea never found out. If she did, I fear for what happened to him." She shook her head and sighed. "The next day I was sent to Lord Latimer's house. But Harry came just in time." She paused reflectively. "He frightened me only a little less than Lord Latimer. Harry was extremely angry. At the time I thought it was directed at me, but now I think it was the situation."

"Guilt often takes the form of anger."

"But I never blamed Harry for what happened to me. I wasn't his responsibility."

Leo's face hardened. "Apparently you were no one's responsibility."

Catherine shrugged uneasily. "Harry didn't know what to do with me. He asked where I wanted to live, since I couldn't stay with him, and I asked if he could send me somewhere far from London. We settled on a school in Aberdeen, called Blue Maid's."

He nodded. "Some of the peerage send their more unruly daughters or by-blows there."

"How did you know about it?"

"I'm acquainted with a woman who attended Blue Maid's. A severe place, she said. Plain food and discipline."

"I loved it."

His lips twitched. "You would."

"I lived there for six years, teaching for the last two."

"Did Rutledge come to visit?"

"Only once. But we corresponded occasionally. I never went home on holiday, because the hotel wasn't really a home, and Harry didn't want to see me." She grimaced a little. "He wasn't very nice until he met Poppy."

"I'm not convinced that he's nice now," Leo said. "But as long as he treats my sister well, I'll have no quarrel with him."

"Oh, but Harry *loves* her," Catherine said earnestly. "Truly he does."

Leo's expression softened. "What makes you so certain?"

"I can see it. The way he is with her, the look in his eyes and . . . why are you smiling like that?"

"Women. You'll interpret anything as love. You see a man wearing an idiotic expression, and you assume he's been struck by Cupid's arrow when in reality he's digesting a bad turnip."

She looked at him indignantly. "Are you mocking me?"

Laughing, Leo tightened his arms around her as she tried to struggle from his lap. "I'm merely making an observation about your gender."

"I suppose you think men are superior."

"Not at all. Only simpler. A woman is a collection of diverse needs, whereas a man has only one. No, don't get up. Tell me why you left Blue Maid's."

"The headmistress asked me to."

"Really? Why? I hope you did something reprehensible and shocking."

"No, I was very well behaved."

"I'm sorry to hear that."

"But Headmistress Marks sent for me to come to her office one afternoon, and—"

"Marks?" Leo glanced at her alertly. "You took her name?"

"Yes, I admired her very much. I wanted to be like her. She was stern but kind, and nothing ever seemed to disrupt her composure. I went to her office, and she poured tea, and we talked for a long time. She said I'd done an excellent job, and I was welcome to return and continue teaching in the future. But first she wanted me to leave Aberdeen and see something of the world. And I told her that leaving Blue Maid's was the last thing I wanted to do, and she said that was why I needed to do it. She had received word from a friend at a placement agency in London that a family of . . . 'uncommon circumstances,' as she put it, was searching for a woman who could act as both governess and companion to pair of sisters, one of whom had recently been expelled from finishing school."

"That would be Beatrix."

Catherine nodded. "The headmistress thought that I might suit the Hathaways. What I never expected was how much they suited *me*. I went for an interview, and I thought the entire family was a bit mad—but in the loveliest possible way. And I've worked for them for almost three years, and I've been so happy and now—" She broke off, her face contorting.

"No, no," Leo said hastily, taking her head in his hands, "don't start that again."

Catherine was so shocked to feel his lips brush her cheeks and closed eyes that the tears instantly evaporated. When she finally brought herself to look at him again, she saw that he was wearing a faint smile. He smoothed her hair, and stared into her grief-ravaged face with a depth of concern she had never seen from him before.

It frightened her to realize how much of herself she had just given away. Now he knew everything she had tried to keep secret for so long. Her hands worked against his chest like the wings of a bird that had found itself trapped indoors.

"My lord," she said with difficulty, "why did you come after me? What do you want from me?"

"I'm surprised you have to ask," he murmured, still caressing her hair. "I want to offer for you, Cat."

Of course, she thought, bitterness welling. "To be your mistress."

His voice matched hers exactly for calmness, in a way that conveyed gentle sarcasm. "No, that would never work. First, your brother would arrange to have me murdered, or, at the very least, maimed. Second, you're far too prickly tempered to be a mistress. You're far better suited as a wife."

"Whose?" she asked with a scowl.

Leo stared directly into her narrowed eyes. "Mine, of course."

Chapter Eighteen

Hurt and outraged, Catherine struggled so violently that he was forced to release her.

"I've had enough of you and your tasteless, insensitive humor," she cried, leaping to her feet. "You cad, you—"

"I'm not joking, damn it!" Leo stood and reached for her, and she hopped backward, and he grabbed, and she flailed. They grappled until Catherine found herself tumbling backward onto the bed.

Leo fell over her in a controlled descent—a pounce, really. She felt him sinking into the mass of skirts, his superior weight urging her legs apart, the muscular mass of his torso pinning her down. She writhed in distress as excitement went skimming and tickling all through her. The more she wriggled, the worse it became. She subsided beneath him, while her hands kept opening and closing on nothing.

Leo stared down at her, eyes dancing with mischief . . . but there was something else in his expression, a purposefulness, that unsettled her profoundly.

"Consider it, Marks. Marrying me would solve both our problems. You would have the protection of my name. You wouldn't have to leave the family. And they couldn't nag me to get married any longer."

"I am illegitimate," she said distinctly, as if he were a foreigner trying to learn English. "You are a viscount. You can't marry a bastard."

"What about the Duke of Clarence? He had ten bastard children by that actress . . . what was her name . . ."

"Mrs. Jordan."

"Yes, that one. Their children were all illegitimate, but some of them married peers."

"You're not the Duke of Clarence."

"That's right. I'm not a blueblood any more than you are. I inherited the title purely by happenstance."

"That doesn't matter. If you married me, it would be scandalous and inappropriate, and doors would be closed to you."

"Good God, woman, I let two of my sisters marry Roma. Those doors have already been closed, bolted, and nailed shut."

Catherine couldn't think clearly, could scarcely hear him through the pounding in her ears, the wild clamor of her blood. Will and desire pulled at her with equal force. Turning her face away as his mouth descended, she said desperately, "The only way you could be certain of keeping Ramsay House for your family is to marry Miss Darvin."

He gave a derisive snort. "It's also the only way I could be certain of committing sororicide."

"Of what?" she asked in bewilderment.

"Sororicide. Killing one's wife."

"No, you mean to say 'uxoricide.'"

"Are you certain?"

"Yes, *uxor* is the Latin word for 'wife.'"

"Then what's 'sororicide'?"

"Killing one's sister."

"Oh, well, if I had to marry Miss Darvin, I'd probably end

up doing that too." Leo grinned down at her. "The point is, I could never have this kind of conversation with her."

He was probably right. Catherine had lived with the Hathaways long enough to fall into their style of banter, slipping into the verbal detours that could start one talking about the increasing problem of the Thames River pollution, and end up debating the question of whether or not the Earl of Sandwich had actually invented sandwiches. Catherine restrained a miserable laugh as she realized that although she might have had a slight civilizing influence on the Hathaways, their influence on her had been much greater.

Leo's head lowered, and he kissed the side of her neck with a slow deliberation that made her squirm. Clearly he had lost interest in the subject of Miss Darvin. "Give in, Cat. Say you'll marry me."

"What if I couldn't give you a son?"

"There are never guarantees." Leo lifted his head and grinned. "But think of how much fun we'll have trying."

"I don't want to be responsible for the Hathaways losing Ramsay House."

A new seriousness infused his expression. "No one would hold you responsible for that. It's a house. No more and no less. There isn't a structure on earth that could last forever. But a family goes on."

The front of her bodice had gone loose. She realized that he had been unbuttoning her as they had been talking. She moved to stop him, but he had already managed to spread the front of her bodice open, revealing her corset and chemise.

"Therefore the only thing you'll be responsible for," Leo said huskily, "is going to bed with me as often as I wish, and participating in all my heir-inducing efforts." As Catherine turned her face away, gasping, he bent to whisper in her ear. "I'm going to pleasure you. Fill you. Seduce you from head to toe. And you're going to love it."

"You are the most arrogant and absurd—oh, please don't do that." He was investigating her ear with the tip of his tongue, a silky-wet tickle. Paying no attention to her protests, he kissed and licked his way along the taut arch of her neck. "Don't," she moaned, but he took her panting mouth with his, and let his tongue play there as well, and the sensation and taste and smell of him made her feel drunk. Her arms groped around his neck, and she surrendered with a weak moan.

After her mouth had been teased, searched, and thoroughly ravished, Leo lifted his head and stared into her dazed eyes. "Do you want to hear the best part of my plan?" he asked thickly. "In order to make an honest woman of you, I'll have to debauch you first."

Catherine was dismayed to hear herself giggle in witless amusement. "No doubt you're good at that."

"Gifted," he assured her. "The trick is for me to find out what you like best, and then let you have only a little of it. I'll torment you until you're absolutely miserable."

"That doesn't sound at all pleasant."

"You think not? Then you'll be surprised when you beg me to do it again."

Catherine couldn't hold back another helpless giggle.

Then they were both motionless, flushed, staring at each other intently.

She heard herself whisper, "I'm afraid."

"I know, darling," Leo said gently. "But you'll have to trust me."

"Why?"

"Because you can."

Their gazes held. Catherine was paralyzed. What he asked was impossible. To give herself over entirely to a man, to anyone, was anathema to her very nature. Therefore, it should have been easy to refuse him.

Except that when she tried to form the word "no," she couldn't produce a sound.

Leo began to undress her, pulling the gown away in rustling armfuls. And Catherine let him. She actually helped him, loosening laces with shaking hands, lifting her hips, tugging her arms free. He unhooked her corset deftly, betraying easy familiarity with women's unmentionables. He was in no hurry, however. He was slow and deliberate as he removed the protective layers one by one.

Finally Catherine was covered in nothing more than a blush, her pale skin scored with temporary marks left by the edges of the corset and the seams of her clothes. Leo's hand descended to her midriff, fingertips moving sensitively along the faint lines like a traveler mapping unexplored territory. His expression was absorbed, tender, as his palm skimmed over her stomach . . . lower . . . softly grazing the fluff of intimate hair.

"Blond everywhere," he whispered.

"Is that . . . does that please you?" she asked bashfully, gasping as his hand ascended to her breast.

There was a hint of a smile in his voice. "Cat, everything about you is so lovely, I can hardly breathe." His fingers caressed the cool rise of her breast, toying with the tip until it was taut and rose-colored. He bent and took it in his mouth.

Her heart missed a beat as she heard a noise from downstairs, a clatter that sounded like dishes being dropped in the tavern, the pitch of a raised voice. It was unimaginable that other people were going about the perfectly ordinary business of their day while she was naked in bed with Leo.

One of his hands slid beneath her hips, aligning her exactly with the hard ridge behind his trousers. She whimpered against his lips, shaken by intense pleasure, wanting to stay against him like that forever. He kissed her deeply, and down below his hand pressed her against him in a corresponding rhythm, the voluptuous nudges driving her into some new dimension of feeling. Closer, closer, lapping waves urging her forward . . . but then he was easing her away. She made an agitated sound, her body aching with unspent sensation.

Leo sat up and stripped his clothes off, revealing a powerful masculine body, efficiently lean and paved with muscle. There was hair on his chest, an intriguing dark fleece, and more of it lower down. His body was ready to couple with hers, she saw. Her stomach clenched in nervous anticipation. He returned to her, gathering her against him, length to length.

She explored him hesitantly, her fingers moving over his chest to the sleek skin of his side. Finding the small scar on his shoulder from their mishap at the ruins, Catherine pressed her lips to it. She heard his rough intake of breath. Encouraged, she inched lower on the bed and rubbed her nose and mouth through the soft mat on his chest. Everywhere their bodies touched, she felt his muscles tighten in response.

Trying to remember Althea's long-ago instructions, she reached down to the upthrust shape of his arousal. The skin was like nothing she had ever felt, thin and silky, moving easily over astonishing hardness. Timidly she leaned down to kiss the side of the shaft, her lips brushing against a strong pulse. She looked up to gauge his reaction, her gaze questioning.

Leo wasn't breathing at all well. A tremor shook his hand as he passed it over her hair. "You are the most adorable woman, the sweetest—" He gasped as she kissed him again, and laughed unsteadily. "No, love—it's all right. No more of that for now." Reaching down to her, he pulled her up beside him.

He was more insistent now, more authoritative, in a way that allowed her to relax completely. How strange that she could so easily relinquish all control to him, when they had been such fierce adversaries. He parted her thighs with his hand, and she felt herself turn wet even before he touched her there. He teased through the protective curls, spreading her intimately. Her head tilted back against his supportive arm, and she closed her eyes, breathing deeply as his finger slipped inside her.

Leo seemed to luxuriate in her response. His head bent to her breast, and he used his teeth gently, licking and gnawing in time to the slow thrust of his finger. It seemed her entire body aligned with that coaxing rhythm, every quiver, pulse, muscle, thought, surging together, and again, until sensation amassed into one exquisite rush of pleasure. She sobbed, riding the swell, letting it take her, letting the heat pump and swirl and ripple all through her . . . then finally she subsided into trembling weakness.

He loomed over her, panting, staring into her dazed face. Reaching up, she pulled him closer, her limbs moving easily to accommodate him. As he pressed against the entrance to her body, a sharp pain burned through her. He went deeper. Too much of him, the intrusion slow and hard and relentless. When he had gone as far as her resisting flesh could take him, he held still and tried to soothe her. His mouth slid gently over her cheeks and throat.

The intimacy of the moment, the sensation of holding him within her body, was stunning. She found herself trying to soothe him as well, her hands stroking his sleek back. Murmuring his name, she slid her palms to his flanks and urged him to continue. He began to thrust cautiously. It hurt, and yet there was something assuaging in the deep, low pressure. She opened to him instinctively, pulling him closer.

She loved the sounds he made, the quiet groans and fragmented words, his roughcast breathing. It became easier to take him, her hips lifting naturally with each forward motion, slippery flesh plunging and grasping. Her knees bent, angling to cradle him. His body trembled roughly, a grunt of something that sounded like pain coming from his throat.

"Cat . . . Cat . . ." Leo withdrew from her abruptly and thrust against her stomach, and she felt heat spill in wet pulses over her skin. He held her tightly, groaning into the joint of her shoulder and neck.

They lay together, trying to catch their breath. Catherine was limp with exhaustion, her limbs heavy. Contentment had saturated and softened her, like water seeping into a dry sponge. For the moment, at least, it was impossible to worry about anything.

"It's true," she said drowsily. "You are gifted."

Leo eased to his side heavily, as if the movement had required great effort. He pressed his lips to her shoulder, and she felt the shape of his smile on her skin. "How delicious you are," he whispered. "It was like making love to an angel."

"Sans halo," she murmured, and was rewarded by his low chuckle. She touched the film of moisture on her stomach. "Why did you do it that way?"

"Withdrawing, you mean? I don't want to get you with child, if you're not ready."

"Do you want children? I mean . . . not because of the copyhold clause, but for their own sake?"

Leo considered that. "In abstraction, not especially. With you, however . . . I wouldn't mind."

"Why with me?"

Taking a handful of her hair, Leo let the pale runners sift through his fingers, playing with it. "I'm not sure. Perhaps because I can see you as a mother."

"Can you?" Catherine had never seen herself that way.

"Oh, yes. The practical kind who makes you eat your turnips, and scolds you for running with sharp objects."

"Is that how your mother was?"

He stretched, his feet reaching far past hers. "Yes. And thank God for it. My father, bless him, was a brilliant scholar one step removed from lunacy. Someone had to be sensible." Rising up on one elbow, he studied her. He used the pad of his thumb to smooth the arc of her eyebrow. "Don't move, love, I'll get a cloth for you."

Catherine waited with her knees drawn up, watching as he left the bed and went to the washstand. He took up a cloth, dampened it with water from a jug, and cleaned himself efficiently. Taking up another cloth, he moistened it liberally and brought it to her. She sensed that he intended to perform the service for her, but she reached for the cloth and said bashfully, "I'll do it."

Leo found his discarded clothing, pulled on his linens and trousers, and returned to Catherine bare-chested. "Your spectacles," he murmured, setting them carefully on her nose. His hands were strong and warm against the humid coolness of her cheeks. Seeing the shiver that went through her, he pulled the quilt up to her shoulders, and half sat on the edge of the mattress.

"Marks," he said soberly. "What just happened . . . am I to take that as a 'yes' to my proposal?"

She hesitated, and shook her head. And then she gave him a wary but resolute glance, as if to indicate that there was nothing he could do or say to change her mind.

His hand found the shape of her hip, squeezing her through the quilt. "I promise it will get better for you, once you heal and have time to—"

"No, it's not that. I enjoyed it." She paused, blushing fiercely. "Very much. But we don't suit in any way other than in the bedroom. We argue so dreadfully."

"It won't be like that now. I'll be nice. I'll let you win every argument, even when I'm right." His lips twitched with amusement. "You're not convinced, I see. What are you afraid we'll argue about?"

Catherine looked down at the quilt, smoothing out a frayed seam. "It is fashionable among the peerage for the husband to take mistresses and the wife to take lovers. I could never accept that." As he opened his mouth to argue, she continued in a rush. "And you've never concealed your aversion to marriage. For you to change your mind so quickly . . . it's impossible to believe."

"I understand." Leo's hand covered hers in a vital grip. "You're right—I've been against the idea of marriage ever since I lost Laura. And I've invented all kinds of excuses to keep from taking such a risk again. But I can't deny any longer that you are entirely worth it. I wouldn't propose to you unless I knew without a doubt that you could satisfy all my needs, and I could satisfy yours." He slid his fingers beneath her chin and urged her to look at him. "As for fidelity—I'll have no difficulty with that." His smile turned wry. "My conscience is burdened enough with past sins—I doubt it could stand any more."

"You would become bored with me," she said anxiously.

That brought a slight smile to his lips. "Obviously you have no idea of the prodigious variety of ways a man and woman can entertain each other. I won't be bored. Neither will you." He stroked her pink cheek with a gentle finger. His gaze was steady. "If I went to another woman's bed, it would be a betrayal of two people—my wife and myself. I wouldn't do that to either of us." He paused. "Do you believe me?"

"Yes," she admitted. "I've always known you to be truthful. Annoying, but truthful."

There was a glint of amusement in his eyes. "Then give me your answer."

"Before I make any decisions, I would like to talk with Harry."

"Of course." A smile played on his lips. "He married my sister, now I want to marry his. If he objects, I'll tell him that it's a fair trade."

As he sat leaning over her, his dark brown hair falling over his brow, Cat could hardly believe that Leo Hathaway was trying to convince her to marry him. Although she was certain that he meant what he said, some promises were broken despite people's best intentions to keep them.

Reading her expression, Leo reached out and pulled her against his warm, hard chest. "I'd tell you not to be afraid," he murmured, "but that's not always possible. On the other hand . . . you've already started to trust me, Marks. There's no point in stopping now."

Chapter Nineteen

Upon learning that the private dining rooms in the tavern would be occupied for some time, Leo requested a tray to be sent up to their room, as well as a hot bath.

Catherine fell asleep beneath the quilt while waiting. She stirred and blinked as she heard the door opening, chairs being moved, the clinking of plates and flatware, the thump of a large tin washtub.

There was a warm, furry weight next to her. Dodger had crawled beneath the quilt and was snoozing beside her shoulder. As Catherine looked at him, she saw the gleam of his bright eyes and heard a tiny yawn before he resettled.

Recalling that she was wearing only Leo's discarded shirt, Catherine hid beneath the quilt and peeked over the edge as a pair of chambermaids set out the bath. Would they suspect what had occurred between her and Leo earlier? She braced herself for a sly or accusing glance, perhaps a contemptuous giggle, but it seemed the chambermaids were too busy to care. They were nothing but businesslike as they tipped two steaming pails into the washtub, and returned with another two pails full. One of the girls set out a three-legged stool piled with folded toweling.

The chambermaids would have left the room without incident, except that Dodger, attracted by the scent of food, emerged from beneath the quilt. He stood tall on the bed and regarded the dinner tray on the small table, his whiskers twitching. *Oh, lovely, I was getting hungry!* his expression seemed to say.

As one of the maids saw Dodger, her face contorted in terror. *"Eeeek!"* She pointed a plump, trembling finger at the ferret. "It's a rat, or a mouse, or—"

"No, it's a ferret," Leo explained, his tone reasonable and soothing. "A harmless and highly civilized creature—the favored pet of royalty, actually. Queen Elizabeth had a pet ferret, and—really, there's no need for violence—"

The chambermaid had picked up a fireplace poker and was raising it in anticipation of an attack.

"Dodger," Catherine said shortly. "Come here."

Dodger slithered up to her. Before she could push him away, he licked her on the cheek in a nuzzling ferret kiss.

One of the chambermaids looked horror-struck, while the other appeared ill.

Fighting to keep a straight face, Leo gave a half-crown to each chambermaid and ushered them from the room. When the door was closed and locked, Catherine lifted the affectionate ferret from her chest and regarded him with a scowl. "You are the most troublesome creature in the world, and not at all civilized."

"Here, Dodger." Leo set out a saucer of beef and parsnips, and the ferret streaked over to it.

While the ferret was busy devouring his meal, Leo came to Catherine and took her face in gentle hands. He lowered his mouth to hers in a brief, warm kiss. "Dinner or bath first?"

She was mortified to hear her stomach tighten with an audible *kworr.*

Leo grinned. "Dinner, it seems."

The meal consisted of beef rounds and mashed parsnips, and a bottle of strong red wine. Catherine ate ravenously, even swabbing the plate with a crust of bread.

Leo was an entertaining companion, telling amusing stories, gently winnowing out confidences, refilling her wine glass. In the light of the single candle that had been set on the table, his face was severely handsome, with thick lashes shadowing incandescent blue eyes.

It occurred to Catherine that this was the first meal she'd ever shared alone with him. Once she would have dreaded the prospect, knowing she would have to be on her guard every second. But there was no conflict in this easy conversation. How remarkable. She almost wished that one of the Hathaway sisters were somewhere nearby, so that she could share this discovery . . . *Your brother and I just spent an entire meal together without arguing!*

It had begun to rain outside, the sky darkening steadily, sprinkles thickening into a steady rush that obliterated the sounds of people and horses and the activity in the carriage yard. Even dressed in the heavy robe that Leo had given her to wear, Catherine shivered and felt gooseflesh rise all over.

"Time for your bath," Leo said, coming to pull her chair back.

Wondering if he intended to stay in the room, Catherine ventured, "Perhaps you might allow me some privacy."

"I wouldn't dream of it," he said. "You may need assistance."

"I can bathe myself. And I would prefer not to be watched."

"My interest is purely aesthetic. I'll imagine you as Rembrandt's *Hendrickje Bathina*, wading in the waters of innocence."

"Purely?" she asked doubtfully.

"Oh, I have a very pure soul. It's only my private parts that have gotten me into trouble."

Catherine couldn't help laughing. "You may stay in the room, as long as you turn your back."

"Agreed." He went to stand by the window.

Catherine glanced at the tub with keen anticipation. She didn't think she had ever looked forward to a bath so much. After securing her hair to the top of her head, she shed the robe, the shirt, and her spectacles, placed them on the bed, and glanced cautiously at Leo, who seemed to have taken a great interest in the view of the carriage yard. He had opened the window a few inches, letting rain-scented air into the room.

"Don't look," she said anxiously.

"I won't. Although you really should discard your inhibitions," he said. "They could get in the way of yielding to temptation."

She sank gingerly into the battered tub. "I would say that I've yielded quite thoroughly today." She sighed in relief as the water soothed all her intimate stings and aches.

"And I was delighted to be of assistance."

"You didn't assist," she said. "You are the temptation." She heard him chuckle.

Leo kept his distance as Catherine bathed, looking out at the rain. After she had washed and rinsed herself, she was so tired that she doubted her own ability to climb out of the bath. Rising on shaking legs, she fumbled to retrieve the folded toweling from the stool next to the tub.

As Catherine stepped out of the water, Leo came to her quickly and held up the toweling, wrapping it around her. Swathing her in a temporary cocoon, he held her for a moment. "Let me sleep with you tonight," he said against her hair, a question in his voice.

Catherine looked up at him quizzically. "What would you do if I refused? Arrange for another room?"

He shook his head. "I would worry about your safety if I were in a different room. I'll sleep on the floor."

"No, we'll share the bed." She pressed her cheek to his chest, relaxing fully in his hold. How comfortable this was, she thought in wonder. How calm and safe she felt with him. "Why wasn't it like this before?" she asked dreamily. "If you'd been the way you are now, I would never have argued with you about anything."

"I tried being nice to you, once or twice. It didn't go well."

"Did you? I never noticed." Her skin, already pink from the bath, turned a deeper shade. "I was suspicious. Mistrustful. And you . . . were everything I feared."

Leo's arms tightened at the admission. He looked down at her with a pensive gaze, as if he were untangling something in his mind, approaching a new realization. The blue eyes were warmer than she had ever seen them. "Let's make a bargain, Marks. From now on, instead of assuming the worst of each other, we'll try to assume the best. Agreed?"

Catherine nodded, transfixed by his gentleness. Somehow those few simple sentences seemed to have wrought a greater change between them than everything that had gone before.

Leo released her carefully. She went to bed while he washed awkwardly in a tub that couldn't begin to accommodate a man his size. She lay and watched him drowsily, the warmth of her body gathering between the sheets of the clean, dry bed. And in spite of all the problems that awaited her, she sank into a deep sleep.

IN HER DREAMS, SHE WENT BACK TO THE DAY SHE HAD TURNED fifteen. She had been parentless for five years, living with her grandmother and Aunt Althea. Her mother had died during that time. She had never known exactly when this event occurred, having been informed well after the fact. She had asked Althea if she might visit her ailing mother, and Althea had replied that she had already died.

Even knowing that her mother had suffered a fatal wasting

disease, knowing there was no hope, the news had come as a shock. Catherine had started to weep, but Althea had grown impatient and snapped, "There's no use crying. It happened long before now, and she's been in the ground since high summer." Which had left Catherine with a bewildering sense of lateness, of off-timing, like a theatergoer who had applauded at the wrong moment. She couldn't grieve properly because she had missed the appropriate opportunity for grieving.

They had lived in a small house in Marylebone, a shabby but respectable dwelling lodged between a dental surgeon's office with a replica of a set of teeth hanging from its sign, and a subscription library supported by private funds. The library was owned and run by her grandmother, who had gone there every day to work.

It had been the most tantalizing place in the world, this heavily frequented building with its vast and hidden collection of books. Catherine had stared at the place from her window, imagining how lovely it would be to browse among rooms of old volumes. Undoubtedly the air had smelled like vellum and leather and book dust, a literary perfume that filled the quiet rooms. She had told Althea that she wanted to work there one day, a declaration that had earned an odd smile from her aunt, and a promise that she undoubtedly would.

However, despite the sign that clearly proclaimed its purpose as a library for the use of distinguished gentlemen, Catherine had gradually realized there was something wrong about the place. No one ever left with any books.

Whenever Catherine mentioned this incongruity, Althea and her grandmother became cross, the same reaction they had displayed when she asked if her father would ever return for her.

On Catherine's fifteenth birthday, she had been given two new dresses. One was blue and one white, with long skirts that had reached all the way to the floor, and waists that had fitted at her own natural waist, instead of childishly high. From now on, Aunt Althea had told her, she would put her hair up and behave as a woman. She was no longer a child. Catherine had absorbed this promotion with pride and anxiety, wondering what would be expected of her now that she had become a woman.

Althea had proceeded to explain, her long, lean face looking harder than usual, her gaze not quite able to meet Catherine's. The establishment next door, as suspected, was not a lending library. It was a house of prostitution, for which she had worked since the age of twelve. It was an easy enough occupation, she assured Catherine . . . let the man do as he pleased, turn your mind elsewhere, and take his money. No matter what his desires or how he used your body, there was relatively little discomfort as long as you didn't resist.

"I don't want to do that," Catherine had said, turning ashen as she realized why the advice was being given.

Althea had raised her plucked, arched brows. "What else do you think you're fit for?"

"Anything but that."

"Mutton-headed girl, do you know how much we've spent on your upkeep? Do you have any idea what a sacrifice it was to take you on? Of course not—you think it was owed to you. But now it's time to repay. You're not being asked to do anything that I haven't done. Do you think you're better than me?"

"No," Catherine said, shamed tears slipping from her eyes. "But I'm not a prostitute."

"Each one of us is born for a purpose, my dear." Althea's voice was calm, even kind. "Some people are born into privilege, some are blessed with artistic talent or natural intelligence. You, unfortunately, are average in every regard . . . average intellect, average wit, and no distinguishable talent. You have inherited beauty, however, and a whore's nature. Therefore, we know what your purpose is, don't we?"

Catherine flinched. She tried to sound composed, but her voice shook. "Being average in most regards doesn't mean I have the makings of a prostitute."

"You're deceiving yourself, child. You are the product of two families of faithless women. Your mother was incapable of being constant to anyone. Men found her irresistible, and she could never resist being wanted. And as for our side . . . your great-grandmother was a procuress, and she trained her daughter in the business. Then it was my turn, and now it is yours. Of all the girls who work for us, you will be the most fortunate. You won't be hired out to any man who comes off the street. You'll be the luminary of our little business. One man at a time, for a negotiated period. You'll last much longer that way."

No matter how Catherine resisted, she had soon found herself being sold to Guy, Lord Latimer. He had been as alien to her as all men were, with his sour breath and scratchy face and crawling hands. Trying to kiss her, forcing his hands into the openings of her clothes, tearing at her like a gamekeeper plucking a dead grouse. He had been amused by her struggles, grunting in her ear about what he was going to do to her, and she had loathed him, loathed all men.

"I won't hurt you . . . if you don't fight me . . ." Latimer had said, grabbing her hands, forcing them down to his groin. "You'll like it. Your little quim knows what's what, I'll show you . . ."

"No, don't touch me, don't—"

She woke up sobbing, straining pitifully against a hard chest. "No—"

"Cat. It's me. Hush, it's me." A warm hand moved over her back.

She went still, her wet cheek pressed to a soft mat of hair. The sound of his voice was deep and familiar. "My lord?"

"Yes. It was just a nightmare. It's over. Let me hold you."

Her head was pounding. She felt shaky and ill, and ice-cold with shame. Leo cuddled her against his chest. As he felt the way she trembled, he smoothed her hair repeatedly. "What were you dreaming of?"

She shook her head with a shuddery sound.

"It had to do with Latimer, didn't it?"

After a long hesitation, she cleared her throat and replied, "Partly."

He caressed her shrinking back in soothing circles, and his lips moved to her damp cheeks. "You're afraid he'll come after you?"

She shook her head. "Something worse."

Very gently he asked, "Can't you tell me?"

Pulling away from him, Catherine curled into a ball, facing the opposite direction. "It's nothing. I'm sorry for waking you."

Leo fit himself against her spoon fashion. She quivered at the sensation of warmth applied all along her back, long hairy legs tucked up beneath hers, a muscular arm thrown across her. All the textures and scents and pulses of him were wrapped around her, his breath falling on her neck. What an extraordinary creature a man was.

It was wrong to take such pleasure in this. Everything Althea had said about her was probably true. She had a whore's nature, a craving for masculine attention . . . she was indeed her mother's daughter. She had repressed and ignored that side of herself for years. But now it was being shown to her, as surely as a reflection in a looking glass. "I don't want to be like her," she whispered without thinking.

"Like who?"

"My mother."

His hand settled on her hip. "Your brother gave me the strong impression that you were definitely not like her." He paused. "In what way are you afraid of being similar?"

Catherine was silent, her breath wavering as she tried not to choke on a new surge of tears. He was undoing her with this newfound tenderness. She would have much preferred the old mocking Leo. It seemed she had no defenses against this one.

He pressed a kiss into the hollow behind her ear. "My dear girl," he whispered, "don't tell me you feel guilty for having enjoyed sexual relations?"

It unnerved her further that he had reached an accurate conclusion so quickly. "Perhaps a little," she said, her voice catching.

"Good God, I'm in bed with a puritan." Leo uncoiled her stiff body and spread her out beneath him, ignoring her protest. "Why is it wrong for a woman to enjoy it?"

"I don't think it's wrong for other women."

"Just you, then?" His voice was gently sardonic. "Why?"

"Because I'm the fourth generation of a family of prostitutes. And my aunt said I had a natural proclivity for it."

"Everyone does, love. It's how the world is populated."

"No, not for that. For prostitution."

He snorted derisively. "There is no such thing as a natural proclivity for selling oneself. Prostitution is forced on women by a society that allows them damned few options to support themselves. And as for you . . . I've never met a woman less equipped for it." He played with the tangled runners of her hair. "I'm afraid I don't follow your logic. It's no sin to enjoy a man's touch, nor does that have anything to do with prostitution. Anything your aunt told you was pure manipulation— for obvious reasons." His mouth lowered to her neck, pressing kisses along the taut surface. "We can't have you feeling guilty," he said. "Especially when it's so misguided."

She sniffled. "Morality isn't misguided."

"Ah. There's the problem. You have morality, guilt, and pleasure all mixed together." His hand went to her breast, cupping tenderly. The sensation shot to the pit of her stomach.

"There's nothing moral about denying pleasure, and nothing wrong about wanting it." She felt him smile against her skin. "What you need is to indulge in several long nights of uncivilized lust with me. It would drive all the guilt out of you. And if that didn't work, at least I would be happy." His hand swept down her body, his thumb brushing the top edge of intimate curls. Her belly tightened beneath his palm. His fingers trailed deeper.

"What are you doing?" she asked.

"Helping you with your problem. No, don't thank me, it's no trouble at all." His smiling mouth brushed against hers, and he moved over her in the darkness. "What word do you use for this, love?"

"For what?"

"For this sweet place . . . here."

Her body jerked at his gentle caress. She could hardly speak. "I don't have a word for that."

"Then how do you refer to it?"

"I don't!"

He laughed quietly. "I know several words. But the French, not surprisingly, have the nicest one. *Le chat.*"

"The cat?" she asked, bewildered.

"Yes, a double meaning for a feline and a woman's softest part. Puss. Pussy. The sweetest fur . . . no, don't be shy. Ask me to pet you."

The words stole her breath away. "My lord," she protested faintly.

"Ask and I'll do it," he prompted, his fingers withdrawing to play in the sensitive hollow behind her knee.

She swallowed back a moan.

"Ask," came his coaxing whisper.

"Please."

Leo kissed her thigh, his mouth soft and hot, his bristle an exciting scrape against the tender skin. "Please what?"

Wicked man. She squirmed and covered her face with her hands, even though they were in complete darkness. Her voice was muffled by the screen of her fingers. "Please pet me there."

His touch came so lightly she could scarcely feel it at first, fingertips stirring, teasing. "Like this?"

"Yes, oh yes . . ." Her hips lifted, inviting more. He fingered the folds of her sex, massaging delicately, tracing the softness within. The skillful caresses brought her body to trembling readiness.

"What else should I do?" Leo whispered, moving lower in the darkness. She felt his breath on her, heat against moisture, a soft intermittent blowing. Her hips arched and strained without volition.

"Make love to me."

He sounded gently regretful. "No, you're too sore."

"*Leo,*" she whimpered.

"Shall I kiss you instead? Here?" His fingertip swirled.

Catherine's eyes widened in the darkness. Stunned and acutely aroused by the suggestion, she licked her dry lips. "No. I don't know." She writhed as she felt him breathe against her, his fingers gently holding her apart. "Yes."

"Ask me nicely."

"Ask you to . . . Oh, I can't."

The teasing fingers left her. "Shall we go to sleep, then?"

She caught his head in her hands. "No."

He was inexorable. "You know how to ask."

She couldn't. The shamed syllables stuck in her throat, and she could only moan in frustration.

And Leo, the monstrous cad, smothered a chuckle against her thigh.

"I'm so glad you find this amusing," she said furiously.

"I do," he assured her, his voice thick with laughter. "Oh, Marks, we have so far to go with you."

"Don't bother," she snapped, trying to move away, but he pinned her legs in place, holding her easily.

"There's no need to be stubborn," he coaxed. "Go on, say it. For me."

A long silence passed. She swallowed and made herself say, "Kiss me."

"Where?"

"Down there," she managed, her voice shaking. "On my pussy. Please."

Leo fairly purred in approval. "What a naughty girl you are." His head lowered, and he nuzzled into the damp softness, and she felt his mouth cover the most sensitive part of her in a wet, open kiss, and the world caught fire.

"Is that what you wanted?" she heard him ask.

"More, more," she cried, gasping.

His tongue traced her in fluid, savoring strokes. Her body drew taut as he began to tug and flick, and the voluptuous expanding pleasure went all through her. She was suffused in wet sensation, each slide of his tongue opening her to greater pleasure. His hands cupped beneath her, making a vessel of her hips, tilting her to meet his mouth. She convulsed in raw shudders, crying out, her nerves dancing with exquisite heat. His mouth lingered softly, as if he were reluctant to stop. For a scalding moment she felt his tongue enter her, teasing out a last few quivers.

She was soon chilled as rain-scented air from the partially open window swept over her skin. She thought Leo would satisfy his own needs then, and she moved toward him in exhausted confusion. But he settled her in the crook of his arm and pulled the quilts over them both. She was replete and enervated, unable to stay awake.

"Sleep," she heard him whisper. "And if you have any more nightmares . . . I'll kiss them all away."

Chapter Twenty

The rainy night had yielded to a damp green morning. Leo awakened to the sounds of the carriage yard coming alive with the whicker and jangling and stomping of horses. A muffled clatter of footsteps advanced along the hallways as people left their rooms and went to the tavern for food.

Leo's favorite part of a romantic rendezvous had always been the moments of anticipation right before lovemaking. His least favorite part had been the morning after, when his first waking thought was how quickly he could leave without causing offense.

This morning, however, was different from any other. He had opened his eyes to discover that he was in bed with Catherine Marks, and there was nowhere else in the world he wanted to be. She was still sleeping deeply, on her side with her hand palm up. Her fingers were curled like the edges of an orchid. She was beautiful in the morning, tumbled and relaxed and sleep-flushed.

His fascinated gaze traveled over her. He had never confided so much in any woman, but he knew that his secrets were safe with her. And hers with him. They were well matched. No matter what happened now, their days of battling were over. They knew too much about each other.

Unfortunately, the question of their betrothal was not at all settled. Leo knew that Cat was not nearly as convinced of the rightness of their match as he was. Furthermore, Harry Rutledge was going to have an opinion about it, and so far Leo had rarely liked his opinions. It was even possible that Harry might encourage Cat in her idea of traveling the Continent.

A frown tugged at Leo's brow as he pondered how she had gone through life virtually unprotected until now. How could a woman so deserving of affection have received so little? He wanted to make up for everything she had missed. He wanted to give her whatever she had been deprived of. The trick would be convincing her to let him.

Catherine's face was peaceful, her lips slightly parted. Curled among the white bed linens, a glimpse of her pink shoulder visible, that golden hair streaming everywhere, she looked like a confection placed amid swirls of whipped cream.

There was a disturbance at the foot of the bed as Dodger hoisted himself up to the corner of the mattress and crept along Catherine's side. She stirred and yawned, and fumbled to pet him. The ferret curled by her hip and closed his eyes.

Catherine awakened slowly, her body lengthening in a trembling stretch. Her lashes lifted. She looked at Leo in bewilderment, clearly wondering why he should be there with her. It was a stare of disarming innocence, those lovely sea-gray eyes contemplating him while her mind collected itself. Hesitantly she reached a cool hand to his cheek, investigating the bristle that had grown during the night. Her voice was low and wondering. "You're as scratchy as Beatrix's hedgehog."

Leo kissed her palm.

Catherine nestled against him cautiously. Her breath stirred the hair on his chest as she asked, "Are we going to London today?"

"Yes."

She was quiet for a moment. "Do you still want to marry me?" she asked abruptly.

He kept her hand in his. "I'm going to insist on it."

Her face was angled so that he couldn't see it. "But . . . I'm not like Laura."

Leo was somewhat startled by the comment. "No," he said frankly. Laura had been the product of a loving family, an idyllic life in a small village. She had known nothing like the fear and pain that had shaped Catherine's childhood. "You resemble Laura no more than I resemble the boy I was then," he continued. "How is that relevant?"

"Perhaps you would be better off with someone like her. Someone you—" She stopped herself.

Leo turned and braced himself on an elbow, looking down into myopic blue-gray eyes. "Someone I love?" he finished for her, and watched her frown and chew her lower lip uncertainly. He wanted to gently bite and suck that perfect little mouth as if it were a fresh plum. Instead he traced the edge of her lower lip with a gentle fingertip. "I've told you before, I love like a madman," he said. "Immoderate, jealous, possessive . . . I'm absolutely intolerable."

He let the backs of his fingers glide over her chin and along the front of her throat, where he felt the swift tattoo of her heartbeat and the flutter of her swallow. No stranger to the signs of feminine arousal, he slid his palm over the front of her body, skimming the hard bud of her nipple, the curve of her side. "If I loved you, Cat, I would have you for breakfast, lunch, and dinner. You'd never have any peace."

"I would set limits. And make you heed them." She drew a sharp breath as he pulled the sheet away from her. "You want a firm hand, that's all."

Annoyed by the disturbance, Dodger slid off the bed indignantly and went to hop into Catherine's carpetbag.

Leo nuzzled the warm curve of her breast and stroked the tip with his tongue. "Perhaps you're right," he said, catching her hand, drawing it down to his hard flesh.

"I . . . I didn't mean . . ."

"Yes, I know. But I'm a terribly literal-minded person." He showed her how to grip and stroke him, guiding her in the ways he liked to be touched. They lay together in the warm bed, both of them breathing fast as she explored him with delicate pale fingers. How many times Leo had fantasized about this moment, the prim and prudish Marks naked in bed with him. It was glorious.

Her hand tightened on his stiff length, and the delicious pressure nearly sent him over the edge.

"*God* . . . no, no, wait . . ." He pried her hand away with a gasping laugh.

"Did I do something wrong?" Catherine asked anxiously.

"Not at all, love. But one rather hopes to last more than five minutes, especially before the lady is satisfied." He reached for her breasts, kneading gently. "How beautiful you are. Bring yourself higher and let me kiss your breast." As she hesitated, he closed his thumb and forefinger over her nipple in a playful pinch.

She jerked in surprise.

"Too hard?" Leo asked contritely, his gaze intent on her face. "Then do as I asked, and I'll soothe it." He didn't miss her quick double-blink, or the altered rhythm of her breathing. Reaching out, he drew his hands slowly over the slender curves of her body, learning more about her by the second.

"You *are* intolerable," she told him unevenly. But she obeyed the encouraging pressure of his palms, and climbed slowly over him. She was light and supple, her skin like silk, the blond thatch of curls brushing crisply against his stomach.

The peak of her breast was already tightly contracted as Leo took it into his mouth. He played with her, dragging the flat of his tongue across the gathered point, relishing the helpless sounds that climbed in her throat.

"Kiss me," he said, slipping a hand behind her neck, pulling her mouth to his. "And rest your hips on mine."

"Stop giving orders," she protested breathlessly.

On impulse, Leo decided to provoke her. He let an arrogant smile touch his lips. "Here in bed, I'm the master. I'll give orders, and you'll follow them without question." He paused deliberately, lifting his brows. "Understood?"

Catherine stiffened. Leo had never enjoyed anything so much as the sight of her struggling between outrage and arousal. He felt the heat rise in her, the excited thrum of her pulse. She took an agitated breath, while gooseflesh rose on her arms. And then her body seemed to lose all its tension, her limbs loosening. "Yes," she finally whispered, not quite able to meet his gaze.

Leo's own heartbeat escalated. "Good girl," he said thickly. "Now spread your thighs so I can feel you against me."

Gradually the angle of her legs widened.

She looked dazed, a little lost, her gaze turning inward as if to contemplate the puzzle of her own reactions to him. Her eyes glittered, an involuntary welling of pleasure and confusion, and the sight sent a tide of lust through him. He wanted to fulfill her beyond imagining, discover and satisfy every need.

"Put your hand beneath your breast," he said, "and bring it to my mouth."

She leaned over him to obey, trembling. And then he was the one who was lost, fiercely absorbed in the sweet softness of her. He lost awareness of everything but instinct, the primitive intent to claim, conquer, possess.

He made her kneel over him, and he followed the intoxicating salt-scented moisture to the tender entrance of her body.

Delving with his tongue, he traced and licked until he felt the long, fine muscles of her thighs tightening rhythmically.

With a hoarse murmur, Leo eased her away and helped her to straddle his hips. He fit himself against the soft slit and clasped her waist to steady her. She quivered as she understood what he wanted.

"Slowly," he murmured as she eased onto him. "All the way down." He barely managed to stifle an agonized groan as he felt her clenching around him, her swollen flesh working to pull him inside. Nothing had ever felt so good. "Oh, sweet Jesus . . . take it all."

"I can't." She writhed and went still, looking disgruntled.

It was inconceivable that Leo should have found any amusement in the moment, when his body was tortured with desire. But she was so adorably awkward astride him. Somehow managing to repress a laugh, Leo put his shaking hands on her, arranging and stroking. "You can," he said huskily. "Put your hands on my shoulders, and lean your sweet little body forward."

"It's too much."

"It's not."

"It *is*."

"I'm the experienced one. You're the novice, remember?"

"That doesn't change the fact that you're too . . . *oh*."

Somewhere in the midst of their debate, he had pressed upward the last crucial distance, and their bodies slid together fully.

"Oh," she said again, her eyes half closing, new color sweeping over her.

Leo felt an explosive climax rolling up to him, requiring only a hint of stimulation to reach irresistible momentum. Catherine's body tightened around him, a voluptuously contained rhythm that threatened to drive him mad. She moved tentatively, the tender friction causing them both to shudder.

"Cat, wait," he whispered through dry lips.

"I can't, I can't . . ." She moved again, and he arched as if on a torture rack.

"Be still."

"I'm trying." But she had begun to rock against him instinctively, and he groaned and took up the rhythm, watching her lips parting with delighted gasps, and as he felt the spasms overtake her, the sensations rushed too powerfully for him to withstand.

With a herculean effort, Leo withdrew and spilled his pleasure on the sheets, while his breath hissed through his clenched teeth. Every muscle screamed in protest at being deprived of the lush warmth that had enclosed him. Panting, blinking against a shower of sparks, Leo felt Catherine curl up against him.

One of her hands came to the center of his chest, pressing over his pounding heart. She pressed her lips to his shoulder. "I didn't want you to stop," she whispered.

"Neither did I." He wrapped his arms around her, and smiled ruefully against her hair. "But that's the problem with coitus interruptus. One always has to exit at the station before one's final destination."

Chapter Twenty-one

Leo proposed twice more to Catherine on the way to London. She refused both times, determined to proceed in a sensible manner and discuss the situation with her brother first. When Leo pointed out that running harum-scarum from Ramsay House in the middle of the night could hardly be characterized as sensible behavior, she allowed that perhaps she shouldn't have acted so impetuously.

"As much as I dislike to admit it," she told Leo as their carriage rolled along the post road, "I haven't been in my right mind since the ball. It was a shock to see Lord Latimer so unexpectedly. And when he put his hands on me, I felt myself shrink down to a frightened child again, and all I could think of was getting away." She paused reflectively. "But I found comfort in knowing I had Harry to run to."

"You also had me," Leo said quietly.

She stared at him in wonder. "I didn't know that."

His gaze held hers. "You know it now."

LET ME BE YOUR BIG BROTHER, HARRY HAD TOLD CATHERINE at their last meeting in Hampshire, making it clear that he wanted to attempt the kind of familial relationship they had never been capable of before. With no small amount of unease, Catherine reflected that she was about to test his claim far sooner than either of them could have expected. And they were still practically strangers.

But Harry had altered greatly during the short time of his marriage to Poppy. He was far kinder and warmer now, and certainly willing to think of Catherine as something more than an inconvenient half sister who didn't belong anywhere.

Upon arriving at the Rutledge Hotel, Leo and Catherine were shown immediately to the sumptuous private apartments that Harry and Poppy shared.

Of all the Hathaways, Poppy was the one Catherine had always felt the most comfortable with. Poppy was a warm and talkative young woman who loved order and routine. Hers was an essentially sunny and accepting nature, providing a necessary balance to Harry's driven intensity.

"Catherine," she exclaimed, embracing her, then standing back to view her with concern. "Why are you here? Is something wrong? Is everyone well?"

"Your family is quite well," Catherine said hastily. "But there was . . . a situation. I had to leave." Her throat became very tight.

Poppy looked at Leo with a frown. "Did you do something?"

"Why do you ask that?"

"Because if there is trouble of any kind, you're usually involved."

"True. But this time I'm not the problem, I'm the solution."

Harry approached them, his green eyes narrowed. "If you're the solution, Ramsay, I'm terrified to hear the problem." He gave Cat an alert glance, and astonished her by bringing her against him in a protective embrace. "What is it, Cat?" he asked near her ear. "What's happened?"

"Oh, Harry," she faltered, "Lord Latimer came to the ball at Ramsay House."

He understood everything from that one sentence. "I'll take care of it," he said without hesitation. "I'll take care of you."

Catherine closed her eyes and let out a slow sigh. "Harry, I don't know what to do."

"You were right to come to me. We'll manage it together." Harry raised his head and glanced at Leo. "Presumably Cat has told you about Latimer."

Leo looked grim. "Believe me, had I known anything about the situation before, he wouldn't have gotten anywhere near her."

Harry kept Catherine in the crook of his arm as he turned to face Leo fully. "Why was the bastard invited to Ramsay House in the first place?"

"His family was invited as a courtesy befitting their social position in Hampshire. He came in their stead. After he tried to force himself on Marks, I booted him from the premises. He won't be returning."

Harry's eyes gleamed dangerously. "I'll put a word in the right ear. By tomorrow evening he'll wish he were dead."

Catherine felt a nervous pang in her stomach. Harry was a man of extensive influence. As well as his hotel dealings, he had access to a great quantity of highly confidential and valuable information. What Harry kept in his head could probably have been used to start wars, fell kingdoms, destroy families, and dismantle the British financial system.

"No, Harry," Poppy said. "If you're planning to have Lord Latimer butchered or maimed, you're going to have to think of something else."

"I like Harry's plan," Leo said.

"It's not up for debate," Poppy informed him. "Come, let's sit and discuss reasonable alternatives." She looked at

Catherine. "You must be famished after traveling so far. I'll ring for tea and sandwiches."

"None for me, thank you," Catherine said. "I'm not—"

"Yes, she wants sandwiches," Leo interrupted. "She had only bread and tea for breakfast."

"I'm not hungry," Catherine protested. He answered her annoyed glance with an implacable one.

It was a new experience, having someone care about the mundane details of her welfare, having him notice what she'd eaten for breakfast. She examined the feeling, tested it, and found it strangely alluring, even as she resisted the idea of being told what to do. The small interaction was similar to a thousand instances she had seen between Cam and Amelia, or Merripen and Win, the way they occasionally fussed over each other. Cared for each other.

After tea was sent for, Poppy returned to the private parlor. Sitting beside Catherine on the velvet-covered settee, Poppy said, "Tell us what happened, dear. Did Lord Latimer approach you early in the evening?"

"No, the ball had been under way for some time . . ."

Catherine relayed the events of the evening in a matter-of-fact manner, her hands clenched in her lap. "The problem is," she said, "that no matter how we try to keep Lord Latimer quiet about the past, he will make it public. A scandal is coming, and nothing will stop it. The best way to throw water on the flames is for me to disappear again."

"A new name, a new identity?" Harry asked, and shook his head. "You can't run forever, Cat. We'll stand and confront it this time—together—as we should have done years ago." He pinched the bridge of his nose, turning various options over in his mind. "I'll start by acknowledging you publicly as my sister."

Catherine felt herself turn ashen. People would be ravenously curious when they learned that the mysterious Harry

Rutledge had a long-lost sister. She was fairly certain she wouldn't be able to bear the scrutiny and the questions.

"People would recognize me as the Hathaways' governess," she said in a suffocated voice. "They would ask why the sister of a wealthy hotelier would have accepted such a position."

"They'll make of it what they will," Harry said.

"It won't reflect well on you."

Leo spoke dryly. "With your brother's associations, Marks, he's accustomed to unflattering rumors."

The familiar way he had addressed her caused Harry's eyes to narrow. "I find it interesting," he said to Catherine, "that you came to London with Ramsay as your traveling companion. When was it decided that the two of you would depart together? And what hour did you leave last night, to reach London by noon?"

All the color that had left Catherine's face earlier now came rushing back at a surplus. "I . . . he . . ." She glanced at Leo, who had adopted an expression of innocent interest, as if he too wanted to hear her explanation. "I left by myself yesterday morning," she managed to say, dragging her gaze back to Harry.

Harry leaned forward, a scowl gathering on his face. "*Yesterday* morning? Where did you spend the night?"

She lifted her chin and tried to sound matter-of-fact. "A coaching inn."

"Do you have any idea how dangerous those places are for a woman alone? Have you taken leave of your senses? When I think of what could have happened to you—"

"She wasn't alone," Leo said.

Harry stared at him incredulously.

It was one of those silences that was far more eloquent than words. One could almost see Harry's brain working like the elaborate mechanisms he liked to construct in his spare time. One could also see the moment at which he reached an accurate and highly unwelcome conclusion.

Harry spoke to Leo in a tone that chilled Catherine to the bone. "Even you wouldn't take advantage of a frightened and vulnerable woman who had just suffered an upheaval."

"You've never given a damn about her," Leo replied. "Why should you start now?"

Harry rose to his feet, his fists clenched.

"Oh, dear," Poppy murmured. "Harry—"

"Did you share a room with her?" Harry demanded of Leo. "A bed?"

"That's none of your bloody business, is it?"

"It is when it's my sister and you were supposed to be protecting her, not molesting her!"

"Harry," Catherine broke in, "he didn't—"

"I'm rarely disposed to listen to a lecture on morality," Leo said to Harry, "when it's given by someone who knows even less about it than I do."

"Poppy," Harry said, his gaze fastened on Leo as if he were contemplating murder. "You and Cat need to leave the room."

"Why must I leave when I'm the subject of discussion?" Catherine demanded. "I'm not a child."

"Come, Catherine," Poppy said quietly, heading to the door. "Let them bluster and brawl in their manly fashion. You and I will go somewhere to discuss your future sensibly."

This struck Catherine as an excellent idea. She followed Poppy from the room, while Harry and Leo continued to glare at each other.

"I'M GOING TO MARRY HER," LEO SAID.

Harry's face went blank. "You despise each other."

"We've come to an understanding."

"Has she accepted you?"

"Not yet. She wants to discuss it with you first."

"Thank God. Because I'll tell her that it's the worst idea I've ever heard."

Leo arched a brow. "You doubt I could protect her?"

"I doubt you could keep from murdering each other! I doubt she could ever be happy in such volatile circumstances. I doubt . . . no, I won't bother listing all my concerns, it would take too bloody long." Harry's eyes were ice-cold. "The answer is no, Ramsay. I'll do what is necessary to take care of Cat. You can return to Hampshire."

"I'm afraid it won't be that easy to get rid of me," Leo said. "Perhaps you didn't notice that I haven't asked for your permission. There is no choice. Certain things have happened that can't be undone. Do you understand?"

He saw from Harry's expression that only a few fragile constraints stood between him and certain death.

"You seduced her deliberately," Harry managed to say.

"Would you be happier if I claimed it was an accident?"

"The only thing that would make me happy is to weight you with rocks and toss you into the Thames."

"I understand. I even sympathize. I can't imagine what it would be like to face a man who's compromised your sister, how difficult it would be to keep from murdering him on the spot. Oh, but wait . . ." Leo tapped a forefinger thoughtfully on his chin. "I *can* imagine. Because I went through it *two bloody months ago.*"

Harry's eyes narrowed. "That wasn't the same. Your sister was still a virgin when I married her."

Leo gave him an unrepentant glance. "When I compromise a woman, I do it properly."

"That does it," Harry muttered, leaping for his throat.

They crashed to the floor, rolling and grappling. Although Harry managed to slam Leo's head on the floor, the thick carpet absorbed most of the impact. Harry sought a chokehold, but Leo ducked his chin and wrenched free. They rolled twice, exchanging blows, aiming for the throat, the kidneys, the solar plexus, in the kind of fight that usually took place in East End slum alleys.

"You won't win this one, Rutledge," Leo panted as they broke apart and lurched to their feet. "I'm not one of your prick-me-dainty fencing partners." He dodged a hard right and took a jab of his own. "I've fought my way in and out of every gaming hell and tavern in London—" He faked a jab with his left and followed with a swift right hook, making a satisfying impact with Harry's jaw. "And aside from all that, I live with Merripen, who has a left uppercut like a kick from a mule—"

"Do you *ever* stop talking?" Harry threw a counterpunch and stepped back before Leo could retaliate.

"It's called communication. You ought to try it sometime." Exasperated, Leo dropped his guard and stood there undefended. "Especially with your sister. Have you ever bothered to listen to her? Damn it, man, she came to London hoping for some kind of brotherly counsel or consolation, and the first thing you do is send her from the room."

Harry's fists lowered. He pinned Leo with a damning glare, but when he spoke, his voice was heavy with self-condemnation. "I've failed her for years. Do you think I'm unaware of all that I could have done for her but didn't? I'll do anything possible to atone. But damn you, Ramsay . . . the last thing she needed in this situation was for her innocence to be taken when she couldn't defend herself."

"It's exactly what she needed."

Harry shook his head in disbelief. "Damn you." He scrubbed a hand through his black hair, and gave a peculiar strangled laugh. "I *hate* arguing with a Hathaway. You all say something lunatic as if it's perfectly logical. Is it too early for brandy?"

"Not at all. I'm feeling far too sober for this conversation."

Harry went to a sideboard and pulled out two glasses. "While I pour," he said, "you can explain why being deflowered by you was so bloody beneficial to my sister."

Shrugging out of his coat, Leo draped it over the back of his chair and sat. "Marks has been isolated and alone for much too long—"

"She hasn't been alone, she's been living with the Hathaways."

"Even so, she's stayed at the edges of the family with her nose pressed against the window, like some Dickensian orphan. A false name, drab clothes, dyed hair . . . she's concealed her identity for so long that she hardly knows who she is. But the real Catherine emerges when she's with me. We've gotten beneath each other's guards. We speak the same language, if you take my meaning." Leo paused, staring into the glowing swirl of his brandy. "Marks is a contradictory woman, and yet the more I know her, the more the contradictions make sense. She's spent too long in the shadows. No matter how she tries to convince herself otherwise, she wants to belong somewhere, with someone. And yes, she wants a man in her bed. Me in particular." Taking the brandy that Harry handed to him, Leo tossed back a swallow. "She'll thrive with me. Not because I'm a stellar example of virtuous manhood, nor have I ever claimed to be. But I'm right for her. I'm not cowed by her sharp tongue, and she can't outmaneuver me. And she knows it."

Harry sat nearby and drank his own brandy. He watched Leo pensively, on one level trying to assess his sincerity, on another judging his veracity. "What would you get from this arrangement?" he asked quietly. "As I understand, you need to marry and sire a child rather soon. If Cat doesn't succeeded in bearing a son, the Hathaways will lose Ramsay House."

"We've survived many things far worse than losing a bloody house. I'll marry Marks and take the risk."

"Perhaps you're testing the waters," Harry said, his face expressionless. "Trying to determine if she's fertile before you marry her."

Instantly offended, Leo forced himself to remember that he was dealing with the legitimate concern of a brother for a sister. "I don't give a damn if she's fertile or not," he said evenly. "If it will settle your concerns, we'll wait however long it will take to make the copyhold clause irrelevant. I want her regardless."

"And what about what Cat wants?"

"That's up to her. As for dealing with Latimer—I've already made him aware that I have leverage against him. I'll use it if he starts to make trouble. But the best protection I can offer her is my name." Finishing his brandy, Leo set the empty snifter aside. "What do you know of this grandmother and aunt?"

"The old crone died not long ago. The aunt, Althea Hutchins, runs the place now. I sent my assistant Valentine to take inventory of the situation, and he returned looking somewhat sickened. Apparently in a bid to revive business, Mrs. Hutchins turned it into a whipping brothel, where any number of depravities are catered to. The unfortunate women who work there are usually too well worn to be employed at other brothels." Harry finished his brandy. "It seems the aunt is ailing, most likely from some untreated bawdy-house disease."

Leo looked at him alertly. "Have you told Marks?"

"No, she's never asked. I don't believe she wants to know."

"She's afraid," Leo said quietly.

"Of what?"

"Of what nearly became of her. Of things Althea said to her."

"Such as?"

Leo shook his head. "She told me in confidence." He smiled faintly at Harry's obvious annoyance. "You've known her for years, Rutledge—what in God's name did you talk about when you were together? Taxes? The weather?" He stood and picked up his coat. "If you'll excuse me, I'm going to arrange for a room."

Harry frowned. "Here?"

"Yes, where else?"

"What about the terrace you usually lease?"

"Closed away for the summer. But even if it weren't, I'd still stay here." Leo smiled slightly. "Consider it yet another chance to experience the joys of a close family."

"It was a far greater joy when the family stayed in bloody Hampshire," Harry said as Leo left the apartment.

Chapter Twenty-two

"Harry was right about something," Poppy told Catherine as they walked through the gardens at the back of the hotel.

In contrast to the modern preference for the romantic appearance in gardening—unstructured, with beds of blossoms that appeared to have sprung up spontaneously, and paths laid out in meandering curves—the Rutledge gardens were orderly and grand. Disciplined hedges formed walls that guided one through a careful arrangement of fountains, statuary, parterres, and elaborate flower beds.

"It is definitely time," Poppy continued, "for Harry to introduce you to people as his sister. And for you to be known by your real name. What is it, by the way?"

"Catherine Wigens."

Poppy considered that. "I'm sure it's only because I've always known you as Miss Marks . . . but I like Marks better."

"So do I. Catherine Wigens was a frightened girl in difficult circumstances. I've been much happier as Catherine Marks."

"Happier?" Poppy asked gently. "Or merely less frightened?"

Catherine smiled. "I've learned quite a lot about happiness over the past few years. I found peace at school, although I was too quiet and private to make friends there. It wasn't until I came to work for the Hathaways that I saw the day-to-day interactions of people who love each other. And then in the past year, I've finally experienced moments of true joy. The feeling that at least for the moment, everything is as it should be, and there's nothing else one could ask for."

Poppy sent her a smiling glance. "Moments such as . . . ?"

They entered the rose garden, filled with a profusion of blossoms, the air heavy with sun-warmed perfume.

"Evenings in the parlor, when the family was together and Win was reading. Going on walks with Beatrix. Or that rainy day in Hampshire when we all had a picnic on the veranda. Or—" She broke off, shaken by the realization of what she had been about to say.

"Or?" Poppy prompted, pausing to examine a large and resplendent rose, inhaling its scent. Her astute gaze darted to Catherine's face.

It was difficult to express her most personal thoughts, but Catherine forced herself to admit the uncomfortable truth. "After Lord Ramsay hurt his shoulder at the old manor ruins . . . he was in bed with fever the next day . . . and I sat with him for hours. We talked while I did the mending, and I read Balzac to him."

Poppy smiled. "Leo must have loved that. He adores French literature."

"He told me about the time he spent in France. He said the French have a marvelous way of uncomplicating things."

"Yes, he needed that very much. When Leo went to France with Win, he was a wreck of a man. You wouldn't have known him. We didn't know whom to fear for more, Win with her weak lungs, or Leo, who was bent on destroying himself."

"But they came back well," Catherine said.

"Yes, both of them were finally well. But different."

"Because of France?"

"That, and also the struggles they'd been through. Win told me that one isn't improved by being at the top of the mountain, one is improved by the climb."

Catherine smiled as she thought of Win, whose patient fortitude had carried her through years of illness. "That sounds exactly like her," she said. "Perceptive. And strong."

"Leo is like that too," Poppy said. "It's only that he's far more irreverent."

"And cynical," Catherine said.

"Yes, cynical . . . but also playful. Perhaps it's an odd combination of qualities, but there's my brother."

Catherine's smile lingered. There were so many images of Leo in her mind . . . patiently rescuing a hedgehog that had fallen into a fencepost hole . . . working on a set of plans for a new tenant house, his face severe with concentration . . . lying wounded on his bed, his eyes glazed with pain as he murmured, *I'm too much for you to manage.*

No, she had replied, *you're not.*

"Catherine," Poppy said hesitantly, "the fact that Leo came to London with you . . . I wonder if . . . that is, I hope . . . is there a betrothal in the making?"

"He has offered for me," Catherine admitted, "but I—"

"Has he?" Poppy astonished her with an enthusiastic embrace. "Oh, it's too good to be true! Please say you'll accept him."

"I'm afraid the situation isn't that simple," Catherine said ruefully, drawing back. "There is much to consider, Poppy."

Poppy's exuberance faded quickly, an anxious pucker appearing between her brows. "You don't love him? But in time you will, I'm sure of it. There is so much about him worth—"

"It's not a question of love," Catherine said with a slight grimace.

"Marriage isn't a question of love?"

"No, it is, of course, but I meant to say that love cannot overcome certain difficulties."

"Then you do love him?" Poppy asked hopefully.

Catherine turned deep red. "There are many qualities I esteem in Lord Ramsay."

"And he makes you happy, you said so."

"Well, on that one day, I'll admit—"

"'A moment of true joy,' was how you put it."

"Heavens, Poppy, I feel as if I'm being interrogated."

Poppy grinned. "I'm sorry, it's just that I want this match so very much. For Leo's sake, and yours, and for the family."

Harry's dry voice came from behind them. "It appears we're at cross-purposes, my love." The women turned as he approached them. Harry regarded his wife warmly, but there was an air of preoccupation about him. "The tea and sandwiches are waiting," he said. "And the brawl is over. Shall we go back to the apartments?"

"Who won the brawl?" Poppy asked impishly.

That earned one of Harry's rare grins. "A conversation broke out in the middle of the fight. Which was undoubtedly a good thing, as it turned out that neither of us knows how to fight like a gentleman."

"You fence," Poppy pointed out. "That's a very gentlemanly way to fight."

"Fencing isn't really fighting. It's more like chess with the risk of puncture wounds."

"Well, I'm glad you didn't hurt each other," Poppy said cheerfully, "since there's a distinct possibility that you may soon be brothers-in-law."

"We're already brothers-in-law."

"Brothers-in-law squared, then." Poppy slipped her arm through his.

Harry glanced at Catherine as they began to walk. "You haven't decided yet, have you? About marrying Ramsay?"

"Certainly not," she said quietly, keeping pace with them. "My head's in a whirl. I need time to think."

"Harry," Poppy said, "when you say that we're at cross-purposes, I hope you don't mean that you're against the idea of Leo and Catherine marrying."

"For the time being," he said, seeming to choose his words carefully, "I believe caution is in order."

"But don't you want Catherine to become part of my family?" Poppy asked, bewildered. "She would have the protection of the Hathaways, and she would be close to your influence."

"Yes, I would like that very much. Except that it would necessitate Cat's marrying Ramsay, and I'm not at all convinced that would be best for her."

"I thought you liked Leo," Poppy protested.

"I do. If there's a man in London with more charm or wit, I have yet to meet him."

"Then how could you have any objections?"

"Because his past doesn't recommend itself as that of a reliable husband. Cat has been betrayed many times in her life." His tone was sober and grim. He looked at Catherine. "And I'm one of the people who failed you. I don't want you to suffer that way again."

"Harry," Catherine said earnestly, "you're far too severe on yourself."

"Now isn't the time to pour sweetener on unpleasant truths," he returned. "If I could change the past, I would go back and do so without hesitation. But all I can do is try to make amends, and do better in the future. And I would say the same of Ramsay."

"Everyone deserves a second chance," Catherine said.

"Agreed. And I'd like to believe that he's turned over a new leaf. But it remains to be seen."

"You're afraid he'll fall back into bad habits," Catherine said.

"He wouldn't be the first. However, Ramsay is nearing the age at which a man's character is more or less fixed. If he continues to avoid his former libertine practices, I think he'll make a fine husband. But until he manages to prove himself, I'm not willing to risk your future as the wife of a man who may prove incapable of keeping his vows."

"He would keep his vows," Poppy insisted.

"How do you know that?"

"Because he's a Hathaway."

Harry smiled down at her. "He is fortunate to have you defend him, sweet. And I hope you're right." His gaze flickered to Catherine's troubled face. "Am I wrong in suspecting that you have the same doubts, Cat?"

"I find it difficult to trust any man," she admitted.

The three of them were quiet as they continued along a neatly edged path.

"Catherine," Poppy ventured, "may I ask something exceptionally personal?"

Cat sent her a mock-worried look, and smiled. "I can't imagine anything more personal than what we've been discussing. Yes, of course."

"Has my brother told you that he loves you?"

Catherine hesitated for a long moment. "No," she said, her gaze fixed on the path before them. "In fact, I recently overheard him telling Win that he would only marry a woman if he were certain *not* to love her." She darted a glance at Harry, who thankfully forbore comment.

Poppy frowned. "He may not have meant it. Leo often jokes about things and says the opposite of how he really feels. One never knows with him."

"Precisely my point," Harry said in a neutral tone. "One never knows with Ramsay."

AFTER CATHERINE HAD EATEN A PLATE OF SANDWICHES WITH an impetus born of a renewed appetite, she went to a private suite that Harry had obtained for her.

"Later, after you've rested," Poppy told her, "I'll send a housemaid down with some of my clothes. They'll be a bit loose for you, but they can be altered easily."

"Oh, there's no need for that," Catherine protested. "I'll send for the things I left in Hampshire."

"You'll need something to wear in the meantime. And I have *scores* of gowns that have never been worn. Harry is ridiculously excessive when it comes to buying things for me. Besides, there's no need for all your stodgy spinster dresses now. I've always longed to see you in beautiful colors . . . pink, or jade green . . ." She smiled at Catherine's expression. "You'll be like the proverbial butterfly emerging from the cocoon."

Catherine tried to respond with humor, although her nerves were strung tight with anxiety. "I was really quite comfortable as a caterpillar."

POPPY WENT TO FIND HARRY IN HIS CURIOSITIES ROOM, where he often went to mull over a problem or work on something in a place where he was certain not to be interrupted. Only Poppy was allowed to come and go as she pleased.

The room was lined with shelves of interesting objects, gifts from foreign visitors, clocks and figurines and odd things he had collected in his travels.

Harry sat at his desk in his shirtsleeves, fiddling with gears and springs and bits of wire, as he did whenever he was deep in thought. Poppy approached him, feeling a little pang of pleasure as she watched the movements of those hands, thinking of how they played on her body.

Harry looked up as she closed the door, his gaze attentive and thoughtful. He discarded the handful of metallic objects. Turning in his chair, he took her by the waist and pulled her between his spread thighs.

Poppy let her hands slide into his shiny dark hair, brown-black silk that curled slightly over her fingers. "Am I distracting you?" she asked as she leaned down to kiss him.

"Yes," he said against her mouth. "Don't stop."

Her chuckle dissolved between their lips, like sugar melting in hot tea. Lifting her head, Poppy tried to remember what she had come there for. "Mmmn, don't," she said as his mouth went to her throat. "I can't think when you do that. I was going to ask you something . . ."

"The answer is yes."

Drawing back, she grinned and looked down at him, her arms still linked around his neck. "What do you really think about this situation with Catherine and Leo?"

"I'm not sure." He toyed with the front of her bodice, running his fingers along the row of decorative buttons.

"Harry, do not pull at those," she warned, "they're decorative."

"What good are buttons that don't do anything?" he asked, looking puzzled.

"It's the fashion."

"How am I to get this dress off you?" Intrigued, Harry began to search for hidden fastenings.

Poppy touched her nose to his. "It's a mystery," she whispered. "I'll let you find out after you tell me what you intend to do about Catherine."

"Scandal burns itself out far sooner when ignored. Any attempt to smother it only fans the flames. I'm going to introduce Cat as my sister, explain that she went to school at Blue Maid's, and subsequently took a position with the Hathaways as a kindness to you and your sister."

"And what about all the uncomfortable questions?" Poppy asked. "How shall we answer?"

"In the manner of politicians. Willfully misinterpret and evade."

She considered that with thoughtfully pursed lips. "I suppose that's the only choice," she said. "But what of Leo's proposal?"

"You think she should accept him?"

Poppy nodded decisively. "I don't see what is to be gained by waiting. One never knows what kind of husband a man will be until one marries him. And then it's too late."

"Poor little wife," Harry murmured, patting her rump over the gathered folds of her skirts. "It's far too late for you, isn't it?"

"Well, yes, I've resigned myself to a lifetime of having to endure your passionate lovemaking and witty conversation." She heaved a sigh. "It's better than being a spinster, I tell myself."

Harry stood and pulled her up against him, kissing her until she was dizzy and pink-cheeked.

"Harry," she persisted, as he nuzzled beneath her ear, "when will you give your blessing to the match between Catherine and my brother?"

"When she tells me that it doesn't matter what I say, she's going to marry him come hell or high water." Lifting his head, he stared deeply into her eyes. "Let's go to the apartment and take a nap."

"I'm not sleepy," she whispered, and he grinned.

"Neither am I." Taking her hand, he drew her out of the room. "Now about those buttons . . ."

Chapter Twenty-three

In the morning, Catherine was awakened by a maid who lit a fire in the grate and brought breakfast. One of the joys of staying at the Rutledge was the delicious food prepared by the talented Chef Broussard. Catherine sighed in enjoyment as she saw the contents of the tray: tea, fresh eggs coddled in cream and sided with pistolettes, small oval-shaped rolls, and a dish of ripe berries.

"There was a note under the door, miss," the maid said. "I put it on the side of the tray."

"Thank you." Picking up the small sealed card, Catherine felt a twinge of pleasure when she saw her name written in Leo's unmistakable style, the neat, semi-joined italic of a trained architect.

"Ring when you're finished with the tray, miss, and I'll run up to get it. And if you need help dressing or arranging your hair, I'm a fair hand at that too."

Catherine waited until the maid had left before opening the note.

Mysterious outing planned for this morning. Be ready at ten o'clock sharp. Wear walking shoes.
—R

A smile broke out on Catherine's face. "Mysterious outing," she said, watching as Dodger hoisted himself up on the bed, his tiny nose working appreciatively as he detected food nearby. "What could he be planning? No, Dodger, don't even think of disturbing my breakfast. You'll have to wait till I'm done. I draw the line at sharing a plate with you."

Seeming to understand her stern tone, Dodger stretched and rolled slowly, completing three revolutions across the mattress.

"And don't expect this to be a permanent arrangement," Catherine added, stirring sugar in her tea. "I'm only taking care of you until you go back to Beatrix."

She was so hungry that she ate every morsel on her plate, except for the small portion she reserved for the ferret. The eggs were perfect, the steaming yellow centers perfect for dipping the crisp pistolette crusts. When she was done, she spooned a coddled egg into a saucer for Dodge, placed a few berries on the side, and went to set it on the floor for him. Happily Dodger circled her, paused for a petting, and went to devour his food.

Catherine had just finished washing and brushing out her hair when there came a knock at the door. It was Poppy, accompanied by the housemaid she had seen earlier. Poppy was carrying at least three dresses draped across her arms, while the maid held a large basket filled with what appeared to ladies' linens, stockings, gloves, and other fripperies.

"Good morning," Poppy said cheerfully, coming in to lay the gown across the bed. Glancing at the ferret eating in the corner, she shook her head and grinned. "Hello, Dodger."

"Are all those things for me?" Catherine asked. "I don't need so much, truly—"

"I'm forcing it on you," Poppy informed her, "so don't dare try to give anything back. I've included a few new underthings from the dressmaker, and a 'reform' corset—do you remember when we saw them displayed at the ladies' outfitter stand at the Great Exhibition?"

"Of course." Catherine smiled. "Impossible to forget a collection of women's private garments being hung out for all the world to view."

"Well, there was a good reason why Madame Caplin won the prize medal at the exhibition. The Caplin corsets are much lighter than the usual ones, and they don't have nearly as many poky, pointy stays, and the whole thing adjusts to the body rather than molding you into an uncomfortable shape. Harry told the hotel housekeeper, Mrs. Pennywhistle, that any of the maids who wished to wear one could charge it to the Rutledge."

Catherine's brows lifted. "Truly?"

"Yes, because it allows them so much more freedom of movement. And you can breathe." Poppy lifted a pale seafoam-green dress from the bed and showed it to her. "You must wear this today, I'm sure it will fit you—we're the same height, only you're slimmer, and I have to tight-lace to fit into it."

"You are too generous, Poppy."

"Nonsense, we're sisters." She sent Catherine an affectionate glance. "Whether or not you marry Leo, we'll always be sisters. Leo told me about your outing at ten o'clock. Did he tell you where you're going?"

"No, did he tell you?"

"Yes." Poppy grinned.

"Where is it?"

"I'll let him surprise you. However, I will say that the expedition has my—and Harry's—full approval."

After the combined efforts of Poppy and the maid, Catherine was dressed in a pale seafoam gown, neither blue nor green but some perfect shade between the two. The bodice was close-fitting, stylishly cut without a waist seam, the skirts plain until the knee, where they draped in rows of flounces. The matching jacket, tailored to the waist, was trimmed with silk fringe in interwoven shades of blue, green, and silver-gray. A small, flirtatious hat was set on the upsweep of her hair, which had been done in a waterfall chignon with the ends tucked up and pinned beneath.

To Catherine, who had gone so long without wearing anything pretty or modish, the effect was disconcerting. She saw a stylishly turned-out woman in the looking glass, decidedly feminine and dashing.

"Oh, miss, you're as pretty as the girls they paint on tins of sweets," the housemaid exclaimed.

"She's right, Catherine," Poppy said, beaming. "Wait until my brother sees you! He'll rue every awful word he's ever said to you."

"I've said awful things to him too," Catherine replied soberly.

"We all knew there was a reason behind the animosity between you," Poppy said. "But we could never agree on what it was. Beatrix was right, of course."

"About what?"

"That you and Leo were like a pair of ferrets, a bit rough-and-tumble in courtship."

Catherine smiled sheepishly. "Beatrix is very intuitive."

Poppy directed a wry glance at Dodger, who was carefully licking the last residue of egg off the saucer. "I used to think Beatrix would outgrow her obsession with animals. Now I realize it's the way her brain works. She sees hardly any difference between the animal world and the human one. I only hope she can find a man who will tolerate her individuality."

"What a tactful way to put it," Catherine said, laughing. "You mean a man who won't complain about finding rabbits in his shoes or a lizard in his cigar box?"

"Exactly."

"She will," Catherine assured her. "Beatrix is far too loving, and worthy of being loved, to go unmarried."

"As are you," Poppy said meaningfully. She went to scoop up the ferret as he proceeded to investigate the contents of the basket. "I'll take Dodger for the day. I'm doing correspondence all morning, and he can sleep on my desk while I work."

The ferret hung limp in Poppy's hold, grinning at Catherine as he was carried away.

LEO HADN'T WANTED TO LEAVE CATHERINE ALONE LAST night. He had wanted to stay beside her, watch over her, like a griffin guarding treasure. Although Leo had never possessed a jealous nature before, it seemed he was quickly making up for lost time. It was particularly annoying that Catherine was so reliant upon Harry. But it was natural that she should want to depend on her brother, especially when Harry had once rescued her from a dire situation and had been her only constant in the years afterward. Even though Harry had shown little love or interest in her until recently, he was all she'd ever had.

The problem was that Leo had a consuming desire to be *everything* to Catherine. He wanted to be her exclusive confidant, her lover and closest friend, to tend to her most intimate needs. To warm her with his body when she was cold, hold a cup to her lips when she was thirsty, rub her feet when she was tired. To join his life with hers in every significant and mundane way.

However, he would not win her with one gesture, one conversation, one passion-filled night. He would have to chip away at her, removing strategic slivers here and there until her objections finally collapsed. That would require patience, attention, time. So be it. She was worth all of that and more.

Arriving at the door of Catherine's suite, Leo knocked

discreetly and waited. She appeared promptly, opening the door and smiling at him. "Good morning," she said with an expectant glance.

Any words of greeting Leo had intended to say vanished instantly. His gaze traveled slowly over her. She was like one of the exquisite feminine images painted on bandboxes or displayed in print shops. The pristine perfection of her made him long to unwrap her, like a bonbon done up in a neat paper twist.

Leo's silence went on so long that Catherine was forced to speak again. "I'm ready for the outing. Where are we going?"

"I can't remember," Leo said, still staring. He moved forward as if to crowd her back into the room.

Holding her ground, Catherine placed a gloved hand on his chest. "I'm afraid I can't allow you inside, my lord. It wouldn't be proper. And I do hope that for this outing you have hired an open carriage instead of a closed one?"

"We can take a carriage if you prefer. But our destination is a short distance, and the walk is pleasant, through St. James's Park. Would you like to go on foot?"

She nodded immediately.

As they left the hotel, Leo took the side nearest the curb. Walking with her hand tucked into the crook of Leo's arm, Catherine told him what she and Beatrix had read concerning the park, that King James had kept a collection of animals there, including camels, crocodiles, and an elephant, as well as a row of aviaries along what became Birdcage Walk. That led to Leo telling her about the architect John Nash, who had designed the central mall through the park. The avenue had become the royal ceremonial route from Buckingham Palace.

"Nash was what they called a coxcomb back then," Leo said. "Arrogant and self-important, which are requirements for an architect of that caliber."

"Are they?" Catherine seemed amused. "Why, my lord?"

"The staggering amount of money expended on an important work, and the public nature of it . . . it's effrontery, really, to believe that a design in one's head has enough merit to be built on a large scale. A painting hangs in a museum where people have to seek it out, or avoid it if they prefer. But there's not much one can do to avoid a building, and God help us all if it's an eyesore."

She glanced at him astutely, paying close attention. "Do you ever dream of designing a grand public palace or monument, as Mr. Nash did?"

"No, I have no ambitions to be a great architect. Only a useful one. I like designing smaller projects, such as the tenant houses on the estate. They're no less important than a palace, in my opinion." He shortened his stride to match hers, and steered her carefully over a rough patch in the pavement. "When I went back to France the second time, I happened to encounter one of my professors from the Académie des Beaux Arts, while I was on a walk in Provence. Lovely old man."

"What a fortunate coincidence."

"Fate."

"You believe in fate?"

Leo gave her a crooked grin. "Impossible not to, living with Rohan and Merripen, don't you think?"

Catherine smiled back, and shook her head. "I'm a skeptic. I believe fate is who we are and what we make of our chances. Go on . . . tell me about the professor."

"I visited Professor Joseph often after that chance meeting, drawing and drafting and studying in his *atelier.*" He pronounced the surname the French way, with the stress on the second syllable. Pausing, he smiled in rueful reminiscence. "We often talked over glasses of *chartreuse.* I couldn't abide the stuff."

"What did you talk about?" came the soft question.

"Usually architecture. Professor Joseph had a pure view of it . . . that a small, perfectly designed cottage has as much value as a grand public edifice. And he spoke of things he'd never mentioned at the Académie; his sense of the connections between the physical and spiritual . . . that a perfect man-made creation, such as a painting, sculpture, or a building, could provide you with a moment of transcendence. Clarity. A key to unlock a glimpse of heaven."

Leo paused as he glimpsed her troubled expression. "I've bored you. Forgive me."

"No, it's not that at all." They walked in silence for nearly a half minute before Catherine burst out, "I've never really known you. You are overturning so much of what I assumed about you. It's very disconcerting."

"Does that mean you're softening toward the idea of marrying me?"

"Not at all," she said, and he grinned.

"You will," he said. "You can't resist my charms forever." He guided her away from the park and onto a prosperous street of shops and businesses.

"Are you taking me to a haberdashery?" Catherine asked, viewing the windows and signs. "A flower shop? A book shop?"

"Here," Leo said, stopping in front of a window. "What do you think of this place?"

She squinted at the printed sign hung inside the window. "Telescopes?" she asked in bewilderment. "You want me to take up astronomy?"

Leo turned her back to the window. "Continue reading."

"'Purveyors of camp, racecourse, opera, and perspective glasses,'" she read aloud, "'by Her Majesty's royal letters patent. Illuminated ocular examinations performed by Dr. Henry Schaeffer with modern devices for the purpose of scientific correction of vision acuity.'"

"Dr. Schaeffer is the finest oculist in London," Leo said. "Some say in the world. He was a professor of astronomy at Trinity, when his work with lenses led him to an interest in the human eye. He was habilitated as an ophthamologist, and has made remarkable strides in the field. I made an appointment for you to see him."

"But I don't need the finest oculist in London," she protested, puzzled that Leo would have gone to such lengths.

"Come, Marks," he said, drawing her to the door. "It's time for you to have proper spectacles."

The interior of the shop was intriguing, lined with shelves of telescopes, magnifying glasses, binoculars, stereoscope instruments, and all manner of eyeglasses. A pleasant young clerk greeted them and went to fetch Dr. Schaeffer. The doctor came out very soon, displaying an expansive and jovial temperament. A handsome set of white whiskers framed his pink cheeks, and a thick snowy mustache curved upward when he smiled.

Schaeffer showed them around his shop, pausing to demonstrate a stereoscope and explain how the illusion of depth was created. "This instrument serves two purposes," the doctor said, his eyes twinkling behind his own spectacle lenses. "First, the stereogram cards are sometimes of use in treating focusing disorders in certain patients. And second, they are helpful in entertaining high-spirited children."

Catherine was cautious but willing as she and Leo followed Dr. Schaeffer to the rooms at the back of his shop. Whenever she had purchased spectacles in the past, the optician had simply brought out a tray of lenses, handed her various ones to hold up to her eyes, and when she felt she had obtained sufficient vision, he had proceeded to make spectacles for her.

Dr. Schaeffer, however, insisted on examining her eyes with a lens he called a "corneal loupe," after putting drops into her eyes to dilate the pupils. After pronouncing that there were no signs of disease or degeneration, he asked her to read letters and numbers from a series of three charts on the wall. She was obliged to reread the charts with various strengths of lenses, until finally they achieved a near-miraculous clarity.

When it came time to discuss the frames for the lenses, Leo surprised both Catherine and Dr. Schaeffer by taking an active part. "The spectacles that Miss Marks wears at present," Leo said, "leave a mark at the bridge of her nose."

"The contour of the support arch must be adjusted," the doctor said.

"Undoubtedly." Leo withdrew a slip of paper from the pocket of his coat and placed it on the table. "However, I have a few more ideas. What if the bridge is built up to hold the lenses a bit farther away from her face?"

"You're thinking of a design similar to the clips of a pince-nez?" Schaeffer asked thoughtfully.

"Yes, they would fit more comfortably and also stay in place."

Schaeffer stared closely at the sketch Leo had given him. "You've drawn curved earpieces, I see. An unusual feature."

"The intention is to hold the spectacles more firmly onto her face."

"This is a problem, keeping them on?"

"Without question," Leo replied. "This is a very active woman. Chasing animals, falling through rooftops, stacking rock—all an average day for her."

"My lord," Catherine said in reproof.

Schaeffer smiled as he examined the contorted shapes of her spectacles. "From the condition of these frames, Miss Marks, one could almost believe Lord Ramsay's claims." His mustache curved upward. "With your permission, I will instruct the jeweler I work with to build the frames you've drawn."

"Make them in silver," Leo said. He paused, regarding Catherine with a faint smile. "And have him put a touch of filigree on the earpieces. Nothing vulgar . . . keep it delicate."

Catherine shook her head immediately. "Such adornment is expensive and unnecessary."

"Do it nevertheless," Leo said to the doctor, his gaze still holding Catherine's. "Your face deserves adornment. I would hardly put a masterpiece in a ordinary frame, would I?"

She sent him a reproving glance. She neither liked nor trusted such outrageous flattery, nor did she intend to melt at his charm. But Leo gave her an unrepentant grin. And as he sat there and surveyed her with wicked blue eyes, she felt a painfully sweet contraction of her heart, followed by the sensation of being knocked off balance. Such a long distance to fall . . . and yet she couldn't seem to back away from the danger.

She could only stay there with her precarious equilibrium, suspended in longing and peril . . . unable to save herself.

Chapter Twenty-four

It has been confirmed by Mr. Harry Rutledge, the London hotelier, that a woman identified as Miss Catherine Marks is in fact a half sister who has heretofore lived in relative obscurity as a companion to the family of Viscount Ramsay of Hampshire. Upon inquiry as to why the young woman was not previously brought out into society, Mr. Rutledge explained the discretion as appropriate to the circumstances of her birth, as the natural child of Mr. Rutledge's mother and an unnamed gentleman. Mr. Rutledge proceeded to emphasize the decorous and refined nature of his sister, and his own pride in acknowledging kinship with a woman he describes as "estimable in every regard."

"How very flattering," Catherine said lightly, setting down the copy of the *Times*. She sent Harry a rueful glance across the breakfast table. "And now the questions will begin."

"I'll deal with the questions," Harry said. "All you have to do is behave in the aforementioned decorous and refined manner when Poppy and I take you to the theater."

"When are we going to the theater?" Poppy asked, popping a last bite of honey-soaked crumpet into her mouth.

"Tomorrow evening, if that pleases you."

Catherine nodded, trying not to look troubled by the prospect. People would stare, and whisper. Part of her shrank at the idea of being on display. On the other hand, it was a play, which meant the audience's attention would focus mainly on the activity within the proscenium.

"Shall we invite Leo?" Poppy asked. She and Harry both looked at Catherine.

She hitched her shoulders in an unconcerned shrug, although she suspected it didn't deceive either of them.

"Would you have any objection?" Harry asked her.

"No, of course not. He is Poppy's brother, and my former employer."

"And possibly your fiancé," Harry murmured.

Catherine looked at him quickly. "I haven't accepted his proposal."

"You are considering it, however . . . aren't you?"

Her heart gave a few thick beats in her chest. "I'm not sure."

"Cat, I don't mean to harass you about this, but how long do you intend to wait before giving Ramsay an answer?"

"Not long." Cat frowned into her tea. "If there's any hope of retaining Ramsay House, Lord Ramsay will have to marry someone soon."

A tap at the door heralded the entrance of Harry's right-hand man, Jake Valentine. He brought Harry a stack of daily manager's reports, as well as a handful of letters. One of these was addressed to Poppy, who received it with a warm smile.

"Thank you, Mr. Valentine."

"Mrs. Rutledge," he said with an answering smile, bowing

before he left. He looked the tiniest bit smitten with Poppy, which Catherine couldn't blame him for in the least.

Poppy broke the seal and read the letter, her fine brows inching higher and higher as she neared the conclusion. "My goodness, this is odd."

Harry and Catherine both looked at her questioningly.

"It's from Lady Fitzwalter, with whom I am acquainted through some charity work. She asks me in this letter, very earnestly, if I will prevail on my brother to call upon Miss Darvin and Countess Ramsay, who are in town. And she provides the address of the house they have let."

"Not so very odd," Catherine said pragmatically, although the news caused a stir of anxiety. "After all, a lady may never call on a man for any reason, and therefore it is certainly not unheard-of for one to prevail upon a mutual acquaintance to arrange the meeting."

"Yes, but why does Miss Darvin wish to speak to Leo?"

"It might be about the copyhold clause," Harry said, looking interested. "Perhaps she wishes to offer some manner of concession."

"I'm sure she means to offer him *something,*" Catherine said sullenly. She couldn't help remembering how beautiful the dark-haired Miss Darvin was, and what a striking couple she and Leo had made as they had waltzed. "However, I doubt she intends to discuss legalities. It's something personal. Otherwise she would allow the solicitors to deal with it."

"Cam and Merripen were terrified by Miss Darvin," Poppy told Harry with a grin. "Amelia wrote that her ballgown was trimmed with peacock feathers, which the Rom view as an omen of danger."

"In some Hindu sects," Harry said, "the peacock's cries are associated with the rainy season, and therefore, fertility."

"Danger or fertility?" Poppy asked dryly. "Well, it should be interesting to see which one Miss Darvin will evince."

"I DON'T WANT TO," LEO SAID IMMEDIATELY UPON BEING informed of the necessity of calling on Miss Darvin.

"That doesn't matter, you have no choice," Poppy said, taking his coat as he entered the apartment.

Seeing Catherine seated in the parlor with Dodger in her lap, Leo came to her. "Good afternoon," he said, reaching for Catherine's hand and brushing a kiss on the backs of her fingers. The feel of his lips, so warm and soft against her skin, caused a quick indrawn breath.

"May I?" he asked, glancing at the place on the settee beside her.

"Yes, of course."

After Poppy was seated in a chair by the hearth, Leo sat beside Catherine.

She smoothed Dodger's fur repeatedly, but he didn't move. A sleeping ferret was so limp and impossible to awaken that one might have reasonably assumed he was dead. One could pick him up, even shake him, and he would slumber on undisturbed.

Leo reached over to toy with the ferret's tiny arms and legs, lifting them gently and letting them drop back into her lap. They both chuckled as Dodger remained unconscious.

Catherine detected an unusual fragrance about Leo, a scent of feed and hay and some pungent animal scent. She sniffed curiously. "You smell a bit like . . . horses . . . Did you go for a ride this morning?"

"It's *eau de zoo*," Leo informed her, his eyes twinkling. "I went for a meeting with the secretary of the zoological society of London, and we toured the newest pavilion."

"Whatever for?" Catherine asked.

"An old acquaintance of mine, with whom I apprenticed

for Rowland Temple, has been commissioned at the Queen's behest to design a gorilla enclosure at the zoo. They keep them in small cages, which is nothing short of cruelty. When my friend complained to me about the difficulty of designing a sufficiently large and safe enclosure without costing a fortune, I suggested that he dig a moat."

"A moat?" Poppy echoed.

Leo smiled. "Gorillas won't cross deep water."

"How did you know that, my lord?" Catherine asked in amusement. "Beatrix?"

"Naturally." He looked rueful. "And now after my suggestion, it seems I've been recruited as a consultant."

"At least if your new clients complain," Catherine told him, "you won't understand what they're saying."

Leo smothered a laugh. "Obviously you haven't seen what gorillas fling when they're displeased." His mouth twisted. "All the same, I'd rather spend my time with primates than pay a call to Miss Darvin and her mother."

THE PLAY THAT EVENING WAS MAWKISH BUT HIGHLY ENTER-taining. The story was about a handsome Russian peasant who was striving for an education, but on his wedding day to his true love, the poor girl was assaulted by the prince of the domain, and while she swooned, was fatally stung by an asp. Before death overtook her, she reached her home and told her fiancé what had happened, whereupon the handsome peasant swore revenge against the prince. These efforts led him to impersonate another nobleman in the royal court, where he happened to meet a woman who looked exactly like his dead love. As it turned out, the woman was an identical twin of the murdered peasant girl, and to further complicate matters, she was in love with the evil prince's honorable young son.

Then it was intermission.

Unfortunately Catherine's and Poppy's enjoyment of the drama was hampered by low-voiced comments from both Harry and Leo, who insisted on pointing out that in her death throes, the asp-stung woman was clutching the wrong side of her body, and furthermore, a person dying of poison probably wouldn't cross the state back and forth while uttering poetic declarations of love.

"You have no romance in your soul," Poppy told Harry at intermission.

"Not in my soul, no," he replied gravely. "However, I have a great deal of it in other locations."

She laughed, reaching up to smooth an imaginary crease in his crisp white cravat. "Darling, would you please have someone bring champagne to our box? Catherine and I are thirsty."

"I'll send for it," Leo said, standing and buttoning his coat. "I need to stretch my legs after an hour and a half in that absurdly small chair." He looked down at Catherine. "Would you care for a promenade?"

She shook her head, feeling much safer in the confines of the theater box than out walking in the crowd. "Thank you, but I am comfortable here."

As Leo pushed aside the curtains at the back of their box, it was evident that the hallways were exceedingly crowded. A pair of gentlemen and a lady came through the curtains and greeted the Rutledges warmly. Catherine tensed as Harry introduced her to Lord and Lady Despencer and Lady Despencer's sister, Mrs. Lisle. She anticipated a cool reception from them, perhaps a dismissive remark, but instead they were polite and affable. Perhaps, she thought wryly, she should stop expecting the worst of people.

Poppy asked Lady Despencer about one of her children, who had been ill recently, and the woman listed all the medications and precautions it had taken for their ailing son to get well. Another cluster of people entered the box, waiting for a turn to speak to Harry, and Catherine moved to make room for them. She stood at the back of the box beside the curtain panels, waiting with forced patience as conversation flowed in currents in the hallway, in the box, large swells of noise rising from the audience below. The relentless clamor and movement irritated her. It was stuffy in the theater, the air warm from the mass of human bodies crowding everywhere. She hoped that intermission would conclude soon.

As she stood with her hands behind her back, she felt a hand reach through the box curtains and close around her wrist. A masculine body pressed behind hers. A smile touched her lips as she wondered what game Leo was playing.

But the voice that slithered into her ear wasn't Leo's. It was a voice from her nightmares.

"How pretty you look in your fine feathers, my pigeon."

Chapter Twenty-five

Catherine stiffened, her hand clenching into a fist, but she couldn't jerk her arm away from Lord Latimer's grasp. He twisted her gloved wrist, forced it an inch or two higher, and continued to speak in a soft undertone.

Stunned and frozen, Catherine could hear nothing at first but the frantic velocity of her heartbeat. Time seemed to flicker, falter, and resume at a crawl. ". . . so many questions about you . . ." he was saying, his voice saturated with contempt. "Everyone wants to know more about Rutledge's enigmatic sister . . . is she fair or ill-favored? Accomplished or vulgar? Endowed or destitute? Perhaps I should supply the answers. 'She's a beauty,' I'll tell my curious friends, 'trained by an infamous procuress. She's a fraud. And most of all she's a whore.'"

Catherine was quiet, breathing through flared nostrils. She couldn't make a scene during her first public outing as Harry's sister. Any conflict with Lord Latimer would expose their past connection, and bring about her social ruin that much faster.

"Why don't you further explain," she whispered, "that you're a filthy lecher who tried to rape a fifteen-year-old girl?"

"Tsk, tsk . . . You should know better, Catherine. People never blame a man for his passions, no matter how perverse. People blame the woman for arousing them. You won't get far, asking for sympathy. The public despises victimized women, especially attractive ones."

"Lord Ramsay will—"

"Ramsay will use you and discard you, which is what he does with all women. Surely you're not so vain or stupid as to think you're different from the others."

"What do you want?" she asked through gritted teeth.

"I want what I paid for," he whispered, "all those years ago. And I'll have it. There's no other future for you, my dear. You were never meant for a respectable life. By the time you've been run through the rumor mills, you'll never have a chance of being received anywhere."

The manacling fingers fell away, and her tormentor disappeared.

Stricken, Catherine stumbled forward to her chair and sat heavily, trying to compose herself. She stared straight ahead, seeing nothing, while the clamor of the theater pressed around her from all sides. She tried to examine her fear objectively, to put a barrier around it. It wasn't that she actually feared Latimer. She loathed him, but he was certainly not the threat to her now that he once had been. She now had sufficient wealth to live as she pleased. She had Harry and Poppy, and the Hathaways.

But Latimer had identified her legitimate worries with cruel accuracy. One could fight a man, but not a rumor. One could lie about the past, but the truth would eventually surface. One could promise fidelity and commitment, but such promises were often broken.

She felt overwhelmed with melancholy. She felt . . . stained.

Poppy sat next to her, smiling. "Nearly time for the second

act," she said. "Do you think the peasant will gain revenge against the prince?"

"Oh, undoubtedly," Catherine replied, trying to sound light, but her voice was forced.

Poppy's smile faded, and she looked at her closely. "Do you feel well, dear? You look pale. Did something happen?"

Before Catherine replied, Leo shouldered his way back into the box, accompanied by a steward bearing a tray of champagne. A little bell rang from the orchestra box, signaling that the intermission would soon conclude. To Catherine's relief, the visitors began to drift out of the box, and the throng in the hallway receded.

"Here we are," Leo said, handing champagne to Poppy and Catherine. "You may want to drink it quickly."

"Why?" Catherine asked, forcing a smile.

"The champagne goes flat much faster in these coupe glasses."

Catherine drained her champagne with unladylike haste, closing her eyes and swallowing against the sparkling burn in her throat.

"I didn't mean that quickly," Leo said, viewing her with a faint, concerned smile.

The lights began to dim, and the audience settled.

Catherine glanced at the silver stand where the bottle of chilled champagne had been placed, a white napkin tied neatly at its neck. "May I have another?" she whispered.

"No, you'll get tipsy if you have it so soon." Leo took the empty glass from her, set it aside, and took her gloved hand in his. "Tell me," he said gently. "What are you thinking about?"

"Later," she whispered back, easing her hand from his. "Please." She didn't want the evening to be ruined for everyone, nor did she want to take the chance that Leo might seek out Latimer in the theater and confront him. There was nothing to be gained by saying anything at the moment.

The theater darkened and the play resumed, although the story's melodramatic charms couldn't pull Catherine out of her frozen misery. She watched the stage with a fixed gaze, hearing the actors' dialogue as if it were a foreign language. And all the while her mind kept trying to find a solution to her internal dilemma.

It didn't seem to matter that she already knew the answers. It had never been her fault, the situation she had once been put in. The blame was Latimer's, and Althea's, and her grandmother's. Catherine could reassure herself of that for the rest of her life, and yet the feelings of guilt, pain, confusion, were still there. How could she rid herself of them? What could possibly free her?

FOR THE NEXT TEN MINUTES, LEO GLANCED AT CATHERINE repeatedly, perceiving that something was deeply wrong. She was trying very hard to concentrate on the play, but it was clear that her mind was consumed with some overpowering problem. She was distant, unreachable, as if she had been encased in ice. Trying to comfort her, he took her hand once more, and ran his thumb above the edge of her wrist-length glove. The iciness of her skin was startling.

Frowning deeply, Leo leaned toward Poppy. "What the devil happened to Marks?" he whispered.

"I don't know," she returned helplessly. "Harry and I were talking to Lord and Lady Despencer, and Catherine was off to the side. Then we both sat, and I noticed that she looked ill."

"I'm taking her back to the hotel," Leo said.

Harry, who had caught the last of the exchange, frowned and murmured, "We'll all go."

"There's no need for any of us to leave," Catherine protested.

Ignoring her, Leo stared at Harry. "It would be better if you stayed and watched the rest of the play. And if anyone asks about Marks, say something about the vapours."

"Don't tell anyone I had vapours," Catherine whispered sharply.

"Then say I had them," Leo told Harry.

That seemed to rouse Catherine from her numbness. Leo was relieved to see a flicker of her usual spirit as she said, "Men can't have vapours. It's a female condition."

"Nevertheless, I do," Leo said. "I may even swoon." He helped her from her seat.

Harry rose as well, looking down at his sister with concern. "Is this what you want, Cat?" he asked.

"Yes," she said, looking annoyed. "If I don't, he'll be asking for smelling salts."

LEO ESCORTED CATHERINE OUTSIDE AND SUMMONED A HACK-ney carriage. It was a two-wheeled, partially open vehicle, with an elevated driver's seat at the rear. One could speak to the driver through a trapdoor at the top.

As Catherine approached the vehicle with Leo, she had a crawling sensation of being watched. Afraid that Latimer had followed her, she glanced to her left, where a man stood beside one of the theater's massive portico columns. To her relief, it was not Latimer, but a much younger man. He was tall, rawboned, and dressed in shabby dark clothing and a tattered hat, with the overall effect of a scarecrow. He had the distinctive London pallor common to those who spent most of their time indoors, whose skin was never touched by sun without the filter of polluted city air. His brows were strong black stripes across his gaunt face, his skin creased with lines that he was too young to have.

He was staring at her fixedly.

Catherine paused uncertainly, aware of a vague sense of recognition. Had she seen him somewhere before? She couldn't fathom where they might have met.

"Come," Leo said, intending to hand her into the carriage.

But Catherine resisted, caught by the riveted stare of the stranger's raven-dark eyes.

Leo followed the direction of her gaze. "Who is that?"

The young man came forward, removing his hat to reveal a mop of shaggy black hair. "Miss Catherine?" he said awkwardly.

"William," she breathed in wonder.

"Yes, miss." His mouth curled upward in the beginnings of a smile. He took another hesitant step, and bobbed in a sort of clumsy bow.

Leo intruded between them protectively and looked down at Catherine. "Who is he?"

"I think he's the boy I once told you about . . . who worked at my grandmother's house."

"The errand boy?"

Catherine nodded. "He was the reason I was able to send for Harry . . . he took my letter to him. My lord, do let me speak to him."

Leo's face was implacable. "You would be the first one to tell me that a lady never stands and converses with a man on the street."

"*Now* you want to pay heed to etiquette?" she asked in annoyance. "I'm going to speak to him." Seeing the refusal in his face, she softened her voice, and surreptitiously touched his hand. "Please."

Leo relented. "Two minutes," he muttered, looking none too happy. He remained right beside her, his eyes ice-blue as he stared at William.

Looking cowed, William obeyed Catherine's motion to

come to them. "You turned into a lady, Miss Catherine," he said in his thick South London accent. "But I knew it was you—that face, and those same little spectacles. I always hoped you was all right."

"You've changed more than I, William," she said, trying to summon a smile. "How tall you've grown. Are you still . . . working for my grandmother?"

He shook his head and smiled ruefully. "She passed on two years ago, miss. Doctor said 'er heart gave out, but the girls at the 'ouse said it couldn't be, she didn't 'ave one."

"Oh," Catherine whispered, her face turning bleached and stiff. It was only to be expected, of course. Her grandmother had suffered from a heart ailment for years. She thought she should feel relieved by the news, but instead she only felt chilled. "And . . . my aunt? Is Althea still there?"

William cast a guarded glance around them. "She's the madam now," he said, his voice low. "I work for her, odd jobs, same as I did for your grandmother. But it's a different place now, miss. Much worse."

Compassion stirred inside her. How unfair it was for him to be trapped in such a life, with no training or education to afford him any other choice. Privately she resolved to ask Harry if there might be some kind of employment for William at the hotel, something that would lead him to a decent future. "How is my aunt?" she asked.

"Ailing, miss." His thin face was sober. "Doctor said she must of got a bawdy-'ouse disease some years back . . . got in 'er joints and went up to 'er brain. Not well in the 'ead, your aunt. And she can't see none too good, neither."

"I'm sorry," Catherine murmured, trying to feel pity, but instead a mass of fear rose in her throat. She tried to swallow it back, to ask more questions, but Leo interrupted brusquely.

"That's enough," he said. "The hackney's waiting."

Catherine gave her childhood friend a troubled glance. "Is

there something I can do to help you, William? Do you need money?" She instantly regretted the question as she saw the shame and offended pride on his face. Had there been more time, had the circumstances allowed, she would have found a better way to ask.

William gave a stiff shake of his head. "Don't need noffing, miss."

"I'm at the Rutledge Hotel. If you wish to see me, if there is something I can—"

"I wouldn't nivver trouble you, Miss Cathy. You was always kind to me. You brought me medicine once when I was sick, 'member? Came to the kitchen pallet where I slept, and covered me wiv one of the blankets from your bed. You sat on the floor and watched over me—"

"We're leaving," Leo said, flipping a coin to William.

William caught it in midair. His fist lowered, and he looked at Leo with a mixture of greed and resentment, his face turning hard. When he spoke, his accent was exaggerated. "Fank you, guvnah."

Leo guided Catherine away with an uncompromising grasp on her elbow, and helped her into the carriage. By the time she had settled in the narrow seat and looked out again, William was gone.

THE PASSENGER SEAT WAS SO SMALL THAT THE MASS OF CATHerine's skirts, layers of pink silk arranged like rose petals, spilled over one of Leo's thighs.

Staring at her profile, Leo thought she looked stern and nettled, like the Marks of old.

"You needn't have dragged me away like that," she said. "You were rude to William."

He gave her an unrepentant glance. "No doubt later, upon reflection, I'll feel terrible about that."

"There were some things I still wanted to ask him."

"Yes, I'm sure there was quite a lot more to be learned about bawdy-house diseases. Forgive me for depriving you of such an enlightening conversation. I should have let the two of you reminisce about the good old times at the brothel while you were standing on a public street."

"William was the dearest boy," Catherine said quietly. "He deserved a better lot in life. He had to work from the time he could toddle, cleaning shoes and carrying heavy buckets of water up and down the stairs . . . he had no family, no education. Have you no sympathy at all for those in unfortunate circumstances?"

"The streets are filled with such children. I do what I can for them in Parliament, and I give to charity. Yes, I have sympathy for them. But at the moment I'm more interested in your unfortunate circumstances than anyone else's. And I have a few questions for you, starting with this: What happened at intermission?"

When Catherine didn't reply, he took her jaw in a gentle but secure grasp, and forced her to look at him. "Let's have it."

She gave him a strained glance. "Lord Latimer approached me."

Leo's eyes narrowed, his hand lowering from her chin. "While you were in the theater box?"

"Yes. Harry and Poppy didn't see. Latimer spoke to me through the curtain at the back of the box seating."

Leo was filled with explosive rage. For a moment he didn't trust himself to speak. He wanted to go back and slaughter the bastard. "What did he say?" he asked roughly.

"That I was a prostitute. And a fraud."

Leo wasn't aware that his grip had tightened until she winced. His hand loosened instantly. "I'm sorry you were subjected to that," he managed to say. "I shouldn't have left you. I didn't think he would dare approach you after the warning I gave him."

"I think he wanted to make it clear that he's not intimidated by you." She drew an unsteady breath. "And I think it hurt his pride all those years ago, to have paid for something he didn't receive. Perhaps I could give him some of the money Harry settled on me, and that might be enough to make him leave me alone. To keep quiet about me."

"No, that would only start us on a course of prolonged blackmail. And Latimer would never keep quiet. Listen to me, Cat . . . Harry and I have discussed how to manage the problem. Suffice it to say that in a few days, Latimer will find himself in a position in which he'll either end up in prison or be forced to flee England."

"For what crime?" she asked, her eyes widening.

"There's a long list to choose from," Leo said. "He's tried nearly everything. And I'd rather not tell you the specific offense, because it's not appropriate for a lady's ears."

"You can make him leave England? Truly?"

"Truly."

He felt her relax a little, her shoulders slumping. "That would be a relief," she said. "However . . ."

"Yes?"

Catherine angled her face away from his searching gaze. "It doesn't really matter. Because what he said was no less than the truth. I am a fraud."

"What self-pitying tripe. You were a fraud as an aspiring prostitute. As a proper and well-mannered lady who holds an irresistible attraction for ferrets, you're completely authentic."

"Not all ferrets. Just Dodger."

"Proof of his excellent taste."

"Don't try to be charming," she muttered. "There's nothing more annoying than someone trying to make one feel better when one wants to wallow."

Leo bit back a grin. "I'm sorry," he said contritely. "Go on and wallow. You were doing so well at it until I interrupted."

"Thank you." She heaved a sigh and waited a moment. "Blast," she finally said, "I can't do it now." Her fingers crept further into his, and he smoothed his thumb over the backs of her knuckles. "I want to correct something," Catherine said. "I was never an aspiring prostitute."

"What did you aspire to?"

"To live somewhere peaceful, and be safe."

"That's all?"

"Yes, that's all. And I haven't managed to do it yet. Although . . . the past few years have been the closest I've ever gotten."

"Marry me," Leo told her, "and you can have both. You'll be safe, and you'll live in Hampshire. And you'll have me, which is obviously icing on the cake."

A reluctant laugh escaped her. "Rather more icing than the cake needs."

"There is no such thing as too much icing, Marks."

"My lord, I don't believe that you sincerely want to marry me as much as you want to have your way."

"I want you to marry me so that I don't have my way all the time," he said, which was the truth. "It's not good for me to be indulged. And you tell me no quite frequently."

She gave a huff of wry amusement. "I haven't said it to you nearly enough lately."

"Then let's practice in your hotel suite. I'll try to have my way with you, and you can try to refuse me."

"No."

"There, you see? You're sharpening your skills already."

Leo directed the driver to take them to the alley that bordered the mews behind the hotel. It was a far more discreet way to enter than parading through the lobby. They went up the back stairs and along the hallway that led to Catherine's suite. The hotel was extraordinarily quiet at that hour, everyone either out for their evening pursuits, or sleeping soundly.

When they reached Catherine's door, Leo waited as Catherine searched for the key in the little knitted silk bag she had looped around one wrist.

"Allow me," Leo said when she had found the key. Taking it from her, he unlocked the door.

"Thank you." Catherine took back the key and turned to face him at the threshold.

Leo stared down into her fine-boned face, reading the emotions that flickered in her eyes: despair, refusal, yearning. "Invite me in," he said softly.

She shook her head. "You must go. It's not seemly for you to stand here."

"The night's still young. What will you do in there, alone?"

"Sleep."

"No, you won't. You'll stay awake as long as possible, worrying about nightmares." Seeing that he had scored a point, Leo pressed his advantage. "Let me in."

Chapter Twenty-six

Leo stood in the doorway, tugging off his gloves casually, as if he had all the time in the world. Catherine went dry-mouthed as she watched him. She needed him. She needed to be held and comforted, and he knew it. If she allowed him into her hotel suite, there was no question as to what would happen next.

She started as the sound of voices came from the end of the long hallway. Reaching out hastily, she grabbed the lapels of Leo's coat, pulled him across the threshold, and closed them both safely inside the room. *"Hush,"* she whispered.

Leo braced his hands on either side of her, caging her against the door. "You know how to keep me quiet."

The voices became louder as people advanced further along the hallway.

Smiling into her tense face, Leo began in a perfectly audible tone, "Marks, I wonder if—"

She drew in an exasperated breath and crammed her mouth against his, anything to shut him up. Leo fell obligingly silent, kissing her with bold and avid pleasure. Even through the elegant layers of his clothes, she could feel the heat and hardness of him. Desperately she fumbled with his clothes, pushing her hands beneath his coat where his body heat had collected.

She moaned, the sound catching between their lips. His tongue went deep, and she felt corresponding twinges of pleasure low in her stomach. Her legs lost their strength, her balance eroding. Her spectacles became dislodged, catching between their faces. Leo reached up to remove them carefully. He slipped them into his pocket. With deliberate slowness, he put the key in the door and locked it from the inside. Catherine stood mutely, torn between desire and caution.

In the silence, Leo went to light a lamp. A rasp, as a match was struck . . . a glow, as the wick kindled. Catherine blinked owlishly at the shadow-crossed room, at the large dark shape of him before her. She ached for him, her body clenching on intimate emptiness. A tremor went through her as she thought of how he had filled her, the sweet heaviness of him inside her.

Blindly she turned to face away from him, offering access to the row of hooks that fastened the back of her dress. The fabric tightened across her breasts as he grasped the dress at the back. There was a series of deft tugs, the garment loosening, slipping lower. She felt his mouth brush the tender nape of her neck, a whisk of exciting warmth. He pushed the gown to her waist and over her hips. She moved to help him, stepping out of the heap of layered pink silk, kicking off her slippers. Turning her around again, Leo unhooked her corset, pausing to kiss each of her shoulders in turn.

"Take down your hair." The touch of his breath on her skin made her shiver.

Catherine obeyed, pulling the pins from her chignon, collecting them in a little bundle. After setting them on the dressing table, she went to the bed and climbed onto the mattress, waiting tensely as he undressed. She couldn't help wishing she had her spectacles back as she stared at the intriguing, hazy shape of him, the play of light and shadow on his skin.

"Don't squint so hard, love. You'll strain your eyes."

"I can't see you."

He approached her, every line of his body replete with masculine grace. "Can you see me at this distance?"

She contemplated him thoroughly. "Certain parts."

Leo gave a husky laugh, crawling onto the bed, over her, bracing his weight on his arms. The tips of her breasts hardened beneath the light veil of her chemise. Their stomachs pressed together, the erect shape of him caught exquisitely against the corresponding notch of her body.

"What about now?" Leo whispered. "Am I close enough?"

"Almost," she managed to say, staring into his face, taking in every breathtaking detail. She had to force out words between uneven breaths. "But not quite . . ."

Leo bent to take her lips, locking his mouth over hers in a blaze of sensation. She lost herself in it, a kiss that was at once giving and demanding. He searched her gently, meeting the shy advances of her own tongue. She tasted inside his mouth for the first time, and felt the jolt of his response.

With a ragged sound, Leo reached for the hem of her chemise. Pulling the garment upward, he helped Catherine to lift it over her head. He untied the tapes of her drawers with torturous slowness, running his fingers along the loosening waist, easing the thin muslin fabric down her hips. Her garters and stockings soon followed, leaving her completely exposed.

Murmuring his name, Catherine twined her arms around his neck and tried to draw him over her again. She arched into him, gasping with delight at the varied textures of him, roughness and silk, smoothness and steel.

He brought his mouth to her ear, his lips toying with the soft lobe before he whispered, "Cat. I'm going to kiss all the way down your body and up again. And I want you to lie perfectly still and let me do as I please. You can do that, can't you?"

"No," she said earnestly, "I really don't think so."

Leo averted his face for a moment. When he looked back at her, his eyes were sparkling with amusement. "That was actually a rhetorical question."

"A rhetorical question has an obvious answer," she argued, "and what you're asking is not—" She broke off, unable to speak or think as she felt him nibble and lick at a sensitive part of her neck. His mouth was hot and silken, the flat of his tongue like velvet. He worked his way along her arm, pausing at the hollows of her inner arm and wrist, caressing the pulse that beat visibly in the fragile skin. Every inch of her body prickled with awareness of him and what he was doing.

His mouth wandered back along her arm to the side of her breast, the trail of his mouth leaving her skin flushed and damp. He kissed all around the rosy peak without touching it, until she felt a whimper climb in her throat. "My lord, *please,*" she gasped, sliding her hands into his hair, trying to guide him.

He resisted, grasping her wrists and pulling them to her sides. "Don't move," he reminded her gently. "Or do you want me to start over?"

She closed her eyes and lay with aggrieved stillness, her chest heaving. Leo had the gall to laugh softly, his mouth returning to nuzzle the undercurve of her breast. A cry escaped her when she felt his lips brush against the gathered crest. Slowly his mouth opened and sealed over her, and he began to suckle. Heat writhed in her stomach, and her hips lifted from the mattress. His hand settled on her taut abdomen, rubbing in a soothing circle, pressing her back down.

It was impossible to lie motionless as Leo tormented her, arousing her skillfully but providing no relief. Impossible to endure . . . but he wouldn't allow otherwise. He made his way down to her stomach, licking and blowing lightly into the hollow of her navel. She was weak and perspiring, wet at the roots of her hair, her body racked with delight that verged on pain.

His mouth glided across the vulnerable softness of her groin to her inner thighs, his tongue playing gently on either side . . . everywhere except the wet pulsing center.

"Leo," she panted. "This . . . is not very nice of you."

"I know," he said. "Move your legs apart."

She obeyed with a shudder, letting him guide her, opening her body in ever more revealing positions. He used his mouth in ways that infuriated and aroused her . . . nibbling along her thigh, investigating the ticklish hollows behind her knees, stringing kisses around her ankles, sucking lazily on her toes. She swallowed back a supplicating moan, and another, impatience thumping through her body.

After an eternity, Leo had finally progressed all the way back to her neck. Catherine parted her thighs, dying for him to take her, but instead he rolled her to her stomach. She whimpered in frustration.

"Impatient wench." Leo's hand smoothed over her bottom and slipped between her thighs. "There, will this satisfy you for now?" She felt him parting her swollen flesh. Her body stiffened in bliss as his fingers entered her, slipping into the wetness. He held them there, deep and flexing, while he kissed along her spine. She found herself grinding against his hand, gasping in pleasure. Closer . . . closer . . . and yet the climax shimmered just out of reach.

Finally Leo turned her to her back again, his features hard and sweat-misted, and it was only then that she realized he had been torturing himself as well as her. He pinned her arms over her head and spread her legs. For an instant she knew a flare of panic at her own helplessness, seeing his powerful body above hers. But then he entered her in a hard, slick plunge, and the fear vanished in a flood of pleasure. He slipped his free arm beneath her neck. Her eyes closed, and her head lolled as he bent to kiss her throat.

She was nothing but feeling, heat coming through her in waves, stronger and stronger as he took her with slow, luscious drives. He rolled his hips with each forward pitch, repeating the movement until she went crimson and whimpered in a last burst of release. And he stayed with her, riding every drawn-out spasm until she was limp and quiet. Murmuring to her, he coaxed her to wrap one leg around his waist, and he lifted her other leg until it hooked over his shoulder. The position opened her, changed the angle between them, so that when he thrust again, it caressed a new place inside her. Another rush of pleasure started, surging so high and fast that she could hardly breathe. She lay still beneath him, her legs trembling as she took him more deeply than she had thought possible. She was propelled into another climax, strong and dizzying, but before the last tremors had faded, he withdrew abruptly to take his own release, his sex throbbing viciously against her stomach.

"Oh, Cat," he said after a while, still over her, his hands gripped in the bedclothes.

She turned her face until her lips brushed the rim of his ear. The erotic perfume of sex and damp skin filled her nostrils. Her palm went to his back, smoothing over the taut surface, and she felt him shiver in pleasure at the gentle scratch of her nails. How remarkable it was to lie with a man, feeling him soften inside her as their pulses slowed. What an astonishing assimilation of flesh and moisture and sensation, the lingering twinges and pulses in the places they pressed together.

Leo lifted his head and looked down at her. "Marks," he said, his voice uneven, "you are not a perfect woman."

"I'm aware of that," she said.

"You have an evil temper, you're as blind as a mole, you're a deplorable poet, and frankly, your French accent could use some work." Supporting himself on his elbows, Leo took her face in his hands. "But when I put those things together with the rest of you, it makes you into the most perfectly imperfect woman I've ever known."

Absurdly pleased, she smiled up into his face.

"You are beautiful beyond words," Leo went on. "You are kind, amusing, and passionate. You also have a keen intellect, but I'm willing to overlook that."

Her smile faded. "Are you leading to another marriage proposal?"

His gaze was intent. "I have a special license from the Archbishop's Court of Faculties. We could wed at any church, whenever we please. We could be married by morning, if you say yes."

Catherine turned her face away from his, pressing a frown into the mattress. She owed him an answer—she owed him honesty. "I'm not certain I'll ever be able to say yes to that."

Leo was very still. "Do you mean only when I propose, or if any man did?"

"Any man," she admitted. "It's only that with you, it's very difficult to refuse."

"Well, that's encouraging," he said, although his tone conveyed the opposite.

Leo left the bed and went to get a damp cloth for her. Returning, he stood beside the bed and watched her. "Think of it this way," he said. "Marriage would change hardly anything between us, except that we would end our arguments in a much more satisfying way. And of course I would have extensive legal rights over your body, your property, and all your individual freedoms, but I don't see what's so alarming about that."

His quip almost made Catherine smile again, despite her encroaching despair. Finishing her ablutions, she set the cloth on the bedside table and pulled the bed linens up to her breasts. "I wish people were like the clocks and mechanisms that Harry is so clever at constructing. Then I could have whatever is wrong with me repaired. As it is, though, I have some parts that aren't working properly."

Leo sat on the side of the bed, his gaze holding hers. He extended a muscular arm and caught the back of her neck in his hand, and held her steady. His mouth possessed hers roughly, until her head swam and her heart pounded. Lifting his head, he said, "I adore all of your parts exactly as they are." He drew back and touched her taut jawline, his fingers gentle. "Can you at least admit that you're fond of me?"

Catherine swallowed against the soft caress. "I . . . it's obvious that I am."

"Then say it," he urged, stroking the side of her throat.

"Why must I say something if it's obvious?"

But he persisted, damn him, seeming to understand how difficult it was for her. "It's only a few words." His thumb brushed the hard, anxious pulse at the base of her neck. "Don't be afraid."

"Please, I can't—"

"Say it."

Catherine couldn't look at him. She went hot and cold. Taking a deep breath, she managed a shaking whisper. "I'm f-fond of you."

"There," Leo murmured, beginning to draw her close. "Was that so bad?"

Her body was wrenched with the longing to huddle against his inviting chest. But instead she put her arms between them, preserving a crucial distance. "It makes no difference," she forced herself to say. "In fact, it makes it worse."

His arms loosened. He gave her a quizzical glance. "Worse?"

"Yes, because I can never give you anything more than that. And regardless of what you claim to the contrary, you'll want the kind of marriage your sisters have. The way Amelia is with Cam, the devotion and intimacy . . . you'll want that too."

"I don't want intimacy with Cam."

"Don't joke about it," she said wretchedly. "This is serious."

"I'm sorry," came his quiet reply. "Sometimes serious conversations make me uncomfortable, and I tend to resort to humor as a result." He paused. "I understand what you're trying to tell me. But what if I say that attraction and fondness would be enough?"

"I wouldn't believe you. Because I know how unhappy you would become, seeing your sisters' marriages, remembering how devoted your parents were to each other, and knowing that ours was a counterfeit by comparison. A parody."

"What makes you so certain that we won't come to care for each other?"

"I just am. I've looked inside my heart, and it's not there. That's what I meant before. I don't think I'll ever be able to trust anyone enough to love them. Even you."

Leo's face was expressionless, but she sensed something dark lurking beneath his self-control, something that hinted of anger, or exasperation. "It's not that you're unable," he said. "It's that you don't want to." He released her carefully and went to retrieve his discarded clothes. As he dressed, he spoke in a voice that chilled her with its pleasant blandness. "I have to leave."

"You're angry."

"No. But if I stay, I'll end up making love to you and proposing to you repeatedly, until morning. And even my tolerance for rejection has its limits."

Words of regret and self-reproach hovered on her lips. But she held them back, sensing that it would only infuriate him. Leo was hardly a man to fear a challenge. But he was beginning to comprehend that he could do nothing with the challenge she presented, some inexplicable quandary that couldn't be solved.

After dressing and shrugging into his coat, Leo returned to the bedside. "Don't try to predict what you're capable of," he murmured, sliding his fingers beneath her chin. He bent to press his lips to her forehead, and added, "You may surprise yourself." Going to the door, he opened it and glanced up and down the hallway. He glanced at Catherine over his shoulder. "Lock the door when I leave."

"Good night," she said with difficulty. "And . . . I'm sorry, my lord. I wish I were different. I wish I could—" She stopped and shook her head miserably.

Pausing a bit longer, Leo gave her a look of amusement edged with warning. "You're going to lose this battle, Cat. And despite yourself, you're going to be very happy in defeat."

Chapter Twenty-seven

Paying a call on Vanessa Darvin the following day was the last thing Leo wanted to do. However, he was curious about why she wanted to see him. The address that Poppy had given to him was of a Mayfair residence in South Audley Street, not far from the terrace he leased. It was a Georgian town house, neat red brick with white trim, fronted by a white pediment with four slender pilaster columns.

Leo liked Mayfair immensely, not so much for its fashionable reputation as the fact that it had once been deemed a "lewd and disorderly" place in the early eighteenth century by the Grand Jury of Westminster. It had been condemned for its practices of gaming, bawdy stage plays, prizefighting and animal baiting, and all the attendant vices of crime and prostitution. Over the next hundred years it had gradually gentrified until John Nash had sealed its hard-won respectability with Regent Street and Regent's Park. To Leo, however, Mayfair would always be a respectable lady with a notorious past.

Upon arriving at the residence, Leo was shown to a reception room overlooking a two-tiered garden. Vanessa Darvin and Countess Ramsay were both present, welcoming him warmly. As they all sat and made the obligatory small talk, inquiring after the health of their family, and his, and the weather, and other safe and polite subjects of an opening acquaintance, Leo found that his impressions of the two women from the ball in Hampshire were unchanged. The countess was a garrulous biddy, and Vanessa Darvin was a self-involved beauty.

A quarter hour passed, and then a half hour. Leo began to wonder if he would ever discover why they had prevailed on him to call.

"Dear me," the countess eventually exclaimed, "I quite forgot that I had intended to consult with Cook about the evening meal. Pardon, I must go at once." She stood, and Leo automatically rose to his feet.

"Perhaps I should leave, as well," he said, grateful for the opportunity to escape.

"Do stay, my lord," Vanessa said quietly. A look passed between Vanessa and the countess before the latter left the room.

Recognizing the obvious pretext to leave them alone, Leo lowered back into the chair. He raised a brow as he regarded Vanessa. "So there is a point to this."

"There is a point," Vanessa confirmed. She was beautiful, her shining dark hair arranged in pinned-up curls, her eyes striking in her porcelain complexion. "I wish to discuss a highly personal matter with you. I hope I may rely on your discretion."

"You may." Leo studied her with a flicker of interest. There was a hint of uncertainty, urgency, beneath her provocative façade.

"I'm not certain how best to begin," she said.

"Be blunt," Leo suggested. "Subtleties are usually wasted on me."

"I would like to put forth a proposition, my lord, that will satisfy our mutual needs."

"How intriguing. I wasn't aware that we had mutual needs."

"Obviously yours is to marry and have a son quickly, before you die."

Leo was mildly startled. "I hadn't planned to expire any time soon."

"What about the Ramsay curse?"

"I don't believe in the Ramsay curse."

"Neither did my father," she said pointedly.

"Well, then," Leo said, both annoyed and amused, "in light of my rapidly approaching demise, we shouldn't waste a moment. Tell me what you want, Miss Darvin."

"I need to find a husband as quickly as possible, or I will soon find myself in a very unpleasant position."

Leo watched her alertly, making no response.

"Although we are not well acquainted," she continued, "I know a great deal about you. Your past exploits are hardly a secret. And I believe all the qualities that would make you an unsuitable husband for anyone else would make you ideal for me. We are very much alike, you see. From all accounts, you are cynical, amoral, and selfish." A deliberate pause. "So am I. Which is why I would never try to change any of those things about you."

Fascinating. For a girl no more than twenty, she possessed preternatural self-confidence.

"Whenever you chose to stray," Vanessa continued, "I wouldn't complain. I probably wouldn't even notice, because I would be similarly occupied. It would be a sophisticated marriage. I can give you children to ensure that the Ramsay title and estate will stay in your line of descent. Furthermore, I can—"

"Miss Darvin," Leo said carefully, "pray don't continue." The irony of the situation was hardly lost on him—she was proposing a true marriage of convenience, free from messy desires and feelings. The diametric opposite of the marriage he wanted with Catherine.

Not long ago, that might have appealed to him.

Settling back in his chair, Leo regarded her with detached patience. "I don't deny the stories of my past sins. But despite all that . . . or perhaps because of it . . . the idea of a sophisticated marriage doesn't appeal to me in the least."

He saw by the frozen stillness of Vanessa's face that he had surprised her. She took her time about replying. "Perhaps it should, my lord. A better woman would be disappointed and shamed by you, and come to hate you. Whereas *I*"—she touched her chest in a practiced gesture, drawing his attention to her round, perfect bosom—"would never expect anything from you."

The arrangement Vanessa Darvin proposed was a perfect recipe for aristocratic domesticity. How fantastically bloodless and civilized.

"But I need someone to expect something from me," he heard himself say.

The truth of that bolted through him like lightning. Had he really just said it? And did he truly mean it?

Yes. Dear God.

When and how had he changed? It had been a mortal struggle to leave behind the excesses of grief and self-loathing. Somewhere along the way he had stopped wanting to die, which was not quite the same thing as wanting to live. But that had been enough for a while.

Until Catherine. She had reawakened him like a cold dash of water in his face. She made him want to be a better man, not just for her, but for himself, as well. He should have known that Catherine would push him over the edge. Good God, how she pushed him. And he loved it. Loved *her*. His small, bespectacled warrior.

I won't let you fall, she had said to him, the day he'd been injured at the ruins. *I won't let you turn into a degenerate.* She had meant it, and he had believed her, and that had been the turning point.

How deeply he had resisted loving someone like this . . . and yet it was exhilarating. He felt as if his soul had been set on fire, every part of him burning with impatient joy.

Aware that his color had heightened, Leo took a deep breath and let it out slowly. A smile twitched his lips as he reflected on the peculiar inconvenience of realizing that he was in love with one woman, when he had just been proposed to by another.

"Miss Darvin," he said gently, "I am honored by your suggestion. But you want the man I was. Not the man I am now."

The dark eyes flashed with malice. "You're claiming to be reformed? You think to disown your past?"

"Not at all. But I have hopes for a better future." He paused deliberately. "Ramsay curse notwithstanding."

"You're making a mistake." Vanessa's pretty features hardened. "I knew you were no gentleman, but I didn't take you for a fool. You should leave now. It seems you'll be of no use to me."

Leo rose obligingly. He paused before taking his leave, giving her an astute glance. "I can't help but ask, Miss Darvin . . . why don't you simply marry the baby's father?"

It turned out to be a very good guess.

Vanessa's eyes flared before she managed to school her expression. "He is too far beneath me," she said in a tight little voice. "I'm rather more discriminating than your sisters, my lord."

"A pity," Leo murmured. "They seem to be very happy in their lack of discrimination." He bowed politely. "Farewell, Miss Darvin. I wish you luck in your search for a husband who's not beneath you."

"I don't need luck, my lord. I will marry, and soon. And I've no doubt my future husband and I will be happy indeed when we come to take possession of Ramsay House."

RETURNING TO THE HOTEL FROM A MORNING DRESSMAKER'S appointment with Poppy, Catherine shivered in pleasure as they entered the Rutledge apartments. It was raining steadily, in fat chilling drops that heralded the approach of autumn. Despite the precautions of cloaks and umbrellas, she and Poppy had not escaped entirely from the damp. They both went to the parlor hearth, standing before the snapping fire.

"Harry ought to be coming back from Bow Street soon," Poppy said, pushing back a wet tendril of hair that had stuck to her cheek. He had gone for a meeting with a special constable and a Bow Street magistrate to discuss Lord Latimer. So far Harry had been maddeningly closemouthed as to the specifics of the situation, promising that after he'd gone to the magistrate's office, he would explain in detail. "And so should my brother, after seeing Miss Darvin."

Catherine removed her spectacles and used a fold of her sleeve to clear the steam from the lenses. She heard a welcoming sound from Dodger, a sort of ferrety chuckling noise, and he came loping toward her out of seemingly nowhere. Replacing her spectacles, she bent to pick him up, and he wriggled into her arms. "You odious rat," she murmured, cradling his long, sleek body.

"He loves you, Catherine," Poppy said, shaking her head and smiling.

"Nevertheless, I'm returning him to Beatrix at the first opportunity." But she furtively lowered her cheek and let Dodger kiss her.

There was a knock at the door, followed by the bustle of someone entering, a masculine murmur, a maid taking his coat and hat. Leo entered the parlor, bringing in the scents of damp wool and rain. His hair was wet at the ends, curling slightly against his neck.

"Leo," Poppy exclaimed with a laugh, "how wet you are! Didn't you take an umbrella?"

"Umbrellas are of little use when it's raining sideways," he informed her.

"I'll fetch a towel." Poppy darted out of the room.

Left alone with Leo, Catherine met his gaze. His smile faded, and he stared at her with alarming intensity. Why did he look at her that way? It seemed as if something had been cut loose in him, his eyes demon-blue and dangerous.

"How was your conversation with Miss Darvin?" she asked, tensing as he approached her.

"Illuminating."

She frowned at the brief reply, taking refuge in a show of exasperation. "What did she ask of you?"

"She proposed a marriage of convenience."

Catherine blinked. It was what she had expected, and yet to hear it caused a stab of jealousy.

Leo stopped beside her, the firelight flickering over his features. Tiny droplets of rain glittered like jewels on his sun-browned face. She wanted to touch that light mist, put her mouth on it, taste his skin.

"What was your response?" she forced herself to ask.

"I was flattered, of course," he said smoothly. "One always appreciates being wanted."

He knew she was jealous. He was toying with her. Catherine struggled to keep her temper from igniting.

"Perhaps you should accept her," she said coolly.

His gaze didn't move from hers. "Perhaps I did."

Catherine drew in a sharp breath.

"Here you are," Poppy said cheerfully, oblivious to the tension between them as she entered the room with a neat stack of toweling. She brought a cloth to Leo, who took it and blotted his face.

Catherine sat on the settee, letting Dodger coil in her lap.

"What did Miss Darvin want?" she heard Poppy ask.

Leo's voice was muffled in the towel. "She proposed to me."

"Good heavens," Poppy said. "She clearly hasn't any idea of what it's like to tolerate you on a daily basis."

"In her situation," he returned, "a woman can't afford to be particular."

"What situation is that?" Catherine asked tersely.

Leo handed the towel back to Poppy. "She's expecting a child. And she doesn't care to marry the father. That's not to go any further than this room, of course."

The two women were silent. Catherine wrestled with a curious mixture of feelings . . . sympathy, hostility, jealousy, fear. With this bit of news, the advantages of a match between Leo and Miss Darvin were abundantly clear.

Poppy regarded her brother gravely. "Her circumstances must be quite desperate, for her to confide in you like that."

Leo's reply was forestalled as Harry entered the apartments, his coat and hat streaming with water. "Good afternoon," Harry said, flashing a smile. The maid took the sodden hat and coat, and Poppy approached him with a fresh towel.

"You walked?" she asked, her gaze sweeping from the sodden hems of his trouser legs to his rain-dappled features. She reached up to dry his face with wifely solicitude.

"I very nearly swam," Harry told her, seeming to enjoy her ministrations.

"Why didn't you take a hackney or send for a carriage?"

"All the hackneys were taken as soon as the rain started," Harry replied. "And it's a short distance. Only a milksop would send for a carriage."

"Better a milksop than to catch your death of cold," Poppy fussed, following as he drew near the hearth.

Harry smiled and leaned down to steal a kiss from her as he worked at the wet knot of his cravat. "I never catch cold." Drawing off the damp length of linen, he tossed it aside and stood by the fire. He glanced at Leo expectantly. "What of your meeting with Miss Darvin?"

Leo sat and leaned forward with his elbows braced on his knees. "Never mind that, tell us about the visit to Bow Street."

"Special Constable Hembrey has considered the information you provided, and he's willing to take up an investigation."

"What kind of investigation?" Catherine asked, looking from Harry to Leo.

Leo's face was impassive as he explained. "A few years ago, Lord Latimer invited me to join an exclusive club. A kind of rakehell society, with secret meetings held in a former abbey."

Catherine's eyes widened. "What is the purpose of the society?"

Harry and Leo were both silent. Eventually Leo replied in a flat tone, his gaze fixed on a distant point outside the rain-streaked windows. "Unmitigated depravity. Mock religious rituals, assaults, unnatural crimes. I'll spare you the details, except to say they were so distasteful that even at the height of my debauchery, I turned down Latimer's invitation."

Catherine watched him carefully. His face was set, a small muscle in his jaw flexing. The firelight gilded the taut lines of his face.

"Latimer was so certain I would want to participate," Leo continued, "that he went into some detail regarding some of the crimes he was involved in. And by some fluke I happened to be sober enough to remember most of what he said."

"Is the information enough to support prosecution?" Catherine asked. "And as a peer, doesn't Lord Latimer have the right of freedom from arrest?"

"Only in civil cases," Harry told her. "Not in criminal ones."

"Then you think he'll be brought to trial?"

"No, it won't come to that," Leo said quietly. "The society can't allow their activities to be exposed. When they realize that Latimer is the focus of an investigation, they'll probably force him to leave England before he can be prosecuted. Or better yet, they'll see to it that he ends up as a floater in the Thames."

"Will Constable Hembrey want to depose me?" Catherine brought herself to ask.

"Absolutely not," Leo said with reassuring firmness. "There's more than enough evidence against him without your involvement."

"However it plays out," Harry added, "Latimer will be far too busy to trouble you further, Cat."

"Thank you," Catherine told Harry. Her gaze flickered back to Leo as she added, "That is a great relief." After an awkward pause, she repeated herself lamely. "A great relief, indeed."

"You don't seem all that relieved," Leo observed lazily. "Why is that, Marks?"

This lack of sympathy, along with his earlier taunts about Miss Darvin, were too much for Catherine's shredded nerves.

"If you were in my position," she said stiffly, "you wouldn't exactly be dancing a jig, either."

"You're in a fine position." Leo's eyes were like blue ice. "Latimer will soon be gone, Rutledge has acknowledged you publicly, you're a woman of means, and you have no obligations or commitments to anyone. What could you possibly want that you don't have?"

"Nothing at all," she snapped.

"I think you're sorry to stop running and hiding. Because now you have to face the unfortunate fact that you have nothing . . . and no one . . . to run to."

"It's enough for me to stay still," she said coldly.

Leo smiled with provoking insouciance. "That brings to mind the old paradox."

"What paradox?"

"About what happens when an unstoppable force meets an immovable object."

Harry and Poppy were both silent, looking back and forth between them.

"I suppose I'm the immovable object?" Catherine asked sarcastically.

"If you like."

"Well, I *don't* like," she said, scowling, "because I've always thought that was an absurd question."

"Why?" Leo asked.

"There is no possible answer."

Their gazes clashed and held.

"Yes, there is," Leo said, seeming to enjoy her rising fury.

Harry joined in the debate. "Not from a scientific standpoint. An immovable object would require infinite mass, and the unstoppable force would require infinite energy, neither of which is possible."

"If you argue in terms of semantics, however," Leo countered with maddening calmness, "there is an answer."

"Naturally," Harry said dryly. "A Hathaway can always find a way to argue. Enlighten us—what is the answer?"

Leo replied with his gaze fixed on Catherine's tense face. "The unstoppable force takes the path of least resistance and goes right around the object . . . leaving it far behind."

He was challenging her, Catherine realized. Arrogant,

manipulative cad, using poor Vanessa Darvin's plight to provoke her *and* implying what might happen if Catherine didn't give in to him. *Go right around the object . . . leave it far behind . . .* Indeed!

She jumped to her feet, glaring at him. "Why don't you go on and marry her, then?" Snatching up her reticule, and Dodger's limp body, she stormed out of the apartments.

Leo was instantly at her heels.

"Ramsay—" Harry began.

"Not now, Rutledge," Leo muttered, striding after Catherine. The door was closed with a force that caused it to tremble in its frame.

In the ensuing stillness, Harry looked at Poppy in bewilderment. "I'm not usually slow-witted," he said. "But what the devil were they bickering about?"

"Miss Darvin, I think." Going to him, Poppy sat in his lap and linked her arms around his neck. "She's with child and wants to marry Leo."

"Oh." Harry leaned his head against the back of the chair. His mouth twisted. "I see. He's using it to try and push Catherine into making a decision."

"You don't approve," Poppy said rather than asked, stroking a damp lock of hair off his forehead.

Harry gave her a wry glance. "It's exactly what I would do in his position. Of course I don't approve."

"Stop following me!"

"I want to talk to you." Leo kept pace with Catherine as she hurried along the hallway, his ground-eating strides accounting for every two of her short ones.

"I have no interest in anything you have to say."

"You're jealous." He sounded more than a little pleased by the fact.

"Of you and Miss Darvin?" She forced a scornful laugh. "I pity the both of you. I can't conceive of a more ill-destined match."

"You can't deny that she's a very attractive woman."

"Except for her neck," Catherine couldn't resist saying.

"What the devil is the matter with her neck?"

"It's abnormally long."

Leo tried, unsuccessfully, to smother a laugh. "I can overlook that. Because if I marry her, I'll get to keep Ramsay House, and we'll have a baby already on the way. Convenient, isn't it? Moreover, Miss Darvin promised that I could philander to my heart's content, and she would look the other way."

"What about fidelity?" Catherine asked in outrage.

"Fidelity is so passé. It's laziness, really, not bothering to go out and seduce new people."

"You told me that you would have no difficulty with fidelity!"

"Yes, but that was when we were talking about *our* marriage. Marriage with Miss Darvin will be another thing entirely."

Leo stopped with her as they reached the door of her suite. While Catherine held the sleeping ferret, Leo reached inside her reticule and extracted the key. Catherine didn't spare him a glance as he opened the door for her.

"May I come in?" he asked.

"No."

Leo pushed his way in regardless, and closed the door behind them.

"Pray don't let me keep you," Catherine said grimly, going to set Dodger in his little basket. "I'm sure you have much to do. Starting with changing the name on the special license."

"No, the license is only good for you. If I marry Miss Darvin, I'd have to pay for a new one."

"I hope it's expensive," she said vehemently.

"It is." Leo approached her from behind and put his arms around her, hauling her back securely against him. "And there's another problem."

"What is it?" she asked, struggling in his grasp.

His mouth touched the edge of her ear. "I want you," he whispered. "Only you. Always you."

Catherine went still. Her eyes closed against a sudden wet sting. "Did you accept her proposal?"

Leo nuzzled tenderly into the hollow beneath her ear. "Of course not, pea-goose."

She couldn't prevent a little sob of angry relief. "Then why did you imply that you had?"

"Because you need to be pushed. Otherwise you'll drag this affair out until I'm too decrepit to be of any use to you." Steering Catherine toward the bed, he scooped her up and tossed her to the mattress. Her spectacles went flying to the side.

"What are you doing?" Catherine struggled indignantly, propping herself up on her elbows. She was buried in the masses of her skirts, with their sodden hems and heavy damp flounces. "My dress is wet."

"I'll help you remove it." His solicitous tone was belied by the wicked gleam in his eyes.

She floundered amid the layers and flounces, while Leo unhooked and unfastened her with astonishing efficiency. One would have thought he had more than two arms, as he turned her this way and that, his hands reaching everywhere. Ignoring her protests, he pulled the heavy skirt, with its stiffened muslin lining, away from the detachable bodice, and tossed it to the floor. Her shoes were removed and dropped over the side of the bed. Flipping Catherine to her stomach, he began on the fastenings of the heavily ruched bodice.

"I beg your pardon, I did not ask to be husked like an ear of corn!" She twisted in an effort to push away his busy hands. A squeak escaped her as he found the tapes of her drawers and pulled them loose.

With a low chuckle, Leo anchored her squirming body with his legs, and kissed the exposed nape of her neck. She felt warm all over, her nerves sparked by the touch of his sensuous mouth.

"Did you kiss her?" she heard herself blurt out, her voice muffled in the bedclothes.

"No, love. I wasn't tempted by her in the least." Leo bit lightly into the soft muscle of her neck, stroked the fine skin with his tongue, and she gasped. His hand slipped inside her drawers and circled over her bottom. "No other woman in the world could excite me as you do. But you're too damn stubborn, and far too good at protecting yourself. There are things I want to say to you . . . do to you . . . and the fact that you're not ready for any of it is going to drive us both mad."

He touched further between her thighs, finding wetness, stroking in soft circles. She moaned and writhed beneath him. Her corset was still snugly laced, the compression of her waist seeming to divert sensation down between her thighs. Although part of her rebelled at the feeling of being held down and caressed, her body reacted with helpless pleasure.

"I want to make love to you." Leo traced the inner structure of her ear with the tip of his tongue. "I want to go as deep as you can take me, and feel you tighten around me, and I want to come inside you." A finger slid inside her, and another, and she whimpered softly. "You know how good it would feel," he whispered, stroking her slowly. "Yield to me, and I'll love you without stopping. I'll stay in you all night."

Catherine gasped for breath, while her heart thumped

madly. "You would have me in the same position as Miss Darvin," she said. "Pregnant and pleading for you to marry me."

"God, yes, I would love that."

She nearly choked with indignation, while his long fingers teased her inside and out. Her body began to clench in a slow, steady pulse of desire. There were great swaths of fabric caught between their bodies, layers of remaining clothing, and all she could feel was his mouth at the back of her neck, and that devilishly persuasive hand.

"I have never said this to anyone before." Leo's voice was like ragged velvet. "But the idea of you with child is the most insanely arousing thing I've ever imagined. Your belly all swollen, your breasts heavy, the funny little way you would walk . . . I would worship you. I would take care of your every need. And everyone would know that I'd made you that way, that you belonged to me."

"You . . . you are so . . ." She couldn't even think of a suitable word.

"I know. Woefully primitive." Laughter threaded through his voice. "But I must be tolerated, because I'm a man and I really can't help it."

He caressed her with gentle, explicit manipulation, his fingers slick and tireless. She felt a new flush of arousal, the liquid heat spreading out to her fingers and toes. Moving behind her, he tugged her drawers to her knees, and fumbled with the fastenings of his trousers. He let his weight settle on her deliciously. A blunt, moist pressure slipped between her thighs, not quite entering. White fire raced through her senses, and her body trembled at the verge of release . . . so close . . .

"You have a decision to make, Cat." Leo kissed the side of her throat hungrily, his mouth strong and wet. "Either tell me to stop right now, or let me take you all the way. Because

I can't withdraw at the last moment any longer. I want you too much. And I probably will make you pregnant, love, because I'm feeling rather potent at the moment. So it's all or nothing. Tell me yes or no."

"I *can't*." Catherine thrashed in frustration as his hips lifted from hers. As he rolled her over to face him, she glared up at him. Unable to stop himself, he lowered his head and kissed her voraciously, savoring the sound of need that came from her throat.

"A pity," he said, breathing heavily. "I was working up to something really lascivious." Rolling off her, he reached for the fall of his trousers, muttering something about the risk of doing himself permanent injury as he tried to fasten them again.

Catherine watched him incredulously. "You're not going to finish?"

He let out an unsteady sigh. "As I said, all or nothing."

She wrapped her arms around herself, trembling with desire until her teeth chattered. "Why are you trying to torture me?"

"It's becoming clear that a lifetime of patience wouldn't be enough to break through your guard. So I'll have to try something else." Leo kissed her gently and left the bed. After he raked both hands through his disheveled hair and straightened his clothes, he gave her a smoldering glance, followed by a grin that seemed to mock both of them simultaneously. "I'm waging war, love. And the only way to win this kind of war is to make you want to lose."

Chapter Twenty-eight

Only a woman made of stone could have lasted against the campaign Leo launched over the next week. It was courtship, he claimed, but there should have been another word for it, the way he kept Catherine constantly off balance with his sweetly subversive charm.

One moment he provoked her into some nonsensical and highly entertaining argument, and the next he was soothing and kind. He whispered whimsical compliments and lines of poetry in her ear, and taught her naughty French words, and made her laugh at inappropriate moments. What Leo did not do, however, was try to kiss or seduce her. At first Catherine was amused by this obvious tactic, and then secretly miffed, and then intrigued. She frequently found herself staring at his mouth, so flawless and firm . . . she couldn't help remembering their past kisses, daydreaming about them.

When they attended a private musical evening at a mansion on Upper Brook Street, Leo stole Catherine away as the hostess led a group of guests on a tour of the house. Following Leo to a private corner behind an arrangement of tall potted ferns, Catherine went eagerly into his arms. Instead of kissing her, however, he pulled her into the warm strength of his body . . . and held her. Simply held her, keeping her warm and close, letting his hands course slowly over her back. He whispered something secretive amid the pinned-up swirls of her hair, the words too soft for her to hear.

What Catherine enjoyed above all was walking with Leo through the Rutledge gardens, where sunlight stuttered through trees and hedges, and the breezes carried the crisp hint of approaching autumn. They had long conversations, sometimes touching on sensitive subjects. Careful questions, difficult answers. And yet it seemed they were both struggling toward the same goal, a kind of connection that neither of them had ever known before.

Sometimes Leo drew back and looked at her for wordless moments as one might stare at a work of art in a museum, trying to discover its truth. It was compelling, the interest he showed in her. Seductive. And he was a wonderful conversationalist, telling her stories about his childhood misadventures, about what it had been like to grow up in the Hathaway family, about the time he had spent in Paris and Provence. Catherine listened carefully to the details, gathering them like quilting scraps, piecing them together to form a better understanding of one of the more complex men she had ever met.

Leo was an unsentimental rogue who was capable of great sensitivity and compassion. He was an articulate man who could use words either to soothe like a balm of honey, or dissect like a surgeon's knife. When it suited him, Leo played the part of a jaded aristocrat, adeptly concealing the quicksilver workings of his brain. But sometimes in unguarded moments, Catherine caught glimpses of the gallant boy he had once been, before experience had weathered and hardened him.

"In some ways he's very much like our father was,"

Poppy told her in private. "Father *loved* conversation. He was a serious man, an intellectual, but he possessed a streak of whimsy." She grinned, remembering. "My mother always said she might have married a more handsome man, or a wealthier one, but never one who talked as he did. And she knew herself to be the kind of woman who would never have been happy with a dullard."

Catherine could well understand that. "Did Lord Ramsay favor your mother in any regard?"

"Oh, yes. She had an artistic eye, and she encouraged Leo in his architectural pursuits." Poppy paused. "I don't think she would have been pleased to learn that Leo would inherit a title—she didn't have a high opinion of the aristocracy. And she certainly wouldn't have approved of Leo's behavior in the past few years, although she would be very glad that he had decided to mend his ways."

"Where did his wicked wit come from?" Catherine asked. "Your mother or your father?"

"That," Poppy said wryly, "is entirely Leo's own."

NEARLY EVERY DAY, LEO BROUGHT CATHERINE A SMALL GIFT: a book, a box of sweets, a collar made of Brussels bobbin lace in a delicate pattern of openwork flowers. "This is the loveliest lacework I've ever seen," she told him regretfully, setting the exquisite gift on a nearby table with great care. "But my lord, I'm afraid—"

"I know," Leo said. "A gentleman shouldn't give personal items to a lady he's courting." He lowered his voice, mindful of being overheard by Poppy and the housekeeper, who were talking by the threshold of the Rutledge apartments. "But I can't take it back—no other woman could do it justice. And Marks, you have no idea of the self-restraint I exercised. I wanted to buy you a pair of embroidered stockings with little flowers that run all the way up the insides of your—"

"My lord," Catherine whispered, a light blush covering her face. "You forget yourself."

"I haven't forgotten a thing, actually. Not one detail of your beautiful body. Soon I may start sketching you naked again. Every time I put a pencil to paper, the temptation nearly overwhelms me."

She tried to look severe. "You promised not to do that again."

"But my pencil has a will of its own," he said gravely.

Catherine's color deepened, even as a smile tugged at her lips. "You're incorrigible."

His lashes lowered fractionally. "Kiss me, and I'll behave."

She made an exasperated little sound. "*Now* you want to kiss me, when Poppy and the housekeeper are standing only a few yards away?"

"They won't notice. They're involved in a riveting conversation about hotel toweling." Leo's voice lowered to a whisper. "Kiss me. One little kiss. Right here." He pointed to his cheek.

Perhaps it was the fact that Leo looked rather boyish as he teased her, his blue eyes alight with mischief. But as Catherine looked at him, she was nearly overwhelmed with a strange new feeling, a warm giddiness that invaded every part of her body. She leaned forward, and instead of kissing his cheek, she put her mouth directly on his.

Leo drew in a surprised breath, letting her take the lead. And, giving in to temptation, she lingered longer than she had intended, her mouth softly teasing, her tongue shyly touching his lips. He responded with a low sound, his arms going around her. She sensed the rising heat in him, the carefully banked urges threatening to flare out of control.

Ending the kiss, Catherine half expected to see Poppy and the housekeeper, Mrs. Pennywhistle, both staring at them with scandalized expressions. But as she peeked over

Leo's shoulder, she saw that the housekeeper's back was still turned toward them.

Poppy had taken in the situation with an astute glance. "Mrs. Pennywhistle," she said glibly, ushering the housekeeper away from the threshold, "do come out into the hallway with me, I thought I saw a dreadful stain on the carpeting the other day, and I wanted to show you . . . is it here? . . . No, perhaps over there . . . Oh, drat, where is it?"

Left in temporary privacy, Catherine looked into Leo's heavy-lidded blue eyes.

"Why did you do that?" he asked, his voice husky.

She tried to think of an answer that would amuse him. "I wanted you to test my higher brain function."

A smile tugged at the corners of his lips. Taking a deep breath, he let it out slowly. "If you have a match when you enter a dark room," he finally said, "which would you light first—the oil lamp on the table, or the kindling in the hearth?"

Catherine squinted as she considered the question. "The lamp."

"The match," he said, shaking his head. His tone was soft and chiding. "Marks, you're not even trying."

"Another one," she prompted, and he complied without hesitation, his head bending over hers. He gave her a long, smoldering kiss, and she relaxed against him, her fingers sinking into his hair. He finished the kiss with a voluptuous nudge.

"Is it legal or illegal for a man to marry his widow's sister?" he asked.

"Illegal," she said languidly, trying to pull his head back to hers.

"Impossible, because he's dead." Leo resisted her efforts and looked down at her with a crooked grin. "It's time to stop."

"No," she protested, straining toward him.

"Easy, Marks," he whispered. "One of us has to have some

self-control, and it really should be you." He brushed his lips against her forehead. "I have another present for you."

"What is it?"

"Look in my pockets." He jumped a little and laughed unsteadily as she began to search him. "No, you little ravisher, not my trouser pockets." Grabbing her wrists in his hands, he held them suspended in the air, as if he were trying to subdue a playful kitten. Seeming unable to resist, he leaned forward and took her mouth again. Being kissed while he held her wrists might have frightened her once, but now it awakened something deep and ticklish inside.

Leo tore his mouth away and released her with a gasping laugh. "Coat pocket. My God, I want to—no, I won't say it. Yes, there's your present."

Catherine drew out an object wrapped in soft cloth. Gently she unwrapped a new pair of spectacles made of silver . . . gleaming and perfect, the oval lenses sparkling. Marveling at the workmanship, she drew a finger along one of the intricate filigreed earpieces, all the way to the curved tip. "They're so beautiful," she said in wonder.

"If they please you, we'll have another pair made in gold. Here, let me help you . . ." Leo gently drew the old spectacles off her face, seeming to savor the gesture.

She put the new ones on. They felt light and secure on the bridge of her nose. As she looked around the room, everything was wonderfully detailed and in focus. In her excitement, she jumped up and hurried to the looking glass that hung over the entryway table. She inspected her own glowing reflection.

"How pretty you are." Leo's tall, elegant form appeared behind hers. "I do love spectacles on a woman."

Catherine's smiling gaze met his in the silvered glass. "Do you? What an odd preference."

"Not at all." His hands came to her shoulders, lightly fondling up to her throat and back again. "They emphasize your beautiful eyes. And they make you look capable of secrets and surprises—which, as we know, you are." His voice lowered. "Most of all I love the act of removing them—getting you ready for a tumble in bed."

She shivered at his bluntness, her eyes half closing as she felt him pull her back against him. His mouth went to the side of her neck.

"You like them?" Leo murmured, kissing her soft skin.

"Yes." Her head listed to the side as his tongue traced a subtle path along her throat. "I . . . I don't know why you went to such trouble. It was very kind."

Leo's dark head lifted, and he met her drowsy gaze in the looking glass. His fingers went to the side of her throat, stroking as if to rub the feel of his mouth into her skin. "I wasn't being kind," he murmured, a smile touching his lips. "I merely wanted you to see clearly."

I'm beginning to, she was tempted to tell him, but Poppy returned to the apartment before she was able.

THAT NIGHT CATHERINE SLEPT BADLY, STUMBLING INTO THE nightmare world that seemed as real, if not more real, than the infinitely kinder world she inhabited in her waking moments.

It was part dream, part memory, the recollection of running through her grandmother's house until she had found the old woman sitting at her desk, writing in a ledger.

Heedlessly Catherine threw herself at her grandmother's feet and buried her face in the voluminous black skirts. She felt the old woman's skeletal fingers slide under her wet chin and lift it.

Her grandmother's face was masked with a sediment of

powder, the ashy whiteness contrasting with her artificially darkened brows and hair. Unlike Althea, she wore no lip rouge, only colorless salve.

"Althea talked to you," Grandmother said, in a voice like dried leaves rubbing together.

Catherine struggled to force out words between sobs. "Yes . . . and I don't underst . . . *understand* . . ."

Grandmother responded with a scratchy croon, pressing Catherine's head on her lap. She stroked her hair, narrow fingers combing lightly through the loose locks. "Did Althea fail to explain adequately? Come, you're not a clever girl, but neither are you stupid. What don't you understand? Stop crying, you know I detest it."

Catherine squeezed her eyes tightly, trying to stop the tears from slipping out. Her throat was tight with misery. "I want something else, anything else. I want a choice."

"You don't want to be like Althea?" The question was spoken with unnerving gentleness.

"*No.*"

"And you don't want to be like me?"

Catherine hesitated and shook her head slightly, afraid to say "no" again. She had learned in the past that the word should be used sparingly with her grandmother. It was an unfailing irritant regardless of the circumstances.

"But you already are," Grandmother told her. "You're a woman. All women have a whore's life, child."

Catherine froze, afraid to move. Her grandmother's fingers became talons, the stroking changing into a sort of slow, rhythmic clawing on her head.

"All women sell themselves to men," her grandmother continued. "Marriage itself is a transaction, in which a woman's value is tied to purposes of copulation and breeding. At least we, in our time-honored profession, are honest about it." Her tone turned reflective. "Men are foul, brutish creatures. But they own the world and always will. And to get the most from them, you must practice submission. You'll be very good at it, Catherine. I've seen the instinct in you. You like being told what to do. You'll like it even more when you're paid for it." Her hand lifted from Catherine's head. "Now, don't trouble me again. You may ask Althea all the questions you like. Mind you, when she began on her career, she was no happier about it than you. But she quickly saw the advantages of her situation. And we all have to earn our keep, don't we? Even you, dear. Being my granddaughter affords you no entitlement. And fifteen minutes on your back will earn you as much as other women earn in two or three days. Willing submission, Catherine."

Feeling stunned, as if she had just fallen from a great height, Catherine had left her grandmother's study. She knew a momentary, mad urge to bolt for the front door. But without a place to go to, without money, an unprotected girl would last only a matter of hours in London. The trapped sobs in her chest had dissolved into shivers.

She went upstairs to her room. But then the dream changed, the memories transforming into dark vagaries of imagination . . . becoming a nightmare. The stairs seemed to multiply, and the climb became difficult and she went upward into deeper and deeper shadows. Alone and shivering with cold, she reached her room, illuminated only by the glaze of moonlight.

There was a man sitting at the window. He was straddling the frame, actually, one long leg placed firmly on the floor, the other swinging negligently outside. She knew him from the shape of his head, from the powerful lines of his silhouette. And from the dark, a velvety voice that lifted the hairs on the back of her neck.

"There you are. Come here, Marks."

Catherine was suffused with relief and yearning. "My lord, what are you doing here?" she cried, running to him.

"Waiting for you." His arms went around her. "I'll take you far away from here—would you like that?"

"Oh, yes, yes . . . but how?"

"We'll go right out this window. I have a ladder."

"But is it safe? Are you certain—"

He put his hand gently to her mouth, silencing her. "Trust me." His hand pressed harder. "I won't let you fall."

She tried to tell him that she would go anywhere with him, do anything he said, but he was covering her mouth too tightly for her to speak. His grip became hurtful, clamping on her jaw. She couldn't breathe.

Catherine's eyes opened. The nightmare fell away, revealing a far worse reality. She struggled beneath a crushing weight, and tried to cry out against the callused hand that covered her mouth.

"Your aunt wants to see you," came a voice in the darkness. "I 'as to do this, miss. I 'as no choice."

IN THE SPACE OF JUST A FEW MINUTES, IT WAS DONE.

William gagged her with a tight cloth that bit into her mouth, a large knot pressing hard against her tongue. After binding her hands and feet, he went to light a lamp. Even without the aid of her spectacles, Catherine perceived that he wore the dark blue coat of a Rutledge Hotel employee.

If only she could get a few words out, plead or bargain with him, but the knotted lump of cloth made coherent sound impossible. Her saliva spiked unpleasantly at the intensely acrid flavor of the gag. There was something on it, she realized, and at that same moment she felt her consciousness breaking into pieces, scattered like an unfinished puzzle. Her heart turned sluggish, pumping poisoned blood through her collapsing limbs, and there was a ballooning, thumping sensation in her head as if her brain had suddenly become too large for her skull.

William came to her with a hotel laundry bag. He began to pull it over her, starting at her feet. He didn't look at her face, only kept his gaze on his task. She watched passively, seeing that he took care to keep the hem of her nightgown primly down at her ankles. Some distant part of her brain wondered at the small kindness of preserving her modesty.

The bedclothes rustled near her feet, and Dodger streaked out with a furious chatter. With quicksilver speed he attacked William's arm and hand, inflicting a series of deep, gouging bites. Catherine had never seen the little animal behave in such a manner. William grunted in surprise and flung out his arm with a low curse. The ferret went flying, slamming hard against the wall and falling limply to the floor.

Catherine moaned behind the gag, her eyes burning with acid tears.

Breathing heavily, William examined his bleeding hand, found a cloth at the washstand to wrap around it, and returned to Catherine. The laundry bag was pulled higher and higher until it went over her head.

She understood that Althea didn't really want to see her. Althea wanted to destroy her. Perhaps William didn't know. Or perhaps he thought it was kinder to lie. It didn't matter. She felt nothing, no fear, no anguish, although tears leaked steadily from the outward corners of her eyes. What a terrible fate to leave the world feeling nothing at all. She was nothing more than a tangle of limbs in a sack, a headless doll, all memories receding, all sensation falling away.

A few thoughts needled through the blanket of nothingness, pinpricks of light in the dark.

Leo would never know that she had loved him.

She thought of his eyes, all those colors of blue. Her mind

was filled with a constellation of high summer, stars in a li-on's shape. *The brightest star marks his heart.*

He would grieve. If only she could spare him that.

Oh, what they could have had. A life together, such a sim-ple thing. To watch that handsome face weather with age. She had to admit now that she had never been happier than in the moments with him.

Her heart beat faintly beneath her ribs. It was heavy, ach-ing with contained feeling, a hard knot within the numbness.

I didn't want to need you, Leo, I fought so hard to stay standing at the edge of my own life . . . when I should have had the courage to walk into yours.

Chapter Twenty-nine

Late in the morning Leo returned from a visit with his old mentor, Rowland Temple. The architect, now a professor at University College, had recently been awarded the Royal Gold Medal for his work in advancing the academic study of architecture. Leo had been amused but hardly surprised to discover that Temple was as imperious and irascible as ever. The old man viewed the aristocracy as a source of patronage to keep him financially solvent, but he had contempt for their traditional and unimaginative sense of style.

"You're not one of those parasitical dunderheads," Temple had told him emphatically, which Leo gathered had been a compliment. And later, "My influence on you cannot be eradicated, can it?" And of course Leo had assured him that it could not, that he remembered and valued everything he had learned from Temple. He hadn't dared to mention the far greater influence of the elderly professor in Provence.

"Architecture is how we reconcile to the difficulties of life," Joseph had once told Leo at his *atelier*. The old professor had been repotting some herbs at a long wooden table, while Leo tried to help. "*Non,* don't touch these, *mon fils,* you pack the roots too tightly, they need more air than you allow them."

He took a pot away from Leo and resumed the lecture. "To be an architect, you have to accept the environment around you, no matter what its conditions. Then, in full awareness, you take your ideals and form them into structure."

"Can I do it without ideals?" Leo had asked, only half joking. "I've learned I can't live up to them."

Professor Joseph had smiled at him. "Neither can you reach the stars. But you still need their light. You need them to navigate, *n'est-ce pas*?"

Take your ideals and form them into structure. Only in that way could a good house, a good building, be designed.

Or a good life.

And Leo had finally found the cornerstone, the essential piece to build the rest on.

A very stubborn cornerstone.

His lips curved as he considered what to do with Catherine that day, how to woo her, or annoy her, since she seemed to enjoy both equally. Perhaps he would start a small argument and kiss her into capitulation. Perhaps he would propose to her again, if he could catch her in a moment of weakness.

Heading to the Rutledge apartments, Leo entered after a careless knock, and found Poppy rushing to the entrance foyer.

"Have you—" she started, then broke off as she saw him. "Leo. I wondered when you'd get back. I didn't know where you were, or I would have sent for you—"

"What is it, sis?" he asked gently, understanding at once that something was very wrong.

Poppy looked wretched, her eyes large in her white face. "Catherine didn't come up for breakfast this morning. I assumed that she wanted to sleep late. Sometimes her nightmares—"

"Yes, I know." Leo gripped her cold hands, staring at her alertly. "Out with it, Poppy."

"An hour ago I send a housemaid to Catherine's room, to see if she needed something. She wasn't there, and these were on the table by the bed." Reaching out with a trembling hand, she gave him the new silver spectacles. "And . . . there was blood on the bed."

It took Leo a moment to contain the rush of panic. He felt it as instant stinging from head to toe, and a heart-thundering blast of energy. A dizzying urge to kill.

"The hotel is being searched," he heard Poppy say over the roar in his ears, "and Harry and Mr. Valentine are talking to the floor stewards."

"Latimer has her," Leo said thickly. "He sent someone for her. I'll rip the filthy whoreson's guts out and hang him with them—"

"Leo," she whispered, her hand fluttering to his mouth. What she saw in his face frightened her. "Please."

Relief partially smoothed Poppy's brow as her husband entered the apartment. "Harry, is there any sign?"

Harry's face was grim and hard. "One of the night stewards said that last night he saw a man dressed as an employee—he assumed he was newly hired—carrying a laundry sack down the back stairs. He noticed it because the housemaids usually take care of laundry, and never at that time of night." He put a restraining hand on Leo's shoulder, and Leo shook him off. "Ramsay, keep your head. I know what you assume, and you're probably right. But you can't go dashing off like a madman. We need to—"

"Try and stop me," Leo said in a guttural tone. There was no controlling what had been unleashed in him. He was gone before Harry could draw another breath.

"Christ," Harry muttered, dragging his hands through his black hair. He gave Poppy a distracted glance. "Find Valentine," he said. "He's still talking with the floor managers. Tell him to go to Special Constable Hembrey—or whoever he can find at Bow Street, and let them know what's happening. Hembrey can start by sending a man to Lord Latimer's house. Tell Valentine to say there's a murder in progress."

"Leo won't kill Lord Latimer," Poppy said, her face blanched.

"If he doesn't," Harry replied with cold certainty, "I will."

CATHERINE AWAKENED IN A STRANGE EUPHORIA, LIGHT-headed and listless, and very glad to awaken from her nightmares. Except that when she opened her eyes, she was still in a nightmare, in a room hazed with sickening-sweet smoke, the windows shrouded with heavy curtains.

She took a long time to collect herself, straining to see without spectacles. Her jaw was sore, her mouth unbearably dry. She was desperate for a sip of cold water, a breath of clean air. Her wrists were fastened behind her back. She half reclined, half sat on a settee, dressed in her nightgown. Awkwardly she used her shoulder to try to push back some of the loose tangles of her hair that had fallen over her face.

Catherine knew this room, blurry as it was. And she knew the old woman sitting near her, stick thin and dressed in black. The woman's hands moved with the delicacy of an insect's pincers as she lifted a thin leather hose attached to a hookah vase. Putting the hose to her lips, she sucked in a breath, held it, and expelled a puff of white smoke.

"Grandmother?" Catherine asked, her voice rough, her tongue thick in her mouth.

The woman moved closer, until her face came into Catherine's limited view. A powdered white face, vermillon lips. Hard, familiar eyes rimmed with kohl. "She's dead. It's my house now. My business."

Althea, Catherine realized in dull horror. A cadaverous version of Althea, the once attractive features shrunken and calcified. The face powder covered the top stratum of skin but hadn't settled into the web of wrinkles, giving her complexion the appearance of crackled glaze on porcelain. She was far more fearsome than even Grandmother had been. And she looked more than a little mad, her eyes bulging and blue-glazed like those of a baby bird.

"William told me he'd seen you," Althea said. "And I said, 'We must fetch her for a long overdue visit, mustn't we?' It took a bit of planning on his part, but he executed it nicely." She glanced into a shadowed corner. "You're a good boy, William."

He replied in an unintelligible murmur. Or at least it was unintelligible to Catherine, through the irregular pulse that thumped in her ears. It seemed the inner systems of her body had been rearranged, a new order of channels and nerves that she couldn't quite integrate.

"May I have some water?" she asked hoarsely.

"William, give our guest some water."

He complied clumsily, going to fill a glass, standing over Catherine. Holding the cup to her lips, he watched as she sipped carefully. The water was instantly absorbed into the parched tissue of her lips, inner cheeks, throat. It carried a dusty, brackish taint, or perhaps that was just the taste of her mouth.

William retreated, and Catherine waited while her aunt puffed thoughtfully on the hookah.

"Mother never forgave you," Althea said, "for running away as you did. Lord Latimer hounded us for years, demanding the return of his money . . . or you. But you don't care about what trouble you caused. You never gave a thought to what you owed."

Catherine fought to keep her head steady, when it kept lolling to the side. "I didn't owe you my body."

"You thought you were too good for that. You wanted to avoid *my* downfall. You wanted a choice." Althea paused, as if waiting for confirmation. When none was forthcoming, she continued with soft vehemence. "But why should you have one when I didn't? My own mother came to my bedroom one night. She said she'd brought a nice gentleman to help tuck me in. But first he was going to show me some new games. After that night, there was no innocent part of me left. I was twelve."

Another long inhalation through the hookah, another dizzying puff of smoke. There was no way for Catherine to avoid breathing in more. The room seemed to sway gently, as Catherine had imagined the deck of a ship would rock at sea. She floated on the waves, buoyant, listening to Althea's seething. And she felt a stirring of sympathy, but like the rest of her emotions, it remained deep under the surface, drowning.

"I thought of running away," Althea said. "I asked my brother—your father—to help me. He lived with us then, coming and going as he pleased. Using the whores for free any time he wanted, and they didn't dare complain to Mother. 'I need just a little money,' I told him. 'I'll go far away to the country.' But he went to Mother and told her what I'd asked. I wasn't let out of the house for months afterward."

From what little Catherine remembered of her father, a brusque and pitiless individual, this story was easy to believe. But she found herself asking distantly, "Why didn't he help you?"

"My brother liked the situation as it was—he had the best of everything without lifting a finger. Mother gave him whatever he wanted. And the selfish pig didn't mind sacrificing me to keep himself comfortable. He was a man, you see." She paused. "So I became a whore. And for years I prayed for rescue. But God doesn't hear the prayers of women. He cares only for those He made in His own image."

Befuddled and squinting, Catherine labored to keep her

thoughts in order. "Aunt," she said carefully, "why did you bring me here? If that was done to you . . . why must it be done to me?"

"Why should you escape when I couldn't? I want you to become me. Just as I became Mother."

Yes . . . this was one of Catherine's fears, the worst one. That if she were put in the wrong situation, the wickedness in her own nature would take over all the rest.

Except . . . it wouldn't.

Catherine's foggy brain seized on the idea and turned it over, examining it. The past was not the future. "I'm not like you," she said slowly. "Won't ever be. I grieve for what was done to you, Aunt. But I didn't make the same choice."

"I have a choice for you now."

Despite Catherine's opiated detachment, Althea's caressing tone made her flesh creep.

"You will either make good on that long-ago arrangement with Lord Latimer," Althea continued, "or you will service customers in the brothel, as I did. Which shall it be?"

Catherine refused to choose. "Doesn't matter what you do," she said, drugged but intractable. "Nothing will change who I am."

"And who are you?" Althea's voice dripped with contempt. "A decent woman? Too good for the likes of this place?"

Catherine's head became too heavy for her to hold up any longer. She lowered herself to the settee, resting her head on the arm. "A woman who is loved."

It was the worst, most hurtful answer she could have given Althea. And it was the truth.

Unable to open her eyes, Catherine was aware of a bustling movement nearby, of Althea's tentaclelike grip on her face, of the leather hose from the hookah shoved between her lips. Her nose was pinched shut, and she breathed in helplessly. A flood of cool, pungent smoke entered her lungs. She coughed, and was forced to draw it in again, and then she wilted into a placid and near-insensible heap.

"Take her upstairs, William," Althea said. "To her old bedroom. Later we'll move her to the brothel."

"Yes, ma'am." William gathered Catherine up carefully. "Ma'am . . . may I undo her wrists?"

Althea shrugged. "She certainly won't go anywhere under her own power."

William carried Catherine upstairs, settled her on the small, musty bed of her old room, and untied her hands. He arranged her arms with her hands touching at her middle, in the position of a body in a casket. "Sorry, miss," he murmured, looking into her half-open, unseeing eyes. "She's all I 'ave. I 'as to do what she says."

Chapter Thirty

Guy, Lord Latimer, lived in a newer section of London on the west side, with a picturesque and peaceful common, and a row of stucco-fronted houses built in a deeply wooded hollow. Leo had visited the house on more than one occasion, several years earlier. Although the street and the house were neatly kept, the place was littered with distasteful memories that would have made an East End slum look like a rectory by comparison.

Dismounting from his horse before it had even halted, Leo raced up to the front door and pounded on it with his fists. All his thoughts had diverted into parallel currents, one occupied with the anguished desperation to find Catherine before harm could come to her. Or, if something already had befallen her—please, God, *no*—how to make her well again.

The other current was directed toward the one goal of turning Latimer into butcher's refuse.

There was no sign of Harry yet—Leo was certain that he was not far behind, but Leo had no inclination to wait for him.

A perturbed-looking butler opened the door, and Leo shouldered his way in. "Sir—"

"Where is your master?" Leo asked brusquely.

"I beg your pardon, sir, but he is not—" The butler broke off with an astonished yelp as Leo grabbed him by the coat and shoved him against the nearest wall. "Good God. Sir, I beg you—"

"Tell me where he is."

"The . . . the library . . . but he's not well . . ."

Leo's lips curled in an evil smile. "I have just the cure for him."

A footman came into the hall, and the butler began to sputter for help, but Leo had already released him. In a matter of seconds he had reached the library. It was dark and overheated, an unseasonably large fire blazing in the hearth. Latimer was slumped in a chair, his chin on his chest, a half-empty bottle in one hand. With his bloated face lit by tongues of yellow and red flame, he looked like a damned soul. His incurious gaze lifted to the harsh contours of Leo's face, and Leo saw from his difficulty in focusing that he was sow-drunk. Too bloody drunk to see a hole in a ladder. It would have taken hours of steady imbibing to arrive at this state.

The realization filled Leo with furious despair. Because the one thing worse than finding Catherine with Latimer was *not* finding her there. He leaped on the bastard, clenched his hands around Latimer's thick, clammy throat, and hauled him to a standing position. The bottle dropped to the floor. Latimer's eyes bulged, and he choked and spat as he tried to pry Leo's hands free.

"Where is she?" Leo demanded, giving him a hard shake. "What have you done with Catherine Marks?" He loosened his bruising grip just enough to allow Latimer to speak.

The bastard coughed and wheezed, and stared at him incredulously. "Sodding lunatic! What the bloody hell are you talking about?"

"She's disappeared."

"And you think I have her?" Latimer let out a disbelieving bark of laughter.

"Convince me that you don't," Leo said, clenching his neck more tightly, "and I may let you live."

Latimer's bloated face turned dark. "I have no use for that woman, or any other harlot, because of the . . . the stew you've put me in! You are tearing my life apart! Investigations, questions from Bow Street . . . allies threatening to turn on me. D' you know how many enemies you're making?"

"Not nearly as many as you."

Latimer writhed in his merciless grasp. "They want me dead, damn you."

"What a coincidence," Leo said through clenched teeth. "So do I."

"What has become of you?" Latimer demanded. "She's *only a woman.*"

"If anything happens to her, I'll have nothing left to lose. And if I don't find her within the next hour, you'll pay with your life."

Something in his tone caused Latimer's eyes to widen in panic. "I have nothing to do with it."

"Tell me, or I'll garrot you until you swell up like a toad."

"Ramsay." Harry Rutledge's voice sliced through the air like a sword.

"He says she's not here," Leo muttered, not taking his gaze from Latimer.

A few metallic clicks, and then Harry placed the muzzle of a flintlock in the center of Latimer's forehead. "Let go of him, Ramsay."

Leo complied.

Latimer made an incoherent sound in the sepulchral quiet of the room. His gaze locked with Harry's.

"Remember me?" Harry asked softly. "I should have done this eight years ago."

It appeared that Harry's ice-cold eyes frightened Latimer even more than Leo's murderous ones. "Please," Latimer whispered, his mouth shaking.

"Give me information about my sister's whereabouts in the next five seconds, or I'll put a hole in your head. Five."

"I don't know anything," Latimer pleaded.

"Four."

"I swear it on my life!" Tears sprang from his eyes.

"Three. Two."

"Please, I'll do anything!"

Harry hesitated, giving him an assessing stare. He read the truth in his eyes. "Damn it," he said softly, and lowered the pistol. He looked at Leo, while Latimer collapsed in a sobbing drunken heap on the floor. "He doesn't have her."

They exchanged a quick, bleak glance. It was the first time Leo had ever felt a kinship with Harry, sharing this moment of despair over the same woman.

"Who else would want her?" Leo muttered. "There's no one with a connection to her past . . . except the aunt." He paused. "The night of the play, Cat happened to see a man who worked at the brothel. William. She knew him as a child."

"The brothel is in Marylebone," Harry said abruptly, heading for the door. He motioned for Leo to follow.

"Why would the aunt have taken Cat?"

"I don't know. Perhaps she's finally gone mad."

THE BROTHEL WAS SAGGING AND FLAT-BREASTED, WITH TRIM that had chipped and been painted a thousand times until someone had finally decided the effort was no longer worth it. The windows were soot-darkened, the front door askew like a lascivious half-smile. The house next door was far smaller, stoop-shouldered, a maltreated child standing next to its promiscuous older sister.

It was often the arrangement that when a brothel was a family business, the owners lived in a separate dwelling. Leo recognized the house from Catherine's description. This was where she had lived as a naïve young girl, unaware that her future had already been stolen from her.

They rode through a cross-street to a fetid alley behind the brothel, a crumbling mews with tilting sides, one of many in the labyrinth of nooks and tiny streets concealed behind the main thoroughfare.

Two men lounged in the doorway of the larger building, the brothel, one of them possessing a massive physical stature that distinguished him as the Bully of the house. In the world of prostitution, the office of Bully was to keep order at a brothel and settle disputes between whores and clients. The other man was small and slight, a hawker of some manner, with a pocketed apron knotted around his waist and a small covered handchaise at the side of the alley.

Noting the attention the visitors paid to the back entrance of the brothel, the Bully spoke in an affable tone. "Sporting ladies aren't working yet, guvnahs, you 'as to come back at nightfall."

Leo summoned all his will to keep his tone pleasant as he spoke to the strongman. "I have business with the mistress of the house."

"She won't see you, I 'spect . . . but you can ask Willy." The Bully gestured toward the dilapidated house with a meaty hand, his manner relaxed, his eyes sharp.

Leo and Harry went to the dilapidated entrance of the smaller house. A cluster of nail holes was all that remained of a long-gone door knocker. Leo struck the door with his knuckles in a controlled hammer, when he longed to kick it down with the full force of his impatience.

In a moment, the door creaked open, and Leo was faced with the pale and undernourished countenance of William.

The young man's eyes dilated in alarm as he recognized Leo. Had there been any color to his complexion, it would have leached out at once. He tried to close the door again, but Leo shouldered his way forward.

Grabbing William's wrist, Leo forced it upward and surveyed the bloodstained bandage on his hand. Blood on the bed . . . the thought of what this man might have done to Cat ignited a rage so violent that it obliterated every other awareness. He stopped thinking altogether. A minute later, he found himself on the floor, straddling William's body and battering him mercilessly. He was dimly aware of Harry shouting his name and endeavoring to pull him off.

Alerted by the fracas, the Bully stormed through the doorway and launched at him. Leo flipped the heavier, larger man over his head, causing his body to slam to the floor with an impetus that shook the house to its frame. The Bully lurched to his feet, and his fists, the size of Sunday roasts, whipped through the air with bone crushing force. Leo leaped back, raising his guard, then jabbed forward with his right. The Bully blocked him easily. Leo, however, did not fight according to the London Prize Ring rules. He followed with a side kick to the kneecap. As the Bully bent over with a grunt of pain, Leo delivered a fouetté, or whip kick, to the head. The Bully toppled to the floor, right at Harry's feet.

Reflecting that his brother-in-law was one of the dirtier fighters he'd ever seen, Harry gave him a short nod and headed into the empty receiving room.

The house was eerily vacant, quiet except for Leo's and Harry's shouts as they searched for Catherine. The place reeked of opium smoke, the windows filmed with such thick grime that curtains were entirely unnecessary. Every room was shrouded in filth. Dust upon dust. Corners clotted with webs, carpets blossomed with stains, wood floors scarred and buckled.

Harry saw a room upstairs where lamplight oozed into the hallway shadows, filtering through a miasma of smoke. He took the steps two and three at a time, his heart hammering.

The form of an old woman was curled on the settee. The loose folds of her black dress couldn't conceal the stick-thin lines of her body, gnarled like the trunk of a crab apple tree. She appeared only half conscious, her bony fingers caressing the length of a leather hookah hose as if it were a pet serpent.

Harry approached her, put his hand on her head, and pushed it back to view her face.

"Who are you?" she croaked. The whites of her eyes were stained, as if they had been soaked in tea. Harry struggled not to recoil at the smell of her breath.

"I've come for Catherine," he said. "Tell me where she is."

She stared at him fixedly. "The brother . . ."

"Yes, where is she? Where are you keeping her? The brothel?"

Althea let go of the leather hose and hugged herself.

"My brother never came for me," she said plaintively, perspiration and tears seeping through the powder on her face, turning it into a creamy paste. "You can't have her." But her gaze chased off to the side, in the direction of the stairs leading to the third floor.

Galvanized, Harry rushed from the room and up the stairs. A blessed waft of cool air and a ray of natural light came from one of the two rooms at the top. He went inside, his gaze sweeping across the stagnant room. The bed was in disarray and the window had been thrown open.

Harry froze, sharp pain lancing through his chest. His heart had stopped with fear. *"Cat!"* he heard himself shout, running to the window. Gulping for air, he looked down at the street three stories below.

But there was no broken body, no blood, nothing on the street below except rubbish and manure.

At the periphery of his vision, a white flutter caught his attention, like the flapping of a bird's wings. Turning his head to the left, Harry drew in a quick breath as he saw his sister.

Catherine was in a white nightgown, perched on the edge of a winged gable. She was only about three yards away, having crept along an incredibly narrow sill that was cantilevered over the second story below. Her arms were locked around her slender knees, and she was shivering violently. The breeze played with the loose locks of her hair, glittering banners dancing against the gray sky. One puff of wind, one momentary loss of balance, would knock her off the gable.

Even more alarming than Catherine's precarious perch was the vacancy of her expression.

"Cat," Harry said carefully, and her face turned in his direction.

She didn't seem to recognize him.

"Don't move," Harry said hoarsely. "Stay still, Cat." He ducked his head inside the house long enough to shout, *"Ramsay!"* and then his head emerged from the window again. "Cat, don't move a muscle. Don't even blink."

She didn't say a word, only sat and continued to shiver, her gaze unfocused.

Leo came up behind Harry and stuck his own head out the window. Harry heard Leo's breath catch. "Sweet mother of God." Taking stock of the situation, Leo became very, very calm. "She's as high as a piper," he said. "This is going to be a pretty trick."

Chapter Thirty-one

"I'll walk along the sill," Harry said. "I'm not afraid of heights."

Leo's expression was grim. "Neither am I. But it won't hold either of us—too much stress on the trusses. The ones above us are rotting, which means they probably all are."

"Is there another way to reach her? From the third-story roof?"

"That would take too long. Keep talking to her while I find some rope."

Leo disappeared, while Harry hung farther out the window. "Cat, it's me," he said. "It's Harry. You know me, don't you?"

"'Course I do." Her head dropped to her bent knees, and she wobbled. "I'm so tired."

"Cat, wait. This isn't the time for a nap. Lift your head and look at me." Harry continued to talk to her, encouraging her to stay still, stay awake, but she barely responded. More than once she altered her position, and Harry's heart plummeted as he expected her to roll right off the winged gable.

To his relief, Leo returned in no time at all with a substantial length of rope. His face was misted with sweat, and he was drawing in deep lungfuls of air.

"That was fast," Harry said, taking the rope from him.

"We're next door to a notorious whipping den," Leo said. "There was a lot of rope."

Harry measured two spans of rope with his arms and began to tie a knot. "If you're planning to coax her to come back to the window," he said, "it won't work. She won't respond to anything I say."

"You tie the knot. I'll do the talking."

LEO HAD NEVER EXPERIENCED FEAR LIKE THIS BEFORE, NOT even when Laura had died. That had been a slow process of loss, watching her life slip away like sand from an hourglass. This was even worse. This was the deepest level of hell.

Leaning out the window, Leo stared at Catherine's huddled, exhausted form. He understood the effects of the opium, the confusion and dizziness, the sense that one's limbs were too heavy to move, and at the same time a feeling of buoyant lightness as if one could fly. And added to that, Catherine couldn't even see.

If he managed to get her to safety, he was never going to let her out of his arms again.

"Well, Marks," he said in as normal a voice as he could manage. "Of all the ridiculous situations you and I have found ourselves in, this one takes the biscuit."

Her head lifted from her knees, and she squinted blindly in his direction. "My lord?"

"Yes, I'm going to help you. Stay still. Naturally you would make my heroic rescue effort as difficult as possible."

"I didn't plan on this." Her voice was slurred, but there was a familiar—and welcome—touch of indignation in it. "Was trying to get away."

"I know. And in just a minute, I'm going to bring you inside so that we can argue properly. For the time being—"

"Don't want to."

"Don't want to come in?" Leo asked, puzzled.

"No, don't want to argue." She lowered her head to her knees again, and gave a muffled sob.

"Christ," Leo said, his emotions nearly getting the better of him. "Darling love, *please,* we won't argue. I promise. Don't cry." He took a shuddering breath as Harry handed him the rope, looped with a perfect bowline knot. "Cat, listen to me . . . lift your head and put your knees down just a little. I'm going to throw a rope to you, but it's very important that you not reach for it, do you understand? Just sit still and let it fall into your lap."

She held obediently still, squinting and blinking.

Leo let the loop swing a few times, testing its weight, estimating how much line to allow. He tossed it in a slow, careful motion, but the loop fell short of its mark, bouncing off the shingles near Catherine's feet.

"You need to throw it harder," she said.

Despite Leo's desperation and bone-deep anxiety, he had to bite back a grin. "Will you ever stop telling me what to do, Marks?"

"I don't think so," she said after a moment's reflection.

He gathered up the rope and tossed the loop again, and this time it caught neatly on her knees.

"I've got it."

"Good girl," Leo said. He fought to keep his voice calm. "Now, put your arms through the circle, and lift it over your head. I want it to go around your chest. Not too fast, keep your balance—" His breath quickened as she fumbled with the loop. "Yes, just so. *Yes*. God, I love you." He let out breath of relief as he saw that the rope was in place, fitting just above her breasts and beneath her arms. He gave the other end of the rope to Harry. "Don't let go."

"Not a chance." Harry quickly tied it around his own waist.

Leo's attention returned to Catherine, who was saying something to him, her face drawn with a frown. "What is it, Marks?"

"You didn't have to say that."

"I didn't have to say what?"

"That you love me."

"But I do."

"No, you don't. I heard you say to Win that . . ." Catherine paused, struggling to recollect. "That you would only marry a woman you were certain never to love."

"I often say idiotic things," Leo protested. "It never crossed my mind that anyone actually listens to me."

A window opened in the brothel next door, and an annoyed prostitute leaned out. "There's girls what's tryin' to sleep in 'ere, and you're shoutin' fit to wake the dead!"

"We'll be finished soon," Leo called back to her, scowling. "Go back to bed."

The prostitute continued to lean out. "What are you doin' wiv a girl on the bleedin' roof?"

"None of your business," Leo said curtly.

A few more windows opened, and more heads stuck out, with incredulous exclamations.

"'Oo is he?"

"Is she goin' to jump?"

"Gor, what a filfy mess that would be."

Catherine didn't seem to notice the audience they had attracted, her squinting gaze fastened on Leo. "Did you mean it?" she asked. "What you said?"

"We'll talk about it later," Leo said, straddling the window-sill, holding on to the frame. "For now, I want you to put your hand against the side of the house and step onto the sill. Carefully."

"Did you mean it?" Catherine repeated, unmoving.

Leo gave her an incredulous glance. "Good God, Marks, do you have to be stubborn now, of all times? You want me to declare myself in front of a chorus of prostitutes?"

She nodded emphatically.

One of the whores called out, "Go on an' tell 'er, dearie!"

The others joined in enthusiastically. "Go on, luv!"

"Let's 'ear it, 'andsome!"

Harry, who was standing just behind Leo, was shaking his head slowly. "If it will get her to come in off the blasted roof, just say it, damn it."

Leo leaned farther out the window. "I love you," he said shortly. As he stared at Catherine's small, shivering figure, he felt his color run high, and his soul open with an emotion deeper than he had ever imagined could reside in him. "I love you, Marks. My heart is completely and utterly yours. And unfortunately for you, the rest of me comes with it." Leo paused, struggling for words, when they had always come so easily to him. But these had to be the right words. They meant too much. "I know I'm a bad bargain. But I'm begging you to have me anyway. Because I want the chance to make you as happy as you make me. I want to build a life with you." He fought to steady his voice. "Please come to me, Cat, because there's no surviving you. You don't have to love me back. You don't have to be mine. Just let me be yours."

"Ohhh . . ." one of the prostitutes sighed.

Another blotted her eyes. "If she won't 'ave 'im," she sniffled, "I'll take 'im."

Before Leo had even finished, Catherine had gotten to her feet and was creeping to the sill. "I'm coming," she said.

"Slowly," Leo cautioned, tightening his grip on the rope as he watched the movements of her small, bare feet. "Do it exactly the way you did before."

She inched toward him, her back to the wall. "I don't remember doing it before," she said breathlessly.

"Don't look down."

"I can't see anyway."

"That's just as well. Keep moving." Gradually Leo gathered the excess rope, as if he were reeling her in. Closer and closer she came, until she was finally within arm's reach. Leo stretched his hand as far as possible, his fingers trembling with effort. Another step, another, and then he finally had his arm around her, and he dragged her inside.

Cheers erupted from the brothel, and the multitude of windows began to close.

Leo sank to the floor with his knees splayed, his face buried in Catherine's hair. Tremors of relief ran through his body, and he let out a shuddering sigh. "I have you. I have you. Oh, Marks. You've just put me through the worst two minutes of my entire life. And for that you're going to spend *years* atoning."

"It was only two minutes," she protested, and he choked on a laugh.

Fumbling at his pocket, he pulled out her spectacles, and placed them carefully on her nose. The world became clear again.

Harry knelt beside them and touched Catherine's shoulder. She turned and put her arms around him, hugging him tightly. "My big brother," she whispered. "You came for me again."

She felt Harry smile against her hair. "Always. Whenever you need me." Lifting his head, he glanced ruefully at Leo as he continued, "You'd better marry him, Cat. Any man willing to put himself through *that* is probably worth keeping."

IT WAS WITH THE GREATEST RELUCTANCE THAT LEO surrendered Catherine to Poppy and Mrs. Pennywhistle when they arrived back at the hotel. The two women brought her to her room and helped her to bathe and wash her hair. She was exhausted and disoriented, and infinitely grateful for the soothing attention. Clad in a fresh nightgown and dressing robe, she sat before the fire while Poppy combed out her hair.

The room had been cleaned and tidied, the bed changed and freshly made. The housekeeper left with an armload of damp toweling, allowing Catherine and Poppy some privacy.

There was no sign of Dodger anywhere. Remembering what had happened to him, Catherine felt her throat clench in grief. Tomorrow she would ask about the gallant little creature, but for now she couldn't quite bring herself to face it.

Hearing her sniffle, Poppy reached around to give her a handkerchief. The comb moved gently through her hair. "Harry told me not to bother you with this tonight, dear, but if it were me, I would want to know. After you left with Leo, Harry stayed behind until the police came to your aunt's house. They went upstairs to find your aunt, but she was dead. They found raw opium paste in her mouth."

"Poor Althea," Catherine whispered, pressing the handkerchief against her welling eyes.

"You're very kind, to have any sympathy at all for her. I'm sure I wouldn't."

"What about William?"

"He ran off before they could arrest him. I heard Harry and Leo discussing it—they're going to commission a runner to find him."

"I don't want that," Catherine protested. "I want them to let him go."

"I have no doubt Leo will agree to whatever you ask," Poppy said. "But why? After what that dreadful man did to you—"

"William was a victim, as surely as I," Catherine said earnestly. "He was only trying to survive. Life was brutally unfair to him."

"And to you, dear. But you made something far better of it than he did."

"But I had Harry. And I had you and your family."

"And Leo," Poppy said, a smile in her voice. "I would say you have him without question. For a man who was so determined to go through life as an observer, he's certainly been pulled back into the stream. Because of you."

"Would you mind if I marry him, Poppy?" she asked almost timidly.

Poppy hugged her from behind, and rested her head briefly against Catherine's. "I'm sure I speak for all the Hathaways in saying that we would be eternally grateful if you would marry him. I can't imagine who else would dare to take him on."

After a light supper of toast and broth, Catherine went to bed and dozed for a while, waking every now and then with a fearful start. Each time she was reassured to see Poppy reading in a chair by the bed, her hair gleaming like mahogany in the glow of lamplight.

"You should go back to the apartment," Catherine finally mumbled, not wishing to seem like a child afraid of the dark.

"I'll stay a little longer," came the soft answer.

The next time Catherine awoke, Leo was sitting in the chair. Her drowsy gaze moved over him, taking in the contours of his handsome face, his serious blue eyes. His shirt was partly unbuttoned, revealing a shadow of chest hair. Suddenly desperate to be held against that hard, strong chest, she reached for him wordlessly.

Leo came to her at once. Wrapping his arms around her, he reclined back against the pillows with her. Catherine luxuriated in the feel and scent of him. "Only I," she whispered, "would feel so safe in the arms of the wickedest man in London."

He made a sound of amusement. "You like them wicked, Marks. An ordinary man would be tame sport for a woman like you."

She snuggled closer, her legs tense beneath the bed linens. "I'm so weary," she said, "but I can't sleep."

"You'll be better tomorrow morning. I promise." His hand settled on her hip, over the covers. "Close your eyes, love, and let me take care of you."

She tried to obey. But as the minutes ticked by, she was plagued by increasing restlessness and irritated nerves, a sense of dryness that permeated to her bones. Her skin clamored to be touched, scratched, rubbed, but even the delicate chafing of the sheets was enough to make her raw.

Leo left the bed and returned with a glass of water, and she drank thirstily. Her mouth tingled agreeably from the cool wetness.

Taking away the empty glass, Leo extinguished the lamp and returned to her. She flinched at the feel of his weight depressing the mattress, the disparate information of her senses distilling into one compelling need. In the darkness, Leo's mouth found hers, tender and gentle, and she couldn't prevent her own exaggerated response. His hand came to her breast, finding the tip already hard beneath the veil of muslin.

"It sometimes happens with opium smoke," Leo said quietly. "Later with habit, it decreases. But when you first try it, it can act upon you this way. As the effects leave your body, your nerves start screaming for more of it, and the result is . . . frustration."

As he spoke, his hand cupped her breast, his thumb gently circling the tight bud. She felt the sensation everywhere, streamers of fire unraveling to the pit of her belly, and along her legs and arms. She panted and squirmed, too desperate to feel embarrassed by her own muffled cries as his hand slipped beneath the covers.

"Easy, love," Leo whispered, caressing the taut plane of her stomach. "Let me help you."

His fingers were gentle on her swollen flesh, stroking and parting and entering, sliding easily into the moisture. She hitched upward, her body craving and willful, every movement enticing him to stroke deeper, harder.

Leo bent his head and kissed her throat. The tip of his thumb rested just above the little spot that burned with white fire, manipulating delicately as his invading fingers stretched her. It sent her into spasms of near-painful release, tearing an unwilling groan from her, and she clutched the back of his shirt in her fists until she felt the fine linen begin to rip. Breathing hard, she let go of the shirt and stammered out an apology. He stripped off the ruined shirt and hushed her with his mouth.

He spread his hand over her intimately, teasing her with exquisite care, while she whimpered and stiffened. Another burst of fire, a series of deep shudders, and she opened her thighs as he slid his fingers in. When the last vibrations had faded, she lay heavily in his arms and let exhaustion overtake her.

In the middle of the night, Catherine pressed against him furtively, needing him again. He rose above her, murmuring that she must relax, he would help her, he would take care of her, and she sobbed openly as she felt him kiss his way down her body. He lifted her legs over his shoulders and cupped her bottom in his hands. His mouth searched gently, his tongue stroking deep into the tender chalice. He did not find a rhythm but instead played with her, pulling softly, licking and nuzzling. The pleasure broke over her in waves, making her gasp in relief.

"Take me," she whispered as he lay beside her again.

"No," Leo said gently, turning to pin her to the mattress. "No chance of that tonight. We'll have to wait until your judgment isn't clouded. By morning, most of the opium will have worn off. If you still want me then, I'll be ready and willing."

"I want you now," she said, but he held her down and pleasured her with his mouth once more.

Catherine woke a few hours later, glimpsing the plum-colored sky as it began to lighten with the premonition of dawn. Leo's long body was tucked comfortably behind hers, one arm beneath her neck, the other draped across her middle. She loved the feel of him, vibrant heat and muscle, his skin like satin in some places, hair-roughened in others. Although she was careful not to move, Leo stirred and murmured.

Slowly she reached for his hand and drew it to her breast. Leo began to fondle her before he was even awake. His lips touched the back of her neck. Feeling him harden against her bottom, she pressed against him. One of his legs intruded between hers, as his hand slid down to the light fleece of curls.

She felt the taut pressure of him, nudging against her entrance, circling into the moisture. He pushed partway inside her and stopped, while her flesh, swollen from the night's excesses, had difficulty accommodating him.

His soft, amused voice tickled her ear. "Mmmn . . . you'll have to try harder, Marks. We both know you can take more than this."

"Help me," she gasped.

With a sympathetic murmur, he lifted her top leg and

adjusted her position. Her eyes closed as she felt him slide inside her.

"There," he whispered. "Is this what you want?"

"Harder . . . harder . . ."

"No, love . . . let me be gentle with you. Just for now."

He moved inside her with slow, deliberate drives, his caressing hand sliding back between her thighs. He took his time, and she had no choice but to let him. She was suffused with warmth, sensation building as he courted her, stroked her. Pressing love words and kisses against her neck, he sank more deeply inside her. She cried out his name, cresting, and he gently urged her even higher. Her shaking hand went to his hip and gripped the flexing surface.

"Don't leave me. Please, Leo."

He understood. As her wet flesh clenched around him once more, delicately wringing and pulling at the hardness, he pumped forcefully, letting himself go. And at last she knew the feel of his release, the way his belly tightened, the trembling of a powerful man rendered helpless in that ultimate moment.

They stayed joined as long as possible, resting together and watching as the dawn seeped through the parted curtains.

"I love you," she whispered, "so dearly, my lord. My Leo."

He smiled and kissed her. Rising, he went to drag on his trousers.

While Leo sluiced his face at the washstand, Catherine reached for her spectacles. Her gaze happened to fall on Dodger's empty basket by the door, and her smile dimmed. "Poor weasel," she murmured.

Leo returned to her, instantly concerned as he saw her watering eyes. "What is it?"

"Dodger," she said with a sniffle. "I miss him already."

Leo sat and drew her up against him. "Would you like to see him?"

"Yes, but I can't."

"Why not?"

Before she could answer, she saw an odd movement beneath the door . . . a furry, skinny body wiggling industriously beneath the ridiculously narrow space. Catherine blinked, afraid to move. *"Dodger?"*

The ferret came loping toward the bed, chuckling and chirping, his eyes bright as he hurried to her.

"Dodger, you're alive!"

"Of course he's alive," Leo said. "We put him in Poppy's apartment last night to allow you some rest." He smiled as the ferret bounded onto the mattress. "Mischievous little beggar. How did you get all the way down here?"

"He came to find me." Catherine held out her arms, and Dodger climbed up to her and snuggled against her chest. She stroked him over and over, murmuring endearments. "He tried to protect me, you know. He bit William's hand quite terribly." She nuzzled her chin against Dodger and crooned, "Good little watch ferret."

"Well done, Dodger," Leo said. Leaving the bed for a moment, he went to his discarded coat and rummaged through the pockets. "I suppose that leads to the question . . . in marrying you, am I going to be gaining a ferret, as well?"

"Do you think Beatrix would let me keep him?"

"There's no doubt of it." Leo returned to sit beside her. "She's always said that he belongs to you."

"Has she?"

"Well, it's rather obvious, in light of his fascination for your garters. And one certainly can't blame him for that." Leo reached for her hand. "I have something to ask you, Marks."

She sat up eagerly, letting Dodger drape around her neck.

"I can't remember if this is the fifth or sixth proposal," he said.

"It's only the fourth."

"I asked you yesterday. Are you counting that one?"

"No, that wasn't really 'will you marry me,' that was more 'will you come down off the roof.'"

One of Leo's brows arched. "By all means, let's be technical." He slid a ring onto the fourth finger of her left hand. It was the most breathtaking ring she had ever seen, a flawless silver opal with flashes of blue and green fire hidden deep inside. With every movement of her hand, the opal glimmered with unearthly color. It was encircled by a rim of glittering small diamonds. "This reminded me of your eyes," he said. "Only not nearly as beautiful." He paused, looking at her intently. "Catherine Marks, love of my life . . . will you marry me?"

"I want to answer another question first," she told him. "Something you asked me before."

He smiled and put his forehead against hers. "The one about the farmer and the sheep?"

"No . . . the one about what happens when an unstoppable force meets an immovable object."

A laugh rustled in his throat. "Tell me your answer, love."

"The unstoppable force stops. And the immovable object moves."

"Mmmn. I like that." His lips brushed hers tenderly.

"My lord, I'd rather not wake up as Catherine Marks ever again. I want to be your wife as soon as possible."

"Tomorrow morning?"

Catherine nodded. "Although . . . I will miss you calling me Marks. I've gotten rather fond of it."

"I'll still call you Marks from time to time. During moments of lurid passion. Let's try it." His voice lowered to a seductive whisper. "Kiss me, Marks . . ."

And she lifted her smiling mouth to his.

Epilogue

The cry of an infant broke through the silence.

Leo flinched at the sound, lifting his head. Having been banished from the bedroom where Catherine was giving birth, he had waited with the rest of the family in the parlor. Amelia had stayed with Catherine and the doctor, occasionally emerging to give a brief report to Win or Beatrix. Cam and Merripen were maddeningly sanguine about the process, both having seen their own wives safely through childbirth.

The Hathaway family was proving remarkably fertile. In March, Win had given birth to a robust boy, Jason Cole, nicknamed Jàdo. Two months later, Poppy had produced a petite red-haired daughter, Elizabeth Grace, upon whom Harry and the entire Rutledge Hotel staff doted.

Now it was Catherine's turn. And while childbirth was a perfectly ordinary event for other people, it was the most nerve-racking experience Leo had ever gone through. The sight of his wife in pain was intolerable, and yet there was nothing he could do. It didn't matter how often he was reassured that the birth was going splendidly . . . endless hours of labor pains did not seem all that splendid to Leo.

For eight hours Leo had waited in the parlor with his head in his hands, brooding and quiet and inconsolable. He was afraid for Catherine, and he could hardly bear to be separated from her. As he had predicted, he loved Catherine like a madman. And as she had once claimed, she was entirely able to manage him. They were different in so many ways, and yet somehow it made them exactly right for each other.

The result had been a remarkably harmonious marriage. They entertained each other with furious, funny bickering and long, thoughtful conversations. When they were alone, they often spoke in a kind of shorthand that no one else would have been able to interpret. They were a physical pair, passionate and affectionate. Playful. But the real surprise of the marriage was the kindness they showed each other . . . they, who had once fought so bitterly.

Leo had never expected that the woman who had formerly brought out the worst in him would now bring out the best in him. And he had never dreamed that his love for her would deepen to such proportions that there was no hope of controlling or restraining it. In the face of a love this vast, a man could only surrender.

If anything happened to Catherine . . . if something went wrong during the childbirth . . .

Leo stood slowly, his fists clenched, as Amelia entered the parlor with a bundled-up newborn. She paused near the doorway as the family gathered around her with soft exclamations. "A perfect little girl," she said, beaming. "The doctor said her color is excellent and her lungs are strong." She brought the baby to Leo.

He was too afraid to move. He didn't take the baby, only stared at Amelia and asked hoarsely, "How is Marks?"

She understood at once. Her tone gentled as she replied. "Absolutely fine. She's quite well, dear, and you can go up to see her now. But first say hello to your daughter."

An unsteady sigh escaped Leo, and he took the baby from her gingerly. He looked down in wonder at the miniature pink face, the rosebud mouth. How light the baby was . . . it was difficult to believe he was holding an entire human being in his arms.

"There's a great deal of Hathaway in her," Amelia said with a smile.

"Well, we'll do what we can to correct that." Leo bent to kiss his daughter's tiny forehead, the wisps of dark hair tickling his lips.

"Have you chosen a name?" Amelia asked.

"Emmaline."

"French. Very pretty." For some reason, Amelia laughed quietly before asking, "What would you have named a boy?"

"Edward."

"After Father? How lovely. And I think it suits him."

"Suits who?" Leo asked, still engrossed in his daughter.

Reaching up to his face, Amelia guided him to look at the doorway, where Win stood with another bundle, displaying it to Merripen, Cam, and Beatrix.

Leo's eyes widened. "My God. *Twins*?"

Cam approached him with a broad grin. "He's a fine-looking boy. You've come into fatherhood with a vengeance, *phral*."

"And Leo," Beatrix added. "You've had an heir just in time . . . with one day to spare!"

"In time for what?" Leo asked dazedly. Handing his daughter back to Amelia, he took his son from Win. Looking down at the infant's face, he fell in love for the second time in the same day. It was almost too much for his overwhelmed heart to endure.

"The copyhold clause, of course," he heard Beatrix say. "The Hathaways will keep Ramsay House now."

"I can't believe you would even think about that at a time like this," Leo said.

"Why not?" Merripen asked, his dark eyes twinkling. "Personally speaking, I find it a relief to know that we'll all be able to stay at Ramsay House."

"You're all concerned about a bloody house, when I've just endured eight hours of sheer hell."

"I'm sorry, Leo," Beatrix said, trying to sound contrite. "I wasn't thinking about what you'd just been through."

Leo kissed his son and handed him carefully to Win. "I'm going to see Marks now. It's probably been difficult for her, too."

"Give her our congratulations," Cam said, a tremor of laughter in his voice.

Taking the stairs two at a time, Leo went to the bedroom where Catherine rested. She looked very small beneath the covers, her face exhausted and pale. A weary grin curved her lips as she saw him.

He went to her and pressed his mouth to hers. "What can I do for you, love?"

"Nothing at all. The doctor gave me some laudanum for the pain. He's coming back in just a moment."

Continuing to lean over her, Leo smoothed her hair. "Damn you for not letting me stay," he whispered against her cheek.

He felt her smile.

"You were frightening the doctor," she said.

"I merely asked if he knew what he was doing."

"Forcefully," she pointed out.

Leo turned to rummage through the articles on the bedside table. "That was only because he'd pulled out a case of instruments that looked more suited to a medieval inquisition than childbirth." He found a little pot of salve and applied a dab of the unguent to Catherine's dry lips.

"Sit with me," she said against his fingertips.

"I don't want to hurt you."

"You won't." She patted the mattress invitingly.

Leo sat beside her with extreme caution, trying not to jostle her. "I'm not at all surprised that you produced two children at once," he said, taking her hand and kissing her fingers. "You're terrifyingly efficient, as usual."

"What do they look like?" she asked. "I didn't see them after they were washed."

"Bowlegged, with large heads."

Catherine chuckled and winced. "Please, please don't make me laugh."

"They're beautiful, actually. My dearest love . . ." Leo pressed a kiss into her palm. "I never fully realized what a woman went through during childbirth. You are the bravest, strongest person who's ever lived. A warrior."

"Not really."

"Oh, yes. Attila the Hun, Genghis Khan, Saladin . . . all milksops, compared to you." Leo paused, a grin spreading across his face. "It was well done of you to make certain one of the babies was a boy. The family is rejoicing, of course."

"Because we can keep Ramsay House?"

"Partly. But I suspect what they're truly ecstatic about is that now I'll have to contend with twins." He paused. "You know they'll be hellions."

"I should hope so. They wouldn't be ours otherwise." Catherine snuggled closer, and he settled her carefully against his shoulder. "Guess what happens at midnight?" she whispered.

"Two hungry infants will wake up screaming simultaneously?"

"Besides that."

"I have no idea."

"The Ramsay curse will be broken."

"You shouldn't have told me. Now I'll be terrified for the

next . . ."—Leo paused to glance at the mantel clock—"seven hours and twenty-eight minutes."

"Stay with me. I'll keep you safe." She yawned and let her head drop more heavily against him.

Leo smiled and stroked her hair. "We'll both be fine, Marks. We've just begun our journey . . . and there's so much we have yet to do." He spoke more softly as he heard her breathing turn even and steady. "Rest against my heart. Let me watch over your dreams. And know that tomorrow morning, and every morning after that, you'll awaken next to someone who loves you."

"Dodger?" she mumbled against his chest, and he grinned.

"No, your confounded ferret will have to stay in his basket. I was referring to myself."

"Yes, I know." Catherine slid her hand up to his cheek. "Only you," she said. "Always you."

Love in the
Afternoon

To my brilliant and utterly fabulous friend Eloisa. If I may paraphrase E.B. White: "It is not often that someone comes along who is a true friend and a good writer. Eloisa is both."

Love always,

L.K.

Prologue

Captain Christopher Phelan
1st Battalion Rifle Brigade
Cape Mapan
Crimea

June 1855

Dearest Christopher,
   I can't write to you again.
   I'm not who you think I am.
   I didn't mean to send love letters, but that is what they became. On their way to you, my words turned into heart-beats on the page.
   Come back, please come home and find me.

—[unsigned]

Chapter One

HAMPSHIRE, ENGLAND
EIGHT MONTHS EARLIER

It all began with a letter.

To be precise, it was the mention of the dog.

"What about the dog?" Beatrix Hathaway asked. "Whose dog?"

Her friend Prudence, the reigning beauty of Hampshire County, looked up from the letter that had been sent by her suitor, Captain Christopher Phelan.

Although it wasn't proper for a gentleman to correspond with an unmarried girl, they had arranged to send letters back and forth with Phelan's sister-in-law as a go-between.

Prudence sent her a mock frown. "Really, Bea, you're displaying far more concern over a dog than you ever have for Captain Phelan."

"Captain Phelan has no need of my concern," Beatrix said pragmatically. "He has the concern of every marriageable miss in Hampshire. Besides, he chose to go to war, and I'm sure he's having a lovely time strutting about in his smart uniform."

"It's not at all smart," came Prudence's glum reply. "In fact, his new regiment has *dreadful* uniforms—very plain, dark green with black facings, and no gold braiding or lace at all. And when I asked why, Captain Phelan said it was to help the Rifles stay concealed, which makes no sense, as everyone knows that a British soldier is far too brave and proud to conceal himself during battle. But Christopher—that is, Captain Phelan—said it had something to do with . . . oh, he used some French word . . ."

"Camouflage?" Beatrix asked, intrigued.

"Yes, how did you know?"

"Many animals have ways of camouflaging themselves to keep from being seen. Chameleons, for example. Or the way an owl's feathering is mottled to help it blend with the bark of its tree. That way—"

"Heavens, Beatrix, do *not* start another lecture on animals."

"I'll stop if you tell me about the dog."

Prudence handed her the letter. "Read it for yourself."

"But Pru," Beatrix protested as the small, neat pages were pushed into her hands. "Captain Phelan may have written something personal."

"I should be so fortunate! It's utterly gloomy. Nothing but battles and bad news."

Although Christopher Phelan was the last man Beatrix would ever want to defend, she couldn't help pointing out, "He is away fighting in the Crimea, Pru. I'm not sure there are many pleasant things to write about in wartime."

"Well, I have no interest in foreign countries, and I've never pretended to."

A reluctant grin spread across Beatrix's face. "Pru, are you certain that you want to be an officer's wife?"

"Well, *of course* . . . most commissioned soldiers never go to war. They're very fashionable men-about-town, and if they agree to go on half pay, they have hardly any duties and they don't have to spend any time at all with the regiment. And that was the case with Captain Phelan, until he was alerted for foreign service." Prudence shrugged. "I suppose wars are always inconveniently timed. Thank heavens Captain Phelan will return to Hampshire soon."

"Will he? How do you know?"

"My parents say the war will be over by Christmas."

"I've heard that as well. However, one wonders if we aren't severely underestimating the Russians' abilities, and overestimating our own."

"How unpatriotic," Prudence exclaimed, a teasing light in her eyes.

"Patriotism has nothing to do with the fact that the War Office, in its enthusiasm, didn't do nearly enough planning before it launched thirty thousand men to the Crimea. We have neither adequate knowledge of the place, nor any sound strategy for its capture."

"How do you know so much about it?"

"From the *Times*. It's reported on every day. Don't you read the papers?"

"Not the political section. My parents say it's ill-bred for a young lady to take an interest in such things."

"My family discusses politics every night at dinner, and my sisters and I all take part." Beatrix paused deliberately before adding with an impish grin, "We even have *opinions*."

Prudence's eyes widened. "My goodness. Well, I shouldn't be surprised. Everyone knows your family is . . . different."

"Different" was a far kinder adjective than was often used to describe the Hathaway family. The Hathaways were comprised of five siblings, the oldest of which was Leo, followed by Amelia, Winnifred, Poppy, and Beatrix. After the death of their parents, the Hathaways had gone through an astonishing change of fortune. Although they were common born, they were distantly related to an aristocratic branch of the family. Through a series of unexpected events, Leo had inherited a viscountcy for which he and his sisters hadn't been remotely prepared. They had moved from their small village of Primrose Place to the Ramsay estate in the southern county of Hampshire.

After six years the Hathaways had managed to learn just enough to accommodate themselves in good society. However, none of them had learned to think like the nobility, nor had they acquired aristocratic values or mannerisms. They had wealth, but that was not nearly as important as breeding and connections. And whereas a family in similar circumstances would have endeavored to improve their situations by marrying their social betters, the Hathaways had so far chosen to marry for love.

As for Beatrix, there was doubt as to whether she would marry at all. She was only half civilized, spending most of her time out-of-doors, riding or rambling through the woodlands, marsh, and meadows of Hampshire. Beatrix preferred the company of animals to people, collecting injured and orphaned creatures and rehabilitating them. The creatures that couldn't survive on their own in the wild were kept as pets, and Beatrix occupied herself with caring for them. Out-of-doors, she was happy and fulfilled. Indoors, life was not nearly so perfect.

More and more frequently, Beatrix had become aware of a chafing sense of dissatisfaction. Of yearning. The problem was that Beatrix had never met a man who was right for her. Certainly none of the pale, overbred specimens of the London drawing rooms she had frequented. And although the more robust men in the country were appealing, none of them had the unnameable *something* Beatrix longed for. She dreamed of a man whose force of will matched her own. She wanted to be passionately loved . . . challenged . . . overtaken.

Beatrix glanced at the folded letter in her hands.

It wasn't that she disliked Christopher Phelan as much as she recognized that he was inimical to everything she was.

Sophisticated and born to privilege, he was able to move with ease in the civilized environment that was so alien to her. He was the second son of a well-to-do local family, his maternal grandfather an earl, his father's family distinguished by a significant shipping fortune.

Although the Phelans were not in line for a title, the oldest son, John, would inherit the Riverton estate in Warwickshire upon the earl's death. John was a sober and thoughtful man, devoted to his wife, Audrey.

But the younger brother, Christopher, was another sort of man entirely. As often happened with second sons, Christopher had purchased an army commission at the age of twenty-two. He had gone in as a cornet, a perfect occupation for such a splendid-looking fellow, since his chief responsibility was to carry the cavalry colors during parades and drills. He was also a great favorite among the ladies of London, where he constantly went without proper leave, spending his time dancing, drinking, gaming, purchasing fine clothes, and indulging in scandalous love affairs.

Beatrix had met Christopher Phelan on two occasions, the first at a local dance, where she had judged him to be the most arrogant man in Hampshire. The next time she had met him was at a picnic, where she had revised her opinion: he was the most arrogant man in the entire world.

"That Hathaway girl is a peculiar creature," Beatrix had overhead him say to a companion.

"I find her charming and original," his companion had protested. "And she can talk horses better than any woman I've ever met."

"Naturally," came Phelan's dry rejoinder. "She's more suited to the stables than the drawing room."

From then on, Beatrix had avoided him whenever possible. Not that she minded the implied comparison to a horse, since horses were lovely animals with generous and noble spirits.

And she knew that although she wasn't a great beauty, she had her own charms. More than one man had commented favorably on her dark brown hair and blue eyes.

These moderate attractions, however, were nothing compared to Christopher Phelan's golden splendor. He was as fair as Lancelot. Gabriel. Perhaps Lucifer, if one believed that he had once been the most beautiful angel in heaven. Phelan was tall and silver eyed, his hair the color of dark winter wheat touched by the sun. His form was strong and soldierly, the shoulders straight and strong, the hips slim. Even as he moved with indolent grace, there was something undeniably potent about him, something selfishly predatory.

Recently Phelan had been one of the select few to be culled from various regiments to become part of the Rifle Brigade. The "Rifles," as they were called, were an unusual brand of soldier, trained to use their own initiative. They were encouraged to take up positions forward of their own front lines and pick off officers and horses that were usually beyond target range. Because of his singular marksmanship skills, Phelan had been promoted to a captaincy in the Rifle Brigade.

It had amused Beatrix to reflect that the honor probably hadn't pleased Phelan at all. Especially since he'd been obliged to trade his beautiful Hussars uniform, with its black coat and abundant gold braiding, for a plain dark green one.

"You're welcome to read it," Prudence said as she sat at her dressing table. "I must repair my coiffure before we go on our walk."

"Your hair looks lovely," Beatrix protested, unable to see any flaw in the elaborately pinned twist of blond braids. "And we're only walking to the village. None of the townspeople will know or care if your coiffure isn't perfect."

"*I'll* know. Besides, one never knows whom one might encounter."

Accustomed as she was to her friend's ceaseless preening, Beatrix grinned and shook her head. "All right. If you're certain you don't mind my looking at Captain Phelan's letter, I'll just read the part about the dog."

"You'll fall asleep long before you get to the dog," Prudence said, expertly inserting a hairpin into a twisted braid.

Beatrix looked down at the scrawled lines. The words looked cramped, tight coils of letters ready to spring from the page.

Dear Prudence,

I'm sitting in this dusty tent, trying to think of something eloquent to write. I'm at wit's end. You deserve beautiful words, but all I have left are these: I think of you constantly. I think of this letter in your hand and the scent of perfume on your wrist. I want silence and clear air, and a bed with a soft white pillow . . .

Beatrix felt her eyebrows lifting, and a quick rise of heat beneath the high collar of her dress. She paused and glanced at Prudence. "You find this boring?" she asked mildly, while her blush spread like spilled wine on linen.

"The beginning is the only good part," Prudence said. "Go on."

. . . Two days ago in our march down the coast to Sebastopol, we fought the Russians at the Alma River. I'm told it was a victory for our side. It doesn't feel like one. We've lost at least two thirds of our regiment's officers, and a quarter of the noncommissioned men. Yesterday we dug graves. They call the final tally of dead and wounded the "butcher's bill." Three hundred and sixty British dead so far, and more as soldiers succumb to their wounds.

One of the fallen, Captain Brighton, brought a rough terrier named Albert, who is undoubtedly the most badly behaved canine in existence. After Brighton was lowered into the ground, the dog sat by his grave and whined for hours, and tried to bite anyone who came near. I made the mistake of offering him a portion of a biscuit, and now the benighted creature follows me everywhere. At this moment he is sitting in my tent, staring at me with half-crazed eyes. The whining rarely stops. Whenever I get near, he tries to sink his teeth into my arm. I want to shoot him, but I'm too tired of killing.

Families are grieving for the lives I've taken. Sons, brothers, fathers. I've earned a place in hell for the things I've done, and the war's barely started. I'm changing, and not for the better. The man you knew is gone for good, and I fear you may not like his replacement nearly so well.

The smell of death, Pru . . . it's everywhere.

The battlefield is strewn with pieces of bodies, clothes, soles of boots. Imagine an explosion that could tear the soles from your shoes. They say that after a battle, wildlflowers are more abundant the next season—the ground is so churned and torn, it gives the new seeds room to take root. I want to grieve, but there is no place for it. No time. I have to put the feelings away somewhere.

Is there still some peaceful place in the world?

Please write to me. Tell me about some bit of needlework you're working on, or your favorite song. Is it raining in Stony Cross? Have the leaves begun to change color?

Yours,
Christopher Phelan

By the time Beatrix had finished the letter, she was aware of a peculiar feeling, a sense of surprised compassion pressing against the walls of her heart.

It didn't seem possible that such a letter could have come from the arrogant Christopher Phelan. It wasn't at all what she had expected. There was a vulnerability, a quiet need, that had touched her.

"You must write to him, Pru," she said, closing the letter with far more care than she had previously handled it.

"I'll do no such thing. That would only encourage more complaining. I'll be silent, and perhaps that will spur him to write something more cheerful next time."

Beatrix frowned. "As you know, I have no great liking for Captain Phelan, but this letter . . . he deserves your sympathy, Pru. Just write him a few lines. A few words of comfort. It would take no time at all. And about the dog, I have some advice—"

"I am not writing anything about the dratted dog." Prudence gave an impatient sigh. "You write to him."

"*Me?* He doesn't want to hear from me. He thinks I'm peculiar."

"I can't imagine why. Just because you brought Medusa to the picnic . . ."

"She's a very well-behaved hedgehog," Beatrix said defensively.

"The gentleman whose hand was pierced didn't seem to think so."

"That was only because he tried to handle her incorrectly. When you pick up a hedgehog—"

"No, there's no use telling me, since I'm never going to handle one. As for Captain Phelan . . . if you feel that strongly about it, write a response and sign my name."

"Won't he recognize that the handwriting is different?"

"No, because I haven't written to him yet."

"But he's not my suitor," Beatrix protested. "I don't know anything about him."

"You know as much as I do, actually. You're acquainted with his family, and you're very close to his sister-in-law. And I wouldn't say that Captain Phelan is my suitor, either. At least not my only one. I certainly won't promise to marry him until he comes back from the war with all his limbs intact. I don't want a husband I would have to push around in an invalid's chair for the rest of my life."

"Pru, you have the depth of a puddle."

Prudence grinned. "At least I'm honest."

Beatrix gave her a dubious glance. "You're actually delegating the writing of a love letter to one of your friends?"

Prudence waved her hand in a dismissive gesture. "Not a love letter. There was nothing of love in his letter to me. Just write something cheerful and encouraging."

Beatrix fumbled for the pocket of her walking dress, and tucked the letter inside. Inwardly she argued with herself, reflecting that it never ended well when one did something morally questionable for the right reasons. On the other hand . . . she couldn't rid herself of the image her mind had conjured, of an exhausted soldier scribbling a hasty letter in the privacy of his tent, his hands blistered from digging the graves of his comrades. And a ragged dog whining in the corner.

She felt entirely inadequate to the task of writing to him. And she suspected that Prudence did as well.

She tried to imagine what it was like for Christopher, leaving his elegant life behind, finding himself in a world where his survival was threatened day by day. Minute by minute. It was impossible to picture a spoiled, beautiful man like Christopher Phelan contending with danger and hardship. Hunger. Loneliness.

Beatrix stared at her friend pensively, their gazes meeting in the looking glass. "What *is* your favorite song, Pru?"

"I don't have one, actually. Tell him yours."

"Should we discuss this with Audrey?" Beatrix asked, referring to Phelan's sister-in-law.

"Certainly not. Audrey has a problem with honesty. She wouldn't send the letter if she knew I hadn't written it."

Beatrix made a sound that could have either been a laugh or a groan. "I wouldn't call that a *problem* with honesty. Oh, Pru, please change your mind and write to him. It would be so much easier."

But Prudence, when pressed to do something, usually turned intransigent, and this situation was no exception. "Easier for everyone but me," she said tartly. "I'm sure I don't know how to reply to such a letter. He's probably even forgotten that he's written it." Returning her attention to the looking glass, she applied a touch of rose-petal salve to her lips.

How lovely Prudence was, with her heart-shaped face, her brows thin and delicately arched over round green eyes. But how very little of a person the looking glass reflected. It was impossible to guess what Prudence truly felt for Christopher Phelan. Only one thing was certain: it was better to answer, no matter how ineptly, than to withhold a reply. Because sometimes silence could wound someone nearly as badly as a bullet.

* * *

IN THE PRIVACY OF HER ROOM AT RAMSAY HOUSE, BEATRIX sat at her desk and dipped a pen nib into a well of dark blue ink. A three-legged gray cat named Lucky lounged at the corner of the desk, watching her alertly. Beatrix's pet hedgehog, Medusa, occupied the other side of the desk. Lucky, being an innately sensible creature, never bothered the bristly little hedgehog.

After consulting the letter from Phelan, Beatrix wrote:

Captain Christopher Phelan
1st Battalion Rifle Brigade
2nd Division Camp, Crimea

17 October 1854

Pausing, Beatrix reached out to stroke Lucky's remaining front paw with a gentle fingertip. "How would Pru start a letter?" she wondered aloud. "Would she call him darling? Dearest?" She wrinkled her nose at the idea.

The writing of letters was hardly Beatrix's forte. Although she came from a highly articulate family, she had always valued instinct and action more than words. In fact, she could learn far more about a person during a short walk outdoors than she could by sitting and conversing for hours.

After pondering various things one might write to a complete stranger while masquerading as someone else, Beatrix finally gave up. "Hang it, I'll just write as I please. He'll probably be too battle weary to notice that the letter doesn't sound like Pru."

Lucky settled her chin beside her paw and half closed her eyes. A purring sigh escaped her.

Beatrix began to write.

Dear Christopher,

I have been reading the reports about the battle of the Alma. According to the account by Mr. Russell of the Times, you and two others of the Rifle Brigade went ahead of the Coldstream Guards, and shot several enemy officers, thereby disordering their columns. Mr. Russell also remarked in admiration that the Rifles never retreated or even bobbed their heads when the bullets came flying.

While I share his esteem, dear sir, I wish to advise that in my opinion it would not detract from your bravery to bob your head when being shot at. Duck, dodge, sidestep, or preferably hide behind a rock. I promise I won't think the less of you!

Is Albert still with you? Still biting? According to my friend Beatrix (she who brings hedgehogs to picnics), the dog is overstimulated and afraid. As dogs are wolves at heart and require a leader, you must establish dominance over him. Whenever he tries to bite you, take his entire muzzle in your hand, apply light pressure, and tell him "no" in a firm voice.

My favorite song is "Over the Hills and Far Away." It rained in Hampshire yesterday, a soft autumn storm that brought down hardly any leaves. The dahlias are no longer in stem, and frost has withered the chrysanthemums, but the air smells divine, like old leaves and wet bark, and ripe apples. Have you ever noticed that each month has its own smell? May and October are the nicest-smelling months, in my opinion.

You ask if there is a peaceful place in the world, and I regret to say that it is not Stony Cross. Recently Mr. Mawdsley's donkey escaped from his stall, raced down the road, and somehow found his way into an enclosed pasture. Mr. Caird's prized mare was innocently grazing when the ill-bred seducer had his way with her. Now it appears the mare has conceived, and a feud is raging between Caird, who demands financial compensation, and Mawdsley, who insists that had the pasture fencing been in better repair, the clandestine meeting would never have occurred. Worse still, it has been suggested that the mare is a shameless lightskirt and did not try nearly hard enough to preserve her virtue.

Do you really think you've earned a place in hell? . . . I don't believe in hell, at least not in the afterlife. I think hell is brought about by man right here on earth.

You say the gentleman I knew has been replaced. How I wish I could offer better comfort than to say that no matter how you have changed, you will be welcomed when you return. Do what you must. If it helps you to endure, put the feelings away for now, and lock the door. Perhaps someday we'll air them out together.

Sincerely,
Prudence

Beatrix had never intentionally deceived anyone. She would have felt infinitely more comfortable writing to Phelan as herself. But she still remembered the disparaging remarks that he had once made about her. He would not want a letter from that "peculiar Beatrix Hathaway." He had asked for a letter from the beautiful golden-haired Prudence Mercer. And wasn't a letter written under false pretenses better than nothing at all? A man in Christopher's situation needed all the words of encouragement one could offer.

He needed to know that someone cared.

And for some reason, after having read his letter, Beatrix found that she did indeed care.

Chapter Two

The harvest moon brought dry, clear weather, and the Ramsay tenants and workers reaped the most abundant yields in memory. Like everyone else on the estate, Beatrix was occupied with the harvest and the local festival that followed. A massive al fresco dinner and dance was held on the grounds of Ramsay House for more than a thousand guests, including tenants, servants, and townspeople.

To Beatrix's disappointment, Audrey Phelan had not been able to attend the festivities, as her husband John had developed a persistent cough. She had stayed home to care for him. "The doctor has left us with some medicine that has already helped John to great effect," Audrey had written, "but he warned that uninterrupted bed rest is important for a complete recovery."

Near the end of November, Beatrix walked to the Phelans' house, taking a direct route through woodlands populated with gnarled oak and wide-gesturing beeches. The dark-branched trees seemed to have been dipped in crushed sugar. As the sun cracked through the veneer of clouds, it struck brilliant glints on the frost. The soles of Beatrix's sturdy shoes bit through the frozen mush of dried leaves and moss.

She approached the Phelan house, formerly a royal hunting lodge, a large ivy-covered home set among ten forested acres. Reaching a charming paved path, Beatrix skirted the side of the house and headed toward the front.

"Beatrix."

Hearing a quiet voice, she turned to behold Audrey Phelan sitting alone on a stone bench.

"Oh, hello," Beatrix said cheerfully. "I hadn't seen you in days, so I thought I would . . ." Her voice faded as she took a closer look at her friend.

Audrey was wearing a simple day gown, the gray fabric blending into the woods behind her. She had been so silent and still that Beatrix hadn't even noticed her.

They had been friends for three years, ever since Audrey had married John and moved to Stony Cross. There was a certain kind of friend one only visited when one had no problems— that was Prudence. But there was another kind of friend one went to in times of trouble or need—that was Audrey.

Beatrix frowned as she saw that Audrey's complexion was bleached of its usual healthy color, and her eyes and nose were red and sore-looking.

Beatrix frowned in concern. "You're not wearing a cloak or shawl."

"I'm fine," Audrey murmured, even though her shoulders were trembling. She shook her head and made a staying gesture as Beatrix took off her heavy wool cloak and went to drape it over Audrey's slender form. "No, Bea, don't—"

"I'm warm from the exertion of the walk," Beatrix insisted. She sat beside her friend on the icy stone bench. A wordless moment passed, while Audrey's throat worked visibly. Something was seriously wrong. Beatrix waited with forced patience, her heartbeat in her throat. "Audrey," she finally asked, "has something happened to Captain Phelan?"

Audrey responded with a blank stare, as if she were trying to decipher a foreign language. "Captain Phelan," she repeated quietly, and gave a little shake of her head. "No, as far as we know, Christopher is well. In fact, a packet of letters arrived from him yesterday. One of them is for Prudence."

Beatrix was nearly overcome with relief. "I'll take it to her, if you like," she volunteered, trying to sound diffident.

"Yes. That would be helpful." Audrey's pale fingers twisted in her lap, knotting and unknotting.

Slowly Beatrix reached out and put her hand over Audrey's. "Your husband's cough is worse?"

"The doctor left earlier." Taking a deep breath, Audrey said dazedly, "John has consumption."

Beatrix's hand tightened.

They were both silent, while a chilling wind crackled the trees.

The enormity of the unfairness was difficult to grasp. John Phelan was a decent man, always the first to call on someone when he had heard they needed help. He had paid for a cottager's wife to have medical treatment that the couple couldn't afford, and had made the piano in his home available for local children to take lessons, and invested in the rebuilding of the Stony Cross pie shop when it had nearly burned to the ground. And he did it all with great discretion, seeming almost embarrassed to be caught in a good deed. Why did someone like John have to be stricken?

"It's not a death sentence," Beatrix eventually said. "Some people survive it."

"One in five," Audrey agreed dully.

"Your husband is young and strong. And *someone* has to be the one out of the five. It will be John."

Audrey managed a nod but didn't reply.

They both knew that consumption was a particularly virulent disease, devastating the lungs, causing drastic loss of weight and fatigue. Worst of all was the consumptive cough, turning ever more persistent and bloody, until the lungs were finally too full for the sufferer to breathe any longer.

"My brother-in-law Cam is very knowledgeable about herbs and medicines," Beatrix volunteered. "His grandmother was a healer in his tribe."

"A Romany cure?" Audrey asked in a doubtful tone.

"You must try anything and everything," Beatrix insisted. "I'll ask Cam to make up a tonic that will help Mr. Phelan's lungs, and—"

"John probably won't take it," Audrey said. "And his mother would object. The Phelans are very conventional people. If it doesn't come from a vial in a doctor's case, or the apothecary's shop, they won't approve."

"I'm going to bring something from Cam all the same."

Audrey leaned her head to the side until it rested briefly on Beatrix's shoulder. "You're a good friend, Bea. I'm going to need you in the coming months."

"You have me," Beatrix said simply.

Another breeze whipped around them, biting through Beatrix's sleeves. Audrey shook herself from her dazed misery and stood, handing back the cloak. "Let's go into the house, and I'll find that letter for Pru."

The interior of the house was cozy and warm, the rooms wide with low timbered ceilings, thick-paned windows admitting the winter-colored light. It seemed every hearth in the house had been lit, heat rolling gently through the tidy rooms. Everything in the Phelan house was muted and tasteful, with stately furniture that had reached a comfortably venerable age.

A subdued-looking housemaid came to take Beatrix's cloak.

"Where is your mother-in-law?" Beatrix asked, following Audrey to the staircase.

"She went to rest in her room. The news is especially difficult for her." A fragile pause. "John has always been her favorite."

Beatrix was well aware of that, as was most of Stony Cross. Mrs. Phelan adored both her sons, the only children she had left after two of her other children, also sons, had died in their infancies, and a daughter who had been stillborn. But it was John in whom Mrs. Phelan had invested all her pride and ambition. Unfortunately no woman would ever have been good enough for John in his mother's eyes. Audrey had endured a great deal of criticism during the three years of her marriage, especially in her failure to conceive children.

Beatrix and Audrey ascended the staircase, past rows of family portraits in heavy gold frames. Most of the subjects were Beauchamps, the aristocratic side of the family. One couldn't help but notice that throughout the generations represented, the Beauchamps were an extraordinarily handsome people, with narrow noses and brilliant eyes and thick flowing hair.

As they reached the top of the stairs, a series of muffled coughs came from a room at the end of the hallway. Beatrix winced at the raw sound.

"Bea, would you mind waiting for a moment?" Audrey asked anxiously. "I must go to John—it's time for his medicine."

"Yes, of course."

"Christopher's room—the one he stays in when he visits—is right there. I put the letter on the dresser."

"I'll fetch it."

Audrey went to her husband, while Beatrix cautiously entered Christopher's room, first peering around the doorjamb.

The room was dim. Beatrix went to open one of the heavy curtains, letting daylight slide across the carpeted floor in a brilliant rectangle. The letter was on the dresser. Beatrix picked it up eagerly, her fingers itching to break the seal.

However, she admonished herself, it was addressed to Prudence.

With an impatient sigh, she slipped the unopened letter into the pocket of her walking dress. Lingering at the dresser, she surveyed the articles arranged neatly on a wooden tray.

A small silver-handled shaving brush . . . a folding-blade razor . . . an empty soap dish . . . a lidded porcelain box with a silver top. Unable to resist, Beatrix lifted the top and looked inside. She found three pairs of cuff links, two in silver, one in gold, a watch chain, and a brass button. Replacing the lid, Beatrix picked up the shaving brush and experimentally touched her cheek with it. The bristles were silky and soft. With the movement of the soft fibers, a pleasant scent was released from the brush. A spicy hint of shaving soap.

Holding the brush closer to her nose, Beatrix drew in the scent . . . masculine richness . . . cedar, lavender, bay leaves. She imagined Christopher spreading lather over his face, stretching his mouth to one side, all the masculine contortions she had seen her father and brother perform in the act of removing bristle from their faces.

"Beatrix?"

Guiltily she set aside the brush and went out into the hallway. "I found the letter," she said. "I opened the curtains— I'll pull them back together, and—"

"Oh, don't worry about that, let the light in. I abhor dark rooms." Audrey gave her a strained smile. "John took his medicine," she said. "It makes him sleepy. While he rests, I'm going downstairs to talk with Cook. John thinks he might be able to eat some white pudding."

They proceeded down the stairs together.

"Thank you for taking the letter to Prudence," Audrey said. "It's very kind of you to facilitate a correspondence between them."

"Oh, it's no bother. It's for Christopher's sake that I agreed. I will admit to being surprised that Prudence took the time to write to Christopher."

"Why do you say that?"

"I don't think she gives a fig about him. I warned Christopher about her before he left, actually. But he was so taken with her looks and her high spirits that he managed to convince himself there was something genuine between them."

"I thought you liked Prudence."

"I do. Or at least . . . I'm trying to. Because of you." Audrey smiled wryly at Beatrix's expression. "I've resolved to be more like you, Bea."

"Like *me*? Oh, I wouldn't do that. Haven't you noticed how odd I am?"

Audrey's smile broadened into a grin, and for a moment she looked like the carefree young woman she had been before John's illness. "You accept people for what they are. I think you regard them as you do your creatures—you're patient, and you observe their habits and wants, and you don't judge them."

"I judged your brother-in-law severely," Beatrix pointed out, feeling guilty.

"More people should be severe on Christopher," Audrey said, her smile lingering. "It might improve his character."

THE UNOPENED LETTER IN BEATRIX'S POCKET WAS NOTHING less than a torment. She hurried back home, saddled a horse, and rode to Mercer House, an elaborately designed house with turrets, intricately turned porch posts, and stained-glass windows.

Having just arisen after attending a dance that lasted until three o'clock in the morning, Prudence received Beatrix in a velvet dressing gown trimmed with spills of white lace. "Oh, Bea, you should have gone to the dance last night! There were so many handsome young gentlemen there, including a cavalry detachment that is being sent to the Crimea in two days, and they looked so splendid in their uniforms—"

"I've just been to see Audrey," Beatrix said breathlessly, entering the private upstairs parlor and closing the door. "Poor Mr. Phelan isn't well, and—well, I'll tell you about that in a minute, but—here's a letter from Captain Phelan!"

Prudence smiled and took the letter. "Thank you, Bea. Now, about the officers I met last night . . . there was a dark-haired lieutenant who asked me to dance, and he—"

"Aren't you going to open it?" Beatrix asked, watching in dismay as Prudence laid the letter on a side table.

Prudence gave her a quizzical smile. "My, you're impatient today. You want me to open it this very moment?"

"*Yes.*" Beatrix promptly sat in a chair upholstered with flower-printed fabric.

"But I want to tell you about the lieutenant."

"I don't give a monkey about the lieutenant, I want to hear about Captain Phelan."

Prudence gave a low chuckle. "I haven't seen you this excited since you stole that fox that Lord Campdon imported from France last year."

"I didn't steal him, I rescued him. Importing a fox for a hunt . . . I call that very unsporting." Beatrix gestured to the letter. "Open it!"

Prudence broke the seal, skimmed the letter, and shook her head in amused disbelief. "Now he's writing about mules." She rolled her eyes and gave Beatrix the letter.

Miss Prudence Mercer
Stony Cross
Hampshire, England

7 November 1854

Dear Prudence,

Regardless of the reports that describe the British soldier as unflinching, I assure you that when riflemen are under fire, we most certainly duck, bob, and run for cover. Per your advice, I have added a sidestep and a dodge to my repertoire, with excellent results. To my mind, the old fable has been disproved: there are times in life when one definitely wants to be the hare, not the tortoise.

We fought at the southern port of Balaklava on the twenty-fourth of October. Light Brigade was ordered to charge directly into a battery of Russian guns for no comprehensible reason. Five cavalry regiments were mowed down without support. Two hundred men and nearly four hundred horses lost in twenty minutes. More fighting on the fifth of November, at Inkerman.

We went to rescue soldiers stranded on the field before the Russians could reach them. Albert went out with me under a storm of shot and shell, and helped to identify the wounded so we could carry them out of range of the guns. My closest friend in the regiment was killed.

Please thank your friend Beatrix for her advice about Albert. His biting is less frequent, and he never goes for me, although he's taken a few nips at visitors to the tent.

May and October, the best-smelling months? I'll make a case for December: evergreen, frost, wood smoke, cinnamon. As for your favorite song . . . were you aware that "Over the Hills and Far Away" is the official music of the Rifle Brigade?

It seems nearly everyone here has fallen prey to some kind of illness except for me. I've had no symptoms of cholera nor any of the other diseases that have swept through both divisions. I feel I should at least feign some kind of digestive problem for the sake of decency.

Regarding the donkey feud: while I have sympathy for Caird and his mare of easy virtue, I feel compelled to point out that the birth of a mule is not at all a bad outcome. Mules are more sure-footed than horses, generally healthier, and best of all, they have very expressive ears. And they're not unduly stubborn, as long they're managed well. If you wonder at my apparent fondness for mules, I should probably explain that as a boy, I had a pet mule named Hector, after the mule mentioned in the *Iliad*.

I wouldn't presume to ask you to wait for me, Pru, but I will ask that you write to me again. I've read your last letter more times than I can count. Somehow you're more real to me now, two thousand miles away, than you ever were before.

Ever yours,
Christopher

P.S. Sketch of Albert included

Albert

As Beatrix read, she was alternately concerned, moved, and charmed out of her stockings. "Let me reply to him and sign your name," she begged. "One more letter. *Please,* Pru. I'll show it to you before I send it."

Prudence burst out laughing. "Honestly, this is the silliest thing I've ever . . . Oh, very well, write to him again if it amuses you."

For the next half hour Beatrix took part in a meaningless conversation about the dance, the guests who had attended, and the latest gossip from London. She slipped the letter from Christopher Phelan into her pocket . . . and froze as she felt an unfamiliar object. A metallic handle . . . and the silk bristle of a shaving brush. Blanching, she realized that she had unintentionally taken the shaving brush from Christopher's dresser.

Her problem was back.

Somehow Beatrix managed to keep smiling and chatting calmly with Prudence, while inside she was filled with turmoil.

Every now and then when Beatrix was nervous or worried, she pocketed some small object from a shop or residence. She had done it ever since her parents had died. Sometimes she wasn't at all aware she had taken something, whereas at other times the compulsion was so irresistible that she began to perspire and tremble until she finally gave in.

Stealing the objects was never any trouble at all. It was only returning them that presented difficulties. Beatrix and her family had always managed to restore the objects to their proper places. But it had, on occasion, required extreme measures—paying calls at improper times of the day, or inventing wild excuses to roam through someone's house—that had only fortified the Hathaways' reputation for eccentricity.

Thankfully, it wouldn't be that difficult to put back the shaving brush. She could do it the next time she visited Audrey.

"I suppose I ought to dress now," Prudence finally said.

Beatrix took the cue without hesitation. "Certainly. It's time for me to go home and attend to some chores." She smiled and added lightly, "Including writing another letter."

"Don't put anything peculiar in it," Prudence said. "I have a reputation, you know."

Chapter Three

Captain Christopher Phelan
1st Battalian Rifle Brigade
Home Ridge Camp
Inkerman, Crimea

3 December 1854

Dear Christopher,

This morning I read that more than two thousand of our men were killed in a recent battle. One Rifle officer was said to have been bayoneted. It wasn't you, was it? Are you injured? I'm so afraid for you. And I'm so sorry that your friend was killed.

We are decorating for the holidays, hanging holly and mistletoe. I am enclosing a Christmas card done by a local artist. Note the tassel and string at the bottom—when you pull it, the merrymaking gentlemen on the left will quaff their goblets of wine. ("Quaff" is such an odd word, isn't it?—but it's one of my favorites.)

I love the old familiar carols. I love the sameness of every Christmas. I love eating the plum pudding even *though I don't really like plum pudding. There is comfort in ritual, isn't there?*

Albert looks like a lovely dog, perhaps not outwardly a gentleman, but inside a loyal and soulful fellow.

I worry that something's happened to you. I hope you are safe. I light a candle for you on the tree every night.

Answer me as soon as you're able.

Sincerely,
Prudence

P.S. I share your affection for mules. Very unpretentious creatures who never boast of their ancestry. One wishes certain people would be a bit more mulish in that regard.

Miss Prudence Mercer
Stony Cross
Hampshire

1 February 1854

Dear Pru,

I'm afraid I was indeed the bayoneted one. How did you guess? It happened as we were climbing a hill to overtake a battery of Russian guns. It was a minor shoulder wound, certainly not worth reporting.

There was a storm on the fourteenth of November that wrecked the camps and sank French and British ships in the harbor. More loss of life, and unfortunately most of the winter supplies and equipment are gone. I believe this is what is known as "rough campaigning."

I'm hungry. Last night I dreamed of food. Ordinarily I dream of you, but last night I'm sorry to say that you were eclipsed by lamb with mint sauce.

It is bitterly cold. I am now sleeping with Albert. We're a pair of surly bedfellows, but we're both willing to endure it in the effort to keep from freezing to death. Albert has become indispensable to the company—he carries messages under fire and runs much faster than a man can. He's also an excellent sentry and scout.

Here are a few things I've learned from Albert—

1. Any food is fair game until it is actually swallowed by someone else.
2. Take a nap whenever you can.
3. Don't bark unless it's important.
4. Chasing one's tail is sometimes unavoidable.

I hope your Christmas was splendid. Thank you for the card—it reached me on the twenty-fourth of December, and it was passed all around my company, most of them never having seen a Christmas card before. Before it was finally handed back to me, the cardboard gentlemen attached to the tassel had done a great deal of quaffing.

I also like the word "quaff." As a matter of fact, I've always liked unusual words. Here's one for you: "soleate," which refers to the shodding of a horse. Or "nidifice," a nest. Has Mr. Caird's mare given birth yet? Perhaps I'll ask my brother to make an offer. One never knows when one might need a good mule.

Dear Christopher,

It feels far too prosaic to send a letter by post. I wish I could find a more interesting way . . . I would tie a little scroll to a bird's leg, or send you a message in a bottle. However, in the interest of efficiency, I'll have to make do with the Royal Mails.

I have just read in the Times that you have been involved in yet more heroics. Why must you take such risks? The ordinary duty of a soldier is dangerous enough. Have a care for your safety, Christopher—for my sake if not your own. My request is entirely selfish . . . I could not bear for your letters to stop coming.

I'm so far away, Pru. I'm standing outside my own life and looking in. Amid all this brutality, I have discovered the simple pleasures of petting a dog, reading a letter, and staring at the night sky. Tonight I almost thought I saw the ancient constellation named Argo . . . after the ship that Jason and his crew sailed in their quest to find the golden fleece. You're not supposed to be able to see Argo unless you're in Australia, but still, I was almost certain I had a glimpse of it.

I beg you to forget what I wrote before: I do want you to wait for me. Don't marry anyone before I come home.

Wait for me.

Dear Christopher,

This is the perfume of March: rain, loam, feathers, mint. Every morning and afternoon I drink fresh mint tea sweetened with honey. I've done a great deal of walking lately. I seem to think better outdoors.

Last night was remarkably clear. I looked up at the sky to find the Argo. I'm terrible at constellations. I can never make out any of them except for Orion and his belt. But the longer I stared, the more the sky seemed like an ocean, and then I saw an entire fleet of ships made of stars. A flotilla was anchored at the moon, while others were casting off. I imagined we were on one of those ships, sailing on moonlight.

In truth, I find the ocean unnerving. Too vast. I much prefer the forests around Stony Cross. They're always fascinating, and full of commonplace miracles . . . spiderwebs glittering with rain, new trees growing from the trunks of fallen oaks. I wish you could see them with me. And together we would listen to the wind rushing through the leaves overhead, a lovely swooshy melody . . . tree music!

As I sit here writing to you, I have propped my stocking feet much too close to the hearth. I've actually singed my stockings on occasion, and once I had to stomp out my feet when they started smoking. Even after that, I still can't seem to rid myself of the habit. There, now you could pick me out of a crowd blindfolded. Simply follow the scent of scorched stockings.

Enclosed is a robin's feather that I found during my walk this morning. It's for luck. Keep it in your pocket.

Just now I had the oddest feeling while writing this letter, as if you were standing in the room with me. As if my pen had become a magic wand, and I had conjured you right here. If I wish hard enough . . .

Dearest Prudence,

I have the robin's feather in my pocket. How did you know I needed a token to carry into battle? For the past two weeks I've been in a rifle pit, sniping back and forth with the Russians. It's no longer a cavalry war, it's all engineers and artillery. Albert stayed in the trench with me, only going out to carry messages up and down the line.

During the lulls, I try to imagine being in some other place. I imagine you with your feet propped near the hearth, and your breath sweet with mint tea. I imagine walking through the Stony Cross forests with you. I would love to see some commonplace miracles, but I don't think I could find them without you. I need your help, Pru. I think you might be my only chance of becoming part of the world again.

I feel as if I have more memories of you than I actually do. I was with you on only a handful of occasions. A dance. A conversation. A kiss. I wish I could relive those moments. I would appreciate them more. I would appreciate everything more. Last night I dreamed of you again. I couldn't see your face, but I felt you near me. You were whispering to me.

The last time I held you, I didn't know who you truly were. Or who I was, for that matter. We never looked beneath the surface. Perhaps it's better we didn't—I don't think I could have left you, had I felt for you then what I do now.

I'll tell you what I'm fighting for. Not for England, nor her allies, nor any patriotic cause. It's all come down to the hope of being with you.

Dear Christopher,

You've made me realize that words are the most important things in the world. And never so much as now. The moment Audrey gave me your last letter, my heart started

beating faster, and I had to run to my secret house to read it
in private.

I haven't yet told you . . . last spring on one of my ram-
bles, I found the oddest structure in the forest, a lone tower
of brick and stonework, all covered with ivy and moss. It
was on a distant portion of the Stony Cross estate that be-
longs to Lord Westcliff. Later when I asked Lady Westcliff
about it, she said that keeping a secret house was a local
custom in medieval times. The lord of the manor might have
used it as a place to keep his mistress. Once a Westcliff
ancestor actually hid there from his own bloodthirsty re-
tainers. Lady Westcliff said I could visit the secret house
whenever I wanted, since it has long been abandoned. I go
there often. It's my hiding place, my sanctuary . . . and now
that you know about it, it's yours as well.

I've just lit a candle and set it in a window. A very tiny
lodestar, for you to follow home.

Dearest Prudence,

Amid all the noise and men and madness, I try
to think of you in your secret house . . . my prin-
cess in a tower. And my lodestar in the window.

The things one has to do in war . . . I thought
it would all become easier as time went on. And
I'm sorry to say I was right. I fear for my soul. The
things I have done, Pru. The things I have yet to
do. If I don't expect God to forgive me, how can I
ask you to?

Dear Christopher,

Love forgives all things. You don't even need to ask.

Ever since you wrote to me about the Argos, I've been
reading about stars. We've loads of books about them, as

the subject was of particular interest to my father. Aristotle taught that stars are made of a different matter than the four earthly elements—a quintessence—that also happens to be what the human psyche is made of. Which is why man's spirit corresponds to the stars. Perhaps that's not a very scientific view, but I do like the idea that there's a little starlight in each of us.

I carry thoughts of you like my own personal constellation. How far away you are, dearest friend, but no farther than those fixed stars in my soul.

Dear Pru,

We're settling in for a long siege. It's uncertain as to when I'll have the chance to write again. This is not my last letter, only the last for a while. Do not doubt that I am coming back to you someday.

Until I can hold you in my arms, these worn and ramshackle words are the only way to reach you. What a poor translation of love they are. Words could never do justice to you, or capture what you mean to me.

Still . . . I love you. I swear by the starlight . . . I will not leave this earth until you hear those words from me.

Sitting on a massive fallen oak deep in the forest, Beatrix looked up from the letter. She didn't realize she was crying until she felt the stroke of a breeze against her wet cheeks. The muscles of her face ached as she tried to compose herself.

He had written to her on the thirtieth of June, without knowing she had written to him on the same day. One couldn't help but take that as a sign.

She hadn't experienced such a depth of bitter loss, of agonized longing, since her parents had died. It was a different kind of grief, of course, but it carried the same flavor of hopeless need.

What have I done?

She, who had always gone through life with unsparing honesty, had carried out an unforgivable deception. And the truth would only make matters worse. If Christopher Phelan ever discovered that she had written to him under false pretenses, he would despise her. And if he never found out, Beatrix would always be "the girl who belonged in the stables." Nothing more.

"Do not doubt that I am coming back to you . . ."

Those words had been meant for Beatrix, no matter that it had been addressed to Prudence.

"I love you," she whispered, and her tears spilled faster.

How had these feelings crept up on her? Good God, she could hardly remember what Christopher Phelan looked like, and yet her heart was breaking over him. Worst of all, it was entirely likely that Christopher's declarations had been inspired by the hardships of wartime. This Christopher she knew from the letters . . . the man she loved . . . might vanish once he returned home.

Nothing good would come of this situation. She had to put a stop to it. She could not pretend to be Prudence any longer. It wasn't fair to any of them, especially Christopher.

Beatrix walked home slowly. As she entered Ramsay House, she encountered Amelia, who was taking her young son Rye outside.

"There you are," Amelia exclaimed. "Would you like to go out to the stable with us? Rye is going to ride his pony."

"No, thank you." Beatrix's smile felt as if it had been tacked on with pins. Every member of her family was quick to include her in their lives. They were all extraordinarily generous in that regard. And yet she sensed herself being cast, incrementally and inexorably, as the spinster aunt.

She felt eccentric and alone. A misfit, like the animals she kept.

Her mind made a disjointed leap, summoning recollections of the men she had met during dances and dinners and soirees. She had never lacked for male attention. Perhaps she should encourage one of them, just pick a likely candidate for attachment and be done with it. Perhaps having her own life was worth being married to a man she didn't love.

But that would be another form of misery.

Her fingers slipped into the pocket of her dress to touch the letter from Christopher Phelan. The feel of the parchment, which he had folded, caused her stomach to tighten with a hot, pleasurable pang.

"You've been very quiet of late," Amelia said, her blue eyes searching. "You look as though you've been crying. Is something troubling you, dear?"

Beatrix shrugged uneasily. "I suppose I'm melancholy because of Mr. Phelan's illness. According to Audrey, he has taken a turn for the worse."

"Oh . . ." Amelia's expression was soft with concern. "I wish there were something we could do. If I fill a basket with plum brandy and blancmange, will you take it to them?"

"Of course. I'll go later this afternoon."

Retreating to the privacy of her room, Beatrix sat at her desk and took out the letter. She would write to Christopher one last time, something impersonal, a gentle withdrawal. Better that than to continue deceiving him.

Carefully she uncapped the inkwell and dipped her pen, and began to write.

Dear Christopher,
   As much as I esteem you, dear friend, it would be unwise for either of us to be precipitate while you are still away. You have my earnest wishes for your well-being and safety.

However, I think it best that any mention of more personal feelings between us should be delayed until you return. In fact, it is probably best that we end our correspondence . . .

With each sentence, it became more difficult to make her fingers work properly. The pen trembled in her fierce grip, and she felt her tears well again. *"Rubbish,"* she said.

It literally hurt to write such lies. Her throat had gone nearly too tight to breathe.

She decided that before she could finish it, she would write the truth, the letter she longed to send to him, and then destroy it.

Breathing with effort, Beatrix snatched another piece of paper and hastily wrote a few lines, only for her eyes, hoping it would ease the intense pain that had clamped around her heart.

Dearest Christopher,
   I can't write to you again.
   I'm not who you think I am.
   I didn't mean to send love letters, but that is what they became. On their way to you, my words turned into heartbeats on the page.
   Come back, please come home and find me.

Beatrix's eyes blurred. Setting the page aside, she returned to her original letter and finished it, expressing her wishes and prayers for his safe return.

As for the love letter, she crumpled it and shoved it into the drawer. Later she would burn it in her own private ceremony, and watch every heartfelt word burn to ashes.

Chapter Four

Later in the afternoon, Beatrix walked to the Phelan home. She carried a substantial basket weighted with the brandy and blancmange, a round of mild white cheese, and a small "homely cake," dry and bare of icing, only slightly sweet. Whether or not the Phelans needed such items didn't matter nearly so much as the gesture itself.

Amelia had urged Beatrix to ride to the Phelan home in a carriage or cart, as the basket was a bit unwieldy. However, Beatrix wanted the exertion of walking, hoping it would help to calm her troubled spirits. She set her feet to a steady rhythm, and drew the early-summer air into her lungs. *This is the smell of June,* she wanted to write to Christopher . . . *honeysuckle, green hay, wet linen hung out to dry . . .*

By the time she reached her destination, both her arms ached from having held the basket for so long.

The house, dressed in thick ivy, resembled a man huddling in his overcoat. Beatrix felt prickles of apprehension as she went to the front door and knocked. She was ushered inside by a solemn-faced butler who relieved her of the basket and showed her to the front receiving room.

The house seemed overheated, especially after her walk.

Beatrix felt a bloom of perspiration emerge beneath the layers of her walking dress and inside her sturdy ankle boots.

Audrey entered the room, thin and untidy, her hair half up, half down. She was wearing an apron with dark ruddy blotches on it.

Bloodstains.

As Audrey met Beatrix's concerned gaze, she attempted a wan smile. "As you see, I'm not prepared to receive anyone. But you're one of the few people I don't have to maintain appearances for." Realizing that she was still wearing the apron, she untied it and rolled it into a little bundle. "Thank you for the basket. I told the butler to pour a glass of the plum brandy and give it to Mrs. Phelan. She's taken to her bed."

"Is she ill?" Beatrix asked as Audrey sat beside her.

Audrey shook her head in answer. "Only distraught."

"And . . . your husband?"

"He's dying," Audrey said flatly. "He doesn't have long. A matter of days, the doctor says."

Beatrix began to reach for her, wishing to gather her in as she might one of her wounded creatures.

Audrey flinched and raised her hands defensively. "No, don't. I can't be touched. I'll break into pieces. I have to be strong for John. Let's talk quickly. I have only a few minutes."

Immediately Beatrix folded her hands in her lap. "Let me do something," she said, her voice low. "Let me sit with him while you rest. At least for an hour."

Audrey managed a faint smile. "Thank you, dear. But I can't let anyone else sit with him. It has to be me."

"Then shall I go to his mother?"

Audrey rubbed her eyes. "You're very kind to offer. I don't think she wants companionship, however." She sighed. "Were it left to her, she would rather die along with John than go on without him."

"But she still has another son."

"She has no affection for Christopher. It was all for John."

As Beatrix tried to absorb that, the tall case clock ticked as if in disapproval, its pendulum swinging like the negative shake of a head. "That can't be true," she finally said.

"Certainly it can," Audrey said, with a faint, rueful smile. "Some people have an infinite supply of love to give. Like your family. But for others it's a limited resource. Mrs. Phelan's love is all poured out. She had just enough for her husband and John." Audrey lifted her shoulders in an exhausted shrug. "It's of no importance whether she loves Christopher or not. Nothing seems important at the moment."

Beatrix reached into her pocket and withdrew the letter. "I have this for him," she said. "For Captain Phelan. From Pru."

Audrey took it with an unreadable expression. "Thank you. I'll send it along with a letter about John's condition. He'll want to know. Poor Christopher . . . so far away."

Beatrix wondered if perhaps she should take the letter back. It would be the worst possible time to distance herself from Christopher. On the other hand, perhaps it would be the best time. One small injury inflicted simultaneously with a far greater one.

Audrey watched the play of emotion on her face. "Are you ever going to tell him?" she asked gently.

Beatrix blinked. "Tell him what?"

That earned an exasperated little huff. "I'm not a half-wit, Bea. Prudence is in London at this very moment, attending balls and soirees and all those silly, trivial events of the season. She couldn't have written that letter."

Beatrix felt herself turn scarlet, then bone-white. "She gave it to me before she left."

"Because of her devotion to Christopher?" Audrey's lips twisted. "The last time I saw her, she didn't even remember to ask after him. And why is it that you're always the one de-livering and fetching letters?" She gave Beatrix a fond but chiding glance. "From what Christopher has written in his let-ters to me and John, it's obvious he's quite taken with Pru-dence. Because of what *she* has written to him. And if I end up with that ninnyhead as a sister-in-law, Bea, it will be your fault."

Seeing the quiver of Beatrix's chin and the glitter in her eyes, Audrey took her hand and pressed it. "Knowing you, I've no doubt your intentions were good. But I rather doubt the results will be." She sighed. "I have to go back to John."

As Beatrix went with Audrey to the entrance hall, she was overwhelmed by the knowledge that her friend would soon have to endure the death of her husband.

"Audrey," she said unsteadily, "I wish I could bear this for you."

Audrey stared at her for a long moment, her face flush-ing with emotion. "That, Beatrix, is what makes you a true friend."

TWO DAYS LATER THE HATHAWAYS RECEIVED WORD THAT John Phelan had passed away in the night. Filled with com-passion, the Hathaways considered how best they could help the bereaved women. Ordinarily it would have fallen to Leo, the lord of the manor, to call on the Phelans and offer his services. However, Leo was in London, as Parliament was still in session. Currently a political debate was raging over the incompetence and indifference that had resulted in the Crimean troops being so appallingly ill supported and badly supplied.

It was decided that Merripen, Win's husband, would go to the Phelan home on behalf of the family. No one had any expectation that he would be received, since the mourn-ers would undoubtedly be too grief-stricken to speak with anyone. However, Merripen would deliver a letter to offer any manner of assistance that might be needed.

"Merripen," Beatrix asked before he left, "would you convey my affection to Audrey, and ask if I might help with any of the funeral arrangements? Or ask if perhaps she wants someone to sit with her."

"Of course," Merripen replied, his dark eyes filled with warmth. Having been raised with the Hathaways since boyhood, Merripen was very much like a brother to all of them. "Why don't you write a note to her? I'll give it to the servants."

"I'll only be a minute." Beatrix dashed toward the stairs, pulling up great handfuls of her skirts to keep from tripping as she hurried to her room.

She went to her desk and pulled out her writing papers and pens, and reached for the top of the inkwell. Her hand froze in midair as she saw the half-crumpled letter in the drawer.

It was the polite, distancing letter she had written to Christopher Phelan.

It had never been sent.

Beatrix went cold all over, her knees threatening to give out from beneath her. "Oh, God," she whispered, sitting on the nearby chair with such force that it wobbled dangerously.

She must have given Audrey the wrong letter. The unsigned one that had started with "I can't write to you again. I'm not who you think I am . . ."

Beatrix's heart pounded, straining with the force of panic. She tried to calm her buzzing thoughts enough to think. Had the letter been posted yet? Perhaps there was still time to retrieve it. She would ask Audrey . . . but no, that would be the height of selfishness and inconsideration. Audrey's husband had just died. She did not deserve to be bothered with trivialities at such a time.

It was too late. Beatrix would have to let it be, and let Christopher Phelan make what he would of the odd note.

"Come back, please come home and find me . . ."

Groaning, Beatrix leaned forward and rested her head on the table. Perspiration caused her forehead to stick to the polished wood. She was aware of Lucky leaping up to the table and nuzzling her hair and purring.

Please, dear God, she thought desperately, *don't let Christopher reply. Let it all be finished. Never let him find out it was me.*

Chapter Five

It occurs to me," Christopher said conversationally as he lifted a cup of broth to a wounded man's lips, "that a hospital may be the worst possible place for a man to try to get well."

The young soldier he was feeding—no more than nineteen or twenty years of age—made a slight sound of amusement as he drank.

Christopher had been brought to the barracks hospital in Scutari three days earlier. He had been wounded during an assault on the Redan during the endless siege on Sebastopol. One moment he'd been accompanying a group of sappers as they carried a ladder toward a Russian bunker, and the next there was an explosion and the sensations of being struck simultaneously in the side and right leg.

The converted barracks were crowded with casualties, rats, and vermin. The only source of water was a fountain at which orderlies queued up to catch a fetid trickle in their pails. As the water was unfit for drinking, it was used for washing and soaking off bandages.

Christopher had bribed the orderlies to bring him a cup of strong spirits. He had sluiced the alcohol over his wounds in the hopes that it would keep them from suppurating. The first time he'd done it, the burst of raw fire had caused him to faint and topple from the bed to the floor, a spectacle that had caused no end of hilarity from the other patients in the ward. Christopher had good-naturedly endured their teasing afterward, knowing that a moment of levity was sorely needed in this squalid place.

The shrapnel had been removed from his side and leg, but the injuries weren't healing properly. This morning he had discovered that the skin around them was red and tight. The prospect of falling seriously ill in this place was frightening.

Yesterday, despite the outraged protests of the soldiers in the long row of beds, the orderlies had begun to sew a man into his own bloodstained blanket, and take him to the communal burial pit before he had quite finished dying. In response to the patients' angry cries, the orderlies replied that the man was insensible, and was only minutes away from death, and the bed was desperately needed. All of which was true. However, as one of the few men able to leave his bed, Christopher had interceded, telling them he would wait with the man on the floor until he had breathed his last. For an hour he had sat on the hard stone, brushing away insects, letting the man's head rest on his uninjured leg.

"You think you did any good for him?" one of the orderlies asked sardonically, when the poor fellow had finally passed away, and Christopher had allowed them to take him.

"Not for him," Christopher said, his voice low. "But perhaps for them." He had nodded in the direction of the rows of ragged cots, where the patients lay and watched. It was important for them to believe that if or when their time came, they would be treated with at least a flicker of humanity.

The young soldier in the bed next to Christopher's was unable to do much of anything for himself, as he had lost an entire arm, and a hand off the other one. Since there were no nurses to spare, Christopher had undertaken to feed him. Wincing and flinching as he knelt by the cot, he lifted the man's head and helped him to drink from the cup of broth.

"Captain Phelan," came the crisp voice of one of the Sisters of Charity. With her stern demeanor and forbidding expression, the nun was so intimidating that some of the soldiers had suggested—out of her hearing, of course—that if she were dispatched to fight the Russians, the war would be won in a matter of hours.

Her bristly gray brows rose as she saw Christopher beside the patient's cot. "Making trouble again?" she asked. "You will return to your own bed, Captain. And do not leave it again . . . unless your intention is to make yourself so ill that we'll be forced to keep you here indefinitely."

Obediently Christopher lurched back into his cot.

She came to him and laid a cool hand on his brow.

"Fever," he heard her announce. "Do not move from this bed, or I'll have you tied to it, Captain." Her hand was withdrawn, and something was placed on his chest.

Slitting his eyes open, Christopher saw that she had given him a packet of letters.

Prudence.

He seized it eagerly, fumbling in his eagerness to break the seal.

There were two letters in the packet.

He waited until the sister had left before he opened the one from Prudence. The sight of her handwriting engulfed him with emotion. He wanted her, needed her, with an intensity he couldn't contain.

Somehow, half a world away, he had fallen in love with her. It didn't matter that he hardly knew her. What little he knew of her, he loved.

Christopher read the few spare lines.

The words seemed to rearrange themselves like a child's alphabet game. He puzzled over them until they became coherent.

"*. . . I'm not who you think I am . . . please come home and find me . . .*"

His lips formed her name soundlessly. He put his hand over his chest, trapping the letter against his rough heartbeat.

What had happened to Prudence?

The strange, impulsive note aroused a tumult in him.

"I'm not who you think I am," he found himself repeating inaudibly.

No, of course she was not. Neither was he. He was not this broken, feverish creature on a hospital cot, and she was not the vapid flirt everyone had taken her to be. Through their letters, they had found the promise of more in each other.

"*. . . please come home and find me . . .*"

His hands felt swollen and tight as he fumbled with the other letter, from Audrey. The fever was making him clumsy. His head had begun to ache . . . vicious throbbing . . . he had to read the words in between the pulses of pain.

Dear Christopher,

There is no way for me to express this gently. John's condition has worsened. He is facing the prospect of death with the same patience and grace that he has shown during his life. By the time this letter reaches you, there is no doubt that he will be gone . . .

Christopher's mind closed against the rest of it. Later there would be time to read more. Time to grieve.

John wasn't supposed to be ill. He was supposed to stay

safe in Stony Cross and father children with Audrey. He was supposed to be there when Christopher came back home.

Christopher managed to huddle on his side. He tugged the blanket high enough to create a shelter for himself. Around him, the other soldiers continued to pass the time . . . talking, playing cards when possible. Mercifully, deliberately, they paid him no attention, allowing him the privacy he needed.

Chapter Six

There had been no correspondence from Christopher Phelan in the ten months after Beatrix had last written to him. He had exchanged letters with Audrey, but in her grief over John's death, Audrey found it difficult to talk to anyone, even Beatrix.

Christopher had been wounded, Audrey relayed, but he had recovered in the hospital and returned to battle. Hunting constantly for any mention of Christopher in the newspapers, Beatrix found innumerable accounts of his bravery. During the months-long siege of Sebastopol, he had become the most decorated soldier of the artillery. Not only had Christopher been awarded the order of the Bath, and the Crimea campaign medal with clasps for Alma, Inkerman, Balaklava, and Sebastopol, he had also been made a knight of the Legion of Honor by the French, and had received the *Medjidie* from the Turks.

To Beatrix's regret, her friendship with Prudence had cooled, starting with the day when Beatrix had told her that she could no longer write to Christopher.

"But why?" Prudence had protested. "I thought you enjoyed corresponding with him."

"I don't enjoy it any longer," Beatrix had replied in a suffocated voice.

Her friend had given her an incredulous glance. "I can scarcely believe that you would abandon him like this. What is he to think when the letters stop coming?"

The question made Beatrix's stomach feel heavy with guilt and wanting. She hardly trusted herself to speak. "I can't continue to write to him without telling him the truth. It's becoming too personal. I . . . feelings are involved. Do you understand what I'm trying to say?"

"All I understand is that you're being selfish. You've made it so that I can't send a letter to him, because he would notice the difference between your penmanship and mine. The least you could do is keep him on the string for me until he returns."

"Why do you want him?" Beatrix had asked with a frown. She didn't like the phrase "keep him on the string" . . . as if Christopher were a dead fish. One among many. "You have many suitors."

"Yes, but Captain Phelan has become a war hero. He may even be invited to dine with the queen upon his return. And now that his brother is dead, he will inherit the Riverton estate. All that makes him nearly as good a catch as a peer."

Although Beatrix had once been amused by Prudence's shallowness, she now felt a stab of annoyance. Christopher deserved much more than to be valued for such superficial things.

"Has it occurred to you that he'll be altered as a result of the war?" she asked quietly.

"Well, he may yet be wounded, but I certainly hope not."

"I meant altered in character."

"Because he's been in battle?" Prudence shrugged. "I suppose that has had an effect on him."

"Have you followed any of the reports about him?"

"I've been very occupied," Prudence said defensively.

"Captain Phelan won the *Medjidie* medal by saving a wounded Turkish officer. A few weeks later, Captain Phelan crawled to a magazine that had just been shelled, with ten French soldiers killed and five guns disabled. He took possession of the remaining gun and held the position alone, against the enemy, for eight hours. On another occasion—"

"I don't need to hear about all that," Prudence protested. "What is your point, Bea?"

"That he may come back as a different man. And if you care for him at all, you should try to understand what he has gone through." She gave Prudence a packet of letters tied with a narrow blue ribbon. "To start with, you should read these. I should have copied the letters that I wrote to him, so you could read them as well. But I'm afraid I didn't think of it."

Prudence had accepted them reluctantly. "Very well, I'll read them. But I'm certain that Christopher won't want to talk about letters when he returns—he'll have me right there with him."

"You should try to know him better," Beatrix said. "I think you want him for the wrong reasons . . . when there are so many right reasons. He's earned it. Not because of his bravery in battle and all those shiny medals . . . in fact, that's the least part of what he is." Falling silent for a moment, Beatrix had reflected ruefully that from then on she really should avoid people and go back to spending her time with animals. "Captain Phelan wrote that when you and he knew each other, neither of you looked beneath the surface."

"The surface of what?"

Beatrix gave her a bleak look, reflecting that for Prudence, the only thing beneath the surface was more surface. "He said you might be his only chance of belonging to the world again."

Prudence had stared at her strangely. "Perhaps it's better after all that you stop writing to him. You seem rather fixed on him. I hope you have no thought that Christopher would ever . . ." She paused delicately. "Never mind."

"I know what you were going to say," Beatrix had said in a matter-of-fact manner. "Of course I have no illusions about that. I haven't forgotten that he once compared me to a horse."

"He did not compare you to a horse," Prudence said. "He merely said you belonged in the stables. However, he is a sophisticated man, and he would never be happy with a girl who spends most of her time with animals."

"I much prefer the company of animals to that of any person I know," Beatrix shot back. Instantly she regretted the tactless statement, especially as she saw that Prudence had taken it as a personal affront. "I'm sorry. I didn't mean—"

"Perhaps you had better leave, then, and go to your pets," Prudence had said in a frosty tone. "You'll be happier conversing with someone who can't talk back to you."

Chastened and vexed, Beatrix had left Mercer House. But not before Prudence had said, "For all our sakes, Bea, you must promise me never to tell Captain Phelan that you wrote the letters. There would be no point to it. Even if you told him, he wouldn't want you. It would only be an embarrassment, and a source of resentment. A man like that would never forgive such a deception."

Ever since that day, Beatrix and Prudence had not seen each other except in passing. And no further letters were written.

It tormented Beatrix, wondering how Christopher was, if

Albert was with him, if his wounds had healed properly . . .
but it was no longer her right to ask questions of him.

It never had been.

To the jubilation of all England, Sebastopol fell in
September 1855, and peace negotiations began in February
of the next year. Beatrix's brother-in-law Cam remarked that
even though Britain had won, war was always a pyrrhic victory, as one could never put a price on each life that had been
damaged or lost. It was a Romany sentiment that Beatrix
agreed with. All totaled, more than one hundred and fifty
thousand of the allied soldiers had died of battle wounds or
disease, as well as over one hundred thousand Russians.

When the long-awaited order was given for the regiments
to return home, Audrey and Mrs. Phelan learned that Christopher's Rifle Brigade would arrive in Dover in mid-April,
and proceed to London. The Rifles' arrival was keenly anticipated, as Christopher was considered a national hero. His
picture had been cut out of newspapers and posted in shop
windows, and the accounts of his bravery were repeated in
taverns and coffeehouses. Long testimonial rolls were written by villages and counties to be presented to him, and no
fewer than three ceremonial swords, engraved with his name
and set with jewels, had been struck by politicians eager to
reward him for service.

However, on the day the Rifles landed at Dover, Christopher was mysteriously absent from the festivities. The
crowds at the quay cheered the Rifle Brigade and demanded
the appearance of its famed sharpshooter, but it seemed that
Christopher had chosen to avoid the cheering crowds, the cer-
emonies and banquets . . . he even failed to appear at the celebration dinner hosted by the queen and her consort.

"What do you suppose has happened to Captain Phelan?"

Beatrix's older sister Amelia asked, after he had gone missing for three days. "From what I remember of the man, he was a social fellow who would have adored being the center of so much attention."

"He's gaining even more attention by his absence," Cam pointed out.

"He doesn't want attention," Beatrix couldn't resist saying. "He's run to ground."

Cam lifted a dark brow, looking amused. "Like a fox?" he asked.

"Yes. Foxes are wily. Even when they seem to head directly away from their goal, they always turn and make it good at the last." Beatrix hesitated, her gaze distant as she stared through the nearby window, at the forest shadowed by a harsh and backward spring . . . too much easterly wind, too much rain. "Captain Phelan wants to come home. But he'll stay aground until the hounds stop drawing for him."

She was quiet and contemplative after that, while Cam and Amelia continued to talk. It was only her imagination . . . but she had the curious feeling that Christopher Phelan was somewhere close by.

"Beatrix." Amelia stood beside her at the window, laying a gentle arm across her shoulders. "Are you feeling melancholy, dear? Perhaps you should have gone to London for the season as your friend Prudence did. You could stay with Leo and Catherine, or with Poppy and Harry at the hotel—"

"I have no interest whatsoever in taking part in the season," Beatrix said. "I've done it four times, and that was three times too many."

"But you were very sought after. The gentlemen adored you. And perhaps there will be someone new there."

Beatrix lifted her gaze heavenward. "There's never anyone new in London society."

"True," Amelia said after a moment's thought. "Still, I

think you would better off in town than staying here in the country. It's too quiet for you here."

A small, dark-haired boy charged into the room on a stick horse, letting out a warlike cry as he brandished a sword. It was Rye, Cam and Amelia's four-and-a-half-year-old son. As the boy sped by, the end of the stick horse accidentally knocked against a floor lamp with a blue glass shade. Cam dove reflexively and caught the lamp before it smashed against the floor.

Turning around, Rye beheld his father on the floor and leaped on him, giggling.

Cam wrestled with his son, pausing briefly to inform his wife, "It's not that quiet here."

"I miss Jàdo," Rye complained, referring to his cousin and favorite playmate. "When is he coming back?"

Merripen, Amelia's sister Win, and their young son Jason, nicknamed Jàdo, had left a month earlier for Ireland to visit the estate that Merripen would someday inherit. As his grandfather was ailing, Merripen had agreed to stay for an indeterminate time to become familiar with the estate and its tenants.

"Not for a while," Cam informed him regretfully. "Perhaps not until Christmas."

"That's too long," Rye said with a wistful sigh.

"You have other cousins, darling," Amelia pointed out.

"They're all in London."

"Edward and Emmaline will be here in the summer. And in the meantime, you have your little brother."

"But Alex is hardly any fun," Rye said. "He can't talk or throw a ball. And he leaks."

"At both ends," Cam added, his amber eyes sparkling as he looked up at his wife.

Amelia tried, without success, to stifle a laugh. "He won't leak forever."

Straddling his father's chest, Rye glanced at Beatrix. "Will you play with me, Aunt?"

"Certainly. Marbles? Jackstraws?"

"War," the boy said with relish. "I'll be the cavalry and you be the Russians, and I'll chase you around the hedgerow."

"Couldn't we reenact the Treaty of Paris instead?"

"You *can't* do a treaty before you have the war," Rye protested. "There would be nothing to talk about."

Beatrix grinned at her sister. "Very logical."

Rye jumped up to grab Beatrix's hand, and he began to drag her outside. "Come, Auntie," he coaxed. "I promise I won't whack you with my sword like the last time."

"Don't go into the woods, Rye," Cam called after them. "One of the tenants said a stray dog came out of the hazel copse this morning and nearly attacked him. He thought the creature might be mad."

Beatrix stopped and looked back at Cam. "What kind of dog?"

"A mongrel with a rough coat like a terrier's. The tenant claims the dog stole one of his hens."

"Don't worry, Papa," Rye said confidently. "I'll be safe with Beatrix. All animals love her, even the mad ones."

Chapter Seven

After an hour of romping along the hedgerow and through the orchard, Beatrix took Rye back to the house for his afternoon lessons.

"I don't like lessons," Rye said, heaving a sigh as they approached the French doors at the side of the house. "I'd much rather play."

"Yes, but you must learn your maths."

"I don't need to, really. I already know how to count to a hundred. And I'm sure I'll never need more than a hundred of anything."

Beatrix grinned. "Practice your letters, then. And you'll be able to read lots of adventure stories."

"But if I spend my time *reading* about adventures," Rye said, "I won't actually be *having* them."

Beatrix shook her head and laughed. "I should know better than to debate with you, Rye. You're as clever as a cart full of monkeys."

The child scampered up the stairs and turned to look back at her. "Aren't you coming in, Auntie?"

"Not yet," she said absently, her gaze drawn to the forest beyond Ramsay House. "I think I'll go for a walk."

"Shall I come with you?"

"Thank you, Rye, but at the moment I need a solitary walk."

"You're going to look for the dog," he said wisely.

Beatrix smiled. "I might."

Rye regarded her speculatively. "Auntie?"

"Yes?"

"Are you ever going to marry?"

"I hope so, Rye. But I have to find the right gentleman first."

"If no one else will marry you, I will when I'm grown up. But only if I'm taller, because I wouldn't want to look up at you."

"Thank you," she said gravely, suppressing a smile as she turned and strode toward the forest.

It was a walk she had taken hundreds of times before. The scenery was familiar, shadows broken by sunlight that came in shards through the tree limbs. Bark was frosted with pale green moss, except for the dark erosions where wood had turned into dust. The woodland floor was soft with mud, overlaid by papery leaves, ferns, and hazel catkins. The sounds were familiar, birdsong and swishing leaves, and the rustlings of a million small creatures.

For all her acquaintance with these woods, however, Beatrix was aware of a new feeling. A sense that she should be cautious. The air was charged with the promise of . . . something. As she went farther, the feeling intensified. Her heart behaved strangely, a wild pulse awakening in her wrists and throat and even in her knees.

There was movement ahead, a shape sliding low through the trees and rippling the bracken. It was not a human shape.

Picking up a fallen branch, Beatrix deftly snapped it to the length of a walking stick.

The creature went still, and silence descended over the forest.

"Come here," Beatrix called out.

A dog came bounding toward her, crashing through brush and leaves. He gave the distinctive bay of a terrier. Halting a few yards away from her, the dog snarled and bared long white teeth.

Beatrix held still and studied him calmly. He was lean, his wiry fur stripped short except for comical whisks of it on his face and ears and near his eyes. Such expressive bright eyes, round as shillings.

There was no mistaking that distinctive face. She had seen it before.

"Albert?" she said in wonder.

The dog's ears twitched at the name. Crouching, he growled in his throat, a sound of angry confusion.

"He brought you back with him," Beatrix said, dropping the stick. Her eyes prickled with the beginnings of tears, even as she let out a little laugh. "I'm so glad you made it through the war safely. Come, Albert, let's be friends." She stayed unmoving and let the dog approach her cautiously. He sniffed at her skirts, circling slowly. In a moment she felt his cold wet nose nudge the side of her hand. She didn't move to pet him, only allowed him to become familiar with her scent. When she saw the change in his face, the jaw muscles relaxing and his mouth hanging open, she spoke firmly. "Sit, Albert."

His bottom dropped to the ground. A whine whistled from his throat. Beatrix reached out to stroke his head and scratch behind his ears. Albert panted eagerly, his eyes half closed in enjoyment.

"So you've run off from him, have you?" Beatrix asked, smoothing the wiry ruff on his head. "Naughty boy. I suppose you've had a fine old time chasing rabbits and squirrels. And there's a damaging rumor about a missing chicken. You had better stay out of poultry yards, or it won't go well for you in Stony Cross. Shall I take you home, boy? He's probably looking for you. He—"

She stopped at the sound of something . . . someone . . . moving through the thicket. Albert turned his head and let out a happy bark, bounding toward the approaching figure.

Beatrix was slow to lift her head. She struggled to moderate her breathing, and tried to calm the frantic stutters of her heart. She was aware of the dog bounding joyfully back to her, tongue dangling. He glanced back at his master as if to convey *Look what I found!*

Letting out a slow breath, Beatrix looked up at the man who had stopped approximately three yards away.

Christopher.

It seemed the entire world stopped.

Beatrix tried to compare the man standing before her with the cavalier rake he had once been. But it seemed impossible that he could be the same person. No longer a god descending from Olympus . . . now a warrior hardened by bitter experience.

His complexion was a deep mixture of gold and copper, as if he had been slowly steeped in sun. The dark wheaten locks of his hair had been cut in efficiently short layers. His face was impassive, but something volatile was contained in the stillness.

How bleak he looked. How alone.

She wanted to run to him. She wanted to touch him. The effort of standing motionless caused her muscles to tremble in protest.

She heard herself speak in a voice that wasn't quite steady. "Welcome home, Captain Phelan."

He was silent, staring at her without apparent recognition. Dear Lord, those eyes . . . frost and fire, his gaze burning through her awareness.

"I'm Beatrix Hathaway," she managed to say. "My family—"

"I remember you."

The rough velvet of his voice was a pleasure-stroke against her ears. Fascinated, bewildered, Beatrix stared at his guarded face.

To Christopher Phelan, she was a stranger. But the memories of his letters were between them, even if he wasn't aware of it.

Her hand moved gently over Albert's rough fur. "You were absent in London," she said. "There was a great deal of hullabaloo on your behalf."

"I wasn't ready for it."

So much was expressed in that spare handful of words. Of course he wasn't ready. The contrast would be too jarring, the blood-soaked brutality of war followed by a fanfare of parades and trumpets and flower petals. "I can't imagine any sane man would be," she said. "It's quite an uproar. Your picture is in all the shop windows. And they're naming things after you."

"Things," he repeated cautiously.

"There's a Phelan hat."

His brows lowered. "No there isn't."

"Oh, yes there is. Rounded at the top. Narrow-brimmed. Sold in shades of gray or black. They have one featured at the milliner's in Stony Cross."

Scowling, Christopher muttered something beneath his breath.

Beatrix played gently with Albert's ears. "I . . . heard about Albert, from Prudence. How lovely that you brought him back with you."

"It was a mistake," he said flatly. "He's behaved like a mad creature ever since we landed at Dover. So far he's tried to bite two people, including one of my servants. He won't stop barking. I had to shut him in a garden shed last night, and he escaped."

"He's fearful," Beatrix said. "He thinks if he acts that way, no one will harm him." Eagerly the dog stood on his hind legs and set his front paws on her. Beatrix bumped a knee gently against his chest.

"Here," Christopher said, in a tone of such quiet menace that it sent a chill down Beatrix's spine. The dog slunk to him, tail between his legs. Christopher took a coiled leather leash from his coat pocket and looped it around the dog's neck. He glanced at Beatrix, his gaze traveling from the two smears of mud on her skirts to the gentle curves of her breasts. "My apologies," he said brusquely.

"No harm done. I don't mind. But he should be taught not to jump on people."

"He's only been with soldiers. He knows nothing of polite company."

"He can learn. I'm sure he'll be a fine dog once he becomes used to his new surroundings." Beatrix paused before offering, "I could work with him the next time I visit Audrey. I'm very good with dogs."

Christopher gave her a brooding glance. "I'd forgotten you were friends with my sister-in-law."

"Yes." Beatrix hesitated. "I should have said earlier that I'm very sorry for the loss of your—"

His hand lifted in a staying gesture. As he brought it to his side, his fingers curled into a tight fist.

Beatrix understood. The pain of his brother's death was still too acute. It was territory he couldn't yet traverse. "You haven't been able to grieve yet, have you?" she asked gently. "I suppose his death wasn't entirely real to you, until you came back to Stony Cross."

Christopher gave her a warning glance.

Beatrix had seen that look from captured animals, the helpless animosity toward anyone who approached. She had learned to respect such a glance, understanding that wild creatures were at their most dangerous when they had the fewest defenses. She returned her attention to the dog, smoothing his fur repeatedly.

"How is Prudence?" she heard him ask. It hurt to hear the note of wary longing in his voice.

"Quite well, I believe. She's in London for the season." Beatrix hesitated before adding carefully, "We are still friends, but perhaps not as fond of each other as we once were."

"Why?"

His gaze was alert now. Clearly any mention of Prudence earned his close attention.

Because of you, Beatrix thought, and managed a faint, wry smile. "It seems we have different interests." *I'm interested in you, and she's interested in your inheritance.*

"You're hardly cut from the same cloth."

Hearing the sardonic note in his voice, Beatrix tilted her head and regarded him curiously. "I don't take your meaning."

He hesitated. "I only meant that Miss Mercer is conventional. And you're . . . not." His tone was seasoned with the merest hint of condescension . . . but there was no mistaking it.

Abruptly all the feelings of compassion and tenderness disappeared as Beatrix realized that Christopher Phelan had not changed in one regard: he still didn't like her.

"I would never want to be a conventional person," she said. "They're usually dull and superficial."

It seemed he took that as a slight against Prudence.

"As compared to people who bring garden pests to picnics? No one could accuse you of being dull, Miss Hathaway."

Beatrix felt the blood drain from her face. He had insulted her. The realization made her numb.

"You may insult me," she said, half amazed that she could still speak. "But leave my hedgehog alone."

Whirling around, she walked away from him in long, digging strides. Albert whimpered and began to follow, which forced Christopher to call him back.

Beatrix didn't glance over her shoulder, only plowed forward. Bad enough to love a man who didn't love her. But it was exponentially worse to love a man who actively disliked her.

Ridiculously, she wished she could write to *her* Christopher about the stranger she had just met.

He was so contemptuous, she would write. *He dismissed me as someone who didn't deserve a modicum of respect. Clearly he thinks I'm wild and more than a little mad. And the worst part is that he's probably right.*

It crossed her mind that this was why she preferred the company of animals to people. Animals weren't deceitful. They didn't give one conflicting impressions of who they were. And one was never tempted to hope that an animal might change its nature.

CHRISTOPHER WALKED BACK HOME WITH ALBERT PADDING calmly beside him. For some reason the dog seemed improved after meeting Beatrix Hathaway. As Christopher gave him a damning glance, Albert looked up at him with a toothy grin, his tongue lolling.

"Idiot," Christopher muttered, although he wasn't certain if the word was directed at his dog or himself.

He felt troubled and guilty. He knew he'd behaved like an ass to Beatrix Hathaway. She had tried to be friendly, and he had been cold and condescending.

He hadn't meant to be offensive. It was just that he was nearly mad with longing for Prudence, for the sweet, artless voice that had saved his sanity. Every word of every letter she'd sent him still resonated through his soul.

"I've done a great deal of walking lately. I seem to think better outdoors . . ."

And when Christopher had set out to find Albert, and found himself walking through the forest, a mad idea had taken hold of him . . . that *she* was nearby, and fate would bring them together that quickly, that simply.

But instead of finding the woman he had dreamed of, craved, needed for so long, he had found Beatrix Hathaway.

It wasn't that he disliked her. Beatrix was an odd creature, but fairly engaging, and far more attractive than he had remembered. In fact, she had become a beauty in his absence, her gangly coltish shape now curved and graceful . . .

Christopher shook his head impatiently, trying to redirect his thoughts. But the image of Beatrix Hathaway remained. A lovely oval face, a gently erotic mouth, and haunting blue eyes, a blue so rich and deep it seemed to contain hints of purple. And that silky dark hair, pinned up haphazardly, with teasing locks slipping free.

Christ, it had been too long since he'd had a woman. He was randy as the devil, and lonely, and filled with equal measures of grief and anger. He had so many unfulfilled needs, and he didn't begin to know how to address any of them. But finding Prudence seemed like a good start.

He would rest here for a few days. When he felt more like his former self, he would go to Prudence in London. At the moment, however, it was fairly clear that his old way with words had left him. And Christopher knew that whereas he had once been relaxed and charming, he was now guarded and wooden.

Part of the problem was that he wasn't sleeping well. Any slight noise, a creak of the house settling, a rap of a branch against the window, woke him to full heart-pounding readiness. And it happened in the daylight hours as well. Yesterday Audrey had dropped a book from a stack she was carrying, and Christopher had nearly jumped out of his shoes. He had instinctively reached for a weapon before recalling in the next instant that he no longer carried a gun. His rifle had become as familiar as one of his own limbs . . . he often felt it as a phantom presence.

Christopher's steps slowed. He stopped to crouch beside Albert, looking into that shaggy fur-whisked face. "Hard to leave the war behind, isn't it?" he murmured, petting the dog with affectionate roughness. Albert panted and lunged against him, and tried to lick his face. "Poor fellow, you have no idea what's going on, do you? For all you know, shells may start exploding overhead at any moment."

Albert flopped to his back and arched up his tummy, begging for a scratch. Christopher obliged him, and stood. "Let's go back," he said. "I'll let you inside the house again—but God help you if you bite anyone."

UNFORTUNATELY, AS SOON AS THEY WENT INTO THE IVY-covered mansion, Albert erupted in the same hostility he had shown before. Grimly Christopher dragged him to the parlor, where his mother and Audrey were having tea.

Albert barked at the women. He barked at a terrified housemaid. He barked at a fly on the wall. He barked at the teapot.

"*Quiet,*" Christopher said through gritted teeth, pulling the crazed canine to the settee. He tied one end of the leash to a leg of the settee. "*Sit,* Albert. Down."

Warily the dog settled on the floor and growled in his throat.

Audrey pasted a false smile on her face and inquired in a parody of teatime manners, "Shall I pour?"

"Thank you," Christopher said in a dry tone, and went to join them at the tea table.

His mother's face pleated, accordionlike, and her voice emerged in a strained tone. "It's leaving mud on the carpet. *Must* you inflict that creature on us, Christopher?"

"Yes, I must. He has to become accustomed to staying in the house."

"*I* won't become accustomed to it," his mother retorted. "I understand that the dog assisted you during the war. But surely you have no need of it now."

"Sugar? Milk?" Audrey asked, her soft brown eyes now unsmiling as she gazed from Christopher to his mother.

"Only sugar." Christopher watched as she stirred a lump of sugar into tea with a little spoon. He took the cup and concentrated on the steaming liquid, while he struggled with a rush of untoward rage. This, too, was a new problem, these surges of feeling that were entirely out of proportion to the circumstances.

When Christopher had calmed himself sufficiently to speak, he said, "Albert did more than assist me. When I spent days at a time in a muddy trench, he kept watch over me so that I could sleep without fear of being taken by surprise. He took messages up and down the lines, so that we didn't make mistakes in carrying out orders. He alerted us when he sensed the enemy approaching, long before our eyes or ears could have detected anyone." Christopher paused as he glanced into his mother's taut, unhappy face. "I owe him my life, and my loyalty. And unsightly and ill mannered though he is, I happen to love him." He slitted a glance at Albert.

Albert's tail thumped the floor enthusiastically.

Audrey looked dubious. His mother looked angry.

Christopher drank his tea in the ensuing silence. It tore at his heart to see the changes in both women. They were both thin and pale. His mother's hair had gone white. No doubt

John's prolonged illness had taken a toll on them before his death, and nearly a year of mourning had finished the job.

Not for the first time, Christopher thought it a shame that the rules of mourning imposed such solitude on people, when it probably would have benefited them to have company and pleasant distractions.

Setting down her half-finished cup of tea, his mother pushed back from the table. Christopher rose to help her with the chair.

"I can't enjoy my tea with that beast staring at me," she said. "At any moment, it could leap forward and rip my throat out."

"His leash is tied to the furniture, Mother," Audrey pointed out.

"That doesn't matter. It's a savage creature, and I detest it." She swept out of the room, her head high with indignation.

Freed of the necessity for good manners, Audrey rested an elbow on the table and leaned her hand on her chin. "Your uncle and aunt have invited her to stay with them in Hertfordshire," she said. "I've encouraged her to accept their offer. She needs a change of view."

"The house is too dark," Christopher said. "Why are all the shutters closed and the curtains drawn?"

"The light hurts her eyes."

"The devil it does." Christopher stared at her with a slight frown. "She should go," he said. "She's been holed up in this morgue for far too long. And so have you."

Audrey sighed. "It's almost been a year. Soon I'll be out of full mourning and I can go into half-mourning."

"What is half-mourning, exactly?" Christopher asked, having only a vague notion of such female-oriented rituals.

"It means I can stop wearing veils," Audrey said without enthusiasm. "I can wear gray and lavender dresses, and ornaments without shine. And I may attend a few limited

social events, as long as I don't actually appear to be enjoy-
ing myself."

Christopher snorted derisively. "Who invents these
rules?"

"I don't know. But heaven help us, we must follow them
or face the wrath of society." Audrey paused. "Your mother
says she won't go into half-mourning. She intends to wear
black for the rest of her life."

Christopher nodded, unsurprised. His mother's devotion
had only been strengthened by death. "It's clear that every
time she looks at me," he said, "she thinks I should have
been the son she lost."

Audrey opened her mouth to argue, then closed it. "It was
hardly your fault that you came back alive," she said eventually. "I'm glad you're here. And I believe that somewhere
in her heart, your mother is glad as well. But she's become
slightly unbalanced during the past year. I don't think she's
always entirely aware of what she says or does. I believe some
time away from Hampshire will do her good." She paused.
"I'm going to leave, too, Christopher. I want to see my family in London. And it wouldn't be appropriate for the two of
us to stay here unchaperoned."

"I'll escort you to London in a few days, if you like. I had
already planned to go there to see Prudence Mercer."

Audrey frowned. "Oh."

Christopher gave her a questioning glance. "I gather your
opinion of her has not changed."

"Oh, it has. It's worsened."

He couldn't help but feel defensive on Prudence's behalf.
"Why?"

"For the past two years, Prudence has earned a reputation
as a shameless flirt. Her ambition to marry a wealthy man,
preferably a peer, is known to everyone. I hope you have no
illusions that she pined for you in your absence."

"I would hardly expect her to don sackcloth while I was gone."

"Good, because she didn't. In fact, from all appearances you slipped from her mind completely." Audrey paused before adding bitterly, "However, soon after John passed away and you became the new heir to Riverton, Prudence evinced a great deal of renewed interest in you."

Christopher showed no expression as he puzzled over this unwelcome information. It sounded nothing like the woman who had corresponded with him. Clearly Prudence was the victim of vicious rumors—and in light of her beauty and charm, that was entirely expected.

However, he had no desire to start an argument with his sister-in-law. Hoping to distract her from the volatile subject of Prudence Mercer, he said, "I happened to meet one of your friends today, when I chanced upon her during a walk."

"Who?"

"Miss Hathaway."

"Beatrix?" Audrey looked at him attentively. "I hope you were polite to her."

"Not especially," he admitted.

"What did you say to her?"

He scowled into his teacup. "I insulted her hedgehog," he muttered.

Audrey looked exasperated. "Oh, good God." She began to stir her tea so vigorously that the spoon threatened to crack the porcelain cup. "And to think you were once renowned for your silver tongue. What perverse instinct drives you to repeatedly offend one of the nicest women I've ever known?"

"I haven't *repeatedly* offended her, I just did it today."

Her mouth twisted in derision. "How conveniently short your memory is. All of Stony Cross knows that you once said she belonged in the stables."

"I would never have said that to a woman, no matter how damned eccentric she was. *Is.*"

"Beatrix overheard you telling it to one of your friends, at the harvest dance held at Stony Cross Manor."

"And she told everyone?"

"No, she made the mistake of confiding in Prudence, who told everyone. Prudence is an incurable gossip."

"Obviously you have no liking for Prudence," he began, "but if you—"

"I've tried my best to like her. I thought if one peeled away the layers of artifice, one would find the real Prudence beneath. But there's nothing beneath. And I doubt there ever will be."

"And you find Beatrix Hathaway superior to her?"

"In every regard, except perhaps beauty."

"There you have it wrong," he informed her. "Miss Hathaway *is* a beauty."

Audrey's brows lifted. "Do you think so?" she asked idly, lifting the teacup to her lips.

"It's obvious. Regardless of what I think of her character, Miss Hathaway is an exceptionally attractive woman."

"Oh, I don't know . . ." Audrey devoted careful attention to her tea, adding a tiny lump of sugar. "She's rather tall."

"She has the ideal height and form."

"And brown hair is so common . . ."

"It's not the usual shade of brown, it's as dark as sable. And those eyes . . ."

"Blue," Audrey said with a dismissive wave.

"The deepest, purest blue I've ever seen. No artist could capture—" Christopher broke off abruptly. "Never mind. I'm straying from the point."

"What *is* your point?" Audrey asked sweetly.

"That it is of no significance to me whether Miss Hathaway is a beauty or not. She's peculiar, and so is her family, and I have no interest in any of them. By the same token, I don't give a damn if Prudence Mercer is beautiful—I'm interested in the workings of her mind. Her lovely, original, absolutely compelling mind."

"I see. Beatrix's mind is peculiar, and Prudence's is original and compelling."

"Just so."

Audrey shook her head slowly. "There is something I want to tell you. But it's going to become more obvious over time. And you wouldn't believe it if I told you, or at least you wouldn't want to believe it. This is one of those things that must be discovered for oneself."

"Audrey, what the devil are you talking about?"

Folding her narrow arms across her chest, his sister-in-law contemplated him sternly. And yet a strange little smile kept tugging at the corners of her lips. "If you are at all a gentleman," she finally said, "you will call on Beatrix tomorrow and apologize for hurting her feelings. Go during one of your walks with Albert—she'll be glad to see *him,* if not you."

Chapter Eight

Christopher walked to Ramsay House the next afternoon. Not because he actually wanted to. However, he had no plans for the day, and unless he wanted to contend with his mother's unforgiving stares, or worse, Audrey's quiet stoicism, he had to go somewhere. The stillness of the rooms, the memories tucked in every nook and shadow, were more than he could face.

He had yet to ask Audrey what it had been like for John the last few days of his life . . . what his last words had been.

Beatrix Hathaway had been right when she'd guessed that John's death hadn't been real to him until he'd come home.

As they went through the forest, Albert bounded this way and that, foraging through the bracken. Christopher felt morose and restless as he anticipated his welcome—or lack thereof—when he arrived at Ramsay House. No doubt Beatrix had told her family about his ungentlemanly behavior. They would be angry with him, rightfully so. It was common knowledge that the Hathaway family was a close-knit, clannish group, fiercely protective of each other. And they had to be, with a pair of Romany brothers-in-law, not to mention their own lack of blood and breeding.

It was only the peerage title, held by Leo, Lord Ramsay, that afforded the family any social foothold whatsoever. Fortunately for them, they were received by Lord West-cliff, one of the most powerful and respected peers of the realm. That connection gave them entrée into circles that otherwise would have excluded them. However, what annoyed the local gentry was that the Hathaways didn't seem to care one way or the other.

As he approached Ramsay House, Christopher wondered what the devil he was doing, calling on the Hathaways unannounced. It probably wasn't a proper visiting day, and certainly not an appropriate time. But he rather doubted they would notice.

The Ramsay estate was small but productive, with three thousand acres of arable land and two hundred prosperous tenant farms. In addition, the estate possessed a large forest that yielded a lucrative annual timber yield. The charming and distinctive roofline of the manor home came into view, a central medieval dormer sided by rows of high peaked gables, Jacobean pierced crestings and strap work, and a tidy square Georgian addition to the left. The effect of mixed architectural features wasn't all that unusual. Many older homes featured additions in a variety of styles. But since this was the Hathaway family, it only seemed to underscore their strangeness.

Christopher put Albert on a leash and proceeded to the entrance of the house with a little stab of dread.

If he were fortunate, no one would be available to receive him.

After tying Albert's leash to a slender porch column, Christopher knocked at the door and waited tensely.

He reared back as the portal was flung open by a frantic-faced housekeeper.

"I beg your pardon, sir, we're in the middle of—" She

paused at the sound of porcelain crashing from somewhere inside the house. "Oh, merciful Lord," she moaned, and gestured to the front parlor. "Wait there if you please, and—"

"I've got her," a masculine voice called. And then, "Damn it, no I don't. She's heading for the stairs."

"Do *not* let her come upstairs!" a woman screamed. A baby was crying in strident gusts. "Oh, that dratted creature has woken the baby. Where are the housemaids?"

"Hiding, I expect."

Christopher hesitated in the entryway, blinking as he heard a bleating noise. He asked the housekeeper blankly, "Are they keeping farm animals in here?"

"No, of course not," she said hastily, trying to push him into the parlor. "That's . . . a baby crying. Yes. A baby."

"It doesn't sound like one," he said.

Christopher heard Albert barking from the porch. A three-legged cat came streaking through the hallway, followed by a bristling hedgehog that scuttled a great deal faster than one might have expected. The housekeeper hastened after them.

"Pandora, come back here!" came a new voice—Beatrix Hathaway's voice—and Christopher's senses sparked in recognition. He twitched uneasily at the commotion, his reflexes urging him to take some kind of action, although he wasn't yet certain what the bloody hell was going on.

A large white goat came leaping and capering and twisting through the hallway.

And then Beatrix Hathaway appeared, tearing around the corner. She skidded to a halt. "You might have tried to stop her," she exclaimed. As she glanced up at Christopher, a scowl flitted across her face. "Oh. It's you."

"Miss Hathaway—" he began.

"Hold this."

Something warm and wriggling was thrust into his grasp, and Beatrix dashed off to pursue the goat.

Dumbfounded, Christopher glanced at the creature in his hands. A baby goat, cream colored, with a brown head. He fumbled to keep from dropping the creature as he glanced at Beatrix's retreating form and realized she was wearing breeches and boots.

Christopher had seen women in every imaginable state of dress or undress. But he had never seen one wearing the clothes of a stablehand.

"I must be having a dream," he told the squirming kid absently. "A very odd dream about Beatrix Hathaway and goats . . ."

"I have her!" the masculine voice called out. "Beatrix, I told you the pen needed to be made taller."

"She didn't leap over it," came Beatrix's protest, "she ate *through* it."

"Who let her into the house?"

"No one. She butted one of the side doors open."

An inaudible conversation followed.

As Christopher waited, a dark-haired boy of approximately four or five years of age made a breathless entrance through the front door. He was carrying a wooden sword and had tied a handkerchief around his head, which gave him the appearance of a miniature pirate. "Did they catch the goat?" he asked Christopher without preamble.

"I believe so."

"Oh, thunderbolts. I missed all the fun." The boy sighed. He looked up at Christopher. "Who are you?"

"Captain Phelan."

The child's gaze sharpened with interest. "Where's your uniform?"

"I don't wear it now that the war is over."

"Did you come to see my father?"

"No, I . . . came to call on Miss Hathaway."

"Are you one of her suitors?"

Christopher gave a decisive shake of his head.

"You might be one," the boy said wisely, "and just not know it yet."

Christopher felt a smile—his first genuine smile in a long time—pulling at his lips. "Does Miss Hathaway have many suitors?"

"Oh, yes. But none of them want to marry her."

"Why is that, do you imagine?"

"They don't want to get shot," the child said, shrugging.

"Pardon?" Christopher's brows lifted.

"Before you marry, you have to get shot by an arrow and fall in love," the boy explained. He paused thoughtfully. "But I don't think the rest of it hurts as much as the beginning."

Christopher couldn't prevent a grin. At that moment, Beatrix returned to the hallway, dragging the nanny goat on a rope lead.

Beatrix looked at Christopher with an arrested expression.

His smile faded, and he found himself staring into her blue-on-blue eyes. They were astonishingly direct and lucid . . . the eyes of a vagabond angel. One had the sense that no matter what she beheld of the sinful world, she would never be jaded. She reminded him that the things he had seen and done could not be polished away like tarnish from silver.

Gradually her gaze lowered from his. "Rye," she said, handing the lead to the boy. "Take Pandora to the barn, will you? And the baby goat as well." Reaching out, she took the kid from Christopher's arms. The touch of her hands against his shirtfront elicited an unnerving response, a pleasurable heaviness in his groin.

"Yes, Auntie." The boy left through the front door, somehow managing to retain possession of the goats and the wooden sword.

Christopher stood facing Beatrix, trying not to gape. And failing utterly. She might as well have been standing there in her undergarments. In fact, that would have been preferable, because at least it wouldn't have seemed so singularly erotic. He could see the feminine outline of her hips and thighs clad in the masculine garments. And she didn't seem at all self-conscious. Confound her, what kind of woman was she?

He struggled with his reaction to her, a mixture of annoyance, fascination, and arousal. With her hair threatening to tumble from its pins, and her cheeks flushed from exertion, she was the epitome of glowing female health.

"Why are you here?" she asked.

"I came to apologize," he said. "I was . . . discourteous yesterday."

"No, you were rude."

"You're right. I'm truly sorry." At her lack of response, Christopher fumbled for words. He, who had once spoken to women so glibly. "I've been too long in rough company. Since I left the Crimea, I find myself reacting irritably without cause. I . . . words are too important for me to be so careless with them."

Perhaps it was his imagination, but he thought her face softened a little.

"You don't have to be sorry for disliking me," she said. "Only for being discourteous."

"Rude," Christopher corrected. "And I don't."

"You don't what?" she asked with a frown.

"Dislike you. That is . . . I don't know you well enough to either like or dislike you."

"I'm fairly certain, Captain," she said, "that the more you discover about me, the more you will dislike me. Therefore, let's cut to the chase and acknowledge that we don't like each other. Then we won't have to bother with the in-between part."

She was so bloody frank and practical about the whole thing that Christopher couldn't help but be amused. "I'm afraid I can't oblige you."

"Why not?"

"Because when you said that just now, I found myself starting to like you."

"You'll recover," she said.

Her decisive tone made him want to smile. "It's getting worse, actually," he told her. "Now I'm absolutely convinced that I like you."

Beatrix gave him a patently skeptical stare. "What about my hedgehog? Do you like her, too?"

Christopher considered that. "Affection for rodents can't be rushed."

"Medusa isn't a rodent. She's an erinaceid."

"Why did you bring her to the picnic?" Christopher couldn't resist asking.

"Because I thought her company would be preferable to that of the people I would meet there." A faint smile played at the corners of her lips. "And I was right." She paused. "We're about to have tea," she said. "Will you join us?"

Christopher began to shake his head before she had even finished. They would ask questions, and he would have to come up with careful answers, and the thought of a prolonged conversation was wearying and anxiety provoking. "Thank you, but no. I—"

"It's a condition of my forgiveness," Beatrix said. Those dark blue eyes, lit with a provocative glint, stared directly into his.

Surprised and diverted, Christopher wondered how an unworldly young woman in her early twenties had the gall to give him orders.

However, it was turning out to be a strangely entertaining afternoon. Why not stay? He wasn't expected anywhere. And no matter how it turned out, it would be preferable to going back to those somber dark rooms at home. "In that case—" He broke off, startled, as Beatrix leaned toward him.

"Oh, bother." She was looking closely at the lapels of his tweed sack coat. "You're covered with goat hair." She began to brush at his lapels vigorously.

It took Christopher a full five seconds to remember how to breathe. "Miss Hathaway—" In her efforts to whisk away the scattering of stray goat hairs, she was standing much too close. He wanted her even closer. What would it feel like to wrap his arms around her, and press his cheek into that mass of shiny dark hair?

"Don't move," Beatrix said, continuing to bat at the front of his coat. "I've almost brushed it off."

"No, I don't . . . that's not . . ." Christopher's control broke. He snatched her slender wrists with his hands, holding them suspended. God, the feel of her . . . the smooth skin . . . the exquisite throb of her veins against his fingertips. A subtle tremor ran through her. He wanted to follow it with his hands, smooth his palms over the supple curves of her. He wanted to wrap her around him, her legs, her arms, her hair

But despite her undeniable attractions, he would never pursue a woman like Beatrix Hathaway, even if he weren't already in love with Prudence. What he truly wanted, needed, was a return to normalcy. To the kind of life that would restore him to peace.

Slowly Beatrix pulled her arms free of his manacling fingers. She stared at him, her gaze wary and intent.

They both started at the sound of approaching footsteps.

"Good afternoon," came a pleasant feminine voice.

It was the oldest Hathaway sister, Amelia. She was shorter and more voluptuous than her younger sister. There was a warm maternal air about her, as if she were prepared to ladle out sympathy and comfort at a moment's notice.

"Mrs. Rohan," Christopher murmured, and bowed.

"Sir," she replied with a questioning lilt. Although they had met before, she clearly didn't recognize him.

"This is Captain Phelan, Amelia," Beatrix said.

The blue eyes widened. "What a lovely surprise," she exclaimed, giving Christopher her hand.

"Captain Phelan and I dislike each other," Beatrix told her. "In fact, we're sworn enemies."

Christopher glanced at her quickly. "When did we become sworn enemies?"

Ignoring him, Beatrix said to her sister, "Regardless, he's staying for tea."

"Wonderful," Amelia said equably. "Why are you enemies, dear?"

"I met him yesterday while I was out walking," Beatrix explained. "And he called Medusa a 'garden pest,' and faulted me for bringing her to a picnic."

Amelia smiled at Christopher. "Medusa has been called many worse things around here, including 'diseased pincushion,' and 'perambulating cactus.'"

"I've never understood," Beatrix said, "why people have such unreasonable dislike of hedgehogs."

"They dig up the garden," Amelia said, "and they're not what one would call cuddlesome. Captain Phelan has a point, dear—you might have brought your cat to the picnic instead."

"Don't be silly. Cats don't like picnics nearly as much as hedgehogs."

The conversation proceeded at such quicksilver speed that there was little opportunity for Christopher to break in. Somehow he managed to find an opening. "I apologized to Miss Hathaway for my remarks," he told Amelia uncomfortably.

This earned an approving glance. "Delightful. A man who's not afraid to apologize. But really, apologies are wasted on our family—we're usually pleased by the things we should be offended by, and vice versa. Come in, Captain, you're among friends."

Christopher found himself being ushered into a bright, cheery house, with abundant windows and piles of books everywhere.

"Beatrix," Amelia said over her shoulder as they proceeded through the hallway. "Perhaps you should reconsider your attire. Poor Captain Phelan may find it somewhat shocking."

"But he's already seen me like this," came Beatrix's voice from behind Christopher, "and I've already shocked him. What is the point in changing clothes? Captain, would you feel more comfortable if I took my breeches off?"

"No," he said hastily.

"Good, I'll keep them on. Really, I don't see why women shouldn't dress like this all the time. One can walk freely and even leap. How is one to chase after a goat in skirts?"

"It's something the dressmakers should consider," Amelia said. "Although my concern is more in the direction of chasing after children, not goats."

They entered a room lined with a semicircular row of tall windows overlooking a spring garden. It was a comfortable room, with overstuffed furniture and embroidered pillows. A housemaid was busy setting out china plates on a tea table. Christopher couldn't help contrasting this cozy scene with yesterday's stilted teatime in the Phelans' immaculate formal parlor.

"Please set another place, Tillie," Amelia said. "We have a guest."

"Yes, mum." The housemaid looked distinctly worried. "Is the goat gone?"

"Entirely gone," came the soothing reply. "You may bring out the tea tray when it's ready." Amelia sent a mock frown to Christopher. "That goat has been nothing but trouble. And the dratted creature isn't even picturesque. Goats resemble nothing so much as badly dressed sheep."

"That's quite unfair," Beatrix said. "Goats have far more

character and intelligence than sheep, who are nothing but followers. I've met far too many in London."

"Sheep?" Christopher asked blankly.

"My sister is speaking figuratively, Captain Phelan," Amelia said.

"Well, I have met some actual sheep in London," Beatrix said. "But yes, I was mainly referring to people. They all tell you the same gossip, which is tedious. They adhere to the current fashions and the popular opinions, no matter how silly. And one never improves in their company. One starts falling in line and baaing."

A quiet laugh came from the doorway as Cam Rohan entered the room. "Obviously Hathaways are not sheep. Because I've tried to herd the lot of you for years, without any success."

From what Christopher remembered of Rohan, he had worked at a London gaming club for a time, and then had made a fortune in manufacturing investments. Although his devotion to his wife and family was well-known in Stony Cross, Rohan was hardly the image of a staid and respectable patriarch.

Approaching Christopher, Rohan exchanged a bow and surveyed him with a friendly gaze. "Captain Phelan. It is good to see you. We were hoping for your safe return."

"Thank you. I hope my presence is not an imposition."

"Not in the least. With Lord Ramsay and his wife still in London, and my brother Merripen and his wife visiting Ireland, it's been far too peaceful here of late." Rohan paused, a glitter of amusement entering his eyes. "Fugitive goats notwithstanding."

The ladies were seated, and finger bowls and napkins were brought out, followed by a sumptuously laden tea tray. As Amelia poured, Christopher noticed that she had added a few crushed green leaves to Beatrix's cup.

Seeing his interest, Amelia said, "My sister prefers her tea flavored with mint. Would you like some as well, Captain?"

"No, thank you, I . . ." Christopher's voice faded as he watched her stir a spoonful of honey into the cup.

"Every morning and afternoon I drink fresh mint tea sweetened with honey . . ."

The reminder of Prudence awakened the familiar yearning, and Christopher steeled himself against it. He forced himself to focus solely on this situation, these people.

In the ensuing pause, he heard the sound of Albert barking outside. With despairing impatience, Christopher wondered if the blasted dog was ever going to be quiet.

"He wants to protect you," Beatrix said. "He's wondering where I've taken you."

Christopher let out a taut sigh. "Perhaps I shouldn't stay. He'll bark for hours."

"Nonsense. Albert must learn to adapt to your plans. I'll bring him inside."

Her authoritative manner rankled Christopher, no matter that she was right. "He might damage something," he said, rising to his feet.

"He can't do any worse than the goat," Beatrix replied, standing to face him.

Politely Rohan stood as well, watching the two of them.

"Miss Hathaway—" Christopher continued to object, but he fell silent, blinking, as she reached out and touched his chest. Her fingertips rested over his heart for the space of one heartbeat.

"Let me try," she said gently.

Christopher fell back a step, his breath catching. His body responded to her touch with disconcerting swiftness. A lady never put her hand to any area of a man's torso unless the circumstances were so extreme that . . . well, he couldn't even imagine what would justify it. Perhaps if his waistcoat was on fire, and she was trying to put it out. Other than that, he couldn't think of any defensible reason.

And yet if he were to point out the breach of etiquette, the act of correcting a lady was just as graceless. Troubled and aroused, Christopher gave her a single nod.

The men resumed their seats after Beatrix had left the room.

"Forgive us, Captain Phelan," Amelia murmured. "I can see that my sister startled you. Really, we've tried to learn better manners, but we're Philistines, all of us. And while Beatrix is out of hearing, I would like to assure you that she doesn't usually dress so outlandishly. However, every now and then she goes on an undertaking that makes long skirts inadvisable. Replacing a bird in a nest, for example, or training a horse, and so forth."

"A more conventional solution," Christopher said carefully, "would be to forbid the activity that necessitated the wearing of men's garments."

Rohan grinned. "One of my private rules for dealing with Hathaways," he said, "is never to forbid them anything. Because that guarantees they'll keep doing it."

"Heavens, we're not as bad as all that," Amelia protested.

Rohan gave his wife a speaking glance, his smile lingering. "Hathaways require freedom," he told Christopher, "Beatrix in particular. An ordinary life—being contained in parlors and drawing rooms—would be a prison for her. She relates to the world in a far more vital and natural way than any *gadji* I've ever known." Seeing Christopher's incomprehension, he added, "That's the word the Rom uses for females of your kind."

"And because of Beatrix," Amelia said, "we possess a

menagerie of creatures no one else wants: a goat with an undershot jaw, a three-legged cat, a portly hedgehog, a mule with an unbalanced build, and so forth."

"A mule?" Christopher stared at her intently, but before he could ask about it, Beatrix returned with Albert on the leash.

Christopher stood and moved to take the dog, but Beatrix shook her head. "Thank you, Captain, but I have him in hand."

Albert wagged his tail wildly at the sight of Christopher and lunged toward him with a bark.

"No," Beatrix scolded, pulling him back and putting her hand briefly to his muzzle. "Your master is safe. No need to make a fuss. Come." Reaching for a pillow from a low-backed settee, she placed it in the corner.

Christopher watched as she led the dog to the pillow and removed the leash. Albert whimpered and refused to lie down, but he remained obediently in the corner. "Stay," she told him.

To Christopher's amazement, Albert didn't move. A dog who thought nothing of running through gunfire was completely cowed by Beatrix Hathaway.

"I think he'll behave," Beatrix said, returning to the table. "But it would be best if we paid him no attention." She sat, placed a napkin in her lap, and reached for her teacup. She smiled as she saw Christopher's expression. "Be at ease, Captain," she said gently. "The more relaxed you are, the calmer he will be."

In the hour that followed, Christopher drank cups of hot sugared tea and let the gently animated conversation flow around him. Slowly, a string of tight, cold knots inside his chest began to loosen. A plate filled with sandwiches and tarts was set before him. Occasionally he glanced at Albert, who had settled in the corner, his chin on his paws.

The Hathaways were new in Christopher's experience.

They were intelligent, amusing, their conversation veering and dashing in unexpected directions. And it was clear to him that the sisters were too clever for polite society. The one subject they didn't tread upon was the Crimea, for which Christopher was grateful. They seemed to understand that the topic of war was the last thing he wanted to discuss. For that reason among others, he liked them.

But Beatrix was a problem.

Christopher didn't know what to make of her. He was mystified and annoyed by the familiar way she spoke to him. And the sight of her in those breeches, her legs crossed like a man's, was unsettling. She was strange. Subversive and half tame.

When the tea was concluded, Christopher thanked them for the agreeable afternoon.

"You will call again soon, I hope," Amelia said.

"Yes," Christopher said, not meaning it. He was fairly certain that the Hathaways, although enjoyable, were best taken in small, infrequent doses.

"I'll walk with you to the edge of the forest," Beatrix announced, going to collect Albert.

Christopher suppressed a twinge of exasperation. "That won't be necessary, Miss Hathaway."

"Oh, I know it's not," she said. "But I want to."

Christopher's jaw tightened. He reached for Albert's leash.

"I have him," Beatrix said, retaining the leash.

Conscious of Rohan's amused regard, Christopher bit back a retort, and followed Beatrix from the house.

AMELIA WENT TO THE PARLOR WINDOWS AND WATCHED THE two distant figures proceed through the orchard toward the forest. The apple trees, frosted with light green buds and white blossoms, soon conspired to hide the pair from view.

She puzzled over the way Beatrix had behaved with the

stern-faced soldier, pecking and chirping at him, almost as if she were trying to remind him of something he'd forgotten.

Cam joined her at the window, standing behind her. She leaned back against him, taking comfort in her husband's steady, strong presence. One of his hands glided along her front. She shivered in pleasure at the casual sensuality of his touch.

"Poor man," Amelia murmured, thinking of Phelan's haunting eyes. "I didn't recognize him at first. I wonder if he knows how much he has changed?"

Cam's lips played lightly at her temple as he replied. "I suspect he is realizing it now that he's home."

"He was very charming before. Now he seems so austere. And the way he stares sometimes, as if he's looking right through one . . ."

"He's spent two years burying his friends," Cam replied quietly. "And he's taken part in the kind of close combat that makes a man as hard as nails." He paused reflectively, "Some of it you can't leave behind. The faces of the men you kill stay with you forever."

Knowing that he was remembering a particular episode of his own past, Amelia turned and hugged herself close to him.

"The Rom don't believe in war," Cam said against her hair. "Conflict, arguing, fighting, yes. But not in taking the life of a man with whom one has no personal grievance. Which is one of many reasons why I would not make a good soldier."

"But for those same reasons, you make a *very* good husband."

Cam's arms tightened around her, and he whispered something in Romany. Although she didn't understand the words, the rough-soft sound of them caused her nerves to tingle.

Amelia nestled closer. With her cheek against his chest, she reflected aloud, "It's obvious that Beatrix is fascinated by Captain Phelan."

"She's always been drawn to wounded creatures."

"The wounded ones are often the most dangerous."

His hand moved in a soothing stroke along her spine. "We'll keep a close watch on her, *monisha*."

BEATRIX KEPT PACE EASILY WITH CHRISTOPHER AS THEY headed toward the forest. It nagged at him to have someone else holding Albert's leash. Beatrix's assertiveness was like a pebble lodged in the toe of his shoe. And yet when she was near, it was impossible to feel detached from his surroundings. She had a knack of keeping him anchored in the present.

He couldn't stop watching how her legs and hips moved in those breeches. What was her family thinking, to allow her to dress this way? Even in private it was unacceptable. A humorless smile curved his lips as he reflected that he had at least one thing in common with Beatrix Hathaway—neither of them was in step with the rest of the world.

The difference was that he wanted to be.

It had been so easy for him, before the war. He had always known the right thing to do or say. Now the prospect of reentering polite society seemed rather like playing a game in which he had forgotten the rules.

"Will you sell your army commission soon?" Beatrix asked.

Christopher nodded. "I'm leaving for London in a few days to make the arrangements."

"Oh." Beatrix's tone was noticeably subdued as she said, "I suppose you'll call on Prudence."

Christopher made a noncommittal sound. Inside his coat

pocket rested the small, tattered note he carried with him always.

I'm not who you think I am . . .
Come back, please come home and find me.

Yes. He would find her, and discover why she had written those haunting words. And then he would marry her.

"Now that your brother is gone," Beatrix said, "you'll have to learn how to manage the Riverton estate."

"Among other things," he said curtly.

"Riverton encompasses a large part of the forest of Arden."

"I was aware of that," Christopher said gently.

She didn't seem to notice the touch of sarcasm. "Some estate owners are overcutting, to supply the local manufacturing businesses. I hope you won't do that."

Christopher remained silent, hoping that would quell further conversation.

"Do you *want* to inherit Riverton?" Beatrix surprised him by asking.

"It doesn't matter whether I want it or not. I'm next in line, and I'll do what is required."

"But it does matter," Beatrix said. "That's why I asked."

Losing his patience, Christopher said, "The answer is no, I don't want it. It was always supposed to be for John. I feel like a bloody impostor trying to assume his place."

With anyone else, the burst of vehemence would have put an end to the questioning. But Beatrix persisted. "What would you have done if he was still alive? You would still sell your commission, wouldn't you?"

"Yes. I've had enough of the army."

"And then? What would you do?"

"I don't know."

"What are your aptitudes? Your talents?"

Their footsteps slowed as they reached the woods. His talents . . . he could hold his liquor, beat a man at billiards or cards, seduce a woman. He was a crack shot and an excellent rider.

Then Christopher thought of the thing in his life he had most been lauded for, and showered with praise and medals.

"I have one talent," he said, taking Albert's leash from Beatrix's hand. He looked down into her round eyes. "I'm good at killing."

Without another word, he left her standing at the edge of the forest.

Chapter Nine

In the week after Christopher had returned to Hampshire, the discord between him and his mother became so pronounced that they found it difficult to occupy the same room for more than a few minutes at a time. Poor Audrey did her best to serve as peacemaker, without much success.

Mrs. Phelan had fallen into a habit of relentless complaining. She couldn't go through a room without tossing out nagging comments like a flower girl flinging handfuls of petals at a wedding. Her nerves were acutely sensitive, obliging her to lie quietly in a dark room in the middle of the day, every day. A collection of aches and pains kept her from supervising the household, and as a result, nothing was ever done to her satisfaction.

During Mrs. Phelan's daily resting period, she reacted to the rattling of plates in the kitchen as if she had been stabbed with invisible knives. The murmur of voices or the thud of feet on the upper floors were agony to her nerves. The entire household had to tread upon eggs for fear of disturbing her.

"I've seen men who had just lost arms or legs and complained far less than my mother," Christopher told Audrey, who had grinned ruefully.

Sobering, Audrey said, "Lately she has become fixed in her mourning rituals . . . almost as if her grieving will keep John with her in some way. I'm glad your uncle is coming for her tomorrow. The pattern of her days needs to be broken."

At least four mornings a week, Mrs. Phelan went to the family burial plot at the graveyard of the Stony Cross church, and spent an hour at John's grave. Since she did not want to go unaccompanied, she usually asked Audrey to go with her. However, yesterday Mrs. Phelan had insisted that Christopher escort her. He had waited for an hour in grim-faced silence while she knelt by John's headstone and let a few tears fall.

After she had finally indicated that she wished to rise, and Christopher had gone to help her to her feet, she had wanted him to kneel and pray as she had.

He hadn't been able to do it, not even to please her.

"I'll mourn in my own way," Christopher had told her. "At a time of my choosing, not yours."

"It's not decent," Mrs. Phelan said heatedly, "this lack of respect for him. Your brother deserves to be mourned, or at least be given a show of it, by the man who has profited so greatly by his death."

Christopher had stared at her in disbelief. "I have *profited*?" he had repeated in a low voice. "You know I never gave a damn about inheriting Riverton. I would give everything I have, if it would bring him back. If I could have sacrificed my life to save his, I would have."

"How I wish that had been possible," she had said acidly, and they had ridden back to the house in silence.

And all the while, Christopher had wondered how many hours she had sat at John's grave and wished that one son were in the place of the other.

John had been the perfect son, responsible and reliable. Christopher, however, had been the wilder, rougher son, sensual and reckless and careless. Like his father, William. Every time William had been caught up in some kind of scandal in London, often involving some other man's wife, Mrs. Phelan had been cold and distant to Christopher, as if he had been the designated proxy of her unfaithful husband. When William Phelan died as a result of being thrown by a horse, it had been whispered in London that the only surprise was that he had not been shot by some outraged husband or father of one of the women he had debauched.

Christopher had been twelve at the time. In his father's absence, he had gradually inhabited the role of wild-living rake. It seemed to have been expected of him. The truth was that he had reveled in the pleasures of the city, no matter that such enjoyments were fleeting and hollow. Being an army officer had been the perfect employment for him . . . he had found it enjoyable in every regard. Until, Christopher reflected with a grim, private smile, he'd actually been called to go to war.

Christopher had been far more effective in combat than he or anyone else had ever expected. And the more successful he'd become at bringing death to others, the more dead he had felt inside.

But there was Prudence. That was the only decent part of him left, the part that loved her. The thought of going to her filled him with agitation.

He still found it difficult to sleep, often waking up bolt upright in the middle of a nightmare. And there were moments in the day when he twitched at a sudden noise and found himself fumbling for a rifle that wasn't there. But he was certain all of that would improve in time.

It had to.

Chapter Ten

Obviously there was no reason to hope for anything, where Christopher Phelan was concerned. Beatrix kept reminding herself of that fact. He wanted Prudence. Beautiful, golden-haired, conventional Prudence.

It was the first time in Beatrix's life that she had wanted to be someone other than who she really was.

"I think you might be my only chance of becoming part of the world again . . ."

Perhaps Prudence, after all, was best suited to help Christopher. She was at ease with society in a way that Beatrix could never be. Very well. If that was best for him, Beatrix could not find it in her heart to blame him for that. The man had endured enough pain and hardship—Beatrix did not want to cause any further difficulties for him.

Except . . . she couldn't stop thinking about him. It was like an illness. It was impossible for her to carry on as usual. She was constantly on the verge of tears. She felt feverish and fatigued and bereft of appetite. In fact, she had become so morose that Amelia had insisted on brewing a pot of sorrel tonic for her.

"You're not yourself," Amelia had said. "You're usually so cheerful."

"Why should I be cheerful if there's no reason for it?" Beatrix had asked sullenly.

"Is there a reason to be miserable?"

Beatrix had longed to confide in her sister, but she had kept silent. There was nothing Amelia could do about the situation. Besides, telling a hundred people, a thousand, wouldn't have made her feel any better. She was pining for a man she could never have, and she didn't want to be told how ridiculous it was. She didn't even want to stop pining. The desperate strength of her wanting was her one frail link with Christopher.

She was so obsessed with him that she had actually considered going to London for the rest of the season. She would be able to visit Audrey, and she would also be able to see Christopher. Except that she would also be forced to see him with Prudence . . . dancing, flirting, courting . . . and Beatrix was quite certain that she couldn't bear that.

No, she would stay in Hampshire where she belonged.

Audrey had said that was a wise decision.

"He has changed, Bea, and not for the better. When Christopher first returned from the Crimea, I was so tempted to tell him the truth about the letters. That you were the one who had written to him, and not Prudence. But now I'm glad I didn't. I wouldn't want to encourage an attachment between you and Christopher. He's not himself. He drinks more than he should. He's easily startled. Sometimes he'll hear or see something that isn't there. And I know he's not sleeping—I often hear him wandering through the house at night. But when I try to talk to him, he brushes my questions away as if I'm being silly. And sometimes a simple question—anything to do with the war, especially—sends him into a rage that he has difficulty controlling. I wonder . . ."

"What?" Beatrix whispered, wrenched with concern.

Audrey had looked at her directly. "I wonder if Prudence can manage him. He's so determined to have her . . . but he's not the man he was. And Prudence won't have the sense to realize it. I even wonder if he'll be a danger to her."

Pondering Audrey's ominous words, Beatrix walked to the Phelans' house with a mission in mind. Although there was nothing she could do for Christopher, there was a great deal she could do for Albert. An aggressive dog was likely to do harm to others, and he would be deprived of necessary love and attention. Dogs were inherently sociable animals, and therefore Albert *must* be taught how to get on with other creatures.

The Phelan housekeeper, Mrs. Clocker, greeted her at the door and said that Audrey was not at home, but was soon expected to return from a visit to the village. "Will you want to wait for her, Miss Hathaway?"

"As a matter of fact, I would like to speak to Captain Phelan on a particular business." Beatrix smiled faintly at the housekeeper's questioning gaze. "I want to offer to look after Albert while Captain Phelan is in London."

The housekeeper's eyes widened. "The master had planned to leave the creature here, and have the servants look after it." Leaning close, she whispered, "He is a hound of Hades, miss. The devil himself wouldn't have such a dog."

Beatrix smiled sympathetically. "I hope that I may influence him for the better. If Captain Phelan allows, I will take Albert with me today, and relieve you of the burden of managing him."

Mrs. Clocker looked positively exuberant. "Oh, that is *very* kind of you, Miss Hathaway! I will inform Captain Phelan immediately." She hurried off as if she feared Beatrix might leave.

When Christopher's tall form entered the front receiving

room, Beatrix was instantly covered with a full-bodied flush. *Stop this at once, Beatrix Hathaway,* she told herself sternly. *If you insist on being idiotic, you will have to go home and drink an entire bottle of sorrel tonic.*

"Miss Hathaway," Christopher said, bowing with meticulous politeness.

The dark smudges of sleeplessness beneath his eyes made him even more appealing, if that was possible, lending a human texture to the hard contours of his face.

Beatrix managed to pull up a casual smile. "Good morning, Captain Phelan."

"It's afternoon."

"Oh, is it?" She glanced over his shoulder at the mantel clock. Half-past twelve. "Good afternoon, then."

One of his brows lifted. "Is there something I may do for you?"

"The reverse, I hope. I would like to keep Albert with me at Ramsay House while you are away to London."

His eyes narrowed. "Why?"

"I want very much to help him adjust to his new life. Albert would receive the best of care, and I would work with him, train him . . ." Her voice faded as she saw his forbidding expression. It had not occurred to her that he might refuse her offer.

"Thank you, Miss Hathaway. But I think it in his best interests to remain here with the servants."

"You . . . you doubt I could help him?" Beatrix managed to ask.

"The dog is excitable. He has need of absolute peace and quiet. I mean no offense in saying that the atmosphere at Ramsay House is too tumultuous for him."

Her brows rushed downward. "I beg your pardon, Captain, but you are entirely wrong. That is precisely the kind of environment Albert needs. You see, from a dog's perspective—"

"I don't need your advice."

"Yes you do," Beatrix said impulsively. "How can you be so certain that you're right? You could at least spare a moment to listen—I daresay I know more about dogs than you."

Christopher skewered her with the hard stare of a man who was not accustomed to having his decisions questioned. "No doubt you do. But I know more about this one."

"Yes, but—"

"It's time for you to leave, Miss Hathaway."

Beatrix was filled with a surge of bitter disappointment. "What do you think your servants will do with him in your absence?" she demanded, and rushed on before he could reply. "They'll keep him shut away in a shed, or locked in a room, because they're frightened of him, and that will make Albert even more of a danger. He's angry and anxious and lonely. He doesn't know what's expected of him. He needs constant attention and care, and I'm the only person who has the time and the willingness to provide those things."

"That dog has been my companion for two years," Christopher snapped. "The last thing I would subject him to is that bedlam of a household. He doesn't need chaos. He doesn't need noise and confusion—"

He was interrupted by an explosion of wild barking, accompanied by an earsplitting metallic crash. Albert had come racing through the entrance hall and had crossed paths with a housemaid bearing a tray of polished silver flatware.

Beatrix caught a glimpse of forks and spoons scattering to the doorway, just before she was thrown bodily to the receiving room floor. The impact robbed her of breath.

Stunned, she found herself pinned to the carpet and covered by a heavy masculine weight.

Dazedly she tried to take in the situation. Christopher had jumped on her. His arms were around her head . . . he had instinctively moved to shelter her with his own body. They lay together in a confusion of limbs and disheveled garments and panting breaths.

Lifting his head, Christopher cast a wary glance at their surroundings. For a moment, the blank ferocity of his face frightened Beatrix. *This,* she realized, was how he had looked in battle. This was what his enemies had seen as he had cut them down.

Albert rushed toward them, baying furiously.

"No," Beatrix said in a low tone, extending her arm to point at him. "Down."

The dog's barking flattened into a growl, and he slowly lowered to the floor. His gaze didn't move from his master.

Beatrix turned her attention back to Christopher. He was gasping and swallowing, struggling to regain his wits. "Christopher," she said carefully, but he didn't seem to hear. At this moment, no words would reach him.

She slid her arms around him, one at his shoulders, the other at his waist. He was a large man, superbly fit, his powerful body trembling. A feeling of searing tenderness swept through her, and she let her fingers stroke the rigid nape of his neck.

Albert whined softly, watching the two of them.

Beyond Christopher's shoulder, Beatrix glimpsed the housemaid standing uncertainly at the doorway, stray forks clutched in her hand.

Although Beatrix didn't give a fig about appearances or scandal, she cared very much about shielding Christopher during a vulnerable moment. He would not want anyone to see him when he was not fully in command of himself.

"Leave us," she said quietly.

"Yes, miss." Gratefully the maid fled, closing the door behind her.

Beatrix returned her attention to Christopher, who didn't

seem to have noticed the exchange. Carefully she drew his head down and turned her cheek against his glinting amber hair. And she waited, letting him feel the even rhythm of her breathing.

The scent of him was clean, summery, like hot sun and saffron. Her eyes closed as she felt his body press along hers with intriguing firmness, his knees digging into the billowing mass of her skirts.

A minute passed, and another. For the rest of her life she would remember lying alone with him in a bright square of sunlight from the window . . . the delicious weight of him, the intimate heat of his breath collecting against her neck. She would have lived in that moment forever, if it were possible. *I love you,* she thought. *I am madly, desperately, permanently in love with you.*

His head lifted, and he looked down at her with bewildered gray eyes. "Beatrix." His ragged whisper thrilled along her nerves. His hands cradled her head, long fingers weaving gently through her tumbled dark locks. "Have I hurt you?"

Beatrix's stomach went tight. She shook her head, unable to speak. Oh, the way he was looking at her, *really* looking at her . . . this was the Christopher of her dreams. This was the man who had written to her. He was so caring, and real, and dazzling, that she wanted to weep.

"I thought . . ." Christopher broke off and drew his thumb over the hot surface of her cheek.

"I know," she whispered, her nerves sparking at his touch.

"I didn't mean to do that."

"I know."

His gaze went to her parted lips, lingering until she felt it like a caress. Her heart labored to supply blood to her nerveless limbs. Every breath caused her body to lift up against his, a teasing friction of firm flesh and clean, warm linen.

Beatrix was transfixed by the subtle changes in his face, the heightening color, the silver brightness of his eyes. Possibilities entered the quietness, like sun breaking through forest canopy.

She wondered if he were going to kiss her.

And a single word flashed through her mind.

Please.

Chapter Eleven

Christopher tensed against the shaking in his muscles. His heartbeat roared in his ears. He struggled to comprehend how he had so utterly lost control of the situation. A noise had startled him, and he had reacted without thinking. He had been aware of nothing until he had found himself lying over Beatrix, trying to protect her, trying to protect them both . . . and when the ferocious heartbeat had faded from his ears, he was suffused with the hideous awareness of what he had done.

Knocking a defenseless woman to the ground. Leaping on her like a madman. *Christ.* He felt disoriented, and more than a little crazed. He might have injured her.

He had to help her up, offer an apology. Instead he watched as his exploring fingertips went to her throat, stroking a tiny pulse. Holy hell, what was he doing?

It had been a long time since a woman had held him. It felt so good that he couldn't make himself release her just yet. Her body cradled his with supple feminine strength. Those slim, gentle fingers continued to stroke the back of his neck. He had never seen such blue eyes, clear and dark like Bristol blue glass.

Christopher tried to remember the reasons why he shouldn't

want her. He even tried to summon thoughts of Prudence, but it was impossible. He closed his eyes and felt her breath striking his chin. He felt her everywhere, with his entire body, her scent in his nose and throat, her warmth sinking into him.

It seemed as if all the months and years of need had distilled to this one moment, this slender form tucked beneath his. He was actually afraid of what he might do to her. He knew he should roll away, put distance between them, but all he could do was gather in the sensations of her, the enticing rise and fall of her breasts, the feel of her legs splayed beneath the layers of her skirts. The stroke of her fingers on his nape raised chills of pleasure, and at the same time turned his flesh hot with need.

Desperately he groped for her hands and pinned them over her head.

Better.

And worse.

Her gaze provoked him, invited him closer. He could feel the force of will in her, radiant as heat, and everything in him responded to it. Fascinated, he watched a blush spread over her skin. He wanted to follow the spreading color with his fingers and mouth.

Instead he shook his head to clear it. "I'm sorry," he said, and took a rough breath. "I'm sorry," he repeated. A humorless laugh scraped in his throat. "I'm always apologizing to you."

Her wrists relaxed in his hold. "This wasn't your fault."

Christopher wondered how the hell she could appear so composed. Aside from the stain of color in her cheeks, she showed no sign of unease. He had a quick, annoying sense of being managed. "I threw you to the floor."

"Not intentionally."

Her efforts to make him feel better were having the opposite effect. "Intentions don't matter when you've been knocked over by someone twice your size."

"Intentions always matter," Beatrix said. "And I'm used to being knocked over."

He let go of her hands. "This happens to you often?" he asked sardonically.

"Oh, yes. Dogs, children . . . everyone leaps on me."

Christopher could well understand that. Leaping on her was the most pleasurable thing he'd done in years. "Being neither a dog nor a child," he said, "I have no excuse."

"The maid dropped a tray. Your reaction was perfectly understandable."

"Was it?" Christopher asked bitterly, rolling off her. "I'll be damned if I understand it."

"Of course it was," Beatrix said as he helped her up from the floor. "For a long time you've been conditioned to dive for cover every time a shell or canister exploded, or a bullet was fired. Just because you've come back home doesn't mean that such reflexes can be easily discarded."

Christopher couldn't help wondering . . . Would Prudence have forgiven him so quickly, or reacted with such self-possession?

His face darkened as a new thought occurred to him. Did he have any right to go to Prudence, when his behavior was so unpredictable? He couldn't put her at risk. He had to gain control over himself. But how? His reflexes were too strong, too fast.

At Christopher's prolonged silence, Beatrix went to Albert and bent to pet him. The dog rolled on his back, offering his tummy.

Christopher straightened his clothes and shoved his hands into his trouser pockets.

"Will you reconsider your decision?" Beatrix asked. "About letting me take Albert?"

"No," Christopher said brusquely.

"No?" she repeated, as if his refusal were inconceivable.

Christopher scowled. "You needn't worry about him. I've left the servants specific instructions. He will be well cared for."

Beatrix's face was taut with indignation. "I'm sure you believe so."

Nettled, he snapped, "I wish I took the same enjoyment in hearing your opinions that you take in airing them, Miss Hathaway."

"I stand by my opinions when I know I'm right, Captain Phelan. Whereas you stand by yours merely because you're stubborn."

Christopher gave her a stony stare. "I will escort you out."

"Don't bother. I know the way." She strode to the threshold, her back very straight.

Albert began to follow, until Christopher commanded him to come back.

Pausing at the threshold, Beatrix turned to give Christopher an oddly intent stare. "Please convey my fondness to Audrey. You both have my hopes for a pleasant journey to London." She hesitated. "If you wouldn't mind, please relay my good wishes to Prudence when you see her, and give her a message."

"What is it?"

"Tell her," Beatrix said quietly, "that I won't break my promise."

"What promise is that?"

"She'll understand."

PRECISELY THREE DAYS AFTER CHRISTOPHER AND AUDREY had left for London, Beatrix went to the Phelans' house to ask after Albert. As she had expected, the dog had set the household into chaos, having barked and howled incessantly, ripped carpeting and upholstery to shreds, and bitten a footman's hand.

"And in addition," the housekeeper, Mrs. Clocker, told Beatrix, "he won't eat. One can already see his ribs. And the master will be furious if we let anything happen to him. Oh, this is the most trying dog, the most detestable creature I've ever encountered."

A housemaid who was busy polishing the banister couldn't seem to resist commenting, "He scares me witless. I can't sleep at night, because he howls fit to wake the dead."

The housekeeper looked aggrieved. "So he does. However, the master said we mustn't let anyone take Albert. And as much as I long to be rid of the vicious beast, I fear the master's displeasure even more."

"I can help him," Beatrix said softly. "I know I can."

"The master or the dog?" Mrs. Clocker asked, as if she couldn't help herself. Her tone was wry and despairing.

"I can start with the dog," Beatrix said in a low undertone.

They exchanged a glance.

"I wish you could be given the chance," Mrs. Clocker murmured. "This household doesn't seem like a place where anyone could get better. It feels like a place where things wane and are extinguished."

This, more than anything, spurred Beatrix into a decision. "Mrs. Clocker, I would never ask you to disobey Captain Phelan's instructions. However . . . if I were to *overhear* you telling one of the housemaids where Albert is being kept at the moment, that's hardly your fault, is it? And if Albert manages to escape and run off . . . and if some unknown person were to take Albert in and care for him but did not tell you about it immediately, you could not be blamed, could you?"

Mrs. Clocker beamed at her. "You are devious, Miss Hathaway."

Beatrix smiled. "Yes, I know."

The housekeeper turned to the housemaid. "Nellie," she said clearly and distinctly. "I want to remind you that we're keeping Albert in the little blue shed next to the kitchen garden.

"Yes, mum." The housemaid didn't even glance at Beatrix. "And I should remind *you,* mum, that his leash is on the half-moon table in the entrance hall."

"Very good, Nellie. Perhaps you should run and tell the other servants and the gardener not to notice if anyone goes out to visit the blue shed."

"Yes, mum."

As the housemaid hurried away, Mrs. Clocker gave Beatrix a grateful glance. "I've heard that you work miracles with animals, Miss Hathaway. And that's indeed what it will take, to tame that flea-ridden fiend."

"I offer no miracles," Beatrix said with a smile. "Merely persistence."

"God bless you, miss. He's a savage creature. If dog is man's best friend, I worry for Captain Phelan."

"So do I," Beatrix said sincerely.

In a few minutes she had found the blue shed.

The shed, built to contain light gardening implements, shuddered as the creature inside lunged against the wall. A fury of barking erupted as Beatrix drew closer. Although Beatrix had no doubt of her ability to handle him, his ferocious baying, which sounded almost unearthly, was enough to give her pause.

"Albert?"

The barking became more passionate, with cries and whimpers breaking in.

Slowly Beatrix lowered to the ground and sat with her back against the shed. "Calm yourself, Albert," she said. "I'll let you out as soon as you're quiet."

The terrier growled and pawed at the door.

Having consulted several books on the subject of dogs, one on rough terriers in particular, Beatrix was fairly cer-

tain that training Albert with techniques involving dominance or punishment would not be at all effective. In fact,
they would probably make his behavior worse. Terriers, the
book had said, frequently tried to outsmart humans. The
only method left was to reward his good behavior with
praise and food and kindness.

"Of course you're unhappy, poor boy. He's gone away,
and your place is by his side. But I've come to collect you,
and while he's gone, we'll work on your manners. Perhaps we
can't turn you into a perfect lapdog . . . but I'll help you learn
to get on with others." She paused before adding with a reflective grin, "Of course, I can't manage to behave properly
in polite society. I've always thought there's a fair amount of
dishonesty involved in politeness. There, you're quiet now."
She stood and pulled at the latch. "Here is your first rule, Albert: it's very rude to maul people."

Albert burst out and jumped on her. Had she not been holding on to the support of the shed's frame, she would have
been knocked over. Whining and wagging his tail, Albert
stood on his hind legs and dove his face against her. He was
rawboned and ragged, and distinctly malodorous.

"My good boy," Beatrix said, petting and scratching his
coarse fur. She tried to slip the leash around his neck, but
was prevented as he wriggled to his back, his quivering legs
stuck straight into the air. Laughing, she obliged him with a
tummy rub. "Come home with me, Albert. I think you'll do
very well with the Hathaways—or at least you will after I've
given you a bath."

Chapter Twelve

Christopher delivered Audrey safely to London, where her family, the Kelseys, had welcomed her eagerly. The large Kelsey brood was overjoyed to have their sister with them. For reasons no one had quite understood, Audrey had refused to allow any of her relations to come stay with her in Hampshire after John's death. She had insisted on grieving with Mrs. Phelan unaccompanied by anyone else.

"Your mother was the only one who felt John's loss as keenly as I did," Audrey had explained to Christopher during the carriage drive to London. "There was a kind of relief in that. Any of my family would have tried to make me feel better, and surrounded me with love and comfort, which would have kept me from grieving properly. The whole thing would have been drawn out. No, it was the right thing to live in grief for as long as I needed. Now it's time to recover."

"You're very good at organizing your feelings, aren't you?" Christopher had asked dryly.

"I suppose I am. I wish I could organize yours. At present they seem to resemble an overturned drawer of neckcloths."

"Not neckcloths," he said. "Flatware, with sharp edges."

Audrey had smiled. "I pity those who find themselves in

the way of your feelings." Pausing, she had studied Christopher with fond concern. "How difficult it is to look at you," she commented, startling him. "It's the resemblance you bear to John. You're more handsome than he was, of course, but I preferred his face. A wonderful everyday face—I never tired of it. Yours is a bit too intimidating for my taste. You resemble an aristocrat far more than John did, you know."

Christopher's gaze darkened as he thought of some of the men he'd fought with, who'd been fortunate to survive their wounds, but had suffered some manner of disfigurement. They had wondered how they would be received upon their return home, if wives or sweethearts would turn away in horror from their ruined appearances. "It doesn't matter what someone looks like," he said. "All that matters is what he is."

"I'm so very glad to hear you say that."

Christopher gave her a speculative glance. "What are you leading to?"

"Nothing. Except . . . I want to ask you something. If another woman—say, Beatrix Hathaway—and Prudence Mercer were to exchange appearances, and all that you esteemed in Prudence was transferred to Beatrix . . . would you want Beatrix?"

"Good God, no."

"Why not?" she asked indignantly.

"Because I know Beatrix Hathaway, and she's nothing like Pru."

"You do not know Beatrix. You haven't spent nearly enough time with her."

"I know that she's unruly, opinionated, and far more cheerful than any reasoning person should be. She wears breeches, climbs trees, and roams wherever she pleases without a chaperone. I also know that she has overrun Ramsay House with squirrels, hedgehogs, and goats, and the man unlucky enough to marry her will be driven to financial ruin from the veterinary bills. Would you care to contradict any of those points?"

Audrey folded her arms and gave him a sour look. "Yes. She doesn't have a squirrel."

Reaching inside his coat, Christopher pulled out the letter from Pru, the one he carried with him always. It had become a talisman, a symbol of what he had fought for. A reason for living. He looked down at the bit of folded paper, not even needing to open it. The words had been seared into his heart.

"Please come home and find me . . ."

In the past he had wondered if he were incapable of love. None of his love affairs had ever lasted more than a matter of months, and although they had blazed on a physical level, they had never transcended that. Ultimately no particular woman had ever seemed all that different from the rest.

Until those letters. The sentences had looped around him with a spirit so artless and adorable, he had loved it, loved her, immediately.

His thumb moved over the parchment as if it were sensitive living skin. "Mark my words, Audrey—I'm going to marry the woman who wrote this letter."

"I am marking your words," she assured him. "We'll see if you live up to them."

The London season would last until August, when Parliament ended and the aristocracy would retire to their country estates. There they would hunt, shoot, and indulge in Friday-to-Monday amusements. While in town, Christopher would sell his army commission and meet with his grandfather to discuss his new responsibilities as the heir of Riverton. He would also renew acquaintances with old friends and spend time with some men from his regiment.

And most importantly, he would find Prudence.

Christopher was uncertain how to approach her, after the way she had broken off their correspondence.

It was his fault. He had declared himself too early. He had been too impetuous.

No doubt Prudence had been wise to break off their communications. She was a gently bred young woman. Serious courtship had to be approached with patience and moderation.

If that was what Prudence wanted of him, she would have it.

He arranged for a suite of rooms at the Rutledge, an elegant hotel favored by European royalty, American entrepreneurs, and British aristocrats who did not maintain town residences. The Rutledge was unparalleled in comfort and luxury, and was arguably worth the exorbitant price of lodging there. As Christopher checked into the hotel and conversed with the concierge, he remarked on a portrait that hung over the marble mantel in the lobby. The subject was a singularly beautiful woman with mahogany-colored hair and striking blue eyes.

"That is a portrait of Mrs. Rutledge, sir," the concierge said with a touch of fond pride. "A beauty, is she not? A better, kinder lady could not be found anywhere."

Christopher regarded the portrait with casual interest. He recalled that Amelia Hathaway had said one of her sisters had married Harry Rutledge, the owner of the hotel. "Then Mrs. Rutledge is one of the Hathaway sisters of Hampshire?"

"Just so, sir."

That had brought a quizzical smile to Christopher's lips. Harry Rutledge, being a wealthy and well-connected man, could have had any woman he wanted. What madness had inspired him to marry into such a family? It was the eyes, Christopher decided, looking closer, unwillingly fascinated. Hathaway blue, heavily lashed. Exactly like Beatrix's.

The day after Christopher took up residence in the Rutledge, invitations flooded in. Balls, soirees, dinners, musical evenings . . . even a summons to dine at Buckingham Palace, where the composer Johann Strauss and his orchestra would play.

After a few inquiries, Christopher accepted an invitation to a private ball that, it was confirmed, Miss Prudence Mercer and her mother had consented to attend. The ball was held at a Mayfair mansion, built on a grand scale in the Italianate style, with an extensive outer forecourt and a central balconied hall that rose three full stories. Populated by aristocrats, foreign diplomats, and celebrated artists in various fields, the ball was a glittering display of wealth and social prominence.

The crowded atmosphere engendered a feeling of vague panic in Christopher's chest. Battening down the anxiety, he went to exchange pleasantries with the hosts. Although he would have preferred to wear civilian attire, he was obliged to wear his dress uniform of rifle green and black, with epaulettes of worsted crescents at the shoulders. As his commission had not yet been sold, it would have caused much comment and disapproval had he not worn the uniform. Worse, he was also obliged to wear all the medals that had been bestowed on him—to leave one off would have been in bad form. The medals had been intended as badges of honor. To Christopher, they represented events he longed to forget.

There were other officers in their various uniforms, scarlet or black trimmed with gold. The attention they garnered, especially from women, only increased Christopher's unease.

He searched for Prudence, but she wasn't in the parlor or drawing room. Minute after painstaking minute he made his way through the crowd, stopping frequently as he was recognized by an acquaintance and forced to make conversation.

Where the devil was Prudence?

"*. . . you could pick me out of a crowd blindfolded. Simply follow the scent of scorched stockings.*"

The thought brought a faint smile to his lips.

Restless and full of wanting, he went into the ballroom. His heartbeat had lodged in the base of his throat.

His breath fractured as he saw her.

Prudence was even more beautiful than he had remembered. She wore a pink gown with lace-trimmed ruffles, her hands tucked into little white gloves. Having just concluded a dance, she stood chatting with an admirer, her expression serene.

Christopher felt as if he had traveled a million miles to reach her. The extent of his own need stunned him. The sight of her, along with the luminous echo of her words, gave him a sense of something he had not felt for a long time.

Hope.

As Christopher reached her, Prudence turned and looked up at him. Her clear green eyes widened, and she laughed with incredulous delight. "My dear Captain Phelan." She extended her gloved hand, and he bent over it and closed his eyes briefly. Her hand in his.

How long he had waited for this moment. How he had dreamed of it.

"As dashing as ever." Prudence smiled at him. "More so, actually. How does it feel to have so many medals pinned to one's chest?"

"Heavy," he said, and she laughed.

"I had despaired of ever seeing you . . ."

Thinking at first that she was referring to the Crimea, Christopher felt a thrill of heat.

But she continued, ". . . since you've been unforgivably elusive upon returning to England." She curved her lips in a provocative smile. "But of course you knew that would only make you more sought after."

"Believe me," he said, "it is not my wish to be sought after."

"You are, however. Every host and hostess in London would love to claim you as a guest." A delicate giggle escaped her. "And every girl wants to marry you."

He wanted to hold her. He wanted to bury his face in her hair. "I may not be fit to marry."

"*La,* of course you are. You're a national hero *and* the heir to Riverton. A man can scarcely be more fit than that."

Christopher stared into her beautiful, fine-featured face, at the gleam of her pearly teeth. She was talking to him as she always had, flirtatious, light, teasing.

"The inheritance of Riverton is hardly a foregone conclusion," he told her. "My grandfather could leave it to one of my cousins."

"After the way you distinguished yourself in the Crimea? I doubt that." She smiled at him. "What moved you to finally make your appearance in society?"

He replied in a low voice. "I followed my lodestar."

"Your . . ." Prudence hesitated and smiled. "Oh, yes. I remember."

But something about that hesitation bothered him.

The hot, joyous urgency began to fade.

No doubt it was unreasonable of him to expect Prudence to remember everything. Christopher had read her letters a thousand times, until every word had been permanently engraved on his soul. But he could hardly expect that she would have done the same. Her life had gone on much the same. His had changed in every regard.

"Do you still like to dance, Captain?" she asked, her long lashes sweeping over vivid green eyes.

"With you as a partner, yes." He proffered his arm, and she took it without hesitation.

They danced. The woman he loved was in his arms.

It should have been the finest night of his life. But in a matter of minutes he began to realize that the long-awaited relief was no more substantial than a bridge made of smoke.

Something was wrong.

Something wasn't real.

Chapter Thirteen

In the weeks that followed, Christopher frequently recalled what Audrey had said about Prudence, that there was nothing beneath the layers of artifice. But there had to be. He hadn't imagined those letters. *Someone* had written them.

He had asked Prudence early on about the last letter she had written . . . *"I'm not who you think I am"* . . . about what she had meant, and why she had stopped corresponding with him.

Prudence had turned red and looked awkward, so different from her usual fetching blushes. It was the first sign of real emotion he had seen in her. "I . . . I suppose I wrote that because . . . I was embarrassed, you see."

"Why?" Christopher had asked tenderly, drawing her farther into the shadowed corner of a balcony terrace. He had touched her upper arms with his gloved hands, exerting the faintest of pressures to bring her closer. "I adored the things you wrote." Longing pressed against his heart and made his pulse unsteady. "When you stopped . . . I would have gone mad, except . . . you asked me to come find you."

"Oh, yes, so I did. I suppose . . . I was alarmed by how I had behaved, writing such silly things . . ."

He eased her closer, every movement careful, as if she were infinitely fragile. His mouth pressed against the thin, delicate skin of her temple. "Pru . . . I dreamed of holding you like this . . . all those nights . . ."

Her arms slid around his neck, and her head tipped back naturally. He kissed her, his mouth gentle and searching. She responded at once, her lips parting softly. It was a lovely kiss. But it did nothing to satisfy him, nothing to ease the angry ache of need. It seemed that his dreams of kissing Prudence had somehow eclipsed reality.

Dreams had a way of doing that.

Prudence turned her face aside with a discomfited laugh. "You're very eager."

"Forgive me." Christopher released her at once. She stayed close to him, the floral scent of her perfume thickening the air around them. He kept his hands on her, his palms curving around her shoulders. He kept expecting to feel something . . . but the region around his heart was locked in ice.

Somehow he had thought . . . but that was unreasonable. No woman on earth could have fulfilled such expectations.

FOR THE DURATION OF THE SEASON, CHRISTOPHER SOUGHT out Prudence, meeting her at dances and dinners, taking her and Mrs. Mercer on carriage drives, scenic walks, and to art and museum exhibits.

There was little that Christopher could fault in Prudence. She was beautiful and charming. She didn't ask uncomfortable questions. In fact, she rarely asked personal questions of him at all. She evinced no interest in the war or the battles he had fought, only in his medals. He wondered if she thought of them as anything more than shiny decorations.

They had the same bland and pleasant conversations, spiced with gossip, that Christopher had had a thousand times before, with other women, during other seasons in London. And that had always been enough for him.

He wished to hell it were enough now.

He had thought . . . hoped . . . that Prudence cared for him in some way. But there was no sign of that now, no tenderness, no trace of the woman who had written *"I carry thoughts of you like my own personal constellation . . ."*

And he loved her so desperately, the Prudence of the letters. Where was she? Why was she hiding from him?

His dreams led him into dark forests, where he searched through bramble and bracken, pushing through the narrow spaces between the trees as he followed the pale form of a woman. She was always just ahead of him, always out of reach. He woke gasping and enraged, his hands clutching on emptiness.

During the days, Christopher kept his business appointments and social engagements. So many tiny, overstuffed, overdecorated rooms. So much pointless conversation. So many events of no consequence. He could not fathom that he had once enjoyed it all. And he was appalled to find himself remembering moments in the Crimea with something like nostalgia, actually yearning for the brief times when he had felt fully alive.

Even with the enemy in battle he had felt some form of connection, in their efforts to understand and reach and kill each other. But with these patricians trussed in elegant clothes and brittle sophistication, he no longer felt kinship or liking. He knew himself to be different. And he knew they sensed it as well.

Christopher comprehended just how desperate he was for something or someone familiar, when the prospect of visiting his grandfather was actually appealing.

Lord Annandale had always been a stern and intimidating

grandparent, never one to spare his withering comments. None of Annandale's grandchildren, including the cousin who would someday inherit the earldom, had ever pleased the demanding old bastard. Except for John, of course. Christopher had deliberately gone the other way.

Christopher approached his grandfather with a mixture of dread and reluctant compassion, knowing that the old man must have been devastated by John's death.

Upon arriving at Annandale's luxuriously appointed London house, Christopher was shown to the library, where a fire had been lit in the hearth despite the fact that it was the height of summer.

"Good God, Grandfather," he said, nearly recoiling at the blast of heat as he entered the library. "You'll have us braised like a pair of game hens." Striding to the window, he flung it open and drew in a breath of outside air. "You could easily heat yourself with a walk out-of-doors."

His grandfather scowled at him from a chair beside the hearth. "The doctor has advised against outside air. I would advise you to negotiate your inheritance before you try to finish me off."

"There's nothing to negotiate. Leave me whatever you wish—or nothing, if it pleases you."

"Manipulative as always," Annandale muttered. "You assume I'll do the reverse of whatever you say."

Christopher smiled and shrugged out of his coat. He tossed it to a nearby chair as he approached his grandfather. He went to shake his hand, enclosing the frail and cold fingers in his own warm grasp. "Hello, sir. You're looking well."

"I am not well," Annandale retorted. "I'm old. Navigating life with this body is like trying to sail a shipwreck."

Taking the other chair, Christopher studied his grandfather. There was a new delicacy about Annandale, his skin like swaths of crumpled silk laid over an iron frame. The eyes, however, were the same, bright and piercing. And his brows, in defiance of the snowy whiteness of his hair, were the same thick black as ever.

"I've missed you," Christopher commented in a tone of mild surprise. "Though I can't decide why. It must be the glare—it brings me back to my childhood."

"You were ever a hellion," Annandale informed him, "and selfish to the bone. When I read Russell's reports of your battlefield heroics, I was certain they had mistaken you for someone else."

Christopher grinned. "If I was heroic, it was purely accidental. I was only trying to save my own skin."

A rumble of amusement came from the old man's throat before he could prevent it. His brows lowered again. "You conducted yourself with honor, it seems. There is talk of a knighthood being bestowed on you. To that end, you might try being receptive to the queen's invitations. Your refusal to stay in London upon your return from the Crimea was not well regarded."

Christopher gave him a baleful glance. "I don't want to entertain people like some trained monkey. I'm no different from thousands of other men who did what they were supposed to do."

"Such modesty is new for you," his grandfather observed idly. "Is it genuine, or merely for my benefit?"

Remaining morosely silent, Christopher tugged irritably at his cravat, untied and unwound it, and let it hang on either side of his neck. When that didn't serve to cool him, he went to the open window.

He looked down at the street. It was crowded and quarrelsome—people lived out in public in the warmer months—sitting or standing in doorways, eating, drinking, and talking while vehicles and hooves stirred up hot fetid dust. Christopher's attention was caught by a dog that sat in the back of a little cart as his master guided a swaybacked pony along the thoroughfare. Thinking of Albert, he was wrenched with remorse. He wished he had brought the dog to London. But no, the hubbub and the confinement would have driven poor Albert mad. He was better off in the country.

He dragged his attention back to his grandfather, realizing that he was saying something.

". . . have reconsidered the question of your inheritance. I had originally set aside very little for you. The lion's share was, of course, for your brother. If there was ever a man who deserved Riverton more than John Phelan, I have not met him."

"Agreed," Christopher said quietly.

"But now he is gone with no heir, which leaves only you. And though your character has shown signs of improvement, I'm not convinced that you're worthy of Riverton."

"Neither am I." Christopher paused. "I want nothing that you had originally intended for John."

"I will tell you what you will have, regardless of what you want." Annandale's tone was firm, but not unkind. "You have responsibilities, my boy, and they are not to be dismissed or evaded. But before I lay out your course, I want to ask something."

Christopher regarded him without expression. "Yes, sir."

"Why did you fight as you did? Why did you risk death so often? Did you do it for the good of the country?"

Christopher snorted in disgust. "The war wasn't for the good of the country. It was for the benefit of private mercantile interests, and fueled by the conceit of politicians."

"You fought for the glory and the medals, then?"

"Hardly."

"Then why?"

Silently Christopher sorted through possible answers. Finding the truth, he examined it with weary resignation before he spoke. "Everything I did was for my men. For the noncommissioned ones who had joined the army to avoid starvation or the workhouse. And for the junior officers who were experienced and long-serving but hadn't the means to buy a commission. I had the command only because I'd had money to purchase it, not for any reason of merit. Absurd. And the men in my company, the poor bastards, were supposed to follow me, whether I proved to be incompetent, an imbecile, or a coward. They had no choice but to depend on me. And therefore I had no choice but to try and be the leader they needed. I tried to keep them alive." He hesitated. "I failed far too often. And now I would love for someone to tell me how to live with their deaths on my conscience." Focusing blindly on a distant patch of carpeting, he heard himself say, "I don't want Riverton. I've had enough of being given things I don't deserve."

Annandale looked at him in a way he never had before, speculative and almost kind. "That is why you will have it. I won't pare a shilling or a single inch of land from what I would have given John. I am willing to gamble that you will care for your tenants and workingmen out of the same sense of responsibility you felt for your men." He paused. "Perhaps you and Riverton will be good for each other. It was to be John's burden. Now it is yours."

AS A SLOW, HOT AUGUST SETTLED OVER LONDON, THE coagulating stench began to drive the town dwellers to the sweeter air of the country. Christopher was more than ready to return to Hampshire. It was becoming apparent that London had done him no good.

Nearly every day was fraught with images that leaped at him from nowhere, startlements, difficulty in concentrating. Nightmares and sweats when he slept, melancholy when he awakened. He heard the sound of guns and shells when there were none, felt his heartbeat begin to hammer or his hands tremble for no reason. It was impossible to lower his guard, regardless of the circumstances. He had visited old friends in his regiment, but when he had tentatively asked if they were suffering from the same mysterious ailments, he was met with determined silence. It was not to be discussed. It was to be managed alone, and privately, in any manner that worked.

The only thing that helped was strong spirits. Christopher dosed himself until the warm, blurring comfort of alcohol quieted his seething brain. And he tried to measure its effects so that he could be sober when he had to. Concealing the encroaching madness as well as he could, he wondered when or how or if he was going to get better.

As for Prudence . . . she was a dream he had to let go of. A ruined illusion. Part of him died a little more each time he saw her. She felt no real love for him, that was clear. Nothing like what she had written. Perhaps in an effort to entertain him, she had culled parts of novels or plays, and copied them into the letters. He had believed in an illusion.

He knew that Prudence and her parents hoped he would offer for her, now that the season was drawing to a close. Her mother, in particular, had been hinting heavily about marriage, a dowry, promises of beautiful children and domestic tranquility. He was in no condition, however, to be a fit husband for anyone.

With mingled dread and relief, Christopher went to the Mercers' London residence to make his farewells. When he asked for permission to speak privately with Prudence, her mother left them in the parlor for a few minutes with the door left conspicuously open.

"But . . . but . . ." Prudence said in dismay when he told her he was leaving town, "you won't go without first talking to my father, will you?"

"Talk to him about what?" Christopher asked, although he knew.

"I should think you'd want to ask for his permission to court me formally," Prudence said, looking indignant.

He met her green eyes directly. "At the moment, I'm not at liberty to do that."

"Not at liberty?" Prudence jumped up, obliging him to stand, and gave him a glance of baffled fury. "Of course you are. There is no other woman, is there?"

"No."

"Your business affairs are settled, and your inheritance is in order?"

"Yes."

"Then there is no reason to wait. You've certainly given every impression that you care for me. Especially when you first returned—you told me so many times how you had longed to see me, how much I had meant to you . . . Why have your passions cooled?"

"I expected—hoped—that you would be more like you were in the letters." Christopher paused, staring at her closely. "I've often wondered . . . did someone help you to write them?"

Although Prudence had the face of an angel, the fury in her eyes was the exact opposite of heavenly serenity. "Oh! Why are you always asking me about those stupid letters? They were only words. Words mean nothing!"

"You've made me realize that words are the most important things in the world . . ."

"Nothing," Christopher repeated, staring at her.

"Yes." Prudence looked slightly mollified as she saw that she had gained his entire attention. "I'm here, Christopher. I'm real. You don't need silly old letters now. You have *me*."

"What about when you wrote to me about the quintessence?" he asked. "Did that mean nothing?"

"The—" Prudence stared at him, flushing. "I can't recall what I meant by that."

"The fifth element, according to Aristotle," he prompted gently.

Her color drained, leaving her bone-white. She looked like a guilty child caught in an act of mischief. "What has that to do with anything?" she cried, taking refuge in anger. "I want to talk about something real. Who cares about Aristotle?"

"I do like the idea that there's a little starlight in each of us . . ."

She had never written those words.

For a moment Christopher couldn't react. One thought followed another, each connecting briefly like the hands of men in a torch race. Some entirely different woman had written to him . . . with Prudence's consent . . . he had been deceived . . . Audrey must have known . . . he had been made to care . . . and then the letters had stopped. *Why?*

"I'm not who you think I am . . ."

Christopher felt his throat and chest tightening, heard a rasp of something that sounded like a wondering laugh.

Prudence laughed as well, the sound edged with relief. She had no idea in hell what had caused his bitter amusement.

Had they wanted to make a fool of him? Had it been intended as revenge for some past slight? By God, he would find who had done it, and why.

He had loved and been betrayed by someone whose name he didn't know. He loved her still—that was the unforgivable part. And she would pay, whoever she was.

It felt good to have a purpose again, to hunt someone for the purpose of inflicting damage. It felt familiar. It was who he was.

His smile, thin as a knife edge, cut through the cold fury.

Prudence gazed at him uncertainly. "Christopher?" she faltered. "What are you thinking?"

He went to her and took her shoulders in his hands, thinking briefly of how easy it would be to slide his hands up to her neck and throttle her. He shaped his mouth into a charming smile. "Only that you're right," he said. "Words aren't important. This is what's important." He kissed her slowly, expertly, until he felt her slender body relax against his. Prudence made a little sound of pleasure, her arms linking around his neck. "Before I leave for Hampshire," Christopher murmured against her blushing cheek, "I'll ask your father for formal permission to court you. Does that please you?"

"Oh, yes," Prudence cried, her face radiant. "Oh, Christopher . . . do I have your heart?"

"You have my heart," Christopher said tonelessly, holding her close, while his cold gaze fastened on a distant point outside the window.

Except that he had no heart left to give.

"WHERE IS SHE?" WERE CHRISTOPHER'S FIRST WORDS TO Audrey, the moment he had reached her parents' home in Kensington. He had gone to her immediately after leaving Prudence. "*Who* is she?"

His sister-in-law seemed unimpressed by his fury. "Please do not scowl at me. What are you talking about?"

"Did Prudence put the letters directly into your hand, or did someone else give them to you?"

"Oh." Audrey looked serene. Sitting on the parlor settee, she took up a small needlework hoop and examined a patch of embroidery. "So you've finally realized that Prudence didn't write them. What gave her away?"

"The fact that she knew the contents of my letters, but nothing of the ones *she* sent." Christopher stood over her, glowering. "It was one of her friends, wasn't it? Tell me which one."

"I can confirm nothing."

"Was Beatrix Hathaway part of it?"

Audrey rolled her eyes. "Why would Beatrix want to take part in something like this?"

"Revenge. Because I once said that she belonged in the stables."

"You denied having said that."

"*You* said that I said it! Set that hoop down, or I swear I'll wrap it around your throat. Understand something, Audrey: I am scarred from neck to foot. I have been shot, stabbed, bayoneted, struck by shrapnel, and treated by doctors so drunk they could barely stay on their feet." A savage pause. "And none of that hurt like this."

"I'm sorry," Audrey said in a subdued tone. "I would never have agreed to any scheme that I thought would cause you unhappiness. It began as an act of kindness. At least that's what I believe."

Kindness? Christopher was revolted by the idea that he had been viewed as the object of pity. "Why in God's name did you help someone to deceive me?"

"I was barely aware of it," she flared. "I was half dead from caring for John—I wasn't eating or sleeping—and I was exhausted. I didn't think much about it at all, other than to decide that it would do no harm for someone to write to you."

"It did, damn you!"

"You wanted to believe it was Prudence," she accused. "Otherwise it would have been obvious that she wasn't the author of the letters."

"I was in the middle of a bloody *war.* I didn't have time to examine participles and prepositions while hauling my arse in and out of trenches—"

He was interrupted by a voice from the doorway. "Audrey." It was one of her tall, strapping brothers, Gavin. He leaned negligently against the frame, giving Christopher a warning stare. "One can't help hearing the pair of you quarreling all through the house. Do you need help?"

"No, thank you," Audrey said firmly. "I can manage this on my own, Gavin."

Her brother smiled faintly. "Actually, I was asking Phelan."

"He doesn't need help, either," Audrey said with great dignity. "Please allow us a few minutes alone, Gavin. We have something important to settle."

"Very well. But I won't go far."

Sighing, Audrey looked after her overprotective brother and returned her attention to Christopher.

He gave her a hard stare. "I want a name."

"Only if you swear that you will not hurt this woman."

"I swear it."

"Swear it on John's grave," she insisted.

A long silence passed.

"I knew it," Audrey said grimly. "If you can't be trusted not to hurt her, I certainly can't tell you who she is."

"Is she married?" A hoarse note had entered his voice.

"No."

"Is she in Hampshire?"

Audrey hesitated before giving him a wary nod.

"Tell her that I'll find her," he said. "And she'll regret it when I do."

In the tense silence, he went to the threshold and glanced over his shoulder. "In the meantime, you can be the first to congratulate me," he said. "Prudence and I are nearly betrothed."

Audrey looked ashen. "Christopher . . . what kind of game are you playing?"

"You'll find out," came his cold reply. "You and your mysterious friend should enjoy it—you both seem to like games."

Chapter Fourteen

W hat the devil are you eating?" Leo, Lord Ramsay, stood in the family parlor at Ramsay House, viewing his dark-haired twins, Edward and Emmaline, who were playing on the carpeted floor.

His wife, Catherine, who was helping the babies to build block towers, looked up with a smile. "They're eating biscuits."

"These?" Leo glanced at a bowl of little brown biscuits that had been placed on a table. "They look revoltingly similar to the ones Beatrix has been feeding the dog."

"That's because they are."

"They're . . . Good God, Cat! What can you be thinking?" Lowering to his haunches, Leo tried to pry a sodden biscuit away from Edward.

Leo's efforts were met with an indignant squall.

"Mine!" Edward cried, clutching the biscuit more tightly.

"Let him have it," Catherine protested. "The twins are teething, and the biscuits are very hard. There's nothing harmful in them."

"How do you know that?"

"Beatrix made them."

"Beatrix doesn't cook. To my knowledge, she can barely butter her bread."

"I don't cook for people," Beatrix said cheerfully, coming into the parlor with Albert padding after her. "But I do for dogs."

"Naturally." Leo took one of the brown lumps from the bowl, examining it closely. "Would you care to reveal the ingredients of these disgusting objects?"

"Oats, honey, eggs . . . they're very nourishing."

As if to underscore the point, Catherine's pet ferret, Dodger, streaked up to Leo, took the biscuit from him, and slithered beneath a nearby chair.

Catherine laughed low in her throat as she saw Leo's expression. "They're made of the same stuff as teething biscuits, my lord."

"Very well," Leo said darkly. "But if the twins start barking and burying their toys, I'll know whom to blame." He lowered to the floor beside his daughter.

Emmaline gave him a wet grin and pushed her own sodden biscuit toward his mouth. "Here, Papa."

"No, thank you, darling." Becoming aware of Albert nosing at his shoulder, Leo turned to pet him. "Is this a dog or a street broom?"

"It's Albert," Beatrix replied.

The dog promptly collapsed to his side, tail thumping the floor repeatedly.

Beatrix smiled. Three months earlier, such a scene would have been unimaginable. Albert would have been so hostile and fearful that she wouldn't have dared to expose him to children.

But with patience, love, and discipline—not to mention a great deal of help from Rye—Albert had become a different dog altogether. Gradually he had become accustomed to the constant activity in the household, including the presence of other animals. Now he greeted newness with curiosity rather than fear and aggression.

Albert had also gained some much-needed weight, looking sleek and healthy. Beatrix had painstakingly groomed him, stripping and trimming his fur regularly, but leaving the adorable whisks that gave his face a whimsical expression. When Beatrix walked Albert to the village, children gathered around him, and he submitted happily to their petting. He loved to play and fetch. He stole shoes and tried to bury them when no one was looking. He was, in short, a thoroughly normal dog.

Although Beatrix was still pining after Christopher, still in despair over him, she had discovered that the best remedy for heartache was trying to make herself useful to others. There were always people in need of assistance, including the tenants and cottagers who resided on the Ramsay lands. And with her sister Win away in Ireland, and Amelia busy with the household, Beatrix was the only sister left who had the time and means for charitable work. She took food to the sick and poor in the village, read to an elderly woman with failing eyesight, and became involved with the causes of the local church. Beatrix found that such work was its own reward. She was far less likely to fall into melancholy when she was busy.

Now, watching Albert with Leo, Beatrix wondered how Christopher would react when he saw the changes in his dog.

"Is he a new member of the family?" Leo asked.

"No, merely a guest," Beatrix replied. "He belongs to Captain Phelan."

"We saw Phelan on a few occasions during the season," Leo remarked. A smile touched his lips. "I told him that if he insists on winning at cards every time we play, I would have to avoid him in the future."

"How was Captain Phelan when you saw him?" Beatrix

asked, striving to sound diffident. "Did he seem well? Was he in good spirits?"

Catherine answered thoughtfully. "He looked to be in good health, and he was certainly very charming. He was often seen in the company of Prudence Mercer."

Beatrix felt a sickening pang of jealousy. She averted her face. "How nice," she said in a muffled voice. "I'm sure they make a handsome pair."

"There is a rumor of a betrothal," Catherine added. She sent a teasing smile to her husband. "Perhaps Captain Phelan will finally succumb to the love of a good woman."

"He's certainly succumbed to enough of the other kind," Leo replied, in a holier-than-thou tone that made her erupt in laughter.

"Pot, may I introduce you to kettle?" Catherine accused, her eyes twinkling.

"That was all in the past," Leo informed her.

"Are wicked women more entertaining?" Beatrix asked him.

"No, darling. But one needs them for contrast."

Beatrix was subdued for the rest of the evening, inwardly miserable at the thought of Christopher and Prudence together. Betrothed. Married. Sharing the same name.

Sharing the same bed.

She had never experienced jealousy before now, and it was agonizing. It was like a slow death by poison. Prudence had spent the summer being courted by a handsome and heroic soldier, whereas Beatrix had spent the summer with his dog.

And soon he would come to retrieve Albert, and she wouldn't even have his dog.

IMMEDIATELY UPON HIS RETURN TO STONY CROSS, CHRISTO-pher learned that Beatrix Hathaway had stolen Albert. The servants didn't even have the decency to look apologetic about it, offering some preposterous story about the dog having run off, and Beatrix having insisted on taking him in.

Although he was weary from the twelve-hour journey from London, and he was starved and travel dusty and in an unbelievably foul temper, Christopher found himself riding to Ramsay House. It was time to put a stop to Beatrix's meddling once and for all.

Dark was lowering by the time he reached Ramsay House, shadows creeping from the woodlands until the trees resembled curtains drawn back to present a view of the house. The last vestiges of light imparted a ruddy glow to the brick and glittered on the multipaned windows. With its charming irregular roofline and sprouting chimneys, the house seemed to have grown from the fertile Hampshire land as if it were part of the forest, a living thing that had sent down roots and was reaching toward the sky.

There was an orderly bustle of outside staff, footmen and gardeners and stablemen, retiring to the indoors after the day's labors. Animals were being led to the barn, horses to the stables. Christopher paused on the drive for a short, staying moment, assessing the situation. He felt apart from the scene, an intruder.

Determined to make the visit short and efficient, Christopher rode to the entrance, allowed a footman to take the reins, and strode to the front door.

The housekeeper came to greet him, and he asked to see Beatrix.

"The family is having dinner, sir—" the housekeeper began.

"I don't care. Either bring Miss Hathaway to me, or I'll find her myself." He had already resolved that the Hathaway household would do nothing to distract or divert him. No doubt after a summer spent with his cantankerous dog, they would hand Albert over without a qualm. As for Beatrix—he only hoped she would try to stop him, so that he could make a few things clear to her.

"Would you care to wait in the front parlor, sir?"

Christopher shook his head wordlessly.

Looking perturbed, the housekeeper left him in the entrance hall.

In no time at all, Beatrix appeared. She was wearing a white dress made of thin, flowing layers, the bodice wrapped intricately over the curves of her breasts. The translucence of her chest and upper arms gave her the look of emerging from the white silk.

For a woman who had stolen his dog, she was remarkably composed.

"Captain Phelan." She stopped before him with a graceful curtsy.

Christopher stared at her in fascination, trying to retain his righteous anger, but it was slipping away like sand through his fingers. "Where are your breeches?" he found himself asking in a husky voice.

Beatrix smiled. "I thought you might come to fetch Albert soon, and I didn't want to offend you by wearing masculine attire."

"If you were all that concerned about giving offense, you would have thought twice before abducting my dog."

"I didn't abduct him. He went with me willingly."

"I seem to recall telling you to stay away from him."

"Yes, I know." Her tone was contrite. "But Albert preferred to stay here for the summer. He has done very well with us, by the way." She paused, looking him over. "How are you?"

"I'm exhausted," Christopher said curtly. "I've just arrived from London."

"Poor man. You must be famished. Come have dinner."

"Thank you, but no. All I want is to collect my dog and go home." *And drink myself into a stupor.* "Where is Albert?"

"He'll be here momentarily. I asked our housekeeper to fetch him."

Christopher blinked. "She's not afraid of him?"

"Of Albert? Heavens, no, everyone adores him."

The concept of someone, *anyone,* adoring his belligerent pet was difficult to grasp. Having expected to receive an inventory of all the damage Albert had caused, Christopher gave her a blank look.

And then the housekeeper returned with an obedient and well-groomed dog trotting by her side.

"Albert?" Christopher said.

The dog looked at him, ears twitching. His whiskered face changed, eyes brightening with excitement. Without hesitating, Albert launched forward with a happy yelp. Christopher knelt on the floor, gathering up an armful of joyfully wriggling canine. Albert strained to lick him, and whimpered and dove against him repeatedly.

Christopher was overwhelmed by feelings of kinship and relief. Gripping the warm, compact body close, Christopher murmured his name and petted him roughly, and Albert whined and trembled.

"I missed you, Albert. Good boy. There's my boy." Unable to help himself, Christopher pressed his face against the rough fur. He was undone by guilt, humbled by the fact that even though he had abandoned Albert for the summer, the dog showed nothing but eager welcome. "I was away too long," Christopher murmured, looking into the soulful brown eyes. "I won't leave you again." He dragged his gaze up to Beatrix's. "It was a mistake to leave him," he said gruffly.

She was smiling at him. "Albert won't hold it against you. To err is human, to forgive, canine."

To his disbelief, Christopher felt an answering smile tug at the corners of his lips. He continued to pet the dog, who was fit and sleek. "You've taken good care of him."

"He's much better behaved than before," she said. "You can take him anywhere now."

Rising to his feet, Christopher looked down at her. "Why did you do it?" he asked softly.

"He's very much worth saving. Anyone could see that."

The awareness between them became unbearably acute. Christopher's heart worked in hard, uneven beats. How pretty she was in the white dress. She radiated a healthy female physicality that was very different from the fashionable frailty of London women. He wondered what it would be like to bed her, if she would be as direct in her passions as she was in everything else.

"Stay for dinner," she urged.

He shook his head. "I must go."

"Have you eaten already?"

"No. But I'll find something in the larder at home."

Albert sat and watched them attentively.

"You need a proper meal after traveling so far."

"Miss Hathaway—" But his breath was clipped as Beatrix took his arm with both hands, one at his wrist, one at his elbow. She gave a gentle tug. He felt it all the way to his groin, his body responding actively to her touch. Annoyed and aroused, he looked down into her dark blue eyes.

"I don't want to talk to anyone," he told her.

"Of course you don't. That's perfectly all right." Another small, entreating tug. "Come."

And somehow Christopher found himself going with Beatrix, through the entrance hall and along a hallway lined with pictures. Albert padded after them without a sound.

Beatrix released his arm as they entered a dining room filled with abundant candlelight. The table was laden with silver and crystal, and a great quantity of food. He recognized Leo, Lord Ramsay, and his wife, and Rohan and Amelia. The dark-haired boy, Rye, was also at the table. Pausing at the threshold, Christopher bowed and said uncomfortably, "Forgive me. I merely came to—"

"I've invited Captain Phelan to join us," Beatrix announced. "He doesn't want to talk. Do not ask him direct questions unless absolutely necessary."

The rest of the family received this unorthodox pronouncement without turning a hair. A footman was dispatched to set a place for him.

"Come in, Phelan," Leo said easily. "We love silent guests—it allows us to talk all the more. By all means, sit and say nothing."

"But if you can manage it," Catherine added with a smile, "try to look impressed by our wit and intelligence."

"I will attempt to add to the conversation," Christopher ventured, "if I can think of anything relevant."

"That never stops the rest of us," Cam remarked.

Christopher took an empty chair beside Rye. A liberally filled plate and a glass of wine were set before him. It wasn't until he began to eat that he realized how famished he was. While he devoured the excellent fare—baked sole, potatoes, smoked oysters wrapped in crisp bacon—the family talked of politics and estate business, and mulled over happenings in Stony Cross.

Rye behaved like a miniature adult. He listened respectfully to the conversation, occasionally asking questions that were readily answered by the others. To Christopher's knowledge, it was highly uncommon to allow a child to sit at the dinner table. Most upper-class families followed the custom of having children eat alone in the nursery.

"Do you always take dinner with the rest of the family?" Christopher asked him sotto voce.

"Most of the time," Rye whispered back. "They don't mind as long as you don't talk with food in your mouth or play with the potatoes."

"I'll try not," Christopher assured him gravely.

"And you mustn't feed Albert from the table, even when he begs. Aunt Beatrix says only plain food is good for him."

Christopher glanced at his dog, who was reclining placidly in the corner.

"Captain Phelan," Amelia asked, noticing the direction of his gaze, "what do you think of the change in Albert?"

"Nearly inconceivable," Christopher replied. "I had wondered if it would be possible to bring him from the battlefield to a peaceful life here." He looked at Beatrix, adding gravely, "I am in your debt."

Beatrix colored and smiled down at her plate. "Not at all."

"My sister has always had a remarkable ability with animals," Amelia said. "I've always wondered what would happen if Beatrix took it in her head to reform a man."

Leo grinned. "I propose we find a really revolting, amoral wastrel, and give him to Beatrix. She would set him to rights within a fortnight."

"I have no wish to reform bipeds," Beatrix said. "Four legs are the absolute minimum. Besides, Cam has forbidden me to put any more creatures in the barn."

"With the size of that barn?" Leo asked. "Don't say we've run out of room?"

"One has to draw the line somewhere," Cam said. "And I had to after the mule."

Christopher looked at Beatrix alertly. "You have a mule?"

"No," she said at once. Perhaps it was merely a trick of the light, but the color seemed to leave her face. "It's nothing. That is, yes, I have a mule. But I don't like to discuss him."

"I like to discuss him," Rye volunteered innocently. "Hector is a very nice mule, but he has a weak back and he's sickle-hocked. No one wanted him after he was born, so Aunt Beatrix went to Mr. Caird and said—"

"His name is Hector?" Christopher asked, his gaze locked on Beatrix.

She didn't answer.

A strange, severe sensation took over Christopher's body. He felt every hair lift, felt every distinct pulse of blood in his veins. "Did his sire belong to Mr. Mawdsley?" he asked.

"How did you know?" came Rye's voice.

Christopher's reply was very soft. "Someone wrote to me about it."

Lifting a glass of wine to his lips, Christopher tore his gaze from Beatrix's carefully blank face.

He did not look at her for the rest of the meal.

He couldn't, or he would lose all self-control.

BEATRIX WAS NEARLY SUFFOCATED BY THE WEIGHT OF HER own worry during the rest of dinner. She had never regretted anything in her life as much as having urged Christopher to stay. What had he made of the news that she had acquired Mr. Caird's mule and given him the same name as the pet mule of his boyhood? He would want an explanation. She would have to pass it off as some bit of information that Prudence had relayed. *I suppose the name stuck in my head when Pru mentioned it,* she would say casually. *And it is a nice name for a mule. I hope you don't mind.*

Yes. That would work, as long as she seemed nonchalant about the whole matter.

Except that it was difficult to appear nonchalant when one was filled with panic.

Mercifully, Christopher had seemed to lose interest in the subject. In fact, he didn't so much as glance at her, but instead launched into a conversation with Leo and Cam about mutual acquaintances in London. He was relaxed and smiling, even laughing outright at some quip of Leo's.

Beatrix's anxiety faded as it became apparent that the subject of Hector was all but forgotten.

She stole surreptitious glances at Christopher, as she had been doing all evening, mesmerized by the sight of him. He was tawny and sun glazed, the candlelight finding threads of gold in his hair. The yellow glow struck sparkling glints in the new growth of bristle on his face. She was fascinated by the raw, restless masculinity beneath his quietness. She wanted to revel in him as one might dash out-of-doors in a storm, letting the elements have their way. Most of all she longed to talk with him . . . to pry each other open with words, share every thought and secret.

"My sincere thanks for your hospitality," Christopher finally said at the conclusion of the meal. "It was much needed."

"You must return soon," Cam said, "especially to view the timber yard in operation. We have installed some innovations that you may want to use at Riverton someday."

"Thank you. I would like to see them." Christopher looked directly at Beatrix. "Before I depart, Miss Hathaway, I wonder if you would introduce me to this notorious mule of yours?" His manner was relaxed . . . but his eyes were those of a predator.

Beatrix's mouth went dry. There would be no escaping him. That much was clear. He wanted answers. He would have them either now or later.

"Now?" she asked wanly. "Tonight?"

"If you don't mind," he said in a far too pleasant tone. "The barn is but a short walk from the house, is it not?"

"Yes," Beatrix said, rising from her chair. The men at the table stood obligingly. "Excuse us, please. I won't be long."

"May I go with you?" Rye asked eagerly.

"No, darling," Amelia said, "it's time for your bath."

"But why must I wash if I can't see any dirt?"

"Those of us who have a difficult time with godliness," Amelia replied with a grin, "must settle for cleanliness."

THE FAMILY MAINTAINED A LIGHT CONVERSATION UNTIL RYE had gone upstairs, and Beatrix and Captain Phelan had left the house with Albert following them.

After a universal silence, Leo was the first to speak. "Did anyone else notice—"

"Yes," Catherine said. "What do you make of it?"

"I haven't decided yet." Leo frowned and took a sip of port. "He's not someone I would pair Bea with."

"Whom would you pair her with?"

"Hanged if I know," Leo said. "Someone with similar interests. The local veterinarian, perhaps?"

"He's eighty-three years old and deaf," Catherine said.

"They would never argue," Leo pointed out.

Amelia smiled and stirred her tea slowly. "Much as I hate to admit it, I agree with Leo. Not about the veterinarian, but . . . Beatrix with a soldier? That doesn't seem a likely match."

"Phelan did resign his commission," Cam said. "He's no longer a soldier."

"And if he inherits Riverton," Amelia mused, "Beatrix would have all that forest to roam . . ."

"I see a likeness between them," Catherine said reflectively.

Leo arched a brow. "How are they alike, pray tell? She likes animals, and he likes to shoot things."

"Beatrix puts a distance between herself and the rest of the world. She's very engaging, but also quite private in nature. I see the same qualities in Captain Phelan."

"Yes," Amelia said. "You're absolutely right, Catherine. Put that way, the match does seem more appropriate."

"I still have reservations," Leo said.

"You always do," Amelia replied. "If you'll recall, you objected to Cam in the beginning, but now you've accepted him."

"That's because the more brothers-in-law I acquire," Leo said, "the better Cam looks by comparison."

Chapter Fifteen

No words were exchanged as Beatrix and Christopher proceeded to the stable. The cloud-hazed moon was low in the sky, insubstantial as a smoke ring in the blackness.

Beatrix was absurdly aware of the sound of her breathing, of her shoes biting into the graveled ground, of the vital male presence beside her.

A stable boy nodded a greeting as they went into the warm, shadowy interior of the stables. Having become accustomed to Beatrix's frequent comings and goings, the stablehands had learned to let her do as she pleased.

The pungent smell of the stables—hay, horses, feed, manure—combined in a familiar and reassuring fragrance. Silently she led Christopher farther into the building, past Thoroughbreds, a cart horse, a matched carriage pair. The animals whickered and turned their heads as they passed.

Beatrix stopped at the mule's stall. "This is Hector," she said.

The small mule came forward to greet them. Despite his flaws, or perhaps because of them, he was an endearing creature. His conformation was terrible, one ear was crooked, and he wore a jaunty and perpetually cheerful expression.

Christopher reached out to pet Hector, who nuzzled against his hand. His gentleness with the animal was reassuring. Perhaps, Beatrix thought hopefully, he wasn't as angry as she had feared.

Taking a deep breath, she said, "The reason that I named him Hector—"

"No." Christopher moved very close to her, his nearness making her blood race. His voice was low and rough. "Let's start with this: did you help Prudence to write those letters?"

Beatrix's eyes widened as she looked into his shadowed face. "No," she managed to say, "I didn't help her."

"Then who did?"

"No one helped her."

It was the truth. It just wasn't the entire truth.

"You know something," he insisted. "And you're going to tell me what it is."

She could feel his fury. The air was charged with it. Her heart thrummed like a bird's. And she struggled to contain a swell of emotion that was almost more than she could bear.

"Captain," she said with exceptional calm. "You won't do either of us good by losing your temper."

His eyes narrowed dangerously. "Don't use your bloody dog-training voice on me."

"That wasn't my dog-training voice. And if you're so intent on getting at the truth, why aren't you asking Prudence?"

"I have asked her. She lied. As you are lying now."

"You've always wanted Prudence," Beatrix burst out. "Now you can have her. Why should a handful of letters matter?"

"Because I was deceived. And I want to know how and why."

"Pride," Beatrix said bitterly. "That's all this is to you . . . your pride was hurt."

One of his hands sank into her hair. A gasp slipped from her throat as he eased her head back.

"Don't try to divert the conversation. You know something you're not telling me." His free hand came to the exposed line of her throat. He caressed her gently, his thumb moving in a subtle swirl in the hollow at the base. The intensity of her own reaction astonished her.

Beatrix's eyes half closed.

Feeling her responsive shiver, Christopher lowered his head until his breath fanned her cheek. "Tell me the truth."

Never. If she told him, he would hate her for the way she had deceived and abandoned him. Some mistakes could not be forgiven.

"Go to hell," Beatrix said unsteadily. She had never used such a phrase in her life.

"I am in hell." His body corralled hers, his legs intruding amid the folds of her skirts.

He was surrounding her, all the strength and force and maleness of him, and she closed her eyes as her senses went quiet and dark in helpless waiting.

And then he was kissing her.

His mouth moved over hers in supple, intimate angles, until he found some perfect alignment that made her weak all over. She reached around his neck to keep from dropping bonelessly to the floor. Gathering her closer into the hard support of his body, he explored her slowly, the tip of his tongue stroking, tasting.

Her body listed more heavily against his as her limbs became weighted with pleasure. She sensed the moment when his anger was eclipsed by passion, desire changing to white-hot need. Her fingers sank into his beautiful hair, the shorn locks heavy and vibrant, his scalp hot against her palms. With each inhalation, she drew in more of his fragrance, the trace of sandalwood on warm male skin.

His mouth slid from hers and dragged roughly along her

throat, crossing sensitive places that made her writhe. Blindly turning her face, she rubbed her lips against his ear. He drew in a sharp breath and kissed her harder, pressing her back against the slatted side of the stall, his hands roaming indecently. Her body was laced and compressed and concealed in layers of feminine attire, frustrating his attempts to caress her.

His garments, however, presented far fewer obstacles. She slid her arms inside his coat, fumbling to touch him, tugging ardently at his waistcoat and shirt. Reaching beneath the straps of his trouser braces, she managed to pull part of his shirt free of the trousers, the fabric warm from his body.

They both gasped as her cool fingers touched the burning skin of his back. Fascinated, Beatrix explored the curvature of deep intrinsic muscles, the tight mesh of sinew and bone, the astonishing strength contained just beneath the surface. She found the texture of scars, vestiges of pain and survival. After stroking a healed-over line, she covered it tenderly with her palm.

A shudder racked his frame. Christopher groaned and crushed his mouth over hers, urging her body against his, until together they found an erotic pattern, a cadence. Instinctively Beatrix tried to draw him inside herself, pulling at his lips and tongue with her own.

Christopher broke the kiss abruptly, panting. Cradling her head in his hands, he pressed his forehead against hers.

"Is it you?" he asked hoarsely. "Is it?"

Beatrix felt tears slip from beneath her lashes, no matter how she tried to blink them back. Her heart was ablaze. It seemed that her entire life had led to this man, this moment of unexpressed love.

But she was too frightened of his scorn, and too ashamed of her own actions, to answer.

Christopher's fingertips found the tear marks on her damp

skin. His mouth grazed her trembling lips, lingering at one soft corner, sliding up to the verge of a salt-flavored cheek.

Releasing her, he stepped back and stared at her with baffled anger. The desire exerted such force between them that Beatrix dazedly wondered how he could maintain even that small distance.

A shaken breath escaped him. He straightened his clothes, moving with undue care, as if he were intoxicated.

"Damn you." His voice was low and strained. He strode out of the stables.

Albert, who had been sitting by a stall, began to trot after him. Upon noticing that Beatrix wasn't going with them, the terrier dashed over to her and whimpered.

Beatrix bent to pet him. "Go on, boy," she whispered.

Hesitating only a moment, Albert ran after his master.

And Beatrix watched them both with despair.

TWO DAYS LATER, A BALL WAS GIVEN AT STONY CROSS Manor, the manorial residence of Lord and Lady Westcliff. It would have been difficult to find a more beautiful setting than the ancient dwelling built of honey-colored stone, surrounded by extensive gardens. The whole of it was situated on a bluff overlooking the Itchen River. As neighbors and friends of Lord and Lady Westcliff, the Hathaways were all invited. Cam in particular was a valued and frequent companion of the earl's, the two having been closely acquainted for many years.

Although Beatrix had been a guest at Stony Cross Manor on many previous occasions, she was still struck by the beauty of the home, especially the lavish interior. The ballroom was beyond compare, with intricately parqueted floors and a double row of chandeliers, two of the long walls fitted with semicircular niches containing velvet upholstered benches.

After partaking of refreshments at the long buffet tables, Beatrix entered the ballroom with Amelia and Catherine. The scene was profligate with color, ladies dressed in lavish ball gowns, the men clad in the formal ensemble of black and white. The sparkle of the crystal chandeliers was very nearly matched by the bountiful displays of jewels on feminine wrists, necks, and ears.

The host of the evening, Lord Westcliff, approached to exchange pleasantries with Beatrix, Amelia, and Catherine. Beatrix had always liked the earl, a courteous and honorable man whose friendship had benefited the Hathaways on countless occasions. With his rugged features, coal-black hair, and dark eyes, he was striking rather than handsome. He wore an aura of power comfortably and without fanfare. Westcliff asked Catherine to dance with him, a mark of favor that was hardly lost on the other guests, and she complied with a smile.

"How kind he is," Amelia said to Beatrix as they watched the earl lead Catherine into the midst of the whirling couples. "I've noticed that he always makes a point of being obliging and gracious to the Hathaways. That way, no one would dare cut or snub us."

"I think he likes unconventional people. He's not nearly as staid as one might assume."

"Lady Westcliff has certainly said as much," Amelia replied, smiling.

A rejoinder faded on Beatrix's lips as she caught sight of a perfectly matched couple on the other side of the room. Christopher Phelan was talking with Prudence Mercer. The scheme of formal black and white was becoming to any man. On someone like Christopher, it was literally breathtaking. He wore the clothes with natural ease, his posture relaxed but straight, his shoulders broad. The crisp white of his starched cravat provided a striking contrast to his tawny skin, while the light of chandeliers glittered over his golden-bronze hair.

Following her gaze, Amelia lifted her brows. "What an attractive man," she said. Her attention returned to Beatrix. "You like him, don't you?"

Before Beatrix could help herself, she sent her sister a pained glance. Letting her gaze drop to the floor, she said, "There have been a dozen times in the past when I should have liked a particular gentleman. When it would have been convenient, and appropriate, and easy. But no, I had to wait for someone special. Someone who would make my heart feel as if it's been trampled by elephants, thrown into the Amazon, and eaten by piranhas."

Amelia smiled at her compassionately. Her gloved hand slipped over Beatrix's. "Darling Bea. Would it console you to hear that such feelings of infatuation are perfectly ordinary?"

Beatrix turned her palm upward, returning the clasp of her sister's hand. Since their mother had died when Bea was twelve, Amelia had been a source of endless love and patience. "Is it infatuation?" she heard herself asking softly. "Because it feels much worse than that. Like a fatal disease."

"I don't know, dear. It's difficult to tell the difference between love and infatuation. Time will reveal it, eventually." Amelia paused. "He is attracted to you," she said. "We all noticed the other night. Why don't you encourage him, dear?"

Beatrix felt her throat tighten. "I can't."

"Why not?"

"I can't explain," Beatrix said miserably, "except to say that I've deceived him."

Amelia glanced at her in surprise. "That doesn't sound like you. You're the least deceptive person I've ever known."

"I didn't mean to do it. And he doesn't know that it was me. But I think he suspects."

"Oh." Amelia frowned as she absorbed the perplexing statement. "Well. This does seem to be a muddle. Perhaps you should confide in him. His reaction may surprise you. What is it that Mother used to say whenever we pushed her to the limits of her patience? . . . 'Love forgives all things.' Do you remember?"

"Of course," Beatrix said. She had written that exact phrase to Christopher in one of her letters. Her throat went very tight. "Amelia, I can't discuss this now. Or I'll start weeping and throw myself to the floor."

"Heavens, don't do that. Someone might trip over you."

Further conversation was forestalled as a gentleman came to ask Beatrix to dance. Although Beatrix hardly felt like dancing at the moment, it was the worst possible manners to refuse such an invitation at a private ball. Unless one had a plausible and obvious excuse, such as a broken leg, one danced.

And in truth, it was no hardship to partner this gentleman, Mr. Theo Chickering. He was an attractive and amiable young man, whom Beatrix had met during her last season in London.

"Would you do me the honor, Miss Hathaway?"

Beatrix smiled at him. "It would be my pleasure, Mr. Chickering." Letting go of her sister's hand, she went with him.

"You look lovely tonight, Miss Hathaway."

"Thank you, kind sir." Beatrix had worn her best gown, made of shimmering aniline violet. The bodice was scooped low, revealing a generous expanse of fair skin. Her hair had been curled and swept up with a multitude of pearl-tipped pins—other than that, she wore no adornment.

Feeling the hairs on her nape prickle with awareness, Beatrix sent a quick glance around the room. Her gaze was immediately caught by a pair of cool gray eyes. Christopher was staring at her, unsmiling.

Chickering gracefully pulled her into the waltz. Following the completion of one turn, Beatrix glanced over her shoulder, but Christopher was no longer staring at her.

In fact, he didn't glance at her even once after that.

Beatrix forced herself to laugh and dance with Chickering, while privately reflecting that there was nothing so trying as pretending you were happy when you weren't. Discreetly she watched Christopher, who was inundated with women who wanted to flirt with him and men who wanted to hear war stories. Everyone, it seemed, wanted to associate with the man whom many were calling England's most celebrated war hero. Christopher bore it all with equanimity, looking composed and courteous, occasionally flashing a charming smile.

"It's hard for a fellow to challenge *that*," Chickering told Beatrix dryly, nodding in Christopher's direction. "Fame, great wealth, and a full head of hair. And one can't even despise him, because he singlehandedly won the war."

Beatrix laughed and gave him a mock-pitying glance. "You're no less impressive than Captain Phelan, Mr. Chickering."

"By what measure? I wasn't in the military, and I have neither fame nor great wealth."

"But you do have a full head of hair," Beatrix pointed out.

Chickering grinned. "Dance with me again, and you can view my abundant tresses at your leisure."

"Thank you, but I've already danced with you twice, and any more would be scandalous."

"You have broken my heart," he informed her, and she laughed.

"There are many delightful ladies here who would be happy to mend it," she said. "Please go and favor them—a gentleman who dances as well as you should not be monopolized."

As Chickering left her reluctantly, Beatrix heard a familiar voice behind her.

"Beatrix."

Although she wanted to cringe, she squared her shoulders and turned to face her former friend. "Hello, Prudence," she said. "How are you?"

Prudence was sumptuously attired in an ivory gown, the skirts a massive froth of blond lace caught up at intervals with pink silk rosebuds. "I am very well, thank you. What a fashionable dress . . . you look very grown-up tonight, Bea."

Beatrix smiled wryly at this bit of condescension coming from a girl who was a year younger than herself. "I'm twenty-three years old, Pru. I daresay I've looked grown-up for quite a while now."

"Of course."

A long, awkward pause ensued.

"Do you want something?" Beatrix asked bluntly.

Prudence smiled and drew closer. "Yes. I want to thank you."

"For what?"

"You've been a loyal friend. You could easily have spoiled things for Christopher and me by revealing our secret, but you didn't. You kept your promise, and I didn't believe that you would."

"Why not?"

"I suppose I thought that you might have tried to attract Christopher's attention to yourself. As ludicrous as that would have been."

Beatrix tilted her head slightly. "Ludicrous?"

"Perhaps that's not the right word. I meant unsuitable. Because a man in Christopher's position needs a sophisticated woman. Someone to support his position in society. With his fame and influence, he may enter politics someday. And he could hardly do that with a wife who spent most of her time in the forest . . . or the stables."

That delicate reminder was like an arrow through Beatrix's heart.

"She's more suited to the stables than the drawing room," Christopher had once said.

Beatrix stretched her lips into a careless grin, hoping it didn't resemble a grimace. "Yes, I remember."

"Again, my thanks," Prudence said warmly. "I've never been happier. I'm coming to care for him very much. We'll be betrothed soon." She glanced at Christopher, who was standing near the ballroom entrance with a group of gentlemen. "See how handsome he is," she said with affectionate pride. "I do prefer him in his uniform, with all those lovely medals, but he looks splendid in black, doesn't he?"

Beatrix returned her attention to Prudence, wondering how to get rid of her. "Oh, look! . . . There is Marietta Newbury. Have you told her about your impending betrothal? I'm sure she would be delighted to hear of it."

"Oh, indeed, she would! Will you come with me?"

"Thank you, but I'm terribly thirsty. I'll go to the refreshment tables."

"We'll talk again soon," Prudence promised.

"That would be lovely."

Prudence left her in a swish of white lace.

Beatrix let out an exasperated puff that blew a stray lock of hair away from her forehead. She stole another glance at Christopher, who was involved in conversation. Although his demeanor was calm—stoic, even—there was a gleam of perspiration on his face. Looking away from his companions for a moment, he discreetly passed a shaking hand over his forehead.

Was he feeling ill?

Beatrix watched him closely.

The orchestra was playing a lively composition, obliging the crowd in the ballroom to talk loudly over the music. So much noise and color . . . so many bodies confined in one place. A percussion came from the refreshment room; clinks of glasses, flatware scratching on china. There came a pop of a champagne cork, and Beatrix saw Christopher twitch in response.

At that moment she understood.

It was all too much for him. His nerves were stretched to the breaking point. The effort at self-discipline was requiring everything he had.

Without a second thought, Beatrix made her way to Christopher as quickly as possible.

"Here you are, Captain Phelan," she exclaimed.

The gentlemen's conversation stopped at this untoward interruption.

"There's no use in hiding from me," Beatrix continued brightly. "Recollect, you promised to stroll with me through Lord Westcliff's picture gallery."

Christopher's face was still. His eyes were dilated, the gray irises nearly extinguished by black. "So I did," he said stiffly.

The other gentlemen acceded immediately. It was the only thing they could do in the face of Beatrix's boldness. "We will certainly not keep you from making good on a promise, Phelan," one of them said.

Another followed suit. "Especially a promise given to a delightful creature such as Miss Hathaway."

Christopher gave an abbreviated nod. "By your leave," he said to his companions, and offered Beatrix his arm. As soon as they were out of the main circuit of rooms, he began to breathe heavily. He was sweating profusely, the muscles of his arm unbelievably hard beneath her fingers. "That did your reputation no good," he muttered, referring to the way she had approached him.

"Bother my reputation."

Being familiar with the arrangement of the manor, Beatrix led him to a small outdoor conservatory. The attached circular roof was supported with slender columns and dimly illuminated with torchlight shed from the surrounding gardens.

Leaning against the side of the house, Christopher closed his eyes and drew in the cool, sweet air. He seemed like a man who had just emerged from a long swim underwater.

Beatrix stood nearby, watching him with concern. "Too much noise in there?"

"Too much of everything," he muttered. After a moment, he slitted his eyes open. "Thank you."

"You're welcome."

"Who was that man?"

"Which one?"

"The one you were dancing with."

"Mr. Chickering?" Her heart felt considerably lighter as she realized that he had noticed. "Oh, he's a delightful gentleman. I'd met him before in London." She paused. "Did you also happen to see that I spoke to Pru?"

"No."

"Well, I did. She seems convinced that you and she will marry."

There was no change in his expression. "Perhaps we will. It's what she deserves."

Beatrix hardly knew how to reply to that. "Do you care for her?"

Christopher gave her a look of scalding derision. "How could I not?"

Her frown deepened. "If you're going to be sarcastic, I may as well go back inside."

"Go, then." He closed his eyes again, continuing to lean against the wall.

Beatrix was tempted to do just that. However, as she looked at his still, gleaming features, a wave of unaccountable tenderness swept through her.

He looked so large and invulnerable, with no sign of emotion save for that indentation between his brows. But she knew that he was overwrought. No man liked to lose control, especially a man whose very life had depended so often on his ability to govern himself.

Oh, how she wished she could tell him that their secret house was close by. *Come with me,* she would say, *and I'll take you to a lovely quiet place . . .*

Instead she fished a handkerchief from a hidden pocket in her gown, and approached him. "Be still," she said. Standing on her toes, she carefully blotted his face with a handkerchief.

And he let her.

He looked down at her when she was done, his mouth grim. "I have these moments of . . . madness," he said gruffly. "In the middle of a conversation, or doing something perfectly ordinary, a vision appears in my head. And then there's a moment of blankness, and I don't know what I've just said or done."

"What kind of vision?" Beatrix asked. "Things you saw in the war?"

His nod was nearly imperceptible.

"That's not madness," she said.

"Then what is it?"

"I'm not certain."

A humorless laugh escaped him. "You have no damned idea what you're talking about."

"Oh, I don't?" Beatrix stared at him intently, wondering how far she could trust him. The instinct of self-preservation struggled with her desire to help him, share with him. *"Boldness be my friend!"* she thought ruefully, summoning her favorite line from Shakespeare. It was practically the Hathaway family motto.

Very well. She would tell him the shameful secret she had never told anyone outside her family. If it helped him, the risk was worth it.

"I steal things," she said bluntly.

That got his attention. "Pardon?"

"Little things. Snuffboxes, sealing wax, odds and ends. Never intentionally."

"How do you steal things unintentionally?"

"Oh, it's dreadful," Beatrix said earnestly. "I'll be in a shop, or someone's home, and I'll see a little object . . . it could be something as valuable as a jewel, or as insignificant as a piece of string . . . and the most terrible sensation comes over me. A sort of anxious, fidgety feeling . . . Have you ever had an itch so awful that you must scratch it or die? And yet you can't?"

His lips twitched. "Yes. Usually in one's army boot, while standing in knee-deep water in a trench. While people are shooting. That absolutely guarantees an unreachable itch."

"My goodness. Well, I try to resist, but the feeling gets worse until I finally take the object and slip it into my pocket. And then later when I return home, I'm overcome with shame and embarrassment, and I have to find ways to return the things I took. My family helps me. And it's *so* much more difficult to put something back than it is to steal it." She grimaced. "Sometimes I'm not even fully aware of doing it. That's why I was expelled from finishing school. I had a collection of hair ribbons, pencil stubs, books . . . and I tried to put everything back, but I couldn't remember where it all went." Beatrix glanced at him cautiously, wondering if she would find condemnation in his face.

But his mouth had gentled, and his eyes were warm. "When did it start?"

"After my parents died. My father went to bed one night with pains in his chest, and he never awoke. But it was even worse with my mother . . . she stopped talking, and hardly ate, and withdrew from everyone and everything. She died of grief a few months later. I was very young, and self-centered, I suppose—because I felt abandoned. I wondered why she hadn't loved me enough to stay."

"That doesn't mean you were self-centered." His voice was quiet and kind. "Any child would have reacted that way."

"My brother and sisters took very good care of me," Beatrix said. "But it wasn't long after Mother was gone that my problem appeared. It's much better than it used to be . . . when I feel peaceful and safe, I don't steal anything at all. It's only at difficult times, when I'm uncomfortable or anxious, that I find myself doing it." She looked up at Christopher compassionately. "I think your problem will fade in time, as mine has. And then it might come back every once in a while, but only briefly. It won't always be this bad."

Torchlight flickered in Christopher's eyes as he stared at her. He reached out and drew her close with slow, stunning tenderness. One of his hands cradled her jaw, his long fingers textured with calluses. To Beatrix's bewilderment, he eased her head against his shoulder. His arms were around her, and nothing had ever felt so wonderful. She leaned against him in a daze of pleasure, feeling the even rise and fall of his chest. He toyed with the tiny wisps at the nape of her neck, the brush of his thumb on her skin sending a rapturous quiver down her spine.

"I have a silver cuff link of yours," Beatrix said unsteadily, her cheek pressed to the smooth fabric of his coat. "And a shaving brush. I went to take back the shaving brush, and stole the cuff link instead. I've been afraid to try and return them, because I'm fairly certain I would only end up stealing something else."

A sound of amusement rustled in his chest. "Why did you take the shaving brush in the first place?"

"I told you, I can't help—"

"No. I meant, what were you feeling anxious about?"

"Oh, that's not important."

"It's important to me."

Beatrix drew back just enough to look up at him. *You. I was anxious about you.* But what she said was, "I don't remember. I have to go back inside."

His arms loosened. "I thought you weren't worried about your reputation."

"Well, it can survive a little damage," Beatrix said reasonably. "But I'd rather not have the whole thing blown to smithereens."

"Go, then." His hands fell away from her, and she began to walk away. "But Beatrix . . ."

She paused and glanced at him uncertainly. "Yes?"

His gaze held hers. "I want my shaving brush back."

A slow grin curved her lips. "I'll return it soon," she promised, and left him alone in the moonlight.

Chapter Sixteen

"Beatrix, see who's here!" Rye came to the paddock with Albert padding beside him.

Beatrix was working with a newly acquired horse, which had been badly trained as a colt and sold by its disgruntled owner. The horse had a potentially fatal habit of rearing, and had once nearly crushed a rider who had been trying to discipline him. The horse started uneasily at the appearance of the boy and dog, but Beatrix soothed him and had him begin a slow circle around the paddock.

She glanced at Rye, who had climbed onto the fence and sat on the top rail. Albert sat and rested his chin on the lowest rail, watching her with alert eyes.

"Did Albert come alone?" Beatrix asked, perplexed.

"Yes. And he wasn't wearing a leash. I think he must have run away from home."

Before Beatrix could reply, the horse stopped and began to rear irritably. Immediately she loosened the reins and leaned forward, sliding her right arm around the horse's neck. As soon as the horse began to come down, Beatrix urged him forward. She doubled the horse in tight half circles, first to the right, then to the left, and began him forward again.

"Why do you double him like that?" Rye asked.

"It's something your father taught me, actually. It's to impress on him that he and I must work together." She patted the horse's neck and kept him at a sedate walk. "One must never pull on the reins when a horse is rearing—it could cause him to fall backward. When I feel him getting light in the front, I urge him forward a little faster. He can't rear as long as he's moving."

"How will you know when he's straightened out?"

"There's never an exact moment when one knows," Beatrix said. "I'll just keep working with him, and he'll improve little by little."

She dismounted and led the horse to the railing, and Rye stroked his satiny neck. "Albert," Beatrix said conversationally, bending to pet the dog. "What are you doing here? Have you run off from your master?"

He wagged his tail enthusiastically.

"I gave him some water," Rye said. "Can we keep him for the afternoon?"

"I'm afraid not. Captain Phelan may be worrying after him. I'm going to take him back now."

The boy heaved a sigh. "I would ask to go with you," he said, "but I have to finish my lessons. I so look forward to the day I know everything. Then I won't have to read any more books or do any more counting."

Beatrix smiled. "I don't wish to be discouraging, Rye, but it's not possible to know *everything*."

"Mama does." Rye paused reflectively. "At least, Papa says we must pretend she does, because it makes her happy."

"Your father," Beatrix informed him with a laugh, "is one of the wisest men I've ever known."

It was only when Beatrix had ridden halfway to Phelan House, with Albert trotting alongside, that she recalled she was still dressed in boots and breeches. No doubt the outlandish attire would annoy Christopher.

There had been no word from him in the week after the ball at Stony Cross Manor. And although Beatrix had certainly not expected him to pay a call on her, it would have been a cordial gesture on his part. They were neighbors, after all. She had gone out walking every day, hoping to encounter him on a long ramble, but there was no sign of him.

It couldn't have been more obvious that Christopher wasn't interested in her, in any regard. Which led Beatrix to the conclusion that it had been a grave mistake to confide in him. She had been presumptuous in assuming that her problem was comparable to his.

"Recently I realized that I'm no longer in love with him," she told Albert as they neared Phelan House. "It's such a relief. Now I'm not at all nervous about the prospect of seeing him. I suppose this is proof that what I felt for him was infatuation. Because it's completely gone now. I couldn't care less about what he does or whom he marries. Oh, what a feeling of utter freedom." She glanced at the dog, who didn't look at all convinced by her statements. She sighed heavily.

Reaching the entrance of the house, Beatrix dismounted and handed the reins to a footman. She suppressed a sheepish smile as she saw how he was gaping at her. "Keep my horse at the ready, please. I'll be only a moment. Come, Albert."

She was met at the front door by Mrs. Clocker, who was taken aback by her attire. "Why, Miss Hathaway . . ." the housekeeper faltered, "you're wearing . . ."

"Yes, I'm so sorry, I know I'm not presentable, but I came in a dash. Albert appeared at Ramsay House today, and I'm delivering him back to you."

"Thank you," the housekeeper said in a distracted manner. "I hadn't even noticed he was missing. With the master not himself . . ."

"Not himself?" Beatrix was instantly concerned. "In what way, Mrs. Clocker?"

"I shouldn't say."

"Yes you should. I'm the perfect person to confide in. I'm very discreet—I only gossip to animals. Is Captain Phelan ill? Did something happen?"

The housekeeper's voice lowered to a whisper. "Three nights ago, we all smelled smoke coming from the master's bedroom. The master was drunk as David's sow, and he had thrown his uniform onto the fire in the hearth, and all his medals with it! We managed to rescue the medals, although the garments were ruined. After that, the master closed himself in his room and began to drink steadily. He hasn't stopped. We've watered his liquor as much as we dared, but . . ." A helpless shrug. "He will talk to no one. He won't touch the dinner trays I sent up. We sent for the doctor, but he wouldn't see him, and when we brought the pastor yesterday, he threatened to murder him. We've been considering the idea of sending for Mrs. Phelan."

"His mother?"

"Dear me, no. Mrs. Phelan the younger. I do not think his mother would be of any help."

"Yes, Audrey is a good choice. She's levelheaded, and she knows him well."

"The problem," the housekeeper said, "is that it would take at least two days for her to arrive . . . and I fear . . ."

"What?"

"This morning he asked for a razor and hot bath. We were frightened to give it to him, but we daren't refuse. I half wonder if he won't do himself harm."

Two things were immediately clear to Beatrix: first, the

housekeeper would never have confided so much in her unless she was desperate, and second, Christopher was in terrible pain.

She felt answering pain, for his sake, piercing beneath her own ribs. Everything she had told herself about her newfound freedom, about the death of her infatuation, was revealed as an absurdity. She was mad for him. She would have done anything for him. Anxiously she wondered what he needed, what words might soothe him. But she was not up to the task. She couldn't think of anything wise or clever. All she knew was that she wanted to be with him.

"Mrs. Clocker," she said carefully, "I wonder if . . . it might be possible for you not to notice if I go upstairs?"

The housekeeper's eyes widened. "I . . . Miss Hathaway . . . I don't think that would be safe. Nor sensible."

"Mrs. Clocker, my family has always believed that when we are faced with large and apparently impossible problems, the best solutions are found by the insane people, not the sensible ones."

Looking confused, the housekeeper opened her mouth to disagree, and closed it. "If you cry out for help," she ventured after a moment, "we will come to your aid."

"Thank you, but I'm certain that won't be necessary."

Beatrix went inside the house and headed to the stairs. As Albert made to follow her, she said, "No, boy. Stay down here."

"Come, Albert," the housekeeper said, "we'll find some scraps for you from the kitchen."

The dog switched directions without pausing, panting happily as he went with Mrs. Clocker.

Beatrix went upstairs, taking her time. How many times, she reflected ruefully, she had sought to understand a wounded wild creature. But it was another matter entirely to penetrate the mystery of a human being.

Reaching Christopher's door, she knocked softly. When there came no response, she let herself inside.

To her surprise, the room brimmed with daylight, the late August sun illuminating tiny floating dust motes by the window. The air smelled like liquor and smoke and bath soap. A portable bath occupied one corner of the room, sodden footprints tracking across the carpet.

Christopher reclined on the unmade bed, half propped on a haphazard stack of pillows, a bottle of brandy clasped negligently in his fingers. His incurious gaze moved to Beatrix and held, his eyes becoming alert.

He was clad in a pair of fawn-colored trousers, only partially fastened, and . . . nothing more. His body was a long golden arc on the bed, lean and complexly muscled. Scars marred the sun-browned skin in places . . . there was a ragged triangular shape where a bayonet had pierced his shoulder, a liberal scattering of marks from shrapnel, a small circular depression on his side that must have been caused by a bullet.

Slowly Christopher levered himself upward and placed the bottle on the bedside table. Half leaning on the edge of the mattress, his bare feet braced on the floor, he regarded Beatrix without expression. The locks of his hair were still damp, darkened to antique gold. How broad his shoulders were, their sturdy slopes flowing into the powerful lines of his arms.

"Why are you here?" His voice sounded rusty from disuse.

Somehow Beatrix managed to drag her mesmerized gaze away from the glinting fleece on his chest.

"I came to return Albert," she said. "He appeared at Ramsay House today. He says you've been neglecting him. And that you haven't taken him on any walks lately."

"Has he? I had no idea he was so loose-tongued."

"Perhaps you would like to put . . . more clothes on . . . and come for a walk with me? To clear your head?"

"This brandy is clearing my head. Or it would if my damned servants would stop watering it."

"Come walk with me," she coaxed. "Or I may be forced to use my dog-training voice on you."

Christopher gave her a baleful look. "I've already been trained. By Her Majesty's Royal Army."

Despite the sunlight in the room, Beatrix sensed the nightmares lurking in the corners. Everything in her insisted that he should be outside, in the open air, away from confinement. "What is it?" she asked. "What's caused this?"

He lifted a hand in an annoyed gesture, as if to bat away an insect.

Beatrix moved toward him cautiously.

"Don't," came his sharp rebuke. "Don't come close. Don't say anything. Just leave."

"Why?"

He gave an impatient shake of his head. "Whatever words would make you go, consider them said."

"Or else?"

His eyes were devil-bright, his face hard. "Or else come to my bed."

Beatrix didn't move.

Christopher came to her and braced his palms on the door on either side of her head. His voice was harsh and low. "I mean it, Beatrix."

Beatrix had to remind herself to start breathing again. The problem was, once she resumed, she couldn't control her lungs, which were working as if she had run miles. Faced with a hard wall of masculine flesh, she could almost feel the heat of his skin.

"Are you afraid of me?" he asked.

She gave a slight shake of her head, her eyes huge.

His hand glided from her waist to the side of her ribs, his breathing deepening as he discovered that she wasn't wearing a corset. His palm moved slowly over her natural shape.

Christopher's lashes half lowered, and his color heightened as he stared at her. His hand came to her breast, lightly shaping the roundness. Beatrix felt her legs threaten to give out beneath her. His thumb and forefinger caught at the rising tip and squeezed gently.

"Last chance," he said in guttural voice. "Get out, or get in my bed."

"Is there a third option?" Beatrix asked weakly, her breast throbbing beneath his touch.

For answer, Christopher picked her up with stunning ease and carried her to the bed. She was tossed to the mattress. Before she could move, he had straddled her, all that sleek golden power poised above her.

"Wait," Beatrix said. "Before we do anything, I would like to have five minutes of rational conversation. Only five. Surely that's not too much to ask."

His eyes were pitiless. "If you wanted rational conversation, you should have gone to another man. Your Mr. Chittering."

"Chickering," Beatrix said, squirming beneath him. "And he's not mine, and—" She swatted his hand away as he touched her breast again. "Stop that. I just want to—" Undeterred, he had gone for the button placket of her shirt. She scowled in exasperation. "All right, then," she snapped, "do as you please! Perhaps afterward we could manage a coherent discussion." Twisting beneath him, she flopped onto her stomach.

Christopher went still. After a long hesitation, she heard him ask in a far more normal voice, "What are you doing?"

"I'm making it easier for you," came her defiant reply.

Another silence. Then, "Why are you facing downward?"

"Because that's how it's done." Beatrix twisted to look at

him over her shoulder. A twinge of uncertainty caused her to ask, "Isn't it?"

His face was blank. "Has no one ever told you?"

"No, but I've read about it."

Christopher rolled off her, relieving her of his weight. He wore an odd expression as he asked, "From what books?"

"Veterinary manuals. And of course, I've observed the squirrels in springtime, and farm animals and—"

She was interrupted as Christopher cleared his throat loudly, and again. Darting a confused glance at him, she realized that he was trying to choke back amusement.

Beatrix began to feel indignant. Her first time in a bed with a man, and he was *laughing*.

"Look here," she said in a businesslike manner, "I've read about the mating habits of over two dozen species, and with the exception of snails, whose genitalia is on their necks, they all—" She broke off and frowned. "Why are you laughing at me?

Christopher had collapsed, overcome with hilarity. As he lifted his head and saw her affronted expression, he struggled manfully with another outburst. "Beatrix. I'm . . . I'm not laughing at you."

"You are!"

"No I'm not. It's just . . ." He swiped a tear from the corner of his eye, and a few more chuckles escaped. "Squirrels . . ."

"Well, it may be humorous to you, but it's a very serious matter to the squirrels."

That set him off again. In a display of rank insensitivity to the reproductive rights of small mammals, Christopher had buried his face in a pillow, his shoulders shaking.

"What is so amusing about fornicating squirrels?" Beatrix asked irritably.

By this time he had gone into near apoplexy. "No more," he gasped. "Please."

"I gather it's not the same for people," Beatrix said with great dignity, inwardly mortified. "They don't go about it the same way that animals do?"

Fighting to control himself, Christopher rolled to face her. His eyes were brilliant with unspent laughter. "Yes. No. That is, they do, but . . ."

"But you don't prefer it that way?"

Considering how to answer her, Christopher reached out to smooth her disheveled hair, which was falling out of its pins. "I do. I'm quite enthusiastic about it, actually. But it's not right for your first time."

"Why not?"

Christopher looked at her, a slow smile curving his lips. His voice deepened as he asked, "Shall I show you?"

Beatrix was transfixed.

Taking her stillness as assent, he pressed her back and moved over her slowly. He touched her with care, arranging her limbs, spreading them to receive him. A gasp escaped her as she felt his hips settle on hers. He was aroused, a thick pressure fitting against her intimately. Bracing some of his weight on his arms, he looked down into her reddening face.

"This way," he said, with the slightest nudge, ". . . is usually more pleasing to the lady."

The gentle movement sent a jolt of pleasure through her. Beatrix couldn't speak, her senses filled with him, her hips catching a helpless arch. She looked up at the powerful surface of his chest, covered with a tantalizing fleece of bronze-gold hair.

Christopher lowered further, his mouth hovering just over hers. "Front to front . . . I could kiss you the entire time. And the shape of you would cushion me so sweetly . . . like this . . ." His lips took hers and coaxed them open, wringing heat and delight from her yielding flesh. Beatrix shivered, her arms lifting around his neck. She felt him all along her body, his warmth and weight anchoring her.

He murmured endearments, kissing along her throat, while he tugged at the buttons of her shirt and spread the fabric open. She wore only a short chemise beneath, the kind commonly used as a corset cover. Pulling down the lace-trimmed strap, he exposed a round, pale breast, the peak already tight and rose colored. His head bent, and he caressed her with his mouth and tongue. His teeth grazed lightly over her sensitive nerves. And all the while, that relentless, rhythmic stimulation below . . . he was riding her, owning her, driving the need to an impossible pitch.

His hands cradled her head as he kissed her again, open-mouthed and deep, as if he were trying to draw the soul from her body. Beatrix answered eagerly, holding him with her arms and legs. But then he let go with a hoarse exclamation, and moved away.

"No," she heard herself moan. "Please—"

His fingers came to her lips, gently stroking her into silence. They lay side by side, facing each other, struggling to regain their breath.

"My God, how I want you." Christopher sounded far from pleased by the fact. His thumb swept over her kiss-swollen lips.

"Even though I annoy you?"

"You don't annoy me." Carefully he rebuttoned the placket of her shirt. "I thought you did, at first. But now I realize it was more like the feeling you get when your foot's been asleep. And when you start moving, the blood coming back into it is uncomfortable . . . but also good. Do you understand what I mean?"

"Yes. I make your feet tingle."

A smile came to his lips. "Among other things."

They continued to lie together, staring at each other.

He had the most remarkable face, Beatrix thought. Strong, flawless . . . and yet it was saved from cold perfection by the lines of humor at the corners of his eyes, and the hint of sensuality edging his mouth. The subtle weathering made him look . . . experienced. It was the kind of face that made a woman's heart beat faster.

Shyly Beatrix reached out to touch the bayonet scar on his shoulder. His skin was like hot pressed satin, except for the dark, uneven gouge of that healed-over wound. "How painful this must have been," she whispered. "Do your wounds still hurt?"

Christopher shook his head slightly.

"Then . . . what is troubling you?"

He was silent, his hand settling on her hip. As he thought, his fingers slipped beneath the untucked hem of her shirt, the backs of his knuckles stroking the skin of her midriff.

"I can't go back to who I was before the war," he eventually said. "And I can't be who I was during the war. And if I'm not either of those men, I'm not sure what I'm left with. Except for the knowledge that I killed more men than I could count." His gaze was distant, as if he were staring into a nightmare. "Always officers first—that sent them into disarray—then I picked off the rest as they scattered. They fell like toys a child had knocked over."

"But those were your orders. They were the enemy."

"I don't give a damn. They were men. They were loved by someone. I could never make myself forget that. You don't know what it looks like, when a man is shot. You've never heard wounded men on the battlefield, begging for water, or for someone to finish what the enemy started—"

Rolling away, he sat up and lowered his head. "I have rages," came his muffled voice. "I tried to attack one of my own footmen yesterday, did they tell you that? Christ, I'm no better than Albert. I can never share a bed with a woman again—I might kill her in her sleep, and not realize what I'm doing until afterward."

Beatrix sat up as well. "You wouldn't do that."

"You don't know that. You're so innocent." Christopher broke off and drew in a shivering breath. "God. I can't crawl out from under this. And I can't live with it."

"With what?" she asked softly, realizing that something in particular was tormenting him, some intolerable memory.

Christopher didn't acknowledge her. His mind was in another place, watching shadows. When she began to move closer to him, he lifted his arm as if in self-defense, palm turned outward. The broken gesture, made with such a strong hand, cut straight to Beatrix's heart.

She felt an overwhelming need to physically draw him closer, as if to ease him away from a precipice. Instead she kept her hands in her lap, and stared at the place where the ends of his hair rested on his sun-browned neck. The muscles of his back were bunched. If only she could smooth her palm over that hard, rippled surface. If only she could soothe him. But he had to find his own way out.

"A friend of mine died at Inkerman," Christopher finally said, his voice halting and raw. "One of my lieutenants. His name was Mark Bennett. He was the best soldier in the regiment. He was always honest. He joked at the wrong times. If you asked him to do something, no matter how difficult or dangerous, it would be done. He would have risked his life for any of us.

"The Russians had set up rifle pits in caverns and old stone huts built in the side of a hill. They were firing directly into our siege batteries—the general decided the Russian position had to be taken. Three companies of Rifles were chosen.

"A company of Hussars was ordered to ride against the enemy if they tried to flank us. They were led by a man I hated. Lieutenant Colonel Fenwick. Everyone hated him. He commanded the same cavalry regiment I had started in when I bought my first commission."

Christopher fell silent, lost in memory. His half-lowered lashes sent spikes of shadow over his cheeks.

"Why was he so hated?" Beatrix eventually prompted.

"Fenwick was often cruel for no reason. Fond of punishment for its own sake. He ordered floggings and deprivations for the most minor infractions. And when he invented excuses to discipline the men, I intervened. He accused me of insubordination, and I was nearly brought up on charges." Christopher let out a slow, uneven breath. "Fenwick was the main reason I agreed to be transferred to the Rifle Brigade. And then at Inkerman I found out I would have to depend on his cavalry support.

"Before the riflemen got to the trenches, we stopped in a ravine where there was shelter from stray shots. Night was coming. We formed into three groups. We opened fire, the Russians returned it, and we pinpointed the positions we had to take. We advanced with guns . . . took out as many as we could . . . then it turned into hand-to-hand combat. I was separated from Bennett in the fighting. The Russians drove us back when their support came . . . and then shell and grape started raining down. It wouldn't stop. Men around me were falling . . . their bodies opening up, wounds breaking out. My arms and back were burning with shrapnel. I couldn't find Bennett. It was dark, and we had to fall back.

"I'd left Albert waiting in the ravine. I called for him, and he came. Through all that hellfire, against every natural instinct . . . Albert came out with me to find wounded men in the dark. He led me to two men lying at the base of the hill. One of them was Bennett."

Beatrix closed her eyes sickly as she drew an accurate conclusion. "And the other was Colonel Fenwick," she said.

Christopher nodded grimly. "Fenwick had been unseated. His horse was gone. One of his legs was broken . . . a bullet wound in the side . . . there was a good chance he would live.

But Bennett . . . his front had been ripped open. He was barely conscious. Dying by degrees. I wanted it to be me, it should have been. I was always taking chances. Bennett was the careful one. He wanted to go back to his family, and to the woman he cared for. I don't know why it wasn't me. That's the hell of battle—it's all chance, you never know if you'll be next. You can try to hide, and a shell will find you. You can run straight at the enemy, and a bullet might jam in a rifle, and you're spared. It's all luck." He clenched his jaw against a tremor of emotion. "I wanted to take them both to safety, but there was no one to help. And I couldn't leave Fenwick there. If he was captured, the enemy would get crucial intelligence from him. He'd had access to all the general's dispatches, knew all about strategies and supplies . . . everything."

Beatrix stared at his partially averted profile. "You had to save Colonel Fenwick first," she whispered, her chest aching with compassion and pity as she finally understood. "Before you could save your friend."

"I told Mark, 'I'll come back for you. I'll come back, I swear it. I'm leaving Albert with you.' There was blood in his mouth. I knew he wanted to say something, but he couldn't. Albert stayed next to him, and I picked up Fenwick, and carried him over my shoulder, and took him back to the ravine.

"When I went back for Bennett, the sky was on fire, the smoke made it difficult to see more than a few feet ahead. The ammunition flashes were like lightning. Bennett was gone. Literally gone. They had taken him. Albert was wounded—someone had jabbed him with a bayonet. One of his ears was half dangling—there's a little ragged place where it wasn't stitched properly afterward. I stayed beside Albert with my rifle, and we held the position until the Rifle companies advanced again. And finally we took the pits, and it was done."

"Lieutenant Bennett was never found?" Beatrix asked faintly.

Christopher shook his head. "He wasn't returned in the prisoner exchange. He couldn't have lived long after he was captured. But I might have saved him. I'll never know. Jesus." Blotting his glittering eyes with his sleeve, he fell silent.

He seemed to be waiting for something . . . sympathy that he would not accept, condemnation that he did not deserve. Beatrix wondered what some person far wiser or more worldly than she might have said. She didn't know. All she could offer was the truth. "You must listen to me," she said. "It was an impossible choice. And Lieutenant Bennett . . . Mark . . . didn't blame you."

"I blame myself." He sounded weary.

How tired of death he must be, she thought compassionately. *How tired of grief and guilt.* But what she said was, "Well, that's not reasonable. I know that it must torment you to think that he died alone, or worse, at the hands of the enemy. But it's not how we die that matters, it's how we live. While Mark lived, he knew that he was loved. He had his family and his friends. That was as much as any man could have."

Christopher shook his head. No good. No words could help him.

Beatrix reached out to him then, unable to hold back any longer. She let her hand glide gently over the warm golden skin of his shoulder. "I don't think you should blame yourself," she said. "But it doesn't matter what I believe. You'll have to come to that conclusion on your own. It wasn't your fault that you were faced with a terrible choice. You must give yourself enough time to get better."

"How much time will that take?" he asked bitterly.

"I don't know," she admitted. "But you have a lifetime."

A caustic laugh broke from him. "That's too damned long."

"I understand that you feel responsible for what happened to Mark. But you've already been forgiven for whatever you think your sins are. You *have,*" she insisted as he shook his head. "Love forgives all things. And so many people—" She stopped as she felt his entire body jerk.

"What did you say?" she heard him whisper.

Beatrix realized the mistake she had just made. Her arms fell away from him.

The blood began to roar in her ears, her heart thumping so madly she felt faint. Without thinking, she scrambled away from him, off the bed, to the center of the room.

Breathing in frantic bursts, Beatrix turned to face him.

Christopher was staring at her, his eyes gleaming with a strange, mad light. "I knew it," he whispered.

She wondered if he might try to kill her.

She decided not to wait to find out.

Fear gave her the speed of a terrified hare. She bolted before he could catch her, tearing to the door, flinging it open, and scampering to the grand staircase. Her boots made absurdly loud thuds on the stairs as she leaped downward.

Christopher followed her to the threshold, bellowing her name.

Beatrix didn't pause for a second, knowing he was going to pursue her as soon as he donned his clothes.

Mrs. Clocker stood near the entrance hall, looking worried and astonished. "Miss Hathaway? What—"

"I think he'll come out of his room now," Beatrix said rapidly, jumping down the last of the stairs. "It's time for me to be going."

"Did he . . . are you . . ."

"If he asks for his horse to be saddled," Beatrix said breathlessly, "please have it done *slowly*."

"Yes, but—"

"Good-bye."

And Beatrix raced from the house as if demons were at her heels.

Chapter Seventeen

Beatrix fled to the one place where she knew he wouldn't find her.

The irony was hardly lost on her, that she was hiding from Christopher in the place she had most longed to share with him. And she was well aware that she could not hide from him forever. There would be a reckoning.

But after having seen his face when he realized that she was the one who had deceived him, Beatrix wanted to put off that reckoning for as long as possible.

She rode pell-mell to the secret house on Lord Westcliff's estate, tethered the horse, and went upstairs to the tower room. It was sparsely furnished with a pair of battered chairs, an ancient settee with a low back, a ramshackle table, and a bed frame propped against one wall. Beatrix had kept the room swept clean and dusted, and she had adorned the walls with unframed sketches of landscapes and animals.

A dish of burned-out candle stubs was set at the window.

After admitting fresh air into the room, Beatrix paced back and forth, muttering frantically to herself.

"He'll probably kill me. Good, that's better than having him hate me. A quick throttling, and it will be over. I wish

I could throttle myself and spare him the trouble. Maybe I should toss myself out the window. If only I'd never written those letters. If only I'd been honest. Oh, what if he goes to Ramsay House and waits there for me? What if—"

She stopped abruptly as she heard a noise from outside. *A bark.* Creeping to the window, she looked down and saw Albert's jaunty, furry form trotting around the building. And Christopher, tethering his horse near hers.

He had found her.

"Oh God," Beatrix whispered, blanching. She turned and set her back against the wall, feeling like a prisoner facing execution. This was one of the worst moments of her entire life . . . and in light of some of the Hathaways' past difficulties, that was saying something.

In just a few moments, Albert bounded into the room and came to her.

"You led him here, didn't you?" Beatrix accused in a furious whisper. *"Traitor!"*

Looking apologetic, Albert went to a chair, hopped up, and rested his chin on his paws. His ears twitched at the sound of a measured tread on the stairs.

Christopher entered the room, having to bend his head to pass through the small medieval doorway. Straightening, he surveyed their surroundings briefly before his piercing gaze found Beatrix. He stared at her with the barely suppressed wrath of a man to whom entirely too much had happened.

Beatrix wished she were a swooning sort of female. It seemed the only appropriate response to the situation.

Unfortunately, no matter how she tried to summon a swoon, her mind remained intractably conscious.

"I'm so sorry," she croaked.

No reply.

Christopher approached her slowly, as if he thought she might try to bolt again. Reaching her, he took her upper arms in a hard grip that allowed no chance of escape. "Tell me why you did it," he said, his voice low and vibrant with . . . hatred? Fury? "No, damn you, don't cry. Was it a game? Was it only to help Prudence?"

Beatrix looked away with a wretched sob. "*No,* it wasn't a game . . . Pru showed me your letter, and she said she wasn't going to answer it. And I *had* to. I felt as if it had been written for me. It was only supposed to be once. But then you wrote back, and I let myself answer just once more . . . and then one more time, and another . . ."

"How much of it was the truth?"

"All of it," Beatrix burst out. "Except for signing Pru's name. The rest of it was real. If you believe nothing else, please believe that."

Christopher was quiet for a long moment. He had begun to breathe heavily. "Why did you stop?"

She sensed how difficult it was for him to ask. But God help her, it was infinitely worse to have to answer

"Because it hurt too much. The words meant too much." She forced herself to go on, even though she was crying. "I fell in love with you, and I knew I could never have you. I couldn't pretend to be Pru any longer. I loved you so much, and I couldn't—"

Her words were abruptly smothered.

He was kissing her, she realized dazedly. What did it mean? What did he want? What . . . but her thoughts dissolved, and she stopped trying to make sense of anything.

His arms had closed around her, one hand gripping the back of her neck. Shaken to her soul, she molded against him. Taking her sobs into his mouth, he licked deep, his kiss strong and savage. It had to be a dream, and yet her senses insisted it was real, the scent and warmth and toughness of him engulfing her. He pulled her even more tightly against him, making it difficult to breathe. She didn't care. The pleasure of the kiss suffused her, drugged her, and when he pulled his head back, she protested with a bewildered moan.

Christopher forced her to look back at him. "Loved?" he asked hoarsely. "Past tense?"

"Present tense," she managed to say.

"You told me to find you."

"I didn't mean to send you that note."

"But you did. You wanted me."

"Yes." More tears escaped her stinging eyes. He bent and pressed his mouth to them, tasting the salt of grief.

Those gray eyes looked into hers, no longer bright as hell-frost, but soft as smoke. "I love you, Beatrix."

Maybe she was capable of swooning after all.

It certainly felt like a swoon, her knees giving way, her head lolling against his shoulder as he lowered them both to the threadbare carpet. Fitting his arm beneath her neck, Christopher covered her mouth with his again. Beatrix answered helplessly, unable to withhold anything. Their legs tangled, and he let his thigh nuzzle between hers.

"I th-thought you would hate me . . ." Her dazed voice seemed to come from far away.

"Never. You could run to the farthest corners of the earth. There's no place you could go where I wouldn't love you. Nothing you could do to stop me."

She shivered at what he was doing, his hands opening her clothes, sliding inside them. Her breasts felt hot, the tips hardening as he touched them. "I thought you were going to murder me," she said with difficulty.

A ghost of a smile came to his lips. "No. That wasn't what I wanted to do." He brought his mouth to hers, kissing her with rough, hungry ardor. Unfastening her breeches, he found the taut surface of her stomach. His hand insinuated farther into the loosened garment, curving around her bare hip. His fingers explored with a gentle but insistent curiosity that made her squirm, gooseflesh rising.

"Christopher," she said brokenly, fumbling with the front of his trousers, but he caught her wrist and pulled it back.

"It's been too long. I don't trust myself with you."

Pressing her burning face against his neck, where his shirt had been laid open, Beatrix felt the strong ripple of his swallow against her parted lips. "I want to be yours."

"You are, God help you."

"Then love me." Feverishly she kissed his throat. "Love me—"

"Hush," Christopher whispered. "I have little enough self-control as it is. I can't make love to you here. It wouldn't be right for you." He kissed her tumbled hair, while his hand smoothed her hip in an unsteady caress. "Talk to me. Would you really have let me marry Prudence?"

"If you seemed happy with her. If she was the one you wanted."

"I wanted *you*." He kissed her, his mouth strong and punishing. "It nearly drove me mad, looking for the things I loved in her and not finding them. And then beginning to see them in you."

"I'm sorry."

"You should have told me."

"Yes. But I knew you'd be angry. And I thought she was what you wanted. Pretty and vivacious—"

"With all the wit of a toasting iron."

"Why did you write to her in the first place?"

"I was lonely. I didn't know her well. But I needed . . . someone. When I received that reply, about Mawdsley's donkey and the smell of October, and the rest of it . . . I started falling in love right then. I thought it was another side of Pru

I hadn't yet seen. It never occurred to me that the letters were written by someone else entirely." He gave her a dark glance.

Beatrix returned his gaze contritely. "I knew you wouldn't want letters from me. I knew I wasn't the kind of woman you wanted."

Rolling Beatrix to her side, Christopher brought her against his aroused form. "Does this feel as if I don't want you?"

The hard pressure of him, the rampant heat of his body, dazzled her senses . . . it was like being drunk . . . like drinking starlight. Closing her eyes, she leaned her face into his shoulder. "You thought I was peculiar," she said in a muffled voice.

His mouth brushed the edge of her ear and settled against her neck. She felt that he was smiling. "Darling love . . . you are."

An answering grin curled her lips. She shivered as Christopher moved over her, pushing her back, using his thigh to part hers. He took her mouth with endless kisses, deep and impatient, turning her blood to fire. He began to caress her with strong, callused hands, a soldier's hands. Her breeches were dragged away from her pale hips.

They both gasped, breath fragmenting, as his palm cupped her intimately. He stroked the humid warmth, parting and spreading her, a fingertip stroking the entrance to her body.

She lay quiet and unresisting, a mad heartbeat resounding everywhere. He touched inside her, his finger pushing gently past the innocent constriction. Lowering his head, he pressed his mouth to the tender curves of her breasts. A moan escaped her as she felt him take a hard bud between his lips. He began to suckle, his tongue lapping between each rhythmic tug. His finger went deeper, the heel of his hand teasing an unspeakably sensitive place.

Beatrix writhed, seeing nothing. Desperate tension folded

in upon itself, and again, centering low and tight. A whimper escaped her as a wave of unimaginable pleasure caught her, and he guided her farther into it. She managed to speak through dry lips, her voice stunned and shaken. "Christopher—I can't—"

"Let it happen," he whispered against her flushed skin. "Let it come."

He stroked her in a wicked, sensual cadence, pushing her higher. Her muscles worked against the alarming rush of sensation, and then her body began pulling it all in, her veins dilating, heat surging. Groping for his head, Beatrix sank her hands into his hair and guided his mouth to hers. He complied at once, drinking in her moans and gasps, his beguiling hands soothing the wrenching spasms.

The delight receded in lazy ebbs, leaving her weak and trembling. Beatrix stirred and opened her eyes, discovering that she was on the floor, half undressed, cradled in the arms of the man she loved. It was a strange, delicious, vulnerable moment. Her head turned in the crook of his arm. She saw Albert, who had fallen asleep in the chair, supremely uninterested in their antics.

Christopher caressed her slowly, his knuckles trailing through the valley between her breasts.

Beatrix tilted her head back to look at him. Perspiration had given his skin the sheen of polished metal, strong masculine features worked in bronze. His expression was engrossed, as if her body fascinated him, as if she were made of some precious substance he had never encountered before. She felt the soft, hot shock of his breath as he bent to kiss the inside of her wrist. He let the tip of his tongue rest against a tiny pulse. So new, this intimacy with him, and yet it was as necessary as the beat of her own heart.

She never wanted to be out of his arms again. She wanted to be with him always.

"When are we going to marry?" she asked, her voice languorous.

Christopher brushed his lips against her cheek. He held her a little more tightly.

And he was silent.

Beatrix blinked in surprise. His hesitation affected her like a splash of cold water. "We *are* going to marry, aren't we?"

Christopher looked into her flushed face. "That's a difficult question."

"No it's not. It's a very simple yes-or-no question!"

"I can't marry you," he said quietly, "until I can be certain that it will be good for you."

"Why is there any doubt of that?"

"You know why."

"I do not!"

His mouth twisted. "Fits of rage, nightmares, strange visions, excessive drinking . . . does any of that sound like a man who's fit for marriage?"

"You were going to marry Prudence," Beatrix said indignantly.

"I wasn't. I wouldn't do this to any woman. Least of all to the woman I love more than my own life."

Beatrix rolled away and sat up, pulling her loosened garments around her. "How long do you intend for us to wait? Obviously you're not perfect, but—"

"'Not perfect' is having a bald spot or pockmarks. My problems are a bit more significant than that."

Beatrix answered in an anxious tumble of words. "I come from a family of flawed people who marry other flawed people. Every one of us has taken a chance on love."

"I love you too much to risk your safety."

"Love me even more, then," she begged. "Enough to marry me no matter what the obstacles are."

Christopher scowled. "Don't you think it would be easier

for me to take what I want, regardless of the consequences? I want you with me every moment of the day. I want to hold you every night. I want to make love to you so badly I can't even breathe. But I won't allow any harm to come to you, especially from my hands."

"You wouldn't hurt me. Your instincts wouldn't let you."

"My instincts are those of a madman."

Beatrix wrapped her arms around her bent knees. "You're willing to accept my problems," she said dolefully, "but you won't allow me to accept yours." She buried her face in her arms. "You don't trust me."

"You know that's not the issue. I don't trust myself."

In her volatile state, it was difficult not to cry. The situation was so vastly unfair. Maddening.

"Beatrix." Christopher knelt beside her, drawing her against him. She stiffened. "Let me hold you," he said near her ear.

"If we don't marry, when will I see you?" she asked miserably. "On chaperoned visits? Carriage drives? Stolen moments?"

Christopher smoothed her hair and stared into her swimming eyes. "It's more than we've had until now."

"It's not enough." Beatrix wrapped her arms around him. "I'm not afraid of you." Gripping the back of his shirt, she gave it a little shake for emphasis. "I want you, and you say you want me, and the only thing standing in our way is *you*. Don't tell me that you survived all those battles, and suffered through so much, merely to come home for *this*—"

He laid his fingers against her mouth. "Quiet. Let me think."

"What is there to—"

"Beatrix," he warned.

She fell silent, her gaze locked on his severe features.

Christopher frowned, weighing possibilities, inwardly

debating the issue without seeming to come to any satisfactory conclusion.

In the silence, Beatrix rested her head on his shoulder. His body was warm and comforting, the deep-flexing muscles easily accommodating her weight. She wriggled to press closer to him, until she felt the satisfying hardness of his chest against her breasts. And she adjusted her position as she felt the firm pressure of him lower down. Her body ached to gather him in. Furtively she brushed her lips against the salt-scented skin of his neck.

He clamped his hand on her hip. Amusement threaded through his voice. "Stop squirming. There is no possible way a man can think when you're doing that."

"Haven't you finished thinking yet?"

"No." But she felt him smile as he kissed her forehead. "If you and I marry," he said eventually, "I would be put in the position of trying to protect my wife against myself. And your well-being and happiness are everything to me."

If . . . Beatrix's heart leaped into her throat. She began to speak, but Christopher nudged his knuckles beneath her chin, gently closing her mouth. "And regardless of what fascinating ideas your family may have about the marital relationship," he continued, "I have a traditional view. The husband is master of the household."

"Oh, absolutely," Beatrix said, a bit too quickly. "That's what my family believes, too."

His eyes narrowed skeptically.

Perhaps that had been taking it a bit far. Hoping to distract him, Beatrix nuzzled her cheek into his hand. "Could I keep my animals?"

"Of course." His voice softened. "I would never deny something so important to you. Although I can't help but ask . . . is the hedgehog negotiable?"

"Medusa? Oh, no, she couldn't survive on her own. She

was abandoned by her mother as kit, and I've taken care of her ever since. I suppose I could try to find a new home for her, but for some reason people don't take readily to the idea of pet hedgehogs."

"How odd of them," Christopher said. "Very well, Medusa stays."

"Are you proposing to me?" Beatrix asked hopefully.

"No." Closing his eyes, Christopher let out a short sigh. "But I'm considering it against all better judgment."

Chapter Eighteen

They rode directly to Ramsay House, with Albert loping happily along. It was nearly time for dinner, which made it likely that both Leo and Cam would have concluded their work for the day. Beatrix wished that she'd had time to prepare her family for the situation. She was fervently glad that Merripen was still in Ireland, because he tended to view all outsiders with suspicion, and he would not have made the situation easier for Christopher. And Leo might have objections. The best option was to approach Cam, who was by far the most reasonable male in the family.

However, when Beatrix tried to make suggestions to Christopher about whom to approach and what to say, he interrupted her with a kiss and told her that he would manage it on his own.

"Very well," Beatrix said reluctantly. "But I warn you, they may be resistant to the match."

"*I'm* resistant to the match," Christopher informed her. "At least we'll have that in common."

They entered the house and went to the family parlor, where Cam and Leo were involved in conversation, and Catherine was sitting at a small writing desk.

"Phelan," Cam said, looking up with an easy smile, "have you come to see the timber yard?"

"Thank you, but I'm here for another reason."

Leo, who was standing near the window, glanced from Christopher's rumpled attire to Beatrix's disheveled condition. "Beatrix, darling, have you taken to going off the estate dressed like that?"

"Only this once," she said apologetically. "I was in a hurry."

"A hurry involving Captain Phelan?" Leo's sharp gaze moved to Christopher. "What do you wish to discuss?"

"It's personal," Christopher said quietly. "And it concerns your sister." He looked from Cam to Leo. Ordinarily there would have been no question concerning which one of them to approach. As lord of the manor, Leo would have been the first choice. However, the Hathaways seemed to have settled on an unconventional sharing of roles.

"Which one of you should I talk to?" Christopher asked.

They pointed to each other and replied at the same time. "Him."

Cam spoke to Leo. "You're the viscount."

"You're the one who usually deals with that sort of thing," Leo protested.

"Yes. But you won't like my opinion on this one."

"You're not actually considering giving them your approval, are you?"

"Of all the Hathaway sisters," Cam said equably, "Beatrix is the one most suited to choose her own husband. I trust her judgment."

Beatrix gave him a brilliant smile. "Thank you, Cam."

"What are you thinking?" Leo demanded of his brother-in-law. "You can't trust Beatrix's judgment."

"Why not?"

"She's too young," Leo said.

"I'm twenty-three," Beatrix protested. "In dog years I'd be dead."

"And you're female," Leo persisted.

"I beg your pardon?" Catherine interrupted. "Are you implying that women have poor judgment?"

"In these matters, yes." Leo gestured to Christopher. "Just look at the fellow, standing there like a bloody Greek god. Do you think she chose him because of his intellect?"

"I graduated from Cambridge," Christopher said acidly. "Should I have brought my diploma?"

"In this family," Cam interrupted, "there is no requirement of a university degree to prove one's intelligence. Lord Ramsay is a perfect example of how one has nothing to do with the other."

"Phelan," Leo said, "I don't intend to be offensive, however—"

"It's something that comes naturally to him," Catherine interrupted sweetly.

Leo sent his wife a scowl and returned his attention to Christopher. "You and Beatrix haven't known each other long enough to consider matrimony. A matter of weeks, to my knowledge. And what about Prudence Mercer? You're practically betrothed, aren't you?"

"Those are valid points," Christopher said. "And I will answer them. But you should know right away that I'm against the match."

Leo blinked in bemusement. "You mean you're against a match with Miss Mercer?"

"Well . . . yes. But I'm also against a match with Beatrix." Silence fell over the room.

"This is a trick of some sort," Leo said.

"Unfortunately, it's not," Christopher replied.

Another silence.

"Captain Phelan," Cam asked, choosing his words with care. "Have you come to ask for our consent to marry Beatrix?"

Christopher shook his head. "If I decide to marry Beatrix, I'll do it with or without your consent."

Leo looked at Cam. "Good God," he said in disgust. "This one's worse than Harry."

Cam wore an expression of beleaguered patience. "Perhaps we should both talk to Captain Phelan in the library. With brandy."

"I want my own bottle," Leo said feelingly, leading the way.

ASIDE FROM LEAVING OUT A FEW INTIMATE DETAILS, CHRIStopher told them everything. He was unsparing when it came to his own flaws, but he was determined to protect Beatrix from criticism, even from her own family.

"It's not like her to play games," Leo said, shaking his head after Christopher told them about the letters. "God knows what possessed her to do such a thing."

"It wasn't a game," Christopher said quietly. "It turned into something more than either of us expected."

Cam regarded him with a speculative gaze. "In the excitement of all these revelations, Phelan, one could easily be swept away. Are you *very sure* of your feelings for Beatrix? Because she is—"

"Unique," Leo supplied.

"I know that." Christopher felt his mouth twitch with a trace of humor. "I know that she steals things unintentionally. She wears breeches, and references Greek philosophers, and has read far too many veterinary manuals. I know that she keeps the kinds of pets that other people pay to have exterminated." Thinking of Beatrix, he felt an ache of yearning. "I know that she could never reside in London, that she could only thrive by living close to nature. I know that she is compassionate, intelligent, and brave, and the only thing she truly fears is being abandoned. And I would never do that, because I happen to love her to distraction. But there is one problem."

"What is that?" Leo asked.

Christopher answered in a bleak syllable. "Me."

Minutes ticked by as Christopher explained the rest of it . . . his inexplicable behavior since the war, the symptoms of a condition that seemed akin to madness. He probably shouldn't have been surprised that they received the information without apparent alarm. But it made him wonder: what kind of family was this?

When Christopher finished, there was a moment of silence.

Leo looked at Cam expectantly. "Well?"

"Well what?"

"Now is the time when you dredge up one of your blasted Romany sayings. Something about roosters laying eggs, or pigs dancing in the orchard. It's what you always do. Let's have it."

Cam gave him a sardonic glance. "I can't think of one right now."

"By God, I've had to listen to hundreds of them. And Phelan doesn't have to hear even *one*?"

Ignoring Leo, Cam turned his attention to Christopher. "I believe the problems you've described will lessen as time passes." He paused. "Our brother Merripen would attest to that, if he were here."

Christopher looked at him alertly.

"He never fought in a war," Cam continued quietly, "but violence and damage are hardly limited to the battlefield. He had his own demons to fight, and he conquered them. I see no reason why you can't do the same."

"I think Phelan and Beatrix should wait," Leo said. "Nothing will be lost by waiting."

"I don't know about that," Cam said. "As the Rom say, 'Take too much time, and time will take you.'"

Leo looked smug. "I knew there would be a saying."

"With all due respect," Christopher muttered, "this conversation is leading nowhere. At least one of you should point out that Beatrix deserves a better man."

"That's what I said about my wife," Leo remarked. "Which is why I married her before she could find one." He smiled slightly as he contemplated Christopher's glowering face. "So far, I haven't been all that impressed by your flaws. You drink more than you should, you have trouble controlling your impulses, and you have a temper. All of those are practically requirements in the Hathaway family. I suppose you think Beatrix should marry a quiet young gentleman whose idea of excitement is collecting snuffboxes or writing sonnets. Well, we've tried that, and it hasn't worked. She doesn't want that kind of man. Apparently what she wants is you."

"She's too young and idealistic to know better," Christopher said. "I fault her judgment."

"So do I," Leo shot back. "But unfortunately none of my sisters let me pick their husbands for them."

"Easy, the two of you," Cam interceded calmly. "I have a question for you, Phelan . . . if you decide to wait indefinitely before proposing marriage to Beatrix . . . do you intend to continue seeing her in the meantime?"

"Yes," Christopher said honestly. "I don't think anything could keep me away from her. But we'll be circumspect."

"I doubt that," Leo said. "The only thing Beatrix knows about being circumspect is how to spell it."

"Before long there would be gossip," Cam said, "and criticism, which would harm Beatrix's reputation. With the result that you would have to marry her anyway. There's not much point in delaying the inevitable."

"Are you saying you *want* me to marry her?" Christopher asked incredulously.

"No," Cam replied, looking rueful. "But I can't say I'm all that fond of the alternative. Beatrix would be miserable. Besides, which one of us will volunteer to tell her that she's going to have to wait?"

All three were silent.

BEATRIX KNEW THAT SHE WOULD GET PRECIOUS LITTLE REST that night, her mind too engaged with worries and questions to allow for sleep. Christopher had not stayed for dinner, but had left soon after his talk with Cam and Leo.

Amelia, who had come downstairs after having put Alex to bed, made no attempt to hide her pleasure in the news. "I like him," she said, hugging Beatrix and drawing back to view her with a smile. "He seems to be a good and honorable man."

"And brave," Cam added.

"Yes," Amelia replied soberly, "one can't forget what he did in the war."

"Oh, I didn't mean that," Cam told her. "I was referring to the fact that he's willing to marry a Hathaway sister."

Amelia stuck her tongue out at him, and he grinned.

The relationship between the pair was so comfortable, and yet spiced with playfulness and flirtation. Beatrix wondered if she and Christopher could ever achieve anything similar, if he would relinquish enough of his defenses to allow her to be close to him.

Frowning, Beatrix sat next to Amelia. "I keep asking about the conversation Cam and Leo had with Christopher, and it seems nothing was decided or resolved. All they did was drink brandy."

"We assured Phelan that we were more than happy to let

him have you and your menagerie," Leo retorted. "After that, he said he needed to think."

"About what?" Beatrix demanded. "What is there to think about? Why is it taking him so long to make a decision?"

"He's a man, dear," Amelia explained kindly. "Sustained thinking is very difficult for them."

"As opposed to women," Leo retorted, "who have the remarkable ability to make decisions without doing any thinking at all."

CHRISTOPHER CAME TO RAMSAY HOUSE IN THE MORNING, looking very . . . well, *soldierly,* despite the fact that he was dressed in informal walking attire. He was quiet and impeccably polite as he asked to accompany Beatrix on a walk. Although Beatrix was thrilled to see him, she was also uneasy. He looked guarded and severe, a man with a possibly unpleasant duty to perform.

This was not at all auspicious.

Still, Beatrix maintained a cheerful façade, leading Christopher to one of her favorite walks in the forest, an outward leg with farmland to the right and woodland to the left. It continued in a loop that cut directly into the forest, crossed over ancient paths, and finished along a creek. Albert crossed back and forth, sniffing industriously as they progressed.

". . . whenever you find a clearing like this," Beatrix said, leading Christopher to a small, sun-dappled meadow, "it's most likely an ancient field enclosure from the Bronze Age. They knew nothing about fertilizing, so when a patch of land became unproductive, they simply cleared a new area. And the old areas became covered with gorse and bracken and heather. And here"—she showed him the cavity of an oak tree near the clearing—"is where I watched a hobby chick hatch in early summer. Hobbies don't build their own nests, they use ones made by other birds. They're so fast when they fly, they look like sickles cutting through the air."

Christopher listened attentively. With the breeze playing lightly in his dark gold hair, and a slight smile on his lips, he was so handsome that it was difficult not to gape at him. "You know all the secrets of this forest, don't you?" he asked gently.

"There's so much to learn, I've only scratched the surface. I've filled books with sketches of animals and plants, and I keep finding new ones to study." A wistful sigh escaped her. "There is talk of a natural history society to be established in London. I wish I could be part of it."

"Why can't you?"

"I'm sure they won't admit ladies," Beatrix said. "None of those groups do. It will be a room full of whiskered old men smoking pipes and sharing entomological notes. Which is a pity, because I daresay I could talk about insects as well as any of them."

A slow smile crossed his face. "I for one am glad you have neither pipe nor whiskers," he said. "However, it seems a pity that anyone who likes animals and insects as well as you shouldn't be allowed to discuss them. Perhaps we could persuade them to make an exception for you."

Beatrix glanced at him in surprise. "You would do that? You wouldn't mind the idea of a woman pursuing such unorthodox interests?"

"Of course I wouldn't. There would be no point in marrying a woman with unorthodox interests and then trying to make her ordinary, would there?"

Her eyes turned round. "Are you going to propose to me now?"

Christopher turned her to face him, his fingers stroking the underside of her chin, coaxing her face upward. "There are some things I want to discuss first."

Beatrix looked at him expectantly.

His expression sobered. Taking her hand in his, he began to walk with her along a grassy path. "First . . . we won't be able to share a bed."

She blinked. Hesitantly she asked, "We're going to be platonic?"

He stumbled a little. "*No.* God, no. What I meant was, we will have relations, but we will not sleep together."

"But . . . I think I would like sleeping with you."

His hand tightened on hers. "My nightmares would keep you awake."

"I wouldn't mind that."

"I might accidently strangle you in my sleep."

"Oh. Well, I would mind that." Beatrix frowned in concentration as they walked slowly. "May I make a request in turn?"

"Yes, what is it?"

"Could you leave off drinking strong liquor, and only have wine from now on? I know that you use spirits as a medicine to treat your other problems, but it's possible that it actually makes them worse, and—"

"There's no need to talk me into it, love. I've already resolved to do that."

"Oh." She smiled at him, pleased.

"There's only one other thing I'll ask of you," Christopher said. "No more dangerous activities, such as climbing trees or training half-wild horses, or removing feral animals from traps, and so forth."

Beatrix glanced at him in mute protest, resisting the prospect of any curtailment on her freedom.

Christopher understood. "I won't be unreasonable," he said quietly. "But I'd rather not have to worry about you being injured."

"People are injured all the time. Women's skirts catch fire, or people are thrown down by vehicles thundering along the road, or they trip and fall—"

"Precisely my point. Life is dangerous enough without your tempting fate."

It occurred to Beatrix that her family had placed far fewer restrictions on her than a husband would. She had to remind herself that marriage would have compensations as well.

". . . I have to go to Riverton soon," Christopher was saying. "I have much to learn about running an estate, not to mention the timber market. According to the estate manager, the production of Riverton timber is inconsistent. And a new railway station is being built in the region, which is to our benefit only if good roads are laid out. I have to take part in the planning, or I'll have no right to complain later." He stopped and turned Beatrix to face him. "I know how close you are to your family. Could you bear to live away from them? We'll keep Phelan House, but our main residence would be at Riverton."

It was a striking thought, living away from her family. They had been her entire world. Especially Amelia, her one great constant. The idea touched a note of anxiety in Beatrix, but also excitement. A new home—new people, new places to explore . . . and Christopher. Most of all, Christopher.

"I believe I could," Beatrix said. "I would miss them. But most of the time I'm left to my own devices here. My siblings are occupied with their families and their lives, which is as it should be. As long as I could travel to see them when I wished, I think I would be happy."

Christopher fondled her cheek, his knuckles sliding delicately against the side of her throat. There was understanding in his eyes, and sympathy, and something else that caused her skin to flush.

"Whatever your happiness requires," he said, "you'll have it." Easing her closer, he kissed her forehead, working down to the tip of her nose. "Beatrix. *Now* I have something to ask you." His lips found the curve of her smiling mouth. "My love . . . I would choose the small sum of hours I've spent with you over a lifetime spent with another woman. You never needed to write that note, asking me to find you. I've wanted to find you my entire life. I don't think there's a man alive who could be all the things you deserve in a husband . . . but I beg you to let me try. Will you marry me?"

Beatrix pulled his head down to hers, and brought her lips close to his ear. "Yes, yes, yes," she whispered, and for no reason at all other than she wanted to, she caught the edge of his ear lightly with her teeth.

Startled by the love nip, Christopher looked down at her. Beatrix's breath quickened as she saw the promises of retribution and pleasure in his eyes. He pressed a hard kiss against her lips.

"What kind of wedding would you like?" he asked, and stole another kiss before she could reply.

"The kind that turns you into my husband." She touched the firm line of his mouth with her fingers. "What kind would you like?"

He smiled ruefully. "A fast one."

Chapter Nineteen

Christopher supposed he should take it as a bad sign that within a fortnight he had become entirely comfortable around his future in-laws. Whereas he had once avoided them for their peculiarities, he now sought out their company, spending nearly every evening at Ramsay House.

The Hathaways squabbled, laughed, and genuinely seemed to like each other, which made them different from any other family of Christopher's experience. They were interested in everything, new ideas, inventions, and discoveries. No doubt the family's intellectual bent was a result of the influence of their late father, Edward.

Christopher sensed that the happy, often chaotic household was doing him good, whereas the clamor of London had not. Somehow the Hathaways, with all their rough edges, were smoothing the broken places of his soul. He liked all of them, especially Cam, who acted as the leader of the family, or the tribe, as he referred to them. Cam was a soothing presence, calm and tolerant, occasionally herding the Hathaways along when necessary.

Leo wasn't quite so approachable. Although he was charming and irreverent, the sharp edges of his humor reminded

Christopher uncomfortably of his own past, when he had often made quips at other people's expense. For example, that remark he had once made about Beatrix belonging in the stables. Which he still didn't remember saying, except that unfortunately it sounded exactly like something he would have said. He hadn't fully understood the power of words then.

The past two years had taught him differently.

In the case of Leo, however, Beatrix assured Christopher that in spite of his sharp tongue, Leo was a caring and loyal brother. "You'll come to like him very well," she said. "But it's no surprise that you feel more comfortable around Cam— you're both foxes."

"Foxes?" Christopher had repeated, amused.

"Yes. I can always tell what kind of animal a person would be. Foxes are hunters, but they don't rely on brute strength. They're subtle and clever. Fond of outwitting others. And although they sometimes travel far, they always like to come back to a snug, safe home."

"I suppose Leo is a lion," Christopher said dryly.

"Oh, yes. Dramatic, demonstrative, and he hates being ignored. And sometimes he'll take a swipe at you. But beneath the sharp claws and the growls, he's still a cat."

"What animal are you?"

"A ferret. We can't help collecting things. When we're awake, we're very busy, but we also like to be still for long periods." She grinned at him. "And ferrets are very affectionate."

Christopher had always imagined that his household would be run with order and precision by a proper wife who would oversee every detail. Instead it seemed there was going to be a wife who strode about in breeches while animals roamed, waddled, crept, or hopped through every room.

He was fascinated by Beatrix's competence at things

women were not usually competent at. She knew how to use a hammer or a plane tool. She rode better than any woman he had ever seen, and possibly better than any man. She had an original mind, an intelligence woven of recall and intuition. But the more Christopher learned about Beatrix, the more he perceived the vein of insecurity that ran deep in her. A sense of otherness that often inclined her toward solitude. He thought that perhaps it had something to do with her parents' untimely deaths, especially her mother's, which Beatrix had felt as an abandonment. And perhaps it was partly a result of the Hathaways' having been pushed into a social position they had never been prepared for. Being in the upper classes wasn't merely following a set of rules, it was a way of thinking, of carrying oneself and interacting with the world, that had to be instilled since birth. Beatrix would never acquire the sophistication of the young women who had been raised in the aristocracy.

That was one of the things he loved most about her.

The day after he had proposed to Beatrix, Christopher had reluctantly gone to talk to Prudence. He was prepared to apologize, knowing that he had not been fair in his dealings with her. However, any trace of remorse he might have felt for having deceived Prudence vanished as soon as he saw that Prudence felt no remorse for having deceived him.

It had not been a pleasant scene, to say the least. A plum-colored flush of rage had swept across her face, and she had stormed and shrieked as if she were unhinged.

"You *can't* throw me over for that dark-haired gargoyle and her freakish family! You'll be a laughingstock. Half of them are Gypsies, and the other half are lunatics—they have few connections and no manners, they're filthy peasants and you'll regret this *to the end of your days.* Beatrix is a rude, uncivilized girl who will probably give birth to a litter."

As she had paused to take a breath, Christopher had

replied quietly, "Unfortunately, not everyone can be as re-fined as the Mercers."

The shot had gone completely over Prudence's head, of course, and she had continued to scream like a fishwife.

And an image had appeared in Christopher's head . . . not the usual ones of the war, but a peaceful one . . . Beatrix's face, calm and intent, as she had tended a wounded bird the previous day. She had wrapped the broken wing of a small sparrow against its body, and then showed Rye how to feed the bird. As Christopher had watched the proceedings, he had been struck by the mixture of delicacy and strength in Bea-trix's hands.

Bringing his attention back to the ranting woman before him, Christopher pitied the man who eventually became Pru-dence's husband.

Prudence's mother had come into the parlor then, alarmed by the uproar, and she had tried to soothe her. Christopher had taken his leave soon after, regretting every minute he had ever wasted in Prudence Mercer's company.

A week and a half later, all of Stony Cross had been star-tled by the news that Prudence had eloped with one of her longtime suitors, a member of the local gentry.

The morning of the elopement, a letter had been delivered to Ramsay House, addressed to Beatrix. It was from Pru-dence. The letter was blotched and angrily scrawled, filled with accusations and dire predictions, and more than a few misspellings. Troubled and guilt-ridden, Beatrix had shown it to Christopher.

His mouth twisted as he tore it in half and gave it back to Beatrix. "Well," he said conversationally, "she's finally writ-ten a letter to someone."

Beatrix tried to look reproving, but a reluctant laugh es-caped her. "Don't make jest of the situation. I feel so awfully guilty."

"Why? Prudence doesn't."

"She blames me for taking you away from her."

"I was never hers in the first place. And this isn't some game of pass-the-parcel."

That made her grin. "If you're the parcel," she said, giving him a suggestive glance, "I would like to unwrap you."

Christopher shook his head as she leaned forward to kiss him. "Don't start that, or we'll never get this done." Putting a board in place, he looked at her expectantly. "Start hammering."

They were in the hayloft, where she had taken him to help repair a nest box that she had constructed herself. Christopher watched, entertained, while Beatrix sank a neat row of nails into the end of the board. He had never expected that a woman's proficiency with tools would be so charming. And he couldn't help but enjoy the way her breeches tightened over her bottom every time she leaned over.

With an effort, he tried to discipline his body, push back the urgent rise of desire, as he'd had to do so often lately. Beatrix offered more temptation than he could bear. Whenever he kissed her, she responded with an innocent sensuality that drove him to the limits of his self-control.

Before he had been called to war, Christopher had never had any difficulty in finding lovers. Sex had been a casual pleasure, something he had enjoyed without guilt or inhibitions. But after prolonged abstinence, he was concerned about the first time he made love to Beatrix. He did not want to hurt or frighten her.

Self-control of any kind was still a struggle.

That was readily apparent on occasions such as the night when one of the twins had accidently stumbled over Beatrix's cat Lucky, who had let out the particular earsplitting screech of an irritated feline. And then both the twins started squalling, while Catherine had rushed to soothe them.

Christopher had nearly jumped out of his skin. The uproar had sent a shock through him, leaving him tense and trembling, and he had lowered his head and squeezed his eyes shut as he was transported in an instant to a battlefield beneath an exploding sky. A few deep breaths, and then he had become aware of Beatrix sitting beside him. She didn't question him, only stayed quiet and near.

And then Albert had come and put his chin on his knee, regarding him with somber brown eyes.

"He understands," Beatrix had said softly.

Christopher reached out to pet the rough head, and Albert nuzzled into his hand, a tongue curling against his wrist. Yes, Albert understood. He had suffered beneath the same rain of shells and cannonfire, knew the feeling of a bullet tearing through his flesh. "We're a pair, aren't we, old fellow?" Christopher had murmured.

His thoughts were wrenched back to the present as Beatrix finished her task, set the hammer aside, and dusted her hands together. "There," she said in satisfaction. "All ready for the next occupant."

She crawled over to where Christopher was half reclining, and stretched out beside him like a cat. His lashes half lowered as he surveyed her. His senses wanted to draw her in, to indulge in the feel of her soft skin, the supple firmness of her beneath him. But he resisted as she tried to pull him closer.

"Your family will suspect we've been doing something other than woodworking," he said. "You'll be covered with hay."

"I'm always covered with hay."

Her slightly crooked grin and lively blue eyes undid him. Relenting, he lowered to her, his mouth covering hers in a warm, lightly probing kiss. Her arms went around his neck. He explored her slowly, taking his time, playing with her until he felt the shy stroke of her tongue against his. The sensation went down to his groin, fueling a fresh wave of erotic heat.

She cradled him, her hips adjusting instinctively beneath his. He couldn't stop himself from pushing against the feminine softness, a pulse of movement that beguiled them both. Murmuring his name, Beatrix let her head fall back on his arm, her throat exposed to the damp caress of his lips. He found sensitive places with his tongue, using the tip of it when he felt her squirm. His hand went to one of her breasts, cupping the natural shape of her through the shirt and chemise, rubbing the tight peak with a warm circling of his palm. Small moans rose in her throat, abbreviated purrs of pleasure.

She was so exquisite, writhing and arching beneath him, that Christopher felt himself begin to drown in lust, his body taking over and his mind going hazy. It would be so easy to open her clothes, free his tortured flesh . . . let himself enter her, and find wholesale relief—

He groaned and rolled to his back, but she stayed with him, clinging.

"Make love to me," she said breathlessly. "Here. Now. Please, Christopher—"

"No." Managing to pry her away, he sat up. "Not in a hayloft, with someone likely to come into the barn at any moment."

"I don't care." Beatrix dove her hot face against his chest. "I don't care," she repeated feverishly.

"I care. You deserve something far better than a tumble in the hay. And so do I, after more than two years of going without."

Beatrix looked up at him, her eyes widening. "Truly? You've been chaste for that long?"

Christopher gave her a sardonic glance. "'Chaste' implies a purity of thought that I assure you does not apply. But I have been celibate."

Crawling behind him, Beatrix began to brush at the straw clinging to his back. "There were no opportunities to be with a woman?"

"There were."

"Then why didn't you?"

Christopher twisted to glance at her over his shoulder. "Are you really asking for the details?"

"Yes."

"Beatrix, do you know what happens to girls who ask such naughty questions?"

"They're ravished in haylofts?" she inquired hopefully.

Christopher shook his head.

Beatrix's arms slid around him from behind. He felt the light, stimulating pressure of her breasts against his back. "Tell me," she said near his ear, the moist heat of her breath causing the hairs on his nape to prickle pleasantly.

"There were camp prostitutes," he said, "who were kept busy servicing the soldiers. But they were none too attractive, and they helped to spread any number of diseases through the regiment."

"Poor things," Beatrix said sincerely.

"The prostitutes or the soldiers?"

"All of you."

How like her, he thought, to react with compassion rather than distaste. Taking one of her hands, Christopher pressed a kiss into her palm. "I also had offers from one or two of the officers' wives who had traveled with the brigade. But I didn't think it was a very good idea to sleep with another man's wife. Especially when I might have found myself fighting side by side with him afterward. And then when I was in the hospital, there were a few nurses who were probably persuadable . . . the regular ones, of course, not the ones who came with the Sisters Of Mercy . . . but after the long sieges and rounds of grave digging . . . and then being wounded . . . I wasn't exactly in an amorous mood. So I waited." He grimaced. "And I'm still waiting."

Beatrix kissed and nuzzled the back of his neck, sending a new rush of arousal through him. "I'll take care of you, poor lad," she murmured. "Don't worry, I'll break you in gently."

This was new, this mixture of desire and amusement. Christopher turned and put his arms around her, toppling her into his lap. "Oh, you will take care of me," he assured her, and crushed his mouth over hers.

LATER IN THE DAY CHRISTOPHER WENT WITH LEO TO SEE THE Ramsay estate timber yard. Although the Ramsay timber business wasn't comparable in scope to the Riverton production, it was infinitely more sophisticated. According to Leo, the Hathaways' absent brother-in-law, Merripen, was the most knowledgeable about estate forestry, including correct procedures for identifying profitable timber, thinning mixed woods, and planting for regeneration.

In the timber yard itself, several technological innovations had been made at the suggestion of Harry Rutledge, Poppy's husband. After showing Christopher an advanced system of rollers and run planks that allowed the cut timber to be moved efficiently and safely, Leo walked with him back to the house.

Their talk turned toward the timber market and arrangements with merchants. "Anything to do with the market," Leo said, "and sales by auction or private treaty, are handled by Cam. He has a better grasp of finance than any man you'll ever meet."

"I find it interesting, the way you and your brothers-in-law have divided the areas of the business, each to his strengths."

"It works well for us. Merripen is a man of the soil, Cam likes numbers . . . and my part is to do as little as possible."

Christopher wasn't deceived. "You know far too much about the entire enterprise for me to believe that. You've worked long and hard on this place."

"Yes. But I keep hoping if I feign ignorance, they'll stop asking me to do things."

Christopher smiled and focused on the ground before them as they walked, their booted feet crossing into the long shadows cast by the sun behind them. "I won't have to feign ignorance," he said, sobering. "I know next to nothing about timber. My brother prepared for it his entire life. It never occurred to me—or anyone—that I would have to fill his shoes." He paused and wished he had kept that last comment to himself. It sounded as if he were asking for sympathy.

Leo, however, replied in a friendly and matter-of-fact manner. "I know that feeling. But Merripen will help you. He's a fount of information, and he's never so happy as when he's telling people what to do. A fortnight in his company, and you'll be a bloody expert on timber. Has Beatrix yet told you that Merripen and Win will return from Ireland in time for the wedding?"

Christopher shook his head. The wedding would be held in a month, at the church on the village green. "I'm glad for Beatrix's sake. She wants the entire family to be there." A brief laugh escaped him. "I only hope we won't have a parade of animals marching through the church along with her."

"Count yourself fortunate that we got rid of the elephant," Leo said. "She might have turned it into a bridesmaid."

"Elephant?" Christopher glanced at him sharply. "She had an elephant?"

"Only for a short time. She found a new home for him."

"No." Christopher was shaking his head. "Knowing Beatrix, I could almost believe it. But no."

"She had an elephant," Leo insisted. "God's own truth."

Christopher still wasn't convinced. "I suppose it showed up at the doorstep one day and someone made the mistake of feeding it?"

"Ask Beatrix, and she'll tell you—"

But Leo broke off as they neared the paddock, where some kind of commotion was taking place. The squeal of an angry horse rent the air. A chestnut Thoroughbred was rearing and bucking with someone on its back.

"Damn it," Leo said, quickening his pace. "I told them not to buy that ill-tempered nag—he was ruined from bad handling, and not even Beatrix can fix him."

"Is that Beatrix?" Christopher asked, alarm jolting through him.

"Either Beatrix or Rohan—no one else is foolhardy enough to mount him."

Christopher broke into a run. It wasn't Beatrix. It couldn't be. She had promised him that she wouldn't put herself at physical risk anymore. But as he reached the paddock, he saw her hat fly off and her dark hair come loose, while the infuriated horse bucked with increasing force. Beatrix clung to the animal with astonishing ease, murmuring and trying to soothe him. The horse seemed to subside, responding to Beatrix's efforts. But in a quicksilver instant he reared impossibly high, his massive bulk balanced on two slender hind legs.

And then the horse twisted and began to fall.

Time itself slowed, while the huge crushing mass toppled, with Beatrix's fragile form landing beneath.

As so often had happened in battle, Christopher's instincts took over completely, prompting action at a speed faster than thought. He heard nothing, but he felt his throat vibrate with a hoarse cry, while his body vaulted over the paddock fence.

Beatrix reacted from instinct as well. As the horse began to fall, she yanked her booted feet from the stirrups and pushed away from him in midair. She hit the ground and rolled twice, thrice, while the horse's body crashed beside her . . . missing her by a matter of inches.

As Beatrix lay still and dazed, the maddened horse struggled to its feet, its hooves pounding the ground beside her with skull-splitting force. Christopher snatched her up and carried her to the side of the paddock, while Leo approached the enraged horse and somehow managed to grab the reins.

Lowering Beatrix to the ground, Christopher searched her for injuries, running his hands over her limbs, feeling her skull. She was panting and wheezing, the breath having been knocked out of her.

She blinked up at him in confusion. "What happened?"

"The horse reared and fell." Christopher's voice came out in a rasp. "Tell me your name."

"Why are you asking me that?"

"Your name," he insisted.

"Beatrix Heloise Hathaway." She looked at him with round blue eyes. "Now that we know who I am . . . who are you?"

Chapter Twenty

At Christopher's expression, Beatrix snickered and wrinkled her nose impishly. "I'm teasing. Really. I know who you are. I'm perfectly all right."

Over Christopher's shoulder, Beatrix caught sight of Leo shaking his head in warning, drawing a finger across his throat.

She realized too late that it probably hadn't been an appropriate moment for teasing. What to a Hathaway would have been a good chuckle was positively infuriating to Christopher.

He glared at her with incredulous wrath. It was only then that she realized he was shaking in the aftermath of his terror for her.

Definitely not the time for humor.

"I'm sorry—" she began contritely.

"I asked you not to train that horse," Christopher snapped, "and you agreed."

Beatrix felt instantly defensive. She was accustomed to doing as she pleased. This was certainly not the first time she'd ever fallen from a horse, nor the last.

"You didn't ask that specifically," she said reasonably, "you asked me not to do anything dangerous. And in my opinion, it wasn't."

Instead of calming Christopher, that seemed to enrage him even further. "In light of the fact that you were nearly flattened like a pikelet just now, I'd say you were wrong."

Beatrix was intent on winning the argument. "Well, it doesn't matter in any case, because the promise I made was for *after* we married. And we're not married yet."

Leo covered his eyes with his hand, shook his head, and retreated from her vision.

Christopher gave her an incinerating glare, opened his mouth to speak, and closed it again. Without another word, he lifted himself away from her and went to the stable in a long, ground-eating stride.

Sitting up, Beatrix stared after him in perplexed annoyance. "He's leaving."

"It would appear so." Leo came to her, extended a hand down, and pulled her up.

"Why did he leave right in the middle of a quarrel?" Beatrix demanded, dusting off her breeches with short, aggravated whacks. "One can't just *leave,* one has to finish it."

"If he had stayed, sweetheart," Leo said, "there's every chance I would have had to pry his hands from around your neck."

Their conversation paused as they saw Christopher riding from the stables, his form straight as a blade as he spurred his horse into a swift graceful canter.

Beatrix sighed. "I was trying to score points rather than consider how he was feeling," she admitted. "He was probably frightened for me, seeing the horse topple over like that."

"Probably?" Leo repeated. "He looked like he had just seen Death. I believe it may have touched off one of his bad spells, or whatever it is you call them."

"I must go to him."

"Not dressed like that."

"For heaven's sake, Leo, just this one time—"

"No exceptions, darling. I know my sisters. Give any one of you an inch, and you'll take a mile." He reached out and pushed back her tumbling hair. "Also . . . don't go without a chaperone."

"I don't want a chaperone. That's never any fun."

"Yes, Beatrix, that's the purpose of a chaperone."

"Well, in our family, anyone who chaperoned me would probably need a chaperone more than I do."

Leo opened his mouth to argue, then closed it.

Rare was the occasion when her brother was unable to argue a point.

Repressing a grin, Beatrix strode toward the house.

CHRISTOPHER HAD FORGIVEN BEATRIX BEFORE HE HAD EVEN reached Phelan House. He was well aware that Beatrix was accustomed to nearly unqualified freedom, and she had no wish to be reined in any more than that devil of a horse had. It would take time for her to adjust to restrictions. He had already known that.

But he had been too rattled to think clearly. She meant too much to him—she was his life. The thought of her being hurt was more than his soul could bear. The shock of seeing Beatrix nearly killed, the overwhelming mixture of terror and fury, had exploded through him and left him in chaos. No, not chaos, something far worse. Gloom. A gray, heavy fog had enclosed him, suffocating all sound and feeling. He felt as if his soul were barely anchored in his body.

This same numb detachment had happened from time to time during the war, and in the hospital. There was no cure for it, except to wait it out.

Telling the housekeeper that he didn't want to be disturbed, Christopher headed to the dark, quiet sanctuary of the library.

After searching through the sideboard, he found a bottle of Armagnac, and poured a glass.

The liquor was harsh and peppery, searing the inside of his throat. Exactly what he wanted. Hoping it would burn through the chill in his soul, he tossed it back and poured a second.

Hearing a scratch at the door, he went to open it. Albert crossed the threshold, wagging and snorting happily. "Useless mongrel," Christopher said, bending to pet him. "You smell like the floor of an East End tavern." The dog pushed back against his palm demandingly. Christopher lowered to his haunches and regarded him ruefully. "What would you say if you could talk?" he asked. "I suppose it's better that you don't. That's the point of having a dog. No conversation. Just admiring gazes and endless panting."

Someone spoke from the threshold behind him, startling him. "I hope that's not what you'll expect . . ."

Reacting with explosive instinct, Christopher turned and fastened his hand around a soft throat.

". . . from a wife," Beatrix finished unsteadily.

Christopher froze. Trying to think above the frenzy, he took a shivering breath, and blinked hard.

What in God's name was he doing?

He had shoved Beatrix against the doorjamb, pinning her by the throat, his other hand drawn back in a lethal fist. He was a hairsbreadth away from delivering a blow that would shatter delicate bones in her face.

It terrified him, how much effort it took to unclench his fist and relax his arm. With the hand that was still at her throat, he felt the fragile throb of her pulse beneath his thumb, and the delicate ripple of a swallow.

Staring into her rich blue eyes, he felt the welter of violence washed away in a flood of despair.

With a muffled curse, he snatched his hand from her and went to get his drink.

"Mrs. Clocker said you'd asked not to be disturbed," Beatrix said. "And of course the first thing I did was disturb you."

"Don't come up behind me," Christopher said roughly. "Ever."

"I of all people should have known that. I won't do it again."

Christopher took a fiery swallow of the liquor. "What do you mean, you of all people?"

"I'm used to wild creatures who don't like to be approached from behind."

He shot her a baleful glance. "How fortunate that your experience with animals has turned out to be such good preparation for marriage to me."

"I didn't mean . . . well, my point was that I should have been more considerate of your nerves."

"I don't have nerves," he snapped.

"I'm sorry. We'll call them something else." Her voice was so soothing and gentle that it would have caused an assortment of cobras, tigers, wolverines, and badgers to all snuggle together and take a group nap.

Christopher gritted his teeth and maintained a stony silence.

Pulling what looked like a biscuit from the pocket of her dress, Beatrix offered it to Albert, who bounded over to her and took the treat eagerly. Leading the dog to the door, she gestured for him to cross the threshold. "Go on to the kitchen," she said in an encouraging tone. "Mrs. Clocker is going to feed you." Albert was gone in a flash.

Closing and locking the door, Beatrix approached Christopher. She looked fresh and feminine in a lavender dress, her hair neatly swept up with combs. One could not fathom a different picture from the outlandish girl in breeches.

"I could have killed you," he said savagely.

"You didn't."

"I could have hurt you."

"You didn't do that, either."

"*God,* Beatrix." Christopher went to sit heavily at a hearth-side chair, glass in hand.

She followed him in a rustle of lavender silk. "I'm not Beatrix, actually. I'm her much nicer twin. She said you could have me from now on." Her gaze flickered to the Armagnac. "You promised not to drink spirits."

"We're not married yet." Christopher knew he should have been ashamed of the sneering echo of her own earlier words, but the temptation was too much to resist.

Beatrix didn't flinch. "I'm sorry about that. It's no fun, caring about my welfare. I'm reckless. I overestimate my abilities." She lowered to the floor at his feet, resting her arms on his knees. Her earnest blue eyes, starred with heavy dark lashes, stared contritely into his. "I shouldn't have spoken to you as I did earlier. For my family, arguing is a sport—we forget that some people tend to take it personally." One of her fingertips drew an intricate little pattern on his thigh. "But I have redeeming qualities," she continued. "I never mind dog hair, for example. And I can pick up small objects with my toes, which is a surprisingly useful talent."

Christopher's numbness started melting like spring ice. And it had nothing to do with the Armagnac. It was all Beatrix.

God, he adored her.

But the more he thawed, the more volatile he felt. Need surged beneath the thin veneer of self-control. Too much need.

Setting the unfinished liquor on the carpeted floor, Christopher drew Beatrix between his knees. He bent forward to press his lips to her forehead. He could smell the tantalizing sweetness of her skin. Settling back in the chair, he studied her. She looked angelic and guileless, as if sugar wouldn't melt in her mouth. *Little rogue,* he thought with tender amusement. He stroked one of her slender hands, which was resting on his thigh. Taking a deep breath, he let it out slowly.

"So your middle name is Heloise," he said.

"Yes, after the medieval French nun. My father loved her writings. In fact, it occurs to me . . . Héloïse was renowned for the love letters she exchanged with Abélard." Beatrix's expression brightened. "I've rather lived up to my namesake, haven't I?"

"Since Abélard was eventually castrated by Héloïse's family, I'm not especially fond of the comparison."

Beatrix grinned. "You have nothing to worry about." As she stared at him, her smile faded. "Am I forgiven?" she asked.

"For endangering yourself? . . . Never. You're too precious to me." Christopher took up her hand and kissed it. "Beatrix, you are beautiful in that dress, and I love your company more than anything in the world. But I have to take you home."

Beatrix didn't move. "Not until this is resolved."

"It is."

"No, there's still a wall between us. I can feel it."

Christopher shook his head. "I'm just . . . distracted." He reached for her elbows. "Let me help you up."

She resisted. "Something's not right. You're so far away."

"I'm right here."

There were no words to describe this infernal sense of detachment. He didn't know why it appeared or what would make it go away. He only knew that if he waited long enough, it would disappear of its own accord. At least, it had before. Perhaps one day it would appear and never leave him. *Christ.*

Staring at him, Beatrix clamped her hands lightly on his thighs. Instead of standing, she hitched her body higher against him.

Her mouth came to his, gently inquiring. He felt a little shock, a sudden pitch of his heart as if it had remembered to start beating again. Beatrix's lips were soft and hot, teasing in the way he had taught her. He felt lust come raging up, dangerously fast. Her weight was on him, her breasts, the mass of her skirts compressed between his thighs. He surrendered for a moment, fusing his mouth to hers and kissing her the way he wanted to take her, deep and hard. Beatrix immediately went pliant, submissive, in a way that drove him mad, and she knew it.

He wanted everything of her, wanted to subject her to every craving and impulse, and she was too innocent for any of it. Tearing his mouth from hers, Christopher held her at arms' length.

Her eyes were wide and wondering.

To his relief, she levered away from him and stood.

And then she began to unfasten her bodice.

"What are you doing?" he asked hoursely.

"Don't worry, the door is locked."

"That isn't what I—*Beatrix*—" By the time he had lurched to his feet, her bodice had listed open. A thick, primitive drumbeat started in his ears. "Beatrix, I'm not in the mood for virginal experimentation."

She gave him a purely ingenuous look. "Neither am I."

"You're not safe with me." He reached for the neckline of her bodice and yanked it together. While he fumbled to fasten it, Beatrix hiked up the side of her dress. A tug and a wriggle, and her petticoat dropped to the floor.

"I can undress faster than you can dress me," she informed him.

Christopher clenched his teeth as he saw her push her dress below her hips. "Damn you, I can't do this. Not now." He was perspiring, every muscle hard. His voice shook with the force of suppressed need. "I'm going to lose control."

He wouldn't be able to stop himself from hurting her. For their first time, he would have to approach her with absolute restraint, give himself release beforehand to take the edge from his lust . . . but at the moment, he would fall on her like a ravening animal.

"I understand." Beatrix pulled the combs from her hair, tossed them into the pile of discarded lavender silk, and shook out the gleaming sable locks. And she gave him a look that caused every hair on his body to lift. "I know you think that I don't understand, but I do. And I need this as much as you do." Slowly she unhooked her corset and dropped it to the floor.

Dear God. How long it had been since a woman had undressed for him. Christopher couldn't move or speak, just stood there aroused and starving and mindless, his eyes eating up the sight of her.

As she saw the way he watched her, she disrobed even more deliberately, drawing the chemise over her head. Her breasts were high and gently curved, the tips rose colored. They bounced delicately as she bent to remove her drawers.

She stood to face him.

Despite her audacity, Beatrix was nervous, an uneven blush covering her from head to toe. But she watched him closely, taking in his reactions.

She was the most beautiful thing he had ever seen, slim and lithe, her legs sheathed in pale pink stockings and white garters. She devastated him. The sable locks of her hair draped over her body, hanging down to her waist. The little triangle between her thighs looked like rich fur, an erotic contrast to her porcelain skin.

He felt weak and brutish at the same time, desire pumping through him. Nothing mattered except getting inside her . . . he had to have her or die. He didn't understand why she had deliberately pushed him over the edge, why she wasn't frightened. A rough sound was torn from his throat. Although he made no conscious decision to move, somehow he had crossed the space between them and seized her. He let his splayed fingers travel over her back, down to the curve of her bottom. Pulling her high and tight against him, he found her mouth, kissing her, almost savaging her.

She yielded completely, offering her body, her mouth, in any way he chose. As his mouth possessed hers, he reached farther between her thighs, forcing them to part. He found the tender pleats of her sex. Parting the softness, he massaged until he found wetness, and slid two fingers into the supple heat of her. Gasping against his mouth, she strained higher on her toes. He held her like that, tightly impaled on his fingers as he kissed her.

"Let me feel you," she said breathlessly, her hands working at his clothes. "Please . . . yes . . ."

Christopher fought with his waistcoat and shirt, sending buttons scattering in his haste. When his upper half was bared, he enfolded her in his arms. They both groaned and went still, absorbing the feel of it, their skin pressed together, her breasts softly abraded by the hair on his chest.

Half dragging, half carrying her to the settee, he lowered her to the cushioned upholstery. She landed in a slow sprawl, her head and shoulders propped against one corner, one foot coming to the floor. He was there before she could close her legs.

Running his hands along the stockings, he discovered they were made of silk. He had never seen pink stockings before, only black or white. He *loved* them. He stroked along her legs, kissed her knees through the silk, untied the garters and licked the red marks they had left against her skin. Beatrix was quiet. Trembling. As he let his lips stray near the inside of her thigh, she squirmed helplessly. That wanton little movement of her hips maddened him, made him frantic.

He unrolled her stockings and stripped them away. Drugged with arousal, he glanced along her body up to her passion-drowsed face, her half-closed eyes, her dark cascading hair. He pushed her thighs open with his hands. Breathing in the erotic perfume of her body, he ran his tongue through the soft triangle.

"Christopher," he heard her beg, and her hands pressed urgently against his head. She was shocked, her face deeply flushed as she realized what he was going to do.

"You started this," he said thickly. "Now I'm going to finish it."

Without giving her a chance to protest, he bent over her again. He kissed his way into the soft, secret hollow, spreading her with his tongue. She moaned and drew up tightly, her knees bending and her spine curving as if she wanted to gather her entire body around him. He pushed her back, pressed her wide, and took what he wanted.

The entire world was nothing but delicate shivering flesh, the taste of a woman, *his* woman, her intimate elixir more powerful than wine, opium, exotic spices. She moaned at the tender traction of his tongue. Her responses became his, her every sound tugging at his groin, her desperate quivers sinking into him with darts of fire. He focused on the most sensitive part of her, tracing slowly, bewitched by the wet silk. He began to flick steadily, taunting her, driving her without mercy. She went still, tensing as the feeling came rolling up to her, and he knew that nothing existed for her except the pleasure he was giving her. He made her take it, and take it, until her sharp breathing turned into repeated cries. The climax was stronger, deeper, than anything he had given her before . . . he heard it, felt it, tasted it.

When the last spasm had left her, he pulled her farther beneath him, his mouth going to her breasts. She slid her arms around his neck. Her body was sated and ready for him, her legs spreading easily as he settled between them. Reaching for the fastenings of his trousers, he fumbled and tore at them, freeing himself.

He had no control left, his entire body an ache of need. He had no words, no way to beg *please don't try to stop me, I can't, I have to have you*. He had no strength to resist any longer. Looking down at her, he said her name, his voice hoarse and questioning.

Beatrix made little crooning sounds and caressed his back. "Don't stop," she whispered. "I want you, I love you . . ." She pulled him closer, arching in welcome as he took her with blunt, insistent pressure.

He'd never had a virgin before, had always assumed it would be a quick, easy breaching. But she was tight everywhere, untried muscles clenching to keep him out. He pushed into the innocent resistance, forcing his way deeper, and she gasped and clung to him. He worked inside her, shaking with the effort to be gentle when every instinct screamed to thrust hard into the luscious heat. And then somehow her muscles accepted the futility of trying to close against him, and she relaxed. Her head rested on his supportive arm, her face turning against the hard curve of his bicep. He began to thrust with a groan of relief, knowing nothing except the blinding pleasure of being inside her, being caressed by her. The rapture was severe, absolute as death, delivering him.

He made no effort to prolong it. The peak came fast, slamming into him with a power that took his breath, and then he tumbled into a violent, shuddering release, the spasms piercing. He came endlessly, cradling her in his arms, hunching over her as if he could protect her, even as he lunged into her with ravenous strokes.

She was shaking in the aftermath, thrills of reaction running through her from head to toe. He held her, trying to comfort her, pulling her head against his chest. His eyes were blurred and hot, and he blotted them against a velvet cushion.

It took a while for him to realize that the trembling came not from her, but him.

Chapter Twenty-one

Minutes passed in sated calmness. Beatrix rested quietly in Christopher's embrace, offering no protest even though his grip was too tight. Gradually she was able to divide the sensation into its parts . . . the heat and weight of his body, the scent of perspiration, the slick of rich moisture where they were still joined. She was sore, but at the same time it was a pleasant feeling, that sense of low, warm fullness.

Slowly Christopher's urgent hold began to loosen. One hand came up to play with her hair. His mouth turned to the tender skin of her neck while his free hand traversed her back and side. A tremor passed through his frame, a slow ripple of relief. He slid an arm behind her back, arched her upward, and his lips went to her breast. She drew in an unsteady breath at the wet pull of his mouth.

He moved, turning them both so she lay atop him. His invasion had slid free, and she felt it against her stomach, an intimate brand. Lifting her head, she looked down into his face, into those silvery eyes, slightly dilated. She relished the feel of him, a great warm creature beneath her. She had the sense of having tamed him, although it was a valid question as to whether it had really been the other way around.

She pressed her lips to his shoulder. His skin was even smoother than hers, tightly stretched satin over the hard swell of muscle. Finding the bayonet scar, she touched her tongue to the unevenly mended skin.

"You didn't lose control," she whispered.

"I did, during parts of it." His voice was that of a man who had just awakened after a long sleep. He began to gather the disparate streams of her hair into a single river. "Did you plan this?"

"You're asking if I deliberately set out to seduce you? No, it was entirely spontaneous." At his silence, Beatrix lifted her head and grinned down at him. "I'm sorry for having set you off earlier. Cam is going to work with the horse from now on. I've never had to answer to anyone before—I'll have to become accustomed to it."

"Yes," he said. "Starting now."

Beatrix might have protested his autocratic tone, except there was still a dangerous glint in his eyes, and she understood that he was chafing just as she was. He wasn't comfortable with any woman having such power over him.

Very well. She certainly wouldn't be submissive to him, but she could yield to him on a few points. "I promise to be more careful from now on," she said.

Christopher didn't smile, precisely, but his lips took on a wry curve. Carefully he deposited her on the settee, went to his discarded clothes, and managed to find a handkerchief.

Beatrix lay half curled on her side and watched him, puzzling over his mood. He seemed as if he were back to himself, for the most part, but there was still a sense of distance between them, of something withheld. Thoughts he wouldn't share, words he wouldn't speak. Even now, after they had engaged in the most intimate act possible.

The distance wasn't new, she realized. It had been there

since the beginning. It was only that she was more aware of it now, attuned to the subtleties of his nature.

Returning, Christopher gave her the handkerchief. Although Beatrix would have thought herself to be far beyond blushing after what she had just experienced, she felt a tide of scarlet cover her as she blotted the sore wet place between her thighs. The sight of blood was not unexpected, but it brought home the awareness that she was irrevocably changed. No longer a virgin. A new and vulnerable feeling came over her.

Christopher dressed her in his shirt, surrounding her in soft white linen that retained the scent of his body.

"I should put on my own clothes and go home," Beatrix said. "My family knows I'm here with you unchaperoned. And even they have their limits."

"You'll stay the rest of the afternoon," Christopher said evenly. "You're not going to invade my house, have your way with me, and dash off as if I were some errand you had to take care of."

"I've had a busy day," she protested. "I've fallen from a horse, and seduced you, and now I'm bruised and sore all over."

"I'll take care of you." Christopher looked down at her, his expression stern. "Are you going to argue with me?"

Beatrix tried to sound meek. "No, sir."

A slow smile crossed his face. "That was the worst attempt at obedience I've ever seen."

"Let's practice," she said, wrapping her arms around his neck. "Give me an order and see if I don't follow it."

"Kiss me."

She pressed her mouth to his, and there was silence for a long time afterward. His hands slipped beneath the shirt, tormenting gently until she pressed herself against him. Her insides felt molten, and she weakened all over, wanting him.

"Upstairs," he said against her lips, and picked her up, carrying her as if she weighed nothing.

Beatrix blanched as they approached the door. "You can't take me upstairs like this."

"Why not?"

"I'm only wearing your shirt."

"That doesn't matter. Turn the doorknob."

"What if one of the servants should see?"

Amusement flickered in his eyes. "*Now* you're worried about propriety? Open the damned door, Beatrix."

She complied and kept her eyes tightly closed as he carried her upstairs. If any of the servants saw them, no one said a word.

After bringing Beatrix to his room, Christopher sent for cans of hot water and a hip bath, and a bottle of champagne. And he insisted on washing her, despite her cringing and protesting.

"I can't just sit here," she protested, straddling the metal tub and lowering herself carefully, "and let you do something I'm perfectly capable of doing myself."

Christopher went to the dresser, where a silver tray bearing champagne and two fluted crystal glasses had been set. He poured a glass for her, and brought it to Beatrix. "This will keep you occupied."

Taking a sip of the cool, bubbly vintage, Beatrix leaned back to look at him. "I've never had champagne in the afternoon," she said. "And certainly never while bathing. You won't let me drown, will you?"

"You can't drown in a hip bath, love." Christopher knelt beside the tub, bare-chested and sleek. "And no, I won't let anything happen to you. I have plans for you." He applied soap to a sponge, and more to his hands, and began to bathe her.

She hadn't been washed by anyone since she had been a

young child. It gave her a curious sense of safety, of being nurtured. Leaning back, she idly touched one of his forearms, trailing her fingertips through a froth of soap. The sponge drew over her slowly, her shoulders and breasts, her legs and the creases behind her knees. He began to cleanse her more intimately, and all sense of safety vanished as she felt his fingers slipping inside her. She gasped and floundered a little, reaching for his wrist.

"Don't drop the glass," Christopher murmured, his hand still between her thighs.

Beatrix nearly choked on her next swallow of champagne. "That's wicked," she said, her eyes half closing as his exploring finger found a sensitive place deep inside her.

"Drink your champagne," he said gently.

Another head-spinning sip, while his invading touch moved in subtle swirls. Beatrix lost her breath. "I can't swallow when you do that," she said helplessly, her hand gripping the glass.

His gaze was caressing. "Share it with me."

With effort, she guided the glass to his lips and gave him a swallow, while he continued to stroke and tease her beneath the water. His mouth came to hers, the kiss carrying the crisp, sweet flavor of champagne. His tongue played in ways that made her heart thunder.

"Now drink the rest," he whispered. She gave him a dazed look, her hips beginning to rise and fall of their own volition, churning the hot soap-clouded water. She was so hot, inside and out, her body aching for the pleasure he withheld. "Finish," he prompted.

One last convulsive gulp, and then the glass was removed from her nerveless grip and set aside.

Christopher kissed her again, his free arm sliding beneath her neck.

Gripping his bare shoulder, Beatrix tried to bite back a moan. "Please. Christopher, I need more, I need—"

"Patience," he whispered. "I know what you need."

A frustrated gasp escaped her as his touch withdrew, and he helped her from the bath. She was so enervated that she could barely stand, her knees threatening to fold. He dried her efficiently, and kept a supportive arm behind her back as he led her to the bed.

He stretched out beside her, cradled her in his arms, and began to kiss and caress her. Beatrix writhed like a cat, trying to absorb the lessons he was intent on teaching her. A new language of skin and hands and lips, more primal than words . . . every touch promise and provocation.

"Don't struggle for it," he whispered, his hand stealing between her straining thighs once more. "Let me give it to you . . ." His hand cupped her and pressed. His fingers entered, teased, played. But he withheld what she wanted, murmuring for her to relax, give in, let go. There was both fear and relief in giving it to him, yielding every part of herself without reserve. But she did. She let her head fall back on his arm, her body turning pliant, legs spreading. Instantly the climax welled, her flesh contracting, all awareness distilled to that secret inner place he stroked.

When Beatrix finally recovered, emerging from the opulent haze, she saw a glow of concern in his eyes. He was looking at her naked side, his hand passing lightly over the large purple bruise from her fall earlier in the day.

"It's nothing," she said. "I nearly always have something bruised or scratched."

The information didn't seem to reassure him. His mouth twisted, and he shook his head. "Stay here," he said. "I'll be back in a moment."

The instruction was entirely unnecessary. Beatrix had no

intention of moving. She crawled farther up to the pillows, letting her cheek press into the down-stuffed linen casing. She sighed and drowsed until she felt Christopher join her on the bed.

His hand settled on her hip, his palm slick with some kind of unguent. She stirred as a strong herbal odor drifted to her nostrils. "Oh, that smells nice. What is it?"

"Clove oil liniment." Carefully he rubbed the balm into her bruise. "My brother and I were covered in the stuff for most of our childhood."

"I know about some of your adventures," Beatrix said. "John told them to Audrey and me. The time the two of you stole the plum tart before dinner . . . and the time when he dared you to jump from the tree limb and you broke your arm . . . John said you were incapable of refusing a dare. He said it was easy to make you do anything, simply by telling you that you couldn't."

"I was an idiot," Christopher said ruefully.

"'Hellion' was the word he used."

"I took after my father."

"You didn't, actually. At least, not according to John. He said it was unfair that you were always cast as your father's son, when you weren't really like him." Beatrix rolled easily as Christopher nudged her onto her front. His strong, gentle hands rubbed the balm into her strained muscles, the hint of clove oil imparting a mild cooling sensation to her skin.

"John always tried to see the good in everyone," Christopher murmured. "Sometimes he saw what he wanted to believe rather than what was truly there."

Beatrix frowned as he worked her shoulder muscles, easing the tension into softness. "I see the good in you."

"Don't harbor illusions about me. In marrying me, you're going to have to make the best of a bad bargain. You don't understand the situation you're in."

"You're right." Beatrix arched in bliss as he massaged the muscles on either side of her spine. "Any woman would pity me, being in this situation."

"It's one thing to spend an afternoon in bed with me," Christopher said darkly. "It's another to experience day-to-day life with a lunatic."

"I know all about living with lunatics. I'm a Hathaway." Beatrix sighed in pleasure as his hands worked the tender places low on her back. Her body felt relaxed and tingly all over, her bruises and aches forgotten. Twisting to glance at him over her shoulder, she saw the austere lines of his face. She had an overwhelming urge to tease him, to make him play. "You missed a place," she told him.

"Where?"

Levering herself upward, Beatrix turned and crawled to where Christopher knelt on the mattress. He had donned a velvet dressing robe, the front parting to reveal a tantalizing hint of sun-browned flesh. Linking her arms around his neck, she kissed him. "Inside," she whispered. "That's where I need soothing."

A reluctant smile lurked at the corners of his lips. "This balm is too strong for that."

"No it's not. It feels lovely. Here, I'll show you—" She pounced for the tin of balm and coated her fingertips with the stuff. The rich scent of clove oil spiced the air. "Just hold still—"

"The devil I will." His voice had thickened with amusement, and he reached for her wrist.

Fleet as a ferret, Beatrix twisted to evade him. Rolling once, twice, she dove for the belt of his robe. "You put it all over me," she accused, giggling. "Coward. Now it's your turn."

"Not a chance." He grabbed her, grappled with her, and she thrilled to the sound of his husky laugh.

Somehow managing to clamber over him, she gasped at

the feel of his aroused flesh. She wrestled with him until he flipped her over with ease, pinning her wrists. The robe had become loosened during their tussle, their naked flesh rubbing together.

Sparkling silver eyes stared into blue. Already breathless with laughter, Beatrix became positively light-headed as she saw the way he was looking at her. Lowering his head, he kissed and licked at her smile as if he could taste it.

Christopher let go of her wrists and rolled to his side, exposing his front to her.

Beatrix gave him a questioning glance. Her fingers waggled slightly. "You want me to . . . to touch you with this?"

He was silent, his gaze daring her.

Shy but curious, she reached down and grasped him cautiously. They both jumped a little at the feel of it, coolness and heat, the frictionless glide of oil and silk and intimidating hardness. "Like this?" she whispered, stroking gently.

An indrawn breath hissed through his teeth, and his lashes half lowered. He made no move to stop her.

She drew the pad of her thumb over the smooth, dark head in a sleek circle. Curling her fingers around the heavy, stiffening shaft, she slid them down, marveling at the feel of him. He let her fondle and explore him at will, while his skin turned fever colored, and his chest rose and fell ever more rapidly. Mesmerized by the power of him barely contained beneath her hands, she spread her fingertips and trailed them down his hips and the front of his thighs. She stroked the rock-hard muscles of his legs, scratched lightly through the scattering of glinting hairs, then glided back to his groin. Delicately she cupped the weight of him below, played with him, gripping both hands around the rigid length.

A guttural sound came from his chest. He shoved the sleeves of the robe off his arms, pushed the garment aside, and clutched her hips. Her heart pounded as she saw the tautness of his features, the primitive intent of his gaze. She was brought over his lap, his shaft opening her, pressing into the stinging softness. A whimper broke from her lips as he pushed her fully down, compelling her to straddle him, to take all of him. He reached a new place inside her, and it felt sore but at the same time so unaccountably good that her flesh throbbed tightly in response.

Christopher went still, his searing gaze fixed on her.

In a matter of seconds the balm had done its work, the cooling spices relieving her heated flesh while simultaneously awakening intimate nerves. She moved restlessly. Grasping her hips, Christopher pushed her back down and thrust upward.

"Christopher . . ." She was unable to stop herself from squirming and lifting again. With every helpless movement she made, he pulled her hips back to his. His thighs braced behind her, and one of his hands went to the place where they were joined. He watched her, played with her, his fingers sliding across her with flirting strokes while his body never relented its deep, provocative grinding.

"Truce," she managed to say. "I can't bear any more."

"But you will." Reaching up to her, he drew her down and kissed her.

"Please. Finish it."

"Not yet." He trailed his hands down her back. "You're so beautiful," he whispered. "So sensitive. I could make love to you forever."

"Christopher—"

"Let me bring you to pleasure one more time."

"No, I'm exhausted." She took his lower lip between her teeth in a gentle nip. "Finish it now," she said.

"Not yet."

"I'll make you."

"How?"

Beatrix considered him, the arrogantly handsome features, the glitter of challenge in his eyes. Lowering herself over him, her body gently rocked by his ceaseless thrusts, she put her mouth near his ear.

"I love you," she whispered, catching his rhythm, riding it. "I love you."

Nothing more was needed. His breath stopped on a groan, and he drove into her and held, his powerful body trembling with the force of his release. Sliding his arms around her, he poured the years of anguished longing into her. And she continued to murmur to him, promising love, safety, new dreams to replace the broken ones.

Promising forever.

Chapter Twenty-two

After the London season had ended, the peerage continued their social amusements in the country. Invitations were sent for balls, dinners, and dances; gamekeepers prepared grouse to be released for shooting; guns were freshly oiled and cleaned for wildfowling; riding courses were trimmed and repaired; and wine and delicacies were brought from the ports of Bristol and London.

The most sought-after invitation in Hampshire was the mid-September soiree to be held at Ramsay House, to announce Beatrix's betrothal to Christopher Phelan. Usually any event the Hathaways hosted was well attended, but this was different. Everyone they had invited had accepted immediately, followed by a flood of letters and inquiries from people asking for invitations. Demanding them, in some instances.

The Hathaways could only attribute their newfound popularity to the fact that Christopher, England's most admired war hero, would be attending. And Christopher, with his unconcealed loathing of crowds, was glum about the entire matter.

"You must admit," Leo remarked, "it's rather amusing that the one of us least inclined to mingle in society is the one all of society wants to mingle with."

"Sod off, Ramsay," Christopher muttered, and Leo grinned.

But the phrase "one of us," used so casually, warmed Christopher's heart. Their relationship had acquired an easy, friendly feeling that reminded Christopher of how it used to be with John. Although no one would ever take John's place, Christopher found a great deal of enjoyment in the company of his future brothers-in-law. At least, he found enjoyment in the company of Leo and Cam. Whether the same liking would extend to Merripen remained to be seen.

MERRIPEN AND HIS WIFE WINNIFRED, OR WIN, AS THE FAMily called her, returned from Ireland with their young son on the first of September. The Hathaways, hardly a subdued lot to begin with, had erupted in a frenzy of joy. Christopher had stayed at the side of the family parlor during the chaotic reunion, watching as the family merged into a tangle of hugs and laughter. Cam and Merripen embraced and thumped each other's backs enthusiastically, speaking in a rapid volley of Romany.

Christopher had met Merripen on one or two occasions before the war. However, Christopher remembered little of him other than as a large and brooding presence, a man of few words. Certainly Christopher had never expected they would belong to the same family someday.

Win was a slim and graceful woman with large blue eyes and light blond hair. She had a fragile quality, almost ethereal, that set her apart from the other Hathaway sisters. Separating from the group in the middle of the room, Win came to Christopher and gave him her hand. "Captain Phelan. How lucky we are to be gaining you as a brother. The men in the family have been quite outmatched—four to five. Now you'll make our total an even ten."

"I still feel outmatched," Leo said.

Merripen approached Christopher, shook his hand with a strong grip, and gave him an appraising glance. "Rohan says you're not bad, for a *gadjo*," he said. "And Beatrix says she loves you, which inclines me to let you marry her. But I'm still considering it."

"If it makes any difference," Christopher said, "I'm willing to take all of her animals."

Merripen considered that. "You can have her."

The discussion at the dinner table was fast-paced and ebullient at first. Eventually, however, the talk turned to Ireland, and the estate Merripen would soon inherit, and the mood became somber.

Approximately ten years earlier Ireland had suffered a prolonged potato blight, leading to a magnitude of disaster the country had still not recovered from. England had offered only minimal assistance in the form of temporary relief measures, assuming that the problem would somehow solve itself through natural means.

Ireland, already impoverished, had fallen into nationwide starvation, followed by a plague of diseases, with the result that entire families had died by the roadside or in their mud huts. And landlords such as Cavan had evicted their penniless tenants, and fought with the ones who remained, resulting in lawsuits and bitterness that would last for generations.

"The Cavan lands and tenants have been neglected for years," Merripen said. "Grandfather was too preoccupied with his properties in England to make improvements or repairs. The land has no drainage, and no machinery for ploughing. The tenants themselves know only the most primitive methods of farming. They live in cottages made of mud and stone. And most of their animals have been sold off to pay the rents." Merripen paused, his face grim. "I met with Cavan before we returned to Stony Cross. He refuses to part with a shilling of his fortune to benefit the people who depend on him."

"How long does he have to live?" Amelia asked.

"Less than a year," Merripen replied. "I would be surprised if he survives past Christmas."

"When he does go," Win interceded, "we'll be free to invest his fortune back into the Cavan lands."

"But it will take far more than money," Merripen said. "We'll have to replace the mud dwellings with sound cottages. We'll have to teach the tenants an entirely new way of farming. They need everything. Machinery, fuel, cattle, seed . . ." His voice trailed away, and he gave Cam an unfathomable glance. "*Phral,* it makes what we accomplished with the Ramsay estates look like child's play."

Cam reached up and absently tugged a forelock of his hair. "We'll have to start preparing now," he said. "I'll need all the information we can obtain on Cavan's finances and holdings. We may sell some of his—your—English properties for capital. You'll have to make estimates for what is needed, and set the priorities. We won't be able to do everything at once."

"It's overwhelming," Merripen said flatly.

From the stunned silence at the table, Christopher gathered that Merripen seldom, if ever, declared that something was overwhelming.

"I'll help, *phral,*" Cam said, his gaze steady.

"I'm beginning to have the unpleasant feeling," Leo said, "that I'm going to be handling the Ramsay estates by myself, while the two of you devote yourselves to saving Ireland."

Beatrix was staring at Christopher, a slight smile on her

lips. "It puts our situation in perspective, doesn't it?" she murmured.

Which was exactly what he had been thinking.

Merripen's alert gaze went to Christopher's face. "You're to inherit Riverton, now that your brother is dead."

"Yes." Christopher's lips twisted in a self-mocking smile. "And while John was thoroughly prepared for the responsibility, the inverse is true for me. I know little more than how to shoot someone or dig trenches."

"You know how to organize men," Merripen pointed out. "How to form a plan and carry it out. How to assess risk, and adapt when necessary." He threw a swift grin in Cam's direction. "When we started to restore the Ramsay estates, we told ourselves the best thing we could do was make a mistake. It meant we would learn something."

It was then that Christopher fully grasped how much he had in common with the men in this family, even though they couldn't have come from more different environments and upbringings. They were all grappling with a rapidly changing world, facing challenges that none of them had been prepared for. All of society was being tumbled and sifted, the old hierarchy crumbling, power shifting to unfamiliar hands. A man could either let himself sink into irrelevance, or step forward to shape the new age that was upon them. The possibilities were both intriguing and exhausting—he saw that in Merripen's face, and in the faces of the others as well. But none of them would shrink from what had to be done.

Christopher contemplated Beatrix, who was sitting a few places away from him. Those eyes . . . midnight-blue, innocent and wise, alarmingly perceptive. What a curious mixture of qualities she possessed. She was capable of extraordinary composure and yet she was willing to play like a child. She was intellectual, instinctive, droll. Talking with her was like opening a treasure box to sort through unexpected delights.

As a man not yet thirty, Christopher was only six years older than Beatrix, and yet he felt the difference between them as a hundred. He wanted, needed, to be close to her, while at the same time he had to close away the worst of what he had seen and done, so that it would never touch her.

He had not made love to her since that afternoon two weeks earlier, having resolved not to take advantage of her until after they were married. But the erotic memory tantalized him constantly. Beatrix was an experience for which he had no reference point or comparison. The women he had known from the prior time in his life had offered easy and sophisticated pleasures. Nothing remotely similar to Beatrix's headlong passion.

She was too innocent, too fine, to be what fate had intended for him. But he wanted her too badly to care. He would take her, and whatever calamity fate might choose to inflict in return, he would keep Beatrix safe from it.

Or from himself, if necessary.

A SHRIEK CAME FROM THE DRAWING ROOM, DISRUPTING ALL conversation at the Ramsay House soiree.

"What the devil was that?" Christopher's grandfather, Lord Annandale, asked with a scowl. He was holding court in the family parlor, occupying a settee while various guests came to offer their homage. The long journey to Hampshire had made him querulous and exhausted. As a result, Annandale had demanded that Audrey, who had accompanied him from London, stay at his side.

Christopher suppressed a grin as he saw his sister-in-law staring at the doorway of the drawing room with patent longing. Although she had always gotten on fairly well with

Annandale, she had spent the entire previous day shut away with the old codger in a private carriage.

"Why would someone scream at a soiree?" Annandale persisted, scowling.

Christopher maintained a bland expression. Since it most likely involved one of the Hathaways, it could have been anything.

"Shall I go and find out?" Audrey asked, clearly desperate to escape her grandfather-in-law.

"No, you may stay here, in case I need something."

Audrey suppressed a sigh. "Yes, my lord."

Beatrix entered the parlor and made her way through the clustered guests. Reaching Christopher, she said in a low tone, "Your mother just met Medusa."

"My mother was the one who screamed?" Christopher asked.

"What was that?" Annandale demanded, remaining seated on the settee. "*My* daughter screamed?"

"I'm afraid so, my lord," Beatrix said apologetically. "She encountered my pet hedgehog, who had escaped from her pen." She glanced at Christopher, adding brightly, "Medusa's always been too plump to climb the walls of her box before. I think her new exercise must be working!"

"Were any quills involved, love?" Christopher asked, repressing a grin.

"Oh, no, your mother wasn't stuck. But Amelia is taking her to one of the upstairs rooms to rest. Unfortunately Medusa gave her a headache."

Audrey glanced heavenward. "Her head always aches."

"Why do you keep a hedgehog as a pet?" Annandale demanded of Beatrix.

"She can't fend for herself, my lord. My brother rescued her from a fencepost hole when she was still a hoglet, and we couldn't find her mother. So I've taken care of her ever since. Hedgehogs make delightful pets, as long as they're handled properly." She paused and regarded Annandale with frank interest. "My goodness, you are an eagle, aren't you?"

"A what?" the elderly man asked, his eyes narrowing.

"An eagle." Beatrix stared at him closely. "You have such striking features, and you exude power even while sitting still. And you like to watch people. You can assess them instantly, can't you? No doubt you're always right."

Christopher began to intervene, certain that his grandfather would incinerate her with his response. To his astonishment, Annandale practically preened under Beatrix's admiring regard.

"I can," the earl allowed. "And indeed, I am seldom mistaken in my judgments."

Audrey rolled her eyes again.

"You look a bit chilled, my lord," Beatrix observed. "You must be sitting in a draft. One moment—" She hurtled off to fetch a lap blanket, and returned to drape the soft blue wool over him.

It wasn't the least bit cool in the room, and there couldn't possibly have been a draft. However, Annandale received the blanket with obvious pleasure. Recalling the overheated rooms in his grandfather's house, Christopher reflected that he probably had been chilled. How Beatrix could have guessed it was a mystery.

"Audrey," Beatrix implored, "do let me sit next to Lord Annandale." As if it were some coveted privilege.

"If you insist." Audrey leaped from the settee as if she had been launched by a spring mechanism.

Before Beatrix took her place, she bent to rummage beneath the settee. Dragging out a drowsing gray cat, she settled it on Annandale's lap. "Here you are. Nothing warms you faster than a cat in your lap. Her name is Lucky. She'll purr if you pet her."

The old man regarded it without expression.

And to Christopher's astonishment, the old man began to stroke the sleek gray fur.

"This cat is missing a leg," he remarked to Beatrix.

"Yes, I would have named her Nelson, after the one-armed admiral, but she's female. She belonged to the cheesemaker until her foot was caught in a trap."

"Why did you name her Lucky?" Annandale asked.

"I hoped it would change her fortunes."

"And did it?"

"Well, she's sitting in the lap of an earl, isn't she?" Beatrix pointed out, and Annandale laughed outright.

He touched the cat's remaining paw. "She is fortunate to have been to able to adapt."

"She was determined," Beatrix said. "You should have seen the poor thing, not long after the amputation. She kept trying to walk on the missing leg, or jump down from a chair, and she would stumble and lose her balance. But one day, she woke up and seemed to have accepted the fact that the leg was gone for good. And she became nearly as agile as before." She added significantly, "The trick was forgetting about what she had lost . . . and learning to go on with what she had left."

Annandale gave her a fascinated stare, his lips curving. "What a clever young woman you are."

CHRISTOPHER AND AUDREY GLANCED AT EACH OTHER IN shared amazement, while Beatrix and Annandale launched into a rapt conversation.

"Men have always adored Beatrix," Audrey said in an undertone, turning toward Christopher. Her eyes sparkled with laughter. "Did you think your grandfather would be proof against her?"

"Yes. He doesn't like anyone."

"Apparently he makes exceptions for young women who flatter his vanity and appear to hang on to his every word."

Christopher stole a glance at Beatrix's glowing face. Of course the earl couldn't resist her. Beatrix had a way of looking at someone with undivided attention, making him feel as if he were the most interesting person in the room.

"I'll never understand why she hasn't married before now," Christopher said.

Audrey kept her voice low as she replied. "Most of the peerage view the Hathaway family as a detraction. And although most gentlemen are delighted by Beatrix, they don't want to marry an unconventional girl. As you well know."

Christopher frowned at the gibe. "As soon as I came to know her, I admitted I was in the wrong."

"That is to your credit," Audrey said. "I didn't think you could ever view her without prejudice. In the past, there have been more than a few men who were quite taken with Beatrix, but they did not pursue her. Mr. Chickering, for example. He absolutely begged his father to be allowed to court her, but his father threatened to cut him off. And so he has had to content himself with adoring Beatrix from afar, and flirting madly with her at every opportunity, knowing it will come to naught."

"Those days are over," Christopher said. "If he ever comes near her again . . ."

Audrey grinned. "Careful. Jealousy is quite unfashionable these days. One must have the sophistication to be amused by the attentions paid to one's wife."

"I'll take great amusement in tossing him through the window." Christopher paused as Audrey laughed. Clearly she thought he was jesting. Deciding to change the subject, he said, "I'm glad to see you're out in society again." He meant it. Audrey had spent nearly her entire marriage taking care of John, who had been diagnosed with consumption soon after their wedding. That, combined with the mourning period, had made it a lengthy and lonely ordeal for her. She deserved to find some enjoyment in life, and most definitely some companionship. "Are there any gentlemen you've taken a liking to?"

Audrey made a face. "You mean the ones my brothers haven't managed to frighten off? No, there's no one who appeals to me in *that* way. I'm sure I could have my choice of nearly any fortune hunter in London, in light of my generous jointure. But it counts against me that I'm barren."

Christopher looked at her alertly. "Are you? How do you know?"

"Three years of marriage to John, and no children. Not even a miscarriage. And it's always said that women are to blame in these matters."

"That's a belief I don't happen to share. Women are not always at fault for infertility—that's been proven. And John was ill for most of your marriage. There's every reason to hope that you'll be able to have children with another man."

Audrey smiled wryly. "We'll see what fate has in store for me. But I don't aspire to marry again. I'm weary to the bone. I feel like a woman of five-and-ninety, instead of five-and-twenty."

"You need more time," Christopher murmured. "You'll feel differently someday, Audrey."

"Perhaps," she said, sounding unconvinced.

Their attention was caught by the increasingly animated conversation between Beatrix and Annandale. ". . . I can climb a tree as well as any of the Ramsay estate woodsmen," Beatrix was telling him.

"I don't believe you," the earl declared, tremendously entertained.

"Oh, yes. Off with the skirts, off with the corset, I put on a pair of breeches, and—"

"Beatrix," Audrey interrupted, before this scandalous discussion of intimate apparel progressed any further. "I just caught a glimpse of Poppy in the next room. It's been ages since I've seen her. And I've never been introduced to her husband."

"Oh." Reluctantly Beatrix turned her attention away from Annandale. "Shall I take you to them?"

"*Yes.*" Audrey seized her arm.

Annandale looked disgruntled, his black brows lowering as Audrey propelled Beatrix away.

Christopher bit back a grin. "What do you think of her?" he asked.

Annandale replied without hesitation. "I would marry her myself, were I five years younger."

"Five?" Christopher repeated skeptically.

"Ten, damn you." But a slight smile had appeared on the earl's time-weathered face. "I commend you on your choice. She's a spirited girl. Fearless. Lovely in her own way, and with her charm she has no need of true beauty. You'll need to keep a firm hand on the reins, but the trouble will be worth it." He paused, looking wistful. "Once you've had a woman like that, you can never be content with the ordinary kind."

Christopher had been about to argue over the question of Beatrix's beauty, which in his opinion was unequaled. But that last sentence caught his attention. "You're referring to Grandmother?" he asked.

"No. Your grandmother was the kind of woman I thought I should marry. I was in love with someone else—a far less suitable girl. And I let her go, to my everlasting regret." He sighed, pondering some distant memory. "A lifetime without her . . ."

Fascinated, Christopher wanted to ask more . . . but this

was hardly the time or place for such a conversation. However, it gave him an unexpected insight into his grandfather. What would it do to a man, to marry a Prudence when one might have had a Beatrix? It would be enough to turn anyone bitter.

Later in the evening, trays of champagne were brought out, and the assembled guests waited expectantly for the betrothal announcement to be made.

Unfortunately, the man designated to do it was temporarily missing.

After a brief search, Leo was found and urged into the drawing room, where he launched into a charming toast and listed any number of amusing reasons for marriage. Although most of the guests listened with close attention and chuckled throughout, Christopher heard a pair of women gossiping nearby, whispering in disapproving undertones.

". . . Ramsay was found flirting in the corner with a woman. They had to drag him away from her."

"Who was it?"

"His *own wife*."

"Oh, dear."

"Yes. How unseemly for a married couple to carry on so."

"I suppose the Hathaways know no better."

Christopher suppressed a grin and fought the temptation to turn and inform the two old hens that the Hathaways actually did know better. They just didn't give a damn. He glanced down at Beatrix, wondering if she had heard, but she was oblivious to the gossip, her attention fixed on her brother.

Leo concluded the toast with heartfelt wishes for the betrothed couple's future happiness and prosperity. The guests raised their glasses and cheered in agreement.

Taking Beatrix's gloved hand in his, Christopher lifted it and pressed a kiss to the back of her wrist. He wanted to carry her away from the crowded drawing room and have her all to himself.

"Soon," Beatrix whispered, as if she had read his thoughts, and he let his gaze caress her. "And don't look at me like that," she added. "It makes my knees wobbly."

"Then I won't tell you what I'd like to do with you right now. Because you'd topple over like a ninepin."

The private, pleasurable moment ended all too soon.

Lord Annandale, who was standing near Leo, pushed his way to the fore, holding up his champagne glass. "My friends," he said, "I hope to contribute to the happiness of this occasion by sharing some news from London."

The crowd quieted respectfully.

A cold feeling slithered down Christopher's spine. He glanced at Leo, who looked bemused and shrugged.

"What is it?" Beatrix whispered.

Christopher shook his head, staring at his grandfather. "God help me, I don't know."

"Before departing for Hampshire," Annandale continued, "I was informed by His Grace the Duke of Cambridge that my grandson is to be invested with the Victoria Cross. The medal, created this January past, is the highest possible military decoration for valor in the face of the enemy. The queen herself will present the medal to Captain Phelan at an investiture ceremony in London next June."

Everyone in the room exclaimed and cheered. Christopher felt all the warmth in his body drain away. This was nothing that he wanted, another bloody piece of metal to pin to his chest, another fucking ceremony to honor events he didn't want to remember. And for *that* to intrude on one of the sweetest moments of his life was revolting. Damn his grandfather for doing this to him without giving him one word of advance warning.

"What will the Victoria Cross be awarded for, my lord?" someone asked.

Annandale sent a smile to Christopher. "Perhaps my grandson can hazard a guess."

Christopher shook his head, regarding him without expression.

Annoyance crossed the earl's face at Christopher's demonstrable lack of enthusiasm. "Captain Phelan was recommended for this honor by a regimental officer who gave an account of seeing him carry a wounded officer to safety under heavy gunfire. Our men had been driven back in an attempt to overtake Russian rifle pits. After rescuing the officer, Captain Phelan held the position until relief arrived. The Russian positions were captured, and the wounded officer, Lieutenant Fenwick, was saved."

Christopher didn't trust himself to speak as a volley of cheers and congratulations filled the air. He forced himself to finish the champagne, to stand still and appear calm, when he could feel himself sliding toward a dangerous precipice. Somehow he found the traction to stop it, to hold the madness at bay, reaching for the sense of detachment he both needed and feared.

Please, God, he thought. *Not for saving Fenwick.*

Chapter Twenty-three

Sensing the explosive quality in Christopher's stillness, Beatrix waited until he had drained his champagne. "Oh, my," she said in a voice loud enough to carry to the people around them. "I fear all this excitement is bringing on a touch of the vapors. Captain Phelan, if you wouldn't mind escorting me to the parlor . . . ?"

The question was greeted with sympathetic murmurs, as any evidence of a woman's delicate constitution was always encouraged.

Trying to look fragile and wan, Beatrix clung to Christopher's arm as he led her from the drawing room. Instead of proceeding to the parlor, however, they found a place outside, a bench set on a graveled walkway.

They sat together in wordless communication. Christopher slid his arm around her, pressing his mouth against her hair. She listened to the night sounds from the nearby wood; peeps and rustlings, the melodious conversations of frogs, the flappings of birds and bats. Eventually she felt Christopher's chest lift and lower in a long sigh.

"I'm sorry," she said quietly, knowing that he was thinking

about Mark Bennett, the friend he hadn't been able to save. "I know why this medal is so odious to you."

Christopher made no reply. From the near-palpable tension he radiated, she understood that of all the dark memories he harbored, this was one of the worst.

"Is it possible to refuse the medal?" she asked. "To forfeit it?"

"Not voluntarily. I'd have to do something illegal or hideous to invoke the expulsion clause."

"We could plan a crime for you to commit," Beatrix suggested. "I'm sure my family would have some excellent suggestions."

Christopher looked at her then, his eyes like silvered glass in the moonlight. For a moment Beatrix feared the attempt at levity might have annoyed him. But then there was a catch of laughter in his throat, and he folded her into his arms. "Beatrix," he whispered. "I'll never stop needing you."

They lingered outside for a few minutes longer than they should have, kissing and caressing until they were both breathless with frustrated need. A quiet groan escaped him, and he tugged her up from the bench and brought her back into the house.

As Beatrix mingled among the guests, chatting brightly and feigning interest in the advice they offered, she kept stealing glances at Christopher whenever possible. He appeared calm to the point of stoicism, maintaining a soldierly demeanor. Everyone fawned on him, even those whose social rank and aristocratic blood far eclipsed his. Despite Christopher's controlled façade, she sensed his unease, perhaps even antagonism, in trying to readjust to a landscape that had once been so familiar. He felt out of place among old friends, none of whom wanted to dwell on the reality of what he had experienced and done in the war. The medals and gold braid and patriotic music were all that anyone felt comfortable discussing. And therefore he could only allow his feelings to show in brief and cautious increments.

"Beatrix." Audrey was at her side, gently drawing her away before she could become involved in another conversation. "Come with me. I want to give you something."

Beatrix took her to the back of the house, to a set of stairs leading to an oddly shaped room on the second floor. It was one of the many charms of Ramsay House, that rooms and eccentric spaces with no apparent purpose seemed to have grown organically from the main residence.

They sat together companionably on the stairs.

"You've done Christopher so much good already," Audrey said. "I thought when he first returned after the war that he had lost all capacity for happiness. But he seems far easier with himself now . . . not nearly so brooding or tightly strung. Even his mother has remarked on the difference—and she is grateful."

"She has been kind to me," Beatrix said. "Even though it's obvious that I am not what she expected of a daughter-in-law."

"No," Audrey conceded with a grin. "However, she is determined to make the best of things. You are the only chance of keeping Riverton in our branch of the family. If you and Christopher produce no offspring, it will go to her cousins, which she could not abide. I think she would have liked me much better, had I been able to conceive."

"I'm sorry," Beatrix murmured, taking her hand.

Audrey's smile turned bittersweet. "It wasn't meant to be. That is the lesson I've had to learn. Some things aren't meant to be, and one can either rail against it, or accept it. John told me near the end that we had to be grateful for the time we had been given. He said he saw things very clearly, as his life drew to a close. Which leads me to what I wanted to give you."

Beatrix looked at her expectantly.

Carefully Audrey removed a neatly folded bit of parchment from her sleeve. It was an unsealed letter.

"Before you read it," Audrey said. "I must explain. John wrote it the week before he died—he insisted on doing it himself—and he told me to give it to Christopher when—or if—he returned. But after reading it, I wasn't certain what to do with it. When Christopher came back from the Crimea, he was so volatile and troubled . . . I thought it better to wait. Because no matter what John had asked of me, I knew above all that I must do no further harm to Christopher, after all he's been through."

Beatrix's eyes widened. "You think this letter might harm him?"

"I'm not sure. In spite of our kinship, I don't understand Christopher well enough to judge." Audrey shrugged helplessly. "You'll know what I mean when you read it. I don't want to give it to Christopher unless I can be sure it will do him good, and not create some unintended torment. I leave it in your hands, Beatrix, and trust in your wisdom."

Chapter Twenty-four

A month later, on a sunny and dry October day, the wedding took place at the parish church on the village green. To the general pleasure of Stony Cross, the ceremony adhered to long-standing village traditions. The wedding party emerged from their carriages a few streets away from the church, and walked the rest of the way along a path heavily strewn with flowers and fertility herbs. More and more people joined them as they passed, until it was less of a wedding procession than a jovial mob.

Additional flowers had been piled into a pair of massive baskets that were strapped across the back of Beatrix's mule, Hector. The little mule led the crowd at a dignified pace, while the women walking beside him reached into the baskets and tossed fresh handfuls of petals and blossoms to the ground. A straw hat festooned with flowers had been tied to Hector's head, his ears sticking out at crooked angles through the holes at the sides.

"Good God, Albert," Christopher said ruefully to the dog beside him. "Between you and the mule, I think you got the best of the bargain." Albert had been freshly washed and trimmed, a collar of white roses fastened around his neck.

The dog looked wary, clearly not liking the close-packed crowd around them any more than Christopher did.

As the women occupied one half of the street, and the men the other, Christopher caught only occasional glimpses of Beatrix. She was surrounded by village girls dressed in white, ostensibly to confuse evil spirits that might have had designs on the bride. Christopher, for his part, was surrounded by an honor guard comprised of friends from the Rifle Brigade, and a few men from his original cavalry unit.

Finally they reached the church, which was already filled. Violin music filled the air in buoyant strains.

While Christopher went to the front of the church to wait at the altar, Beatrix remained at the back with Leo.

"Beatrix," her brother asked, "what did you do to Hector?"

"He's a flower mule," she said reasonably.

"I hope it won't distress you to learn that he's eating his hat."

Beatrix stifled a giggle.

Bending his head over hers, Leo murmured, "When I give you away at the altar, Bea, I want you to remember something. I'm not really giving you away. I'm merely allowing him the chance to love you as much as the rest of us do."

Beatrix's eyes watered, and she leaned against him. "He does," she whispered.

"I think so, too," her brother whispered back. "I wouldn't let you marry him otherwise."

The rest of the morning and afternoon passed in a daze of happiness. After they exchanged vows, they left the church beneath an arch of swords held up by the honor guard. The front gate was closed—another Stony Cross tradition—and would not be opened until the groom paid the toll. Christopher reached into a velvet bag, pulled out a fistful of gold coins, and tossed them to the crowd. The shower of coins elicited squeals of glee. Three more handfuls were sent into the air, most of the glittering pieces caught before they ever reached the ground.

When every last coin had been retrieved, the assemblage swarmed to the village green, where long tables had been piled high with cakes brought by everyone in Stony Cross. Beatrix and Christopher fed each other bites of cake, while villagers showered them with crumbs to ensure the couple's fertility.

The crowd continued their celebration on the green as the wedding party departed for Ramsay House. A massive wedding breakfast ensued, with endless rounds of toasting and merriment.

When the lengthy affair was finished, Beatrix was relieved to be able to go upstairs and remove her wedding dress. As Amelia and a housemaid helped to remove the voluminous dress, the three of them started laughing as a shower of cake crumbs fell to the floor.

"That is my least favorite Stony Cross wedding custom," Beatrix said ruefully, brushing at the remaining few crumbs that clung to her arms. "On the other hand, it's probably made more than a few birds happy."

"Speaking of birds, dear . . ." Amelia waited until the maid had gone to draw a bath. "That brings to mind the line from Samuel Coleridge's poem about spring, 'The bees are stirring—birds are on the wing—'"

Beatrix gave her a quizzical glance. "Why do you mention that? It's autumn, not spring."

"Yes, but that particular poem mentions birds *pairing*. I thought you might have some questions for me on that topic."

"About birds? Thank you, but I know far more about birds than you."

Amelia sighed, giving up the attempt to be delicate. "Forget the blasted birds. It's your wedding night—do you want to ask me anything?"

"*Oh*. Thank you, but Christopher has already, er . . . provided the information."

Amelia's brows lifted. "Has he?"

"Yes. Although he used a different euphemism than birds or bees."

"Did he? What did he reference, then?"

"Squirrels," Beatrix said. And she turned aside to hide a grin at her sister's expression.

ALTHOUGH THEY WOULD BE LEAVING ON THE MORROW FOR A fortnight in the Cotswolds, Beatrix had assumed that they would spend their wedding night at Phelan House. She had sent a trunk containing some clothes, toiletries, and a nightgown to Christopher's home. She was surprised, therefore, when Christopher informed her that he had different plans in mind.

After bidding her family good-bye, Beatrix went out to the front drive with Christopher. He had changed from his uniform, with its gleaming jangle of medals, and wore simple tweed and broadcloth, with a simple white cravat tied at his neck. She much preferred him this way, in rougher, simpler clothing—the splendor of Christopher in military dress was nearly too dazzling to bear. The sun was a rich autumn gold, lowering into the black nest of treetops.

Instead of the carriage Beatrix had expected, there was a single horse on the drive, Christopher's large bay gelding.

Beatrix turned to give him a questioning look. "Don't I get a horse? A pony cart? Or am I to trot along behind you?"

His lips twitched. "We'll ride together, if you're willing. I have a surprise for you."

"How unconventional of you."

"Yes, I thought that would please you." He helped her to mount the horse, and swung up easily behind her.

No matter what the surprise was, Beatrix thought as she

leaned back into his cradling arms, this moment was bliss. She savored the feel of him, all his strength around her, his body adjusting easily to every movement of the horse. He bade her to close her eyes as they went into the forest. Beatrix relaxed against his chest. The forest air turned sweeter as it cooled, infused with scents of resin and dark earth.

"Where are we going?" she asked against his coat.

"We're almost there. Don't look."

Soon Christopher reined in the horse and dismounted, helping her down.

Viewing their surroundings, Beatrix smiled in perplexity. It was the secret house on Lord Westcliff's estate. Light glowed through the open windows. "Why are we here?"

"Go upstairs and see," Christopher said, and went to tether the horse.

Picking up the skirts of her blue dress, Beatrix ascended the circular staircase, which had been lit with strategically placed lamps in the wall brackets where ancient torches had once hung. Reaching the circular room upstairs, Beatrix crossed the threshold.

The room had been transformed.

A small fire glowed in the formerly dark hearth, and golden lamplight filled the air. The scarred wooden floors had been scrubbed clean and covered with rich, thick Turkish carpets. Floral tapestries softened the old stone walls. The ancient bedframe had been replaced by a large chestnut bed with carved panels and spiral columns. The bed had been made up with a deep mattress and luxurious quilts and linens, and plump white pillows piled three deep. The table in the corner was draped in mauve damask and laden with covered silver trays and baskets spilling over with food. Condensation glittered on the sides of a silver bucket of iced champagne. And there was her trunk, set beside a painted dressing screen.

Stunned, Beatrix wandered farther into the room, trying to take it all in.

Christopher came up behind her. As Beatrix turned to face him, he searched her face with a gently quizzical gaze. "If you like, we can spend our first night together here," he said. "But if this doesn't suit you, we'll go to Phelan House."

Beatrix could hardly speak. "You did this for me?"

He nodded. "I asked Lord Westcliff if we might stay the night here. And he had no objections to a little redecorating. Do you—"

He was interrupted as Beatrix flung herself at him and wrapped her arms tightly around his neck.

Christopher held her, his hands coursing slowly over her back and hips. His lips found the tender skin of her cheeks, her chin, the yielding softness of her mouth. Through the descending diaphanous layers of pleasure, Beatrix answered him blindly, taking a shivering breath as his long fingers curved beneath her jaw. He shaped her lips with his own, his tongue questing gently. The taste of him was smooth and subtle and masculine. Intoxicating. Needing more of him, she struggled to draw him deeper, to kiss him harder, and he resisted with a quiet laugh.

"Wait. Easy . . . love, there's another part of the surprise that I don't want you to miss."

"Where?" Beatrix asked drowsily, her hand searching over his front.

Christopher gave a muffled laugh, taking her by the shoulders and easing her away. He stared down at her, his gray eyes glowing.

"Listen," he whispered.

As the thrumming of her own heart quieted, Beatrix heard music. Not instruments, but human voices joined in harmony. Bemused, she went to the window and looked out. A smile lit her face.

A small group of officers from Christopher's regiment, still in uniform, were standing in a row and singing a slow, haunting ballad.

> *Were I laid on Greenland's coast,*
> *And in my arms embrac'd my lass;*
> *Warm amidst eternal frost,*
> *Too soon the half year's night would pass.*
> *And I would love you all the day.*
> *Ev'ry night would kiss and play,*
> *If with me you'd fondly stray.*
> *Over the hills and far away . . .*

"Our song," Beatrix whispered, as the sweet strains floated up to them.

"Yes."

Beatrix lowered to the floor and braced her folded arms on the windowsill . . . the same place where she had lit so many candles for a soldier fighting in a faraway land.

Christopher joined her at the window, kneeling with his arms braced around her. At the conclusion of the song, Beatrix blew the officers a kiss. "Thank you, gentlemen," she called down to them. "I will treasure this memory always."

One of them volunteered, "Perhaps you're not aware of it, Mrs. Phelan, but according to Rifle Brigade wedding tradition, every man on the groom's honor guard gets to kiss the bride on her wedding night."

"What rot," Christopher retorted amiably. "The only Rifles wedding tradition I know of is to avoid getting married in the first place."

"Well, you bungled that one, old fellow." The group chortled.

"Can't say as I blame him," one of them added. "You are a vision, Mrs. Phelan."

"As fair as moonlight," another said.

"Thank you," Christopher said. "Now stop wooing my wife, and take your leave."

"We started the job," one of the officers said. "It's left to you to finish it, Phelan."

And with cheerful catcalls and well wishes, the Rifles departed.

"They're taking the horse with them," Christopher said, a smile in his voice. "You're well and truly stranded with me now." He turned toward Beatrix and slid his fingers beneath her chin, nudging her to look at him. "What's this?" His voice gentled. "What's the matter?"

"Nothing," Beatrix said, seeing him through a shimmer of tears. "Absolutely nothing. It's just . . . I spent so many hours in this place, dreaming of being with you someday. But I never dared to believe it could really happen."

"You had to believe, just a little," Christopher whispered. "Otherwise it wouldn't have come true." Pulling her between his spread thighs, he wrapped her in a comforting hug. After a long time, he spoke quietly into her hair. "Beatrix. One of the reasons I haven't made love to you since that afternoon is that I didn't want to take advantage of you again."

"You didn't," she protested. "I gave myself to you freely."

"Yes, I know." Christopher kissed her head. "You were generous, and beautiful, and so passionate that you've ruined me for any other woman. But it wasn't what I had intended for your first time. Tonight I'm going to make amends."

Beatrix shivered at the sensual promise of his tone. "There's no need. But if you insist . . ."

"I do insist." He smoothed his hand over her back and continued to hold her, making her feel safe. And then he began to kiss his way along the side of her neck, his mouth hot and deliberate, and she began to feel not entirely safe. She drew in a quick breath as he lingered at a sensitive place.

Feeling the ripple of her convulsive swallow, he lifted his head and smiled down at her. "Shall we have supper first?" Standing in an easy movement, he pulled her up with him.

"After that enormous wedding breakfast," Beatrix replied, "I'll never be hungry again. However . . ."—she gave him a brilliant grin—"I wouldn't mind a glass of champagne."

Taking her face in his hands, Christopher kissed her swiftly. "For that smile, you can have the entire bottle."

She pressed her cheek into his palm. "Would you unfasten my dress first?"

Turning her away from him, he began on the row of concealed hooks that held the back of her dress together.

It felt like a husbandly act, this unfastening of her dress, both comforting and pleasant. As he bared her nape, he pressed his lips to the delicate skin, and strung more lingering kisses to the top of her spine.

"Shall I do the corset as well?" he asked, his voice close to her ear.

Beatrix was privately amazed that her legs were still supporting her. "No, thank you, I can manage that by myself." She fled to the privacy of the dressing screen, and tugged her trunk behind it. Opening the lid, Beatrix found her neatly folded clothes and a drawstring muslin bag containing a brush and a rack of hairpins, and other small necessities. There was also a package wrapped in pale blue paper and tied with a matching ribbon. Picking up a small folded note that had been tucked under the ribbon, Beatrix read:

A gift for your wedding night, darling Bea. This gown was made by the most fashionable modiste in London. It is rather different from the ones you usually wear, but it will be very pleasing to a bridegroom. Trust me about this.
    —Poppy

Holding the nightgown up, Beatrix saw that it was made of black gossamer and fastened with tiny jet buttons. Since the only nightgowns she had ever worn had been of modest white cambric or muslin, this was rather shocking. However, if it was what husbands liked . . .

After removing her corset and her other underpinnings, Beatrix drew the gown over her head and let it slither over her body in a cool, silky drift. The thin fabric draped closely over her shoulders and torso and buttoned at the waist before flowing to the ground in transparent panels. A side slit went up to her hip, exposing her leg when she moved. And her back was shockingly exposed, the gown dipping low against her spine. Pulling the pins and combs from her hair, she dropped them into the muslin bag in the trunk.

Tentatively she emerged from behind the screen.

Christopher had just finished pouring two glasses of champagne. He turned toward her and froze, except for his gaze, which traveled over her in a burning sweep. "My God," he muttered, and drained his champagne. Setting the empty glass aside, he gripped the other as if he were afraid it might slip through his fingers.

"Do you like my nightgown?" Beatrix asked.

Christopher nodded, not taking his gaze from her. "Where's the rest of it?"

"This was all I could find." Unable to resist teasing him, Beatrix twisted and tried to see the back view. "I wonder if I put it on backward . . ."

"Let me see." As she turned to reveal the naked line of her back, Christopher drew in a harsh breath.

Although Beatrix heard him mumble a curse, she didn't take offense, deducing that Poppy had been right about the nightgown. And when he drained the second glass of champagne, forgetting that it was hers, Beatrix sternly repressed a grin. She went to the bed and climbed onto the mattress, relishing the billowy softness of the quilts and linens. Reclining on her side, she made no attempt to cover her exposed leg as the gossamer fabric fell open to her hip.

Christopher came to her, stripping off his shirt along the way. The sight of him, all that flexing muscle and sun-glazed skin, was breathtaking. He was a beautiful man, a scarred Apollo, a dream lover. And he was hers.

She reached for him, a breath catching in her throat as her hand flattened on his chest. She let her fingertips trail through the crisp, glinting fur. He bent over her, his eyes heavy lidded, his mouth firming in the way it did when he was aroused.

Overwhelmed by a mingling of love and desire, she said breathlessly, "Christopher—"

He touched her lips with a single finger, stroking the tremulous curves, using the tip of his thumb to part them. He kissed her, fitting his mouth to hers at varying angles. Each kiss delivered a deep, sweet shock to her nerves, spreading fire inside her, making it impossible to think clearly. His hands swept over her with a sensitive lightness that promised rather than satisfied. She was being seduced, quite skillfully.

She felt herself being pressed to her back, one of his legs pushing between hers. His fingers smoothed over her breast, finding the aching point of a nipple veiled in silk. His thumb prodded the bud, swirled lightly, stroked with a softness that made her writhe in agitation. Taking the tip of her breast in his thumb and forefinger, he squeezed gently through the gossamer, sending a bolt of desire through her. She moaned against his lips and broke their kiss as she struggled to draw in more air.

Christopher bent to her chest, the mist of his breath penetrating the shimmering fabric and heating the skin beneath.

His tongue touched the taut peak, flickered wetly over the silk, the gauzy stimulation affording both frustration and pleasure. Beatrix reached with shaking hands to push the nightgown out of the way.

"Slowly," he whispered, trailing his tongue across her skin, not quite reaching the place where she most wanted it.

Her fingers went to his cheeks and jaw, the abrasion of his shaven bristle like raw velvet against her palms. She tried to guide his mouth, and he laughed quietly, resisting. "Slowly," he repeated, brushing kisses in the soft space between her breasts.

"Why?" she asked between agitated breaths.

"It's better for both of us." He cupped beneath her breast and shaped it in gentle fingers. "Especially you. It makes the pleasure deeper . . . sweeter . . . let me show you, love . . ."

Her head tossed restlessly as his tongue played on her flesh. "Christopher . . ." Her voice was trembling. "I wish . . ."

"Yes?"

It was so terribly selfish, and yet she couldn't help from blurting out, "I wish there had been no other women before me."

He looked down at her in a way that made her feel as if she were dissolving in honey. His mouth descended, caressing hers with tender, urgent warmth. "My heart belongs only to you," he whispered. "It was never lovemaking before. This is a first for me, too."

She puzzled over that, staring into his bright, lambent eyes. "Then it's different, when one is in love?"

"Beatrix, dearest love, it's beyond anything I've ever known. Beyond dreams." His hand glided over her hip, fingers gently tugging the black gossamer aside to reach her skin. Her stomach tightened at the temptation and knowledge in his touch. "You're the reason I live. If it weren't for you, I never would have come back."

"Don't say that." It was unbearable, the thought of anything happening to him.

"'It's all come down to the hope of being with you,' . . . Do you remember when I wrote that?"

Beatrix nodded and bit her lip as his hand slid farther beneath the transparent silk panels.

"I meant every word," he murmured. "I would have written much more, but I didn't want to frighten you."

"I wanted to write more, too," she said shakily. "I wanted to share every thought with you, every—" She broke off with a gasp as he found the vulnerable place between her thighs.

"You're so warm here," he whispered, stroking her intimately. "So soft. Oh, Beatrix . . . I fell in love with you by words alone . . . but I have to admit . . . I prefer this way of communicating."

She could barely speak, her mind dazzled by sensation. "It's still a love letter," she said, sliding her hand over the golden slope of his shoulder. "Only in bed."

He smiled. "Then I'll try to use proper punctuation."

"And no dangling participles," she added, making him laugh.

But she lost all reason for amusement as he stroked and cradled and tormented her. Too many sensations, coming from different directions. She twisted in the gathering heat. Christopher tried to ease her as the rapture rose too high, too fast, his hands gentle on her quivering limbs.

"Please," she said, perspiration gathering on her skin and at the roots of her hair. "I need you now."

"No, love. Wait just a little longer." He caressed her thighs, his thumbs stroking up to the humid folds of her sex.

She discovered that the most impossible thing in the world was to hold climax at bay, that the more he told her not to, the more powerfully it surged toward her. And he knew it, the devil, a teasing light in his eyes as he whispered to her . . . "Not yet. It's too soon." And all the while, his fingers stroked idly between her thighs, and his mouth grazed over her breast. Every part of her body was filled with desperate craving. "Don't give in to it," he said against her twitching skin. "Wait . . ."

Beatrix panted and stiffened, trying to hold back the rush of sensation. But his lips opened over her nipple, and he began to tug gently, and she was lost. Crying out, she hitched upward against his mouth and hands, and let the wrenching delight overtake her. She jerked and moaned as the voluptuous spasms went through her, while tears of chagrin filled her eyes.

Looking down at her, Christopher murmured sympathetically. His hands moved over her body in soothing strokes, and he kissed away an escaping tear. "Don't be upset," he whispered.

"I couldn't stop it from happening," she said in a plaintive voice.

"You weren't supposed to," he said tenderly. "I was playing with you. Teasing you."

"But I wanted it to last longer. It's our wedding night, and it's already over." Pausing, Beatrix added glumly, "At least my part of it is."

Christopher averted his face, but she could see that he was struggling to contain a laugh. When he had mastered himself, he looked down at her with a slight smile and smoothed her hair back from her face. "I can make you ready again."

Beatrix was quiet for a moment as she evaluated her spent nerves and limp body. "I don't think so," she said. "I feel like a wrung-out kitchen mop."

"I *promise* to make you ready again," he said, his voice threaded with amusement.

"It will take a long time," Beatrix said, still frowning.

Gathering her into his arms, Christopher crushed his mouth over hers. "I can only hope so."

After undressing them both, Christopher kissed her sated body everywhere, tasting her leisurely. She stretched and arched, her breath quickening. He followed the subtle signs of her response, coaxing out heat as if he were nurturing a flame set to kindling. Compulsively her hands wandered over the masculine textures of him, the rough hair and hard satiny muscles, the scars that were slowly becoming familiar.

Turning Beatrix to her side, he pulled her top knee upward. She felt him enter her from behind, the pressure of him opening her, stretching her impossibly tight. Too much, and yet she wanted more. She dropped her head to his supportive arm, and sobbed as he bent to kiss her neck. He surrounded her, filled her . . . she felt her flesh swelling with heat and sensation, her body adjusting instinctively to his.

He whispered in her ear, words of lust and praise and adoration, telling her all the ways he wanted to pleasure her. Very gently he pushed her onto her stomach, and kneed her thighs wider. She groaned as she felt one of his hands slide beneath her hips. He cupped her sex, stroking in counterpoint as he began a deep, insistent rhythm. Faster than before, deliberate . . . ruthless. She moaned and gripped the quilt in handfuls as the sensation blazed.

When she was at the verge of another peak, he stopped and turned her over. She couldn't look away from the molten silver of his eyes, storms stirred by lightning.

"I love you," he whispered, and she jolted as he entered her again. Wrapping her arms and legs around him, she kissed and bit the thick, enticing muscle of his shoulder. He made a low sound, almost a growl, and cupped her bottom to lift her more tightly into his thrusts. Every time he lunged forward, his body rubbed intimately against hers, stroking her sex over and over, sending her into a climax that shimmered through every cell and nerve.

Christopher buried himself and held, letting the convulsions of her body pull at him wetly, severely, the mutual release exacting groans from them both. And yet the need didn't stop. The physical release opened into a craving for even more intimacy. Rolling them both to their sides, Christopher cradled her with their bodies locked together. Even now, he wasn't close enough to her, he wanted more of her.

They emerged from the bed some time later to feast on the delectable cold supper that had been left for them, slices of game pie, salads, ripe black plums, cake soaked in elderflower cordial. They washed it all down with champagne, and took the last two glasses to bed, where Christopher made any number of lascivious toasts. And Beatrix made a project of applying her champagne-chilled mouth to various parts of his body. They played, and made each other laugh, and then they were silent for a while, watching the candles burn down.

"I don't want to fall asleep," Beatrix mumbled. "I want tonight to last forever."

She felt Christopher smile against her cheek. "It doesn't have to last. I'm personally quite optimistic about tomorrow night."

"In that case, I'm going to sleep. I can't keep my eyes open any longer."

He kissed her gently. "Good night, Mrs. Phelan."

"Good night." A drowsy smile curved her lips as she watched him leave the bed to extinguish the last of the candles.

But first he took a pillow from the bed, and dropped it to the carpet along with a spare quilt.

"What are you doing?"

Christopher glanced at her over his shoulder, one brow

arching. "You'll recollect that I told you we can't sleep together."

"Not even on our wedding night?" she protested.

"I'll be within arm's reach, love."

"But you won't be comfortable on the floor."

He went to snuff out the light. "Beatrix, compared to some of the places I've slept in the past, this is a palace. Believe me, I'll be comfortable."

Disgruntled, Beatrix drew the covers around herself and lay on her side. The room went dark, and she heard the sounds of Christopher settling, and the measured sound of his breathing. Soon she felt herself slipping into the welcoming blackness . . . leaving him to contend with the demons of his sleep.

Chapter Twenty-five

Although Beatrix considered Hampshire to be the most beautiful place in England, the Cotswolds very nearly eclipsed it. The Cotswolds, often referred to as the heart of England, were formed by a chain of escarpments and hills that crossed Gloucestershire and Oxfordshire. Beatrix was delighted by the storybook villages with their small, neat cottages, and by the green hills covered with plump sheep. Since wool had been the most profitable industry of the Cotswolds, with profits being used to improve the landscape and build churches, more than one plaque proclaimed, THE SHEEP HATH PAID FOR ALL.

To Beatrix's delight, the sheepdog had a similarly elevated status. The villagers' attitude toward dogs reminded Beatrix of a Romany saying she had once heard from Cam . . . "To make a visitor feel welcome, you must also make his dog feel welcome." Here in this Cotswold village, people took their dogs everywhere, even to churches in which the pews were worn with grooves where leashes had been tied.

Christopher took Beatrix to a thatched-roof cottage on the estate of Lord Brackley. The viscount, an elderly friend and connection of Annandale's, had offered to make the place available to them indefinitely. The cottage was just out of sight of Brackley Manor, built on the other side of an ancient tithe barn. With its low arched doors, sloping thatched roof, and twice-flowering pink clematis climbing the outside walls, the cottage was enchanting.

The main room featured a stone fireplace, beamed ceilings and comfortable furnishings, and mullioned windows overlooking a back garden. Albert went to investigate the upstairs rooms, while a pair of footmen carried in trunks and valises.

"Does it please you?" Christopher asked, smiling as he saw Beatrix's excitement.

"How could it not?" she asked, turning a slow circle to view everything.

"It's a rather humble place for a honeymoon," Christopher said, smiling as she bounded to him and threw her arms around his neck. "I could take you anywhere—Paris, Florence—"

"As I told you before, I want a quiet, snug place." Beatrix pressed impulsive kisses on his face. "Books . . . wine . . . long walks . . . and *you*. It's the most wonderful place in the world. I'm already sorry to leave."

He chuckled, endeavoring to catch her mouth with his own. "We don't have to leave for two weeks." After he captured her lips in a long, searing kiss, Beatrix melted against him and sighed.

"How could ordinary life possibly compare to this?"

"Ordinary life will be just as wonderful," he whispered. "As long as you're there."

AT CHRISTOPHER'S INSISTENCE, BEATRIX SLEPT IN ONE OF two adjoining upstairs bedrooms, separated only by a thin wall of lath and plaster. He knew it bothered her not to share a room with him, but his sleep was too restless, his nightmares too unpredictable, for him to take any chances.

Even here, in this place of unfolding happiness, there were difficult nights. He woke and sat bolt upright from dreams of blood and bullets, of faces contorted with agony, and he found himself reaching for a gun, a sword, some means of defending himself. Whenever the nightmares were especially bad, Albert always crept onto the foot of the bed and kept him company. Just as he had during the war, Albert guarded Christopher while he slept, ready to alert him if an enemy approached.

No matter how troubled the nights were, however, the days were extraordinary . . . pleasure filled, serene, imparting a sense of well-being that Christopher hadn't felt in years. There was something about the light in the Cotswolds, a smooth opalesence that covered the hills and farmland in a soft binding. The morning usually began with sun, the sky gradually thickening to clouds in the afternoon. Later in the day, rain fell on the brilliant autumn leaves and gave them a boiled-sugar glaze, and drew out a dark, fresh scent from the loam and clay.

They quickly fell into a pattern of things, a simple breakfast followed by a long ramble with Albert, and then they ventured out to visit the nearby market town with its shops and bakeries, or to explore old ruins and monuments. One could not employ a purposeful stride with Beatrix. She stopped frequently to look at spiderwebs, insects, moss, nests. She listened to out-of-doors sounds with the same appreciation that other people showed while listening to Mozart. It was all a symphony to her . . . sky, water, land. She approached the world anew each day, living fully in the present, keeping pace with everything around her.

One evening they accepted an invitation from Lord and Lady Brackley to have dinner at the manor. Most of the time, however, they secluded themselves, their privacy disrupted only when servants came from the nearby manor to bring food and fresh linens. Many an afternoon was spent making love before the hearth or in bed. The more Christopher had of Beatrix, the more he wanted.

But Christopher was determined to shelter her from the darker side of himself, the memories that he couldn't escape. She was patient when they came to stumbling blocks in their conversations, when one of her questions had veered close to dangerous territory. She was equally forbearing when a shadow crossed his mood. And Christopher was ashamed that she had to accommodate such complexities in his nature.

There were moments when her gentle prying spurred a flare of irritation, and rather than snap at her, he withdrew into a cool silence. And their sleeping arrangements were a frequent source of tension. Beatrix could not seem to accept the fact that he wanted no one near him while he slept. It wasn't merely his nightmares—he was literally incapable of falling asleep if there was someone else next to him. Every touch or sound would jolt him awake. Every night was a struggle.

"At least take a nap with me," Beatrix had coaxed one afternoon. "One little nap. It will be lovely. You'll see. Just lie with me, and—"

"Beatrix," he had said in barely contained exasperation, "don't badger. You won't accomplish anything except to drive me mad."

"I'm sorry," she had replied, chastened. "It's only that I want to be close to you."

Christopher understood. But the uncompromised closeness she desired would always be impossible for him. The only thing left was to make it up to her in every other way he could think of.

His need for her ran so deep that it seemed to be part of his blood, woven into his bones. He didn't understand all the reasons for such mysterious alchemy. But did reasons really matter? One could pick apart love, examine every filament of attraction, and still it would never be fully explained.

It simply was.

UPON THEIR RETURN TO STONY CROSS, CHRISTOPHER AND Beatrix found Phelan House in disorder. The servants were still accustoming themselves to the new residents of the stables and the house, including the cat, hedgehog, goat, birds and rabbits, the mule, and so forth. The main reason for the disarray, however, was that most of the rooms at Phelan House were being closed and their contents stored in preparation for the household to be moved to Riverton.

Neither Audrey nor Christopher's mother intended to take up residence at Phelan House. Audrey preferred to live in town with her family, who surrounded her with affection and attention. Mrs. Phelan had elected to remain in Hertfordshire with her brother and his family. The servants who were either unable or unwilling to move away from Stony Cross would remain behind to care for Phelan House and its grounds.

Mrs. Clocker gave Christopher a detailed report of what had occurred in his absence. "More wedding gifts have arrived, including some lovely crystal and silver, which I have placed on the long table in the library along with the cards that accompanied them. There is a stack of correspondence and calling cards as well. And sir . . . there was a call paid by an army officer. Not one of those who attended your wedding, but another. He left his card and said he would return soon."

Christopher's face was expressionless. "His name?" he asked quietly.

"Colonel Fenwick."

He gave no response. However, as Beatrix stood beside him, she saw the twitch of the fingers at his side, and the nearly imperceptible double blink of his lashes. Looking grim and distant, Christopher gave the housekeeper a short nod. "Thank you, Mrs. Clocker."

"Yes, sir."

Without a word to Beatrix, Christopher left the parlor and strode to the library. She was at his heels immediately.

"Christopher—"

"Not now."

"What could Colonel Fenwick want?"

"How should I know?" he asked curtly.

"Do you think it has something to do with the Victoria Cross?"

Christopher stopped and turned to face Beatrix with an aggressive swiftness that caused to her fall back on her heels. His eyes were hard, bladelike. She realized that he was overwhelmed with one of the rages that happened when his nerves had been stretched to the breaking point. The mere mention of Colonel Fenwick had overset him completely. To his credit, Christopher took a few deep breaths and managed to control his raging emotions. "I can't talk now," he muttered. "I need a reprieve, Beatrix." And he turned and strode away.

"From *me*?" Beatrix asked, frowning after him.

The coolness between them persisted for the rest of the day. Christopher was monosyllabic at dinner, which made Beatrix miserable and resentful. In the Hathaway family, whenever there was conflict, there was always someone else in the house to talk to. When one was married and childless, however, quarreling with one's husband meant one was, for all purposes, friendless. Should she apologize to him? No, something in her balked at the idea. She had done nothing wrong, she had only asked a question.

Just before bedtime, Beatrix recalled something Amelia had advised: never go to bed angry with your husband.

Dressed in nightgown and robe, she went through the house until she found him in the library, sitting by the hearth.

"This isn't fair," she said, standing at the threshold.

Christopher looked at her. Firelight slid over his face in washes of yellow and red, gleaming in the amber layers of his hair. His hands were joined together neatly, like a folding knife. Albert was stretched on the floor beside the chair, resting his chin between his paws.

"What have I done?" Beatrix continued. "Why won't you talk to me?"

Her husband's face was expressionless. "I have been talking to you."

"Yes, as a stranger would. Completely without affection."

"Beatrix," he said, looking weary, "I'm sorry. Go to bed. Everything will be back to rights tomorrow, after I go to see Fenwick."

"But what have I—"

"It's nothing you've done. Let me deal with this on my own."

"Why must I be shut out? Why can't you trust me?"

Christopher's expression altered, softening. He regarded her with a hint of something like compassion. Standing, he came to her slowly, his form large and dark against the glow of the hearth. Beatrix set her spine against the doorjamb, her heartbeat quickening as he reached her.

"It was a selfish act to marry you," he said. "I knew you wouldn't find it easy to settle for what I could give you, and not push for more. But I did warn you." His opaque gaze slid over her. Bracing one hand on the jamb above her head, he brought the other to the front of her robe, where a hint of her white lace nightgown spilled over the neckline. He toyed with the bit of lace, and bent his head over hers. "Shall I make love to you?" he asked softly. "Would that suffice?"

Beatrix knew when she was being placated. She was being offered sexual pleasure in lieu of real communication. As far as palliatives went, it was a very good substitute. But even as her body responded to his nearness, kindling at the warm scent of him and the sensual promise of his touch, her mind objected. She did not want him to make love to her merely as ploy to distract her. She wanted to be a *wife*, not an object to toy with.

"Would you share my bed afterward?" she asked stubbornly. "And stay with me until morning?"

His fingers stilled. "No."

Beatrix scowled and stepped away from him. "Then I'll go to bed alone." Giving in to momentary frustration, she added as she strode away from him, "As I do every night."

Chapter Twenty-six

"I am cross with Christopher," Beatrix told Amelia in the afternoon, as they strolled arm in arm along the graveled paths behind Ramsay House. "And before I tell you about it, I want to make it clear that there is only one reasonable side of the issue. Mine."

"Oh, bother," Amelia said sympathetically. "Husbands do make one cross at times. Tell me your side, and I will agree completely."

Beatrix began by explaining about the calling card left by the Colonel Fenwick, and Christopher's subsequent behavior.

Amelia sent Beatrix a wry sideways smile. "I believe these are the problems that Christopher took pains to warn you about."

"That's true," Beatrix admitted. "But that doesn't make it any easier to contend with. I love him madly. But I see how he struggles against certain thoughts that jump into his head, or reflexes that he tries to suppress. And he won't discuss any of it with me. I've won his heart, but it's like owning a house in which most of the doors are permanently locked. He wants to shield me from all unpleasantness. And it's not really marriage—not like the marriage you have with Cam—until he's willing to share the worst of himself as well as the best of himself."

"Men don't like to put themselves at risk in that way," Amelia said. "One has to be patient." Her tone became gently arid, her smile rueful. "But I can assure you, dear . . . no one is ever able to share only the best of himself."

Beatrix gave her a brooding glance. "No doubt I'll provoke him into some desperate act before long. I push and pry, and he resists, and I'm afraid that will be the pattern of our marriage for the rest of my life."

Amelia smiled at her fondly. "No marriage stays in the same pattern forever. It is both the best feature of marriage and the worst, that it inevitably changes. Wait for your chance, dear. I promise it will come."

AFTER BEATRIX HAD LEFT TO VISIT HER SISTER, CHRISTOPHER reluctantly contemplated the prospect of visiting Lieutenant Colonel William Fenwick. He hadn't seen the bastard since Fenwick had been sent back to England to recover from the wounds he'd received at Inkerman. To say the least, they hadn't parted on good terms.

Fenwick had made no secret of his resentment toward Christopher, for having gained all the attention and homage that he felt he had deserved. As universally loathed as Fenwick had been, one thing had been acknowledged by all: he had been destined for military glory. He was an unequaled horseman, unquestionably brave, and aggressive in combat. His ambition had been to distinguish himself on the battlefield, and gain a place in Britain's pantheon of legendary war heroes.

The fact that Christopher had been the one to save his life had been especially galling for Fenwick. One would not have been far off the mark to guess that Fenwick would rather have perished on the battlefield than see Christopher receive a medal for it.

Christopher couldn't fathom what Fenwick might want of him now. Most likely he had learned about the Victoria Cross investiture, and had come to air his grievances. Very well. Christopher would let him speak his piece, and then he would make certain that Fenwick left Hampshire. There was a scrawled address on the calling card Fenwick had left. It seemed he was staying at a local inn. Christopher had no choice but to meet with him there. He'd be damned if he would let Fenwick into his house or anywhere near Beatrix.

The afternoon sky was gray and wind whipped, the woodland paths choked with dried brown leaves and fallen branches. Clouds had veiled the sun, imparting a dull blue cast. A damp chill had settled over Hampshire as winter shouldered autumn aside. Christopher took the main road beside the forest, his bay Thoroughbred invigorated by the weather and eager to stretch his legs. The wind blew through the lattice of branches in the woodland, eliciting whispery movements like restless ghosts flitting among the trees.

Christopher felt as if he were being followed. He actually glanced over his shoulder, half expecting to see death or the devil. It was the kind of morbid thought that had plagued him so mercilessly after the war. But far less often lately.

All because of Beatrix.

He felt a sudden pull in his chest, a yearning to go wherever she was, find her and draw her tightly against him. Last night it had seemed impossible to talk to her. Today he thought it might be easier. He would do anything to try and be the husband she needed. It would not be done in one fell swoop. But she was patient, and forgiving, and dear Lord, he loved her for it. Thoughts of his wife helped to steady his nerves as he arrived at the inn. The village was quiet, shop doors closed against the November bluster and damp.

The Stony Cross Inn was well-worn and comfortable, smelling of ale and food, the plastered walls aged the color of dark honey. The innkeeper, Mr. Palfreyman, had known Christopher since his boyhood. He welcomed him warmly, asked a few jovial questions about the honeymoon, and readily supplied the location of the room that Fenwick occupied. A few minutes later, Christopher knocked on the door and waited tensely.

The door opened, one corner scraping against the uneven hallway flooring.

It was jarring to see Lieutenant Colonel William Fenwick wearing civilian attire, when all Christopher had ever seen him in was the scarlet and gold cavalry uniform. The face was the same, except for a complexion faded to an indoors pallor that seemed utterly wrong for a man who had been so obsessed with horsemanship.

Christopher was instinctively reluctant to go near him "Colonel Fenwick," he said, and he had to check himself from saluting. Instead he reached out to shake hands. The feel of the other man's hand, moist and cool, gave him a creeping sensation.

"Phelan." Fenwick moved awkwardly to the side. "Will you come in?"

Christopher hesitated. "There are two parlors downstairs, and a taproom."

Fenwick smiled slightly. "Unfortunately, I'm troubled by old wounds. Stairs are an inconvenience. I beg your indulgence in remaining up here." He looked rueful, even apologetic.

Relaxing marginally, Christopher entered the room.

Like the other sleeping rooms in the inn, the private space was commodious, clean, and sparely furnished. He noticed as Fenwick took one of the chairs that he didn't move well, one leg noticeably stiff.

"Please be seated," Fenwick said. "Thank you for coming to the inn. I would have called at your residence again, but I'm glad to have been spared the effort." He indicated his leg. "The pain has worsened of late. I was told it was miraculous to have kept the leg, but I've wondered if I wouldn't have been better served by amputation."

Christopher waited for Fenwick to explain why he was in Hampshire. When it became clear that the colonel was in no hurry to address the subject, he said abruptly, "You're here because you want something."

"You're not nearly as patient as you used to be," the colonel observed, looking amused. "What happened to the sharpshooter renowned for his ability to wait?"

"The war is over. And I have better things to do now."

"No doubt involving your new bride. It seems congratulations are in order. Tell me, what kind of woman managed to land the most decorated soldier in England?"

"The kind who cares nothing for medals or laurels."

Giving him a frankly disbelieving glance, Fenwick said, "How can that be true? Of course she cares about such things. She is now the wife of an immortal."

Christopher stared at him blankly. "Pardon?"

"You'll be remembered for decades," Fenwick said. "Perhaps centuries. Don't tell me that it means nothing to you."

Christopher shook his head slightly, his gaze locked on the other man's face.

"There is an ancient tradition of military honor in my family," Fenwick said. "I knew that I would achieve the most, and be remembered the longest. No one ever thinks about the ancestors who led small lives, who were known principally as husbands and fathers, benevolent masters, loyal friends. No one cares about those nameless ciphers. But warriors are revered. They are never forgotten." Bitterness creased his face, leaving it puckered and uneven like the skin of an overripe orange. "A medal like the Victoria Cross—that is all I've ever wanted."

"A half ounce of die-stamped gunmetal?" Christopher asked skeptically.

"Don't use that supercilious tone with me, you arrogant ass." Oddly, despite the venom of the words, Fenwick was calm and controlled. "From the beginning, I knew you were nothing more than an empty-headed fop. Handsome stuffing for a uniform. But you turned out to have one useful gift— you could shoot. And then you went to the Rifles, where somehow you became a soldier. When I first read the dispatches, I thought there had to be some other Phelan. Because the Phelan of the reports was a warrior, and I knew you hadn't the makings of one."

"I proved you wrong at Inkerman," Christopher said quietly.

The jab brought a smile to Fenwick's face, the smile of a man standing at a distance from life and seeing unimaginable irony. "Yes. You saved me, and now you're to get the nation's highest honor for it."

"I don't want it."

"That makes it even worse. I was sent home while you became the lauded hero, and took everything that should have been mine. Your name will be remembered, and you don't even care. Had I died on the battlefield, that would have at least been something. But you took even that away. And you betrayed your closest friend in the process. A friend who trusted you. You left Lieutenant Bennett to die alone." He watched Christopher keenly, hunting for any sign of emotion.

"If I had it to do again, I would make the same choice," Christopher said flatly.

An incredulous look came over Fenwick's face.

"Do you think I dragged you off the battlefield for either of our sakes?" Christopher demanded. "Do you think I gave a damn about you, or about winning some godforsaken medal?"

"Why did you do it, then?"

"Because Mark Bennett was dying," Christopher said savagely. "And there was enough life left in you to save. In all that death, something had to survive. If it was you, so be it."

A long silence passed, while Fenwick digested the statement. He gave Christopher a shrewd look that raised the hairs on his neck. "Bennett's wound wasn't as bad as it must have appeared," he said. "It wasn't mortal."

Christopher stared at him without comprehension. He shook himself a little and refocused on Fenwick, who had continued to speak.

". . . a pair of Russian Hussars found Bennett and took him prisoner," Fenwick was saying. "He was treated by one of their surgeons, and sent to a prison camp far inland. He was subjected to hardships, lacking proper food or shelter, and later he was put to work. After a few unsuccessful escape attempts, Lieutenant Bennett finally managed to free himself. He made his way to friendly territory, and was brought back to London approximately a fortnight ago."

Christopher was afraid to believe his ears. Could it be true? Steady . . . steady . . . his mind was buzzing. His muscles had gone tense against the threat of deep tremors. He couldn't let the shaking start, or it wouldn't stop.

"Why wasn't Bennett released in the prisoner exchange at the war's end?" he heard himself ask.

"It seems his captors were trying to negotiate his exchange for a stipulated sum of money, along with provisions and weapons. I suspect Bennett admitted under questioning that he was the heir to the Bennett shipping fortune. In any event, negotiations were problematic, and it was kept secret from all but the highest levels at the War Office."

"Damn those bastards," Christopher said in anguished fury. "I would have rescued him, had I known . . ."

"No doubt you would have," Fenwick said dryly. "However, difficult as it is to believe, the matter was resolved without your heroic efforts."

"Where is Bennett now? What is his condition?"

"That is why I've come to see you. To warn you. And after this, I am no longer in your debt, do you understand?"

Christopher stood, his fists clenched. "Warn me about what?"

"Lieutenant Bennett is not in his right mind. The doctor accompanying him on the ship back to England recommended a stay in a lunatic asylum. That is why Bennett's return has not been reported in the gazettes or newspapers. His family desires to maintain absolute privacy. Bennett was sent to his family in Buckinghamshire, but subsequently disappeared without a word to anyone. His whereabouts are unknown. The reason I'm warning you is that according to his relations, Bennett blames you for his ordeal. They believe he wants to kill you." A cold, thin smile split his face, like a crack in a sheet of ice. "How ironic, that you're being given a medal for saving a man who despises you, and you'll probably be murdered by the one you should have saved. You had better find him, Phelan, before he finds you."

Christopher stumbled from the room and went along the hallway in swift strides. Was it true? Was this some obscene manipulation by Fenwick, or was Mark Bennett truly unhinged? And if so, what had he endured? He tried to reconcile his memories of the dashing, good-humored Bennett with what Fenwick had just told him. It was impossible.

Holy hell . . . if Bennett was looking for him, it would be an easy matter to find Phelan House.

A new kind of fear came over him, more piercing than

anything he had ever felt. He had to make certain Beatrix was safe. Nothing in the world mattered beyond protecting her. He went down the stairs, his heart thundering, the pounding of his feet seeming to echo the syllables of her name.

Mr. Palfreyman was standing near the inn's entrance. "A tankard of ale before you leave?" he suggested. "Always free for England's greatest hero."

"No. I'm going home."

Palfreyman reached out to stop him, looking concerned. "Captain Phelan, there's a table in the taproom—come sit for a moment, there's a good lad. You're a bit gray around the gills. I'll bring out a good brandy or rum. One for the stirrups, eh?"

Christopher shook his head. "No time." No time for anything. He ran outside. It was darker, colder than it had been before. The late afternoon sky was nightmare colored, swallowing up the world.

He rode for Phelan House, his ears filled with the ghostly cries of men on the battlefield, sounds of distress and pleading and pain. Bennett, alive . . . how was it possible? Christopher had seen the wound in his chest, had seen enough similar injuries to know that death had been inevitable. But what if by some miracle . . .

As he neared the house, he saw Albert bounding out of the woods, followed by Beatrix's slender form. She was returning from Ramsay House. A strong gust of wind blew against her wine-colored cloak, causing it to flap wildly, and her hat flew from her head. She laughed as the dog went to chase it. Seeing Christopher approach on the road, she waved at him.

He was nearly overcome with relief. The panic eased. The darkness began to recede. *Thank you, God.* Beatrix was there, and safe. She belonged to him, she was beautiful and vibrant, and he would spend his life taking care of her. Whatever she desired of him, whatever words or memories she asked for, he would give. It almost seemed easy now—the force of his love would make anything easy.

Christopher slowed the horse to a walk. "Beatrix." His voice was carried away in the wind.

She was still laughing, her hair having come free, and she waited for him to come to her.

He was startled by a streak of bright pain in his head. A fraction of a second later, he heard the crack of a rifle shot. A familiar sound . . . an indelible tattoo on his memory. Shots and the whistling of shells, explosions, men shouting, the screams of panicked horses . . .

He'd been unseated. He was tumbling slowly, the world a confusion of sight and sound. The sky and ground had been reversed. Was he falling up, or down? He slammed against a hard surface, the breath knocked from him, and he felt the hot trickle of blood sliding along his face into his ear.

Another nightmare. He had to wake up, get his bearings. But oddly, Beatrix was in the nightmare with him, crying out and running toward him. Albert reached him in a fury of barking.

His lungs strained to take in a breath, his heart leaping like a fish freshly pulled from water. Beatrix dropped to her knees beside him, her skirts a billow of blue, and she tugged his head to her lap.

"Christopher—let me—oh, God—"

Albert bayed and snarled as someone approached. A momentary pause, and then the dog's ferocious barks were mingled with high-pitched whines.

Christopher levered upward to a sitting position, using his coat sleeve to blot the rivulet of blood that rolled from his temple. Blinking hard, he saw the rawboned, disheveled figure of a man coming to stand a few yards away from them. The man held a revolver.

Instantly Christopher's brain made an assessment of the weapon—a cap-and-ball revolver, five-shot percussion. British military issue.

Before he glanced up at the man's haggard face, Christopher knew who he was.

"Bennett."

Chapter Twenty-seven

Beatrix's first instinct was to interpose herself between her husband and the stranger, but Christopher shoved her behind him. Breathing hard from fear and shock, she looked over his shoulder.

The man was dressed in civilian clothes that hung on his near-skeletal limbs. He was tall and large framed, looking as if he hadn't slept or eaten well in months. The shaggy layers of his dark hair badly needed cutting. He regarded them with the wild, unnerving stare of a madman. Despite all that, it wasn't difficult to see that he had once been handsome. Now he was a barely salvaged wreck. A young man, with an old face and haunted eyes.

"Back from the dead," Bennett said hoarsely. "You didn't think I'd make it, did you?"

"Bennett . . . Mark." As Christopher spoke, Beatrix felt the fine, nearly undetectable tremors running through his body. "I never knew what happened to you."

"No." The revolver shook in Bennett's grip. "You were too busy rescuing Fenwick."

"Bennett, put that damn thing down. I—*quiet,* Albert—it nearly killed me to leave you there."

"But you did. And I've gone through hell ever since. I rotted and starved, while you became England's great hero. Traitor. Bastard—" He aimed the pistol at Christopher's chest. Beatrix gasped and huddled against his back.

"I had to save Fenwick first," Christopher said coolly, his pulse racing. "I had no choice."

"Like hell. You wanted the glory for saving a superior officer."

"I thought you were done for. And if Fenwick had been captured, they would have dragged all kinds of damaging intelligence out of him."

"Then you should have shot him, and taken me out of there."

"You're out of your bloody mind," Christopher snapped. Which probably wasn't the wisest thing to say to a man in Bennett's condition, but Beatrix could hardly blame him. "Murder a defenseless soldier in cold blood? Not for any reason. Not even Fenwick. If you want to shoot me for that, go ahead, and the devil take you. But if you harm one hair on my wife's head, I'll drag you down to hell with me. And the same goes for Albert—he was wounded while defending you."

"Albert wasn't there."

"I left him with you. When I came back for you, he was bleeding from a bayonet wound, and one of his ears was nearly cut off. And you were gone."

Bennett blinked and stared at him with a flicker of uncertainty. His gaze moved to Albert. He surprised Beatrix by lowering to his haunches and gesturing to the dog. "Come here, boy."

Albert didn't move.

"He knows what a gun is," Beatrix heard Christopher say curtly. "He won't go to you unless you set it aside."

Bennett hesitated. Slowly he set the revolver on the ground. "Come," he said to the dog, who whimpered in confusion.

"Go on, boy," Christopher said in a low tone.

Albert approached Bennett warily, his tail wagging. Bennett rubbed the shaggy head and scratched the dog's neck. Panting, Albert licked his hand.

Leaning against Christopher's back, Beatrix felt some of the tension leave him.

"Albert was there," Bennett said in a different voice. "I remember him licking my face."

"Do you think I would have left him with you, if I hadn't meant to come back?" Christopher demanded.

"Doesn't matter. If the situation were reversed, I would have shot Fenwick, and saved you."

"No you wouldn't have."

"I would," Bennett insisted unsteadily. "I'm not like you, you fucking honorable sod." He sat full on the ground, and buried his face in Albert's shaggy coat. His voice was muffled as he said, "You should have at least finished me off before you let them capture me."

"But I didn't. And you survived."

"The price of surviving wasn't worth it. You don't know what I went through. I can't bloody live with it." Bennett let go of Albert, his tortured gaze alighting on the revolver beside him.

Before Bennett could reach for the weapon, Beatrix said, "*Fetch,* Albert." Instantly the dog took up the revolver and brought it to her. "Good boy." She took careful possession of the gun and patted him on the head.

Bracing his arms on his knees, Bennett buried his face on them, a broken posture that Beatrix recognized all too well. He let out a few incoherent words.

Christopher went to kneel beside him, laying a strong arm across his back. "Listen to me. You're not alone. You're with friends. Damn you, Bennett . . . come to the house with us. Tell me what you went through. I'll listen. And then we'll find some way for you to live with it. I couldn't help you then. But let me try to help you now."

THEY BROUGHT BENNETT TO THE HOUSE, WHERE HE COL-lapsed from exhaustion, hunger, and nervous distress. Before Christopher could begin to tell Mrs. Clocker what needed to be done, she had taken stock of the situation and marshaled the servants to action. This was a household well accustomed to illness and the needs of an invalid. A bath was drawn, a bedroom was prepared, and a tray of bland and nourishing food was brought up. After Bennett was taken care of, Mrs. Clocker dosed him with tonic and laudanum.

Going to Bennett's bedside, Christopher stared down at the nearly unrecognizable features of his old friend. Suffering had altered him, within and without. But he would recover. Christopher would see to that.

And with that hope and sense of purpose, Christopher was aware of a new and fragile feeling of absolution. Bennett wasn't dead. With all the sins on his conscience, at least that one had been taken from him.

Bennett looked up at him drowsily, his once-vibrant dark eyes now dim and dull.

"You're going to stay with us until you're better," Christopher said. "You won't try to leave, will you?"

"Nowhere else to go," Bennett mumbled, and went to sleep.

Christopher left the room, closed the door with care, and walked slowly toward the other wing of the house.

Medusa the hedgehog was wandering casually along the hallway. She paused as Christopher approached. A faint smile touched his lips. He bent to pick her up as Beatrix had showed him, inserting his hands beneath her. The hedge-hog's quills flattened naturally as he turned her up to look at him. Relaxed and curious, she viewed him with her per-petual hedgehog smile.

"Medusa," he said softly, "I wouldn't advise climbing out of your pen at night. One of the maids might find you, and then what? You might find yourself taken to the scullery and used to scrub a pot." Taking her to the private upstairs receiving room, he lowered her into her pen.

Continuing on to Beatrix's room, he reflected that his wife viewed poor Bennett as yet another wounded creature. She had shown no hesitation in welcoming him into their home. One would expect no less of Beatrix.

Entering the room quietly, he saw his wife at her dressing table, carefully filing the claws of Lucky's remaining paw. The cat regarded her with a bored expression, tail flicking lazily. ". . . you must stay away from the settee cushions," Beatrix was lecturing, "or Mrs. Clocker will have both our heads."

Christopher's gaze traveled over the long, elegant lines of her figure, her silhouette revealed in the lampglow that shone through her muslin nightgown.

Becoming aware of Christopher's presence, Beatrix stood and came to him with natural, unselfconscious grace. "Does your head pain you?" she asked in concern, reaching up to touch the small plaster at his temple. In all the commotion of bringing Bennett to their home, there had been no opportunity for private conversation.

He bent to brush a soft kiss on her lips. "No. With a head as hard as mine, bullets merely bounce off."

She let her hand linger at the side of his face. "What happened when you spoke to Colonel Fenwick? Did he try to shoot you, too?"

Christopher shook his head. "Only my friends do that."

Beatrix smiled slightly, then sobered. "Lieutenant Bennett isn't mad, you know. He'll be well again, with time and rest."

"I hope so."

Her blue eyes searched his. "You blame yourself, don't you?"

He nodded. "I made the best decision I could at the time. But knowing that doesn't make the consequences any easier to bear."

Beatrix was momentarily still, appearing to consider something. Pulling away from him, she went to the dressing table. "I have something for you." Busily she rummaged through the small drawer in the front of the table, and extracted a folded piece of paper. "It's a letter."

He gave her a warm, quizzical glance. "From you?"

Beatrix shook her head. "From John." She brought it to him. "He wrote it before he died. Audrey was reluctant to give it to you. But I think it's time that you read it."

Christopher made no move to take it, only reached out and pulled her close. Picking up a handful of her flowing brown hair, he rubbed it gently against his cheek. "Read it to me."

Together they went to the bed and sat on the mattress. Christopher kept his gaze on Beatrix's profile as she unfolded the letter and began to read.

Dear Christopher,

It seems I have less time than I had hoped for. I confess I find myself surprised by how short this life has been. As I draw back to view it, I see that I spent too much time dwelling on the wrong things, and not enough on what mattered. But I also see that I have been blessed far beyond other men. I needn't ask you to look after Audrey and Mother. I know that you will do so to the extent that they will allow.

If you are reading this, it means you have returned from the war and are facing responsibilities that you have never been prepared for. Let me offer a few words of counsel. I have watched you for your entire life . . . your restless nature, your lack of satisfaction in anything. You put the people you love on pedestals, and are inevitably disappointed by them. And you do the same to yourself. My dear brother, you are your own worst enemy. If you can learn to stop expecting impossible perfection, in yourself and others, you may find the happiness that has always eluded you.

Forgive me for not being able to survive . . . and forgive yourself for surviving.

This is the life you were meant to have. Not a single day should be squandered.

John

Christopher was silent for a long time, his chest tight. It sounded like his brother . . . that loving, slightly lecturing tone. "How I miss him," he whispered. "He knew me well."

"He knew you as you were," Beatrix said. "But I think you've changed. You don't expect perfection now. How else could you explain your attraction to me?"

Christopher gently took her face in his hands. "You are my idea of perfection, Beatrix Heloise."

She leaned forward until their noses touched. "Have you forgiven yourself?" she asked softly. "For surviving?"

"I'm trying to." The proximity of her warm, scantily clad body was too much for him to resist. He slid his hand behind her neck, and kissed her throat. A little shiver chased over her skin. He undressed her carefully, fighting to contain a need that threatened to rage out of control. He kept every movement gentle, light, while his body ached with the violent desire to possess her. His hands swept over her, mapping the physical contours of what words had already expressed.

Making love, creating it, letting sensation flow over both of them. Emotion became movement. Movement became pleasure.

He let his tongue explore her mouth at the same time he entered her, his hands clutched in the pouring dark silk of her hair. She tried to move, but he held her still, feeding more pleasure into her, and more, until her every breath was a moan, and she trembled without stopping.

Beatrix dug her heels into the bedclothes, her fingertips digging into his back. He relished the little crescents of pain, loving the dazed, lost look on her face. The rhythms of her body gathered in one impetus, a delicate watercolor flush spreading across her fine skin. But he didn't want it to end yet, despite his own ravening hunger. With agonized effort, he forced himself to hold still inside her.

She cried out, her hips lifting against his weight. "Christopher, please—"

"Shhh . . ." He pressed her down, kissed her neck, worked slowly to her breasts. He pulled her nipple into his mouth, caressing her with his teeth and tongue, leaving a residue of damp heat. Small hungering sounds came from her throat, and her inner muscles clasped him in a helpless rhythm. He began to follow the tender pattern, pressing forward, letting her clasp him on each withdrawal stroke. "Look at me," he whispered, and her lashes lifted to reveal the depths of her soul.

Cupping a hand beneath her head, he fused his lips to hers, while he entered her more deeply than ever before. She took him, wrapping her arms and legs around him, holding him with her entire body. He let the rhythm roughen, quicken, his lovemaking turning wild and unrestrained as he rode the fast, relentless rhythm of her hips. Arching upward, she convulsed violently, her flesh gripping him in tight, wet ripples that drew out a wrenching release.

They were both too love dazed to move for a while. Saturated in the feeling of being open, unguarded, Christopher let his hand wander over her, not with sexual intent, but reverence. She stretched and moved to trap his legs beneath a slender thigh, her arm slung across his chest. Climbing farther atop him, she rubbed her mouth and nose lightly through the hair on his chest. He lay still beneath the warm scaffolding of her body, letting her play and explore as she would.

When they finally left the bed, they were giddy. Christopher made a project of bathing her, drying her, even brushing her hair. She brought his robe and sat beside the bathtub as he washed. Occasionally she leaned downward to steal a kiss. They invented endearments for each other. Small marital intimacies that meant nothing and everything. They were collecting them, just as they were collecting words and memories, all of it containing special resonance for the two of them.

Beatrix turned down all the lamps except the one on the night table. "Time for bed," she murmured.

Christopher stood at the threshold, watching his wife slip beneath the covers, her hair falling in a loose braid over one shoulder. She gave him the look that by now had become familiar . . . patiently encouraging. A Beatrix look.

A lifetime with such a woman was not nearly enough.

Taking a deep breath, Christopher made a decision.

"I want the left side," he said, and turned down the last lamp.

He got into bed with his wife, taking her into his arms.

And together they slept until morning.

Epilogue

Christopher waited with the Rifle Brigade in a large space on the northern side of Hyde Park, a half mile broad and three quarters of a mile long, reserved for nine thousand men of all arms. There were Marines, Dragoons, Rifles, Hussars, Life Guards, Highlanders, and more, all glittering in the abundant sun. The morning was hot and breezeless, promising to roast the hundred thousand people in attendance at the very first Victoria Cross ceremony.

The soldiers in their full dress uniforms were already miserable, some from the heat, others from envy. "We've got the bloody ugliest uniforms in the Empire," one of the Rifles muttered, casting a glance at the infinitely more splendid dress of the nearby Hussars. "I hate this gloomy dark green."

"Pretty target you'd make, crawling forward of the front lines in bright red and gold," another Rifle replied in a scornful undertone. "You'd have your arse shot off."

"I don't care. Women like red coats."

"You'd choose a woman over not having your arse shot off?"

"Wouldn't you?"

The other man's silence conceded the point.

A faint smile curved Christopher's mouth. He glanced at the enclosure near the Grosvenor Gate galleries, where seven thousand ticket holders had been seated. Beatrix and the rest of the Hathaways were there, as well as his grandfather, and Audrey, and several cousins. After this elaborate and unwanted presentation was over, Christopher and the entire mass of his family and in-laws would return to the Rutledge Hotel. There would be a private dinner with feasting and merriment, and Harry Rutledge had hinted at some special entertainment. Knowing Rutledge, it could be anything from a trio of opera singers to a troop of performing monkeys. Only two things were certain—the Hathaways were in London, and it would be a wild, mad romp.

Another guest would attend the family dinner at the Rutledge—Mark Bennett, who had sold his army commission and was preparing to take the reins of his family shipping business. It had taken months for Bennett to recover from the trauma of his wartime experiences, and the process was far from complete. However, a long stay in the Phelan household had done him a world of good. Piece by piece, Bennett had put his psyche back together in a necessary but painful process. With the support of understanding friends, he had gradually come back to himself.

Now more and more, Bennett resembled the dashing and quick-witted rogue he had once been. During long vigorous rides through the countryside, he had acquired healthy color and vitality, and had regained lost muscle. Even after returning to his family estate in Gloucestershire, Bennett often visited Christopher and Beatrix at Riverton. It so happened that during one of these visits, he had met Audrey, who had come to stay a fortnight.

Audrey's reaction to the tall, dark-haired ex-soldier had been more than a little perplexing. Christopher hadn't understood why his normally sanguine sister-in-law became so shy and clumsy whenever Bennett was near.

"It's because he's a tiger," Beatrix had explained in private, "and Audrey is a swan, and tigers always make swans nervous. She finds him very attractive, but she doesn't think he's the kind of gentleman she should keep company with."

Bennett, for his part, seemed quite taken with Audrey, but every time he had made a careful advance to her, she had retreated.

And then with startling quickness, the two of them seemed to have become fast friends. They went on rides and walks together and corresponded frequently when they were apart. When they were both in London, they were always seen in each other's company.

Mystified by the change in their formerly awkward relationship, Christopher asked Bennett what had happened to alter it.

"I told her I was impotent from old war wounds," Bennett said. "That calmed her nerves considerably."

Taken aback, Christopher had brought himself to ask gingerly, "Are you?"

"Hell no," came Bennett's indignant reply. "I only said it because she was so skittish around me. And it worked."

Christopher had given him a sardonic glance. "Are you ever going to tell Audrey the truth?"

A mischievous smile had played at the corners of Bennett's lips. "I may let her cure me soon," he admitted. Seeing Christopher's expression, he had added hastily that his intentions were entirely honorable.

It was a good match. And in Christopher's opinion, his brother would have approved.

The Royal Salute was sounded, the heavy artillery guns booming. The national anthem played as the inspection of the ranks commenced, the entire force lowering colors and presenting arms. Slowly the royal party rode along the lines. At the conclusion of the inspection, the queen, her escorts, and a detachment of Royal Horse Guards proceeded to the center of the galleries between the Legislature and the *Corps Diplomatique.*

A minor commotion occurred when the queen did not dismount at the center dais as planned, but instead remained on her charger. It appeared she intended to award the Victoria Crosses from her seat on horseback, with the prince consort on her left.

The medal recipients, sixty-two in all, were summoned to the dais. Like many of the other men, Christopher was dressed in private clothes, having left the ranks at the conclusion of the war. Unlike the other men, Christopher was holding a leash. Attached to a dog. For reasons that had not been explained, he had been told to bring Albert to the presentation. The other Rifles whispered encouragement as Albert walked obediently beside Christopher.

"There's a good boy!"

"Look smart, fellow!"

"No accidents in front of the queen!"

"And all that goes for you too, Albert," someone added, causing the lot of them to snicker.

Giving his friends a damning glance, which only amused them further, Christopher took Albert to meet the queen.

Her Majesty was even shorter and stouter than he had expected, her nose hawklike, her chin nonexistent, her eyes penetrating. She was dressed in a scarlet riding coat, a general's sash over one shoulder, and a general's plume of red and white feathers on her open riding hat. A band of black mourning crepe, a customary token of military mourning, had been tied around one plump arm. On horseback beside the dais, she was at the same level as the medal recipients.

Christopher was gratified by the businesslike manner with which she conducted the ceremony. The men filed past her, each stopping to be presented and have the queen pin a bronze cross with a red ribbon to his chest, and then he was efficiently ushered away. At this rate, the entire process wouldn't take more than a quarter hour.

As soon as Christopher and Albert stepped up to the dais, he was disconcerted to hear a cheer rising from the crowd, spreading and growing until the noise was deafening. It wasn't right for him to receive more acclamation than the other soldiers—they deserved just as much recognition for their courage and gallantry. And yet the ranks were cheering as well, humbling him utterly. Albert looked up at him uneasily, staying close to his side. "Easy, boy," he murmured.

The queen regarded the pair of them curiously as they stopped before her.

"Captain Phelan," she said. "Our subjects' enthusiasm does you honor."

Christopher replied carefully. "The honor belongs to all the soldiers who have fought in Your Majesty's service—and to the families who waited for them to return."

"Well and modestly said, Captain." There was a slight deepening of the creases at the corners of her eyes. "Come forward."

As he complied, the queen leaned from the horse to pin the bronze cross with its crimson ribbon to his coat. Christopher made to withdraw, but she stopped him with a gesture and a word. "Remain." Her attention switched to Albert, who sat on the dais and cocked his head as he regarded her curiously. "What is your companion's name?"

"His name is Albert, Your Majesty."

Her lips quirked as if she were tempted to smile. She slid a brief glance to her left, at the prince consort. "We are informed that he campaigned with you at Inkerman and Sebastopol."

"Yes, Your Majesty. He performed many difficult and dangerous duties to keep the men safe. This cross belongs partly to him—he assisted in recovering a wounded officer under enemy fire."

The general charged with handing the orders to the queen approached and gave her a curious object. It looked like . . . a dog collar?

"Come forward, Albert," she said.

Albert obeyed promptly, sitting at the edge of the dais. The queen reached over and fastened the collar around his neck with a deft efficiency that revealed some experience with the procedure. Christopher recalled having heard that she owned several dogs and was partial to collies. "This collar," she said to Albert, as if he could understand her, "has been engraved with regimental distinctions and battle honors. We have added a silver clasp to commend the valor and devotion you have displayed in our service."

Albert waited patiently until the collar was fastened, and then licked her wrist.

"Impertinent," she scolded in a whisper, and patted his head. And she sent a brief, discreet smile to Christopher as they left to make way for the next recipient.

"ALBERT, FRIEND TO ROYALTY," BEATRIX SAID LATER AT THE Rutledge Hotel, laughing as she sat on the floor of their suite and examined the new collar. "I hope you don't get above yourself, and put on airs."

"Not around your family, he won't," Christopher said, stripping off his coat and waistcoat, and removing his cravat. He lowered himself to the settee, relishing the coolness of the room. Albert went to drink from his bowl of water, lapping noisily.

Beatrix went to Christopher, stretched full length atop him, and braced her arms on his chest. "I was so proud of you today," she said, smiling down at him. "And perhaps a tiny bit smug that with all the women swooning and sighing over you, I'm the one you went home with."

Arching a brow, Christopher asked, "Only a tiny bit smug?"

"Oh, very well. *Enormously* smug." She began to play with his hair. "Now that all this medal business is done with, I have something to discuss with you."

Closing his eyes, Christopher enjoyed the sensation of her fingers stroking his scalp. "What is it?"

"What would you say to adding a new member to the family?"

This was not an unusual question. Since they had established a household at Riverton, Beatrix had increased the size of her menagerie, and was constantly occupied with animal-related charities and concerns. She had also compiled a report for the newly established natural history society in London. For some reason it had not been at all difficult to convince the group of elderly entomologists, ornithologists, and other naturalists to include a pretty young woman in their midst. Especially when it became clear that Beatrix could talk for hours about migration patterns, plant cycles, and other matters relating to animal habitats and behavior. There was even discussion of Beatrix's joining a board to form a new natural history museum, to provide a lady's perspective on various aspects of the project.

Keeping his eyes closed, Christopher smiled lazily. "Fur, feathers, or scales?" he asked in response to her earlier question.

"None of those."

"God. Something exotic. Very well, where will this creature come from? Will we have to go to Australia to collect it? Iceland? Brazil?"

A tremor of laughter went through her. "It's already here, actually. But you won't be able to view it for, say . . . eight more months."

Christopher's eyes flew open. Beatrix was smiling down at him, looking shy and eager and more than a little pleased with herself.

"Beatrix." He turned carefully so that she was underneath him. His hand came to cradle the side of her face. "You're sure?"

She nodded.

Overwhelmed, Christopher covered her mouth with his, kissing her fiercely. "My love . . . precious girl . . ."

"It's what you wanted, then?" she asked between kisses, already knowing the answer.

Christopher looked down at her through a bright sheen of joy that made everything blurred and radiant. "More than I ever dreamed. And certainly more than I deserve."

Beatrix's arms slid around his neck. "I'll show you what you deserve," she informed him, and pulled his head down to hers again.